GHOSTLY MAGIC

Hwyn tossed the stone high in the air, above Lord Dannoth's head. He had to release me to catch it, lest it fall to the stone floor. As soon as I felt his grip slacken I sprang away. I turned to confront the man who still held Trenara.

"Release her," I said in the most menacing tone I could manage. To my surprise, he dropped his sword and let the lady go, a look of dread on his face. But he was not looking at me. I turned and followed his gaze to Lord Dannoth Kelgarran.

The lord held the white stone but looked as though he would gladly drop it. Vapors rose from the gem and formed themselves into the semblance of men: tall, solidly built swordsmen still bearing what must have been their death wounds. Slashed throats and torn chests oozed spectral blood.

Lord Kelgarran shrieked and wailed, holding the stone as far from his body as he could, trying vainly to cast it aside. By the time he managed to release his grip, I smelled burnt flesh. He sank to the floor whimpering as seven ghostly warriors glowered at him from all sides.

THE EYE OF NIGHT

PAULINE J. ALAMA

BANTAM BOOKS

THE EYE OF NIGHT
A Bantam Spectra Book / July 2002

SPECTRA and the portrayal of a boxed "s" are trademarks of
Bantam Books, a division of Random House, Inc.

ISBN 0-553-58463-4

Published simultaneously in the United States and Canada

Bantam Books are published by Bantam Books, a division of Random
House, Inc. Its trademark, consisting of the words "Bantam Books"
and the portrayal of a rooster, is Registered in U.S. Patent and Trademark Office and in other countries. Marca Registrada. Bantam Books,
1540 Broadway, New York, New York 10036.

PRINTED IN THE UNITED STATES OF AMERICA
OPM   10 9 8 7 6 5 4 3 2 1

THE EYE OF NIGHT is dedicated to my beloved Paul and my great friend Susan, who followed the quest since it was a short story, demanded more, gave advice when I needed it and refrained when I didn't, and always asked the right questions, especially "What happens next?"

To my great friend Elizabeth Edersheim (1963–1992), who never saw this story, but left her mark on it nonetheless.

And to those who made me a writer: the teachers of Yantacaw Elementary School, first and foremost my mother, Lottie Zachai Alama. Love always.

Acknowledgments

Special thanks to Warwick Daw for help with sailing terms; to Kendra Adema for information on rural life; to the staff of the Rutherford Free Public Library; to Alan Lupack and Diana Beach for great discussions; to Chris Nugent and Sarah Higley, who understood why I had to tell them about the gods of the World-Wheel one day before *Beowulf* seminar; to Sally and Joe Cunneen for introducing me to the perfect agent; to Hy Cohen for being the perfect agent; and to editor Juliet Ulman for making me write more.

"Indeed, all creation groans and is in labor, even until now."

—Romans 8:22

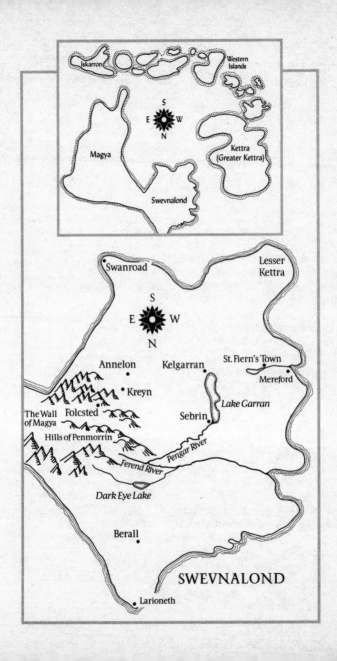

Iskarron

Western Islands

S
E · W
N

Magya

Kettra
(Greater Kettra)

Swevnalond

Swanroad

Lesser
Kettra

S
E · W
N

Annelon

Kelgarran

St. Fiern's Town

Kreyn

Mereford

The Wall
of Magya

Folcsted

Sebrin

Lake Garran

Hills of Penmorrin

Pengar River

Ferend River

Dark Eye Lake

Berall

SWEVNALOND

Larioneth

1

KELGARRAN HALL

I little thought, when I begged shelter at Kelgarran Hall one rainy night, that I should take part in its downfall.

It happened the night of St. Bridwen's Day, in the year of my pilgrimage. I had left the Tarvon Order and taken my troubles to the Lake-Shrine of St. Fiern, as so many god-haunted wanderers do. I was traveling back toward what I could no longer call my home when I came, a disappointed pilgrim, to Kelgarran Hall.

It was a generous hearth in those days, the grand days of Lord Dannoth Kelgarran: Dannoth the Mighty, Dannoth the Bountiful. Some lords honor St. Bridwen's Day by doling out bread at the gate, but Lord Dannoth opened his doors and larder to all travelers, high- or lowborn. I was abjectly grateful; it was the first thing I'd found to praise that whole unfruitful year.

A sorry pilgrimage that had been! I'd seen nothing in the still pool they call the Mirror of St. Fiern, *nothing*: not even my own reflection, for rainstorms had drowned the pool in dull, blackish mud. That featureless blackness, more than any evil vision I might have seen, seemed to pass a death sentence over me: my life was a void, a starless night. For a moment, I felt I must cast myself into the depths and drown, as though the saint herself had urged it. I'd never felt less inclined to return to the Order, but neither had I any glimmer of a new life outside it.

I arrived at Kelgarran Hall a lost man, and they welcomed me. Whatever has been said of them since then—whatever I myself am compelled to say—let this kindness be set in the balance.

The holiday took me by surprise. I had lost count of days in the long footsore passage from St. Fiern's Town eastward to Lake Garran, with an anxious detour into the marshy wastes to avoid a small war between two of the cities of the plain. Even when I'd passed the marshes, the damp clung to me. It was late spring, but a spring almost stillborn, cold and meager—a sign of the Troubles, people said. When I slogged through the mud to the gates of Kelgarran City one rainy afternoon, it puzzled me to see festal banners of green and gold exposed to the rain, and the populace in a chilled and damp procession toward the town square for the St. Bridwen's Day pageant. Only by counting days on my fingers could I convince myself that it was, indeed, the saint's day, with summer and the Feast of the Bright Goddess close at hand.

Under the pavilions hastily set up in the town square against the weather, I watched the pageant with only half an eye for it. St. Bridwen's legendary openhandedness was all very well in ancient days, but I'd found precious little of it among the people I met along the road from St. Fiern's Town to Kelgarran. The little money I had been granted for the pilgrimage was spent, and I had been sleeping in the temple courts with other travelers and beggars, eating whatever crust would be spared to me. Like many in the crowd, I looked forward to the culmination of the pageant, when St. Bridwen's mysterious well gives ale and bowls are handed round to the populace. I was hungry, and even a mouthful of ale is at least something in the belly.

But the man who passed me the bowl, a thin blond youth with a Kettran accent and the white robes of the Order of St. Rann, laughed at my eagerness. "This is breakfast for you, too?" he said.

I grimaced. "It's been a hard pilgrimage."

"Mine, too," he said. "But they say that travelers are welcome at the lord's table tonight. I am Brother Ennes, priest of the Order of St. Rann. Pass the bowl and come with me; we'll see if it's true."

"I'm Jereth," I told him, and added no more, unsure whether I dared any longer to add any suffix to my bare given name. Order, profession, patronym, hometown—any of these seemingly innocent additions might drag along in their train the whole story of my failed priesthood and failed pilgrimage. My very appearance must have told part of that story: I looked scarcely more than a common beggar, my hair grown out of tonsure. A travel-worn cassock belted in rope was the only remaining mark of my abandoned order. The wooden emblem of a key that hung from my belt was scarcely recognizable, half broken the night before when I'd had to scramble under a hedge, driven from my sleeping place by a guard dog. It had been a hard pilgrimage indeed.

Grateful for any slim chance of shelter, I followed Ennes through the stone streets of Kelgarran, past shops decked in gold and green for the holiday, past the tall houses of the wealthy citizens, on an ever-climbing road to the castle door. I was surprised by the beauty of the structure: having heard of the might of the House of Kelgarran, I had expected a stark fortress, blank-faced and harsh as a cliff; but here was a many-towered cloud-castle of silvery-pale stone that gleamed even in the dull light of a rain-drenched day.

I shook my head as Ennes strode boldly to the door, answering the sentry's cry with a few words, "In St. Bridwen's Name." But little as they seemed, those words gained us entry. At the guard's request, Ennes left his sword and bow at the door; having no weapon to leave, I entered freely as the flies that had taken refuge from the rain.

I could scarcely believe our good fortune when Lord Dannoth's servant led us, not to some nook of the scullery to gnaw crust amid the noise of pot-scraping, but to the lord's feast-hall, to share in the plenty among his own kindred and retainers, mingling among them as if St. Bridwen's name obliterated all distinction of rank.

Dazed as sleepwalkers, Ennes and I made our way to the purple-draped dais at the head of the hall to bow before our host, Lord Dannoth Kelgarran, a broad-shouldered man dressed in the colors of the holiday with a robe of grass-green and a close-fitting jacket of gold brocade, a crown of new leaves pressing down the iron-gray hair that still curled thickly down to his collar. I had expected him to look older; my father, sixty when he died, had been young when Dannoth was crowned.

His lady sat by his side, also decked out in the green and gold of approaching summer, a crown of flowers in her butter-blond hair. She looked young and fresh, but that is no rare thing in the wife of a prosperous man. They bid us welcome, and a liveried servant ushered us to seats at a huge table that was fast filling with people of every station: Lord Dannoth's own kin in silks, merchants in velvet caps, laborers in homespun, priests and priestesses of all four Great Ones wearing the garb of some dozen different orders.

The warmth and brightness of the feast-hall seemed to me to hold all the delights of the fabled womb of the world. I had been shivering ever since I woke, but here was a hearty fire; here were walls warm and festive with tapestries, red and gold; here were folk at ease around an oak table broad as the deck of a trading ship, laden with enough food to provision a journey to the world's end. The scents made me dizzy: thick stew steamed in wooden bowls, roast meats smoked on silver plates, and spiced wine raised its languid perfume from gilded flagons. And the sounds intoxicated me: the sound of laughter around the table, like a music I had half forgotten, heard long ago in a life I could scarcely call mine.

I spoke little, but listened to Ennes chatter with the merchant and scholar on his other side. He said he'd been sent from Kettra by the Order of St. Rann to guard the great trading road of northern Swevnalond. Now he was returning to his homeland, for with the Troubles in the North, no one went that way anymore. "Even if the traders came north again, what could I do for them? Guard them against ghosts, and wave my sword at apparitions? It's no place for a living man anymore," he said. "I believe the gods themselves have condemned it."

It was only later that I noticed the discrepancy in his story: earlier, he had as good as told me he was on a pilgrimage, like me. I had been startled by the habit of St. Rann; my father once employed a guard from that notorious band of Kettran warrior-priests, as strong as a blacksmith and about as scrupulous as an assassin. Ennes looked at once too slight and too innocent for the robes he wore. Now, looking back, I wonder if he was lying, wearing a dead man's habit and name to deter highwaymen and overawe chance acquaintances on the road home. Perhaps I was the innocent, to accept without question the face each passerby chose to wear. More likely I never had time to consider Ennes's story, for the last guest to arrive that evening put him clean out of my mind.

The meal had begun already when the carved oaken doors of the hall opened to the Lady Trenara. There was a little servant with her—not a child, I mean, but a woman shorter than many of the children about the table. The maidservant wore the bewildered expression of a simpleton in a face oddly lopsided, like an image in troubled water. As they passed the foot of the great table, she looked wildly about, stammering, "Beg of your kindness, please sir, some shelter, for my lady's sake, kind sir," to no one in particular, unable to tell who was the lord of the hall or whom she should ask. The lady placed a gentle hand on her shoulder, calming her confusion, and together they walked to the head of the hall to bow deeply before Lord Dannoth.

The lord smiled down from his oaken throne. "All travelers are welcome in St. Bridwen's name," he said. "What is your name, good gentlewoman?"

"I am the Lady Trenara of Larioneth. My family was scattered by the Troubles in the North."

"I'm Hwyn," the servant said, squinting up from the floor where she still knelt.

"Larioneth!" exclaimed Lord Dannoth Kelgarran. "I had not thought any still lived of that land's best blood. Is it true what they say—that even the dead are cast out of their graves and walk the earth?"

Trenara nodded gravely.

"I heard the King of Larioneth tore his own eyes out, ghost-ridden, years ago," Ennes muttered to the scholar.

Lord Kelgarran frowned. "These days I even fear for my own land. The Troubles are reaching farther and farther; as Larioneth is today, all Swevnalond may be tomorrow—gods defend us! A madness is sweeping down over the land. They say a rioting crowd in Helmstrang slew their Count and all his family; that the Crown Prince of Adelwic killed his own kin and himself. But enough of these forebodings. My home is yours for as long as you need it, noble cousin—for a cousin you must be at long remove, like all the house of Larioneth. Have a seat: my people will serve you, and you'll lack nothing."

"*I* serve Trenara," the little servant grumbled, and without waiting for the household people to set a place for them at table, began helping the lady out of her long cloak and traveling boots, unveiling a little more of the beauty that held every eye in the hall.

How shall I begin to describe Trenara? She was majestic. Her deep-dyed violet surcoat and indigo gown were a little worse for the journey, frayed at the cuffs and trodden on at the hem; but a little outward shabbiness could not trouble the serenity of her splendor. Her servant was sodden and bedraggled from the stormy night, but the Lady Trenara seemed not to have walked under the same rain. She was a vision, a dream, too perfect for this heavy world of mud and work and loss. Her knowing dark eyes were measureless as the star-filled ocean of the night sky, her smile as mysterious as the Hidden Goddess, her high forehead unmarred by a wrinkle of earthly care. Her glossy black hair was wet, but no less lovely for that, falling in loose curls over her perfect shoulder and breast. Tall and slim as a young tree, she might be a sylph, a spirit of the wood. But more than that, she seemed to me a spirit of pure air, for she moved with a fluid, effortless grace as though there were no weight of earth in her whole body.

They set a place for her—oh unmerited gift of the gods!—beside me. Ennes kept leaning over me to look at her, and I suppose I must have looked equally silly to other eyes, but she did not laugh at us.

"Have you had a long journey?" I asked, trying to draw her out.

"Ah, yes. Very long." She paused, black lashes drooping on her fair cheek, as though these words stirred some secret thought in her, before returning to the conversation. "Have you?"

"From the Abbey of St. Tarvi in Annelon to the Lake-Shrine of St. Fiern, and halfway back. Long enough, I think."

"Long enough," she sighed. She looked as though she'd have spoken more, but the servant Hwyn returned then with food for her and distracted us by waiting on Trenara with great energy and little direction, cutting meat on her plate, buttering bread, jostling me and her lady, arranging the food fussily on the plate. She rarely seemed to look at her work, and spilled a good deal. Trenara took it in good part, smiling her thanks, ignoring the grubby fingers on her meat and the crumbs in her servant's hair, waiting patiently till Hwyn had finished fussing before beginning her meal, as serene as a painted image on a temple wall. I was half surprised to see that she did eat, nibbling delicately at a pale half-moon of fine white bread.

"Why did you leave home?" Trenara asked me.

"You mean the monastery?" I asked, and she nodded. "It's not really home anymore," I said. "I've left the Order for life. I went to the Mirror of St. Fiern in hope of finding a new calling. Have you ever been to the Lake-Shrine?"

She shook her head.

"They say some have wept for joy at what they saw in the waters, and others laughed aloud. One merchant gave away his fortune because of a vision in St. Fiern's Mirror. A knight-at-arms cast his sword into the waters, never to fight again. Only last year a woman left her husband at the Mirror's bidding, and even the priests dared not call it sin. They say there that children have looked into the waters and walked away strangely grown; that the old and hardened have come away childlike."

Trenara's eyes were on me with a look of troubled knowledge. *She says nothing, but she knows something of this,* I thought. With a subtle nod of her head, she motioned for me to continue.

"I had heard all about the Mirror, or so I thought. I was prepared for anything but—"

At this I was cut off by a cry from Trenara and a shout from one of Lord Dannoth's young kinsmen, seated at her other side. Hwyn, reaching awkwardly past me to fill Trenara's wineglass, had upset a full pitcher of red wine over Trenara and the lordling.

"Stupid oaf!" The young lord slapped Hwyn's face with a beefy hand. The servant began to cry.

"Don't you touch her!" The lady sprang to her feet to confront him, and I jumped up too, without any clear idea of what I meant to do. The whelp stood a hand span taller than I, his shoulders broad as an ox yoke. But Lord Kelgarran spoke out before either of us could act: "Nephew, I will not tolerate brutality. You have no right to chastise any servant in *my* house: surely not a guest's servant, and least of all for an honest mishap. You can see the simpleton means no harm. Now beg pardon of the lady, and give place for her handmaid to sit at table. My own servants are enough for all my guests."

The lordling made a grudging apology and inched away from Trenara, leaving a little space at the table, but Hwyn, trembling and weeping, wedged herself between Trenara and me. Trenara watched anxiously until her servant was settled with a bowl of stew and a bit of bread. The witling hunched over the bowl, salting it liberally with tears, looking up furtively now and again as if to prevent anyone from stealing it. At last she stopped crying and dug in with one bony, clawlike hand. Trenara stroked Hwyn's ragged light hair and looked up at me, waiting for me to continue my story. Continue I did, but the lady seemed distracted by the events of the night, and made little response. Nor could I coax her to tell her own story. However I might hint or pry, she answered with a wistful smile and a bare word that gave nothing away.

The meal soon ended, and we guests were shown to sleeping quarters. Again, I was gratified at the lord's magnanimity: instead of being left to bed down on the floor of the room where we'd eaten, with our cloaks for pillows, Ennes and I were treated like cousins of the House of Kelgarran; we were given a real bedchamber to share. It was a snug room with a featherbed in a nest of brocaded curtains: just the thing for an unjustifiably cold spring night; and if I little relished sharing it with a stranger, it was better than sharing a thin pallet on the floor with three quarrelsome fellow-monks. A housekeeper led Trenara and Hwyn to a room in another wing amid the castle's maze of passageways. As she left the hall, Trenara turned once and gave me a look that sent blood rushing through me like a sudden spring thaw.

Sleep did not come easily. Though the bed was the first good one I'd lain in those past seven years, perhaps some old monkish guilt kept me from enjoying it. Or perhaps I was disturbed by feelings of a less ascetic cast. When I slept at last, I dreamed a woman's voice was calling me down the corridors of Kelgarran Hall. As I followed the voice, it seemed to change: now cold and commanding, now throaty, warm, enticing. Reaching its source at last I found not a woman but a caged bird, an enormous raven pent up cruelly in a sparrow-cage. "Help me!" she cried in her human voice. I reached out to open the cage, but the raven shrank back into an egg.

The dream dissolved then into my old, familiar nightmare, the bodies washing up on the shore, bloodless lips and lightless eyes seeming to curse me. I woke, as always, sick and shivering.

It was still night, but for me there was no question of sleeping. Beside me, Ennes was snoring thunderously, and the noise seemed to mock my own wakefulness. I got up, pulled on my cloak and boots against the chill of the night, and lit a candle from the embers of the fire. Shielding the flame with my hand, I padded out into the corridors of the castle as silently as I could manage, past a drunken guard who snored even louder than Ennes, into the silence of the sleeping castle.

My fingers, curved around the candle flame, cast weird shadows on the stones of the hall. If I'd hoped to dispel the visions of my dream, this was not the way to do it. I began chanting St. Tarvi's invocations of the Four Great Ones—intended to ward off evil spirits, not nightmares, but years of haunted nights had blurred the distinction in my mind. My candle flickered in a breeze sweeping down from a narrow, high window in the right branch of the hallway. The storm must have ended and the sky cleared, for moonlight streamed down through the window. It illuminated a small, bent figure walking without a candle away from me. I followed, my heart beating so hard that I think its pounding must have alerted her, for the servant Hwyn turned to face me, wide-eyed.

"I'm lost," she said, holding up the pitcher she'd been carrying. "I need to get water. I spilled what we had."

I had to smile to myself, that fancy had made me fear this figure in the shadows. "If water's what you need, you certainly are lost," I said. She wrinkled her forehead in dismay. "No matter," I said, "I'm sure we can find the scullery together."

She nodded and fell into step beside me. "What's your name, priest man?" she asked, tugging my cassock with her one free hand. In the candlelight I could see the stump of a severed finger as she drew her hand away again.

"My name's Jereth," I said, "and I'm no priest anymore."

She looked up at me so earnestly that I was sure she'd miss her step from inattention to the path before her. I noticed for the first time that her eyes were crossed; one lid habitually dragged half closed over an eye misaligned and probably useless. They were dark eyes, incongruous with her light hair, which shone almost white in the candlelight. She seemed to be made of the ill-assorted parts of various bodies, all stitched together with noticeable seams. She looked neither young nor old—probably about thirty, like me—but in some ways she seemed half child, half crone, not full-grown but as faded and worn as her colorless, threadbare sack of a garment. Along with the finger, a canine tooth was missing. Her misshapen face was so heavily scarred that there could be no question whether its deformity were natural: she had been ravaged by wounds, crushed and torn like a defeated warrior's shield. On her bare neck the candlelight revealed what was unmistakably a whip-welt. Was that another one on her cheek? I shuddered, and for the first time began to doubt if Hwyn's mistress were all she seemed.

"Have you been with Lady Trenara for long?" I probed awkwardly.

"Oh, pretty long," Hwyn said. She pointed at me, grinning. "You like my lady. I know."

"Pretty well," I said, making an effort to smile back.

We trudged on in silence a while until we came to the scullery. I helped Hwyn fill her pitcher—not quite full, remembering the spills at supper—and persuaded her to let me carry it as I guided her back to the room she shared with Trenara. It seemed improper for me to go with her all the way to their bedroom, so I took her to the end of that wing and pointed out the way. She took back her pitcher, flashed a snaggletoothed grin, and proceeded on in the dark, guiding herself with one hand on the wall as I retreated through the maze of corridors to my bed.

I dozed a while, tired by the night's wandering, but I don't think it was for long. There was a rumble of thunder and I woke quivering, every hair standing on end, not in fear but in a strange expectancy. I rose, and when I reached to steady myself against the wall I could have sworn that it, too, was trembling. All thought of sleep gone, I regained my clothes and my candle, and stepped out again, scarcely even noticing whether I left the door open or shut. Unsure what to look for, I took a random course through the corridors, straining my ears for any new sound. I did not go far before I saw the candle of another night walker approaching me. I continued toward the light until I could see a face clearly illuminated in the halo of light around the candle: the Lady Trenara.

"I'm looking for Hwyn," she said.

"What! Is she still lost?"

"I don't know," Trenara said.

It struck me as an odd response, so I explained myself: "I saw her earlier in the night. She said she was looking for water, but she was hopelessly lost—not far from here, in fact. I led her to the scullery, then most of the way back to your room. Didn't she return then?"

The lady shrugged.

"I can't believe she could get lost again! I pointed the way out to her; it was straight down the corridor. And that might have been hours ago. I've slept since then. How long has she been gone?"

"A long time." She fixed me with the same profound gaze that had fascinated me at dinner, but now it only puzzled me.

"I guess you must be used to this," I said.

"Oh, yes," she said in her refined, musical voice. "But I get frightened by myself. She won't like it that I came out to look. She told me to wait for her, when she was pouring the water on the floor."

"What?"

"She told me to wait for her. She won't like it that I came out here."

"No, after that. What was it you said she did?"

"She poured the water on the floor. Then she left," Trenara said, so calmly that I thought there must be some logic to the statement.

"Why did she do that?" I asked.

"I don't know. She didn't tell me. She told me to wait," said Trenara.

"She poured the water on the floor? You mean, on purpose?"

Trenara nodded serenely, and fixed me with that same gaze of measureless compassion. At that my sight finally cleared. A thousand pieces of a great puzzle suddenly turned in my mind and settled into a picture of such clarity that I felt I'd been a dunce not to see it earlier. Trenara's look of profound understanding changed in my mind to a fool's uncomprehending stare. Her serene, smooth brow was unclouded by thought. There had never been any sense, I realized, in anything she had said to me—only what I had read into her eyes. And if Trenara were a fool, then Hwyn could not be one. I remembered how Hwyn waited on Trenara hand and foot, cutting her meat for her, unlacing her boots for her; and inwardly, I cursed myself for the biggest fool of the lot.

"Trenara," I said, "can you wait here for me? I'm going to look for Hwyn." I left her on a bench in the corridor, and tore off down the passageway Hwyn had taken when I first saw her on her pretended errand for water.

2

THE RAVEN'S EGG

After a long while, the passageway branched, offering a path to the right and a stairway straight ahead. The right turn, I thought, seemed unlikely: it probably led back to the same rooms Hwyn must have passed on the way from her quarters. So I began spiraling slowly up the staircase, until a faint noise below me made me change my course. Hwyn was coming up from the underground chambers, panting with either exertion or fear. I emerged onto the landing to confront her just as she reached it. Her pitcher was still at her hip, and she still had no candle.

"You find your way well in the dark," I said.

She smiled, and said nothing.

"You're no idiot," I said.

"Thank you," said Hwyn, in a tone I had not heard before, a laugh lingering at the edge of her voice.

"You're no faithful family servant, either."

"Never said I was," she said.

"Why the masquerade?"

"Oh, it's not much of a masquerade. Trenara *is* a lady, as far as I know. At least, I didn't teach her those high-table manners, as you can well believe. And when I said I serve her, it was no more than the truth. I do everything for her, though no one compels me."

"You're using her for cover," I pressed.

"Oh, you righteous soul!" she spat back. "Using Trenara? If you could care for her better, please, take her. I don't need lords' hospitality, and in my own class I can make my way easier without her. Why, where do you think she'd be if I left her? How do you think she got her living before she met me, this unworldly beauty?"

With this, she tried to push past me and leave. Daunted by her fury, and sensible of my own audacity in accusing her, I almost let her go; but just as she might have escaped me, something impelled me to reach out and touch her arm. She jumped as if stung.

"Hwyn," I said, "I'm sorry. I had no right to say such a thing."

She turned back toward me, but did not stand too close. I continued, "All the same, it seems very strange that a woman who is no idiot could be so badly lost twice in one night."

"It takes no idiot to be lost in the dark, in a strange house."

"And to search for water up and down the house only to pour it out on the floor? Come, Hwyn. What are you roaming the halls for, really?"

"Maybe I'm meeting a lover. Why should you care? I might as well ask why you're out walking the halls tonight. It seems to me you're up and about quite a bit, for a weary stranger who had to beg lodging. What honest purpose could *you* have, eh?"

"Me? I had a strange dream—"

"Well, so did I," Hwyn said. She pushed past me again and went on down the hallway; I followed, keeping at arm's length but determined not to let her get away without some answers. Abruptly she turned to me again and said, "Did your dream, by any chance, include a raven's egg?"

"Holy saints!" I seized her by the shoulder. "How do you know what I dreamed?"

But even as the words left my mouth, Hwyn started at some sound I could not hear, and motioned me to be still. As soon as I stopped speaking I could hear it too: a distant scream.

"It's Trenara!" shrieked Hwyn, and broke into a run. The pitcher dropped to the floor and shattered. I took off after her, stumbling on shards of pottery, wondering where we were heading and what I would do when we got there. My candle went out, and I was left to navigate by sound. The screams continued, and I heard them more clearly as I neared the place, even above the noise of Hwyn's cursing.

I lost my bearings in the dark, and so was surprised to find myself not far from my own room—not far from where I left Trenara on the bench, either. As Hwyn began pounding on one of the doors, I tripped over a body in the hall. Lifting it in my arms, I found that it was Ennes, dead, bleeding from the chest. Poor boy—had he fallen in Trenara's defense?

Meanwhile, Trenara was sobbing behind the door that Hwyn pounded with both fists. "Let me in!" Hwyn shouted. "You've got the wrong person. *I* stole the Eye of Night!"

She had to repeat herself a few times before anyone responded—perhaps the noise of her pounding drowned out her words. When the door finally opened, I followed her in to find Trenara bound to a chair, and a guardsman in the Kelgarran livery threatening her with a hot poker. Presiding over this scene was our gracious host, Lord Dannoth Kelgarran.

"Let her go!" Hwyn cried. "Can't you see she knows nothing? I'm the one you want." The lord seized her roughly, twisting her arm behind her, and called the man with the poker to bind her. I threw myself at Lord Dannoth with all my force, and managed to make him drop Hwyn as he and I fell to the floor in a heap. With more luck than skill, I kicked away the blade he tried to draw. But the advantage of surprise gone, I was not strong enough. Lord Dannoth might be more than twice my age, but his reflexes were sharp as a youth's, the force of his arm like the grip of fear. The lord recovered himself, pinned me to the ground, and grasped me by the throat, so that I was sure the end had come.

"Don't harm him," Hwyn said behind him. I saw him stiffen, and though I didn't quite put it together then, I knew later that she'd been holding a knife at his back. The man with the poker hovered, but would not strike for fear she'd kill his lord.

"Do as I say," said Hwyn, "or you'll never see the Eye of Night again. Only I know its hiding place. These two had nothing to do with the theft: let them go. I won't show you the stone until I'm sure they're free. Jereth, will you guide Trenara out to safety? I can deal with this alone."

But Dannoth Kelgarran would have none of it. "Drop your blade, or one of your friends will get a poker through the skull."

"If you kill either of my friends, you'll never find the Eye of Night. I might surrender it for their lives, but not for my own. Do you think I treasure my life so highly, marred as I am? I'd die before I'd give the Eye of Night to a man who'd killed my friends; then the secret would die with me."

I wondered whether she meant these passionate words; wondered, too, when I had become one of her "friends." Most pressingly, I wondered if Lord Dannoth believed her threat.

"Bring me the Eye of Night," said the lord, "and I will release them; but not before I see it."

"You must follow me to its hiding place," countered Hwyn. "My friends must be with me and able to walk. Otherwise, I can only assume that you mean to kill us all after regaining the Eye. In that case, it would be better for us to die now for the Eye of

Night than to die later for nothing. If I'm to surrender the Eye, all three of us must be free to escape."

Lord Dannoth's knee was on my chest, and his tremendous hands half gagged me. I began to expect that, regardless of the outcome, I'd suffocate by the time they finished arguing, never to know in what battle I had perished.

"Agreed," said Dannoth. "But first you must drop your blade. I can't have you killing me the moment I get the Eye back."

"Untie Trenara first," said Hwyn.

The lord gave the order, and after a pause, I heard Hwyn's blade clatter to the floor. In one quick movement, the lord took his hand from my neck and scooped up the knife. He moved back a step. "Get up," he said to me. I got up. He waved the dagger at me: "Turn around." I turned, and he pinned my right arm neatly behind my back, using his other hand to hold the knife poised at my throat. The other man held Trenara at sword's point. He motioned to her to pick up a candle to light our way, but she did not understand; at last he thrust it into her hands, spilling hot tallow on her fingers, so that she cried out and I almost got myself stabbed moving instinctively to help her. "Enough. Let's go," said Lord Kelgarran. We filed out of the room, first Hwyn, arms clasped nervously in front of herself; then Lord Kelgarran, holding me in front of him; then the other man with the whimpering Trenara.

We pushed on in silence a while. Hwyn began guiding herself with one hand along the wall, as she had done the first time I met her in the corridor. In the terrible quiet, I could hear the soft scrape of her fingernails, searching. "Hurry," said the lord.

"It's close," Hwyn said, "very close." We reached an intersection of two corridors. "Yes, let me see." She groped along the wall with one hand as though she were counting the bricks to find her stash, but I thought I saw her other hand slip something out of her pocket: a luminous white stone the size of a robin's egg. She turned to Lord Dannoth Kelgarran: "Here—catch!"

She tossed the stone high in the air, above Lord Dannoth's head. He had to release me to catch it, lest it fall to the stone floor. As soon as I felt his grip slacken I sprang away. I turned to confront the man who still held Trenara.

"Release her," I said in the most menacing tone I could manage. To my surprise, he dropped his sword and let the lady go, a look of dread on his face. But he was not looking at me. I turned and followed his gaze to Lord Dannoth Kelgarran.

The lord held the white stone but looked as though he would gladly drop it. Vapors rose from the gem and formed themselves into the semblance of men: tall, broad-shouldered swordsmen still bearing what must have been their death wounds. Slashed throats and torn chests oozed spectral blood.

Lord Kelgarran shrieked and wailed, holding the stone as far from his body as he could, trying vainly to cast it aside. By the time he managed to release his grip, I smelled burnt flesh. He sank to the floor whimpering as seven ghostly warriors glowered at him from all sides.

He had dropped the dagger, and Hwyn lost no time in snatching it up. She dared not touch the white stone, but hovered over it lest anyone else should take it. Trenara ran to her side. I meant to join them, but I felt somehow transfixed, fascinated by the seven phantoms. All I could do was to stare at them, at their flashing swords and burning eyes. They did not look at me, however: all seven grim faces turned toward Lord Dannoth Kelgarran.

At last the tallest and grimmest of them spoke: "For thirty years we have been your prisoners, Dannoth. Now you are ours." The specter pointed a long finger at his prey, and Lord Kelgarran winced and moaned from some unseen wound. He seemed to shrivel with age even as I watched him. "You will suffer as we suffered for your profit."

"Mercy! I did not understand—" the lord protested.

"You understood enough," the ghost said. "You knew you held us bound. You used us for your power. You kept us from the wanderings by which we must earn our peace at last. You understood all this, even if you did not know the full measure of our pain. Now your stronghold shall fall shattered, and you with it."

"Lord Conor Kelgarran," I addressed the ghost, "what do you mean to do? Surely you will not sweep away your liberator along with your jailer."

Despite my fear, it was gratifying to see the look of astonishment on the ghost's face. "You know me."

"And all your brothers: Tellion, Mirron, Delvon, Tor, Tabon, and Garrith of Kelgarran." With each name I pointed to one of the phantoms. "The Seven Slaughtered Brothers, brought low by the treachery of his ancestor," I pointed to Lord Dannoth, "some two centuries ago."

"Ah, Tarvon priest, the Gift of Naming has not failed you," the ghost said. "Ask what you will of me: I am bound to answer."

"I'm not a priest now," I muttered compulsively.

"What's a vow more or less? You have the gifts of one," Conor said. "Surely you don't mean to give up the right it gives you?"

I shook my head, and met the ghost's challenging eyes. "What is that stone, and what power does it have over you?"

"You disappoint me, to ask a spirit what any of these mortals could no doubt answer. How were you caught up in this struggle, if you knew not the Eye of Night, the Sky-Raven's Egg? Nothing within the wheel of the world is beyond its power. But it is no tool for the hands of mortals, as our kinsman will learn to his grief." Conor pointed with his sword at the cowering Dannoth. "This wretch, true descendent of the cousin who slew us, heir of the land usurped from us, has imprisoned our spirits for thirty years by power of the Eye of Night enclosed in a magic circle. Our spirit-force upheld his power and his prosperity. Although the Eye of Night could not have stayed in his power forever, it might have continued much longer, at terrible cost to us and to the world. But someone has taken it out of the Circle of Power. That was not you, Tarvon priest, for you did not even know the Eye when you saw it. Who took it?"

"I did," Hwyn spoke forth.

"She speaks the truth," I said.

The seven phantoms turned and bowed to her. "We owe our freedom to you; you shall have a gift in return. Take the Eye of Night now. We will not hinder you," Conor said.

"Your pardon, sirs, but that I would have done with or without your permission," Hwyn said as she slipped the white gem back into her pocket. "It is no more yours to give than it was his," she pointed at Dannoth, "to keep. It is not mine either, but I take it only to set it free."

Conor scowled, but another of the phantoms spoke up: "Well spoken, wise maiden," said silver-eyed Mirron of Kelgarran, the sole diplomat in a family of warriors. "We would not give you what is not ours. Take it by right. You know well what must be done with it."

Conor spoke again. "The Eye of Night is not the gift I offer. Choose what you would ask of us: our power is great tonight, in the first rush of freedom. One boon, too, we grant to the Tarvon Priest who restored our names to us."

"We need safe passage away from here," I said when Conor turned to me. "These two women and I will have enemies enough in Kelgarran when this night's deeds are known. Will you help us escape?"

"That is a small thing to ask," said Conor. "And you, my liberator? What will you have?"

"Mercy for the people of this house," Hwyn said, her voice shaking. "Most of them must be innocent of your torment: Dannoth kept his secret well. But even for the guilty, I ask some share of clemency. It becomes you well, Lord Conor: you were always known as a merciful lord."

"*That* is a hard request," the phantom said. "Think well: would you have me spare the man who nearly killed you and your friends?"

"I don't ask you to release him *armed*. But I owe him at least some gentleness in return for two favors: he stopped his kinsman from beating me, and invited me to sit at his table. Honor binds me to remember these things. For that kindness, be lenient with him."

"What good can be said of a man who is kind in the great hall and cruel in the secret chamber?"

"For your own sake, then—for you will come nearer to your long-denied peace by mercy than by vengeance," Hwyn persisted.

"For your sake, rather," Conor said, "I will be lenient. I cannot forestall his doom: he has meddled with the Eye of Night, and must fall as deep as the height to which he raised himself."

Dannoth looked up from the floor, and it seemed that he had already aged twenty years since the ghosts had appeared. He cast a pleading look on Conor with bleary, sunken eyes.

"Nevertheless," Conor continued, "I will not prolong his pain, for your sake alone, my friend." He bowed again to Hwyn. "Because you have not sought power over us, as you might have done, you will be well provided. Go to the shore of Lake Garran. Under a clump of willows you will find a boat prepared with all you need. Now make haste."

We fled down the corridor to the front gate. As we ran, the

walls of the house began to shake and a wind seemed to rise within its halls. When we reached the gate, the guards had abandoned their posts. The very stones of the stronghold seemed to be howling in pain, the seven towers shaking in fear. We ran through the drowsing streets of the city, spiraling down toward the lakeside, watching as one by one shutters opened and bleary-eyed citizens gaped at the towers of Kelgarran Hall in horror. When I looked back once I saw people pouring out of the castle gates in a disordered mob.

Hwyn grabbed me by the arm and pulled me on with her. Only when we reached the shelter of the willows at the lakeside did she herself look back. On the heights, the spires of Kelgarran Hall loomed somber in the dawning light. But even as we watched, one of its towers began to totter and crumble until it fell, scattering the escapees farther from their former home. The wind lifted their cries to us. I looked at Hwyn, and saw a shiver run through her at the sound.

"Let's go," she said, brushing away tears with her sleeve. "Someone may think of connecting the night's guests with the night's trouble."

I nodded, and we turned to inspect the boat that awaited us as Conor had promised: a clinker-built boat with a broad, flat bottom, a single mast, and one square sail. I waded into the reedy water and lifted Trenara aboard, then little Hwyn. Then, up to my thighs in Lake Garran, I examined the boat from stem to stern before climbing aboard. Despite what I had seen of the boat, its rocking comforted me, as though some part of me felt that for years the world had been all too still under my feet. I was raised on the seaside, and coming aboard was like coming home.

"Look—there's traveling packs with food and water-skins—even a tinderbox—everything we need for the journey, as he promised," Hwyn gloated.

"Everything but a rudder," I said. "That Conor's an old joker. Has he at least given us an oar to steer with?"

Hwyn gave me a look as blank as Trenara's. There was no oar.

As I examined the boat further to make up my mind how to proceed, Hwyn fussed over the burn Dannoth's henchman had left on Trenara's hand, cooling it with wet leaves. Then, without warning, the boat unfurled its own sail, cast off, and lurched away from shore, steered by no mortal hand.

"Did you—?" Hwyn began.

"I haven't done a thing," I said.

"The ghost's at the helm, then," she said. "Nothing for us to do but sit back and try to enjoy it." So we did sit back—it was a good-sized boat for three—and we tried to keep our heads as the craft skimmed along at an alarming speed, churning the placid lake-water to spume.

"He's taking us northward. That doesn't bother you?" I said.

"Should it?"

"It bothers plenty of people these days."

"You among them?" she asked.

"Not me. What have I got to lose?" I said. She scrutinized my face a moment with that sort of desperate squint that marks weak eyes, but said nothing. For a while we only watched the boat's rough progress and the sun's struggle over the horizon.

"Look," Hwyn said after a while, pointing at Trenara with a grin. The lady was sleeping in the bow, undisturbed by the spray that kissed her dark hair. "Only Trenara could fall asleep at a time like this."

"Maybe she's the wisest of us," I said. "Lake Garran goes a long way north; even at this pace, we have a long journey ahead of us, with none of the sailor's work to do ourselves. What can we do but sleep?"

"Talk," said Hwyn. "I so rarely have anyone to talk to. How did you know the seven ghosts? That was a fine piece of work."

"The Gift of Naming was something I learned in the Tarvon Order. Or rather, something that comes to you in the Order. I never thought it would stay with me when I left for good.

"Unfortunately," I said, "it only seems useful for disembodied spirits—not fellow travelers. I misnamed you most foully, and judged you most unjustly."

"Don't speak of it. You risked your life for us! That was magnificent, you know, when you threw yourself at Lord Dannoth."

"I thought it was rather inept," I said, my face hot.

"But don't you see, that's the glory of it. A man who knows nothing of fighting hurls himself unarmed at a belted knight. That's courage," she laughed, looking at me through the lashes of her right eye. The left one was permanently turned inward, no doubt blind as a stone.

"You took some fool's chances yourself," I said. "Talking back to the phantom warrior. And tossing the Eye of Night to your enemy—or did you know, then, that the phantoms would come out of it?"

"I gambled," she said. "At least I knew it wouldn't break if it fell—which Dannoth seems not to have known, the way he dove for it."

"What will you do with this Eye, now that you have it?"

"Take it where it wants to go," Hwyn said, looking away from me.

"You don't want to tell me, do you? Well, that's all right. We all have our secrets. But you must tell me something, at least, about yourself. For instance, is Hwyn your real name? It isn't, is it?"

She laughed again. "Are you sure your gift doesn't apply to the living? When I passed through the town of Gwilth, a man spotted me from a distance and ran toward me, waving his arms and shouting, 'Hwyn! Is it really you?' But of course, once he came within a few yards of me he said, 'You're not Hwyn.' He sounded so downcast, and it had been so good to see him running toward me, calling and waving, that I said, 'I'll be Hwyn if you want me to.' We went to a tavern then, laughing and telling stories, and got as full of ale as St. Bridwen's Well. I hoped he might come with me, but we parted company the next day. I kept the name. I wonder who it was that he could have been so glad to see, that looked like me." She bit a fingernail, studied it, then continued.

"Instead of him, I got Trenara as a companion," Hwyn said. "She had me fooled, all right, just as she fooled you. I sat half the night in a pub in Torun, telling her my troubles as she gave me that understanding smile. I thought she was such a good listener. It took hours for me to realize that she was just listening to the sound of my voice."

I didn't blame her. Hwyn's voice, I had begun to notice, was as beautiful as her face was ugly, when she wasn't distorting her speech to play the fool. It had a fluid, warm tone, like the large end-blown flute my little brother used to play, which had washed ashore sodden and useless with his body seven years before.

"I stayed in Torun a while. I had work there, at decent wages," Hwyn went on. "I knew the ways of the town, and it didn't shock me to learn what a pretty girl like Trenara did to get by. What did make me lose control one day was to see her bawd clout her for losing money. I told him to take his hands off her; he laughed, and challenged me to stop him. And I . . . I let things get out of hand.

"I'm talking too much," Hwyn broke off suddenly, turning away from me. "It's been so long since I've had anyone to talk to. So much silence—it eats away at the soul." She looked at me sidelong, furtively, then turned away again. "Sometimes I think the day I was born, a sword-blade was set between me and humankind to keep me apart, alone. And now I am on a journey that will take me even further from any hope of companionship, so that I sometimes think I will die with all my words trapped unspoken inside me like unquiet ghosts. And sometimes I wonder if it even matters. It's not as if anyone would mourn for me. I am scarcely human, after all."

I could tell by her voice that she was weeping again, though she still faced away from me. I laid a hand on her shoulder. I was unused to such gestures, and it felt awkward to me, like a priest's ritual blessing where a friend's touch is needed. Still, her hunched shoulders seemed to relax under my hand, and at last she spoke again. "You see I cry easily," she said. "That part of the idiot act was real."

"It's *not* idiotic," I said almost fiercely. "As for me—I couldn't even cry when my family drowned."

She turned to me, startled. "How did that happen?"

"We were merchants, returning from a trading voyage to Iskarron, when the ship sank. I was the only survivor."

"I'm sorry," she said. "How can you sit so calmly on this boat? It must speak death to you!"

I shrugged. "I was born on shipboard. I grew up on ships and boats and shipyards. They are birth, life, and death to me—and even I am not so far gone as to fear all three.

"But it was different seven years ago. I turned my back on the sea, gave away everything I had inherited, and joined the Tarvon Order to serve the Upright God."

"That's one of the celibate orders? Poverty, chastity, and whatnot?" Hwyn said with a sardonic smile.

"And obedience—you left the worst for last," I said. "Luckily in my order final vows are taken after seven years, and I stayed for six. I began to wonder whether holiness lay as close to order as I'd been taught."

"I offer you chaos," Hwyn said, "and the chance for new life." She slipped the Eye of Night into my hand.

The lustrous white stone looked cool, but felt warm, and seemed to stir ever so slightly in my hand. "It feels alive!" I gasped.

"It is alive. It is an egg, the Sky-Raven's Egg."

"When will it hatch?" I asked.

"I don't know. Not today. Perhaps this year; perhaps many years in the future. Lord Dannoth, and others before him, kept the life within it from growing by imprisoning it in magic circles. I am trying to set it free."

"By bringing it into the North, into the Troubles," I guessed. "Isn't that your destination?"

"Yes—and Trenara's as well, I think. I've tried more than once to leave her in a safe place—with an order of penitent ladies, or a couple whose only daughter had died—but she followed me each time," Hwyn spoke softly, looking anxiously at Trenara to make sure she remained asleep. "She slows me down, and she's about as much company as a statue, but until I reach Larioneth I may be stuck with her. I've come to think she has a quest of her own. Maybe she'll find her lost wits in the north country."

"And you—what will you find? What drives you into the North?" I pressed.

"Dreams have chased me there," she said. "These past seven years I've been driven by dreams—as you have." She paused, and I thought she was closing up again, but soon she spoke:

"What's really happening in the North? Trouble, they say. Chaos. Rulers cast from their thrones; tremors in the earth and sky; graves thrown open, and the dead walking about.

"Maybe I can say what's happening there. Night is falling; nothing worse," she declared, her voice level but tense with feeling. "Night has a bad name on the earth; we fear the dark as children, and scarcely put away that fear when we come of age. But what would become of the world without night?" Hwyn demanded of me.

"No rest for the weary laborer," I said, "and no cool nights to relieve the summer's heat."

"Very true," she said, "yet there is more: no private time for wife and husband, no sheltering darkness for lovers. And graver: every flowering plant and seed-bearing tree on the earth times its seasons of flower and fruit by the changing cycle of night and day. Without night there can be no flowers, no fruits, no grains.

Picture the earth barren, hungry, and hot under an endless, weary day.

"Whatever hatches from this egg," Hwyn said, "will be a child of Night. It may be terrible; I may be cursed for releasing it. I fear it as a child fears the dark. But I know this much: it cannot be held back. Like the night, it is necessary. Dannoth Kelgarran and other learned fools have been trying to hold back the nightfall—to hold back the Trouble. And how can I blame them? Who wouldn't want to hold back pain?"

"That's what I was doing in the Tarvon Order," I said, "holding back the pain of my family's deaths, praying when I couldn't weep, learning to discern strange spirits but unable to lay my own ghosts to rest. Of course, it was doomed to failure."

"Then maybe you can understand," Hwyn said, "why I'm running headlong into the Troubles; why I have to release the hatchling from the Raven's Egg, even though I fear it. Why I'll consent to be a midwife to the Night.

"Childbirth, after all, is a fearful trouble. Women suffer pain in childbirth that would undo strong men. Women often die in childbirth, or labor in vain to bring forth a dead child. But what if some magician had the power to hold back this deadly pain, to keep the troublesome child trapped in the womb? Both mother and child would die, and not alone, but the human race with them. No less with the Troubles in the North. The mighty cast down from their pride, the dead cast up from their graves: are these the pangs of death, or of birth?"

"I believe you," I said. "I don't know how you know these things, but they ring true. And I, too, have dreamed of the Raven's Egg; it means something to me. Let me go with you into the North. I may be able to help you."

"You will, I'm sure." Hwyn smiled. "Now that you've stopped suspecting me, I think I couldn't ask for a better companion."

"If it makes any difference," I said, "I mistrusted Trenara for a while as well. When I noticed your scars I began to suspect her of mistreating you. But I trusted Dannoth, and would have sung his praises all the way back to Annelon if I hadn't happened to wake in the night and see his secrets unmasked. Was there a person I didn't misjudge?"

"Why do you trust me now?" Hwyn asked, only half smiling.

"I saw you risk the Eye of Night, and your life, to save

Trenara. I heard you ask mercy for your enemy. What room is left for doubting you?"

"Then you really will rush off with us into the darkness? We may never return alive," she said.

"Where else should I go?" I said. "I'm finished with the Order. My family is dead. My patrimony is long gone. Any friends I ever had lost patience with me either when I joined the Order or when I left it. What door did I leave open for myself but death? You at least have offered me life—with chaos. And I'm determined not to part company until I've guessed your name—which must be a name of power, because you've told me nearly everything else."

She gestured me to silence with one finger poised over my lips, almost but not quite touching. "Hush. I've certainly told you too much; I've been trusting you in spite of myself. Yes, come with me, by all means—please come. Who knows but the gods may have sent you to Kelgarran Hall for just that purpose?"

I laughed dryly. "If they care which way I go, or whether I live or die, they have an odd way of showing it. They told me nothing at the Mirror of St. Fiern, you know. Or didn't you hear that part of my story?"

"I did," Hwyn said. "You were too drunk on Trenara's presence to notice how my ears almost stood up like a cat's when you spoke of the Mirror. I hung on every word.

"You see, I used to live in St. Fiern's Town. Don't think you were the only pilgrim ever to walk away disappointed. We townspeople have seen them all: the ones who slink away downcast, the ones who tell transparent lies about wonders they claim to have seen. We approach the Mirror more cautiously, less hopefully than you pilgrims do; in fact, the townspeople rarely seek its wisdom. It's not only the disappointments. We've seen those changed souls who rise laughing or weeping from the lakeside, the ones whose stories make the Lake-Shrine famous. And they frighten us.

"After all, merchants don't want to give up their wealth at a vision's command. Think what it took to make you give away your goods: was theirs, too, a vision of death that made wealth seem contemptible? And a warrior who casts his sword into the waters to live peaceably—how will he earn his bread? For us, the Mirror is as full of dread as of wonder. But after some years I, too, summoned the courage to approach the pool.

"I am half blind," said Hwyn, "and I feared I might see nothing. So when I bent over the pool and no clear vision appeared, I lost patience and cast myself in.

"Under the murky water there was no light, but a thousand voices. I stayed listening until I nearly drowned. Some pilgrim pulled me out by the hair, senseless and all but dead. I had such dreams." She shook her head and looked at me searchingly with her right eye, the left one as always impenetrable. "People pumped water out of my lungs and demanded what I had seen, but I couldn't find the words to tell them. Ever since then I've had what they call the 'second sight,' the dreams that have turned my path to the North—though what I *saw,* with my eyes, was no more than the blank blackness under the water. No more than you saw."

I drew in a slow breath, as though I had discovered breathing for the first time. "You are the Mirror of St. Fiern to me," I said. "You have turned my darkness into vision. I will follow you to the world's end."

"To the world's beginning," Hwyn corrected me, as the ghostly craft carried us into the unknown.

3

WHITE CATS
AND GOLDEN CHAINS

The ghost-pilot sailed us northward for a day and a night as we lived off the dried meat and biscuits in the packs and wondered where we would reach land. There were fishing-nets in the boat, and I trailed them over the side experimentally, without much hope: fishing needs stillness, and we never stopped. On the morning of the second day, I could see the roofs of a city before us to the northeast, set afire by the rising sun.

"It's a walled city—see there?" I pointed into the brightness.

Hwyn shook her head. "I can't see that far."

"Sorry!"

"No need to be squeamish about it," she said. "It's a fact of my life. It will be good to have someone to be eyes for me, now and then. Is it a big city?"

"Not as big as Kelgarran, I think. It's still a long way from here, so it's hard to tell. I think it must be Sebrin. I'll know when I see the shape of the harbor."

"You've been there?"

"No," I said. "But I can recall seeing a map of these parts. The Pengar River feeds Lake Garran at Sebrin; the harbor is in an inlet below the falls. We won't be able to go farther north by boat from here, but we may sell the boat and buy provisions for an overland journey. That is, if we can find some buyer willing to overlook the lack of a rudder."

But the ghost had other ideas. With the town in sight, the boat becalmed itself in the shallows under another clump of willows as perversely as it had unfurled its own sail. As I fiddled with the sheets to see whether I could take control of the craft myself, the boat abruptly vanished under us, leaving us to fish out all our worldly possessions: the packs, the tin cups, the fishing-nets, and the water-skins. These, at least, showed no sign of dissolving into air: Conor had left us with something after all. "Well," I said, "we won't be selling any boat."

"We can get a few days' labor in town," Hwyn said. "We'll re-provision ourselves, then find out the lay of the land for the next stage of the journey."

"What sort of day-labor will we find?" I said. "I've been relying on the Key of the Tarvon Order to bring me to shelter—in monasteries, temples, and pious households. But I can't bring two women into a house of celibate brothers."

Hwyn laughed. "With a few stolen clothes, I could pose as a boy—but Trenara, never."

"And to tell you the truth, I'm not sure I could pass as a priest anymore," I said, "or that I could stomach it. My tonsure's grown out, my beard's grown back, my habit's in ruins, and to restore it all would seem a sort of hypocrisy."

"But honesty has its cost," said Hwyn. "What kind of work can you do?"

"That's the terrible question," I said. "There's a Tarvon house in Sebrin, so I'll never find work as a scribe. I kept my father's account ledgers, but no merchant could be mad enough to entrust that task to a stranger. I've done almost everything there is to do on a ship or a shipyard—except cooking, the only thing likely to be of use here. Even building boats will be different here than at the seashore. I've never farmed, never hunted, never herded, never been in service. What about you? What work have you done?"

"None of the things you've done and most of the ones you haven't. Can you sing?" Hwyn said.

"Sing? Of course. Any priest can sing. What earthly use is that?"

"The Feast of the Bright Goddess isn't far away," she said. "If we can scrape by till then hauling loads or scrubbing pots, we might get a hatful of silver singing in the streets."

"Are you a minstrel, then?"

"Among other things," she said. "It's not a steady living by itself, but when the great feasts roll around, there's no pleasanter way to earn your bread. Not just in coin, either: before Trenara came with me, I tricked my way into strongholds as a player, not a servant—though to tell the truth, the rich treat the two much the same."

"Does it get you into walled cities, too?" I said, gesturing at the formidable gate looming up ahead of us with the falcon crest of the Counts of Sebrin painted over it and a guard in purple livery holding a spear across the entryway.

"Sometimes," Hwyn said. "More often on the holiday itself than before it. But if we can find work on one of the farms outside the walls, at least we will not be penniless when we reach the wall. They'll let you in sooner if they think you have money to spend; two coins to jingle against each other are sometimes enough."

Neither of us had so much as a farthing, so we set about looking for day-labor. The first few farmhouses were discouraging: in one fly-infested kitchen, the franklin's wife told us they had no shortage of hands; in a neater, more prosperous-looking farmhouse, they said that idiots were all right with proper supervision, but they'd sooner throw fresh cream to the hogs than hire a lazy priest. Outside a third farmhouse, the landowner gave Trenara such a leer that Hwyn, without any pretense of civility, grabbed us both by the arm and hurried us back to the road.

"If you steer clear of everyone that leers at Trenara, the only work you'll find will be in a house of holy sisters," I said, "and maybe not there, either."

"If that were all that bothered me, I'd resign myself," Hwyn said. "But that man—that man had a smell of blood about him.

Truesight is a chancy thing, so it may mean much or little, but that man looked at her as prey, and I will not lead her across his threshold."

I nodded, out of my depth, and we walked on, the stone walls of Sebrin growing larger before us.

Just outside the walls stood a slate-roofed three-story house of sturdy fieldstone, strangely out of keeping with its surroundings: a townsman's house out of town. There were no sprawling grainfields about it, but a neat kitchen-garden, a small chicken shed, a cow-byre, and an ample stable. On the gray stone wall hung a painted sign of a plump, contented white cat. So far it looked promising enough, but I had to ask myself why such a prosperous-looking inn was outside the town wall when the best-heeled customers would want to be in the center, close to the market or the count's hall.

The answer was immediately apparent when I stepped in the door. A languid girl in a green Iskarrian robe and several ropes of pearls stretched across a divan, her yellow hair disordered. At the sight of me, she started up indignantly: "What, already? It's early for trade."

A black-haired woman in purple Magyan silks, a gaudy belt about her hips, grinned wolfishly as the innkeeper brought her a breakfast of beer and cheese. "A holy brother goes about his devotions early, Aude, don't you know?" Taking a swallow of beer, she stared at me over the rim of her tankard. "You'll have to wait till after breakfast, Tarvon." Even in the dim light, I could see the emeralds dangling from her ears in the Iskarrian fashion, the bright chips of crystal glued to each fingernail in the manner of the Western Islanders.

"It's the innkeeper we're looking for," said Hwyn, emerging from behind me. "With the festival at hand, a few extra hands at sweeping and scrubbing won't come amiss, will they?"

"Hwyn," I said, grabbing her shoulder as forcefully as she had seized my elbow at our last stop. Was it possible she didn't know what all this exotic finery meant? Even if she could not see, could she not guess what lay behind the second woman's taunt?

The innkeeper, undismayed, looked us over like merchandise. "Penny apiece plus table-leavings for today, noon to midnight. We'll talk about tomorrow when I see how you work."

"Excuse me, sir," I said, "but I need to talk this over with my—" I stumbled on what to call Hwyn and Trenara: *sisters* would not be believed, and anything else would sound, in that place, too much like a smirking euphemism for something else.

"We'll let you know," Hwyn told the innkeeper sweetly, then went outside without any further arm-twisting, Trenara following silently.

"Look, Hwyn," I said when the thick oaken door closed solidly behind me, "I may not have truesight, but I haven't been away from the ports long enough to have forgotten what sort of trade those ladies must be expecting."

"I know," said Hwyn calmly.

"I'm not trying to be monkish about this," I said, "but if you're worried about Trenara—"

"Trenara's in no danger here," Hwyn said, "and this time I'm not speaking from truesight, but from plain experience. Those ladies are courtesans, not slaves of some bawd. Did you notice how the innkeeper waited on them? How he didn't speak till they'd spoken? They may be prostitutes, but they sell themselves for gold and rent rooms with silver, and they'll quit their costly quarters sooner than let a stranger be sold in this inn to undercut their trade. No whoremaster will cross this threshold while they lodge here, and if Trenara were capable of going into the trade on her own, they'd prevent it. They'll protect her better than I can."

"Oh," was all I could say, after opening and shutting my mouth a couple of times like a fish.

To my surprise, Hwyn didn't laugh at me. She reached out tentatively, almost fearfully, with one spidery hand, placing it on my arm only when she could see that I wasn't retreating from her. "This really isn't your world, is it?" she said. "Not even in your seafaring days."

"It's all one world," I said. "I have to learn to live in it. I haven't given enough thought to how I shall earn my keep without my father's trading ships, without the Order."

"It doesn't have to be here," Hwyn said. "I didn't choose this place as some sort of cruel test. It's a long fall from priest in a monastery to drudge in a brothel, and if you can't bear it—"

That touched off some small flare of pride in me. "I can bear it," I said. "What do you think? Are his terms fair?"

"It's not what I might have hoped," Hwyn said, "but it may be the best we can get, for now. They won't be quite desperate till the festival's on, and you can see by our reception in the farmsteads that we don't cut a promising figure: I'm too small, Trenara's too fine, and you're at once too clerical and not clerical enough, if you follow my line of thought."

"Yes," I said, "I think you're right. Too priestly for farm work and not enough to look trustworthy."

"We'll have to explain about Trenara," Hwyn said, "and talk one of the courtesans into guarding her. If there's no problem with that, I think we should take the penny and hope for better another day. What do you say?"

My heart sat low in my stomach, but I had already spoken, and would not take it back. And so in the heat of the afternoon, we were scrubbing last night's beer-stains off the sticky public-room floor while Trenara watched dreamily, as though this were a feat of skill and daring scarcely glimpsed in the world. Blond Aude and black-haired Grana had vanished upstairs to their scented and cushioned rooms, so at least there was none to taunt me as I wrung out the sodden sleeves of my cassock on the gummy floor and tried for the hundredth time to roll them out of the way. I could not help noticing that little Hwyn had covered twice the length of floor I had covered, and that the sleeves of her colorless shift stayed rolled up. There's an art to everything, I thought. It's bound to get better with practice.

By nightfall, we'd helped the more regular drudges sweep out the perfumed boudoirs of the inn's eight courtesans, wash linens stiff and musky with old pleasures, air out little-used rooms in the attic for the festival travelers, dust the great bedsteads, spread fresh coverlets, fill pallets with fresh straw for common-room sleepers, shovel the muck from the stable and spread it in the kitchen-garden, and fill the kitchen's huge cauldrons with water from a well that seemed too far away. The first time I saw Hwyn laboring under a yoke of buckets that looked like they must be heavier than herself, I hurried to her aid, cursing the innkeeper under my breath for sending her on such an errand. I was ashamed to find that I could walk no faster under them than she, and spilled more trying to prove myself stronger. Either she was made of stronger stuff than I had recognized, or years of copying old scriptures had made me too soft for the world. In furious whispers I cursed the Order and myself for making me unfit for the life I must lead.

After a few trips with the yoke, I was ready to drop, and the first customers had scarcely begun pounding mugs on the table for refills of the inn's watery excuse for beer. The innkeeper, Morvath, manned the tap himself, no doubt from the misguided impression that his drudges were dying to steal the sickly yellow fluid he sold as beer. His daughter and another maid wore themselves out running to and fro with full mugs and empty mugs, but there was still enough fetching and carrying left to exhaust me and Hwyn. I toted so many trenchers of chicken stew that I stopped being hungry long before I found the chance to take any of the promised table-leavings. Trenara fared better: Grana, not wanting another dark-haired beauty on display, had paid the scullery maid to keep her out of sight and content, which she did by feeding her tidbits and filling her lap with a cat as sleek and spoiled as the one painted on the inn's sign. Whenever my work brought me through the scullery, I could see the two of them, Trenara and the cat, tranquil amid the commotion of the inn's nightly work.

Once I stole a moment there to lean on the wall and catch my breath, but the sight of Hwyn lugging another heavy bucket of water shamed me back to work, feet throbbing, back aching, head pounding. I had worked this hard before—there were no idle hands on my father's trading ships—but that had been when the wind and weather demanded it, when every ounce of strength was needed to keep the ocean beneath us instead of above us. To throw this sort of killing effort into sating the greed of old tradesmen for overpriced stew, execrable beer, and expensively perfumed womanhood seemed disproportionate, ludicrous, insane. And at every turn I was chided: I folded the sheets wrong, left muddy footprints on the floor I'd washed, splashed too much water, spilled the precious beer, didn't come fast enough when someone shouted.

A voice inside my head mocked, *This is the life you've chosen?*

"*Monk!*" shouted Morvath. "Take that trencher to those soldiers by the door. Quick, now, or I'll have a war on my hands."

I followed his pointing finger to the kitchen door, where the cook held out a wooden trencher of stew, anxious to get it off her hands and get back to her pots. I took it and ran off toward the knot of soldiers who sat at ease, boots up on the carved oak chairs, cloaks thrown back to reveal the gleaming hilts at their hips. Ahead of me, Hwyn carried a pitcher of beer in the same direction. A sound broke through the clamor: a chord struck on the harp, sweet as daylight, out of place in the tumult.

Hwyn stopped in midstride and turned to stare at the harpist by the hearth, her face upraised, lips parted, like a child given an unexpected gift. I can still see her like that in my mind's eye; strange, for in the moment, I did not see her soon enough. Before I'd quite grasped the notion that she'd stopped in front of me, one of my longer strides sent me careening into her, the trencher of stew flying over her head to crash on the floor near the soldiers' table while I myself landed hard, catching my knee painfully on the buckler one of the soldiers had left on the floor. I let loose the long catalog of obscenities I'd learned in twenty-three years on ships and shipyards, not just in plain Swevnian but Iskarrian, Kettran, High Magyan, Demotic Magyan, and that trade jargon that the Western Islanders use to keep filthy foreigners from sullying their sacred language. The whole room was laughing—whether at my pratfall or at the spectacle of a priest in the Tarvon cassock letting loose a strain of full-throated profanity, I'm not sure. After a while, I began helplessly laughing with them, hoping all the while that I hadn't lost us our jobs.

Hwyn had somehow managed to keep most of the beer unspilled; I wasn't sure whether to credit this to experience or preternatural ability. She deposited it on the soldiers' table before joining me on the floor to clean up the mess. "I'm sorry," she said, "that was all my fault."

"Not all," I said. "I should have noticed you sooner." In reality, once the shock of the fall was past, I was too relieved to realize I wasn't the only fallible one to hold it against her.

"You, Half-Pint," shouted the cook to Hwyn, "let the priest clean up. Take the gentlemen another trencher." She scurried off, leaving me to mop up the mess of broth and boiled greens and meat scraps. And so I was on my knees with a wet rag and a brush when one of the inn's guests nearly fell over me.

"Tarvons!" he spat, catching himself on the counter.

"Excuse me?" I said.

"What have I done to deserve to be surrounded by Tarvons?" the man growled. "They're in Ectirion, filling my firstborn's head with ruinous notions. They're in Sebrin. They're in every decent trading town, even in the very counting-houses—keeping trade honest, they say! Pah! And even when I get to this town too late and the gate is locked, so I have to put up in a whorehouse, for the gods' love, fit to put ideas in the other boy's head, what do I find but a Tarvon cleaning the public-room floor?"

"Sorry," I said, and went on slopping up the mess.

"Sent my boys to the Tarvon school. Thought it would give them some mathematics, some languages, some knowledge that's worth something. Now the oldest, the heir, says he wants to shut himself up in a monastery," the man grumbled on.

"Hmm," I said, not knowing how else to respond.

"What in the Bright Goddess's bum-hole are you doing here?" he said.

"I left the Order," I said. "I have to do *something* for a living."

"This might be informative for my son to see," the man mused. He was a stout, solid-looking man in a rich robe of deep green serge and a close-laced black jacket, the kind with reinforced pockets too tough for a pickpocket's knife. The leather purse that hung from his belt had the same sort of trick catch my father's had. All in all, though I had never seen him before, I felt I knew him well enough: the same sort of prosperous merchant my father had dealt with. He was looking me over the way my father might have eyed some dusty wares that he suspected of having real rubies under the grime. "Was that you I heard cursing in Magyan?" he said.

"Yes," I said. "Would you mind, sir?" I pointed at his black leather boot—costly Kettran leatherwork—which was on top of a smashed leek.

"Hmm?" He moved the foot absently, then said in High Magyan, with the stilted cadence of one who has learned at school and not from a native, "Do you know the tongue thoroughly, or only to curse in?"

I replied in the same language, "I had a Magyan tutor for three years."

"And Kettran?" he asked in that language.

"Kettran is easy," I said. It is an insolent tongue as well, at least as spoken in the trading circles I remembered; the term I used for *easy* was scatological. It did not deter the merchant.

"You had a family that went to some expense to educate you," he said, switching back to his school-taught Magyan. "But perhaps they're not too eager to take you back?"

"They are dead," I told him in the same language.

"You might become a tutor yourself," said the merchant, "instead of a drudge in a whorehouse. I might be willing to offer a good living to an able tutor who's not in the Order anymore."

"What makes you think I'm looking for a position?" I said, looking up at him with a smile of bemused innocence that might have done Hwyn proud.

The merchant laughed heartily. "If you think of the reason, look for me in the Street of the Weavers, and I'll see what you can teach. Turl of Ectirion, son of Tarrow, dealer in cloth and clothing." He stared at me a while longer. "What's your name, ex-Tarvon?"

"Jereth," I said unwillingly.

"Jereth of where? Son of whom?" he pried.

"Of the White Cat, son of another cat," I said, switching back to Kettran; it is easy to be insolent in Kettran.

Then the innkeeper bawled "Monk!" again, and I ran to fetch and carry for another eternity, till the last of the drunken soldiers, insensible on the table, was dragged to the common room to sleep it off. I would have loved to lie down next to them, but our pay did not include shelter, and besides, there was work still to be done. By the time we'd helped the scullery maid clean the last of the crockery, I was too numb with fatigue to hear Hwyn's haggling with the innkeeper over the price of our next day's labor. I would have missed my share of the table-leavings but that Hwyn insisted I eat.

"You have to live on this," she said in an undertone. "If we spend the money for food for now, we'll have none for the journey." She stuffed her pockets with broken ends of bread and cheese, and picked at the burnt crust of stew at the bottom of a pot.

Wearied into submission, I ate a little of the cold and clammy leavings before resigning the stew-pot to the scullion's eager grasp. Clearly the poverty of the monastery had not prepared me for the real thing, for my gorge rose at the thought of eating any more. If I were hungry the next day, I thought dejectedly, it would be instructive for me. I scrubbed my last pot and let myself be led like a sleepwalker, like helpless Trenara, out of the inn.

"We ought to have picked ourselves a sleeping spot by day," Hwyn said. "I might have thought of it before we took work."

"Maybe we could have found a place to hide the packs, too," I said, weary of carrying anything and chafing under the small burden. "We could find one tomorrow."

"So close to the city, it's hard to find a place no one else would come upon," Hwyn said.

"Well, don't you know some sort of—I mean—" I groped about for a word, wondering if it were impolite to say *magic* or *sorcery* to a mage's face. "What you did in Kelgarran Hall surely took some knowledge of hidden things."

"I'm not really a mage," Hwyn said softly. "What little I know of such things is too dangerous for everyday use. I'm afraid we're stuck carrying everything we have. There were some shrubs by the lakeshore; maybe there we can find a bit of cover to sleep under, some shred of privacy."

"I hope you can find it in the dark; I have no idea where we are," I said. "I can't believe you're still so awake. I could fall asleep standing up."

"Well, it's better if you drop off as soon as we make camp," Hwyn said. "We'll need to be up early tomorrow, if we're to have any chance to try singing before we go back to work. After all, we don't want to be doing *this* for the whole festival."

"Certainly not," I said.

"But one thing I wanted to ask you before we sleep—what was that inn-guest on about, talking to you in some other language?"

"Amused to see a Tarvon priest cleaning a brothel," I said. "His son wants to join the Order; I think he was half ready to take me on as tutor, as a sort of living proof of the Order's hollowness."

"Well," Hwyn said, "it would be better work than this."

"But not day-labor," I pointed out.

"How's this for a campsite?" Hwyn said, stooping to touch the earth.

"Good," I said, without bothering to look or feel around me. I sank to the ground, managing by sheer luck not to be tangled in the branches that sheltered us from the wind off the lake. "Gods! If I hadn't given away my father's property, we could scorn to stay in the White Cat, much less work there."

"Jereth," laughed Hwyn, "if you had kept your father's property, you wouldn't have met me at all. Now get some sleep."

It was strange to wake in the broken light of the copse at dawn and see them beside me: Trenara still sleeping, her long dark curls fallen across her face like a veil; Hwyn sitting cross-legged at a little distance, half turned away, worrying at something with her hands, her face furrowed in concentration. "Sky-Raven's Bones!" she cursed softly. I wondered whether her cursing had awakened me.

I rose, but she did not notice me till I moved silently around in front of her to see what absorbed her concentration. "Good morning," I said.

She startled at my voice, then looked up at me, a smile stretching across her crooked face, as though my company were an unexpected pleasure. "Ah, Jereth, you're awake." She'd removed the left sleeve from her shift and held it in her lap, knotting and unknotting it.

"What's that you're working on?" I said.

"I'm trying to make a sort of pocket I can carry about my neck, out of sight," she said.

"For the Eye of Night?" I said softly.

She nodded. "Why keep it in a side-pocket where any pick-pocket could make off with it, taking it for a hen's egg? And besides," she said, dropping her eyes a little, "I think it belongs over my heart. It seems to want that."

"Like an infant," I mused, dredging up memories from far back in childhood: the nursemaid holding one of the twins and teaching me to hold the other.

"Is it?" Hwyn said. "I've never held one."

"Never?" I said. "Didn't you have any brothers or sisters, then?"

"Not really," she said, staring at her hands. She picked up the sleeve. "I'm trying to find a way of turning this into a pocket. I could cut here, and make the rest into strips to bind it around my neck. But I don't want to make a mistake, and have to rip the other sleeve to redo it."

As things stood, she had one arm bare; the shift, a knife-belt, and a worn pair of soft boots seemed to be all her clothing. Luckily the weather had taken a decided turn toward summer since St. Bridwen's Day, or the breeze from the lakeshore would have struck her cruelly. Even so, she could ill afford to lose any more clothing. "Do you mind if I look at it?" I said, putting out my hand.

Reluctantly, she handed me the sleeve. I turned it inside-out and noted with satisfaction that it was two pieces of cloth stitched together, not one closed on itself. The elbow was darned very untidily, making an unsightly weal of wool, but the whole looked sturdy enough to serve. "All right," I said, "the most basic job will be easy. We can take the stitches out from shoulder to elbow. Then you have two straps at the top, from the two sides of the sleeve. You have a needle and thread?"

"I have a needle in my knife-belt," she said. "There's the thread I took out at the shoulder."

"We'll need more than that," I said. "Let's see. Your hair's longer than mine; could you spare a few?" It was thin, ragged hair, falling unevenly over her shoulders, but mine, newly grown out of tonsure, could not have yielded a piece long enough to thread a needle with. She took out her knife, cut a few hairs near her scalp, and handed them to me.

"Anyway," I said, "once we have the thread it's an easy job. Close the two ends at the top, close the wrist for the bottom of the pocket, reinforce the sides so the rest of the thread doesn't unravel. As soon as we can get a patch about this big," I gestured a double hand span, "sew it into the bottom, across the wrist-opening, to guard against a split seam. It'll be a good enough pouch for the time being, and we won't cut any cloth, so we can still make the sleeve back into a sleeve if you want."

"You keep saying *we*," Hwyn said.

"I'll do it myself, if you like," I said.

"What, you can sew?"

"Of course. Every sailor can sew," I said. "Months at sea, and my mother the only woman in a crew of forty when she came at all, we'd be in a fix if we waited for her to mend every split sail."

"Why didn't you tell me that when we were looking for work?" Hwyn said.

"I didn't think it was unusual. I thought everyone could do it."

"I'm not very good at it," Hwyn grimaced.

"Give me the needle," I said. She handed it over, a little sliver of bone. "That's a pitifully small one."

"If you're used to working in sailcloth, it is," Hwyn said. "For old worn homespun, believe me, this will do."

I threaded it with hair, made a knot, and began.

"How quickly your fingers go," Hwyn said. "Maybe I could have gotten us better jobs than the inn. What else can you do that you didn't think worth mentioning? What else do sailors do? Fishing?"

"Yes," I said, "but we've got no boat to fish in, since Conor took back his loan, and the area within wading distance of shore will be overfished, so close to a city."

"Fixing things, maybe?"

"I can fix a boat," I said. "I suppose I could learn to fix other things." I came to the end of the hair, and threaded on another. "I'll have to redo this with real thread when we can get some. Hair may get brittle."

"Will the Eye of Night be safe?"

I shrugged. "It'll be inside your shift. Tie your belt tightly, so if the pouch breaks, the stone will stay inside. Let's see how long this needs to be." I went behind her to hold the makeshift pouch around her neck, under her straw-colored hair. I could feel the delicate down on the back of her neck, and it felt strange to touch a woman like that, after all those cloistered years. Hwyn seemed to feel the same awkwardness; I could feel the sinews in her neck tighten with apprehension.

"Perhaps you'd better show me," I said, and let her take the sleeve. "Fold the ends to the right length, and I'll sew them to fit."

She held it, adjusting the ends till the pouch fell between her small breasts, then handed it back to me with the ends pinched to the length she wanted. "It looks like you're almost done. This would have taken me all day, you know. Thank you."

"I'm glad I can do something competently," I said, "besides making the drunks laugh with my pratfalls, and cursing in Magyan."

"Well, I was the one that tripped you," Hwyn said. "I probably lost us an extra farthing from today's pay; it's nearer the festival, so I should have been able to haggle the price up. I have half a mind not to go back. We might find something better by noontime."

"I thought we were going to try singing together," I said. "If it's not going to work out, we may as well find out now: no sense paying festival prices for food if we're not profiting. And if it will work out, we'll need practice before the festival."

"Yes," said Hwyn, "and I'll need to teach you some songs not fit for celibates."

"Ha! I grew up at sea, remember?" I said. "Maybe I can teach you some. Do you know 'The Captain and the Mermaid'?"

"No," Hwyn said. "You start, and I'll join in when I start to pick it up."

So I launched into the old sailors' drinking-song, beginning with the refrain:

*"She may be only half a wench
Half a fish and half a wench
But half a wench is better than none."*

Then came the tale of the captain's long frustration, months at sea without a woman in sight, with the surprising and inventive catalog of things he tries to use as substitutes before seeing the mermaid. She lures him into the water, of course, and then leaves him plugging a leak in the bottom of his ship, where he must stay till he reaches port.

I made my way through most of the verses blushing furiously. Hwyn had been right about me: even in my seafaring days there had been a little of the monk about me, and in my eagerness to prove myself not wholly naive I had chosen a song that I'd always found a little embarrassing. Furthermore, it was a song I'd never heard sung in the company of a woman. I had to shut my eyes to keep myself unperturbed by Hwyn's laughter—and then, when another voice joined mine on the last chorus but one, I had to open them to see who in the World-Wheel was singing with me, because I could scarcely believe it was Hwyn.

It was, and I fell silent in wonder to hear that voice coming from that body. To the eye, she was a fragile thing, like the tiny bone needle she'd given me to work with, pinched and meager in every particular: limp, lusterless pale hair; bony fingers; misshapen bones standing out sharply under the windburned skin of her face. All the strength, all the richness, all the luxuriance, all the life her form seemed deprived of was abundant in her voice. Had I heard that voice in the fabled Palace of Earthly Delights, I would have cared for nothing else there. Had I heard it from the sea, like the mermaid's voice in the song, I would have leapt in without hesitation.

She finished the refrain, stopped, and opened her eyes. "You left off singing," she said.

"I don't think I'm fit to sing with you," I said.

"Nonsense," she said, turning scarlet. "Besides, if you don't finish the song, I'll never find out what happened to the captain."

"What do you think?" I said. "You're the mermaid, to sing your hearers overboard. No wonder you went into a dream at a few notes of music, there in the tavern last night. It's your element, the air you breathe. What could draw you away from it?"

She smiled at the memory. "I do go into the song and out of the world, don't I?"

"My brother was like that, too," I said, "the younger one, Saeverth. Everywhere we traveled, he would pick up a different sort of flute, and by the next voyage he'd have mastered it. If only he could be here; to hear the two of you together would be the world's wonder!"

Hwyn, knowing that the brother I spoke of was dead, reached out shyly to put a hand over mine. "I'm sorry," she said. "Still, he was not the only musician in your family. I have not heard a false or faltering note in all the song. Once we've learned to harmonize, I think we'll take the festival by storm. Finish the song, now, and begin again so I can join you."

So I gathered my courage and my breath, closed my eyes, and sang the end of the tale. When I began again, I was struck with how much of the song Hwyn had already learned on one hearing. By the time Trenara woke, she was beginning to test out counterpoints to the refrain, and I was beginning to like "The Captain and the Mermaid" better than I ever had at sea.

We paused to share last night's leavings of bread with Trenara, washed down with water from the skins Conor had given us, then hurried back to our singing, all thought of seeking new day-labor gone. Even when noon brought us back to the White Cat, we remained in the music, scrubbing floors to "The Captain and the Mermaid," washing sheets to a sheep-shearing song Hwyn had taught me that morning, scouring pots to "The Drunken Sailor and the Wooden Lady." The courtesans who'd been piqued by the thought of a Tarvon in their inn were greatly amused by the mermaid song and began requesting it over again. After the eleventh repetition, the innkeeper bawled, "Sing something else, for the gods' sakes!"

Hwyn considered, then began tossing out verses two by two about a white cat. At first I puzzled over whether I might have heard the song anywhere, but when the white cat had gobbled up a mermaid, thinking it just another fish, I realized that it was all a joke on the name of the inn that Hwyn was making up as she went along: a couplet, then a pause to think, then another couplet, hands busy all the while with the scrubbing brush. I can't remember the words now—it was a song of the moment only, never repeated—but I remember well the glint in her eye and the smile of complete abandon stretching across her angular face as each new couplet was born in her brain. The white cat climbed the Tree of the Moon and sharpened her claws on the moon. She could not get down until she fell with the nuts in autumn. At Aude's urging, she tired out all the tomcats in Sebrin. There was much more, some of it clever, some of it dreadful, but I had never before heard anyone spin verses out of nothing while polishing tankards; it was all I could do to keep my eyes on my job as I listened.

At the end of our third night at the White Cat, when Morvath again offered the same terms for the next day's work, Hwyn shook her head. "Penny and a half each. The festival's three nights away, and work will be plentiful. Besides, we've given you music as well as labor."

"I didn't ask for the music," the innkeeper said. "Only one kind of pleasure my customers come for. Same terms or nothing."

"The providers of the other sort of pleasure seemed to be enjoying the music," Hwyn said. "They won't be pleased when we go."

"They'll forget," Morvath predicted implacably.

"Fine," said Hwyn. "We'll find better work than this. Trenara, Jereth, come." We gathered up our things to go. As we reached the threshold, Hwyn said over her shoulder, "The White Cat song could be altered into a satire, you know."

The next morning, after very little sleep, we were up with the birds to steal some time for singing together before setting out to look for more work.

"Do you know 'The Female Cabin Boy'?" I said.

"Another seagoing song? No," said Hwyn. But when I'd sung the first verse and refrain, she cried, "It's 'The Lady Knight-at-Arms'!" She sang a verse to show me; the tune was the same, and the exploits of the disguised heroine seemed to run along parallel paths.

"All right," I laughed. "You do know this one. Let me finish it the way I know it, and then hear yours. We'll see which we want to use at the festival." The question was not resolved before we had to break camp and enter the walls of Sebrin to seek work inside.

Following the plan Hwyn and I had discussed, I led the way to the massive gate, chanting a simple prayer to the Rising God as I went. Hwyn followed with bowed head, carrying our packs, my cloak over her head like a hood, Trenara at her arm.

A sentry at the door, dressed in the purple livery of the Count of Sebrin, demanded our business.

"These two penitents and I have been on a long pilgrimage," I said. "Can we find any harbor in this town?"

The sentry peered suspiciously at Hwyn and Trenara, but found the two women busy attending to a couple of the beggars who lingered near the gate. Hwyn gave each of them one of the twelve farthings she'd earned in three days' toil at the White Cat. The sentry noted this with a grunt and said, "They're not worth your pity, good sister. But let's see. The Tarvon Monastery will welcome you, of course, good brother. It's a little way down the East Way, near the Lane of the Potters: you can't miss it. These pious ladies will have to see whether the Order of St. Rignid by the northern gate can put them up, or lodge at an inn. They'll all be full by festival-time, so hurry."

"Thank you, good sir. I should escort these women first. By the north gate, you said?"

"Yes, in the weavers' district," said the sentry. "Good day."

"May the Rising God bless your vigil," I said, and we passed through the gate, holding our breaths and our air of piety until we were well away from him.

Sebrin looked unremarkable, a town like many others I had known: whitewashed timber houses of two and three stories with thatched roofs and kitchen-gardens, some boasting little cherry-orchards bloody with ripening fruit and alive with bees. A few women and children bent over the kitchen-gardens in nothing but their shifts, sleeves rolled up to their elbows, feet bare, prepared for what promised to be a hot day.

Yesterday's table-leavings seemed a distant memory, and we eyed the fallen cherries hungrily, but even these were already claimed: hogs scavenged under the trees, or dogs guarded the orchards. When we reached a corner onto a side lane, the houses were smaller and shabbier, the garden-plots narrower, the children in them skinnier. There was no fruit on the ground, for the children had eaten it all.

We moved toward the center of the city, stopping at the odd shop to ask if any day-labor were wanted. A tailor, plying her trade under the sign of the shears, said frostily that she had use for apprentices, not day-laborers. Nonetheless, shaking her head at Hwyn's incomplete garment, she called us back when we had almost shut the door. "I have an extra bit of woolen, not enough for much, but it might make a sleeve for you, little one. Can you attach it yourself?"

"I can," I said, then made bold to add, "if I have thread."

She gave us a little skein of thread and a scrap of woolen cloth unevenly dyed red, then swept us out the door as though she might regret her generosity. I folded it all together carefully and stashed it in my pack for later.

"It's red," Hwyn said admiringly. "This dress was blue once, but the color's all weathered out. Well, it's not a job, but it's something."

"I'll piece it together later," I said. "Shall we try another shop, or an inn?"

In the end, we settled for more inn-labor, at scarcely better wages than Morvath had paid us. The innkeepers were sadly unimpressed with my languages, for few foreigners came to Swevnalond in the shadow of the Troubles. However, one was piqued when Hwyn walked in singing her satire of the White Cat—the beds were its furballs, the beer was its urine, the food was the mice it caught. Harwel, the proprietor of the Golden Chain, offered us six farthings a day to work, amuse the guests, and mock the competition, agreeing to let Trenara spoil the inn's elderly cat in the kitchen while we worked, so long as she stayed out of the way.

The Golden Chain harbored no obvious courtesans, but a number of mice kept apartments deep in its foundations, venturing out at times to sample the fare. We sounded off to set them scurrying, refilling sleeping-pallets to "The Mowing of the Hay," polishing the decorative shields that hung round the public room to "The Battle of Hamford," scrubbing floors to "The Long Gray Tides." The other drudges would laugh at us as we faltered through a song for the first time, making me all the more flustered and prone to mistakes in both the song and the task at hand. But as we went on, I become more used to both the laughter and the work, more able to become caught up in the song while my hands worked without me. Once, as I swept out the kitchen hearth, I was startled out of the song we were singing by the applause of the cook and scullion. I looked up to see Hwyn juggling onions from the pile she'd been set to chopping, the motions of her hands keeping perfect time with the song.

This time, as the supper-guests trickled in, the innkeeper urged us to keep up the flood of song as we moved among the tables with trenchers of roast fowl and pitchers of honey-colored beer. Hwyn managed it well enough; but I soon lost the thread of the song, my attention caught up in shuttling from table to table, remembering who wanted five courses and who just wanted beer, avoiding the outstretched feet, knapsacks, and dogs that thrust out treacherously into my path. She was the better part of the duet, anyway; I overheard an old man look up from his beer to sigh, "Gods, she must have traded her face to a sorcerer for that voice. And it may have been worth it."

"Enjoy it while you can," said his companion. "It may be the best you get all holiday. All the clever folk go south, these days."

"Small wonder," said another. "There's war in Brunfells, insurrection in Branwith, and all sorts of madness—stirred up by ghosts, they say. The whole North is moontouched."

"More than that," said the second man. "The very land is going mad. They say in Lastweard, it was summer all year."

"I'd like summer all year," said the first man. "Here, it's cold too long."

"You don't know what you're wishing for," the second man said. "The streams dried up; the grain parched; the apples rotted on the tree; the flies and ants and crawling things teemed beyond all imagining. I heard this from a man that fled. The town is empty now—as all the North will be empty before long, if things don't change."

They were not the only ones speaking of the Troubles. As I dished out the first of five courses, mushroom soup, to a couple of merchants in a table half hidden by a painted screen, I heard one of them say, "I heard that in Branwith, the mob rules now; the royal family all butchered, the prince's head on a pike at the city gate. He was no more gentle with his foes while he lived—but all the same, it's a shocking thing to hear of, the fall of a household honored since the time of the High King."

It was none of my business, but after six years copying chronicles in the monastery, I could not resist saying, "The High King is a myth. There was never one king over all Swevnalond."

"What do you mean, a myth?" said the merchant, a wiry, sharp-faced man with an aquiline nose and gray hair. "Everyone knows the High King fought the Kettran invasion."

"The Chronicle of St. Hiugod dates from the time of the invasion, and has been copied and continued faithfully ever since," I said. "If there had been a High King, St. Hiugod would surely have mentioned him. He did not. It was then as now, a king or count or lord for every petty town in Swevnalond, all fighting each other when they weren't fighting the Kettrans. The High King was a tale spread by the House of Larioneth to rally opposition to the Kettrans under their own banner."

The hawk-nosed merchant gave me a skeptical look. His companion, whose face had been hidden from me, turned toward me then to exclaim, "You again!" It was Turl of Ectirion, the same merchant who'd bent my ear in the last inn. "Jereth of the White Cat. What are you doing here?"

"I swear I'm not following you," I said. "The pay's better here."

"So's the food," grunted Turl. Turning to one of the skinny boys who sat beside him, he said, "See, Torrin, this man once thought joining the Tarvon Order was a good plan, and now he'd rather scrub inn floors than go back."

The boy to whom these remarks seemed directed, a sallow-faced, black-haired lad of twelve or thirteen, evaded his father's gaze, solemn black eyes wandering off at an angle to stare at nothing, unable to resist but refusing to acquiesce with even a glance. That little trick of the eyes sent a shudder of recognition through me. Had I looked like that eighteen years ago? "Well," I said, "each man must find his own calling—or his own name, as St. Tarvi said." At these words, the boy's scorched-black eyes fixed on me till I thought they might burn a hole in me. The smaller boy, meanwhile, stared intently into his soup, as if it were the only thing in the room not likely to resent his attention.

"A man's name must be found with those that named him," Turl said. "He's my boy. I named him."

I said in the Old Tongue, "We think we name our children, but the gods have been there before us." Neither father nor son showed any sign of comprehension. "Excuse me, sirs," I added in Swevnian, "I hear the cook calling me to fetch the next course."

When I returned to the half-curtained table with fish baked in cabbage leaves, the dark-eyed boy blurted out, "Was that the Old Tongue?"

"Don't speak till you're spoken to, Torrin," chided Turl.

"Yes, lad: Golden Age dialect, just before the Kettran invasion," I said.

"How many languages do you know?" Turl said, as curious as his son.

I set down the last plate of fish to count on my fingers. "Aside from Swevnian, six, counting High and Demotic Magyan separately."

"Why would you want to know demotic?" said Turl. "Isn't that the jargon of the filthy mob?"

"Yes, but even the cleanest-fingered Magyans will use it among themselves before your face to deceive you if they think you don't know it," I said.

"When were you in Magya?" said Turl.

"Many times," I said. "I was born halfway there."

The boy who'd been staring into his dish, looked up, hazel eyes round as soup bowls. "What, on the mountaintop? Or in the sea?"

"Tadric!" his father warned.

But I laughed. "In the sea, of course—with a ship's hull under me." With that I had to scurry off to fetch a drink for one of the locals.

When time came to bring the merchants the main course of roasted quail, I noticed the dark-eyed boy, Torrin, staring fixedly at me as I set each dish down. *Don't speak till spoken to,* I thought. "Young sir," I said, "why do you stare? Do you require anything else?"

He turned red. "No, I—I wanted to know what you were saying. In the Old Tongue. I haven't had very much schooling."

"It was a saying of St. Elfrith of Larioneth: We think we name our children, but the gods have been there before us."

"But what does that mean, really?" the boy persisted.

Gods, I thought, he's a Tarvon from the cradle: always another question, another meaning to be found. "If you find the answer, tell it to me," I said, avoiding his father's eyes as I rushed away to refill the tankards of the locals by the door for what seemed the hundredth time. When I returned with the fourth and fifth courses, cheese and seed-cake, Turl was in deep discussion of the price of brocaded indigo silk, and posed me no more questions. Dark-eyed Torrin gave me about half a smile, furtive as a prisoner's knock on the wall.

At the frayed end of the night, Hwyn and I took our six farthings each and our table-leavings—better this time than at the White Cat. Hwyn particularly pursued the sweet seed-cakes, pocketing the smallest fragments, even from the floor, as though they were gold for the taking. Then we collected Trenara and crept off to sleep in the temple courts, three among dozens of paupers and transients in the one part of the city where we could not be turned away.

I woke to the sound of the Dawn Chant to the Rising God, for though this was a lunar temple, consecrated to the Turning God and the Hidden Goddess, every priest must at least nod to all the Four Great Ones who surround the world. My old order had been devoted to the Rising or Upright God, and the song emanating from the temple was a familiar touchstone among so many unfamiliar things. Almost without realizing it I began singing with the unseen priests—and though the chant was a prayer for the blessings of wakefulness, to join my soft voice to the chorus was almost to lose myself in a dream that nothing had changed, that I would rise from this unaccustomed bed to prayers in the temple, bread and water in the refectory, and a long day's work in the scriptorium, copying the Chronicle of St. Hiugod.

Then Hwyn's voice softly joined mine, like a stream of bright water cutting through the languid heat of the morning. I faltered and almost lost the thread of the melody, but then found the fit of it, my deep voice moving under her high one like the shadow under a bird in flight. Trenara opened her eyes and watched us solemnly. Around us, our fellow paupers were waking.

"What do they think—" one blustered.

"Shh," hissed his companion. "Listen."

Caught up in the lift and swoop of the melody, when the singing in the temple ceased, I continued through the longer version I'd learned in the monastery. Hwyn did not follow, and the strangers around us began chattering and bustling about their business. Hwyn, nonetheless, listened in silence, her good eye fixed on me. When I had finished, she said, "That was beautiful. I didn't know there were so many verses. Will you teach them to me?"

"I thought we were working on songs not fit for celibates," I laughed.

"Oh, not for the festival. I just want to know it," she said. "Is it something from the monastery?"

"Yes," I said, "but it's not forbidden to lay singers, if that's what you mean. Certainly I could teach you. But I doubt it will play as well in the Golden Chain as 'The Lady Knight-at-Arms.'" Being asked about the monastery reminded me of Turl and Torrin. "By the way," I said, "did you notice who was at the screened table last night at supper? That merchant I met at the White Cat. He keeps asking me questions."

"What sort of questions?" Hwyn said. "Do you think he suspects—"

"Nothing of that sort," I reassured hurriedly. "Questions about me, my education, what languages I know. I don't think he even noticed y— noticed we were together."

She caught the slip, smiling sardonically. "Sometimes there are advantages to being beneath notice."

"Well, if he didn't notice you last night, he has no ear for music," I said.

"Is he still trying to hire you to tutor his son?"

"More like toying with the idea. He'd be mad to suggest it seriously, with nothing to tell him what I'd been or what I was running from but a patched clerical cassock."

"All the same," Hwyn said, squinting at me as if to see into me, "he'd be right if he did. He could trust you. And you'd be good at it."

It seemed a strange thing to say, unless she were having second thoughts about our partnership. Small wonder if she were; I could not deny that she bore the greater weight of both work and song. "Well," I said uncomfortably, "that may be so, but he'll never find out."

On our third evening in the Golden Chain, as I was bringing the locals their fourth or fifth beers, I heard the door bang open and a familiar voice call, "Well, ex-priest, I hope you've saved some of that for us! It's thirsty weather." Turl and his sons swept into a table just quitted by a handful of students. I was grateful when Hwyn launched into one of the seafaring songs I'd taught her, so that I could join in singing and be unable to answer questions as I brought the merchant strong beer for himself and small beer for the boys.

Later in the evening, however, as I brought him the fish course and retrieved the empty soup bowls on a broad tray, Turl said without preamble, "You're from a sea-trading family, aren't you?"

"Yes, sir," I said. "More beer?"

"One more, yes. But tell me, did you learn that new mathematical navigation?"

"It's not so new, really," I said.

"Would that mean yes?" Turl probed.

I nodded, frowning at the scarcely touched beet soup in Torrin's bowl—a fine table-leaving, but difficult to claim at the busiest part of the evening without eating in front of the customers, which was forbidden to us. The scullion would get it. I sighed hungrily, and met the merchant's probing eyes again. "Yes, sir. Why are you interested?"

"Why not?" Turl countered, unanswerably. I turned away to carry the dirty bowls to the scullery and the empty tankards to the cask for refilling. At a nearby table, Hwyn was amusing the guests with a rare display, juggling a plate, a spoon, and a seedcake. I had passed her before Turl called after me, "Why not take an interest in the son of Garmund the Sea-Trader?"

I might as well have been struck in the face. I whirled around, tray in hand, to answer him, crashing into Hwyn and sending her and the things she'd been juggling, as well as my own tray of unfinished bowls of beet soup, careening into a table-full of well-dressed burghers. Hwyn began cursing loudly, and the burghers, beet soup dripping down their costly brocaded jackets, sprang to their feet, calling for the innkeeper. The next thing we knew, we were thrown out into the street, Trenara crying after us. Hwyn screamed back at the innkeeper that if he didn't pay us for eight hours' labor, she could sing satires about his inn as well as any other. In the end, we were lucky to be allowed to gather up our things before retreating into the night.

"I'm sorry," I told Hwyn as we wandered toward the temple courts for the night. "That one was all my fault."

She shrugged. "We're even, then. It's hard to lose today's pay, with the night so nearly through; but tomorrow's the festival, and we'll have better work to do."

"We missed the table-leavings," I said.

"I have a few morsels in my pockets," said Hwyn, "though I've been unlucky enough to miss those seed-cakes. We'll survive till tomorrow—and then there may be bread given out at the temple door. Meanwhile, we can claim a decent sleeping spot—no small feat, with the holiday crowd—and practice our songs for tomorrow."

"Not 'The Captain and the Mermaid,' so close to the temple," I laughed.

"Well, I think we could sing that one in our sleep," Hwyn said, giving me one of those lopsided smiles that I was coming to like so well. "Meanwhile, you can finish teaching me the Dawn Chant to the Rising God."

"All right," I said. "I guess there are some rewards to being thrown out of work, after all."

"By the way," Hwyn said, "what did that merchant say that startled you so?"

"My father's name," I said.

"How did he know?"

I shrugged. "I never met this fellow before, I'm sure. He may have traded with my father. I didn't think I looked that much like the old man." But why not, I thought: even in Torrin's pensive face were the lines of Turl's complacent one.

"I suppose you've strayed far from your father's world," Hwyn said.

"Not far enough, apparently," I said. "What do you think of this for a campsite?" I gestured to a lilac bush spreading over a little hollow in the temple grounds. The roots would be lumpy under us, but if the heavy moisture in the air turned to rain, we would be sheltered.

Hwyn nodded approvingly, and we hurried to claim the hollow before any of the other travelers spotted it. We sat down to share the greasy bits of meat and cheese Hwyn had stashed in her pockets, stuffed into bits of mangled bread-roll. None of us had our fill, but there was hope for the morning, and we soothed ourselves with song far into the night.

As I taught Hwyn the Dawn Chant to the Rising God, my hands were busy with the needle and thread. Hwyn had insisted I strengthen the pouch for the Eye of Night with the thread the tailor had given us, adding a patch of the precious red cloth to nest the Raven's Egg more securely. When I had done that, and we had changed to more secular songs, I began making a little sleeve of the rest of the fabric, testing out the cloth for size on Hwyn's arm, then stitching mostly by touch in the dying light.

By the time Hwyn finished the seventh of the "Battles of Calenholt" and I finished the sleeve, it was pitch-dark, the waning moon half veiled in cloud. "I'd better put off attaching this till tomorrow," I said. "I wouldn't want to slip with the needle right against your shoulder." Just then song spilled from the temple again: the Night Chant to the Hidden Goddess. This time Hwyn knew more of the verses than I did.

"Where did you learn all those verses?" I asked.

"Places like this," she said. "Sleep now; we'll want to get an early start tomorrow."

4

THE UNLUCKY WORD

On the first day of the festival, the longest day of the year, I woke to the sight of Hwyn bending over me, looking at me curiously. I was about to ask what was the matter when the sounds of the morning hymn began drifting out of the temple. As if by unspoken agreement, we both sang with the unseen priests, our voices at first thick and clumsy with sleep, but gradually gaining strength and assurance. By the time we finished we were singing out boldly, and we had an audience. Thus began our Feast of the Bright Goddess.

We scarcely paused for food, and we collected more coins for the first morning's song than for twelve hours' toil in either inn. We left off singing only to follow the crowd to the courts of the solar temple for the noon rites of the Bright Goddess, praising her for her gifts of flowers and fruit, grain and gladness and song. When the high priestess sang the goddess's call to all living things to arise and grow, Hwyn stood with her head tipped back, her face glowing, rapt as a child too young to remember the last feast, drinking it in as if for the first time. Trenara flowed into a stately dance, oblivious of the worshipers she bumped and jostled, lost in a world no one could fathom. As for me, I had eyes only for them: these unearthly wonders who shared table-leavings with me.

All afternoon and into the late midsummer twilight, the festival crowd seemed almost as taken with them as I. Though we could not persuade Trenara to dance while we were singing, even her quiet presence, beautiful as she was, seemed part of the spectacle we brought to the Feast of the Bright Goddess. As for Hwyn, though passersby looked uneasily at her and away again, her voice could not be ignored even among the many minstrels at this festival of song. The crowd showered us with applause and honey-cakes, and sometimes with coins; and we sang longer hours than we'd worked, too delighted to be weary.

When we finally sank to sleep for a few hours on the same corner of the market-square where we'd been singing, it was with a sense of triumph. I had no doubt the remaining three days of the festival would be as successful as the first one; we could fill our pockets with coins, buy what we needed for the journey, and make unhindered progress northward. On the second day of the festival, when buying and selling were allowed to resume, I began scanning the stalls in the marketplace for things we might need for the journey north: warmer clothes, sturdier boots, a cooking-pot, a better knife than the one I carried. I bought nothing yet, awaiting Hwyn's counsel, for she had traveled more by land and knew the ways of the roads. Nonetheless, I spent a farthing—three hours' toil at the White Cat—to have my old knife sharpened. The rest, I thought, could wait till our true prosperity came in.

But the afternoon did not go as we'd planned. We had scarcely retuned our voices after the noon rites when a passing drudge, distracted by our song from the path before his feet, tripped and fell, kicking our cup of money over so the coins rolled out of sight, and tumbling an armload of heavy crockery right over Hwyn.

"Sky-Raven's Bones!" she cursed.

The drudge cried out sharply, and pulled a hunting knife from his belt.

"Hwyn!" I thrust myself between them as Trenara shrieked and the assailant snarled with rage. "You, *boy*," I spat, "what do you think you're doing?"

"Step aside or, gods help me, I'll cut through you to get to her!"

"Madman!" I had only my eating-knife, but I drew it out as a better weapon than my bare hands.

It was fortunate, then, that another voice broke from behind the boy: "Klem! Hothead, what are you up to now?" The attacker turned to see, and I took the opportunity to seize his arms from behind. The newcomer—the drudge's master, as I surmised—asked us, "What trouble has my boy been making here?"

"He dropped a load of crockery on my partner and then, instead of asking her pardon, he pulled a blade on her," I answered.

"She swore by—by—a thing I cannot name," the wretch protested.

The master put a weary hand to his temple. "Klem, you mad dog, put your knife away."

"But—"

"*Now,* Klem. Do you think you can leave this place alive if you harm a minstrel in the Festival of Song?"

The man's arms slackened in my grasp. At last he dropped the knife. I pocketed it, then stepped back to show that if he left us alone, I would return the courtesy. I collided with Hwyn behind me, and reflexively put a protective arm about her shoulders, as though she were the child she sometimes seemed. The too-ready tears sprang to her eyes.

The merchant approached to claim his servant. "Has this wastrel hurt you, songbird?"

"No," Hwyn said, "only frightened me. And it seems I frightened him first, unwittingly. Klem," she addressed her astonished enemy, "what do you know of—of what I swore by?"

The servant's eyes widened, and his mouth opened, but he could not seem to summon the words.

"He's as superstitious as a child," the merchant said. "He's from Kreyn; they're all like that there. If you don't stumble on his bugbears and goblins, he's a good enough fellow, but it seems you've said an unlucky word. I'm glad he didn't harm you. My name is Edwold; will you come with me to a tavern and let me recompense you for your fright?"

Hwyn nodded, but a hush was on her, and as far as I could follow her cross-eyed gaze, she seemed to be looking at crazy Klem rather than his master.

Edwold seemed to notice it; he turned to the servant and said, "See, Klem, these are peaceable folk. Can't you come share a meal with them in peace, and give them a chance to prove your forebodings wrong?"

"Klem," Hwyn said, "I swore as people do in St. Fiern's Town—at least, in the hottest fury. But if you know a reason why it is wrong to swear thus, tell me, and I will mend my ways."

At that Klem's face softened. "I almost killed you," he whispered.

Hwyn nodded. "I know. I need to know why."

"You're not even angry?" said Klem.

Hwyn shrugged. "I'm a peculiar type of fool. I see you thought you were doing right, and now I'm more curious than angry." She put out her hand and after some hesitation Klem took it, squeezed it for a moment, then let it go.

"I'm sorry," he said. "I see I must have been wrong."

"Well, come along, then," Edwold said. "A few rounds of ale, and all will be forgiven and forgotten."

We followed him eagerly enough. On the way Hwyn leaned close to me. "You protected me," she murmured wonderingly. "Thank you."

"Someone has to," I said, "since you won't protect yourself. Why are you taking this so calmly?" But she only shrugged and smiled as Edwold led us into the Lark Tavern.

It was a good inn—far better than either of the ones we'd slaved at—and Edwold was a generous host, so that the feast set before us was enough to ease many hurts, and the ale plentiful enough to loosen even Klem's tongue. When his hunched shoulders relaxed, Hwyn took it as her cue to question him: "Tell me frankly, Klem, why it was wrong to swear by that thing you will not name."

He scrutinized her a moment, perhaps trying and failing to read her purpose in her eyes. At last he spoke: "To swear by a thing is to call it."

"That is often so," Hwyn admitted. "But what if I do call it? Was not the—the bird I spoke of—was it not a friend to our kind? The priests say that it spread its wings between heaven and earth when the sun would have scorched the earth barren."

"I too have heard that tale," Klem said cautiously. "And yet they say that its second flight will be the coming of the great darkness."

"That may be true," Hwyn said, "but seeds send out roots in darkness. A child grows in the darkness of the womb. Children fear the dark, but we cannot, to comfort them, hold the sun bleeding on the horizon and refuse the night."

"Do you call my people children?" Klem bristled.

"I am taken for a child so often myself that the word has no sting for me anymore," Hwyn said. "And I fear the dark as well, but I expect no good to come of fearing it."

Klem shook his head. "I cannot answer you wisely. I only know what I have heard from childhood, passed down from mouth to ear. But the Lady of Kreyn—the Guardian of Day—has in her chapel a speaking stone that, I have heard, prophesies strange fates to follow the Bearer of Night, who summons the bird into our land at the end of things. The Guardian of Day could answer you."

Hwyn laughed. "And would this great lady spare any words for a vagabond like me?"

Klem blushed. "I suppose not."

"And I would not advise you to try," Edwold said. "It is the cruelest town I ever visited."

Klem protested, "It is my home!"

"And what kindness did you ever know there? What did you take with you from Kreyn but whip-scars and bad dreams?"

"My master there was a hard one," Klem acknowledged. "But the place is no less home to me. Still," he turned to Hwyn, "Master Edwold is right: I would not advise you to travel there. The Guardian is wise, but proud, and might not see what you are."

"A priestess, surely," Edwold put in.

I leaned forward to hear Hwyn's answer, but she only smiled. It was Klem who framed an answer: "More than that, I think: she is one of those that the gods ride hard, a prophet or a lunatic. Hwyn, I'm sorry I attacked you. As I remember with a cooler head, not even the prophecy can excuse me—for it speaks of one who calls the bird into Kreyn, and you have never been there."

"Then there is peace between us?" Hwyn said. "I am glad of it."

"You are a generous foe, to be sure," he said.

"You are a strange one to remark on my generosity, Klem," Hwyn said softly. "You have come into servitude through your own generosity, and been betrayed by the one you saved."

Klem's eyes widened. "Do you see further?"

She nodded. "You think that by going back you can mend

what remains; but do not go back. The one you love most has left. You will not find him there."

"Will I ever see him again?"

Hwyn sat silent a while, then spread her hands apologetically. "I don't know. I sense him seeking something; he may be seeking you or seeking himself, for all I can see. The gift is not at my command: it comes as it will, a glimmer of light, then nothing."

Edwold, discomfited, changed the topic to music, and we talked of inconsequential things until the meal was over and we staggered back into the streets, drunk and well fed, to rejoin the festival. But Hwyn's attention flagged, and even her singing seemed to lack its usual fire, as if her mind were far away. I managed to secure her agreement to buying a cooking-pot with some of our earnings, but even preparing for the journey north seemed far from her mind.

The following morning, I woke to find Hwyn already awake, regarding me with eyes that seemed red at the rims. "Hwyn, are you all right?"

"Yes," she said, her voice husky.

"You are not still worrying about what that madman Klem said of you, are you?"

"No, it isn't that," she said, which was as good as admitting that something was indeed wrong.

"What, then?" I said softly.

"Nothing, really," she said. But I was more convinced than ever that she had been weeping.

Uncertain what to say, whether to simply touch her shoulder as I had in the boat, I noticed her bare left arm and remembered that I had a promise to fulfill. "I've been forgetting to attach your sleeve," I said, rummaging for it in my pack. "Shall I try it now?"

"All right," she said.

I moved toward her, needle in one hand, cloth in the other. She shied a bit as I reached for her shoulder. "Come now, hold still," I said. "I'll be careful. But I can't do a thing if you're afraid of the needle—I doubt you want to take off your shift in full view of the street so I can work on it."

"No, of course not," she said, reddening. "I'm not afraid, really. I'm just not used to this."

I worked cautiously, drawing the needle toward myself lest any sudden motion on her part should plant it in her neck or shoulder. Holding the fabric taut around the armhole, I noticed again the whip-marks that had alarmed me the night I met her, extending from her shoulders down out of sight. They were healing and fading, but still unmistakable. "You've been hurt here," I said.

"It's nearly healed," she dismissed it.

"I noticed those that night in Kelgarran Hall," I said, "when I still thought you were the servant girl. It made me think Trenara must have had you whipped."

Hwyn cast an eye on the lady, who still slept with her dark locks tumbled over her fair face, as elegantly disordered as the rambling roses in the temple court. "Gods! Trenara cries over a squashed spider. She couldn't hurt anyone."

I pulled the thread taut delicately, and spoke as carefully as I worked. "Who did this?"

"Why do you need to know?" she demanded.

"Never mind," I retreated. "I was just concerned."

"Klem would not be surprised at those," she mused. "There are some very harsh places to live in Swevnalond; I guess Kreyn is one of them. It's not always so easy as we've had it in Sebrin. Festivals are the best times for roaming; between them it's lean, hungry traveling. I was sorry to miss singing at St. Bridwen's Day, but I had bigger things to do, and couldn't risk making myself noticeable. Still, it's a grand feast for a player and it stung to miss playing it."

"Well, we'd better stir ourselves to make the most of this one," I said, though I was still nettled by her evasion and disturbed to hear our time in Sebrin called easy; the playing, certainly, was pure joy, but the early days in the inns had been back-breaking drudgery. "We only have two days left."

"Maybe only one," Hwyn said faintly, avoiding my gaze. "I may want to slip out of town quietly before the festival ends."

"Why?" I said. "The brawl seemed to end peacefully enough."

"True," she said, "but it would not do to have Klem know I am going to Kreyn."

"To Kreyn!" I said, dropping the needle and thread, which dangled uselessly from the half-attached sleeve. "You are madder than he is!"

"Have you just discovered it?" She smiled crookedly.

"After all Edwold said—and more, after all Klem almost did—"

"I know. It's pure folly. But—"

"The prophecy," I finished for her. "You need to know it—or simply can't resist it."

"How could I?" she said. "It's out of the way, but there's much to be gained. How much have you ever heard of the Sky-Raven, beyond the sparse tale told over midwinter fires? The tale is so old it is half forgotten—and I hold the dark half of it sleeping in my pocket. I know so little about this thing I've taken into my care."

"You knew enough," I said, "to find it when it was hidden, to set it free from necromancy, to know when it was safe to let your enemy get his hands on it, to talk back to the ghosts that came out of it and leave with their blessing. Why should this Speaking Stone hold any prophecy you don't already know?"

"All I know is by touch, as it were, one step at a time, the way I grope through a strange house in the dark."

"You do that well enough," I remembered.

"But the prophecy could let me see a long way down the road," she said. "I don't know what the end of this journey will be."

"Do you mean we might not be headed north after all?"

"No, that much I'm sure of," she said. "All the dreams say *north*. The thing itself urges me north, ever since I touched it."

"Then why go off the path?" I said. Kreyn, I knew from maps, lay almost due east of Sebrin, across the rugged land north of Annelon. It would not be an easy detour. Nor would there be an easy route north from Kreyn, for it lay just south of the Hills of Penmorrin, which rose toward the impassable mountain range of the east, the Wall of Magya.

"It's a detour, I know," Hwyn said. "I should take it alone; you might stay here with Trenara till I find out the prophecy and return."

"Oh, I see," I said. "All this talk of traveling together has just been to trick me into taking Trenara off your hands. We can wait forever in this nondescript middle-Swevnian town while you travel light—"

"You don't understand!"

"No, I don't," I said. "Maybe if you told me something,

anything, instead of hiding behind cryptic hints, always asking more questions than you answer, repaying my questions with an evasion or a lie—"

"I've *never* lied to you," she spat back.

Trenara, lying just beyond her, stirred uneasily.

Hwyn's body was tensed as for a fight, her chest heaving with furious breath, but the look she gave me was not of anger but of pain. Slowly, as if I were coaxing a shy animal out of its hole with a bit of food, I lifted my hand, opened it, brought it toward her till I touched her crumpled left cheek, gently tracing the scars under her misaligned eye. My thumb found a drop of brine. "I'm sorry," I said very quietly, "but you did, this morning, when I asked you if you were all right. You have been weeping."

As slowly and cautiously as I had touched her cheek, she raised her hand to place it over mine, holding it against her face. "I'm sorry," she said. "There was one other time, also, now I re-member: I told you I was looking for water. Pity: I thought that if I had lied to all the world, at least I had a clear conscience with one man. I swear by the Sky-Raven's Egg that in all the great things, I have dealt honestly with you. But there are things I can-not speak of, and things I simply don't want to speak of. Klem is right, in a sense: to name something is to call it, and there are ghosts I fear to raise. Can you accept a few evasions if I promise you no lies?"

"All right," I said, then looked down at the dangling needle. "I'd better finish that sleeve."

"I'm hungry," said Trenara, sitting up and rubbing her eyes.

"All right, Trenara," I said, "I'll finish this and then find us some food."

Hwyn complied docilely as I fitted the underside of the sleeve; it looked funny, a fresh scarlet patch on an old gray sack, like wild plumage on a sparrow's wing. Most likely it would need to be reattached when it shrank out of proportion to the old garment. But seeing Hwyn finger the new wool and hold up her arm to admire the rich color, I felt this was far better than reat-taching the old sleeve. It was probably the first pretty thing she'd had to wear.

I left her and Trenara to guard our patch of the market-square against other performers, while I went off to the victualers' booths to get us some breakfast. After starting the day with jan-gled nerves and hurt feelings, I felt we needed some sort of treat.

I remembered Hwyn's fondness for the sweet seed-cakes at the Golden Chain; in sharing table-leavings with her, I also noticed that she seemed partial to cheese. I made up my mind to see what I could find in this line without spending too much of our song-money. Some decent dark ale, if I could find it, would go well with the cheese and cakes, and go a long way toward assuaging my own ruffled feelings. I was not sure what Trenara would like best, but as far as I could see, she ate anything we gave her with equal relish, and would probably be pleased with the same things we chose.

I was deep in contemplation of the wares in a baker's cart, wondering whether the cakes were made with the same sort of seed as the ones I remembered, when a voice behind me made me whirl around in alarm.

"By all the gods on the Wheel," said Turl of Ectirion, "Jereth son of Garmund!"

"Hidden Goddess," I swore, "if my father's ghost sent you to haunt me, he's done a rare job of it."

"I thought it was a sign from the gods that we should meet three times by chance," said Turl. "But I'm sorry I startled you so with your father's name, last time we met. You looked like you'd seen a ghost indeed. I know I cost you your job, and I mean to offer you something to make up for it. Come, this inn on the corner's not bad. I'll buy us a bit to eat while I explain myself."

For what I realized was the first time, I met Turl's eyes, noticing the soft lines of humor and worry around them, counterbalancing his hard jawline. "It's kind of you to offer," I said, "but I'm not alone in Sebrin. I was just buying breakfast for myself and two friends; they'll be expecting me."

"In that case, I'll buy what you came for, if you'll hear me out," said Turl, "but I want to speak to you apart. Pick what you'll have."

"My friend liked those sweet seed-cakes they had at the Golden Chain. If those are the same—"

"Not that," Turl said, pointing to what I'd almost bought. "Those are bitter. I know where you can find them—without going back to the inn." So we set off across the lane.

"I still don't understand why you should take an interest in me," I said. "I thought I'd been fairly rude to you."

Turl laughed. "Smooth words I can get anywhere. When people fawn on me, I know they lack buyers for whatever they're selling. You've never shown the least interest in anything I might have to give you, so I have to wonder what you have that's worth more than anything you think I could pay."

I had to smile at that. "Gods! You sound like my father. But even so, I can't understand— You seem, almost, to be offering me a position tutoring your sons."

"There, you've cut to the heart of the matter," said Turl.

"But how can you trust me? For all you know, I could have been turned away from the monastery for stealing the alms-money or molesting the village girls—or boys."

"Wrong," said Turl. "At first, it's true, I was playing a hunch. But since then, I have heard quite a solid report of your character."

"Not from the innkeepers, surely!" I said.

"Oh, no," said Turl. "From Brother Becmon of the House of the Tarvon Order at Annelon."

"What?"

"Among the merchandise I brought with me was a chest of plain sheep-gray woolen cloth for the Tarvon House here in Sebrin," Turl said, grinning at my bemused appearance. "Now, from my first glimpse of you, I'd wondered about you. Despite the clerical dress, you were once obviously a seaman or a merchant; no one else speaks that horrid trading-tongue of the islanders. And by the Upright God, you meet few people in this whole godforsaken, Trouble-ridden land anymore that speak anything but Swevnian. The foreigners are all going home— have you noticed? Even the Kettrans, who still think they own this land, centuries after their stinking empire fell—they're giving up on it. They're too cunning to stay in a doomed land. Little Kettra may not be Northern, but it's the first place in the South to see the sort of migrations we've heard of from the North. They're getting out of Swevnalond, back to the mother country.

"Anyway, there you were, cleaning a tavern floor in your cassock, a man of learning, an ex-priest and ex-merchant, as I had no doubt once I'd spoken to you. And I put it together with a terrible story that made the rounds of the fairgrounds a couple of years ago, the sort of story that travels far because it sounds like our worst nightmares: how in the height of his wealth, Garmund the Sea-Trader went to the bottom of the sea with his best ship and his whole family, save one son, the sole heir, who gave away everything and buried himself in a monastery."

I stared at him, open-mouthed.

"A dozen of those," Garmund said to the baker, pointing at just the sort of little cakes Hwyn had liked. "What now?" he said to me.

"Excuse me?"

"What else were you going to buy?"

"Cheese and ale," I said tonelessly, putting the cakes into my pack. "Brown ale, preferably. How did you hear our story?"

"Lad, your father was no market-square peddler," Turl said impatiently. "When a great man falls, there's talk of it."

I rolled my eyes to hear that "great man" again; I'd thought I was long quit of it.

"At any rate," Turl said, "I asked about you at the monastery when I came to sell the cloth: did they know a Brother Jereth who had left the Order? The Sebrin monks didn't, but as it turned out, they had a visitor from Annelon, the Scriptorium Master, who confirmed my hunch: Jereth son of Garmund the Sea-Trader joined the Order after his family drowned, but was never cut out for it; he had left this year, as anyone should have predicted, before the Feast of the Rising God, with the snow still on the ground and the ruts in the road still frozen, like a man fleeing destruction. He said you should never have been allowed to join in the height of grief, when no man can see his path clearly."

"It wasn't so simple as that," I muttered, but Turl paid no heed.

"Brother Becmon described you as a master of languages, a clear thinker, and the sort of man who could be trusted with his enemy's purse or an absent friend's wife, without reservation," Turl said. "And I was looking for a trustworthy tutor, fluent in several languages, who would not nudge Torrin toward the abbey. That is not an easy thing to find in the shadow of the Troubles; with all the foreigners gone, the only teachers worth a wooden farthing are hopelessly mired in monastic orders."

"Don't be so sure I'd be your ally in making a merchant of Torrin," I said. "Most likely the lad already knows his own mind. He'll find his own way into the Order or away from it; by pushing, you may make him a bitter and half-hearted merchant or an angry and rebellious priest. If the advice of a stranger is worth anything, I'd say, let him choose whether to accept his birthright or give it to his brother."

"Well," Turl said, "you're frank with me, as I've been frank with you. We may not agree, but at least we know where we differ. Isn't it better that way?"

"I suppose," I said.

"And whether you think he should be monk or merchant, you'll be able to teach him what he needs for both paths," Turl said, steering me away from a clean-looking brewer's stall to a dirty but agreeable-smelling one. "There, that's a better buy; trust me. Anyway, it's not just the languages—or the navigation. You're the son of Garmund; you must have learned something from him. Besides," Turl said, wrinkling his face in the most vulnerable look I'd seen on him, or on any of the merchants whose ghosts he'd raised in my memory, "you remind me of Torrin, somehow. You might understand the boy. I don't; I understand him only well enough to know that. And he likes you already. That boy doesn't like many people, Jereth. Gods know he doesn't like me right now, any more than you do. Did you think I didn't know that? And what do you think, eh? Do you think that means I don't love my son?"

I stood gaping at him, more amazed by this display of feeling than by his deduction of my identity. He put a jug of ale in my hand and steered me toward a dairyman's cart without further speech. I let him choose for me, and accepted the leaf-wrapped bundle as if I had forgotten what I had wanted it for.

"Where are you staying?" Turl asked.

"Northwest corner of the market-square," I said.

"There's no inn there," Turl said.

"Who said anything about an inn?"

"Gods on the Wheel!" said Turl. "If your father could see you now—" My grin cut him short. "Maybe that's not the best thing to say," he conceded. "I know if you'd wanted the merchant's life, you'd have it already. But you don't have to be a merchant. You could teach. You'd like my boys. They're good children. Think about it."

He had known which notes to sound. I did think I'd like the boys, from the little I'd seen of them; they stirred memories in me of the boy I had once been and the brothers I had once had. I'd loved my tutors then—except the Magyan, who had been abruptly substituted for a great favorite of mine, a one-legged bard with a dry sense of humor and a great wealth of stories. To become a tutor myself seemed so natural that I wondered why I had never thought of it before. But I shook my head. "I'm touched by the offer, and I wish your sons every blessing of the gods: they seemed like fine lads. But I never meant to settle here—or in Ectirion, either; I'm only here for the festival. I can't stay in one place."

"We're going, too," Turl said. "I can feel which way the wind's blowing. The foreigners have the right of it: the Troubles of the North are sweeping down over all Swevnalond."

I looked at him with more interest.

"I've always been a landlocked trader, small-time, just up and down the Pengar River, not a seafarer like your father," Turl said. "But the future is at sea. I want to take my family to Magya or Iskarron, take the leap into sea-trading. You could help us. I know my Magyan's piss-poor; I saw it in your face when I spoke to you. You could teach me, too. And I could give you a steady place, a home. After all, we're going the same way, aren't we?" He turned to look at me, then burst out, "Curse it, man, why are you leering at me like that again, like a man that has something I couldn't buy with all I have?"

"You wouldn't understand," I said.

"Gods, you sound like Torrin," he said. "You may be thirty years old, and he thirteen, but you're still just a lad that's run from his father's home and not been found yet. Is this your corner?"

"Yes," I said, for we had reached my friends, Hwyn squinting up at us curiously, Trenara toying with a dandelion growing between the cobbles.

Turl looked at Hwyn, then at me, with a mixture of horror and pity. "If you change your mind, you can find me in the Street of the Weavers, near the Spinners' Lane." Then he left us to divide the little feast in peace.

I set down the bottle of ale, opened my pack to reveal the rest of the booty, took out the leaf-wrapped bundle of cheese, and spread it on the cleanest cobblestone I could spy.

Hwyn asked, "What did he mean, 'If you change your mind'?"

"He offered me a position," I said, "partly for being my father's son." I uncorked the ale. "Seven years dead and the old man's still chasing me." I took a swig of the good malty brew; in this, at least, Turl had steered me right.

"Why, was it a bad position?" Hwyn said.

"Hmm? Oh, no." I stuck my knife in the cheese and took another swig of ale as Hwyn sliced off a piece and broke it in half to share with Trenara. "You don't understand, do you, why it galls me to come to a strange town and find I'm still that son of Garmund the Sea-Trader, the one that survived?"

"Maybe I'd understand," Hwyn said, "if you told me."

"You tell me first," I said, my nerves thoroughly jangled, "something—anything—who your parents were, why you were weeping—what your *name* is, for the gods' sake."

"I can't tell you that," she said.

"Fine, then." I took another pull at the ale-jug, but it wasn't improving my mood.

"Oh—seed-cakes!" Hwyn said, finally noticing the contents of my pack. "How did you know what I wanted?" At that, even I had to laugh.

When the feast had been reduced to table-leavings, we eased into our day's performance, first tuning our voices together on the easiest children's counting song, heedless of whether anyone listened or not, then working toward some of the showier pieces and putting out the cup for coins as passersby began to linger near. But I was not up to the mark of the previous day's singing, distracted by thoughts of Hwyn's secrecy and her moods and Turl's pitying look and the road ahead, where things would be harder than they had been so far. Once I fell so badly behind on a round that Hwyn broke off with a baleful look.

"For the gods' love, what's gotten into you?" she snapped. "Yesterday you could count!"

"Sorry," I said, but it only drove me further into my thoughts. What was I doing here, playing the minstrel, sleeping in the street, following a couple of strangers, one that couldn't have told me where we were going, one that wouldn't tell me where she'd come from? *She doesn't even need me,* I thought, hearing Hwyn's voice change one of my everyday sea chanteys into a strange mermaid-call. *She's done Trenara's share of the work and half of mine; and if I dropped out of the song now, it would be much the same to the listeners. At least I can offer Turl and his family something they don't have.*

As if in answer to my thoughts, a barley-sugar sweet plunked into the cup from thin young fingers. I looked up to see solemn black eyes fixed on me.

Just as I thought: rich, but no pocket-money, I ruminated. When the song was done, I said, "Torrin son of Turl, what brings you here?"

"What did you mean about naming?"

"Hmm?"

"What you said in the Golden Chain: that the gods have named us first. What did you mean by it?" the boy said.

"What do you think I meant by it?" I said, sounding like one of my old tutors.

Hwyn looked at the boy, then at me, with a strangely wistful look. The audience, finding no new song forthcoming, began to drift away.

"That my father is wrong?" the boy said hopefully. "That I should join the Tarvon Order?"

I smiled. "I scarcely know where I belong, myself, let alone you. It's not so simple. St. Elfrith said we think we name our children, but the gods have been there first. You are your father's son, but that's not all you are. He did name you, but only the gods know what that name means in full. Whether your name calls you to the Tarvon Order, to trade, or to weaving North Magyan saddle-cloths is the great question that I cannot answer for you. Nor, I think, can your father, though he may try. In that we disagree."

"Then that is why he will not make you my tutor, though he said he would," Torrin said.

"Not so," I said. "He offered me the position. He said you and I would get along—and I think, in that, he was right."

"But then—" the boy hesitated, "aren't you coming with us?"

"Torrin, your father can't buy me for you like a handful of sweets. I have other work."

"Here?" The boy's gaze took everything in: the rotted vegetables left in the gutter near the stones that had been our bed; the flies; the tin cup for coins; the two meager bundles containing all our possessions.

"Jereth," Hwyn cut in, "you should consider the position. There's no other festival till St. Katred's Day, and the work will be worse, not better, where I'm going."

I spun toward her. "Why do you keep pushing me away?"

"Will you listen to reason?" she said. "I'm not pushing you away. I'm trying to give you a choice. You said, when you joined me, you had nowhere else to go. Now you have another choice."

"I made my choice," I said to her, half forgetting Torrin, who stood fidgeting with embarrassment before us. "I said I would follow you. Did you think that meant nothing?"

"Well, I'm not holding you to it," she said. "I'm not dragging you along on the strength of words spoken in haste. We were equal then: neither of us had anything to lose. We're not now." With that, she picked up her pack and began striding away, leaving our patch of the market-square. Trenara, bewildered, got up and followed.

"Hwyn!" I called after her.

She cast a glance over her shoulder, but did not stop. A voice in my head said, *you will not hear her voice again, or know whether she lives or dies, or how her mad quest ends.* I glanced at the merchant's son, at my open pack and our performance spot; deciding quickly that the one could take care of himself and the others were unimportant, I ran after her.

"Hwyn! For the gods' love," I said, grasping her by the arm, "don't leave me like this."

She turned to face me. "Jereth, these are your people, your world. I don't want you to regret too late giving it up for a hasty promise to me. For the gods' sake, if you're going to leave me, leave now, while I still remember how to go on alone."

"Do you still remember that?" I said. "I don't. I'm begging you not to leave me; what language do I have to speak for you to hear me?"

"The marks on my back were thirty lashes for theft," she said. "There was no honest work for a stranger in Fledley, and I was caught with my hand in a merchant's pocket. I begged the constable to let me take off my shift, as I would have nothing to wear if the lash tore it; so by his mercy I was whipped naked before the market-square. That is the life I'm leading you into, if you follow me."

"Gods on the Wheel," I said, "I wish we were going to Fledley, so I could beat the constable senseless. I wish I were a stronger defender for you. I know I'm not much use to you—"

"Gods, Jereth," said Hwyn, "is that what you were thinking?"

"Isn't that what *you* were thinking, telling me how much harder things could be?"

"*No,*" she said. "Honestly! What a thought!"

"What a muddle," I said. "Now someone more desperate will have taken our cup of coins. If only they've had the decency to leave the cup behind—"

"You left the cup when you ran?"

"Of course I did," I said. "You were disappearing into the crowd."

"And your pack—with the cook-pot and the leftover cakes and ale," she said.

"I wasn't going to stop to bundle it up," I said.

"And your would-be student will have left by now," she said. The crowd milled thick between us and the place we had been; I could not see whether everything was gone, but it seemed more than likely.

"If Torrin could find us by himself, he can find his way back," I said.

"Bright Goddess, Jereth," Hwyn said, "for the second time in your life, you've left all your possessions." A smile slowly spread across her face.

It took me a while to understand what she was smiling at. "It was a better choice the second time," I said. "The Tarvon Order is an armload of dead rules walled up in stone houses like great tombs. You are alive. I don't want to burden you—"

Just then, I heard a tentative voice at my side: "Brother Jereth?"

Torrin son of Turl, red-faced and hesitant, stood clutching our cup of coins in one hand, my pack in the other, the ale-jug under his arm. "I saved your things for you. You can't leave *anything* unwatched in a place like this."

His father's words, I thought, accepting our things and bundling them up properly. "Thank you, Torrin. That was kind of you. Is there anything I can do for you in return?"

"You're not going to come with us?"

"No, lad," I said. "It's a fine offer, but I have a better one."

He looked at me skeptically.

"The Magyans have a legend," I said, "of a firebird that makes its nest in the heart of a burning mountain. There is only one in all the world, so if you see it once in your life, you can be sure it will not come again. Its plumes, they say, are like the fire at the heart of the world. And some see the firebird and let it pass, holding it in memory, while they live out their lives as before; but maybe afterward everything they see seems dim beside that single fiery vision. Others see it and follow after it; they leave the life they have known and inherit a world of trouble, and hardship, and danger, and wonder, and joy." I fixed my eyes on

Hwyn as I spoke, but I could not tell from her expression what she heard in the story. "Only by journeying into trouble can you find the joy at the heart of the world—if you survive the journey. For some, it is better to stay in the known life. For others, the journey is the only life. Do you know what I mean?"

"Yes—well, I think—no. Are you speaking of your journey or mine?" said Torrin. "You're speaking in symbols; you haven't seen any firebird. How do you know where to go?"

"You don't," I said. "You guess. You dream, or you listen to those who dream. You trust and risk betrayal. You make mistakes, and you try not to make the same ones twice. Torrin, this is all I can teach you. The Tarvon Monastery is not hard to find: down the Eastern Way, near the Potters' Lane. If your name leads you there, you don't need my guidance: go there. If you go of your own accord, they may accept you as an acolyte with or without your father's blessing. But beware of exchanging one false life for another. Ask yourself always—before you go there, before you are initiated, and especially, before you take vows—do you go there to follow your calling, or only to leave your father's world?"

"Was that why you went?" the boy said.

"In a sense," I said. "My father was dead already. But a dead father can be a more relentless pursuer than a live one."

"Do you regret joining the Order?" said Torrin.

I surprised myself by saying, "No, not now. Three months ago, when I left, I regretted it. I hated the high walls, the rules, the pieties that had become meaningless to me. But it was what I needed. A trapped animal will gnaw its own leg off, and the Order was the wound I had to give myself to break free. I can't say I recommend it, but it was the way I found out of my trap."

For a long while, the boy looked out in the direction I had pointed out to him. When he turned back to me, he wore a look of resolution. "Thank you," he said. "You've been the best tutor I've ever had." With that, he turned eastward, weaving his way through the crowd so nimbly that he was lost from sight before I could call him back.

"What have I done?" I said.

"Set him free?" Hwyn suggested.

"Maybe," I said. "Or maybe helped him into a new prison. Does he know what he's doing?"

"Did you?" Hwyn said.

"Not in the least," I said.

"Maybe that's why they give you seven years," said Hwyn. "He'll have time to work it out."

"I hope so," I said.

"You told him the truth," Hwyn said. "You told him what he needed. I think you did the best thing possible."

"His father won't see it that way when I tell him."

Hwyn stared at me, much as I had at her when she spoke of going to Kreyn.

"Well, someone has to tell him where the boy went," I said. "Torrin won't think of it; he thinks the old man doesn't care. I'm afraid that leaves me."

"He'll think it's your fault," Hwyn said.

"True," I said, "but he can't kill me for it in front of the marketplace. The sooner I break the news, the better. You *will* be here when I come back, won't you?"

"Of course," she said. "I promise. You *will* come back, won't you?"

"Nothing could keep me away."

The Street of the Weavers was a chaos of color and motion, great shops and small stalls jostling elbows to offer bolts of wool and linen and even the odd elusive glimpse of silk to dressmakers, tailors, upholsterers, drapers, housewives, ladies' maids, and ladies themselves, as well as to traders bound for places the weavers would never see. I stood wondering where in all this commotion to ask for Turl, when I heard his voice: "What do you mean you haven't seen him? Did I or did I not pay you extra to make sure the boys didn't leave the shop till I returned?"

Fists clenched at his sides, Turl glowered over a spindly couple, simply dressed, with faces faded as Hwyn's shift. The woman ventured to speak: "He's so quiet. We could hear Tadric asking the dyers questions all the while, so we thought they were both there."

"Excuse me, sir," I said. I had to say it three times before Turl spun around to confront me.

"Garmund's son!" he sputtered. "You've picked the worst of all times to reconsider my offer. Torrin—"

"I've seen Torrin," I said.

"He's gone, slipped off—" Turl blustered before my words sank in. "What?"

"Torrin came to speak to me," I said.

"Well? Where is he?"

"He went to join the Tarvon Order," I said.

"Bright Goddess's buttocks!" Turl sputtered. "What did you say to him?"

"I told you before what I thought: the boy already knows his own mind," I said. "I told him as much: that if he were called, he didn't need me to tell him what to do."

The words were barely out of my mouth before Turl's fist connected with my chin, sending me careening into a cart full of bolts of linen. I struck the back of my head sharply on a scale for weighing coins and sank to the cobblestones, dimly aware of an agitated tradesman scrambling about on the other side of the cart to rescue his precious wares from the dirty road.

"Is that how you repay the interest I took in you?"

"I gave Torrin the truth as best I could. I have given you the same," I said, rubbing my head and rising stiffly to face him. He was half a head shorter than I; there was nothing to fear in him, but I did not want a fight. I held my hands before me, ready but open. "I know this news distresses you, but at least now you know where to find him."

"Who in the bum-hole of the world are you?" Turl sputtered, his hands still clenched at his sides. "Why don't you fight back or run? Why did you come to tell me this at all?"

"I don't fight back because I know I gave first injury, although unwillingly. I don't run because I came here for a purpose. I came to tell you because you said you loved your son, and I did not want you to think he was dead in an alley—and because Torrin thinks you hate him, and won't imagine that you might worry over him."

Turl frowned. "So you think you've done me a service, telling me this?"

I shrugged. "I don't expect you to see it as such."

"Well, what did you expect?"

"More or less what I got," I said. "If I thought my advice were worth anything to you, I would counsel you to go to Torrin and say nothing for or against his choice. He may not be certain yet, but opposition will harden him. But as it is, my part here is done: you need no more words from me, and I need no more reminders of my childhood. I'd best go."

Turl's hands unclenched at his sides. "Jereth son of Garmund, you're a strange man. You didn't have to come here. You knew what I was likely to do—".

"More or less," I said. "If I'd known exactly, I'd have ducked. But I suppose the Rising God protects his own; he sent me to take that blow in place of Torrin."

"Is that what you think?" Turl said. "That if I couldn't vent my rage on some stranger, I'd be beating Torrin about the head for thwarting me?"

I did not answer.

"Gods! I hope the lad doesn't think the same. Well. I am sorry I struck you. I'm not myself." Turl put his thick hands over his eyes. "Gods! I can hardly think. Everything is overturned. I can't leave Swevnalond now: not with Torrin stuck here, rooted in that monastery. There are no Tarvon houses outside Swevnalond—but then, you knew that, didn't you? I suppose I'll have to give those grasping priests some sort of donation as well; it will shame me if they take him in as a beggar. And half my worth tied up in provisions for a sea-voyage that will never come—and the Troubles sweeping down from the North to overtake us all—"

"They are sweeping down over all the world," I said softly. "You would not have escaped forever in Magya or Iskarron, I believe. Better to meet them boldly."

Turl took his hands from his face to stare at me. "Don't tell me you're a prophet!"

"No, but I travel with one," I said. "Tell me, will you really give up your plans of sea-trading for Torrin?"

"Unless he comes to his senses, what else could I do?" said Turl.

For that, I had no answer. "I'd best go, and let you go to him. I'd give you my hand in peace, but I doubt you'd take it."

"What do you know of me, ex-Tarvon?" said Turl. "Here's my hand. Now, let's find you something for that bump on the head."

I limped back to our corner in the square in midafternoon, holding a spirit-soaked rag to the back of my head. I could not see through the crowd whether my friends were still there, but gradually I began to hear over the clamor a high, clear voice that permeated the summer air like the scent of lilacs.

I quickened my step toward the sound, threading through the crowd as eagerly as Torrin had when he slipped away from us. I saw Trenara first, swaying slightly to the music in some unfathomable dream of her own; Hwyn must be near, but still hidden by the heads of bystanders.

The song grew in my ears: one of the sea-songs I had taught Hwyn, the lament of a sailor's wife while her man is away at sea. It was well suited to her voice, and she even had the player's trick of putting a slight sob in her voice without losing the purity of the melody. When I glimpsed her between the listeners standing about her, she seemed unaware of my presence. I joined the song and watched her turn toward my voice, her face brightening. *There is only one in the world,* I thought, *and when you have once seen it, you can be sure it will never come again.* I did not know whether Torrin had chosen right or wrong, but for myself, I was certain.

5

THE SPEAKING STONE

We took the eastward road toward Kreyn the next morning, slipping away while the Feast of the Bright Goddess still flourished lest we meet Klem and Edwold in the departing crowds when it was done. Nursing regrets for the lost fourth day of the festival, I looked back many times, sorry to leave the site of our undreamt-of success, the first I'd known in years. And Trenara, as well—Trenara, so docile in Sebrin, caught a mood of rebellion on the road. Though she made no move to leave Hwyn, she did everything in her power to delay her: casting off bits of her clothes at the roadside, unpacking the knapsacks, whining and dragging her feet. After a few days of it, Hwyn lost her temper and harangued her, until the sheer futility of it made her laugh despite herself. "I might as well be talking to a tree," she said. "It's scarcely worth the effort. To think she was as sweet as you please, all that wild ride on Lake Garran! I almost wish we'd continued north instead of turning aside."

"We can turn any time you choose," I reminded her.

She considered the possibility, upending her boot to shake out a pebble. "Am I being a fool?"

"How could I possibly tell?" I said. "Visions, voices, prophecies, the end of the world—nothing in the Tarvon Order quite prepared me to deal with any of these outside a book. You're the seer."

"A half-blind seer," she said with a sardonic twist of her long mouth. "It never ceases to amaze me how much the Second Sight leaves dark. The prophets in the holiday pageants always seem so sure, so complete in their knowledge. As for me, I know my path leads into the Troubles, but I don't know what I'll do when I'm there. I don't know what will happen afterward. It's not knowledge my dreams give me; it's a gadfly driving me, a scent on the wind to lure me. Can you understand how it feels to find your way by bare intuition, without a shred of reason to cover yourself with?"

"I'm following you," I said. "Need I say more?"

She stared at the dirt between her feet. "You can turn away whenever you choose."

"I don't," I said. "Come on, before Trenara gets her boots off again."

The way to Kreyn was hilly and hard. Worst of all were the long stretches of arid land where we sweated ourselves dry, drained our water-skins, and kept anxious watch for any little spot of greenery that might signal a trickle of water, or hold enough moisture in fruits or stems to keep us going till the next stream. Trenara whined; Hwyn cursed; I set my teeth against complaint, determined to prove to Hwyn that I would not repent my decision or weaken under the hardships of the journey.

As we wound our way down the thousandth brown hill in a row, Hwyn said, "You haven't said a word in hours."

"Well," I said, "in all that time, you've said, 'Sky-Raven's Bones!' and, 'Curse this dust!' and, 'I'd give my other eyetooth for a drink of fresh water,' several times each. And I couldn't argue with any of those, so there wasn't much to say."

"You don't have to argue," she said with a sly smile, the first I'd seen in miles of dusty road.

"Could I ask questions, then?" I said.

"You could," she said, "as long as you know I may not answer."

"You don't have to tell me a great thing, a secret thing," I said. "But surely there's something you could tell me about yourself that wouldn't touch on those things you can't speak of. About your childhood, maybe."

She looked at the dust. "That's where the ghosts are."

"All right," I said, "then tell me about the place where you were happiest."

She tipped back her head, not seeming to see the bright hot sky over us, but some shining vision out of the past. "All right: St. Fiern's Town, when I was very small. The whole town was like a year-round festival, with the pilgrims coming in from everywhere, and the minstrels following the pilgrims in and out of town—no end of music and pageants and strange stories. I learned to sing from the minstrels, and the pilgrims would fuss over me and give me sweets." She smiled at the memory. "That was before I was deformed, of course. I went back, years later— ah, gods! There's no going back." The smile faded, and she was silent a while. At last she said, "What about you? Where were you happy?"

I thought about it long. "I don't know," I said finally. "Gods, that's pathetic. I've been almost everywhere—Swevnalond, Magya, Greater and Lesser Kettra, Iskarron, the Islands—and I don't know. Wherever I was, I always wanted to be somewhere else."

Hwyn squinted up at me, looking puzzled or perhaps distressed. "Why did you ask me that question if you couldn't answer it?"

"On the boat," I said at last.

"On boats?"

"I mean, on the rudderless boat on Lake Garran, escaping from Kelgarran Hall, with the whole world ahead of us. That was where I was happy."

"Really?" she said, with that puzzled squint again. "Escaping a ruined castle, jammed in a defective boat with two strangers at the whim of a ghost?" She considered it a while, then smiled. "So was I."

"I wish Lake Garran were in front of us right now," I said. "I'd drink it."

As we neared Kreyn, the land turned greener, fed by streams flowing south from the Hills of Penmorrin. Our water-skins were full, but our money drained away. The folk along the road, cowherds and vineyard-keepers, would give no crust of bread for work, much less for song, but would eagerly take the coins we'd earned at the festival, hoarding them away for rare trips to the market, sure to buy twice the goods that they'd doled out to us. By the time we reached Kreyn, our pockets and stomach were empty, our spirits low.

"We'll eat at the lady's table tonight, or I'll be hanged for forcing my way," Hwyn boasted on our first day in Kreyn. But the city was large, and there were many splendid houses—their high walls painted rose or gold, their glazed windows reflecting the sun—that were nonetheless not Kreyn Hall. Of poor hovels there were also many, scraps of wood patched together with mud like birds' nests. Among the tangle of streets and alleys without coherence, we poor strangers could not find the hall of the Guardian of Day.

Small help we had from the passersby! Not a soul would give us directions, much less anything else. They would neither stop for Hwyn's singing—a sign of either dull ears or impoverished souls—nor pity her seeming helplessness in idiot's guise; minstrels and beggars were both too plentiful to regard. They wanted no day-labor from foreigners; poor laborers were plentiful as well, willing to work for food or the hope of it. Ragged children thronged the roads, begging for crumbs, clinging to Trenara's skirt with a pleading look, offering to fetch and carry. Hwyn found one girl's hand in her pocket. She caught it and extracted it emphatically, giving the child a grave look. "Now, learn by this," she began, but the child twisted away and ran, leaving Hwyn staring after her with haunted eyes.

Toward the end of the day, when Hwyn made a motion to leave the town limits, I thought perhaps she'd given up—and to be honest, my heart rose at the prospect, despite the harsh road we'd have to follow to retrace our steps. But when we camped in the shelter of a brushy hollow, she pulled from her pockets the reason for our retreat: a few crumbly seed-cakes of the kind she liked, which I'd heard hawked in the Kreyn market-square at an alarming price.

"Where did you get those?" I asked stupidly.

"Corner booth at the market. Poorly guarded," she said. "The merchant can afford the loss, I assure you: his purse was bulging, and his prices were robbery of the purest kind." I must have looked disapproving, for she added defensively, "We tried all else. I won't beg when I can earn, and I won't steal when I can beg. But I won't starve when I can steal, either."

"I understand," I said hesitantly. "You and Trenara divide them: you're hungrier than I."

Hwyn opened her mouth as if to make a rebuttal, then stopped herself, reconsidering. Finally she bowed her head. "All right, then. I understand." She gave most of the booty to Trenara, saving only one cake for herself. I tried not to stare at them as they ate, but without success; and all the while she ruminated over her one cake, crumbs in her skirt, a sheen of butter on her fingers, Hwyn eyed me with a strange solemn stare—I might almost have said a hungry look. I went off to search the brush for wild berries, but found none. There was a clump of what looked like blackberry bushes, but other scavengers had picked them clean.

That night I lay long awake, stomach twisted with its emptiness. After trying valiantly to will myself to sleep by staying still—or at least to lie quiet for the others' sake—I lost patience. I writhed and curled myself around my crying stomach, muttering curses.

"Are you all right?"

The voice came so unexpectedly that I jumped up, quivering in every nerve, before my eyes adjusted to the pale starlight and my reason caught up with me. I saw Hwyn before me, sitting uncomfortably upright, one hand pressed to her chest. Trenara, of course, slept soundly.

"Yes," I lied. "Are you?"

I would not believe her if she said yes. Hwyn's brow was knotted with worry, and though the night was warm, she shivered. "I feel—strange—that's all," she stammered.

"Is it a pain in your chest?" I pried, suspecting that such a hard-used creature might well be consumptive.

But she looked blankly at me. "No. Why should you think—? Oh!" Noticing as if for the first time the position of her hand, she extended and uncurled it to reveal the Eye of Night. "It's this. I think it's speaking to me."

"Of what?"

"I can't tell. It's like a thousand voices calling all at once and none in unison: no clear words, just a babble of tongues. But it calls to me. Maybe in time I'll understand."

I nodded.

"Or maybe—" She held it out to me. "Take it. Can you hear them?"

I hesitated. She put the stone in my hand, curled my fingers around it; I was startled to feel the Eye, curiously warm, and her fingers, curiously cool in the humid night. I felt life in the stone. Then, moved by much the same instinct that draws one to babies or kittens, I pressed it to my heart. Hwyn leaned toward me, avid, hopeful. But I shook my head. "No voices. A faint sense of life, nothing more." I put it back in the hollow of her hand.

"Are you sure?" she asked, as she returned it to the breast of her smock.

"I have no ear for such things. But you surprise me: you thought I might hear what eluded you?"

"I had some hope," she said. "I don't know yet what you are, and what deeper purpose there might be in your coming with me. You might have held the key."

"And you trusted me to take the Eye of Night and return it, even if my powers had been great?"

"Yes," she said without hesitation. "If you'd understood its message, you would have told me."

"How do you know?" I challenged, though of course it was perfectly true.

"Because you're defenseless."

"Thank you very much," I drawled.

"I mean that in the best sense," she amended. "You have no guile, no stratagems; you go at things headfirst. You get a lump on the head from a self-deluded man and accept it as the wages of truth-telling. You'd set your bare heart as a shield between a child and a wolf. I'd trust you with my life."

"But not your name?" I couldn't resist adding.

Hwyn shrugged, opened her empty hands to the starlight. " 'A name is more than life; for what shall you hope to gain when you have lost yourself?' Revelations of St. Ligaiya."

I could not, at some hour past midnight, on an empty stomach, recall a trenchant commentary to that scripture, so I only grunted, wrapped my arms around my middle, and rocked myself like a discontented infant.

Suddenly Hwyn tipped back her head like a dog scenting the wind. Her gesture made me notice that there was, indeed, a spicy scent in the air that I had thought the product of my hungry imagination. She rose and beckoned me to follow her into the brush. Tangled in the bare branches of a dead bush, she showed me a vine, invisible in the dark thicket but plain to the touch and scent. "Wild slakings," she said, plucking a few leaves and thrusting them into my hand. "Nothing to fill the belly, but they'll calm its complaining a while."

They had a comforting smell, like an herb my parents' cook had called gammage—perhaps it was the same thing. "Thank you," I said, and pressed her hand before I put one of the leaves in my mouth. It was soothing, not all at once but little by little. In time fatigue took its rightful place over hunger. My head drooped. Thickly I realized that Hwyn was saying something, and I jerked awake. "Hmm?"

But she laughed softly. "Never mind. Go to sleep, righteous man." She'd called me something similar once before, in mockery; the laugh was still in her voice, but now she spoke the words gently.

"What about you?" I said.

"Either I'll learn to ignore the voices, or listen till I understand them," she said. "I'll tell you which in the morning."

But when I awoke in the morning she was sound asleep, one arm flung out carelessly, looking as defenseless as she claimed I was, looking so fragile that the sight caught at my heart. Trenara never looked fragile in sleep; she looked perfectly whole, an enchanted maiden sleeping a hundred years under a guardian's spell, a forest asleep under snow. It was with an effort that I turned away from them to look for more gammage. When I returned I sat quietly chewing a leaf, watching my companions sleep, marveling what a strange fate had brought such a pair together—and how much stranger that I should be their companion.

We returned to the city in the day, to be met by frustration. Our luck had not improved. If Hwyn filled her pockets with anything, she did not show me, and I did not ask. In the heat of the day, I pulled her aside into a shaded alley and whispered, "Could you teach me to steal? I don't think I can hold out much longer." She looked so horrified that I almost laughed. "Come now, you can't disapprove of my doing what you do yourself. You laughed at my overscrupulousness; well, it's worn thin quickly enough."

"Do you think I'm eager to see you as marred as I am?" she whispered back. "Never mind learning. Next time I offer you something, don't ask where I found it."

"No. I can't let you take risks for both of us. Teach me."

"You'd never learn; you're too old. You'd get caught. Everyone does, at first. Look at this," she held up her right hand, displaying the stump of her severed finger. "They did this to me for theft. And I was a child then. You're a grown man: they'd take your whole hand. This town is not gentle."

"All the more reason not to let you take risks for me," I said. "Forget that I asked. I'll manage." I walked out into the crowd again, and she followed. Luck was with me, for I was in time to see a mangled bread-roll tumble from a merchant's basket into the roadside dirt. I dove for it with an ardor I'd have found comic a few days earlier, then retreated into a corner with my quarry, dusting it off as best I could. Hwyn settled down beside me, and I offered her half, Trenara being somewhere astray out of sight.

Hwyn took the offered morsel absentmindedly, but did nothing with it. As I attacked my half of the bread, scarcely pausing to rub the grime away on my sleeve, she squinted up at me. "You shouldn't be here," she said. "I did wrong to ask you to come with me."

"Why? Do you have someone better?" I retorted, missing for a moment the sorrow in her voice.

She responded at once: "No, Jereth, of course not. But look at you! You didn't have to be here, scrounging bread out of the gutter, starving on a fool's errand. You weren't brought up to this."

"And you were?"

She shrugged. "I don't know. I suppose I wouldn't call anything that happened to me 'bringing up.' But that's not quite what I mean, anyway. Trenara and I—we're marked, set aside, ruined already. What's a few more scars? But you're different. You weren't brought up to this. I brought you to this."

"I came here on my own legs," I said. "You couldn't have brought me anywhere without—what's this?"

A herald came elbowing past the people in the market-square. "Make way! Make way for Her Resplendence!" Pushed as far back against a glove-shop wall as we could be, we still had to flatten ourselves thinner against the press of people clearing out of the street. I stood, as much to get my long legs out of people's way as to see what was coming. Mounted guards rode by, splendid in white and gold livery, followed by four milk-white horses bearing an ornate litter. On it reclined a graceful lady dressed in yellow silk, her fair hair sparkling with jeweled combs. The people bowed before her, grubby beggars and plumed gentry alike. But in the midst of her procession she called to the horsemen to stop and, to their astonishment, leapt down from the litter, shouting, "Cousin Luith!"

I gripped Hwyn's arm and whispered: "Look: it's Trenara!"

We wove our way closer to see. My eyes had not deceived me. Amid open-mouthed guards, the lady clung to Trenara, crying, "Cousin Luith! By the Hidden Goddess! How you've surprised me! Why have you come all this way? Is there trouble in Quinth?"

Trenara embraced her with all the grace she could so well command. I could hear Hwyn's breath drawn in slowly; I could almost hear her hoping this would last. But Trenara spoke as calmly and musically as ever: "I am the Lady Trenara of Larioneth. I come from the Troubles in the North."

"Larioneth!" the stranger exclaimed. "You *are* a long way from home! Forgive me: I mistook you for a kinswoman of mine. But come with me anyway. I am eager to hear all the tale you must have to tell me. I am Lady Goldifer, Guardian of Day—surely you have heard of me? I have long taken an interest in the fate of your land."

Trenara looked about for us, then turned back to the lady, saying, "I must bring my Hwyn."

At these words Hwyn reached Trenara's side, and in a heartbeat I saw her transformed into the half-wit she had seemed when I first saw her. "M-m-m'lady?" she stammered. I managed not to burst out laughing.

"Your servant, of course, must come with you, noble sister," Lady Goldifer said. "Have you any other retinue?"

That was my cue, and I summoned my wits as hurriedly as Hwyn had hidden hers. "My lady, will you require my services, or shall I attend my meditations in the temple till you send for me?" I spoke to Trenara, who only smiled graciously, as ever; but I awaited an answer from Her Resplendence.

She took the bait. "Your chaplain travels with you?" Lady Goldifer said to Trenara. "Ah, but of course. You are a lady of piety as well as beauty. He is welcome as well. Of which order is he?"

Trenara only cocked her head to one side with a dreamy look. I said, "My Lady is tired from a hard journey. We have lost all our goods on the road, and have scarcely eaten these three days; it's no wonder she is half in dreams by now. Is there a place she can rest?"

"She shall share my own litter and rest in Kreyn Hall," the fair-haired lady declared. "You, reverend sir, may take one of my guards' horses. The servant can follow."

That plan was not to my liking. "Begging your pardon, my Lady," I said, "let me walk, or let Hwyn ride with me. She is a distant kinswoman of mine, and it would dishonor my forebears to accept such distinctions from her."

"As you wish," the lady said. "She will be no great burden to the mount." At her command, one of the guardsmen relinquished his horse. I mounted cautiously—it had been years upon years since I'd been on horseback, and I'd never been much of a rider. As for Hwyn, she showed no sign of knowing what to do, and she was too short anyway to put her foot in the stirrup to be pulled up; in the end I had to dismount and lift her up into the saddle while the impatient guard held the reins. By the time I regained my seat, the procession had almost gone without us. But then we were on our way through the market-streets of Kreyn, and all was well. The busy crowd cleared before us at the demand of the heralds. Hwyn let go of the horse's mane just long enough to squeeze my arm briefly, as if to reassure me that behind the fool's mask, she still remained. It seemed I could feel both our spirits lifting, and with good cause: we had found a way in to the stronghold, and more than that, we would surely be given something to eat.

Kreyn Hall was magnificent—not after the regal manner of Kelgarran Hall, with its huge oaken table and mighty hearth, but in a glorious disorder, like a field of summer blossoms. Lady Goldifer's feasting-hall was hung with jeweled draperies and furnished with an array of soft divans—crimson, sapphire, gold brocade—around a series of low tables of various sizes. One table, carved with intricate filigrees, stood on a dais before an ample couch. Here the Guardian of Day led the Lady Trenara to sit with her; at her sign, servants brought a footstool for me. As for Hwyn, she scurried off with the servants, who disappeared into the kitchen almost without any word of command. They reappeared with golden flagons of Iskarrian green wine, platters of cold spiced meats, fragrant cheeses, glistening fruits, fine white bread. It was not the hour for the household meal, so the expanse of the room was empty, but I could well imagine it cluttered with guests and swarming with a hive of these quick-footed servants, shuttling back and forth from kitchen to table to kitchen with steaming trenchers on their shoulders, melting away like morning dew at a clap of their mistress's hands. As it was, we were more than well attended to, and Hwyn looked more unnecessary than ever, fussing over Trenara's plate, cutting her meat, getting in the way, hearing things meant for other ears.

Lady Goldifer eyed Hwyn as she would a fly on the meat, but she spoke only to Trenara: "Noble cousin, how is it that I found you in a situation so beneath you? Could you not have come to me at once when you reached Kreyn?"

"I do not know this place," said Trenara.

"But surely anyone on the street could have directed you to the great hall," Lady Goldifer said.

Trenara shrugged, nibbling a bit of meat in that delicate, maidenly way of hers. By then I had watched that elegant nibbling enough to be impressed by how much food she could make disappear without ever seeming to gluttonize. "I didn't know," she murmured, when her mouth was empty.

I explained for her: "The streets are full of strangers, and without gold or goods we had little to capture their attention or sympathy. We'd lost our valuables when a ferry sank and we had to swim for our lives. By the time we reached your city, we had to beg for sustenance—but there are too many beggars in this town for anyone to regard a few more." I took a wedge of cheese from the tray, trying not to attack it with noticeable desperation.

Lady Goldifer shrugged. "There are not more beggars here than in another town." From this I judged that either she'd never seen another city, or she'd never seen her own.

Trenara interrupted, "My city is Larioneth"—a bald non sequitur, which I was sure would give her away.

But before I could make a lame attempt to rescue her, Lady Goldifer took the fool's gold for true coin, and repaid it. "Ah yes: tell me of your troubled land."

"It is not like this place," Trenara said, a melancholy chime. "I miss it."

"How long ago did you leave?" Goldifer pursued.

"Long," Trenara sighed musically, "long and long years ago. My family were scattered by the Troubles."

"The Troubles! Are they all the tales speak of? The earth in upheaval, the dead pitched from their graves, kings cast down, all order lost?"

Trenara looked solemn.

"Ah, these are dark times, dark times indeed!" Lady Goldifer cried. "But let me ask you: have you had any peculiar dreams—I mean, any visions, dreams sent by the gods to illumine the Troubles?"

Trenara nodded slowly. I held my breath; *what would she say?*

But the Guardian of Day burst out eagerly, "So have I! I meditate on the mysteries, and I dream things...Do you know what I think is happening in the North? It is really quite simple. Night is falling."

Hwyn spilled the wine she had been pouring. Mopping it up with my napkin, I kept my mind on the conversation taking place past us, lest we miss the sequel to this revelation. Before resuming, the Guardian of Day clapped for servants, who cleaned the table and replaced the food that had been flooded.

Lady Goldifer repeated, "Night is falling: the night of the world. That's why it is important, above all, to reflect light—to reflect *on* the light—to meditate on the sun and its gifts. So I tell my people. The laborers used to sleep through the noon of the day, but now, by my decree, all must be out of doors under the noonday sun. We need its blessing. And these—" she raised the pendant she wore at her throat, a crystal stone that flashed in the sunlight streaming from the windows above her. It was the same sort of gem that ornamented her golden hair and the belt at her hips. "See how it sends the light everywhere? We *must* reflect the light. It is our weapon against the darkness. I have decreed the wearing of these crystals as the duty of the commonwealth. The laborers cannot comply, of course, but all the citizens of any worth join me in this. I have charged the merchants of the town with procuring them. We need them more than any other goods. We need them to reflect the light, to dispel the darkness."

Hearing her impassioned speech, watching her pendant flash with each emphatic movement of her head, I could not resist asking, "Your Resplendence, if you send your merchants east and west to procure these gems, will not other lands be defenseless against the darkness?"

Hwyn gave me a warning nudge. But the Guardian of Day

missed the edge to my voice. "Other peoples do not know what to do with them," she said. "In other lands these are mere baubles. Here, they are the prayer of pure light. I have many of them in my chapel, along with other holy things. In sight of them, my chaplain and I gather the best citizens each day to praise the dawn. The power of our light together—ah, you shall see it, priest, and doubt no longer: we shall drive off the darkness, not just from Kreyn but from all Swevnalond, from all the world."

"That—that is indeed admirable," I stammered, my mind racing for a strategy. Those "other holy things" in the chapel ought not to escape Hwyn's scrutiny. "I long to see this chapel," I said, "to feel the power gathered there. Must I wait till dawn?"

Goldifer began smiling her consent, but my goal was scarcely half achieved. Of course I, as Trenara's chaplain, would easily make my way to the chapel, but Hwyn? Furiously I cast my mind back over my years in the Tarvon Order for some grounds for bringing her along—and it was as if St. Tarvi, like his image on our crest, handed me the key of wisdom. I smiled. "With so many tokens of light gathered in one place, and holy things—healing things, I dare say—perhaps we may find in the chapel some healing power for my afflicted kinswoman's eyes." With that I brushed back the wisps of hair from Hwyn's eyes so their abnormality was plainly visible.

"Ah yes—she has need of light," said Lady Goldifer. "Perhaps even her wits may be bettered by it. Can she be trusted to behave fittingly in a place of worship?"

I assured her she could.

"Good," said the lady. "If her lady needs her during the day, we will send a servant to call her back. Meanwhile, my chaplain will show you the way."

The chaplain appeared almost as rapidly as the servants had; one of them must have been dispatched for him in the same silent way they'd been sent for food. He was a stoop-shouldered man with gray hair tonsured across the back of the head, just as my own had recently been; but his cassock, unlike my drab one, was brilliantly white. I could not identify his order. He bowed deeply to his lady, smiled at me, and with a few soft words, conducted me down a corridor as I led Hwyn by the hand. He pulled open a heavy arched door and gestured us in. "Now tell me, have you ever seen the like?"

"It—it's astonishing," I gulped.

The chapel was indeed a startling sight. Light streaming in from high glazed windows struck sparks from crystals on all sides, so that the room glittered like snow in sunlight. The broken light of the crystals cast strange colors on the faces of the gods above and below and around them. And indeed, there seemed to be more gods in that room than anywhere on the World-Wheel.

Single icons of the Bright Goddess predominated, portrayed in all the classic ways: embracing the sun, clothed in the sun, clothed in flowers, scattering flowers on the earth, releasing doves from her hand, blessing fruit-trees. But there were also more icons of the Upright or Rising God than in my whole abbey, which had been devoted to his worship. And there were a number of World-Wheels with the Four Great Ones portrayed in various styles, old and new. One of them must have come from the Western Islands, where men are beardless and both sexes wear the same loose robes; this icon was hung wrong, with the Rising and Turning Gods at the top and bottom, where the goddesses belonged. Some of them were badly drawn, faces distorted pitifully, but none were adorned with less than four gems, and one was made entirely of crystals of various colors. There was also a wheel without any proper icons; the four directions were marked instead by four gems, amethyst for the Hidden Goddess, emerald for the Rising God, diamond for the Bright Goddess, and for the Turning God a garnet. My eyes were dazzled by the glitter.

"It's awe-striking, isn't it?" the chaplain said, misreading my glazed expression. "Sometimes I stand here so lost in wonder that the sunset comes before I can fathom how the time slipped by. It's like being out of the world."

"That it is," I breathed. "The townspeople come here—they are allowed?"

"Two or three dozen each morning," the chaplain said.

There were two cushioned benches, enough for eight or ten to have seats; the rest must stand or sit on the tiled floor, and they must be crowded quite close to the riches on the walls. "But these jeweled things—doesn't her ladyship fear theft?"

"What! Steal a sanctified relic from the temple? Who could be so mad?"

There was nothing here that I'd have called a relic, none of the brittle locks of centuries-old hair, the bones full of mystery, the rags of cloth or clay cups once handled by an ancient saint, that I'd seen enshrined in the Tarvon Monastery or the sea-cliff temple at Swanroad. "Gems make many mad," I said, "and there are many poor."

"This is a god-fearing city," the priest said, "and what is more, the people reverence the Guardian of Day for her piety. Why, they'd as soon—" he broke off suddenly. "*Must* that serving-maid handle the icons?"

"Hwyn!" I pulled her away by the hand. "I'm sorry, your reverence. She's nearly blind, you see: she only knows things by feeling them. Where we stayed at Annelon, there were many born blind, and the temple had icons entirely made for the touch, so the blind could feel the love of the gods. She's used to being able to touch them."

"What her ladyship might say—" the priest muttered, but his shoulders sagged, as if he disliked forbidding. "Ah, well, I suppose, if her hands are clean..."

And so, as he and I chanted prayers together and the sunlight in the high windows faded to twilight, Hwyn fingered everything in the room. I noticed that the chaplain kept his eyes shut to avoid seeing her at it. Mine were wide open in fear that Her Resplendence would walk in and see her gems getting dulled by finger-streaks—or worse still, that the Speaking Stone would start babbling prophecies and give us away. I could barely conceal my joy when the chaplain ended his interminable prayers and made a move toward the door. "I must go to bless the evening meal for the noble family, and then spend the night with my own wife and children," he said.

Not celibate, I noted compulsively. *Order of St. Hubon?*

"You two may come with me or stay here, as you please," he continued.

"We will stay. We may need to meditate through the night," I said. "This is a healing place, and gods alone know when we will find another in our travels."

The chaplain nodded approvingly. "I will see that no one disturbs your meditation."

For that, I prayed the gods bless him eternally. I thanked him, accepted his blessing, and breathed a great sigh of relief when the door closed behind him.

Hwyn drew close enough to whisper to me, "For an honest man, you lie well."

"Hush," I laughed. "You're lucky you weren't thrown out onto the streets, putting your grubby hands on her ladyship's crystals."

"My hands are clean," she protested. "But this place—these crystals—" She shook her head. "They're not what I'm looking for. There must be another place—a secret altar somewhere. What do you think?"

"What do *I* think?" I said. "I think her taste in icons is appalling. What more do I know of these matters?"

"Really? Are they ugly? Most are just a blur of color to me," Hwyn said. "But you *do* know something of these things—enough to be flippant about Her Resplendence's piety."

"I finally understand," I said, "why the Tarvon Order was so given to plainness—and what the abbot meant about people who try to buy the gods. But there was one thing the Lady said, that you said before—"

" 'Night is falling,' " Hwyn whispered back. "Yes. She came this close to the truth—" she held her fingers a pinch apart, "—and then sailed on past it as fast as ever a thought could carry her. At least, so it seems to me. Unless I'm the one that sailed past the truth and went on going."

"When one woman's vision sets her in luxury amid the misery of her people, and another's leads her into hardship, I know which vision I trust. 'The gods are not easy comrades,' " I said, quoting St. Ligaiya back at her. "But tell me, what do you find here?"

"Nothing," Hwyn whispered furiously. "None of these 'holy things' have a glimmer of power, any more than my old boot. But there's *something* of real power in this house—nearby, but not in this room. That must be the Speaking Stone."

"Unless Klem was mistaken," I cautioned.

"Maybe," she said, "but I feel some trace of power, not far away."

"I don't know. How would I know?" I muttered. Then something came to me. "You don't think the Speaking Stone could be the one on the lady's neck?"

"No," Hwyn said. "If it were, it would be speaking constantly. It's always touching her skin."

"Is that what a Speaking Stone does?"

"So I've heard," Hwyn said. "At the temple in St. Fiern's Town, a priestess told me of them."

"Well, you know more than I," I said. "Perhaps I'd best go back to praying."

"Yes: chant some prayers, so no one will hear me scuffling about."

She paced the room, touching the walls here and there: the west wall, with its door to the outside world, where the townspeople must enter for their morning prayers; the south wall, painted with the largest icon of the Bright Goddess; the east wall, hung with a tapestry of the Rising God. There she paused and gazed a long while at the image, squinting to see. Then she groped behind the hanging purposefully for far too long. All my attention was on the northern door, the one to the other rooms of Kreyn Hall, lest anyone enter and catch her in this un-simpleton-like behavior. After a time Hwyn dropped to her knees before the tapestry, but not in prayer. She felt the floor, chose a flag-stone, and pulled with all her might, but the stone would not give way. Instead, with a tremendous tug, she unbalanced herself and went careening into the wall below the tapestry, which shifted with a small creaking sound. Hwyn opened her mouth as though to cry out, then stopped it with her fist. It was all I could do to keep up my chanting as she pried the section of wall open. The secret door was so low that even Hwyn had to bend her head to enter. She waved a hand at me, then disappeared through the doorway. I prayed fervently that no one would come and ask for an explanation: all my clever lies were spent.

The sun was sinking low before Hwyn reappeared.

"Did you find it?" I whispered frantically as soon as I could decently end my chant.

"That idiot Klem!" she hissed. "That ignorant, meddlesome bundle of lead-brained piety! He got it all wrong. A Speaking Stone, indeed!"

"You mean you didn't find it? Then what was the power you sensed?"

"Oh, it's there, all right," she said. "And I suppose in a manner of thinking, it's a speaking stone. It doesn't *speak* when you touch it. It has *writing* carved in it. What the power's for, I don't know, but it's not for speech."

"What does the writing say?" I pressed.

"How should I know?" said Hwyn.

"Why, can't you read?" I said.

"Of course I can't! What did you think I was—a priestess?"

"Priestess of the Hidden Wisdom, I guessed," I said. "You haven't told me a thing about yourself. But if you can't read—"

"*You* can!" Hwyn suddenly gripped my arm with hard, wiry fingers. "Come with me. Come on!"

Just then the door creaked—the northern door, the one to the hall. We froze: the secret passage was still open for all to see. I moved frantically to shut it; it proved heavier than I expected. My heart almost burst before I saw that the intruder was only Trenara. "I missed you," she said to Hwyn. "Are you well?"

"Fine, Trenara," Hwyn said softly. "Would you like to come and explore with us? You'll have to be very quiet."

Trenara nodded silently.

There was nothing for it, then, but for the three of us to go down the tunnel. Hwyn led the way, Trenara crowded after her, and I brought up the rear, shutting the door most of the way behind us. For the first several yards I had to crawl, holding Trenara's skirt for guidance. Then the path sloped sharply downward into a big, echoing corridor. There was no light; Hwyn skimmed the wall with one hand, Trenara held her other arm, and I held Trenara's.

"We're almost there," Hwyn said at last. "Here: the secret altar. The stone. We're here." In the deep gloom of an underground chamber, she found my hand and placed it on a pillar of stone. Whatever power might be in it, I could not feel it; I did feel the carvings, but that was not enough. "Hwyn, you didn't tell me it was in a dungeon. There's not even moonlight here; it's as if my eyes were shut. I haven't got a candle. I'll have to go back for one," I said. This, I thought, is what happens when you let a blind guide lead you.

"Can't you feel the writing?" she asked.

"I'm not used to reading by touch," I said. "It's not intelligible to me. I need light."

"Wait: how about this?" I saw a soft glow as she drew the Eye of Night from her pocket. As she held it up before the Speaking Stone, the light grew, illuminating the stone and the inscription on it.

"It might be enough," I said. "There: I can make some of it out. It's in the Old Tongue. Move the Eye to the left; I can't see the beginning."

She moved it, but as she did so, smoke began to rise from the stone, blurring my sight. "What's that?" I grumbled, and fanned the smoke away. It took me a few tries to realize that the words were fading, turning to dust under the light. "Wait! Stop!" I cried foolishly, as though the stone or the light might obey me. "Oh, Sky-Raven's Bones!" I cursed as Hwyn had, for darkness ceased to be the problem: flames burst from the Speaking Stone. Hwyn pocketed the Eye of Night as quickly as possible, muttering imprecations, and smothered the fire—as I later found, with a curtain hanging at the altar's side—but it was too late. I ran my fingers over the hot stone: smooth as a new-laid egg. "Nothing. The writing's gone."

"Dear gods! I destroyed it," Hwyn said.

"Let's go," Trenara whimpered.

"Trenara, I think you're right," I said. All the way back up the corridor my heart was in my mouth, and I could feel Hwyn's hand shaking as she pulled me along. The soft scraping of our feet along the floor echoed against the walls till it sounded like pursuing footsteps. My awkward crouching posture, an annoyance on the way down, became a torment, a knife in the back. By the time Hwyn opened the secret door, I was sure we were about to be caught. I was so relieved when we emerged into an empty chapel that I didn't notice anything wrong. "Empty!" I whispered ecstatically, forcing the door closed with all my might. "Thank the gods! It's all behind us now."

"What's that smell of smoke?" Hwyn said.

"It must have clung to us from the cellar," I said, but then my eyes adjusted to the light, and I saw. "Hidden Goddess!" I gasped. "The icons! What happened to them?" We stood among the smoldering ruins of Lady Goldifer's holy things. Even the gems, which by nature should not have burned, were ashes.

"Burnt," Hwyn breathed.

"Did the lamp flare up? No, that's absurd," I babbled, "nothing else is burnt. What in the gods' names happened here?"

Trenara pointed at the northeast alcove of the temple. "Black bird," she said. Sure enough, just where the gaudiest of the jeweled icons had been was a smoke-stain in the shape of a bird.

Hwyn put a hand over the pocket where she carried the Eye of Night. "When the true appears, the false will pass away," she murmured—another verse of the Revelations of St. Ligaiya.

"Well, we'd better pass away from this place before anyone comes looking for us," I said.

"But how can we leave here? This treasure-trove must be well guarded." Hwyn bit her knuckle, thinking.

I considered the problem a moment. "At least the guards would be thinking to keep thieves out, not in."

Hwyn shook her head. "Do you think she trusts her servants so well?"

For a moment my mind was filled with the image of the sort of treatment that might make the servants heed Lady Goldifer's least gesture. But this was no time for such speculations. Instead I considered the layout of the room. "We'll never get to those windows," I said, craning up at them far above us.

"Just as well," Hwyn said. "Once we got out of them, we'd have a real tumbler's trick to do to get down—at least until the guards thoughtfully brought us down with arrows. It's either the west door or the hall door."

"The west door, surely," I said.

"Yes—no," said Hwyn. "That's where they'd expect a thief to come out. And besides, there's the wall around the courtyard—"

"But the *hall* door?" I put to her, incredulous.

Trenara broke in to whimper, "We must *go*."

"We know," I said soothingly, then fretted to Hwyn, "If only she could tell that to Her Resplendence."

"At this hour?" Hwyn said, for it had been dark for long. "And yet—oh, gods be with us, it's our only hope. Goldifer trusts her. Trenara," she took the lady's arm and spoke gravely, "You are right. We *must* go. We must go *now*. Can you tell that to them? Can you lead us out, and tell them all that we *must* go?"

Trenara did not answer, but seemed cheered by Hwyn's words. She straightened, walked to the hall door, and waited, her head regally high, for Hwyn to open it for her. Hwyn turned to show me her slack-jawed fool's face for an instant before opening the door and holding it wide for the lady and her chaplain. I took up a torch and, taking my cue from Hwyn, assumed an expression of preoccupied piety, my role in our little pageant. I did not need to pretend to be praying; I'd been at sea in tempests that scared me less than this walk through the corridors—perhaps because then, at least, I could do something to fend off death, mend sails or pump water, but now my life and Hwyn's rested in Trenara's hands. My heart was in my mouth when we reached the great door of the hall and a sentry demanded, "Who goes there?"

"I am the Lady Trenara of Larioneth," she chimed in her usual tones.

"Good Lady, you must be lost in the corridors. We will call a servant to guide you to a bedchamber."

"No. We must go," Trenara said.

"What?" the guard said, bewildered. "Have you already taken leave of Her Resplendence, then?"

"Tell her. We must go now," Trenara said. "We must."

There was a silent pause, when I could only imagine the look of profound knowledge she bound him with. At last the sentry called out, "Gerd!" A servant sprang into being, it seemed, from some nook unseen. "See if Her Resplendence will receive her guest now, so she can take leave of her."

We were led through corridor after corridor and passed from servant to servant till a perfumed and silk-clad bower-maid bade Hwyn and me wait outside the chamber of Lady Goldifer. We never heard Trenara's leave-taking, but whatever she said and whatever Lady Goldifer read into it must have sufficed, because we were given our packs, full water-skins, and torches and led out through the great gate.

We stayed silent and let Trenara lead until we were far enough from the great hall to discreetly douse our torches and disappear into the night.

"Thank the gods the city's not walled," Hwyn said. "We can slip out through the fields at the edge of town and be gone by the time they see the chapel."

"Which way?" I asked.

"North," Hwyn said firmly. "It's the way they'll least suspect. And it's the way we're headed, in the end."

It was also the way to the Hills of Penmorrin, rising eastward in a long swath till they joined the impassable mountains of eastern Swevnalond on the Magyan border, the Wall of Magya. It was known far and wide as cruelly hard traveling land, beside which a sea-journey to Magya was a stroll in the garden. But I said nothing, knowing Hwyn was right: the northern paths would be least watched.

We turned northward and crept through the silent streets, ever alert for signs of another waking footstep. Twice sounds in the street sent us scuttling for alleys—an old beggar and a stray dog, as it turned out. At length the houses thinned and we broke and ran between rows of crops until these, too, gave way to low hills and woody downs. We wound northeast to skirt a hill, hoping its bulk would hide us a while.

A sliver of sun squeezed over the rugged horizon. "They'll be finding out now," Hwyn said.

I nodded and kept going. So did the sun, relentless pursuer, stealing the cover of night from our escape.

Threading a copse, Hwyn stumbled and caught herself with one hand against a thick gray trunk. She hung there a while, panting. "I can't go much farther."

"We've gotten a head start, at least," I said, relieved that she had yielded before I was forced to beg a rest. "Can you go on as far as that ridge?" I pointed to a line of garish yellow gorse on a green hill ahead of us.

"Where?" Hwyn squinted.

"Halfway up the next rise ahead of us there's a row of bushes on an outcropping. It would shelter us, but not so I couldn't keep watch on the land below."

"Lead on. You're my eyes," she said.

I put an arm across her shoulders, got her moving again. We climbed the slope almost on hands and knees till we found the perfect spot, well hidden from below unless we chose to peer over the bushes. It was a hard, sloping bed with thorns to one side and rocks to the other—but we were in no mood to quarrel with it. We threw ourselves down, breathing heavily as though we'd forgotten to breathe till then. "Oh," I gasped, "my feet."

"My stomach," Hwyn groaned. "I scarcely had time to eat, serving at table. They told me to fill my pockets for later." She pulled out her small takings, fried hearth-cakes, odd scraps of cheese and meat from the cutting-board, and the best bit, a squashed cheese-filled roll that she broke in half to share with me, Trenara being already asleep.

I waved it away, though the scent of it teased me. "If you didn't have a chance to eat at the hall, you should have it all. Keep your strength up."

"*Please,*" she said, so I took half and thanked her for it.

"Don't mention it," she said. "I'm so sorry I brought you here—both of you." She turned to include the oblivious Trenara. "I could have gotten us all killed—and all for nothing! So stupid of me!"

"It's all right," I said. "But please tell me something. If you can't read, how on earth do you know the Revelations so well?"

"Easy," she said. "I've heard them recited in the temple often enough. But honestly, can you really have thought me a priestess? Scrubbing tavern floors and stealing cakes? What order would that be, my good priest?"

"The Priestesses of the Hidden Wisdom often have interesting interpretations of the vow of poverty," I said, "which might stretch to condone theft. Scrubbing tavern floors, certainly— they might elevate that to a sacred rite of humility. They take no vows of obedience or chastity. I've met a few, but not many. They make most Tarvons nervous."

"But not you," Hwyn laughed. Then, anxiously, she asked the question I'd been dreading: "Did you read any of the inscription before it burned away?"

"Two words," I said, "and without knowing the rest, I can only guess what they mean."

"And what is it you guess?"

I hesitated. "*Sith morum*," I said. "If it's the Golden Age dialect, it would mean 'journey by sea.'"

"And if it isn't?" Hwyn pressed.

I hesitated again.

"Tell me. It can't hurt me more known than unknown," she said.

"If it's Silver Age dialect," I said, "it might mean 'journey to death.'"

She bowed her head. "Thank you. For being honest, I mean. And for not reproaching me for the whole misadventure. I did wrong to bring us here. I should have known better."

"Why should I reproach you?" I said. "It was all for your quest, wasn't it?"

"No," she said. "It was for my fear. I know what I have to do. But I hoped I'd find out what will happen to me. I shouldn't have staked so much on finding out. Why should I want to know for certain what I already feared? It's too late to look back now, come what may."

"If it's a journey by sea," I said, "at least you've got a competent sailor with you."

"It may not be," she sighed. "But mean what it may, this prophecy was not for my knowing, and I should not have pried into it. I took this quest upon myself, unurged, alone; the time to wonder about consequences is past. The burden was my own choice, and it's mine to bear, to whatever end it takes me."

I almost wished I'd lied about what I'd read on the stone. I did not know how to comfort her. But silence seemed too cruel, so I filled it as best I could. "For what it's worth," I stammered, "I will be with you. Whatever we journey toward."

She did not speak, but pressed my hand so hard that I felt it to my heart.

6

THE SMALL END

OF THE CHISEL

I kept vigil while Hwyn dropped off to sleep sitting up. Her head lolled against me till I eased it into my lap with a familiarity that might have seemed awkward when she was awake, but that felt natural in the half-real world of guarding a sleeper.

With her small body curled against me, her face turned away, she looked like a child. I saw again my little brother, twenty years before, curled up like that, worn from playing, the rhythm of his sleeping breaths as steady as the sea below our window. A wave of fear came over me, as though that moment's resemblance to my dead brother had proven the futility of all my efforts to protect anyone I cared for. Thrusting away these thoughts, I stirred myself to do the one thing I could do at the moment. Cradling Hwyn's head cautiously so as not to wake her, I raised myself a little to peer through the brambles at the land below. All was still.

I settled myself again; Hwyn stirred in her sleep but did not wake. It would be easy to fall asleep myself, leaving us all unguarded. I began to mouth the Dawn Chant to the Rising God for vigilance and awareness, hoping he would not take it amiss if I meant it more literally than strict theology might countenance. When I reached the end, I began again.

The sun rose higher, and my eyes stung and watered. I wondered whether, in time, I might steal a bit of sleep in safety, letting the other two watch; Trenara could see, and Hwyn could hear and interpret, though inevitably something would be lost when no one could both see the land below and plan a route of escape. Eventually, I thought, there would be no avoiding it. But before the sun neared its zenith, I peered over the fringe of brambles to see movement on the road below.

I rubbed Hwyn's head till her eyes opened. "Hwyn, they're coming."

"What?"

"Four riders in the valley below, headed this way. I see spears glinting at the horses' sides. It's too far to tell if they have bows, as well."

"Sky-Raven's Bones!" she cursed softly. Trenara opened a sleepy eye, saw the two of us in anxious conference, and seemed to catch our mood of vigilance, rising to sit on her heels.

"There seems to be more cover to the east of this hill," I said. "We might circle round and down into the wooded vale without showing ourselves. It seems to go on a long way to the east, into the cleft of the hills."

"Very well," said Hwyn, "you lead the way."

We crept along the brushy slope on hands and knees lest the riders see our heads above the gorse. At last our path dropped low and the greenway rose on either side, aspen trees raising a silver-green canopy over us, flowering thorns now blocking our path, now sheltering it. Secure from detection for the moment, we quickened our pace.

"How close were they when you looked?" Hwyn whispered.

"Just barely in sight," I said. "But how much lead that gives us, it's hard to judge. What took us hours to cross on foot may be an easy canter on horseback."

"And me with my little legs," Hwyn grimaced, "slower than most afoot." In truth, she scrambled quickly over roots and rocks, but her speed was hard won. I had to agree with her unspoken fear that our pursuers would overtake us before long.

"We'll have to find a way to make them lose our trail," I said. "If only it would rain!" But the sun glared down on the dusty ground, where our footprints were all too plain.

"We could part ways—you, alone, might have a chance with the Eye of Night—"

"*No,*" I said. "What use would that be? There are four of them, enough to pursue all of us separately, even if the Eye of Night could run off on its own legs."

"Oh. Of course. Good," said Hwyn, negotiating a great tree fallen across our path. "I didn't want to, anyway."

I hoisted her over, then gave a hand to Trenara, who stood delicately waiting her turn. "Maybe we could turn our smallness to advantage," I said, "find a pass too narrow for their horses—or for the men, even." Though tolerably tall, I was narrow-shouldered, and months on the road had left me looking like a cassock hanging on a few sticks. I had little doubt of being smaller than Lady Goldifer's soldiers, and I was the largest of our little band.

"That would have to be in rockier ground," Hwyn said. "We'd best head for the hills."

I nodded wearily. I had not slept, and as the day advanced, it grew harder to keep hastening on, even in the soft valley, in the shade of the aspen trees. I had no stomach for the hills that loomed to our north. Nonetheless, I noted where the moss grew on the trees and angled our path due north.

The land rose and grew rockier; the trees thinned. We walked on rocks when we could to leave as little trace as we might. Slender birch and pine gave little cover, and I hurried on, feeling naked. At the crest of a rise, I motioned the others to lie low as I scouted the area. I looked back to see a rider emerge from the woods, armed with both sword and bow.

"Holy Saints!" I said. "They're closing on us."

"Gods on the Wheel," Hwyn murmured, "the quest is lost."

"Not quite," I said, though my heart echoed her despair. I pointed ahead, to the north. "That ravine—the horses could never go there."

"Can we?" gasped Hwyn.

"We'll have to—so we will," I said.

The hill dropped off steeply into a gully cut by a little stream. Clinging to earth and the roots of gnarled saplings half unearthed in the stream bank, I dropped myself into the gully, then reached up to help Hwyn down after me. Trenara slipped over the edge with a dancer's grace, landing easily as a cat. We stood in a shallow rill that scarcely wet our feet, but that a heavy rain must swell as high as our shoulders, to judge by the water-weeds on the banks. From the walls of earth on each side, roots trailed toward the water like reaching fingers.

"Upstream, we may find an easier pass to the north bank," I said, hoping I was right. "Meanwhile, if we stay in the stream, it may confuse our tracks." For all that matters, I thought silently; soon enough they might be able to see us in the flesh. We slogged along the muddy streambed, not daring to look behind us or at anything but our feet. There were fish passing below us, and a joint-legged creature like a dwarfed lobster; a pity I could not stop to catch some, I thought, for if we weren't caught, we'd need food before long.

The stream snaked through the hills so that I could not see the road behind us, but sometimes I thought I heard echoes of voices, and I feared we had not shaken our pursuers.

At last we came to the falls from which the brook issued: a nearly vertical cliff looming high above us, with a thin stream of water spilling over the rocks, dead ahead of us. To our right, the bank we had come from bowed gently toward the water.

"We could climb that easily, but—" Hwyn said.

"We can't go back the way we came," I finished for her. "Maybe we can get a handhold on the other side." The far bank looked daunting, but was still our best hope of escape. I tested it for handholds, but the mud slipped between my fingers, leaving me nothing. Grasping for the vines that cascaded down the precipice of the falls, I was startled to see my hand sink deep behind them into a crevice I had not noticed. "It's a cave!"

"What?" Hwyn said.

I drew aside the vines. "Just what we were looking for: a crevice big enough to hide us, but not much wider. Come on!"

Hwyn, needing no second urging, plunged through the falling water to slide under the falls and into the crevice. Trenara followed like a shadow, and I came after them, ducking through the entrance. "How far back does it go?" I said, my soft voice echoing strangely on the stone.

"I'm not sure," Hwyn whispered. "It seems to widen a bit as I go in. Let's rest and adjust to the darkness, then feel our way forward. If there's a second outlet on the far bank, that would be perfect."

We settled ourselves on the damp cavern floor where the passage widened, out of view of the opening but within earshot of any who might follow us to the falls. Sitting with my back to the stone wall, I closed my eyes and was nearly asleep when Hwyn passed me the water-skin she had been carrying. I had been too tired to think of thirst, but I drank gratefully enough. Trenara, prompted by Hwyn's gesture, produced some candied fruits she must have carried from Kreyn Hall and shared them with us. We ate in silence, listening for sounds of pursuit.

Hwyn leaned close to me to whisper, "You might as well sleep now. If the guards pass by, I will hear them and mark which way their footsteps go so we can take the opposite path."

"And if they find us?" I whispered back.

She sighed. "If they find us, there's little we can do, unarmed and weary and small. You've done all you can to preserve us, Jereth; for the rest, we can only pray the gods favor fools. They sometimes do. Sleep, Jereth."

So I slept.

I awoke to a commotion of voices that mixed strangely with my dream. "What?" I groaned through the thickness of long-denied sleep.

Some way down the passage, a loud, deep voice was blustering about spies and informers. Then Hwyn's voice hissed, "Let go of her! Can't you see she's simple?" At that moment I struggled to my feet to confront the intruders at the entrance—only to realize, slowly and groggily, that the voices came from deeper within the cave, not outside. I shifted my weight suddenly to change directions and found myself skidding toward them on the slimy floor of the cave, catching myself on my hands. I peered up through the gloom, and could barely make out a burly man trying to shake an answer out of poor unresisting Trenara: "Who told you we were here? Who sent you to spy on us?"

Hwyn was jumping up and down beside him, waving her knife, which might as well have been a wisp of straw for all he noticed her. "Let her go, I tell you! Don't be ridiculous. No one sent us. Who would send *us*?"

No sooner did I open my mouth to add my voice to her pleas, another man's voice came from beyond them: "What's this? Enough now, Wilgar! We fight men, not girls."

Wilgar, hearing my first groggy utterings and his comrade's admonitions, turned instead on me: "What are you doing in our cave?"

"Sleeping, until just now," I said.

"We didn't know it was yours," said Hwyn, "or anyone's. We meant no harm."

"They were spying out our stronghold," Wilgar said stubbornly to the second stranger.

"We were resting," I said. "It was the only shelter we could find."

"I found this woman creeping down the passage toward us," said Wilgar.

"Trenara is simple," Hwyn said. "She tends to wander off. Sir," she said to the second stranger, "you seem a reasonable man. You can see well that no one would send us to spy out anything: Trenara is moontouched, I am nearly blind."

"What of him?" said Wilgar, pointing in my direction with his sword.

"Jereth is a scholar from the Tarvon Monastery in Annelon," said Hwyn. "He is no one's spy."

"*Priests*," spat the second stranger. "I've had my fill of Goldifer's holy hypocrites—"

I could not let that sit. "I am none of Goldifer's carping sycophants—"

"Never mind whose you are," the man interrupted. "I need no war with tattered vagrants. Wilgar, you can see how harmless they are by how easily you've shaken them. But this place is mine and my men's, and not a way-house for travelers. Leave the way you came, and no harm will—"

"Listen!" Hwyn hissed. In the hush that followed, we all heard it: men's voices echoing in the ravine, not quite close but growing closer.

"Who have you brought here?" said the second man.

"Hush! That's Lady Goldifer's men," Hwyn said.

"You brought them against us?"

"No, no! They're hunting us," she said.

Wilgar's voice, too, dropped to a whisper. "Hunting *you?* Why, what did you make off with?"

But Hwyn ignored him, speaking only to the other: "If we leave now, they will see where we have been and know your hiding place. And if you slay us, they will hear us cry out. We have a common enemy; why should we fight each other?"

As the man hesitated, I peered desperately through the gloom to read his face, but in the darkness of the cavern, I was blind as Hwyn. After some moments I heard, "Very well. An enemy of Goldifer's is a friend of mine. Wilgar, fetch Lok and my bow, quickly." Wilgar followed his orders swiftly, as if accustomed to obeying him. The captain—for so I could not help but think of the second man—turned again to me with the same air of practiced command. "How many guards did you say were chasing you? With what arms?"

"Four riders," I said. "I saw spears at their sides, and one, at least, had a bow."

"We'll avoid making a target for him," the outlaw said. "Were they in mail?"

"I saw breastplates and helmets."

"We outnumber them, then, by strict count," said the outlaw, "but if you three were fighters, Wilgar would not have had all three of you at his mercy so painlessly." Wilgar returned with a third man, and the leader accepted his bow with thanks before issuing his orders for the battle: "Lok, come with me to the fore, just short of the mouth—if they have not marked us, we will let them pass, but if they try to enter, we will shoot. You vagabonds, if you have arms, draw them and stand by Wilgar. If not, stay out of our way."

I drew my knife, for all the good that might do; it would scarcely cut hair anymore. Hwyn shepherded Trenara backward into the cave with our parcels and returned to stand beside me, knife in hand. And thus, in silence, we waited as the guards' footsteps drew closer.

"Where can they have gone?" one said, "the bank's too steep."

"Look: a cave behind the vines," said another, and the passage lightened for an instant as he parted them. His cry of surprise was cut short by an arrow from the leader's bow. Moments later, I knew by Lok's cry of triumph that his shot also hit its mark. As they nocked second arrows, another guard entered. I heard our protector gasp, "Kelman?" and the intruder, "Warfast?" equally shocked. "Deserter, you were not the quarry we sought, but by the gods—"

They grappled till Wilgar rushed forward to join the fray. Their struggle blocked the passageway so that all I could see was a dark beast with more heads and feet than a man, thrashing about the stone corridor. At last, when the one dark shape split, half falling to earth, I heard Wilgar murmur, "Ah, Kelman, you should have joined us years ago."

"Our own company!" Lok exclaimed, staring down at the body.

"Hush, friend," Warfast said. "Vagabond, you said *four* guards."

"And four they were," I said. "One must have stayed to guard the horses on the far bank."

"Ill luck," said Warfast. "He can ride back home and give us all away—unless we stop him. Lok and Wilgar, take the upper passage and scout out the land from above. You, priest, take arms from the dead and come with me through the falls. The women can stay here; you, little one, keep the fool out of trouble."

Afraid of disgracing myself if I so much as hesitated, I took the sword of the man Wilgar had killed—for all the good I might do with it, having as much notion what to do with one as with the oracle-bones of St. Argode—and rushed out the mouth of the cavern. No sooner had I passed through the curtain of vines and water than I felt something sting the skin above my left brow. I dropped to the streambed, rolled, and came right-side-up again to see the fourth guard training a second arrow down at me from the southern bank.

Warfast, crouched low under the bank, used a crevice as an archer's slot and took aim at the guard in turn. "Shoot again and, gods help me, I'll shoot you."

The guard called down to him. "What are these three vagabonds to you, Warfast? They are not even people of Kreyn. What have they to do with you and your precious ancient rights and Laws of Antir?"

"What are they to *you,* Heregar?" the outlaw said.

"They are enemies of the Guardian of Day," said Heregar.

"Ah, yes. They are that to me, too," said Warfast without moving his bow. "What threat can these pitiful scarecrows have posed to Her Resplendence?"

"They have defaced the holy chapel in Kreyn Hall," said Heregar.

"When did you begin caring for such things?" said Warfast. "When did you fall so far as to be hunting threadbare beggars up and down the hills—and for Lady Goldifer's sake? You should have joined us from the first. You don't like the new ways any more than I do, do you?"

"When did you start concerning yourself with what I like or loathe? You never asked my counsel when you deserted, and now that you've killed three of my comrades—your comrades that once were—it is late to begin," said Heregar. He did not shoot, nor did Warfast, but neither one lowered his bow or the deadly arrow nocked to the string. My head spun with pain and I felt hot blood running down the left side of my face, but I strained every nerve to stay awake and aware. Not quite trusting the success of Warfast's parley, I began quietly groping in the mud of the streambed for a stone to throw.

"I'm sorry for your men, Heregar, but they left us no choice. They'd have killed us all; you know they would. I don't want to kill you. But I will defend myself and my comrades."

"I know, and I honor that," said Heregar, "but this man and the two women are none of yours. Let us call a truce. Though we are foes now, Warfast, I did not come hunting you. Give up the three wanderers and I may choose to forget I have seen you."

"I dislike giving up helpless creatures to slaughter," Warfast said. "I never thought it was your way, either, old comrade. Let me propose a better settlement: a contest of strength, unarmed, you against me. You always fancied yourself a great wrestler. Best of three throws has his way. If you win, I'll go back with you as your prize. If I win, you'll join us, as you should have done from the first—or at least sit with us in peace long enough to let me argue with you why you should be one of us."

"Very well," said Heregar. "It's a fool's bargain on your part; you know you could never best me. But lower your weapon and I'll lower mine."

Slowly, slowly, the bows lowered. Standing aslant of them, I watched incredulous through the haze of pain in my head. Could it all, indeed, end peacefully?

A quick move from Heregar caught my eye, then. I cast my stone at the first quick darting move, before the flash of the knife caught the sun, but dizzy with my wound, I threw far wide of the mark. Still, the stone caught his eye; the guardsman turned to me and wavered an instant where to throw the knife. That instant was enough; his knife planted itself harmlessly in the streambed as Lok's arrow flew from the heights straight into Heregar's side. As the guard fell bleeding from the bank, Warfast caught him, murmuring, "I'm sorry, Heregar, truly I am. You should have been one of us."

Lok leapt down to help Warfast heave the guard's body into the cave, then disappeared somewhere. It all began to blur before my eyes; I crouched with my head in my hands, blood welling up between my fingers.

I felt a hand on my shoulder. "Are you still living? Come inside with us," said Warfast, and half pulled me through the crevice in the rock. "We'll find a rag to bind your head. Priest or no, you're a brave enough fool—leaping straight out into the face of your foe, without even looking for cover! But I'd advise you to stay out of trouble till you learn to guard your head."

"I'll try," I said through gritted teeth.

"That was a well-timed throw," he said.

"But an ill-aimed one," I said ruefully.

"That I won't deny," said the outlaw. "But without it, Heregar would not have missed, and I would be dead."

"You knew that man," I said—obvious enough, I suppose, but it seemed to need acknowledging.

"Yes," he said heavily. "All of us knew all of them."

We followed the upward slope of the stone floor to the broadest part of the cavern, a chamber lit by a single torch, its uneven floor now mostly taken up by the bodies of the dead laid side by side, hands clasped on their chests. At their heads, Wilgar sat in silent gloom like a chief mourner, with Lok a little distance away. Behind them, the torch barely illuminated a heap of coffers and sacks. This, then, was a storeroom for the outlaws, a hiding place for booty and weapons. Perhaps we had interrupted them in stowing their latest take. Strange luck, caught between enemies, to be alive at all. Unutterably weary, I sank down at the dead men's feet.

Hwyn, who had crouched in a corner with Trenara, hastened toward me. "You're hurt!" she cried, and insisted on washing my wound with water from the water-skins and bandaging my head with the rag Warfast found for me. Before I quite knew how it had happened, whether it was my doing or hers, I found I had laid my head in her lap; as she made no objection, I stayed thus, dizzy and weak and glad for the comfort in the dark. Against the dank air of the cave, now almost a grave, the homespun wool under my cheek smelled of meadow grass and life.

Across the length of the dead men's bodies, the outlaws sat staring at our fallen enemies in a sort of uneasy mourning.

"I never thought I'd see such a day," Wilgar said. "To think I should have to kill Kelman with my own hands!"

"And I Heregar," Lok lamented. "Remember, Warfast, the time he wrestled you for a jug of ale, and no one could declare a winner?"

Warfast nodded. "My ribs still ache at the thought."

Wilgar groaned, "Why couldn't he have joined us?"

"They must have a proper burial," Lok said.

"They will," said Warfast. "We will wait till nightfall, in case any others are on the hunt. You," he addressed me, "what's your name? As you're a priest, you might chant a prayer over the grave."

"I *was* a priest," I corrected. "I left the Tarvon Monastery after six years, initiated but not fully consecrated. But I can serve in the place of one, if you choose. As for my name, it's Jereth, son of Garmund."

The outlaw chief made a sound of surprise. "Fitting. That man—the second to your left—was named Garmund." He pointed to each in turn: "Nevan. Garmund. Kelman. Heregar. Will you remember their names for the rite?"

I shuddered, but only said, "I will do them all the honor I can."

"Good," said Warfast. "They were old comrades of ours. I was sorry to become their enemy."

"For my part," I said, "I am sorry our flight brought them to your door. And I thank you for refusing to buy peace with our lives."

The man waved that away. "As for that, I doubt Heregar would have kept his promise to leave us be. Either he was for us or against us; if I could not persuade him to join us, I knew he would kill us. But I did not know which until he asked me to hand you over. The Heregar who once fought beside me would never have proposed such a dishonorable bargain; in that, I had my answer."

"You were a guard, then, once," I said. "How did you come to leave them?"

"No, stranger," Warfast said in a sharper tone, "I'll answer no questions. You know enough of me already: my name and one of my strongholds. If I were as ruthless as some believe me, you would be dead. I think it's you three that owe me and my men some answers, now that we've rescued you from men we once called brothers. And what I'd most like to know now is how three such scrawny little vagabonds can cause so much trouble."

"Does that surprise you?" Hwyn spoke. "Bees killed the giant Bleobis, that no warrior dared face. A mouse gnawed the hangman's rope and saved Saint Gueneos from death. A loose pebble betrayed the great army of Kettra, and turned back an empire. And mere words killed the tyrant Ryons, when the taunting of an old woman drove him to such fury that his heart burst. It is the small end of the chisel that cleaves the stone, after all. So small things and small people may sculpt the world, once they find the spot where the gods wait to strike a blow."

Warfast squinted at her curiously through the darkness. "Who are you?"

She shrugged. "A minstrel, a scullery maid, a beggar, sometimes a thief at need. A scrawny little vagabond, as you say. I am called Hwyn."

"And do you withstand the hammer-blows of the gods, little Hwyn?"

She hesitated, as if embarrassed by the audacity of her own words. "I am still moving into place for the blow."

"Is that what brought you to Kreyn?" Again she hesitated. Warfast continued, "Did you really deface Lady Goldifer's chapel?"

I could hear the grin in her voice as she answered: "We burned it as empty and barren as her seeming piety."

"Did you indeed? Well, it's time someone stripped off her fine mask. It's almost worth being caught up in your defense to hear that news," said Warfast. "I salute you, Hwyn—and Jereth—and your fair friend, what was her name again?"

"I am the Lady Trenara of Larioneth," said Trenara regally.

"Are you really?" laughed Warfast. "How came you here, Your Ladyship?"

Trenara did not answer, but walked toward him, skirting the dead bodies with all imaginable grace. When she reached out to touch his face, he leapt back as if unused to being touched. "What is it?"

"You have kind eyes," she said, and stroked back his hair.

"Ah, Warfast, you have all the luck with women," said Lok, "and we're left lonely as monks."

"Poor boy," said Trenara, and as gracefully as she had gone to him, she left Warfast to put her arms around Lok.

Warfast seemed almost as relieved as Lok at this abrupt shift of attention. "Moontouched," he murmured. "What a strange lot you are! Why have you come here? You're not from Kreyn; your accents make that unmistakable. What did you want with burning Lady Goldifer's chapel?"

"We didn't exactly plan it," said Hwyn. "We came seeking a sign. That was the one given to us."

"Visionaries!" Warfast exclaimed. "I am a plain man of action, and if I could penetrate Kreyn Hall, I would act to more purpose."

"What would you do?" asked Hwyn coolly.

"I'll ask the questions," he snapped, as if she had touched a sore point. "What made you come seeking signs and wonders in Kreyn, of all places?"

"It was a mistake, I confess," Hwyn said. "I had heard of an oracle there that I hoped might tell me what lay at the end of my journey. But I should have let it alone. It mattered little: I already know which way I must go, and what will happen there is in the gods' hands."

"Where do you go, then? What do you journey toward?"

"We go north," said Hwyn, "into the Land of Troubles."

Warfast laughed. "Of course: to the very place all the world flees from. Why north?"

"Why did you leave your hometown and make your stronghold in the wilderness?" Hwyn said. "Times of trial call for bold journeys; you know that. Not all of us can flee from trouble if any are to overcome it in the end."

"You could see plainly enough in the guards' enmity why I had to leave and gather my forces outside Kreyn," Warfast said. "Your cause is less clear. What battle are you gathering forces for in a land more desolate than this?"

"Why do you ask?" said Hwyn, a note of challenge in her voice. "Are these idle questions to pass the time till dark, or will you do something with the knowledge? If my answers are bold enough for your heart, will you join us? Will you come away from this barren place where you no longer have a task to do?"

I stiffened and half raised my head from her lap: what was she thinking?

"What's she raving about?" Wilgar almost echoed my thoughts. "You wouldn't leave here!"

"No, of course not, cousin," said Warfast. "Hwyn, what in the Wheel of the World makes you dream I would even think of joining you?"

"I don't know," she said. "But since I drank prophecy from St. Fiern's Lake, when I-don't-know speaks so loudly in my ear, it is usually for a reason. And you have let on more about yourself than you believe. You rebelled against the one who calls herself Guardian of Day."

"Her mother put on no such airs," Warfast muttered.

Hwyn nodded agreement and went on: "What would you say if I told you that night is falling—the night of the whole world?"

"What do you mean?" Warfast said. "That Goldifer is destined to fall, as night must follow day?"

"Nothing so particular about one petty ruler," she said. "But the world is changing, and many in high places will be shaken down. Some great change is coming down from the North—whether for good or ill may depend on how we rise to meet it. Heavy hammer-strokes are coming: are you in the right place to sculpt the stone?"

"Why? Where else should I be but here? Kreyn is my heart and the hills about it my bones. What might I shape in the world beyond it if I left all this behind?"

"What can you shape here if you never leave?" she countered. "How long have you been here? How long since you've been able to so much as chip the stone toward the shape you hoped for? Does the Guardian of Day still fear you? Or does she rather stir the people's fear of you to tighten her hold on them? Haven't you fallen a long way from your oath to the gods?"

"What do *you* know about me or any oath I may have sworn?"

"Perhaps nothing, perhaps much," she said in a softer tone. "Shall I tell you what I guess? I think you've turned so far from your intention that you no longer recognize your face in the water. It takes no guessing and no prophecy to know why you left: your adversary named it the Laws of Antir. Goldifer's intransigence turned you from guardian of law into outlaw. From rebellion you turned to robbery by degrees, never meaning it to become your life. Over the years your band has dwindled, some slain, some gone by the roads you dare not take, for to leave this countryside now would be to confess all has been for naught. Yet somewhere in the depths of your heart you envy the ones that leave; maybe you even envy the dead, for you ache so for times past that each turn of the World-Wheel seems only to drag you further away from your heart. You cannot bear to see that you must go forward to go back; to return to Kreyn you must leave it behind."

"Silence, doomsayer!" roared Wilgar and rushed at us. I sprang to my feet and stood before Hwyn to defend her with what little strength I had.

Warfast grabbed Wilgar's arm, saying, "Cousin, I'll deal with this." To Hwyn he said, "Who are you to speak this way to me? If not for me and my men, the guards would have spitted you and your two friends like rabbits for roasting. You've acquired a costly taste for walking into the halls of power and flinging sand in the faces of the mighty, all in the name of some coming hammer-stroke of the gods that will *not* defend you, that did *not* defend you today—"

"Perhaps it did," she mused. "Perhaps it found you to defend us."

"Bright Goddess's back-end!" Warfast exploded, "Was there ever such a presumptuous, infuriating, bold-faced little creature since—since—" He waved a hand in place of words, as if unable to think of any example to league with Hwyn. "Who are you anyway to tell me what I have done, what I would do, what I dare not do, or what the gods, *if* they still live, would have me do? What right have you to weave my life into your own strange designs?"

"Forgive me," Hwyn replied quietly. "You asked me what I knew of you, and I told you what I guessed. But perhaps I guessed badly."

The outlaw stopped where he stood as if her words were a stone wall he could not pass. "Very well," he said sullenly, and stalked away to the far end of the cavern, till he tripped on something: a tangle of arms, legs, hair, bodies. "Lok, *what* are you doing there?" he sputtered.

Hwyn, realizing who the other half of the tangle must be, called "Trenara!" in disapproving tones. The lady disengaged herself delicately from Lok's embraces and went to sit by Hwyn's side, a conciliatory arm around her shoulder. Displaced from my favored spot, I went off in the corner to rest my aching head till nightfall and the burial. Around me, my companions and our hosts were nearly as silent as the waiting dead.

After dark, Warfast woke me to help carry the four bodies to their burial place. It needed two trips, for two of us had to carry each one, and Hwyn was too small to pair with another bearer. Lok and Wilgar between them carried one body, Warfast and I another, while Hwyn and Trenara waited in the cavern. I was led out a different passageway than the one we had entered, longer and steeper. As Hwyn had hoped, it did lead to the far bank, to a place high above the ravine. From there we trekked across little rises and falls to a sheltered glade that Warfast had chosen for the grave. We set down the first two bodies and returned for the other two, and for my companions. Hwyn and Trenara were given spades to carry in our grim procession.

We dug one grave for the four in the rocky earth of the glade; it was hard labor, and though the mountain wind made even a summer night chilly, we were all soon sweating. Hwyn did her part with a strength surprising in one so small; Warfast even remarked on it. Only Trenara took no part in the work. Instead she crouched near the dead men, softly singing a weird, wordless tune. The sound startled me, and I realized that I had never heard her sing before.

"What's she doing?" said Wilgar.

"Maybe she's trying to sing the burial chant," I said. "She must remember some funeral from among her own people." The others looked at her uneasily, and I could hardly blame them: in the wild land by night, with the moon half veiled by gathering clouds, her white face and solemn dark eyes looked ghostly, and her mournful voice woke echoes of fearful dreams. I had more reason than they to be displeased by it; it was long since I had sung any kind of rites, and I thought that with Trenara keening in counterpoint, I might forget what to do.

I needn't have worried about that, at least. When the grave was dug and I stood poised on the rim of crumbling earth, Trenara was as still as the others, awaiting my chant. I looked down at the four bodies stretched out beneath me, and it all came back with a force more than memory. My family's sodden, fish-belly-white bodies had been stretched before me thus, in one joint grave from which only I was missing. I had not sung that service, of course—I had only entered the Order after it was done—but every word, every gesture of it was scarred into me.

I picked up a handful of earth from the grave, marked east by the position of the moon, and held out the earth in that direction, like a gift. "Rising God, righteous one, open our eyes." Then to the south: "Bright Goddess, beauty's light, console us." To the west: "Turning God, traveler, guide our steps." Finally, to the north, where I remained: "Hidden Goddess, hearth of the dead, give us hope. Hold these, our lost and broken comrades: Nevan,

Garmund, Kelman, and Heregar. Heart of the world, cherish them, children of your womb."

As I sang, I could hear under my voice a soft sobbing. It moved me to think the outlaws could feel such grief for long-ago comrades who had become their mortal enemies. But as I continued the invocation the sobbing grew louder, and I realized it came from Trenara. In the wan moonlight, only a sliver of white face showed between the dark wings of her hair; I could not see her tears, but her whole body shook with them. Hwyn reached up to clasp her arm, trying to soothe her, but Trenara wept on. Only when the last chant was finished did she surrender herself to Hwyn's comforting arms. "Peace, Trenara. It's done; long done, no doubt. What memories wring your heart?" But Trenara could not answer.

I kissed the handful of blessed earth and sprinkled it over the bodies. Then, my role as priest done, I took my part with the spade to fill the grave. After the last spadeful of soil was packed firmly over them, we returned to the cavern to gather up our few belongings as Warfast and his men also made ready to leave. They had the guards' horses, secured while I'd been busy about my wound, so they would have much the easier trip.

"Which way will you travel?" Warfast asked us.

"North into the hills," said Hwyn.

"It's a hard land, that way; it doesn't stoop down to a human-like height till the Graves of the Mountains, miles away, and even that stretch is the hardest flat land you ever want to see."

"But no one will hunt us there," Hwyn said.

"True enough," Warfast admitted. "If that's what it must be, then take the upper passage, the way we went out to the graves, and—"

Wilgar interrupted him: "Are they to pay no fee for their protection?" There was a note of triumph in his voice as though no matter what came of this question, he knew he would win the game he was playing.

"Hold still, Wilgar," said Warfast irritably.

"We have taken protection-money from better ladies than that half-wit, from better priests than that skinny beggar. Why should these three give nothing?"

"We have nothing," I said. "If we had even food, we would have offered it in gratitude."

"And for this we killed Kelman, Heregar?"

"I am more sorry than I can say that our flight brought them to you as enemies," I said. "But what you have lost, no fee could restore."

"Peace, friend. I'll handle this," said Warfast to me, and then turned to Wilgar: "Cousin, you know I took up their defense not for pay but for common enmity to Goldifer and common defense of our safety. And what the priest says is true: harassing these travelers for gold they don't have won't ease your heart. Let them go."

"Oh, yes, let them go," Wilgar sneered. "They have seen our stronghold; they know the lower passage and the upper passage; they know our names and our story. And you will let them go. You trust them."

"I doubt they'll go crying our names to Goldifer," Warfast said. "What other danger is there?"

"Are you sure they have not robbed us?" Wilgar said, as if exploring every door till one broke open. "The women were alone in the stronghold while we carried the bodies uphill. Plenty of time for opening sacks and coffers and lightening their load. Will you not even search them before you let them go?"

"Don't be absurd, Wilgar," Warfast said. "The fine lady's too moontouched to pick up ready money off the street in broad daylight."

"But the other is crafty enough," said Wilgar. "She admitted herself a thief."

"Oh, *that* was crafty indeed," Warfast sneered. "Would she say so if she meant to steal from us?"

"If it puts you off your guard now, then yes, it was crafty of her," Wilgar persisted. "But *you* will not suspect her, oh no. You hold her above suspicion. What is she, your love? Your heart's desire? Have you and Lok been away from women so long that at the first sight of them you must dote like sailors just ashore, one on a fool, one on a freak, and let them play you for the biggest fools of all? Will you let this little woman twist you around with her riddling words, telling you what you are and what you must do?"

"Enough!" Warfast said. "Hwyn, you can see we'll have no peace from this hothead until his suspicions are satisfied. You'd best turn your pockets out to set his mind at rest, or I won't answer for his actions."

I froze, and I could see Hwyn hesitating: if she resisted, she'd increase Wilgar's suspicions, most likely even set Warfast on his guard. But dared she show the Eye of Night?

She exhaled a slow sigh. "All right, then." With exaggerated care, she turned out her left side pocket. "See? Only the crumbs of yesterday's meal." Just as slowly, she turned out her right side pocket. "There's my handkerchief and some string."

"There's another pocket inside your shift, between your teats," said Wilgar menacingly.

"Wilgar," Warfast said warningly, but without the vehemence of his earlier objections.

"What? I've not moved to turn it out for her," said Wilgar. "But she's gone to some trouble to hide it."

"Show him," said Warfast.

Hwyn sighed. "I suppose there's no asking you to turn modestly aside while I unlace my clothes."

"Take your time and arrange yourself as you need," Warfast said. "There's no hurry."

Slowly, slowly, with much muttering, she unlaced her shift as far as the heart and turned out the little pouch I had made for her. As she opened her clothing, I glimpsed a rose-tipped breast and averted my eyes, but Wilgar did no such thing. "What's that you're palming behind the handkerchief?" Wilgar shouted, and lunged at her.

"Ow! Get away, that's nothing of yours!" Hwyn shrieked, but it was no use. He pulled away from her with a wad in his hand—the handkerchief with the Eye of Night inside—and the force of his motion sent her toppling to the floor.

I hurried to help her up, then confronted Wilgar, shouting, "That's not a gem! Drop it, for the gods' sake!"

Holding the stolen booty in one hand, he swatted me with the other, right across the arrow-cut on my head. I sank to the floor, able to do nothing but hold my head and curse.

Through the fog of pain I heard Trenara wail wordlessly and Hwyn appeal to Warfast, "Make him drop it. It's not what he thinks it is, nothing to sell: it's a living thing."

"How dare you ask my help now?" he cried. "You've begged my protection, harangued me, gone high and holy with me, and all the while lied to me! What have you been hiding from me?"

Her answer was drowned out by Wilgar's scream. His eyes bulging, he held the Eye of Night rigidly over his head, the handkerchief now fallen to the ground at his feet. "What would you do with me?" he called out in a strange keening voice. "Stronger men have wrecked themselves upon me."

"Wilgar?" stammered Warfast, uncertain.

Wilgar's mad eyes fixed on his leader. "You! Why are you here?"

"Wilgar? Is it you speaking, or—"

"No," said Lok in a hoarse whisper. "It's something else."

"You were not always brigands!" Wilgar shouted. "What have you become? Must what began in honor end in greed? You swore your life to the gods for justice. Will you die for a handful of coins or a bright trinket?"

"What have you done to him?" Warfast asked Hwyn.

"I've done nothing," she said. "It's his own grasping fingers. Make him drop it!"

Wilgar continued, "I see a rope swinging with the weight of a man. Leave this road!"

"Can't you—" Warfast stammered.

"Make him drop it!" Hwyn repeated. "He's too big for me."

Warfast lunged at Wilgar, wrestled with him for some anxious moments, then got the bigger man's arm twisted around behind his back till the fingers spasmed and the Eye of Night rolled loose on the floor. Both men shrank from it.

Hwyn picked it up, retrieved her handkerchief, and tucked them both away in her pockets.

Wilgar huddled on the floor, sobbing in Warfast's arms. "Gods on the Wheel, what things I saw! What have we become?"

"Peace, cousin," murmured Warfast soothingly.

"I'm sorry," Hwyn said, crouching at Warfast's side. "I couldn't tell you. I didn't know what you might try to do with it if you knew. But you've seen now what drives us, what burned Goldifer's chapel, what tells me that change is coming. And it has spoken to you."

Warfast turned on her with a snarl of animal fury: "Haven't you done enough harm? Go! Go, before I make you wish the guards had killed you before you saw us. Take your magic stone and your half-wit whore and go!"

We snatched up our things and scrambled through the upward passage without looking back. In the utter dark, I let Hwyn lead, keeping a hand on her shoulder, with Trenara clinging to my belt. Once I tripped on a jagged edge of rock and caught myself painfully on my hands, stifling an urge to cry out. Hwyn offered me a hand and pulled me along as if our lives depended upon it; and so terrible had been Warfast's anger that I was ready to believe they did. I scarcely breathed until we were out in the night air in the Hills of Penmorrin. The moon peered through a gap in the cloud, lending just enough light to stumble forward, cursing the roots that caught at our feet, the ups and downs of the land that deceived us. We crested the hill and descended into the valley beyond it almost too fast for safety, anxious to leave our pursuers and our grudging rescuers both far behind us. Not until we stopped to rest by a pleasant brook that wound its way through the glens did we notice that in the uproar we had left our waterskins behind.

"Sky-Raven's Bones!" swore Hwyn.

"I'm sorry. I can't believe I forgot them," I said.

She dropped disconsolately to the mossy stream bank. "I forgot them, too. It was as much my fault—"

"You had the Eye of Night to worry about. The rest should be my responsibility."

"You had a wound to distract you," she observed in my defense. Then she shrugged. "Well, at any rate, I don't think either of us should go back for them."

Wearily, I dropped down to the bank beside her. "What should we do now?"

"Drink our fill from the stream and move on," she said.

With the cool voice of the water before us and the fragrance of a linden tree over us, the glen seemed for the moment like the blissful Womb of the World. Yet I knew she was right: we dared not linger here. We stayed long enough to drink, wash the sweat off our bodies, pull a few edible rushes Hwyn found on the bank, and drink again. Then we followed the stream to its source, up a steeper slope than the last one.

The rocks grew rugged under our feet, and the clouds closed over the moon, blinding us. I wrenched my ankle on an unexpected drop, but continued to limp on into the gray dawn, leg throbbing, head throbbing, using hands where I must to supplement my failing feet.

Soon after daybreak, the sky darkened again and we had the rainstorm I had wished for the previous day. It came down suddenly, a few drops and then, a heartbeat later, a torrent, soaking us almost to our bones and making the rocky slopes slick and treacherous. We labored on till we found a shallow outcropping of stone to cower under. I dug our one cooking-pot out of my pack and set it out to catch rainwater; Hwyn put out a tin cup for the same purpose. We nibbled a bit on the rushes we'd gathered, which were sharp-tasting and stringy. "Are you sure these are edible?" I asked.

"They're better cooked," Hwyn said, "but with this rain, it'll be a time before we can find enough dry wood for a fire."

"At least it will hide our trail," I said, watching the silvery sheet of rain splash down over the lip of stone, inches from my face. The land was shrouded in gray, low clouds kissing the stones. We were safe from pursuit, if not from the blind cruelty of nature.

Hwyn nodded. "They won't find us now. I only hope we can find our way through these highlands."

"We'll manage," I said. "When the sky clears, we can get our bearings. Eastward is the Wall of Magya, the mountains too high to scale. To the north, also, the land must grow more rugged before the end of the hill country, but if we bear northwest we should be able to regain our course without crossing the worst of the highlands. At least, I expect so. I never studied inland geography very well."

"At least it's a plan," said Hwyn.

Lightning cracked somewhere nearby. We jumped, and Trenara stirred in her sleep, but that was all.

"How's your head?" said Hwyn.

"It wasn't a deep cut," I said, "so I'm not much worried. But the skin burns under the bandage, even with the rainwater to cool it. And I can still feel the print of Wilgar's fist."

"Should I have a look at it?"

"No," I said. "What's the use? We have no clean bandages, no herbs to poultice it. Besides, I'd rather it wasn't touched."

"Sorry." She stared moodily out into the rain. "It shouldn't have ended this way. Until Wilgar began badgering me, I was hoping Warfast might be about to propose guiding us for at least the next day's journey—I'm sure he knows more of these hills than we can find out any way but the hardest one. Maybe I should have told Warfast what I was carrying. But I wasn't sure I could trust him. I knew he was not like Goldifer—he longs for change—but that longing could be for good or ill: longing to set things right, or just to come out on top. I don't know whether he himself knows how to separate those two dreams. And the dream of power can do so much harm with the Eye of Night."

"*I* wouldn't have trusted him," I said, surprising myself with my vehemence.

"Why?" said Hwyn. "Because he's a highwayman?"

"Isn't that enough?"

"Perhaps. But he did protect us, after all, and it seemed he might have done more if I'd been more careful of his feelings. I was so clumsy!"

"What made you want to take him with you?" I said.

"I wouldn't exactly say *want*," said Hwyn. "I had a strange feeling that he ought to travel with us. As if, perhaps, the Eye of Night wanted him."

"Did you have that feeling when you met me?" I said, and instantly wanted to stuff the words back into my mouth and swallow them.

Hwyn squinted at me curiously. "If I were any other woman, I might think you were jealous," she said. "I don't know, Jereth. It was more complex with you. You see," she looked off into the rain again, "I wanted you to come with me from the first. I thought you'd be—well—good company, everything Trenara was not. It seemed right, somehow, but I couldn't know whether there were any truesight about it or just my own wishes, my longing for a friend to come with me."

At first I did not know what to say, so I took her hand and held it a while in silence, feeling her cool fingers tighten around my warmer ones. At last I said, "I confess I was afraid that if Warfast came with you, you wouldn't need me anymore."

"Don't be ridiculous," she said. "I would have needed you twice as much. He would have been an awkward comrade, especially if his men came with him. He would have wanted to lead, and I would have quarreled with him from here to the north end of nowhere, for if I follow anything but the vision that was given to me, I might as well have stayed in St. Fiern's Town, safe until the Troubles came to meet me. I would have needed your clear eye for the truth—and your friendship—to survive such a partnership. But all the same, I felt he was meant to come with us—more for his sake than for ours." She laughed. "Is that not presumptuous? Can you imagine what he would say if he could hear me?"

"If you wanted to say something to change his mind, those are not the words you're looking for," I said.

"Nonetheless, they're true," Hwyn said. "All I said of him was true. If I had any doubts when I said it, I have none left. He raged at the things I said of him, but refuted none of them, as if he could not find one fact to fling in my face against my words. He's at an impasse, and he must know it: he can do no good where he is, nor can he turn back. We could have broken that impasse for him. But it would have meant giving up all his years of struggle as lost."

"That would be hard," I said. "I remember when I left the Tarvon Order: if the time hadn't come when they asked me to take vows, I can well imagine I might have stayed on, always delaying the decision to leave. But there are no final vows for failed insurrectionists, no moment of truth when you must either go forward or take another road. I can feel for him."

"You see, then, why I kept trying to open the door for him?"

"Yes," I said. "I suppose you were right. He seemed a decent sort—for an outlaw. He was fair to his enemies, almost to the point of losing his life. And he seemed, in his odd way, drawn to you, for all his anger. He rose to the bait a little too quickly when Wilgar taunted him with being in love with you."

"Do you think so? Strange notion," said Hwyn. "Still, I guess he never saw me by daylight."

"Not so very strange," I said. "What could be more natural than to love someone who offers you the key to your prison?"

"He might also resent them for proving he couldn't find it himself," she mused. "He might fear the power they might have over him."

"Then he made the coward's choice," I said passionately. "Let him find his own way out of the impasse: he has underprized you, and we are better without him."

Hwyn gave me one of those crooked smiles of hers, and it was well worth huddling on a windy mountain ledge, chewing inedible rushes in the rain, to see it.

7

THE HILLS OF PENMORRIN

We waited out the storm, Hwyn and Trenara napping in the cliff's shelter while I tried vainly to ease the pain in my head. By the time the rain had abated, I felt my very eyesight had been affected by it: there seemed to be a shadow in the corner of my left eye, narrowing my field of vision. When Hwyn woke, even she could see the problem: "Jereth, the whole side of your head is swollen."

"I know," I said. "I wonder—did they fear us enough to poison their arrows?"

Hwyn washed the wound again, but if washing had failed to clean out the poison when the wound was still bleeding, I doubted it could help a closed, day-old sore. Besides, every touch made me clench my teeth against the pain. I waved away Trenara, who seemed to want to help with the rebandaging, and gingerly bound it myself.

"Are you well enough to travel?" Hwyn asked.

"No point in staying here," I said. And so, slower than before, I followed the easiest of all the hard paths the mountain presented to us, trying to wend our way toward the north side. I set my feet carefully, wary of stones made slick by rainwater, going on hands and knees when footing seemed too perilous and staying behind my companions on upward slopes lest I fall and bring them down with me. From time to time, Hwyn would stoop to examine the little plants squeezing through cracks in the stone or growing on brushy ridges, in hopes of recognizing one with healing properties. Many of them were strange to her; one smelled a bit like heal-all, she said, but not enough like it to be trusted. Nonetheless, she found some wild currants and edible greens that made a far better meal than uncooked rushes. Fueled by these finds, we carried on through the long summer day.

The greenery of the hills was not ours alone: birds wheeled down to seize the berries we also sought, and one stand of blackberry bushes had been savaged, branches broken here and there, with bear tracks in the mud. Unarmed as we were, we took care to avoid the path those paw-prints had taken.

Nor would the bear have had to confine itself to fruit: once when we pushed our way into a thicket, a mountain deer sprang away from us in panic and sped out of sight; and from time to time, flocks of wild goats mocked our slow progress, skipping up rocky passages we could never attempt. Once a great crowd of them blocked our path, forcing us to sit on a rock and rest till they had gone by. Watching the parade of slim-legged nimble creatures amble past us, I noticed something odd about a white one nibbling a shrub nearby: "They're not all wild. That one has a notch in its ear that it couldn't have gotten by chance."

"Who would live in this hard land?" Hwyn said.

"Goatherds, apparently. But the hills are so vast, we may never meet them."

As we journeyed onward through the day, the air cleared till I could see a long stretch of land behind us—and often, a frightening depth of canyon below us. What I could not see was any end to the mountain above us. It was higher than I had reckoned; I wondered whether we had strayed farther east toward the Wall of Magya than we ever intended. I tried to lead us westward and downward when possible, but the land itself chose our path as often as not, throwing impossible gaps or sheer walls of rock or thickets of thorns in our way, forcing us to turn east or climb upward against our will, then struggle to regain what we had lost. When we found ourselves near water, rarely could we follow the stream, for it cut channels treacherous to our feet.

As the sun angled low in the west, we came upon some wind-twisted little mulberry trees, spilling their bounty prodigally on a high meadow. We ate as many as we could gather ripe from the branches and even some from the ground, for our climb had left us hungry and tired. Then we collapsed to the grassy slope to rest as the sun vanished behind the mountain. There was no talk of traveling by night now, with our pursuers safely behind us and the very earth under our feet chancy and treacherous. Hard as the day's climb had been, I could have thanked the mountain for its harshness and the night for its darkness, so glad was I not to have to pretend I had strength to walk any longer.

I awoke at daybreak, scarcely less weary than I had been at evening. My head seemed to weigh more than all the gold Warfast's band had ever taken. "Hwyn, I'm not sure I can go anywhere," I said. By now my injury caricatured her own, my face lopsided, one eye swollen shut.

"I'll look again for herbs," she said. "There must be something to help you." The search was laborious for her with her dim eyesight. I watched her in the morning mist, poring over the meadow pace by pace, dropping often to hands and knees to look more closely at leaf or flower. Trenara drifted after her as if bound to her by invisible threads. When they disappeared into a thicket, I closed my one good eye again and rested my burning head on the dewy grass.

They returned without herbs but with fresh mulberries heaped up in Hwyn's threadbare skirt. I ate a few, slowly, and pretended they made me feel better. The crimson juice on our hands and Hwyn's skirt looked so much like blood that it almost turned my stomach. When my gorge rose at the thought of another berry, I forced a smile, said I was full, and wearily rose with the others to press onward.

It would not do. With only one eye open, I could scarcely judge the depth of each little fall or rise of the ground. I stumbled dangerously, then dropped to all fours, my head reeling.

"Do you need help?" Hwyn said.

I shook my head, making myself even dizzier. What help could she give me? What I needed was someone of my own height to lean against. No, I reflected, what I needed was a bed to lie in and a physician with a thorough knowledge of poisons and a good stock of antidotes. "I just needed to touch the earth to be sure of it. With only one good eye, I can't see to judge my steps. How do you manage it?" I blurted out, then instantly regretted having called attention to her lack.

But Hwyn only mused, "I'm not sure what I do. I never think of it—it's been so long since I've had to think of it."

"One gets used to it then," I said, though I inwardly thought it might have taken Hwyn months or years to acquire her unconscious ease in the world of half-sight.

"In time," Hwyn said, as if guessing my thought, "one grows used to anything. Should we rest here?"

"Hardly a place to rest," I said, for we were on a jagged spur of rock among dozens of broken crags, like the rotten uneven teeth of a giant, sticking out at all angles with broad gaps between them. I ached with regret for the mulberry grove we'd left behind, like Mereforth the Mariner pining for the Island of the

Innocent that, once left behind, could never be found again. "I can go on a little way, if I keep my hands close to the ground. You go ahead and talk or sing so I can follow your voice."

"If that will help you," she said unsteadily. "I hate to leave you crawling on the ground. If only I could support you—but oh, gods, what use would I be, with my head lower than your armpit? All right, then, I'll go ahead. But cry out if you need anything." So she started along the way, slower than before, and she sang, looking over her shoulder every couple of measures to see if I were following. In her place, I might have chosen a marching song or a minstrel's calling-on song as most compatible with a hard hike over the rocks. I was startled by the exquisite, fluid strains of a song I'd rarely heard outside a temple:

> *"Arise, arise, my own, my love,*
> *Earthly joy of my heavenly heart,*
> *Stretch toward me if you long for me:*
> *I am here, here for your growing,*
> *Here for your knowing,*
> *Here for your loving,*
> *Here for your living,*
> *Here for your having.*
> *Golden joy of my blue eye,*
> *Grow toward me if you love me,*
> *Grow to the sky that knows me,*
> *Grow to the sun that shows my love,*
> *Grow to the height that is in you, waiting to show.*
> *Grow, though you grow to be cut down;*
> *Grow though you know the grinder's stone*
> *Waits to make dust of your growing;*
> *Though I will mourn at the mowing,*
> *I give you, grain of my fields,*
> *Joy of the sweetness of summer,*
> *Oblivion of autumn's doom,*
> *New life in the creatures you nourish,*
> *New life in the next planting,*
> *When brightness shall sing you alive again:*
> *Grow to me, earthly love."*

It was the Bright Goddess's song to the growing grain, and I had never heard any but a priestess sing it—for aught I knew, it might have been forbidden. Where had she learned to sing like that? Her voice was like the bright water springing over the rocks to the grateful pool, or like the sunlight on that water; yet there was a tremor in it, as though she might at any moment have begun sobbing for the grain cut down and sacrificed for our food. It was splendid: I caught Trenara looking wonderingly at her as she sang, and I fancied even the wild goats paused a little to listen before gamboling up and away from us. It made the hairs rise on the back of my neck; at the same time, it made me feel I could follow her forever. But the song ended, and she seemed to forget to begin again, looking back over her shoulder as much as forward, watching me toil on behind her, a furrow of concern deepening on her brow. At last we came to a grassy stretch that was nearly level along the western face of the hill. "Hwyn," I said, weakly at first, then again, "*Hwyn,*" till she turned again: "Hwyn, this is where I stop."

She came back to kneel in the grass by my side, her face drawn. "Of course. This is a good spot; we can rest a while. Then—"

"No," I said. "No *then*. I can go no farther until something draws the poison from me. You have a quest to complete, and its end lies over the mountains to the north. I can never complete that journey in this state. I cannot go on." My head spun, and the sun's glare seemed to oppress me; I curled on the ground, burying my hot face in my hands.

Hwyn's cool fingers glanced lightly over my hair. "I can't leave you."

"Then we are at an impasse," I said, raising my head to look her in the eye—aptly phrased, one eye to one eye, some relentlessly ironical part of my mind said. "Let me think."

That was not easy: my head would not stop pounding, nor the ground stop spinning under me, and my mind seemed distracted, as though I kept passing into dreams and out again without entirely falling asleep. Through it all, Hwyn's hand was on my shoulder, and that gentleness was all I wanted of life at that moment: to surrender myself to her care, as I had in the robbers' cave, and lie peacefully with my head in her lap, her voice in my ears, till I died of whatever poison or sickness had entered that trifling arrow-cut, for in my fevered state I could scarcely imagine surviving. But if I were dying, it would be worse than useless for Hwyn to linger without hope in this barren place with no food, no water, no shelter against a storm. I must not tempt her with my weakness to stay in this poor harbor. Certainly we would have been better off in the mulberry grove, but I was loath to ask Hwyn to turn backward—or, in truth, to raise myself off the ground and walk anywhere, forward or back, without some prospect of help from a more skilled hand than hers or mine.

"Perhaps I can break the impasse," I said at last. "There must be herdsmen in these hills, for it was not another goat that marked that white goat's ear. Where they live in all these hills I cannot say, but they must be where there is water. Go find a stream you can follow. You can move faster without me, and will have more hope of finding whatever there is to be found while I stay here. If you find help in the next day, you can come back for me."

"What if it takes longer?"

"If you find no help by then, there will be no point turning back," I said as firmly as I could.

"Hidden Goddess!" Hwyn swore in a choked voice. "You promised to be with me to my journey's end."

"And you told me," I said with growing strength, "that if you followed anything but the vision given to you, you might as well have stayed in safety. Very true: and if I tempt you to follow anything but that vision, I should never have come with you. If you stay here, where there is no hope, I will be ashamed, for I will have turned you from your true path. Go now. May the gods go with you."

She seized both my hands and pressed them to her face. "Forgive me."

I felt her tears, and strange to say, they gave me strength not to hold her there any longer, seeking another sign of regard. "My friend, there is nothing to forgive. I know if there is help for me, you will find it. Go quickly."

She pressed into my hand a handkerchief full of currants she'd been saving for later; I tried to refuse, having no stomach for them, but it distressed her too much to leave me with nothing, and in the end I took them so as not to weaken her resolve to go. Then I watched them depart, the little drab figure and the tall splendid one retreating into the sunlit haze and dropping out of sight. They looked so defenseless, I found myself wishing Warfast had gone with them after all, so they would have some protector all the rest of their journey. I gazed out along a greensward dotted with white and gold flowers, as if Hwyn's tears had taken root in the sunshine, until it all blurred in my eye. For a time I knew nothing.

I was awakened by a moist nudge at my face that sent a spasm of pain through my head. I opened my right eye and was too alarmed even to cry out at the sight of an enormous animal's black muzzle. I froze, trying to imagine what sort of hideous beast was about to assail me, as the creature kept sniffing at me with a motion that I dimly recognized as familiar.

"Heel, Seeker," said a tenor voice somewhere beyond the huge black dog—for that, of course, was the true nature of the monster. The dog retreated, and a young man's round, genial face appeared over me, frank blue eyes searching me as avidly as the dog had sniffed. His hair, black as the dog's fur, hung in two braids, an ancient style long disused in the lands I knew. "Are you alive, stranger?"

I struggled up on one elbow. "Did Hwyn send you?"

"Did who?"

"Hwyn—my friend—a little woman, very small, with light hair, in old gray clothes with one red sleeve. She went to look for help."

"No, good brother, no one sent me. I hunt on this mountain often. What brought you here? And what's that great sore on your head?"

"One of the guards of Kreyn grazed me with an arrow—a shallow wound, but it festered. I couldn't walk any farther. Even lifting my head like this makes the mountain seem to tilt and spin."

"Could you walk with me for support?"

He looked about my height; it might help. "I'll try."

"I can take you to Folcsted; the healer-priestess will know what to do for you."

"Thank the gods you're here—and thank you for your willingness to help a stranger," I said. "But I had rather you find Hwyn and Trenara. They have nearly as much need of help as I, and more hope of surviving."

"Take heart, man. You're not dead yet," said the youth. "As for your friends, if you have something of theirs, show it to Seeker and he'll find them soon enough."

Glad, then, for the handkerchief full of currants, I emptied the fruit into one hand, gave it to the boy, then presented the cloth to the dog's snout, half afraid it would only send him into the next stand of currant bushes. But the beast started instead in the direction Hwyn and Trenara had taken when I had last seen them. With a triumphant nod, the young man pulled me to my feet and led me down the same pathway, supporting me all the way, his quiver of arrows jostling against me uncomfortably, his longbow hanging from his other shoulder. "What's your name, traveler?" he asked as we went along.

"Jereth," I said. "And yours?"

"Ethwin the Hunter," he said. "You're a priest?"

"No," I said, "I left the Tarvon Order without vows."

"Pity," said Ethwin. "It would have been a better story to tell—a priest forced to flee the city guards like a thief, and me there to rescue him."

"You can tell it that way if you like," I said, ready to agree to anything, for I needed the strong arm under my shoulder so badly it shamed me.

"What are you, then? Since you're not a priest?"

I was not sure what to say—pilgrim, minstrel, merchant's son? "Hwyn's follower," I mused to myself, and dazed by pain, said it aloud without further explanation.

"Then what is Hwyn?" the youth said as we followed Seeker around an outcropping of gray stone. Just then my bleary eye caught a blur of violet and a flash of red—Trenara's surcoat, and Hwyn's mismatched sleeve.

"There they are!" I said. "Or do my hopes deceive me? Do you see them, the two women—a little one with light hair and a tall dark one in blue and violet?"

"Yes," said Ethwin. "There they are, coming up to meet us."

Trenara hastened toward me first; Hwyn, still unseeing, lagged a little behind. "Hwyn!" I called weakly. When Ethwin echoed me in stronger tones, she quickened her step toward us. We met on a grassy slope, where Ethwin gradually lowered me to earth. "I thought to see you walking away from us," I said.

She held out a handful of rough gray peelings. "Willow bark," she explained, "to ease the pain. I found it near a stream I meant to follow downhill, looking for dwellings. I thought there would be no harm in bringing it to you first. Here, take a strip and chew on it."

I did as she said. The bark had a bitter, ashy flavor, but I was too pleased to see her returning to me to complain of anything.

"Now that you've found your friends, Jereth, maybe I can leave you in their care and fetch a donkey from Folcsted to carry you," Ethwin said. "I can go faster alone. Unless, perhaps," he turned to Trenara, "this lady will bear me company? She seems a good walker." The lad was gawking at Trenara with the same dreamy expression she'd inspired in Lok. But Trenara only smiled demurely and clung to Hwyn's arm. "Not without Hwyn."

"Hwyn, I see you have many followers," Ethwin said, "and I none. I will leave you one more. Seeker," he called to his dog, "guard them." He pointed at us. The dog trotted to Trenara's side—as its master might have liked to—and remained with her as the young man vanished down the hillside.

"How did you find him?" Hwyn asked me as he disappeared.

I laughed weakly. "Everything happens while I'm asleep. The dog found me, and I gave him your handkerchief to pick up your scent so we could follow you."

"Then I needn't have left you at all," she fretted.

"You wouldn't have found this bark without leaving," I reminded her. "It does seem to help." It was true: for all its bitterness, I had to admit it seemed to have eased the pain in my head. "Thank you for these. And for coming back."

I rested with my head in her lap until Ethwin returned, better than his word, with two donkeys, one for me, the other for Hwyn and Trenara to take turns, one riding, one walking. Though it shamed me to ride while either of them went on their own weary feet, I had little choice: every jolt along the way made the world blur and swim before my eyes, and it was all I could do to stay mounted, much less walk.

Nimble as the mountain goats, Ethwin led us downhill and northward, now by stony ridges, now by nearly flat stretches of meadow, now by thickets of birch and thorn. It was well that the donkeys were surefooted beasts, for some of the drops were steep enough to trouble my weak stomach. We went a long way through a narrow, rocky pass, gray stone rising on both sides like walls of a passageway, so that I half expected to descend into a cave. But after we rounded a bend, the walls of stone fell back, the land opened out before us, and I was almost blinded by the brilliance of a lake in the valley below us, blazing under the setting sun like a mirror on fire. A narrow band of plowed fields and a few stone houses huddled between the lakeshore and the wooded slopes beyond the valley.

We descended sharply, picking our way between birches and brambles until we reached the flat cleared land. "Here we are," Ethwin said, "Folcsted by St. Arin's Lake. You are in luck today," he added, "for Mother Halred's in the valley, not out among the flocks. I told the good mother you were coming, and she bade me take these donkeys and bring you back to her house."

We were passing by plowed land worked anxiously by women and some children, all bent low over the soil. An old woman straightened to call a greeting to Ethwin, and a few children stared and pointed at us, jumping up and down and calling to their elders in piping voices. Most of the others raised their heads for a bemused glance, then returned to their work.

On the opposite side of our path, on the lakeshore, a knot of men wrestled boulders into place to reinforce an embankment. Most of them, like the farming women, only glanced up fleetingly before resuming work. But one gray-haired man broke from the group and strode toward us, calling, "Ethwin! Ethwin, I'm talking to *you*." Our guide ignored him, looking straight before him, hands clenching at his sides.

"Your father?" I murmured to Ethwin.

He nodded sullenly and continued on, letting his father hurry panting after him. The old man caught up with us as we neared the first building, a simple long house of lime-washed stone, its door and window-shutters moss-green. "You're not bringing those strangers into our house," he said without preamble.

"No, Father," the youth said, "to Mother Halred's."

"It's no difference," said his father. "We've none of us got anything extra to go around. If you're responsible for bringing the Folc three beggars to feed—"

"The good mother bade me bring them," Ethwin said.

"—it's out of our own mouths you're taking their keep," his father continued.

As we passed more grainfields, the workers looked up at the sound of the older man's voice, shook their heads, then looked down again.

"What would you have me do?" Ethwin shot back.

"Your duty, like the rest of us. You've brought home nothing from the hunt today, unless you mean us to eat these three skinny vagabonds—"

"Should I have left them to die of wounds and thirst? Is that the way of the Folc?"

"Is it the way of the Folc to starve our own to feed strangers?"

"They can have my portion, if it comes to that," Ethwin shouted, making heads lift again to stare.

His father seemed about to retort, but stopped silent in mid-stride as a woman stepped forward to meet us. There was little remarkable in her appearance—she looked fifty or sixty years old, a little above middle height, as lean and angular as any of the people I had seen, but not more so. Her gray-black hair hung down her back and shoulders in long tangles. Her tunic of undyed wool draped loosely over her thin frame, and her feet were bare, with knobbly toes caked in mud. Nonetheless, there was something about her that stopped Ethwin and his father in midretort, and would have stopped me, too. Her steel-gray eyes held us like a wall of spears.

"Ethwin, there you are at last," she said. "So these are my guests—the wounded man and his friends?"

"Yes, Good Mother," Ethwin said, and I could tell from his tone that he did not call her "Mother" in the same sense as he called the man "Father." "They are Jereth, Hwyn, and—and—"

"I am the Lady Trenara of Larioneth," the lady said as he stood stammering and blushing beside her.

"May the gods smile on our meeting," said the woman. "I am Halred, priestess and healer. Ethwin, thank you for the time you've spent bringing them."

"It is our part to thank Ethwin for rescuing us in distress," Hwyn said, "and you for calling us your guests."

"It was never the way of my people to turn aside strangers," Halred said over our shoulders at Ethwin's father, whose angry glare I could almost feel burning the back of my head. "You are welcome to Folcsted on St. Arin's Lake. Edwach," she spoke past us again, "you disapprove of this welcome?"

"Mother Halred, you know how it stands with us in this lean year. Priestess though you are, even you cannot act as one alone. You must bring them before the Assembly."

"I will, Edwach. Tomorrow," said the healer. "Now let me do my work. You strangers, come with me."

She led us to a round cottage of gray fieldstone, its door and windows open to the air. Ethwin helped me dismount and went to tether the donkeys as the rest of us followed the healer into her home. It was nearly as bare as my cell in the Tarvon Monastery: two plain pinewood chests were the only furniture, their tops smooth and flat to double as worktables. The low sun slanting in the westward window illuminated pots, cups, and bowls piled on the stone floor to one side of the cold hearth, a pair of well-worn boots to the other.

The healer opened one of the chests, took out a sheepskin bedroll, shook it out, and spread it near the hearth. At her gesture, I sank gratefully down on it. "Thank you, Good Mother," I said. "I am sorry to cause you trouble—"

"Edwach is causing me trouble," she said sharply, but then sighed, "and the late spring, and the poor soil, and the leanness of the flocks—I am not insensible to these things, whatever Edwach may believe. But turning away wounded travelers will not restore the land."

"I am loath to burden you in hard times," Hwyn said. "But for Jereth's wound, I would take my chances in the hills, foraging like the wild goats. But I can work while he mends—weed fields, tend beasts—"

"Tomorrow," Halred told her. "Tonight we will tend to your friend."

She took flint and steel from the hearthstones and lit a lamp, for the russet glow of the setting sun was dying to embers. Then she knelt on the floor by my side and, holding the lamp over me with one hand, she pulled the bandage away from the wound with the other. It stuck to the wound, crusted with blood; as it tore free, I gasped involuntarily.

"What are you doing?" Hwyn said, hovering anxiously nearby.

Ignoring the interruption, Halred explored my swollen head with her fingers, making me flinch again. "Hold still!" she chided, prodding at the wound all the while. "How did you come by this wound?"

"An arrow grazed my head," I said. "It may have been poisoned, or the sore may have festered of its own."

Halred nodded approvingly. "You answer well, Jereth. You've passed the first test, for if you'd pretended it was anything but an arrow-wound, I'd never have trusted another word from your mouth. You do not look like a soldier, nor yet like a huntsman. What brought you in the path of that arrow?"

I glanced at Hwyn, who looked uncertain, then back at Halred. And not a movement of my eyes had escaped the healer. She turned to Hwyn and demanded, "Why does he look to you for words? What secret are you holding between you with your conspiratorial glances?"

"None that mean harm to you or to any of your people," Hwyn said. "But as St. Ligaiya said, all things have their secrets, whether for good or ill: a white hare hides in the snow or a brown toad in the mud like an innocent heart in the world."

Halred regarded her with a bemused smile. "Are you that innocent heart, then?"

Hwyn looked abashed. "Who is wholly innocent? Trenara, perhaps, in her way; not I. But my secrets, at least, are innocent ones, and I have reasons for keeping them that bind me like the laws of your order, Good Mother. Or at least they *ought* to bind me. But now I am at your mercy, and cannot cling to principle: Jereth is hurt, and I will tell what I must to pay the price of his healing."

Halred stiffened. "I did not say there was a price. Keep your secrets, then, snow hare."

She turned to me again with a professional eye, like my father sizing up merchandise. Ethwin crept in with a bucket of water, but Halred paid him no heed. After some moments of silent scrutiny, she said, "There is some impurity in the wound; all your flesh is struggling to push it out. You would not think this swelling a sign of health, would you? But it is your body fighting back. Heat may help it along."

She moved along the wall to a series of hooks, from which bundles of herbs hung drying, and chose a leaf here, a bulb there, an ominous-looking bit of white fungus. She put the herbs into a hammered metal bowl poised on a tripod, ladled a little water over them, then set her lamp under the bowl so its flame heated the bottom. The smell that rose from this brew made me queasy.

She turned, then, to my friends and Ethwin. "There's been no fire in this hearth for a month or more, but we will need a fire tonight. You three may as well set about getting fuel and kindling. Ethwin, you might show Hwyn where to find some." So the hunter and Hwyn went out, and Trenara drifted after them.

Halred stared after them until they were well out of earshot. "Well, I wouldn't have believed it," she said then. "That great lady with her rich clothes and refined manners—gone to help them fetch peat or dung to burn!"

"Trenara's simple," I explained. "She may not actually help. But where Hwyn goes, she goes."

"And you too?" Halred smiled slyly at me as she knelt on the hearthstones, stirring her concoction.

"When I can," I said, staring off through the dark door where my friends had disappeared.

"I confess, I sent Hwyn off for more reasons than to fetch peat," Halred said. "She's protective of you, which is of course a good thing, taken by itself—but she also seems distrustful by nature or habit, and I can't be distracted with questions and protests during a delicate task. And it will be delicate: I will have to reopen your wound. Do you understand?"

"You said something needed to be pushed out," I said. "But the wound has already opened more than once. I caught a fist half as big as my head right on the sore, bursting it open. It bled a fountain."

"I'm sure it did," Halred said. "But since then, it looks as though you've been sleeping in the dirt, and keeping the same foul rag on your head till it crusted to the sore. It's had plenty of chances to fester since then. And Jereth, you must know something has to be done. If not, you wouldn't have been lying on that hillside, helpless, till Ethwin carried you here."

As she spoke, she opened one of the chests and drew out her materials: a little clay jug with a stopper, clean linen cloths, and a delicate knife, its blade bright in the lantern light. "I will open the wound and wash it with sour wine, and I warn you, the washing will hurt more than the cut itself. Then I will put the hot poultice on the sore and bind it with linen. After that, I may have to let you drink the rest of the wine to dull the pain. Will you consent to all this?"

It did not take much thought. "Yes," I said. "It can't be worse than going on as I am."

"Good," the healer said. "The mixture's bubbling; let's begin before your friends come sticking their heads in the way. First," she poured off a bit of broth from the heating flask into a clay cup, "drink this."

Of all the unpleasant things she'd promised to do, none stands out in my memory so horribly as that mouthful of herb broth, which stank like the hold of a ship that has been calmed for too long with too many people aboard. After that ordeal, the quick burning cut of the flamed knife on the old sore, the acidic sting of the wine in the open wound, and the hot poultice slimy with the sediment of the heating-flask were nothing to complain about. I had meant to refuse the wine, for I doubted she could easily replace her stock and I had already taxed her resources more than I wished. But in the end I weakened and drank a little, not only to numb the pain but to wash the taste of the broth from my mouth. The wine was nearly vinegar, but it was a cleaner sort of bad taste than the herbs. Fortunately, with nothing in my stomach all day but a few mulberries and a strip of willow bark, a quick swallow of wine was enough to send me to sleep.

I woke once during the night to find Hwyn sitting on the floor by my side. I reached out, clumsy with sleep, and felt her thin, strong fingers clasp mine.

"Peace, now," she murmured. "Rest."

"Will you sing to me?" I said. "Sing what you sang on the way."

Softly, softly she sang to me, as to the summer grainfields we had passed in the last leg of our journey, and though the goddess called the grain to awaken, before the song was done I was blissfully asleep.

8

THE ASSEMBLY

OF THE FOLC

When I woke again to the full light of afternoon and saw Hwyn slumped against the stone wall, asleep sitting up, her straw-colored hair disordered as an abandoned nest, I wondered whether her night singing had been real or a dream.

"She kept watch over you all night."

I turned toward the voice. Halred stood on the hearthstones, looking down at us. She pointed toward Hwyn with a long-handled spoon before crouching back down to stir a pot over the fire. "A very tenacious woman, that one. She only fell asleep well into the morning, and then not by design, as you can tell by the way she's propped up."

"She'll get a crick in her neck from sleeping like that." I pulled myself up onto my knees, feeling a slight lightness in my head, but nothing compared to the day before. There was a shadow in the corner of my left eye, but the very fact that I noticed it meant I could see with both eyes again. I crept toward Hwyn without any of yesterday's half-blind fumbling, and slid an arm between her back and the wall, shifting her weight onto my shoulder to ease her down onto the end of my bedroll. I was not careful enough, however, for she woke.

"Jereth!" Her head on my shoulder, she looked into my face with her one good eye, then reached up to touch my left temple with cool fingers, light as dreams. "It's less swollen. Do you feel better?"

"Yes. Weak, still, but the hammering pain is gone. Whatever Halred did to the sore was well done."

"With the gods' help, lad," Halred crouched nearby, "you're past the crisis."

"When I came back," Hwyn said, "you were already asleep with a poultice on your head. We built a fire, and then Ethwin went back to his clan's house, while Mother Halred put herbed water in the tripod to heat."

"For the healthful steam," Halred explained, and indeed, there was a comforting scent in the air, overpowering even the dung-smoke and the smell of the sheepskin.

Hwyn went on, "Then she cast other herbs on the fire as a sacrifice and began invoking the Four Great Ones."

Trenara wandered in from the front garden and knelt near me, reaching out to stroke my face. I had recovered well enough that her touch did not make me flinch. Nonetheless, her gesture surprised me: for the most part, after the first night of our acquaintance, Trenara had ignored me entirely, behaving as though Hwyn were her only companion—as I suppose I too did, in my own way.

"My Lady," I said to her, "why this tenderness?"

Trenara, as usual, only smiled inscrutably.

"You knew Jereth was in danger, didn't you, Trenara?" Hwyn said to her, and Trenara nodded solemnly—though she might have done so regardless of what was said to her.

Halred put in, "All the while I was chanting the prayers of healing, she knelt by your head with her hands open before her. I half expected she would begin chanting with me—but I take it she doesn't speak much."

"Very little," Hwyn admitted. "I don't know how much of these ceremonies she understands, but someone raised her to be reverent. And I sometimes think she has sat by many sickbeds and stood by many graves in her young life."

"Here I thought she had always been in your care! You speak as though you had not known her long."

"Not above a year or so," she said.

"And yet she follows where you go—even to this lonely land," said Halred.

Hwyn shrugged. "I defended her once. I doubt anyone had done so before."

Halred shook her head. "No, I doubt they had. It's always the weak who defend the weak—if you'll pardon my calling you so."

Hwyn stretched her long mouth in a crooked smile, sweeping her arms out as if to lay bare all her smallness and brokenness. "Truth needs no pardon, Good Mother. And even if it did, I would be loath to blame you, when you have spent your precious herbs, your labor, and your prayers for us, vagabonds unwelcome in your land."

"There would have been a time," Halred said, "when no one would have questioned your welcome here. When strangers were sacred. When they would have been clustering about you for news instead of debating your right to stay in my house and share my portion of bread."

"But these are lean times," I said, "and bread is hard-won. I can understand them well."

Halred frowned. "No one has starved. But we have had three years of dry summers and poor harvests, three years of thin forage for the animals, three years when we had to live off the meat of our flocks, not the milk, slaughtering more than the year's births could replace. Now the flocks are dwindling, not growing.

"And now we have had another late spring with too little rain; the meadow grass is thin, and the crops are not as high as they should be now, in the prime of summer.

"As if that were not enough, some among us have grown

grasping, saying 'this is mine,' not 'this is ours.' One shepherd quarrels with another, 'The ewe that miscarried was yours; mine has the live lamb. If some must starve, that is the will of the gods, but it shall not be my household.' That was not always our way. We held flocks in common, and marked them only with the mark of the valley. Now the heads of the four clans each have their own marks, and some of the sons of each clan have begun devising their own variations on the clan-mark, so brother can hoard sheep from brother and cousin from cousin—as if all were not needed to drive the wolves from the flocks together!

"At this rate they will take to building fences and enclosing pastures, like the outlanders our ancestors fled from; the flocks will not be free to move to untasted pastures as summer grows old, and all will have less so each can guard his own. Thus the blight of the land is matched by a blight on our ways that may starve us even if the land's sickness does not."

I smiled bitterly. "And here we have come in the midst of this quarrel over wants, with our hands empty. Will it save you strife if we leave at once? You have been kind to us, and I hate to cause you more trouble. Though I would rather repay you, if it's better to leave I may be strong enough to go on my own two feet."

Halred shook her head. "No, Jereth. As my guest and my patient you may not go. Though you feel stronger now, you have not yet tried to walk as far as the door; I doubt you are ready to cross the hills afoot. And besides," she said, "I want to challenge the naysayers among us, not hide from them. After all, I am their priestess."

I nodded, my eyes drawn again to a sight that had piqued my curiosity on the wall across from where I sat: a broad shield-shaped icon of the Hidden Goddess, depicted as a woman looking away into the starlit distance, the flow of her straight black hair merging into the stark slopes of a dark mountain with a blue lake at its base. It was artfully drawn, though the paints looked like the same simple colors found on the doors of the Folcsted houses, blue, berry-red, green, black, and lime-wash white.

"You are given to the Hidden Goddess?" I remarked, gesturing toward the icon. "All the healing orders I know are vowed to the Bright Goddess."

"Look above you," Halred said, pointing. I turned to crane at the wall I'd been leaning on, and there indeed the Bright Goddess smiled down on us, trailing a cloak of summer flowers over the green hillsides. On either side of her, a white goat followed her up the hill. I gazed long, then turned from the rejoicing goddess's face to her dark sister's back and Halred's smiling eyes.

"Why not both?" the priestess said. "After all, Night too is a healer. Are you not strengthened by your long night's rest and quiet? Could the sun do more for your wounds than darkness did? And though the sun ripens the herbs that soothe and heal, they begin in the dark earth. The wine I use to cleanse wounds begins in sunlit fields, but is completed in dark casks. Who can heal without one or the other?"

Hwyn looked up at the priestess with new appreciation. "If that is the custom in the Hills of Penmorrin, then it is high time the people of the flatlands came to the mountains for wisdom."

Mother Halred smiled ruefully. "It was never the way of the Folc till I made it my own way. Indeed, many called it unseemly when I would not choose between the priestesses of the Bright and Hidden Goddesses, but remained the acolyte of both. Well for the Folc that I was so stubborn, for no other priestess is left in this valley. The other acolyte of the Bright Goddess ran away with a handsome stranger in our youth, and the young priestess of the Hidden Goddess died soon after our teacher. I alone preserve the teachings of both orders in this valley.

"I am teaching two acolytes now—you will meet them later; I left them with my other patient, for they are well able to handle a simple childbirth without me. I call them Day and Night, and though I teach them both all I know, I hold each one to the test for her half of the lore, Bright or Hidden. In another year or so, they will be ready to change places and learn the other half of wisdom, both from me and from each other."

Halred's eye seized on my cassock. "Your garb has a clerical plainness to it, though your hair is not tonsured. You would not be a priest of the Turning God, would you?"

"No," I said.

"Pity. We have none now. Old Father Wendlac was such a rough old bear that he could not keep an acolyte from one feastday to the next; and our priest of the Rising God, Anlaf, is not of my way of thinking."

"I was in the Tarvon Monastery, devoted to the Rising God—but I left without final vows," I said.

"And now you follow Hwyn," Halred mused, "who has secrets to keep. I wonder—I have heard tales of the Priestesses of
the Hidden Wisdom..."

"The likeness has been observed before," I said, with a sly
smile at Hwyn.

"And in error," Hwyn concluded. "I have no order, nor any
learning at all. I wish I had been taught by you, Good Mother. I
might then be better able to understand the dreams that drive
me." She looked up at Halred like a schoolchild at a favorite
teacher. Their eyes seemed to meet, and I watched her shed yesterday's suspicious like unneeded winter garments in the sunshine. "Maybe you could explain what has eluded me, even
now."

"I won't deny you pique my curiosity," Halred said. "Do you
mean to speak of these dreams, then, or only to add riddles on
riddles, like St. Lar's Vision of the Hidden Goddess?"

"I think now that I was wrong to mistrust you," Hwyn said.
"And yet it is hard to speak plainly of what is still misty and
dreamlike to me. So much of what I know seems to lie below
speech, out of my willing grasp."

"That must burden you," Halred said softly. "And it may be
true, as you say, that learning would have made all clearer and
simpler. Yet dreams and visions are not given amiss: they are
given to those they are meant for, whether scholars or plain laborers or outright fools. It might be that the hand of a teacher
would have lain too heavy on you to let you feel the subtle pull
of your own calling—or that understanding the portents too
clearly would only frighten you from the course you must take."

Hwyn smiled ruefully. "Now you speak as if you knew the
last twists of my journey. I went to Kreyn because I heard that an
oracle-stone kept by Lady Goldifer Kreyn held some prophecy
about—about me, it might be.

"I went there seeking answers; what I found was almost death
for all three of us, for in seeking the stone we offended Lady
Goldifer, who reigns almost as a priest-queen, high in the reverence of the people. Her guards chased us into the hills. Now,
thanks to my curiosity, Jereth has been hurt, we have strayed far
from the path I must travel, and what little I have learned at this
cost can only frighten me—it cannot help me complete my task."

"Nor may my counsel help you," Halred admitted. "I am not a
visionary; my wisdom is in things I can touch with my two

hands. And though you may be untaught, no one who heard you bolster your case for secrecy with verses of St. Ligaiya would call you unlearned. You may have gleaned your knowledge by following the reapers, but it is as much as many have harvested with a teacher's help. It may be that what you know is enough, if you could but trust your own knowing."

"Maybe," said Hwyn softly.

The healer moved closer to Hwyn. "You said you had strong reasons to keep your secrets. Now, I won't lie to you: everything you say makes me hungrier to know what you're hiding. I am one of those people whose appetite to know is never satisfied. And besides, if you are some kind of prophet, you may have some knowledge that would help my people. But I would be ashamed to coerce that knowledge from you. You must not feel you owe me your secrets because I poulticed your friend's wound."

"It was not that—or not *only* that," Hwyn said. "But something you said made me think you might understand, as so few can understand."

Halred smiled. "Maybe so. But I admit you touched a sore point when you said you would tell me what you must to pay for Jereth's healing—to *pay!* Bright Goddess defend us!

"My teacher in the mysteries of the Bright Goddess took her lore from a long tradition of healer-priests, stretching back before the dawn of memory, and none have ever asked payment for healing. We lived on the free bounty of the Folc. But if the changes I see run their course, I will need to ask payment; everything will be mine or yours or his or hers, nothing everyone's or no one's, no free bounty for healing or worship.

"But enough talk for now," she said, returning to her kettle by the hearth. "We must hasten, for we have an ordeal ahead of us. Jereth, I am sorry: I ought to be able to promise you a day and night of uninterrupted rest, at least. But with the Folc in disagreement over you, you must appear at the Assembly Stone to be judged. Let me give you a bit to eat before we go. There will be more time to talk along the way."

She ladled porridge from the cauldron into clay bowls and set them on a closed chest as on a table. We sat on the floor around it and dug in eagerly with our fingers, for we'd been half starved ever since we left faraway Sebrin, and my appetite was returning with my health. Not entirely returned, however: the thick porridge of oats and peas seemed so heavy after days of berries and odd leaves that I found it slow work to eat it. "I'm not sure I need this much," I told Halred.

"Finish it," she commanded with a healer's authority.

As they waited for me, Hwyn began tentatively to speak: "I've been thinking about what you said—that night is a healer as well as day. And I wonder, in this remote land, have you heard of the Troubles in the North?"

"That we have," Halred said. "We see few strangers, but in recent years, most have come down from the North, fleeing from earthquakes or angry ghosts or towns fallen into lawlessness—or telling stranger tales than those.

"One hunter said the paths turned under his feet, more and more with each passing day, till he could not find his way home again. Farmers said that when spring bothered to come at all, they could not be sure that what followed it would be summer. And we ourselves, with three years' late springs and three years' lean harvests, fear that we feel the first blows of whatever destruction is coming down from the North."

Hwyn paused a while, and I watched her as eagerly as Halred to see what she would say. "Whether your land's troubles are part of the same upheaval, I cannot say," she said. "But since I half drowned in a sacred pool, I have had a sort of dark sight, a knowledge of things beyond the grasp of reason. And whatever fills my night with visions has taught me to see the Troubles not as destruction, but as the coming of Night over the world."

Halred shook her head. "If it is, it is a crueler night than I want to imagine. You don't know what it means to live in a land that is dying, among a people that is losing its soul."

"Maybe not," Hwyn said. "I have rarely stayed in one place for long. But everywhere I have traveled, I have found things stirring like the air before a storm that will wash away all before it: old ways and new, rulers and subjects, kings and priests, wrestling each other to a stalemate, neither able to gain the upper hand, neither able to surrender. In every city, in every least village, I feel something about to burst.

"It is like the moment before the clouds open with rain, the moment before the dam bursts, the moment before the fever breaks, the moment before the womb opens. And the only thing that keeps me from running mad in this chaos—save Jereth's friendship—is something that whispers to me that these are the pangs of birth."

"I want to believe you," Halred said. "I want desperately to believe that you have some power to help my people, when we most need it. And there is some power in you, I am certain. I felt it when you sang the Bright Goddess's call to Jereth last night, in half-voice, as if hardly using your strength, and yet I half expected the green shoots to pierce through the stone floor in response. And I want to believe that the power you bring is for the good of this land. But what I see around me looks like the pangs of death, not birth. Though I have attended many a desperate-seeming childbirth, I can see no new life amid this darkness."

"Here," said Hwyn, "is new life in the darkness." And to my amazement, she drew forth the Eye of Night from its hiding place. "Any power you sensed from me must be traced to this."

"Why? What is it?" Halred breathed, stretching out a hand toward it hesitantly, as if she longed to touch it, but dared not.

"It is the egg of the Sky-Raven that sheltered the world in the dawn of time," Hwyn said.

"Gods on the Wheel!" Halred gasped, backing away from Hwyn. "There are prophecies about you: Bearer of Night."

"Not evil ones, I hope," said Hwyn with a nervous smile.

"Some good and some ill," Halred said, "and taken together, impossible to fathom. Some say the Bearer of Night will come in a time of confusion, and all will be made clear. Some say you will bring division, doubt, and strife. Some say that the Bearer of Night will restore what was lost—or take away what we most desire. Some say the visitation betokens the end of the world." She looked at Hwyn, who sat on the floor with eyes downcast, shoulders hunched, as if ashamed. "Mind, it does not say any of this will be your fault, but that your coming foreshadows things to come—what things, I can hardly say. There is also a prophecy that your coming foretells the coming of the gods—whether that means the world's end or something else, my two teachers could not agree."

Hwyn looked up again, half smiling. *"People say, 'Where are the gods?' and, 'Will the gods return to us?' But the gods are always among us.* St. Ligaiya, of course. As for the end of the world—I don't know. There is so much I don't understand. Change is coming, and it may be the end of the world—or the end of one and the beginning of the next. But this—" she held out the Eye of Night in a cupped palm, "this, this living thing, this child, it calls me, it murmurs to me in language I scarcely understand. I feel it yearning, longing to be free, longing to be born, and I cannot deny it. And it gives me hope: blind, unreasoning hope. Do you understand?"

Halred was silent a while, looking at Hwyn with curiosity and kindness in her eyes. "I see that a heavy destiny has been laid on you," she said at last, "and to harden you to endure it, some rare understanding or some rare madness has been given along with the burden. It may not be mine to understand. And yet—I often feel my wisdom is in my hands. May I touch the egg?"

Hwyn held it out farther toward the healer. Halred hesitated, uncertain, before covering Hwyn's hand with her own. Only slowly did her fingers relax, curling around the white stone, touching Hwyn's bony, calloused hand. For a moment, they held the Eye of Night between them. I held my breath, wondering whether Halred would sense something that had been hidden from me when Hwyn had placed the strange stone in my hand.

Slowly, Halred withdrew her hand, shaking her head. "It feels, as you say, alive, like a small creature in need of healing. Beyond that, I cannot say. Its language is not for me."

For a time she brooded, staring at her hands as though to find the defect in them that could not sense what Hwyn did. But as Hwyn returned the stone to its hiding place, Halred roused herself and pulled on her worn boots. "Enough time in the misty heights of prophecy. You've slept away the day, and now we must go, or the Assembly will begin without us—and decide against us."

"But do you still want to defend us before your people, now that you know what I am?" Hwyn said.

"You are my guests," Halred said firmly. "That much I understand; let the rest fall as it may. And you, Hwyn, though you may be the Bringer of Night, I cannot see how I should blame you for it. Some god's hand is on you; should I stand against it? Besides, if I learned nothing from the Raven's Egg, I may have learned something from the hand that held it: and I sensed there an innocent heart."

We made our way up the feet of Summerbride, the mountain north of the valley. As we neared the meeting place, we began to see the flocks of the Folc, small soft-eyed sheep and wiry white goats munching the grass and wildflowers. The first dog I saw among them, I took for Seeker: as large as any I'd ever seen, with the same blunt black snout and thick black coat. But when I'd seen more of the formidable creatures running about the edges of the flock, keeping the sheep within bounds, I realized that it was simply a local type, as common here as skinny yellow dogs had been on the wharves of Swanroad in my childhood.

Most of the shepherds, too, were of a type: tall, spare, and big-boned, with large hands and feet, high cheekbones and a low-bridged nose. Most had hair as straight and black as any Magyan's, though there were also a handful as redheaded as the Bright Goddess in Halred's icon, and some with hair like rich brown earth broken with veins of clay-red and loam-black. The women wore their hair in one braid down the back, the men in two over each shoulder, like Ethwin and his father. All their eyes were blue or light gray; Hwyn's dark gray, my hazel, and Trenara's brown eyes were the darkest to be seen. Their clothes, too, showed little variance: sturdy knitted woolen tunics of green, rust-red, ochre, or blue, with patterns of leaves or flowers stitched at the wrists and throat, over undyed shifts or breeches or bare legs.

They called to Halred as they saw her, "Good day, Good Mother!" or, "Blessings on the day, Mother Halred!" One drew her aside to ask her advice on an ailing ewe. She bent over the animal as attentively as she had examined my wound, prodding at its sores and forcing its mouth open to look at its tongue in a way that made me feel for the beast, fellow-sufferer of her healing arts. She and the shepherd spoke some time about what the sheep might have eaten, and what it might be given, while Trenara, suddenly taken with the animal, petted it and made much of it.

The shepherd turned from Halred little by little to stare at the elegant lady kneeling in the grass. "So this is the reason for our Assembly," he said at last, gesturing at the lady.

"These are my guests," Mother Halred said emphatically. "This kind gentlewoman is the Lady Trenara. Hwyn, here, is a wise woman—perhaps a prophet, as the gods may choose to reveal—and may bring some sign for our enlightenment in this time of fear. And Jereth, who was found sick and hurt on Wildhelm, brings knowledge from the Tarvon Monastery. My friends, this is Aldworth of the Ashwood Clan."

Hwyn extended a hand to him, and when Aldworth's eyes had strayed from Trenara enough to notice it, he clasped it hesitantly. "Are you indeed a wise woman?" he said.

Hwyn shrugged. "I'd better say no, lest I disappoint you."

He smiled, then, as though that moment of uncertainty touched him. "Never mind that, good sister. You are welcome to this land."

Halred smiled in return. "I knew we could count on your kindness, Aldworth."

And so, as we met the Folc along the way, Halred mustered her allies: as one asked advice for a lame sheepdog, another for her husband's aching back, another for his wife's late childbirth, she introduced us to all who sought her counsel, and we entered the gathering-place in the company of Drict, the largest man in the village and a person of some influence, once Halred had given him something for his headache. In fact, it was Hwyn's own willow bark she gave him; I wondered, idly, whether Hwyn might in other circumstances have been like Halred, healer-priestess of some village, living on the gratitude of her neighbors instead of the scraps she could beg or steal from strangers. Surely she was a likelier priest than I had ever been.

One by one the Folc gathered, shepherds leaving their flocks in a common paddock nearby or under the care of their sons or daughters; tillers of the soil climbing the same donkey-trails we had followed; mothers with babies at their hips; old women with distaffs busy in their fingers, old men mending harnesses while they waited for the meeting to begin. Yet I did not see our first friend among the Folc. "Where can Ethwin be?" I asked Halred.

"As far away as his father can send him, if I know Edwach," Halred answered.

We clustered on a high meadow ending in rocks and rubble before a sheer wall of stone cleft with the mouth of a cave. A few yards before this gateway into darkness, a huge, flat-topped stone marked the boundary between the stony waste and the grassy stretch beyond it. Even lying on its longest side, the stone stood shoulder-high to the tall men of the Folc.

As we entered the crowd, people made way before us, bowing to Halred or greeting her warmly, calling merrily to Drict, staring at us travelers in unconcealed curiosity. Someone took the donkey's reins, and Drict unassumingly helped me to dismount and half supported me through the press of people, who gave way without ado, to sit on the thinning grass before the great stone.

On the broad face of the Assembly Stone, I saw a single emblem: a circle graven with four leaves of different shapes at its compass points. By its narrower ends, smaller slabs of stone were piled like stairs. To one side, the crowd cleared around what I now saw was a small fire-pit.

As the sun sank low on the western slopes, a powerfully built man in a berry-red tunic noted the position of the Assembly Stone's shadow and raised a leafy branch above his head as a symbol to the crowd. Three other men approached, carrying branches of their own. With a start, I recognized one of them as Ethwin's father, Edwach. He seemed to catch my eye, but did not return my nod of acknowledgment.

A man in a plain undyed cassock now threaded his way through the crowd, which parted around him as it had around Halred and Drict. He mounted the Assembly Stone from the edge of the fire-pit and stood stone-still, waiting for the people to seat themselves and be silent.

"Anlaf," Halred whispered to me, "our Priest of the Upright God."

She had no need to tell me his vocation, nor would I have been in much doubt even if he had changed clothes with one of the shepherds. If he were not a priest of the Rising God, he could only be a minstrel playing the part of one. He was the very type and caricature of my own order: his back straight as a temple pillar, as if he took the epithet "Upright God" too literally and made a spiritual exercise of good posture; his whole frame gaunt and ascetic as his undyed clothing; his jaw, stripped of its beard, too narrow; his head too bony, shaved high up the back to leave only a pitiful fringe of white hair; his gaze abstracted, as if he were unused to contemplating anything in the visible world but books. This man might never have left the Hills of Penmorrin, where I had never been before—yet I had met him countless times before.

Standing atop the Assembly Stone, the priest called out to the crowd, "My neighbors and kin of the Folc of St. Arin's Lake, do you come together before the gods for honest speech and sober judgment, after the ways of our ancestors? Who comes to this Assembly? Is the Holly Clan present and spoken for?"

"Yes!" shouted a portion of the people around us; then one of the men by the fire-pit raised a holly branch aloft, saying, "I, Holt, Elder of the Holly Clan, speak for my people." With that, he cast his branch into the fire-pit.

"Is the Ashwood among us and spoken for?" the priest intoned.

"Yes!"

"I, Aldworth, Elder of the Ashwood Clan, speak for my people." I was startled to recognize the quiet-spoken shepherd in the elder who held aloft his branch; Halred had been cultivating well-placed allies indeed.

"Is the Linden among us and spoken for?"

This time it was Edwach who claimed the right to speak for his people and cast a linden branch on the fire-pit.

"Is the Red Oak among us and spoken for?"

"I, Guthlac, Elder of the Red Oak Clan and Headman for the year, speak for my household and for the weaponed-men of the Folc." The man in the red tunic who had signaled the start of the Assembly tossed his branch on the fire-pit.

"Who speaks for the women?"

A small, white-haired woman with a distaff and a stalk of grain stepped forward. "I, Maethild of the Ashwood Clan, widowed from the Linden Clan, Headwoman for the year, speak for the women of the Folc."

"Arise, Guthlac and Maethild," said the priest, "and take my place upon the Assembly Stone."

Maethild tossed the stalk of grain onto the fire-pit and stood with her foot on the stone step, waiting for the priest to make way. As soon as he descended the other side, she strode to the top with energetic movements, her long white braid swinging as she climbed; Guthlac followed her with strides measured to hers, not to catch up too fast for all his length of leg.

When they stood together atop the stone, Maethild brandished her distaff like a weapon and demanded, "Who comes to light the fire?"

"I, Halred, Priestess of the Hidden Goddess," said our host, moving to the fire-pit. She knelt and struck sparks with flint and steel until one caught. She fanned the fire till it blazed steadily, spreading across all four woods. Then she rose and stood over it, her proud face illumined in its glow.

Only then did Guthlac speak. "We, the four clans of the Folc of St. Arin's Lake, meet in the sight of the Four Gods of the

World-Wheel. We salute the hearth of the Hidden Goddess. But who is here for the Rising God?"

"I, Anlaf, listen for the voice of the Rising God," said the priest.

"And who is here for the Bright Goddess?" said Maethild.

"I, Halred, listen for the voice of the Bright Goddess," said Halred, as Anlaf sighed audibly.

"And who is here for the Turning God?" said Guthlac.

Silence fell, and the Folc bowed their heads.

"We have no priest of the Turning God," Maethild answered—a ritual response, for of course all had known this before. "Let the god himself choose by lot who shall listen for his voice. Let Red Oak provide the choosing straws."

Guthlac descended from the Assembly Stone and took from the hand of one of his kinsmen a bundle of straws. He moved through the crowd, offering the bundle to each to take a straw. It surprised me to see that he offered the bundle to Hwyn, who raised her eyebrows, then drew a straw like all the others. Next he thrust the bundle at me: "Take one, stranger."

Hesitantly, I put my hand forward and drew a straw half the length of Hwyn's.

Guthlac smiled fiercely, straightened, and called aloud, "The god has chosen!"

"Who? What?" The people crowded closer, nearly trampling me. Halred gasped and pushed her way back toward us.

"What's your name?" Guthlac asked me.

"Jereth," I said. "Are you sure—"

"Jereth the Outlander, guest of Halred, is here for the Upside-Down God," Guthlac proclaimed.

"What?" Edwach shouted above the babble of the crowd. "Guthlac, what foolery is this? How can he stand for the god?"

"I can't even stand," I muttered, but no one listened.

"He's not even one of us," Edwach said.

"He's one of the gods' children," Guthlac retorted. "The priests speak for them, not for us."

"This is an Assembly of the Folc," Edwach protested. "How can a stranger have a voice in our councils when his very right to be among us is in question?"

"The priests speak for the gods, not the Folc," Guthlac repeated. "We can bind him by the same oath we'd ask of any neighbor that drew the short straw: to choose only as the god prompts him. What, would you go against the lots and discard the traditions of our people?"

"He should never have been offered the choosing straws," Edwach said. "This is your fault, Guthlac—your plot, maybe."

"Do you accuse me of falsifying the god's choosing, Edwach? For generations there has been no war between two houses of the Folc, but—"

Halred cut in, "Guthlac, my friend, think what you say—though you do so in my own cause, I beg you—"

"Good sirs," I said from my spot on the ground, "do not fight on my account—"

"IF I had wanted to cheat," Guthlac roared, "which I did NOT, I would have wanted one of my OWN clan to support me in the final choice. The stranger belongs to none of our clans. It could not have fallen out better."

"Anything YOU like so well cannot be good for MY clan," Edwach shouted back. "You know it was my son who brought him among us. You want him to stay and burden my household. And if you want a fight, my lord of the Oaken Skull—"

"QUIET!" shrieked Maethild from atop the stone.

The noise on all sides subsided, save for the distant bleating of the flocks.

"Let's solve this like kin and neighbors, not barbarians," said Maethild. "The Upright God and the Upside-Down God can be no less in harmony than the Bright and Hidden Goddesses—is that not so, Mother Halred?"

Halred gave her assent.

"Then let the Priest of the Upright God decide whether a stranger can stand for the Upside-Down God in our Assembly," she said. "My cousins, my neighbors, can we agree to that?"

There was a murmur of agreement, with some muted grumbling from Halred who, caught with her own words, could now do nothing.

Anlaf ascended the Assembly Stone again, and looked out at us all with an expression of utmost gravity—my old abbot to the ends of his fingers. At last he spoke. "While the stranger is undoubtedly a child of the gods, that does not give him the right to a share in the councils of the Folc," he said. "My answer is no. Gather the straws again and choose one of our own."

"Old hypocrite," Halred muttered.

I handed my short straw back without protest as Guthlac gathered them up, grateful to be spared this unsought honor. I'd been a priest of the Upright or Rising God, at the furthest extreme of the Wheel from the Upside-Down or Turning God, and whatever Halred might say, there was little harmony between the two gods' priesthoods. I knew no more of his worship than we were taught to avoid the deadly sin of slighting one of the Four Great Ones. I breathed a sigh of relief as the lots were redone and Athel of the Linden Clan drew the short straw, taking the priest's role for the evening. He was another of the farmers who had sought Halred's help along the way.

"Well, at least he's a man I trust," Halred whispered to me. "In Edwach's own clan, as well, so he can hardly complain."

I nodded distractedly. Athel recited the oath from memory without prompting, as though he had heard it many times or even spoken it many times before: "I pledge to the Turning God, the Upside-Down God, Lord of Change and Time, to listen for his voice during this Assembly and speak or be silent as he bids me, not seeking my own gain or my clan's advantage but the god's working in the world."

What would that mean in reality, I wondered? Would Athel be silent, awaiting the divine word, or assume that anything that passed through his head was the god's prompting? I had always wondered about such things, even when I had given my life over to the Tarvon Order. Well, small matter, so long as it was not my burden anymore. I watched Athel move to the front rank of the crowd, near where I sat. With all the powers of the Wheel and of the Folc accounted for, the Assembly could now begin in earnest.

"My kin and my neighbors," Guthlac called, standing once again atop the Assembly Stone. "We are gathered here to settle the dispute between Mother Halred, Priestess of the Bright and Hidden Goddesses and healer of the Folc, and Lord Edwach, Elder of the Linden Clan. We are come to judge whether the three strangers should be allowed to shelter among us—and if they are, on what terms they may stay.

"Edwach, as the discontent, speak first or give up your complaint."

These seemed to be rote words only, for Edwach took no offense at the brusque demand. He stood and spoke: "My friends, you know as well as I that these are lean times. We have had three poor harvests, and the late spring and scant rain do not augur well for the one we can expect this year.

"Our flocks have dwindled: our goats are drier, our sheep smaller, their wool thinner than of old. And we have slaughtered too many for lack of fodder for them or food for ourselves through the winters.

"To take in strangers in time of plenty is a kindness. To do so in time of hunger is a cruelty to our own people: our kin and the sharers in our toil and our harvest. We must keep our own for our own. The strangers must go."

Guthlac turned to Halred: "Mother Halred, how do you answer? Speak now, or yield to the complaint against you."

Halred rose. "Is anyone here hungry? These are lean times, but if anyone had yet run out of food, I would think I as healer would have heard of it. And if we do find hunger among us, we should bring it to the Assembly and amend it.

"Together our ancestors came into this land from the Ferend River Valley, depending on one another for survival, whatever their clan. And we still depend on each other. All shepherds run to guard the flocks if a wolf appears, not asking whose sheep are threatened. All pray together; all feast together; and if we starve, all shall starve together, for there are too few of us to keep the wolf away if the Folc dwindles smaller than we are now. And so if anyone starves among us, it is matter for the whole Folc to learn how we can draw more nourishment from the land or, if it will not support us, to leave together for some more fruitful land. And so I ask, is anyone hungry now?"

For a moment there was silence. Then Edwach objected: "Of course no one is hungry now, in high summer, now that milk is as plentiful as it will be all year and fruits are ripening at last, not only in our gardens but in the wild hillsides. It is in the winter and the spring to follow that we must fear the cost of sheltering these strangers."

Halred replied, "Still, none have yet starved, and none need starve: before winter, there is still a harvest to be won from the land, with the gods' good will. And we will not gain their good will by turning away three hapless travelers, one of them injured. Hard hearts, greed, and cowardice, neglect of the guest-code and the ways of our saints and forebears—those will plead poorly for the blessing we seek. Better to court the gods' favor with hearts bent to their will, generosity, courage, sacrifice.

"We must return to the holy ways: share what we have as one Folc, welcome guests in the gods' names. We must return to what is good in us, what is true to the way of the Folc. Leave such alien ways as ear-marking of beasts by clan and shepherd, and share like the kinfolk we are. Only then will the gods hear us."

"You speak glibly of the old ways of the Folc," said the old priest, Anlaf, "but it was not our tradition of old for one priest to take vows to two of the Four Great Ones on opposite sides of the Wheel."

Halred answered, "Nonetheless, we call it sin to slight any of the Four Great Ones who embrace our world together. Why, then, should priests not learn the lore of all four, save that human life is too short? If I'd had my will, I would have learned at the feet of your master and Wendlac of old, and we would not now need to cast lots to represent the Turning God."

"And you would hold three portions of the judgment of the Folc instead of two. Yes, Halred, I see through your pious talk to what lies beneath: the hunger for power."

"If you envy me such power, study from me and be priest of two Great Ones yourself—"

"And take on your corruption?"

"Corruption! Dear gods, give me patience!"

The hubbub rose around them as all order broke down. These people really are one family, I thought; any dispute brings back all the old grievances, right to the beginning of time. If it goes on much longer, we'll hear who pulled whose hair when they were toddlers. Who but a family could fight like that? At least they weren't confined together in a ship's cabin, as my family had often been—though perhaps living alone in this lonely land might be much the same. My head began aching again to listen to them, and I was thankful when Guthlac and Maethild, as one, shouted, "ENOUGH!" and, "QUIET!"

The din died down to a murmur, and Halred and Anlaf stopped, red-faced and trembling, in midsentence.

"Small wonder the gods frown on us, when the only priests we have profane our place of Assembly, squabbling like ill-taught children," Maethild scolded.

This may not have been her best tactic: indeed, it threatened

154 · PAULINE J. ALAMA

to start everything over again. Both priests opened their mouths to protest, as if one thought guided them both.

But Guthlac cut in: "We have strayed far from the matter we came to settle: the harboring of three strangers among us. Halred, you have argued in their favor that need is not dire enough to justify denying them; that our oldest customs demand hospitality to strangers; and that the gods will smile on generosity and frown on hard-heartedness. Do you have anything to add to your plea, or will you give way to the free parley of the assembled Folc?"

"There is more," Halred said. "Helpless as they seem now, the strangers may be a help to us in the end. We are short hands, with so many young of all houses gone over the hills to seek their fortune. We are too few to turn any away lightly."

"Why, what can a wounded man do for us?" laughed Edwach.

"He will recover soon, if the gods smile upon it, and if my good neighbors and kin will allow him a few days' rest under my care," said Halred. "And his companions are unhurt. But it is not only labor of the body we lack. We have not had news from outside the valley all year, and these have traveled far. More than that, I have spoken to them, and I doubt they are ordinary wanderers. Be wary of turning a stranger away, for if the old tales are true, St. Tarvi came among our people as a beggar, and none would have expected anything of him at first sight."

"Well, let us see these strangers," called a voice from the far end of the crowd. "Let their leader rise and speak."

"You speak for us, Hwyn," I urged.

Hwyn got to her feet. "What would you ask me?"

Again the voice came from the back, "Stand up so we can see you."

"I *am* standing," Hwyn said. Half-smothered laughs began to ripple out around us; Halred tried futilely to hush them.

"Come up on the Assembly Stone with us," said Guthlac.

Hwyn scrambled up the stone stairs, onto the broad back of the stone, and stood with her arms crossed over her chest, her face darkening to crimson as the laughter reached the back of the crowd. Standing next to Guthlac—a powerfully built man, one of the tallest of the Folc—she scarcely came higher than his waist.

"Go on, laugh," she said at last. "It is nothing new to me. Someone told me the Folc were a people apart, but in this, at least, you are like all others."

That stilled the laughter, for the most part. From the back of the crowd, a man rose to speak: "Good sister, I at least see nothing to laugh at. You have crossed the Hills of Penmorrin to come here, as I did once, and must have more strength in you than any wise man can laugh at. What shall I call you?"

"I am called Hwyn. My friends are Jereth and Trenara."

"My name is Paddon," the man said. "I came to the Folc as a stranger in better times, five years ago. Then there was no need for an Assembly to argue my fate: they gave me food and water when I had none, and I worked the fields, was adopted by the Red Oak Clan, and married a woman of the Linden Clan. I am one of the Folc now—and if any says I am not, he may do my share of the hay-making tomorrow. But do you and your companions mean to stay on as kin and neighbors, or to leave when you no longer need our help?"

"You ask fair questions, Paddon," Hwyn said. "In truth, I must confess we never meant to make a home here. We were on a journey when we were attacked; Jereth was wounded, and we had to flee into the Hills of Penmorrin without stores of food or water. We became lost, and Jereth's wound festered till he seemed likely to die of it. We would not have prevailed on you for so much as a crumb if our case had been less desperate. But neither do we mean to take and give nothing in return. I can do work of many kinds. Don't let my size deceive you: heavy loads and long days' labor are no strangers to me. When Jereth is recovered, he can work as well, until we work off our debt to the Folc. We will do what we can to requite your kindness to us, but we cannot abandon our journey."

"Why, where are you going?" said Paddon.

But Edwach cut in, "You say you and the wounded man will work. But there are three of you. What of the third?"

"Trenara is simple," Hwyn said. "There's not much she can do. We will have to bear her share of the burden."

"Fine lot you've taken into our land, Halred," scoffed Edwach. "One invalid, one fool, and the best of them no bigger than a child."

"Hwyn and Jereth share with Trenara without hope of recompense," Halred said. "Their generosity should shame us if we turn them away. But beyond that, whatever weaknesses you may see, look deeper. Jereth is a scholar from the Tarvon Monastery, and may bring wisdom of use to us in dark times. And Hwyn has something of the prophet about her; I have heard her singing a holy hymn, and the power gathered about her like thunder-clouds."

"Have a care, Halred," said Father Anlaf. "There are more kinds of power than one, and not all are holy. Power may come from the gods, from hidden natures of things, or from ghosts of the unquiet dead and such unclean necromancy—"

"Wherever it comes from, we will test it in holy rites," Halred said. "The new moon will be time for the Rite of Increase. I mean to use Hwyn's voice for the ceremony."

"That ceremony needs more than singers," said Anlaf. "If you hold a Rite of Increase, four men must bleed for the land. And where will you find four to bleed in these lean times, when none have strength to spare?"

"If a stranger may ask," I said, "what is this rite? It sounds like none we had at the monastery at Annelon." It sounded, how-ever, like the dark tales I had read about the ancient blood-rites in barbarous days; it unsettled me to find such customs still living.

"It is an old rite of the Folc to wake the land from its sleeping and bring life to barren soil," said Halred. "Traditionally the priesthoods of the Bright and Hidden Goddesses perform it together to invoke the seen and unseen powers that give life to the land. As I am all we have left of both priesthoods, I have brought my two acolytes into it; still, a fourth celebrant would fill out the holy number, and let us perform the rite as it was meant to be.

"Four men of the Folc must give a bowlful of blood to the land," she continued. "They must come forward willingly to make this sacrifice for the good of all, so Anlaf taunts me that I will not find four willing to give their blood in the rites I must lead."

"I bled last summer," said a voice somewhere behind me, "and we were no better off for it."

I was skeptical, myself, and furthermore, the very sound of it made my flesh crawl. Those four bowls of blood, I knew, stood for the whole life-blood of one man sacrificed in harsher times to appease the gods.

And yet this seemed the answer to our problems. "If that is what you need, then very well: I will bleed for the land," I said. "If that is not enough to make us, for a little time, one with the

Folc, maybe at least it will make the gods pity us more as we stagger away hungry and thristy over the hard hills."

But the end of my sentence was scarcely heard for Halred gasping "Jereth!" and Hwyn shouting "No!" right over my words.

"Jereth, you've bled more than enough of late," Hwyn said. "That bowlful might kill you! Halred, you must not listen to him. Take my blood instead; I can better spare it."

"No, Hwyn—" I began.

Halred cut both of us short. "It's no use, Hwyn. The blood must come from weaponed-men, not women who bleed with each moon."

"Not when you've been traveling half starved as long as I have," Hwyn muttered.

Halred disregarded this. "Hwyn, even if I could accept your blood, it would not substitute. Jereth, my lad, you've put me between the horns of a dilemma. As healer, I should forbid you to offer yourself for bleeding. It won't kill you—gods willing—but it will weaken you more than I care to see, sick as you are. The new moon is only three nights away; you won't have time to gather your strength. But as priestess, I have no power to refuse what has been offered to the gods. You have already committed yourself; it is not mine to undo."

As I digested that inevitability, Halred spread her hands theatrically to address the full Assembly: "And if this bond of blood does not give Jereth the right to stay among us till he is strong enough to travel, then I might as well give up both priesthoods for despair of teaching you anything. What say you, my cousins, my neighbors?"

"He is one of us," said Drict, "and in fellowship, I offer myself to bleed at the Rite of Increase."

"And I," said Paddon. "I offer myself in brotherhood, for the honor of the Folc not born of the Folc, few though we be."

"What say all the powers of the Folc?" called Guthlac, falling into ritual speech again, his deep voice ringing almost musically on the mountainside. "Priest of the Upright God, what say you?"

Anlaf paused, regarding us with an abstracted air. At last he spoke: "Though I admire the spirit of the stranger who offers his blood in our rites, I do not agree that our priestess is bound to accept it. The stranger remains a stranger; he does not even mean to stay among us. Neither his blood nor the sorcerous voice of his companion are ours. I say, let them depart at once."

"Priestess of the Bright Goddess, what say you?"

"Let them stay," said Halred.

"Voice of the Upside-Down God chosen by lot, what say you?"

"Let them stay," said Athel.

"Priestess of the Hidden Goddess, what say you?"

Halred said again, "Let them stay."

"Headwoman of the Folc, what say you?"

Maethild hesitated, looking from Anlaf to Halred and back again, then, unnervingly, straight into my eyes. At last she nodded. "Very well. Let them stay."

"Elder of the Ashwood Clan, what say you?"

"Let them stay," said Aldworth, smiling at Halred as he did so.

"Elder of the Linden Clan, what say you?"

Edwach stood scowling a while. He's lost, I thought, and trying to work a way around it. At last he said, "I, too, offer myself to bleed at the Rite of Increase. Now let another of the Folc come forward, so we have no need of these strangers, and can bid them leave!"

"No, Edwach," said Halred, "that is not the way."

"You've had your turn—more than once," Edwach said. "Let me speak now. I say we are better without them. Let them depart."

Of all the "powers," there remained only Guthlac. He paused a while, surveying the crowd with cool gray eyes, his sense of ritual drama better than Edwach's or the priest's. All fell silent, awaiting his word. "As Elder of the Red Oak and Headman of the Folc," he said slowly, "I say, shame on me if I stint food to one who has offered blood! Let the traveler Jereth stay—and though he entered through the Linden, let him be counted one of the Red Oak Clan. Hwyn, as acolyte to the priestess for the duration of the rite, should belong to no clan and stay with the priestess. The simpleton may accept my hospitality or any other's, as the gods please, for a fool is everyone's child.

"So say I and so says the Folc under my headship. If any disagree, let brotherhood guard your tongue and stay your hand, for you have had your chance to speak. The Assembly is ended."

The throng slowly trickled away, but Halred remained to tend the fire until the last ember died. As we waited for her, Hwyn seized my arm with talon-hard fingers. "What a fright you gave me, offering yourself for the blood rite! Gods, Jereth, what have you done to yourself?"

"I've won." I grinned, feeling in command of my destiny for the first time since I could not say when.

She looked at me curiously, scrutinizing my face as if she saw something there she had not seen before. "You seem so sure of yourself," she said, "that I wonder whether you've seen something more clearly than I have, or ignored what I see."

"I know not," I said, "but this is what I see: we had little to offer them but our secrets, which might have hurt as much as helped us. I have done what I could to gain a few days' rest without sacrificing our secrets or our quest."

"I know. It was a bold gambit," she said. "And yet—Jereth, I am to act as one of the four celebrants of the rite, and I will *not,* I will refuse, if it means shedding your blood."

In fact, I had not thought of that possibility, and her distress, her real anguish caught me short. I caught her hands in midgesture and held them still. "Hwyn, gentle soul, don't worry so. I will not die of this, I promise. And I know you would not willingly hurt me. If it falls to you during the ceremony to—"

"I will not!" she said again.

"Will not what?" Halred, overhearing, raised her voice to carry over to us from where she sat watching the embers of the fire.

"Mother Halred," said Hwyn, "this ritual will not force me to draw blood from Jereth, will it?"

Halred raised her eyebrows. "No, child. That burden falls to me, as the only fully consecrated priestess in the village. And it is not a light one for me, either, I assure you. But at least you can rest easy that as a healer, I know how to mend what I must do."

"It will be all right," I said, still buoyed up by the energy of decision.

"With the gods' help, yes," said Halred. "Now leave me in peace a little space as I make one last prayer over the embers." We retreated a bit from the fire. Drict was off in a knot of Folc talking some distance away; shy of interrupting them and uncertain where to go, we sat on the grass to wait.

"Excuse me," said a man's voice beside me. I looked up and

saw by the dying light a man who must be conspicuous among the Folc, but nowhere else: a compactly built man with sandy hair and pale, freckled skin.

Though I had not seen him clearly before, I recognized his voice. "Paddon?"

He nodded. "I wanted to meet you and welcome you. It's not always easy to be a stranger among the Folc—or an adopted countryman, even."

"Thank you for speaking on our behalf," said Hwyn.

He smiled. "I speak as I see fit, here among the Folc. That is why I stayed here, even though in some ways I will always be a stranger. But I think often of the country I was born in. They say you came from southward. Do you have any news of Kreyn?"

"We passed through the city," I said cautiously.

"Is that cursed hypocrite Goldifer still queen?" he said, removing our cause for fear.

"Alas, she is," said Hwyn. "We were found lacking in reverence for her and fell afoul of her guards, who chased us into the hills and wounded Jereth. We might not have escaped but that chance brought us to the lair of an outlaw with even more reason to hate Her Resplendence than we had."

"What—Warfast the Firebrand?" Paddon said.

"Yes, Warfast was his name," Hwyn said.

"He is still living, then—and still at his old games," Paddon half smiled. "Is Wilgar still his right-hand man?"

"There were two men with him, Wilgar and Lok," Hwyn said.

"And Lok will have been intoxicated with your fair friend." Paddon gestured at Trenara with his head.

"You know them well," Hwyn said.

"I was one of their band," Paddon said. "I rose against Goldifer with them, leaving my home and my kinsmen when we lost the battle. I can never return to Kreyn now. And I can never return to Warfast, either—Wilgar has a short way with deserters. The gods know I miss my old comrades, but I could not stay with them any longer. They will never win, and I did not sacrifice all I had to become a mere highwayman. But I am glad the old fox is still alive, for all the danger he has courted these seven years. And he protected you?"

"Yes," Hwyn said.

"I am glad. Perhaps outlawry has not changed him much, after all. He was always the sort of man who keeps to his code:

the Law of Antir commands protection to supplicants, and so it must be, whatever the cost."

"He is not much changed, then," Hwyn said. "And here, among the Folc, as well—"

"The Folc keep to their code, and I honor them for it," Paddon said, nodding. Then, softer, "And yet—here as anywhere—the high-minded reasons are not the only ones. My Lord Guthlac of the Red Oak is a generous man, and it is his good nature to take in strays like you and me. But in your case, it also shames Edwach, who ought to have taken you in himself—and that is a fine sauce for Guthlac to digest his sacrifice. Nor should you take it for granted that Father Anlaf hates you; he has been arguing with Mother Halred so long that opposing her is only a habit."

"And Halred," I said very quietly. "Edwach's hostility makes us dearer to her, doesn't it? What is it between them?"

Paddon grinned. "The Folc say a priest has no clan or family; to say otherwise is forbidden. Yet it is hard to conceal—indeed, they have both blurted it out by accident—"

"Gods on the Wheel," I whispered. "Are they brother and sister?"

"You see clearly," said Paddon.

"What are you three whispering about?" Guthlac, Elder of the Red Oak, put a big hand on Paddon's shoulder—but he was smiling broadly.

"Someone has to tell them the things everyone else has known since cradle days," Paddon said.

"Ah, Paddon, if you start that, you'll be here talking till harvest," said Guthlac. "The night is brief enough without prolonging the Assembly. Let's bring the travelers inside and give them some rest." He extended a hand to me. "Welcome to our family, Jereth. For a man distracted by illness you spoke boldly, and I think you will do us proud."

I clasped his hand gratefully.

"And Hwyn, is it? You too showed a bold spirit. Give me your hand. You are of no clan, but you may as well come with us."

"Thank you. But as acolyte, I must lodge with the priestess, mustn't I?"

"True enough. But while Jereth is ill, the healer will lodge where he does. She'll be along soon enough, I judge. As soon as the fire dies, we can be on our way."

He brought us to the house of the Red Oak Clan—a sheep paddock and barn with a stone house added on as an after-thought, it seemed, where the whole clan shared a great hall and a kitchen, with a small chamber at the end for the elder and his wife. Some of the household who had not gone to the Assembly were already bedded down on sheepskins on the floor of the great hall, scattered here and there like sleeping cats. Indeed, not all were sleeping; some of the sheepskins, wrapped around more than one body, moved in a suspicious rhythm. Taking my cue from my host, I trained my eyes to the way before me till we left the dark hall for the kitchen.

There we were welcomed by Guthlac's wife, Girnhild, a woman well matched to him, with broad shoulders and big, workmanlike hands. Their daughter Godrun, a red-haired girl with intelligent eyes, gave us each a bowl of curds and a care-fully rationed, precious mouthful of last autumn's ale. Between the ale, my ill-health, and the trying Assembly, I scarcely waited to be given a bedroll before sinking deep into slumber.

9

THE RITE OF INCREASE

During the days that followed, I recovered my strength, rest-ing in the Red Oak Clan's house while Hwyn milked goats, picked strawberries, joined in the hay-making, and generally tried as hard to prove herself worth her keep by labor as I had by offering to bleed for the Rite of Increase. Trenara followed wherever she went, and I saw little of my companions until the swift sunset brought all the laborers home for the brief summer night.

Halred's ministrations continued: she would change my poul-tice, make me drink something nasty, grudgingly admit I was mending, and forbid me to stir farther than the privy. Notwith-standing her prohibitions, I began gradually mingling into the life of the Folc. Most were outdoors in the day, for all the Folc, from the Headman to toddling children, worked on the land or with the livestock. Even Halred spent part of each day among the flocks with a pot of salve for fleabites and sores. Nonethe-less, the house and its courtyard were never quite empty; someone would always be there churning butter, setting cheeses, stirring a pot of last summer's oats and new peas in the kitchen, braiding baskets in the shade of the eaves, or fixing the roof.

On my first day in the House of the Red Oak Clan, I was happy enough to sleep; on the second day, however, I stumbled to the kitchen, where a knot of women and girls were engaged in making cheese. They left off their gossiping to stare up at me where I stood in the doorway. "Sit down, traveler," said Girnhild, pushing a sawn-log stool toward me, "or Mother Halred will be cross with me for tiring her patient."

"Thank you," I said. "I came to ask what I can do here. I'm not going to sleep away another day, and you must have some chore fit for an invalid—something even a very ignorant person can't spoil," I added, for the things they were then doing were as mysterious to me as any mage's art.

"Why, you can't be so very ignorant," said Godrun. "What have you done all your life?"

I laughed. "Little of use here. I was a priest once, but no longer. And you already have enough priests here to keep on arguing till the gods call the world home for supper."

One of the older women—Wylf, they called her—laughed at that. "You've come to know them well already. But don't flatland priests work like other people?"

"It depends what you call work," I said. In theory, of course, all in the Tarvon Order worked in simple humility on the farms that fed us. In practice, we had the best libraries, schools, and scriptoria in all Swevnalond; most of us only dirtied our hands with ink. I had entered with the resolution to embrace the land, but I was found out for a quick and accurate copyist—a skill I had learned by the rod and lash, keeping my father's account ledgers. "I copied books in the monastery. Before that I was at sea. There's nothing much I can do that's of use here, except— well, you're land-folk, so you'll laugh at this, but at sea, any boy can mend a sail."

"Mending? With needle and thread?" one of the girls giggled, and I reddened, though in truth I still can't understand why it should be any funnier for a man to sew than to copy books or count coins.

At any rate, the women did not laugh too much to find me all the mending they'd put off for more urgent tasks. So I set about making myself useful, all the while watching them at their strange tasks and learning from them. Their talk was full of the missing Folc—mostly young men who had gone off to seek their fortunes and not returned.

"They go off seeking brides, but who's to come seeking us?" lamented a dark-haired woman of about twenty.

"Small wonder if no outlanders come," I said, "when a stranger must stand before the Assembly to be allowed a few days' stay."

"That wasn't always the way," said Girnhild. "Paddon of Kreyn faced no Assembly. He came in harvest time, when an extra pair of hands is a godsend; no one even cared that he was an outlaw. We simply adopted him, and that was that."

"Those were better times," said Wylf. "These valleys used to feed so many. As we have dwindled, the land has dwindled; it's hard to say which came first. Sometimes I think the land has given up because so many of us gave up."

"How many were you?" I said. "I've seen no empty houses in Folcsted. Were others torn down as the Folc dwindled?"

"St. Arin's Lake was not the only place of the Folc in olden times," said Wylf. "In my great-grandfather's day, the four clans were four villages, each ruled by its own elder. As our numbers dwindled, we drew together, for too few hands cannot keep the fields, the flocks, the orchards, all that is needed to survive."

"Mother Halred's right in that," said Girnhild. "We need each other too much to fly apart."

"But her talk of the old ways of the Folc—" I began, then hesitated.

Wylf smiled. "True enough, in the old days, sheep were marked for the valley, not the clan; but today's clans were of four valleys, and each had its own mark. Halred's 'old ways' are not very old. But what of that? A straight path is only as straight as the hills allow it to be, but it is straight enough for everyday use; nor is the truth any straighter than the ground it has to run on. Living as one Folc is our way now; if our ancestors lived apart, they left those ways for good reason. Calling common flocks 'the old way of the Folc' is true enough for everyday use."

"You reason like a Tarvon priest," I said, gambling that the order's reputation for too-clever argument had penetrated even this remote country. By the women's smiles, I saw that it had.

"Nonetheless, your words seem wise to me. But others must remember this, too; I wonder why Edwach did not call Mother Halred a liar in Assembly when she spoke of the old ways."

"Well, the guest-code really is ancient—for all I know," said Wylf.

"And if he spoke of the four valleys, his real wishes would be too naked," said Girnhild. "St. Arin's Lake was the place of the Linden Clan—did you notice how many lindens grow in the valley? It was the best of the four settlements, so naturally, it was the one to be kept alive. But Edwach thinks his forbear foolish to let the other clans share it so easily. He thinks that Linden should rule the other clans, and he should be Headman always, not just one year in four."

Godrun put in, "Well, let him keep the land himself, then. His sons have all left but Ethwin. He would be crying for our help before long."

"We all may be crying for help soon if the land is not kinder," reminded Girnhild, silencing the conversation.

At night when we gathered in the great hall for a meal, these worries surfaced again. "Here it is, twelve days past the Longest Day, and the lambs as small as they should have been in spring," complained a shepherd.

"The milk's down to a trickle," Paddon said.

"The grain's barely sprouted," said his wife, Sigrun of the Linden.

Ethwin, who was visiting to stare at Trenara and avoid his father, said, "Maybe it's time we should all leave this land together."

"Would you really?" Hwyn asked. "The whole Folc, leave St. Arin's Lake?"

"Or the Hills of Penmorrin entirely," Ethwin said. "They say the lowlands are easier." He himself had never seen any flat ground larger than the lakeshore.

"It's been talked of," Guthlac admitted. "The last Assembly but yours, we spoke of leaving. If this harvest isn't better than the ones before it, we may be forced to go."

"Our people were not always here," said Girnhild. "We came east from the Ferend River Valley. Our ancestors, oppressed by the Kettran conquerors, fled to the mountains for freedom."

"That must have been ages ago," I said. "The Kettran Empire hasn't stretched so far east in over three hundred years."

"Maybe it's time to return, then," said Ethwin. "Maybe that's what the land is telling us."

"Maybe," Guthlac said doubtfully. "But there would be war and strife, with or without the Kettrans. We would be aliens there, just as these travelers were among us. Why should the lowlanders welcome four whole clans of vagabonds when we could scarcely welcome three souls?"

"You might go north," Hwyn said. "Enough people have fled from there to leave plenty of farms untended, plenty of villages needing fresh hands."

"What—go from the frying pan to the fire?" said Guthlac. "Who goes to the very place all the world flees?"

"Those that are different from all the world. Those that fled to a harsh land for freedom and learned to live there," Hwyn said. "Don't tell me you fear ghosts more than hunger!"

"Ghosts! Those are nothing," said Guthlac. "It's the stranger stories I'm thinking of: summer not following spring, harvest not following summer. We're far enough along that path ourselves. Last year's harvest was so small that Edwach of the Linden tried to tell me that autumn had not come and his year as Headman had not ended."

"Edwach *would* say that," put in Girnhild.

"Of course, I told him that if the harvest was poor in his year, he should not profit from it by keeping the headship." Guthlac sighed. "Now I wish I'd chosen other words. The way this year's begun, I don't want to be judged by the harvest of my own year as Headman. Better to think it had not really begun! And I have better cause to say so than Edwach, for the Longest Day passed before we even dared shear the sheep."

"Perhaps the Rite of Increase will wake the gods to our plight," said Girnhild.

Paddon shook his head. "The gods are far away at the rim of the world, with the dead and the unborn. What do they even see of these little gestures we call rites of the gods?"

"Why did you volunteer to bleed, then?" I asked.

"For the reason I gave," Paddon said. "In solidarity with a newcomer willing to be generous with the Folc. I don't really believe the gods require it, or that they will notice what we do here."

"You may be right," said Guthlac slowly. "But then again, there are moments." His eyes strayed toward my face. "In the Assembly, when we drew lots for the Upside-Down God, I brought the choosing straws to the travelers on a whim—"

"To gall Edwach," Girnhild cut in.

"All right, woman, all right," he said with mock-exasperation. "That may have entered my head. But even as I did so, I remember thinking, *If any of the strangers draws the one short straw in a hundred, then the god's hand really is in it.*" He looked levelly at me.

"Strange coincidence," I said uneasily.

"You hated being chosen, didn't you?" Guthlac said. "To my mind, it only makes the god's hand clearer."

I rolled my eyes toward Paddon, who returned a sardonic smile.

Meeting Guthlac's steely eyes again, I said evenly, "And if the gods did have a hand in it—the better to annoy Edwach!"

Girnhild laughed heartily, and that was the end of the topic. But I could see from Hwyn's face that she at least took the sign seriously.

The eve of the Rite of Increase came swiftly. Despite Halred's pessimism and Hwyn's fears, I felt by then quite recovered, the wound sealing neatly over unswollen flesh, my eye unaffected and my face no worse than it ever was.

This was fortunate, for the night before the rite we were required to sleep with the flocks—not only the four men who were to bleed, but the four women who would perform the ritual. Although each clan had its own paddock, all the flocks had been herded together in the common paddock near the Assembly grounds for the night. All four elders were to stand guard over them, save that Edwach, who like me was one of the "beasts" for the night, had to leave that task to Ethwin. And so it was a strange gathering, our chief friends among the Folc and our chief enemy together with all three travelers—for though Trenara had not been asked, she went where Hwyn did.

At the paddock, I also met Halred's two acolytes, graceful, quick-witted, sharp-tongued maids of some twenty summers who laughed when they told me the names Halred had given them, Day and Night, but declined to give any other. Day was tall and broad-shouldered, with a thick red braid and round aster-blue eyes; she would take vows to the Bright Goddess the next summer. Night was small and black-haired, with long silver-gray eyes and a low-bridged nose like a Magyan; she would soon be consecrated to the Hidden Goddess. These girls had been rehearsing the rite with Hwyn while I had been cooped up in Red Oak house, and so they knew her a little by then, but their close camaraderie with each other left Hwyn on the outside. As much as ritual propriety allowed, she stayed by me.

We stood a while watching Trenara playing with the sheep, stroking their patient heads, feeling the fleece just starting to grow back from the shearing, gazing into their quiet brown eyes. Hwyn watched her a bit wistfully. "Thank the gods we're not here at slaughtering time. It would distress her too much to see—and me to take part in it again, if the truth be told."

"You've done it before?"

"Too many times. I remember when I was a little girl, very young, I had been feeding the lambs since spring, and I'd given them all names. And someone thought it instructive, or maybe just amusing, to make me hold a bowl for blood while he slaughtered my favorites, the ones I'd begged him to spare. I never gave a name to an animal again."

"Who would do that to a child?"

She looked away. "It doesn't matter. I don't know why I remembered it just now."

"Maybe," I said softly, "because you're worried about tomorrow."

She said nothing, but I saw her shoulders tremble as though a chill had gone through them.

I put a hand on her shoulder, very carefully. "Hwyn, it's all right. No one is going to die. This isn't a human sacrifice."

"But it was once," she said. "I can feel the ghosts gathering near the place of slaughter, waiting, waiting for something to happen."

As she spoke it seemed that I too could feel something like names whispered at the edges of my consciousness, where I could not quite discern one from the other. "Yes, they are here," I said. "What are they waiting for?"

She shook her head. "I only feel a sense of expectancy, nothing more."

"If they rage, I can call them by name and reason with them. It seemed of some use with Conor of Kelgarran."

Hwyn squinted up at me. "You are not the least bit uneasy, are you?"

"For once in my life, no," I said. "When I first volunteered for the Rite of Increase, it was a desperate stratagem, but almost as soon as the words were out of my mouth it all seemed strangely right. I can't tell you why, but I feel perfectly sure of what I'm doing."

"Then I have to trust you," she said.

"It will all be well," I said. "No one will die. It's like Halred's argument against marking what's mine and what's yours: if all four share the sacrifice, none need die."

Hwyn smiled. "That's a fine thought. Have you told it to Halred?"

I shook my head. "When I see her, she's prodding me and making me drink reeking brews. *You* tell her. But listen, will you be all right bearing your part in the ceremony as temple-singer as I—as I bear my part?"

"Jereth," said Hwyn, smiling shamefacedly, "you are my great friend, and I hate to think of you hurt, but I may as well confess that when I sing, I think of nothing but singing."

Halred called her then to stand guard with Night, and I lay down to take what little sleep I could on the close-cropped turf, among the warm bodies of the beasts.

I dreamed of a heart beating deep under the hill, where no men heard it. But all the beasts that fed on the hillside grasses, tame and wild, stood still to listen, and the dull passivity of the sheep, which I had taken for stupidity, was really the silence of waiting.

I woke to a cool, misty dawn, the trilling of birds, and the barking of sheepdogs. The other three men marked for the ritual were already on their feet. Rubbing my eyes, I too rose and waited for the rites to begin. I could not see Hwyn, but I knew the priestess and acolytes stood around the flocks, for Halred was plainly visible a short distance away, her face impassive as the mountains, and Day's red hair stood out like a beacon-fire at some distance across the sea of animal bodies. The elders, too, stood silent around us; Ethwin, in his father's place, looked nervous and very young.

As the red light blossomed in the east, the lonely song of the reed pipes rose slowly toward us. The three elders and Ethwin moved to meet the sound, their pace dreamlike. The piper led a procession of shepherds, whom the Elders met at the paddock gate. I heard Guthlac's voice ring out, "Who seeks entry?"

"Shepherds of the Folc," said the second in line behind the piper.

"Whose sheep are these?"

"They are the gods' but we tend them," said the shepherd.

"Enter, then, and tend them."

They entered, and I expected the ceremony to begin, or rather continue from there. But for a long while, nothing followed but the routine morning tasks, the milking of ewes, the tarring of sores. The other three men marked for the ritual stood passive as sheep themselves, so I followed their example.

At last the shepherds drove the flocks out, and us with them. To my surprise, they took us to the ground around the Assembly Stone and let the sheep graze there, on what had seemed sanctified ground. On the Assembly Stone, a bowl, a candle, and a large jug stood amid coiled vines.

For a long time, again, we waited in silence. I looked around, feeling foolish, but Paddon, Drict, and Edwach seemed unperturbed, so the delay must have been normal.

I could see Halred, Day, and Night by the Assembly Stone, but Hwyn was still out of my sight, and Trenara also. I began to doubt that they had been with us when I woke in the sheep-fold. Where could they have gone? Cut off from my companions, the only people in the whole Hills of Penmorrin I'd known more than a few days, I felt a sudden surge of panic. Then reason returned: Halred had been counting on Hwyn's participation in the rite, and she would not survey the scene so calmly if any of the pieces in her pageant were out of order. Hwyn was wherever Halred had sent her, and Trenara with her as always.

A hollow pattering sound announced a second procession, led by a young woman deftly worrying a goat-hide drum with a polished bone held loosely between her fingers.

"Who comes to this place of Assembly?" Guthlac called out to her.

"We are the farmers and other hands of the Folc," she said.

"And whose beasts, and whose fields, and whose crafts have you just left?"

"They belong to the Four Great Ones; we are honored to keep them."

"Come, then, and let your labors be blessed."

They came and dispersed among the sheep and shepherds already on the green, and now all the Folc were together. I realized then what we had been waiting for: just as the shepherds had to work their morning tasks into the morning rite, so too the others had tasks that could not be left undone, rite or no rite. No one had spoken of it because everyone but me—even Hwyn, maybe even Trenara—had known the rhythms of farming life too well to remark on it. Only I was as out of place here as a seal among goats.

Halred climbed up onto the Assembly Stone and called out, "Sunlight ripens the grain, but dark earth bore it. May the Bright Goddess and the Hidden Goddess extend their hands over this land and give life to it. May our hands, too, always be open to give what we can for the life of all. Who comes to give of himself for the life of this land?"

"I, Edwach of the Linden."

"I, Drict of the Holly."

"I, Paddon Outlaw, adopted by the Red Oak."

I took my cue from the others, and called out my name.

"Come, then, to the gate of the mountain and prepare yourselves."

I followed the others to the cave behind the Assembly Stone. Halred led us in, and her acolytes followed us till we stood muffled in dark and silent stone. I could see nothing. I felt the warmth of Paddon's body recede before me, and put out a hand to orient myself. On either side were cool walls of hewn stone. I hesitated, then felt a hand reach out and draw me forward: Hwyn's hand, I knew instinctively, though I could not have said how I knew. I dared not speak; even Halred was silent. But if I had dared, I would have asked Hwyn whether she felt what I sensed: the dead gathered around us, waiting.

At last Halred broke the silence: "Hidden Goddess, hear us, your children! We neither understand what makes the earth barren nor what makes it bear, why we die nor why we are born. All we know is our yearning. Accept our longing; accept the blood-offering of our men in atonement for the life we have taken from the land. Lead us in the dark passage before us. Bear us to life again or give us hope even in death."

Someone began sobbing, then—a familiar voice. I heard Hwyn hushing her softly and knew it must be Trenara. I tensed, afraid the Folc might take it as a profanation of their holy place, but either it seemed well enough in keeping with the mournful prayer or they deemed it greater offense to reprimand her in the holy cave than to let her be, for none disturbed her, and at length even Hwyn stopped trying.

After some time, Halred spoke again: "We thank you, Goddess, for your presence in the dark, even as we move into the light. In darkness, the seed wakens and grows toward light." We crept out again through the walls of stone. I had lost Hwyn's hand in Trenara's disruption, so I stumbled out alone into the light of day, where the Folc awaited us. When we stood before the Assembly Stone and faced the mountain again, I saw that Hwyn had not followed.

Halred took her place atop the stone and called out, "Bright Goddess, ripener of fruit and grain, lifter of hearts, we rejoice in your warmth, in the splendor of the sun, in the richness of the earth. We have sung your praise in your summer festival. Now we beg your aid in our time of travail. Join hands across the Wheel with the Hidden Goddess, and come among us with your power to heal, with your warmth to swell the fruits, with your gentleness to make the land gentle to us.

"And you, Hidden Goddess, secret of the earth's inner depths, well of life, join hands across the Wheel with the Bright Goddess, and come among us with your silent call to the hidden sources of life.

"We need you both, for it is not sun alone nor rain alone, not leaf alone nor root alone, not earth alone nor air alone, not day alone nor night alone that brings forth life, but both together.

"But my people, cast your eyes down! The Four Great Ones bring life to the land, but we have wearied this land with our greed. We have plucked its fruits, fished its waters, hunted its wild beasts, cleared its fields for plowing and filled them with grain only to empty them at harvest. We have slain the tame beasts that trusted us, and eaten their flesh. All this we have done to live, but we ask pardon for it. We ask pardon for the times when we have taken too much, slaughtered lambs we could have bred, plucked fruit and let it spoil, cleared land we might have left in the gods' hands and not labored hard enough to make it fruitful."

I could not think offhand of any people I had met that wasted less or labored more than the Folc, but the herders and farmers around me bowed their heads and I bowed mine, ashamed in truth, for I had been rich once, and in my youth I had probably squandered more than all these good folk, taken together, had in their whole lives.

As we stood in silence, Day ascended the stone and began to sing the Lament of the Bright Goddess for the Felled Wheat:

"Tall to the sun you were,
Gracious and golden as sunlight
Tall to the sun you were
Till reapers cut you low.
Skyward you stretched your head
Skyward you yearned to light
Ruthless the reaper's blade
That laid you low.
Glad to my touch you grew
Glad to my light you rose
Barren the fields again
Your beauty shorn."

Her voice was warm and bright, its pitch steady and true, its tone strong and full. And yet, I thought, Hwyn could have given that song a fire beyond anything this girl could find inside her, and I wondered why the part had not been given to Hwyn. And then from somewhere out of sight came another song in answer, the Hidden Goddess's Lament for the Slain Lambs:

"In the dark of the womb I knew you,
Stirred your limbs, taught you life,
Dear was your stirring to me,
Dear was the rush in your veins to me,
The rush of life in your limbs.
Dark was the passage I showed you,
Dire was your journey to birth,
Dear was your warm breath to me
When first you drew milk of my breasts
Fair was the life in you,
Your body lithe in motion,
Your eyes soft as twilight,

As the night I wrapped around you.
Fair was your body, sacrificed
To nourish other lives.
Deep in the dark I know you,
Deep in the stillness of death,
Still in the darkness I know you."

It was Hwyn's voice, and it seemed to come from the mountain itself, echoing everywhere. The downcast faces of the Folc lifted in wonder, and for all the solemnity of the moment I could not help smiling. Of course they'd had no idea what to expect; they had never heard her, perhaps never heard any singer better than Day. Of course Hwyn's voice must dazzle them: it dazzled me, who had heard it often before. Its heights were nightingale-song, its depths were the sighing of the sea, and it filled the valley as the voice of the sea fills the world of the sailor. To those who did not know her, the unseen voice might have been the voice of the whole world's longing.

When the last heart-tearing echoes had died away, Halred spoke again. "We seek pardon for the life we have taken from the land. Let us not give in sacrifice what is not truly ours. All we have to give is ourselves. Oh Great Ones, four men among the Folc place themselves in your hands, offering blood of their bodies to feed your earth in prayer that it may feed us. We pray you accept this offering in token of all our hearts. Take pity on us in our weakness, and heal the land touched by their blood."

Halred took from the stone a knife and a bundle of vines and descended to the ground; Night came after her, carrying a clay bowl. Together they processed toward us, as Day lit a small candle and stuck it on the stone next to a larger urn. At the priestess's sign, we turned to face the people; all eyes were on us.

Halred went first to Edwach, bound his arm tightly with a length of vine, and stood a while looking him in the eye. "Edwach, have you freely consented to give your blood to the land?"

Sister and brother, I thought in wonder, wishing I could see the look that passed between the gray eyes and the blue. "Yes," was all he said, but the fierce pride in his voice made the word a gauntlet thrown down before battle. Halred cocked her head to one side for an instant, as if trying to see something else in him—the little boy she had played and fought with, perhaps?

But at last she took his arm firmly and scored a small, precise cut below the pressure-line where she had bound it.

Night held the bowl to catch the blood that spurted forth. When it was full, Halred unbound the vine and stanched the flow of blood with a leaf. Then the two women returned to the stone, where Halred cleansed the knife in the candle flame and Night poured the blood into the urn.

As she did so, the Lament for Slain Lambs began again, the two voices blended together, Hwyn's and the acolyte's, though only Day was visible atop the great stone.

I watched Halred bind and bleed Drict's muscular arm, while another part of my mind wondered at my own calmness—not because of the cut, which would be quick and clean, but simply for the strangeness of the blood-rite I had propelled myself into. I remembered how, after my hasty speech, Halred had said she could not refuse me—I was already given to the gods, the decision already made. Perhaps that is the way with all our decisions: made in a moment, unconscious of their full weight, they are already given to the gods before we know them. After that, there is no use wavering, nothing to do but accept what you have chosen with whatever grace you can muster, and pray that if you chose badly, the gods may still make of it more than it is. My old order may have been right, and this blood unnecessary; yet as I watched Paddon next to me offering his arm for bleeding, I prayed: *take this slight thing, this impulse of mine, impure though my motives were; take what was best in it, and make of it more than it was.* I was ready.

I watched Halred and Night retreat to the urn and the flame, then return to me with the same measured pace. Halred's gray eyes searched my face as if to see whether I were truly prepared for the loss of blood, still seeing me as an invalid under her charge. Without wanting to disturb the solemnity of the rite, I managed a half-smile to reassure her. She answered with a quizzical look, but proceeded.

"Jereth, have you freely consented to give your blood to the land?"

"Yes," I said levelly.

The same dry fingers that had poulticed my head now bound my left arm tightly with thick, coarse vines. I felt the blood pooling below the knotted vine until it felt like the pent-up force of water just before the ice breaks, freeing the cascade. Halred looked up at me shrewdly once more, and I thrust my arm toward her. She grasped it with her left hand and held it over Night's bowl. A quick flash of the knife freed a bright stream of blood.

The bowl seemed to fill slowly. I was suddenly aware that the sun had burned away the cool mist, that I had not drunk anything all morning, that my mouth was dry as the inside of the old wooden chests in Halred's hut. Darkness floated before my eyes, and I swayed. A hard-boned hand gripped me under the right arm; dragging my eyes open, I saw Halred supporting me. "Breathe," she hissed.

Remembering Brother Beylor's first lesson in singing, I drew in air slowly, starting with the abdomen till my whole body seemed filled with it. That cleared my head, so I was able to stand still and straight as the blood reached its measure in the catch-bowl. Halred untied the vine and stanched the flow. She reached up to touch my face—a motherly sort of gesture—before returning to the flame with the knife. Then she and Night brought before the people the urn of blood.

"Blood of four men is one in this vessel, and no man can divide one from the others," she said. "In this we are all one, our hearts bleeding with them in fellowship. Let us be one with the land that nourishes us, and with all those nourished by the land, grass and grain, beast and bird, Folc of all clans and folk of no clan. May the hands of the Bright and Hidden Goddesses work as one to give life to the land we share: the land that feeds us, houses us, holds us, buries us. Give life to the land; give life to us in the land. We commit the blood of our brave ones to the land in token of our love for it."

Night slowly poured the blood into the earth, beginning in front of the Assembly Stone and continuing a long way into the crowd, which parted around her. Darkness once again rose before my eyes; I heard Halred pronounce another prayer, but my slow-moving brain did not decipher the words.

Then a sound broke through the darkness in my head: Hwyn's voice, at first as meaningless as birdsong. At length words and meaning returned to me, and I heard the Call of the Hidden Goddess to the buried seed:

"Deep in the dark I know you
Deep in the night I name you

In the silent earth I call you
In the womb of earth, I call you
In the grave of earth, you answer.
Stir at the sound of my calling
Break the shell that binds you
Reach down your roots to my waters
Drink of me, deep in the darkness
Draw your life from my darkness
Draw yourself from my wellsprings
Drink of my secret depths.
Deep in the dark I know you
Drink of my secret knowing.
Drink your own name from my darkness;
Rise, knowing your way."

The song twined around me, over me, under me, bearing me safely through the darkness behind my eyes, holding out to me a lifeline no thicker than a taproot—but this lifeline led down into the darkness.

I let go and sank to my knees, feeling the weight of earth, feeling the blessed coolness of dewy grass under my palms. In the darkness, water. I raised a trembling hand to my lips to moisten them—whether sacrilege or sacred gift-exchange, tasting the blood of the land that had tasted mine, I was unsure.

Hwyn's voice was joined by the acolyte's, and as they sang again the call to the buried seed, I heard soft sobbing and felt hands struggling to lift me. There was Trenara, gathering me in her arms as she had done to Aldworth's sick sheep. I said nothing, inwardly praying this breach of decorum wouldn't be seen as sacrilege. I found her hand and pressed it softly to reassure her I was all right, but she did not leave me, keeping a hand on my arm, making soft sounds of encouragement.

The two voices lifted into the other hymn, the one Hwyn had sung to me on the mountain, "Arise, arise, my earthly love," the Bright Goddess's call to the grain, calling me out of the darkness, singing me up and out of my grave, singing the sun up the mountainside toward the noon, singing my heart into rapture. If there were no other sign the gods lived, that song would have convinced me. Breathing deep into my abdomen the sweet breaths of linden and meadow flowers, I struggled to my feet.

Trenara twirled away like a dancer, her movements matched to the swooping and soaring of the two voices calling to the grain, calling to the waking life in all things.

The song ended, and Halred pronounced some final blessing, but I scarcely heard it, savoring the echoes of song in my memory. I was aware that the rite had ended less by Halred's words than by the sudden rush of people offering assistance they had not dared give while the ceremony continued. Paddon took me by the arm to lead me into the shade, Halred felt my pulse and produced a welcome flask from her pocket, and Hwyn came running out of the mouth of the cave where she had been hidden, calling, "Jereth! Are you all right?"

"I'll be fine," I said. "I just need to sit down—and drink some more, if I can. I've never been so thirsty." I sank to the ground and sat with my back to a linden tree. Godrun of the Red Oak came with a bucket of water and handed the dipper to me, first of all the men who had bled.

"Why this flood of kindness?" I said, smiling. "Didn't I fail?"

"What do you mean?" Halred said. "Oh—your fall? That's quite usual. Typically one in four men will fall." She paused to feel my pulse, frowned a little, then handed me her flask again. "You didn't by any chance have a vision?"

"A vision? Not exactly," I said, taking a quick swallow of the unknown liquid, some sort of herb brew with a faint taste of mead. "And yet—something happened." I fixed my eyes on Hwyn. "The sound of the singing was like a revelation. I was dreaming in the sound. Hwyn, when you sang of the water deep in the darkness, I seemed to fall into it, falling on the dewy grass. Whether that might betoken anything—I mean, for anyone but myself—I don't know."

"I dreamed," Hwyn said so softly that I was at first not sure she meant anyone to hear. "In the cave."

Halred seized on her words. "You saw something?"

"I heard something. Mother Halred, that cave—what is it? Is it a tomb?"

"You didn't know?" Halred said. "It is the Hall of the Dead, the home of our ancestors' ashes. Have you nothing like it in the lowlands?"

"No. That is, of course we have tombs, but I never heard of anyone singing out of one," said Hwyn. "It was like nothing else. There are ghosts on this mountain."

"Did they speak to you?" Halred asked.

"I heard a babble of voices. Only a few words came clear through the confusion. 'I am nearer than you think. The time will not be long.' I don't know whether the message is for me and my companions or for the Folc."

"The time will not be long," Halred echoed. "Time for what, I wonder? Is that a threat or a reassurance?"

"That I do not know," Hwyn said. "But the voice did not sound unfriendly."

Halred gazed into the tomb's entrance. "St. Arin's ashes lie there. I wonder...But it is so little to judge by. At any rate, I thank you for your listening, as for your voice in this rite." She turned to me. "And thank you, Jereth. Your gift was a great one."

I stared at my feet, remembering uncomfortably the motives that had driven me to this rite. "It was what I had to do to become less alien here, less of an intruder."

"You are one of us now," Halred said, "one blood, one land."

"And what now?" I said. "What happens next?"

"Now, the feast," grinned Day. "Always, after the rite, the feast."

"Not much of a feast in these times," said Godrun, handing me the water-dipper again as if she read my mind. "But we are putting out the last of the ale in the Red Oak stores. That will be the last till harvest, brother, so you'd better not miss it. Come along!" With a toss of her long braid, she dropped the dipper back into the nearly empty water-bucket, and grabbed me by the hand to pull me along after her. As I rose, helpless to resist, I glanced back at Hwyn to see her looking up at me anxiously. I stretched a hand toward her to add her to the chain, but could not catch her before I was swept away.

They led me back to the great hall of the Red Oak Clan, which had assumed responsibility for the day's hospitality—a defiant gesture, as Paddon explained to me in an undertone when he followed us in. "Summer feasts should be Linden's responsibility. Guthlac is flaunting his generosity in Edwach's face. At least it will not decrease his flock, as this is a fleshless feast. Still, it's no small thing to lay out the last of the beer so early in summer."

The tables were spread with cheeses, smoked lake-fish, summer fruits, nuts carefully preserved since the past autumn, and fried cakes with honey. It was, as Godrun had warned, a limited feast—in my richer days, I would have taken such fare for granted—but after even a few days among the Folc, I could appreciate the recklessness of Red Oak's generosity; the time till harvest might be lean and anxious after this display. I accepted almost with reverence a wedge of cheese and a cake with fresh cream and honey.

True to her word, Godrun put one of the first mugs of dark ale in my hand, and another in Paddon's. "Those that spared blood should not be cheated of ale," she said. Guthlac presided over the barrel of ale with a similar play of images, telling the feasters that "in the spirit of sacrifice, it seemed right to kill off the last barrel." I appreciated the gesture, but light-headed as I was, ale was not what I most needed; a small amount was enough to set me spinning over the depths of half-dream I'd plumbed in the rite.

Casting my eye about the crowded hall for a safe harbor, I saw Hwyn and Trenara with Halred and her acolytes. I crossed the room toward them unsteadily, almost upsetting the precious mug of ale. "Hwyn!" I plunked down the mug on the board before her. "You must share this. I think people are making a game of trying to make me drunk in this weakened state."

"Not a bit of it," Hwyn said. "Surely you must see you're getting a hero's homecoming, with the Headman's daughter taking you by the hand to give you drink?"

"Do you think so?" I said. "I was a public burden a few days ago. All I've done since then is to fall down. But you—" I shook my head, feeling too befuddled to say half of what I had wanted to tell her since the rite concluded. "Do you know how you startled me?"

"I guess I shouldn't have reached out for you so suddenly. I was afraid of that, but I wanted you to know where I was," she said.

"No, I don't mean in the cave," I said. "I mean your voice. Of course I knew you sing beautifully—you always have—but—" I stopped for breath. Somehow I'd had a better way of saying this in my head while they were pouring beer for me. "You were the Hidden Goddess. I thought you would sing the Bright Goddess's part again."

"Me? Stand and face the people as Beauty's Light? What a thought," she said, looking down at her hands. "The people would laugh. Of course I would have to be Hidden."

"You could be both," Halred cut in. "There is enough height and depth in your soul for both teachings, both devotions. Do you think the Bright Goddess's beauty is only a fair face and an easy smile? Then you have much to learn. But you could learn: you have the mind and heart for it."

"Do you mean you would teach me?" Hwyn said, putting down her bit of honeyed cake to turn all her attention to the priestess.

Halred said, "I would take you on as both my student and my teacher. There is much you could learn from me: the art of healing; the rites of the goddesses; the lore of the saints—not to mention book-reading. But I am no prophet, and we have had none among us for generations—till you came."

I saw Day raise her eyebrows, but she said nothing.

Halred continued, "Each of my acolytes is now on the verge of becoming a priestess and teacher to each other—and to me, too, for each of them has her own way of knowing, and may see what I miss. But you bring a fourth kind of wisdom. You would make the circle complete. Stay among us a while and learn with us."

Hwyn looked at Halred hopefully, and my heart sank, for I had lost the chance to say to her what I had meant to say, and the words were floating fast away on a tide of beer and blood-loss.

At last Hwyn said, "I don't know how long we can stay."

"You travelers are truly of the Folc now," said Drict from a little way down the bench. "After the Rite, I think none would dare challenge your right to stay."

I noticed a slight frown furrow Day's fair face. *Jealousy,* I thought. For all that she stood before the people, atop the Assembly Stone, with Hwyn hidden from sight; for all the beauty that made the eyes of every man follow her; for all her laughing command of life, she fears to lose her prominence—to Hwyn of all people, the scarred outcast. And Hwyn, so used to the cold corner farthest from favor, may slip dutifully away and lose her one chance to shine. That goaded me to speak: "Well, Hwyn, we have to stay a little while at least. We promised to work beside the Folc for a time before we move on. Surely you'll have time for some learning while we stay."

Hwyn looked at me quizzically, then back at Halred.

"Surely you never meant to leave so soon," Halred said.

What Hwyn might have answered was lost in a din of pipes

and drums as the shepherds' piper, the farmers' drummer, and Ethwin with a shrill whistle marched into the room. They made their way to our corner and demanded the participation of Hwyn and Day in particular, and all in general, in their music.

To my astonishment, I saw a multitude of instruments appear from the pockets of rough-handed herders and from storage-chests in the hall: reed pipes, flutes, harps, a lute, a gittern. Music, like work, was the birthright of all the Folc, and if the feast of food was not great, the feast of music more than compensated. Even dour Anlaf sang with abandon.

Hwyn and I joined with the rest when we knew the songs, and were urged up onto a tabletop to perform a few of our own, not just once but over and over till the others could sing them.

We sang until the work of the Folc could no longer be postponed, feast or no feast. As the gathering broke apart, Paddon called me to follow him. "Come on, traveler. You're one of the Folc now, as I am, and that means tending the livestock. I'll claim you as my apprentice for the evening. I tend the Red Oak Clan's cows. You can learn to milk, while you're here."

Hwyn came along as well. "I've wondered before—it's strange to see cows here," she said. "It doesn't seem quite the countryside for them."

"It's not, really," Paddon admitted. "I brought the cows. When the blight started, and many of the goats died, I made a foray out to a farm in the Kreyn holdings and raided their cattle. I just took a few—as many as I thought I could drive to St. Arin's Lake without losing any. I gave most to Guthlac, and the rest to the Linden Clan as a peace offering so I could marry Edwach's niece. Other than marrying Sigrun, though, the raid doesn't seem to have been such a good idea," he admitted. "They're a nuisance. They have to be pastured apart from the sheep, you know."

I didn't, but let it pass.

"And they eat more than the goats, and besides, they're not thriving here. But I'm more used to keeping them than sheep or goats. And what else was an outlaw to do for his adopted homeland in times of hardship?"

We reached the cow-byre then, and even to my inexpert eye, the cows looked stringy and miserable, like beggars on four hooves. Nonetheless, Hwyn and Paddon made a merry enough time of the milking, laughing at my awkwardness till they could scarcely show me the right way, as Trenara hovered about making friends with the cows.

After that there were harder chores, the stalls to be cleaned, the manure to be hauled out for mulch or set to dry for fuel. At the end of it, when we dove in the lake, clothes and all, to wash ourselves, I was too exhausted to pay back their laughter with the sort of water-tricks my seafaring youth might have made easy. The climb back to the Red Oak house seemed long.

"You're still recovering," Hwyn told me, when Paddon had left us to confer with his wife about a salve for fly-bitten beasts. "Time enough tomorrow to learn other tasks. You should rest now; I'll see you in the morning."

"Won't you be in the Red Oak house tonight?" I said.

"No," she said, "I must rejoin Halred now; there are other rites to be performed in the darkness, and then we spend another night among the flocks."

"Oh," I said, brought up short, for I had counted on having time to talk to her at night. "I should have expected that. I knew you were more a priest already than I ever was."

"Do you think so? I had expected something to happen in the rite, more than a few ghostly words in the cave."

"Something happened. Did you not feel it? When you sang the words of the goddess, I believed you."

"The lament for slain lambs," she mused. "I have always felt that I knew it from the inside, knew how the goddess must feel, if I dare say so. I have wept for the deaths that nourish life. I knew I could sing her part."

"Not just the lament, not just the Hidden Goddess," I said. "Halred is right. They are both in you. Go to your evening rites, and may they bear fruit for this land."

I fell asleep to the drumming of rain on the roof of the Red Oak house. I dreamed of the rain washing the blood over the fields and down to the sleeping roots in the stony ground.

When Paddon woke me at dawn, the rain was dwindling away. We went out into the silvery mist to meet Hwyn and Trenara in the cow-byre for the morning's milking. I expected it to seem easier the second time. When the first encouraging stream of milk came foaming into the pail, I thought I would soon be done. But I kept on until my hands ached, and the cow showed no sign of drying. "This seems to take forever."

"It's more than we had yesterday," Paddon said, busy with another animal. "At this rate, I may even prove my raid worthwhile." True enough, the milk we brought in that morning was half again what we'd had the evening before.

We had no time to marvel on it, though, for in my eagerness to learn the tasks of farm and herd that would earn my keep, I'd promised to help Hwyn clean out the Red Oak Clan's chicken-shed and then help Godrun in the kitchen-garden before returning to the byre for the second milking. These were children's tasks, both women had told me teasingly. Still, I had to start somewhere.

Hwyn managed to find a great deal of hilarity in my tentative way with the hens, and we both laughed to see Trenara skipping after the ungainly birds like a child after butterflies. The cleaning was dirty, mucky, hot work in the humid morning, but there was the lake to cool us afterward and the satisfaction of carrying a good-sized heap of eggs back to the kitchen—Hwyn juggling three of them, to the alarm of Girnhild and the delight of the children.

In the afternoon heat, Hwyn went off to the wooded hillsides with Halred to gather wild herbs and learn their virtues. I spent the afternoon learning when and how to pick and store beans, peas, radishes, cucumbers, onions, and strawberries. My teachers, Godrun and a gang of her nieces and nephews, were even more amused by my ignorance of the obvious than Hwyn had been by my first attempt to find an egg under a hen. Nonetheless, when we sat shelling beans into a bowl, I could recuperate some of my dignity by telling them tales of faraway places I'd sailed to: the ancient cities of Magya, the flowery islands of Iskarron, the rich ports of the Kettrans on both sides of the western sea— the *wicked* Kettrans, as the children of the Folc would say, historical memory being unforgiving.

As I reached the end of a particularly satisfying tale of a tempest we'd sailed through when I was fourteen, I noticed that Ethwin had been standing by listening for some time. Over his shoulder he carried a chamois carcass; he'd shot two, he said, and thought it only right to offer one to our household after our hospitality at the feast. Still, after handing over the chamois to Godrun to present to Girnhild, he lingered about until at last he asked to speak to me apart.

"I thought your friends would be with you," he said. "I was so glad to be done early, so I could steal a moment here."

"Hwyn is gathering herbs with the priestess, and Trenara goes wherever she goes," I said. "They should be back for the evening milking—I don't think they'd pass up another chance to laugh at me."

"Will they take supper with the Red Oak Clan? Having brought the meat, I could easily stay."

"I don't know," I sighed. "They've been spending so much time with Halred that you might do better to feign sickness and call for the healer."

"I was so hoping she'd be here," he said, worrying at the slight dark down of new beard on his chin. "Ah, well. I shouldn't weary you with my complaints. You're in love with her too, aren't you?"

"What?"

"Every man that looks at Trenara must be."

"Ah, Trenara," I chuckled. "Don't worry, lad, I'm not your rival—not that such a poor rival as myself would worry you if I were. I grant you, she's beautiful—"

"Oh, but there's so much more than her beauty," he said. "Her tenderness for all creatures—the way she'll touch Seeker, or one of the lambs, as gentle as—as—as starlight."

Hidden Goddess, I thought, he's got the worst case of Trenara I've ever seen. She's turned him into a poet. Small wonder, when he's seen precious few women before that he couldn't call "cousin." Poor boy; I'd encourage him to marry her and solve both our problems at once, but his father would kill him if he bred the elder-line of the Linden Clan with an idiot. Could the lad really be too love-struck to notice she was simple, even after so many days? Unable to think of a kind or tactful way of raising the issue, I only nodded sympathetically.

"I guess it's no use," he said. "You three are not here to stay, and she will be off to lands I'll never see."

"Sometimes that's the best thing that can happen to the beautiful ideal," I said, remembering my older brother's ardent courtship of a nearly inaccessible lady he only saw in a certain port, and the mutually disappointing marriage that had come of it. "Starlight isn't made to be touched."

"You don't understand. I could grow to be worthy of her," he said desperately.

I gave up all hope of talking sense to him. "Ethwin, I certainly never meant to say you were anything but worthy. Contrive an excuse to drop by at milking time, and Trenara should be there. Now I must get back to the pea-pods, or Godrun and an entire clan of children will come after me."

He returned for the milking as I bade him, just as Hwyn and Trenara came herb-scented from the cool woods. Paddon raised an eyebrow to see him mooning about while we worked, but smiled tolerantly and said nothing. Soon enough we were all too busy to mind Ethwin, for the milk seemed practically endless.

"This isn't natural," Paddon said flatly as he set aside another pailful. "How could she be giving so much? She was nearly dry on the eve of the Rite of Increase." He stopped, his eyes wide as full moons. "Gods on the Wheel," he breathed.

"The rite," I completed his thought. "What else could it be?"

"What's this?" Ethwin said, startled out of his rapt contemplation of Trenara.

"Linden Clan or not, you'd better stop loafing and help us, Ethwin," said Paddon. "These cows must be relieved of their milk, and there seems to be no end of it."

And so even Ethwin the Hunter sat down to the milking with us and worked diligently, scarcely raising his head to contemplate Trenara as she fed the cows bits of clover she'd stowed in her pockets.

"Where's an empty pail?" Hwyn said after a time.

"Gods, they're all full," said Paddon. "Go in to Girnhild and put some of this milk in jugs, churns, anything." And so, soon enough, Girnhild and Godrun were rushing back and forth, wide-eyed, stowing the milk wherever they could.

When there were no more jugs, Girnhild said, "Ethwin, why don't you run back home and have your kin bring jugs to fill? There's enough here for two houses today; it shouldn't go to waste."

"What if they're in the same situation?" mused Hwyn.

But when Ethwin returned, he came in a knot of people, each with an empty jug: his mother, Sibfrith, his cousin Holdwin, and two skinny Linden children. "Is it true?" Sibfrith burst out. "Did the goddesses free your cattle of the curse on the land?"

"More than free of the curse," Girnhild said, "they're flowing like spring thaw in the mountains. Have some milk, neighbor, or we'll never be through with the cheese-making."

"Will Guthlac agree to this?" Sibfrith frowned. "He and my husband—"

"If he doesn't agree, he'll have the rough side of me to deal with," Girnhild said. "Besides, your son has been generous to us with his extra game, and my husband swears by the return of hospitalities. I have no fear of giving this. Have you of accepting it?" She looked shrewdly, and perhaps a bit pityingly at the Linden elder's wife. Sibfrith had a defeated look about her, like a faded banner, like my mother. But she shook her head, and began filling her jugs.

"Lady Sibfrith," Hwyn said hesitantly, "forgive my curiosity, but I thought—are not all the cattle of the Folc affected by the rite?"

"Hardly," Holdwin answered for her. "Ours are as bad as they've ever been in the green time of year. Uncle Edwach will run mad when he hears of your good fortune."

"Halred will love it," Paddon muttered very low.

"I wonder," Hwyn mused to herself, but she did not finish the sentence, nor could I catch her eye to see if her thoughts matched mine.

"I knew we should never have turned you travelers away," Sibfrith said to Hwyn and me. "But there's no speaking to my husband at these times, no speaking to him at all. Will you forgive us and lift the curse?"

Hwyn and I stared at her, then looked at each other. Finally Hwyn spoke. "My Lady, we can surely have no ill will against you or your house after your son rescued us in the hills. Nor do we know what makes the milk flow so freely here and not from the Linden cattle. It may only be that what started here must spread slowly outward; the Red Oak holding is, after all, closest to the place where the rite was performed. Your house may not have long to wait."

"Your words are kind," said Sibfrith, "and yet my heart misgives me. I must speak to Mother Halred about this."

"May I go with you?" Girnhild said.

Sibfrith smiled. "Of course, cousin. We have been too much apart these twenty years or more."

"It's a sin that we have let it be so, and I mean to reform my ways," Girnhild said. "Before the summer is out, we'll make our stubborn husbands sit down like neighbors at the same table, and end this foolishness."

"If that happens, I will truly know the gods have not forgotten us," said Sibfrith. And so they left together with Holdwin and the children, each carrying a jug of milk. Godrun dashed off to tell the rest of the household, leaving the same little gathering that had come for milking.

"Well," Paddon said as he returned to cleaning the stalls, "I think it's time for me to eat my words: the rite had more power than I guessed."

"I wonder whether anything else will have increased since the rite," Hwyn said, picking up a spade to help him.

"Nothing at our house had increased," said Ethwin without rancor.

"Hwyn, I would bet all my money, if I had any," I said, "that the hens you worked among will be laying more eggs than seems quite normal, and the groves where you searched for herbs will be flourishing. The kitchen-garden where I worked without you, however, will be much the same as it has been."

Paddon leaned on his spade. "Hwyn—you?"

"Not me, but what I carry," Hwyn said. "I have not told anyone but Halred, and she seemed to think it unwise to tell the others. But I trust you two, Paddon and Ethwin—and I think you are not inclined to distrust me."

"What is it?" said Ethwin.

"I carry the Eye of Night," she said, "the Sky-Raven's Egg. I am taking it into the North, where it will hatch and change the world—in what way, I don't know."

Paddon let out his breath slowly. "You're lucky I'm not easily given to believing old legends. I have heard dark tales of you since cradle days, Bearer of Night. Somehow, I expected you to be eight feet tall, with an army at your back and blood dripping from your claws. How much is true? Is this the end of the world?"

"I don't know," Hwyn said. "Sometimes I think that if I don't take this egg where it must hatch, the world will burst like an overripe fruit. Then again, the world might not end outright: we might all go on living, but with the spirit dead inside us like an undelivered stillbirth. I scarcely know which to fear the more."

"I thought you were supposed to *bring* the world's end, not avoid it," said Ethwin, then hastily added, "Not that I believe it now, you know."

Hwyn shrugged. "What do we mean by the world's end? When three tribes left their valleys to join the Linden Clan at St. Arin's

Lake, it must have been the end of the world to them. Now Mother Halred sees the world's end in the dying of the customs born in that union: the shared flocks of the Folc. And if the Folc now leave Penmorrin, that will be the world's end for many of you."

"Not for me," muttered Ethwin, but Paddon spoke over him: "What world ended in Kreyn when you were there?"

"Lady Goldifer's chapel burned," said Hwyn. "All its icons were destroyed. We tricked our way into it seeking a prophecy, and the Eye of Night turned it to ashes."

"Are you sure it was your doing?" laughed Paddon. "Some would say that's all there ever was of her piety. Well, I have been wrong before—I was wrong about the ritual—but I trust your living voice better than the dead voice of ancient prophecy. In the end, neither the wonders I have seen nor the strange tales of the Night-Bearer can change what I think of you. Now come, friends: the lake is waiting for us."

The rain had begun again, so we only splashed in and out of the lake to clean ourselves, then climbed back toward the Red Oak house, hoping that the excitement had not delayed the evening meal. As we slogged along the muddy path, it gradually sank into our heads that for all the ominous tales he had heard, Paddon treated us the same as ever. As for Ethwin, if he were at all changed toward us, it was only in being more willing to look at someone other than Trenara, even when the lake-water and rainwater plastered her clothing tantalizingly close around her form.

"You two seem to have recovered quickly from the legends," Hwyn said.

"What else can we do?" said Ethwin.

"Some might have driven us from the village," Hwyn said.

"What? And chase away the first luck we've seen in years?" said Paddon. "Everyone will want you to stay forever."

When we reached the Red Oak house, we were so beset with Folc clustering round us to ask about the miracle, to bask in whatever good luck might radiate from us, or simply to congratulate us, that we were in danger of never getting a chance to eat. The aromas of roast chamois and stewed berries mocked us a long time before Girnhild sent children diving through the crowd with steaming bowls for us.

Halred had come back to see the strangely blessed cattle for herself, and to call all the Folc to an Assembly of thanksgiving the following night. When she saw Hwyn, she ran toward her beaming. "I knew you had not been sent to us in vain," she said. "Your message in the cave was for us, after all: 'The time will not be long,' it said, and here it has scarcely been two days before we see the rebirth we hoped for."

"That may be," Hwyn mused. "It is still dark to me, like so many of the dreams that drive me."

"We will pray over it, and learn what we can from my lorebooks," Halred said. And so, at the meal's end, Hwyn and Trenara went off to the priestess's house again, leaving me among my new brethren of the Red Oak. Ethwin at least could escort them, as the little round house lay on his way home; I could only look toward the morning.

Morning proved me almost prophetic: milk continued to flow like the watercourse that fed St. Arin's Lake, and the chickens had outdone themselves. Furthermore, Guthlac swore that the sheep among which Hwyn had spent two nights were regrowing their fleece faster than he had ever seen before.

Nor were the beasts all that had changed: the Folc had changed toward us. While no one called Hwyn the Bearer of Night, all seemed to have noticed a pattern in the unexpected blessings and traced it to the stranger who had sung the Rite of Increase so movingly. As we wheeled a barrow of manure out to mulch the fruit-trees, everyone we passed on the way smiled or bowed or lingered to ask whether Hwyn might look in on a kitchen-garden or a goat tethered by a house for morning milk. She always complied, when it did not take us too far from the task we'd promised to do.

"How wonderfully tenacious they are, to stand chatting with us beside a wheelbarrow of manure on a humid day," I said as soon as we were out of earshot of the latest petitioner.

"Success has been known to make worse things smell good," Hwyn said.

But soon there was no space for wry remarks, because by the time we reached the orchard, several of the Folc were following us as if they expected to see the fruit swell on the branch before their eyes. No such sudden wonders were revealed, but things went well enough anyway. The Folc were too used to work to simply watch: spades and wheelbarrows appeared as if by magic from any shed along the way, and every watcher lent a hand, making short work of the mulching.

After we and our spontaneous following had gone to the lake

o bathe off the streaks of sweat and mulch, we emerged dripping to find Edwach regarding us with a nervous, uncertain look. After hemming and hawing, and ordering away any Linden kin among the bathers to suddenly urgent errands, he spoke to us in an undertone, so that we had to strain to hear. "My wife bade me—that is, we thought—I was looking for you, to apologize to you." He looked daggers at the remaining followers, and they slowly dispersed. "I'm sorry I spoke so rashly when—when my son brought you to the valley. I only—you must understand, with three years' bad harvests, I had to think of the survival of my people, my house. But I should have thought better, and invited you in."

"It's all right," Hwyn said. "We understood. Hunger's a hard master."

"Then will you lift the curse on my house?" Edwach said.

"We put no curse on you," Hwyn said.

"That's not what I mean," he said. "They've convinced me now—my wife and son, that is—that my sister was right: I brought this on myself when I broke the guest-code. I should have given you shelter. Jereth is of the Red Oak Clan now, and that can't be taken back, but Hwyn—you have no clan, and yet you're not under vows; you could have one. And my house is half empty. I have but the one son left, Ethwin; he's the youngest, but the others ran off and he will be Elder after me. He's a good lad, as you know; for all that we fight, I know it too. We are so few now, and though I would not have Guthlac know it, we are poor: half our flock miscarried this year. Whatever this luck, this blessing is, we need it more than the others. If anyone needed a Rite of Increase, we did." He trailed off as if exhausted by the mere words.

For all the venom that had begun our acquaintance, I could not help pitying this defeated man, sent out by his meek wife to beg aid of the beggars he'd turned away. Hwyn seemed to feel it too; backing away a bit, she spoke gently: "There is no curse on you, for all I know, nor am I in power to judge you, sir. I cannot change my habitation here; the priestess has offered to teach me while I remain here, and I must go where she sends me. But I bear you no ill will, and the luck I carry is not to be hoarded. I think I can be spared for the evening milking."

"Thank you," he said. "You don't know what this means to us." Then he slunk away like a dog with its tail between its legs.

When he was out of earshot, Hwyn said, "I'm not sure

whether he was trying to adopt me, or to marry his son to me gods forbid."

"I couldn't swear it wasn't the latter," I said. "And Ethwin's in love with Trenara."

Trenara, walking a little off the path to pick red clover scarcely looked up at the sound of her name.

"Naturally," Hwyn said. "Mercy of the gods, what hideous things hardship brings people to! What should I do with this tangle?"

"Exactly what you proposed," I said. "Who could be offended by it? Except myself, of course, for I'll miss seeing you at milking-time. Are you spending the whole afternoon with Halred again?"

"I have to practice hymns for the thanksgiving rite," Hwyn said, "and then if there's time, she promised to begin teaching me letters."

"Letters! If I'd known you wanted to learn, I'd have taught you at once," I said.

She squinted up at me. "Strange that I never thought of asking you. But they're the key to much of Halred's lore."

"I know there are things she can teach you that are dark to me," I said. "But I grew so used to being with you."

Hwyn smiled. "So did I, Jereth. It's just that there's so much here, so much I can do. But it's not like that for you, is it?"

I shook my head. "Little use here for a scholar or a sailor, though I seem to be serving as a sort of jester by my amusing attempts to be useful. And I'm learning things that will be useful for picking up day-labor along the road. But—" I laughed bitterly, "the only thing of use I could offer the Folc was my blood."

She put a hand on my arm lightly. "I'm sorry, Jereth. I thought you wanted to stay longer. Why were you so quick to second Halred's urging that we stay?"

"To get for you what Halred promised. To see you admired for your gifts, honored, valued by someone besides me and Trenara. To give you your due."

She looked at me with wonder. "I hardly know what to say. You're so kind."

"No," I said. "This is no gift to a beggar. It's— It delights me to see you loved and valued. It would delight my heart to see you become what you long to be. And it is foolish of me to grudge you the time to do it."

"Thank you," she said quietly. "Thank you, my friend, my true comrade. I—" she broke off, as if she could scarcely speak. "No one has taken your place, you can be sure. When we leave, it will be together."

"Good," I said. "I'll be patient till then."

"Where are you bound for now?" she asked.

"To the high pastures," I said. "They've all been teasing me with my ignorance about sheep. I think they've decided I'll be most comical there."

"It's early still," she said. "I can go with you and still return to Halred in time. And now that they believe I carry luck, no one will call it idle of me to pay a visit to the pastures."

But when we met Guthlac on a flowery high meadow, he was deep in discussion with one of the Red Oak Clan followers that Edwach had dispersed with his stare; and Guthlac's eyes looked almost as baleful as his rival's had. "What's this I hear? You're going over to the Linden Clan?" he barked at Hwyn.

"What?"

"What has Edwach offered you to tend his cows instead of mine?"

"He offered me nothing," Hwyn said, the fire rising in her voice to match Guthlac's. "He asked my help, and I felt sorry for him."

"You felt sorry for him! *He* didn't feel sorry for Jereth when he came wounded and sick into the valley, or for you without food or water in a strange land. You thought my house good enough when you came as beggars, pleading for shelter. Now that your luck has returned, will you bring it to Edwach instead?"

"How can you think I would rather bring it to Edwach?" By now, Hwyn was red in the face. "You sheltered me, which is a great gift. You sheltered my friends, which is more. And I would rather bring blessings to you than to any of the elders. But I was not warned that the *price* of your hospitality was to do good to no one else." She leaned on the word *price* a little, and it had much the same effect on Guthlac that it had on Halred: his look of angry self-assurance wavered. She went on: "Guthlac, this thing I carry, this luck as you call it, is *not* to be hoarded. The last man that tried to hoard it ended ghost-addled, whimpering on the floor—not by my action, mind, but by his own. If you begin this way at the first taste of power, you will fall as far. And

that will break my heart, my lord of the Red Oak, for I though
better of you, far better."

For a while they only stared at each other, a fire looking into
fire.

"I'm sorry," said Guthlac at last. "There are old grievance
between me and Edwach, and where he is concerned, I am apt t
see treachery in every corner. And there is still fear of anothe
kind, for one or two days' bounty of milk is not enough to que
my worries: we emptied our stores for the feast. But you ar
right: you hold some power I cannot understand, and I shoul
not expect to put my mark on its ear and call it mine."

"And I am sorry," Hwyn said, "that I did not foresee wha
should have been plain: if it's true that the—that my quest, m
calling brought the blessing on your cows, then wherever I brin
that blessing, I must cause envy elsewhere. While I carry it, I an
not free to choose my path for myself. Can you call an Assembl
to decide what must be done?"

"What—to divide you like a deer between four hunters?"
Guthlac said with a sour laugh. "Would you abide by that?"

Hwyn hesitated. "Not in everything," she said. "In the end
my path is plain: I must continue my journey. But while I stay,
must not cause strife among the Folc. It will be better if every
one agrees what is best for me to do here."

Guthlac nodded. "I cannot call the Assembly, for all th
elders are parties to the dispute. But at Halred's Assembly o
thanksgiving, the priests may judge all claims."

"That will be best," Hwyn said. "I will tell her." With that sh
was off down the green mountain path to rejoin her mentor.
spent the afternoon learning the mysterious ways of sheep an
goats, looking forward to the evening.

That evening's Assembly began much as the first had, with th
ritual calling of the four clans, the lighting of the hearth, th
naming of priests to listen for the voices of the Four Great One
But this time no one challenged our right to be counted amon
the Folc. When the time came to choose the representative of th
Upside-Down God, no one cried foul as Guthlac presented th
choosing straws to Hwyn. She drew out a long straw. Next to her
Trenara stared at the choosing straws a long time, as if uncertain

what to do with them. "Take one, Trenara," Guthlac urged. "Or would you like me to give you one?"

Trenara shook her head, reached out with a delicate forefinger and thumb, and drew out a straw—the shortest one. Smiling broadly, she turned and gave it to me.

"You again, Jereth?" said Guthlac, his grin as broad as the fool's.

"No: it was Trenara," I said emphatically. "Trenara, this is yours. You have to keep it. You stand for the Turning God tonight." I tried to put it in her hand, but she pushed it away.

"What! The imbecile?" cried Anlaf. "Why did you give her the choosing straws? It's an affront to the god."

"If you cared so much about affronts to the Upside-Down God, why didn't you learn his lore while Wendlac lived, so it would not die with the old priest?" Halred cut in.

Anlaf opened his mouth to reply, but Guthlac was faster. "Mother Halred, *please* set aside that old quarrel till we have settled some new ones. How can we look to you and Father Anlaf to keep peace among the four clans if you are still at each other's throats?

"And Father Anlaf, with all respect to the Rising God and his priesthood, I must protest on behalf of the Upside-Down God, the patron of my clan. Twice he has chosen one of these newcomers—can this be mere chance? Twice you have rejected his choice. This time I dare not choose again. That, to me, would seem the greater affront to the god. He has chosen; who are we to put his choice aside?"

"If, indeed, it is *his* choice," Anlaf said. "The straws were in your hands."

"Do you call the Elder of Red Oak a cheat, a blasphemer?" roared Guthlac.

"Brothers, be still!" cried Maethild. "We have gathered to thank the gods for a great blessing. At this rate, they may never give us another. Make peace, for the sake of the land."

That silenced them a while. Maethild continued: "Let us consider this carefully. Can Trenara fulfill the duties of the Turning God's representative?"

"Can any of us?" called a voice just behind us; I turned and saw Night rising to speak. "If the duty is to stand in the god's place, listen for his voice, and act only as the god would, all of us

must ask ourselves whether we can hope to fulfill those duties
being only human. All of us, chosen by lot or schooled in the lore
of the saints, are unready. That is not in question. The question is
whether the god can make his will known through Trenara—or
through any of us. I say he can. Who says otherwise?"

A little silence followed her words. Then Anlaf, without
speaking, threaded his way through the crowd toward Night. He
extended a hand to her. "Well spoken, acolyte," he said. "You
are well prepared, I see, to take the vows of the Hidden Goddess, and to take your place as one of the nine voices in our
Assembly."

She seemed half disbelieving as she clasped the proffered
hand.

"I will concede," the old priest said, "if I can be satisfied on
one point: can Trenara swear the oath required of the Upside-
Down God's representative?"

Guthlac turned to Trenara: "Lady Trenara, listen. Can you
pledge to the Upside-Down God, the Turning God, to listen for
his voice in the Assembly and speak or be silent as he bids you?"

Trenara gave him one of her profoundly blank looks.

Hwyn touched her arm. "Trenara, can you promise for
tonight to say only what the Upside-Down God bids?"

"No," said Trenara, then tugged at my sleeve.

"Yes, Trenara, I picked the short straw last time," I said. "This
is a new time. You won this time."

"*No,*" said Trenara, a bit more impatiently.

"She can't understand," Hwyn said. "I'm sorry. We've had a
fine theological discussion over it, but she just can't."

"Very well," said Guthlac, "Hand back your straws, everyone,
and be quick, or the Assembly will last till dawn."

In the second drawing, Night chose the short straw. As she
solemnly took her place on the Assembly Stone with Halred and
Anlaf, I saw the old priest regard her with the sort of look my abbot used to give a particularly puzzling text.

Halred began the Assembly: "We have gathered the Folc to
give thanks for the wonders you have all heard of, the miraculous
increase in the sheep and goats of the Folc, the milk of Red Oak's
cattle, and the eggs of Red Oak's hens."

"The fish in the lake have also increased," Anlaf added.

Halred nodded in acknowledgment, and went on. "This is
wonderful indeed, and yet we must do more than give thanks

The gifts of the gods are not to be hoarded, nor to be fought over. We must choose wisely what is to be done with these gifts for the good of the Folc.

"Many of you know that the newcomer Hwyn, who sang in the Rite of Increase, seems to be followed by these wondrous events. Some of you have begun vying for her attention to get some of the new blessings for your own clan. But it is not right for blessings to be given only to the most insistent, or for their bearer to be torn to pieces by demands from all sides. What, then, must we do?"

Anlaf broke in, "Are we certain that these changes really do follow Hwyn?"

"Nothing is certain," Halred said, "but—"

"Forgive me," Hwyn cut in, "but—"

"Hwyn," Halred said in a tone of warning, "let me speak. As I was saying, we have no certain knowledge of what caused these wonders, or whether they will continue in the same manner. But it takes no extraordinary penetration to see Hwyn's movements at the heart of the pattern. The cows that give double milk and the hens that lay eggs in abundance are those she helped care for. As for the sheep and goats, all those that were driven together to the common pasture where Hwyn spent two nights showed signs of increase. The lake has thrived since she swam in it. If it were only the sheep and goats, I would say their part in the ritual gained them this favor. If it were just the cows and hens, I would say the Red Oak Clan had been peculiarly blessed. But Hwyn links all these things—and more: the wild herbs she gathered with me have grown back overnight."

There was a murmur in the crowd, and at this interruption, Hwyn tried again to speak, and Halred again signaled her to be silent. "Hwyn, I know it troubles you to be singled out so. I am not saying you caused all these wonders; the hands of the Bright and Hidden Goddesses are behind them. I know you did not expect this blessing, do not control it, and cannot promise it will last. But whatever the reason the goddesses have chosen to work through you, it little matters. What does matter is that the Folc must not quarrel over you or put more demands on you than it is fair to ask of a guest."

Hwyn said nothing, but bit her lip.

Halred continued: "Let me propose a solution, and then all of you can say whether it seems fair to you. While these wonders continue, let the ritual nights among the flocks continue too. Let all clans bring their flocks to a common paddock by night for the blessing.

"Let us hold the grainfields in common, and let Hwyn work in the fields by morning. And if the blessing she carries is needed on any other thing, let the holder of it agree that whatever is blessed shall be held in common.

"But let her be given time as well to study and pray with me and my acolytes, to better understand the gift that has been entrusted to her.

"My neighbors and cousins, does this seem fair to you? What say you?" Halred called.

Paddon stood to respond. "Does Hwyn agree to all that she's asked to do? We should not portion her out like a quartered loaf, without her consent."

Hwyn smiled. "Thank you, Paddon. I am well willing to do what has been asked of me while I remain here, in gratitude for the welcome of the Folc. But I ask you all to remember that I was on a journey when I came here, and in time I must go."

"We remember," said Anlaf. "I would add, too, that anything we Folc agree to now should not be taken as standing for all time; we do not know what may come to light about these marvels we have seen. But for the time being, Halred," he said, "whatever our reputation for quarreling, I can see no reason to oppose your plan."

And so it was accepted; all that remained was the ritual agreement of the Voices of the Folc, and the chants of thanksgiving that had been prepared for the Assembly. Hwyn sang her part with the priestess and her acolytes, in counterpart to Anlaf and his acolyte, a young man called Tarvas whose rich baritone voice I recognized from the singing at the feast.

When the chants were done and Halred settled down to guard the embers of the fire, Hwyn whispered to me, "Don't go. I need to speak to Halred apart from the Folc, and I'd like you to be with me."

Unsurprised, I pressed her hand in answer, and waited with Trenara a little distance from those who kept vigil by the fire. Halred's eyes were alight with triumph; Day and Night, on either side of her, watched the embers solemnly, lips moving in prayer. When the red glow died and a crescent moon shed the only light, Halred at last looked up at me. "Jereth, are you going to join us with the flocks?"

I shook my head. "I will need to be at the Red Oak house for the early milking; I can only linger a little while with Hwyn—fitting as it would seem to re-create the eve of the rite. But before I was one of the Red Oak Clan, I was Hwyn's follower on a great journey. And we need to speak to you on matters of that journey."

Halred nodded as if she had been expecting this. Turning to Day and Night, she said, "Go on ahead. I will follow you soon." With many glances back, they went.

"Mother Halred, I see you have kept my secrets well," Hwyn began. "You haven't told even them, have you?" She gestured with her head at the retreating forms of Day and Night. "But why did you silence me in the Assembly? I was ready to speak openly."

"I knew you were about to speak of the Eye of Night," said Halred. "When you first came here, you told me you had strong reasons to keep it secret. I have come to believe you were right. Why have you now changed your mind?"

"When I came here, I did not know whether we would be welcomed, or left to starve, or stoned to death as bringers of bad fortune," Hwyn said. "All that has changed. They call us neighbor, cousin, sister, brother. They are beginning to call us bringers of good luck; at this rate, it will be saint or hero before long. Don't they have the right to know what I am and what I bring among them? What right have I to distrust the Folc now?"

"If you have no right to distrust them, I do. I know them better," said Halred. "Anlaf and Tarvas are not to be underestimated. If they believe the more ominous prophecies about the Raven's Egg, they might take it to destroy it."

"It is not so easily destroyed as all that," said Hwyn.

"Nonetheless," said Halred, "they might throw it in the lake or drop it in a crevice in the mountains, where you could not get it. And if the elders knew this luck you carry is a physical talisman, they might steal it to wield for themselves rather than leave it for the good of all. You have already seen the envy and rivalry among them."

Hwyn weighed these words carefully before she answered. "True enough. And there would be a terrible price on any who tried to wield it thus—not at once, but in the long run, when it was too late for warnings. I suppose you are right. Still, it troubles me to have the Folc hold me in awe, as if I were working these wonders of myself."

"Remember this, and you will not become too proud," Halred said. "I can keep your secret because I trust you to remember where this power comes from, even if no one else does."

In the days that followed, I saw little of Hwyn. She no longer came to the Red Oak Clan's cow-byre for milking, but busied herself in the common fields and in study, while I became immersed in the herding life, chasing stray sheep up and down the high pastures of Summerbride, venturing out farther every day as the summer progressed. Sometimes I would linger at the common paddock at day's end to speak to Hwyn as she came to bed down among the beasts; at other times, Guthlac would send me for a day's labor in the fields by Hwyn's side.

As the oats had grown unnaturally, so had the weeds; though women did most of the Folc's farming, I was not the only man helping out with the harrowing in this season of increase. It was back-breaking labor under a high sun, but no amount of toil could dim Hwyn's glow as she spoke of the things she was learning from Halred, the powers of herbs, the long festival chants, the lore of saints.

How things had changed for her! Everyone was glad to see her; she was greeted, courted constantly. Even her meals had to be portioned among the four clans' halls to prevent envy, or eaten in Halred's round hut as the priestess and her acolytes debated questions of theology. As a one-time priest of the Tarvon Order, I might have tried to insinuate myself into these discussions, but that part of my life was past, and I had not left one Order to find another.

One evening as I sat in the Red Oak Hall, disconsolately eating without Hwyn or Trenara, Ethwin came by. Invited in hastily by Guthlac, he sat gloomily near me and picked at a bowl of fresh curds. When the others about us were engaged in a tale from Paddon's outlaw days, Ethwin said to me quietly, "I thought your friends would be here."

"They're with the priestess," I said. "I see so little of them since the wonders began."

"At least you will be with them when you go," he said. "As for me, they'll leave me behind without a thought, on to foreign places, wonderful places. I was born here and I've never been farther than a day's hunt away from here and I'll probably die without going any farther."

"I don't at all know that the places we're going will be wonderful. We may find ourselves in quite terrible places," I said, though I realized as soon as the words were out of my mouth that they would only make our travels more intriguing to him.

"You *are* going, though? There's no chance you'll stay here?" he asked forlornly.

I shrugged. "I don't know. They seem so content here, as if this were the place they'd been meant all along to find," I said, voicing aloud for the first time what had been troubling me. "Sometimes I wonder whether we will leave at all."

"That displeases you," the boy said. "Have we been such poor company?"

"Not at all," I said, "but I'm so unneeded here. It's hard not to be needed."

"It's hard to be needed, sometimes," he replied, and I agreed with him, thinking of Hwyn, before it dawned on me that he might mean himself. "I'd best go," he added, "or they'll be looking for me at home."

"You know where you can always find them, don't you," I said.

"The common paddock at night, of course," he said.

"I'll be there too," I said.

But the evening was like to turn me into a liar. As darkness gathered in the sapphire sky, Hwyn interrupted me along the winding path, Trenara trailing after her. "Will you come with me to the cave beyond the Assembly Stone?" she said. "I know it seems foolhardy to go into a grave at night, but with your Gift of Naming, I'll have less fear of the ghosts."

"I'll go with you," I said. "But why this hurry and secrecy? Don't you want to bring the priestess?"

"No," said Hwyn. "I have learned wonderful things from her, and yet I need to remember how to hear for myself. That voice that spoke to me in the darkness dwells there. Tonight there is no rite to prompt its speech, yet in a sense I have been living in the Rite of Increase ever since I first heard it, sleeping among the beasts, working the earth, studying the wild herbs of the mountain. Perhaps it is still waiting to speak to me again." She sighed. "And besides, that cave is the only private place in the valley."

"I'll come," I said. "But could we not leave Trenara in a safer place?"

"Where?" Hwyn said.

"With Ethwin," I said. "He is coming to the paddock in the hope of meeting her, and I think if we can slip away while they're together, he at least will ask no questions."

As luck would have it, Ethwin chose that moment to come bounding up the mountain path with Seeker at his side. When Trenara was sufficiently distracted—less by poor Ethwin than by the dog—we slipped away to the cave together.

Hwyn took my hand at the threshold of the cave and went in first, pulling me after. I skinned an elbow on the rough cool stone of the passageway, following her to a more open space. I smelled moisture, a buried stream somewhere deep in the mountain, but I saw nothing, the stubborn grip of Hwyn's four-fingered hand becoming all I perceived of the world.

Though I saw nothing, I knew plainly where the dead were: their ashes lay ahead of us in great clay urns, and their spirits hovered all around us, not all of them at peace. Nonetheless, I felt strangely in my element, holding Hwyn's hand in the dark, the turbulent spirits around us like the sea through which our boat was bound. "Peace to all here," I said softly, "and may the Hidden Goddess be gentle to all the dead of the Folc. But forgive me if I speak to one of the living in this holy place. Hwyn, has something happened to drive you to seek a sign?"

"No sudden calamity," she said, "and yet I am troubled. The grain and the flocks are not all that has increased. The Eye of Night has grown." She drew it out of its hiding place, and its light went out across the dim underground chamber.

I gasped and for some moments was distracted by my first sight of the chamber. Intricate carvings covered almost all the walls: a tall, graceful tree with the moon in its branches, which snaked and spiraled everywhere like reaching fingers. Its roots too became a fantastic tangle of branching paths over the whole lower half of the chamber. Only a row of fine clay urns broke the endless spirals of root and branch, and these too were painted with the Tree of the Moon. "Hidden Goddess!"

"May she be gentle with us," Hwyn completed the ritual invocation. "But yes: what splendor!" She touched the wall, her thin fingers following the carvings. "And how much I see of it! I swear I see better by the light of this stone than by daylight."

"That's not unlikely," I said. "It has a voice for you: why not a light as well?"

"Yes, its voice is much with me now," she said, "and I have come to love it, like a creature I have fed from my hand. I could not let it come to harm. I have come to love the Folc as well, but the time may be coming when I must choose between them and the Eye of Night."

"It's hatching?" I asked.

"Not yet. But it has swelled with life, and I think we have far to go to reach its proper place. The time will not be long, the voice said. We must not delay much longer. Or so I think; Halred has her own interpretation. I thought if I returned here, I might hear some clearer message. I could not come with Halred: she wants too badly for all signs to tell me to stay."

"But I, too, have wants," I said gently.

"I know, Jereth. But you call your wants your wants, not the will of the gods or the good of the Folc. You can help me do the same." She held the Eye of Night higher and called out, "Spirit that spoke to me in this place, whether you be ghost or god, we beg your friendship. If you have any more to say to me, I will listen."

We waited long in silence. All around me I seemed to feel the ghosts, too, awaiting an answer. But at length Hwyn shook her head. "It's no use. The moment of revelation is past: all that remains is the everyday confusion of thought and will and hope."

"Should we leave the cave, then?" I said.

"I'm afraid so," said Hwyn. "But thank you for coming with me."

As we emerged from the cave into the light of the waxing moon, I said, "What will we do now?"

"I don't know," Hwyn said. "I must wrestle with this."

"You don't want to leave, do you?"

"In the end, I don't think what I want is the question."

"Does it always have to be that way?"

She shrugged and said nothing.

"Hwyn!" Trenara rushed to embrace her. Following her path backward with my eye, I saw Ethwin coming out of a thicket. "Where were you?" he said. "Trenara was frightened without Hwyn."

Again I found myself looking to Hwyn for permission to reveal our secrets, but she was swallowed up in Trenara's long arms. I shrugged; we had trusted Ethwin with every secret so far, and never been betrayed. "We went to the cave—the Hall of the Dead."

He smirked, and my puzzlement must have shown on my face, because he said, "Don't you know how we use that cave?"

"For burials and rituals, I thought," I said.

"And for wedding nights, friend." He grinned.

I felt the blood rush to my face, but that would not be seen by moonlight. At any rate, we were coming to the paddock, where Halred stood waiting for us, Day and Night somewhere beyond her among the flocks. "There you are," Halred said. "I was afraid you would not come, Hwyn. Are we taxing you too hard, between work and study and nights with the flocks?"

"All the Folc work hard," Hwyn said. "That is nothing. And to study is a great gift, not a burden. Yet I need time to speak with Jereth about the journey we have postponed. And I think the journey must not be postponed much longer."

"Surely you will not leave now, when you have barely begun the good you could do in this land," Halred said.

"Not today or tomorrow," Hwyn said, "but soon. The oats and barley have grown apace, the sheep have grown—and the Eye of Night has grown. If I do not leave soon, I will not reach the North before it hatches. As the voice in the cave told me, 'The time will not be long.' I now see the warning in those words."

"But you also heard, 'I am nearer than you think,'" said Halred. "I have thought much of your prophecy, and I believe this valley is the goal of your journey, not some far-off land to the north. What you seek is nearer than you think. Surely the hand of one of the Four Great Ones steered you to the Hills of Penmorrin, and urged Ethwin to hunt on the mountain where he met you. What else could have brought you to this remote place where you had no thought to go? Why else would the thing you carry join so powerfully with our rites, rites you did not know, to heal our land? How else can you explain all that has happened?"

"I don't know," Hwyn said. "But I do hear the living creature inside the Eye of Night crying, urging me northward. I am nearer than you think, it says: nearer in time, I now believe. It says, I am nearer completion than you think: be ready for me. The time will not be long."

"That seems a finely cut quibble on *near*." Halred frowned.

Hwyn sighed. "I don't know. You may be right. I will ponder

it and pray over it. I went just now to the Hall of the Dead to listen for any further message, but none came."

"If the gods meant you to leave, would not the voice have
spoken again?" Halred said.

"I don't know," Hwyn said. "I don't know. It's not that I want
to leave, you understand." She sighed again. "Well, it will not be
the decision of one night. I may as well sleep now. Perhaps there
will be dreams."

The next morning, Halred surprised me on my way out of the
cow-byre. "I need to speak to you, Jereth," she said. "Where are
you bound this morning?"

"To the fields, for the harrowing," I said.

"Surely that can wait a little while you speak to me," she said,
and I nodded: the weeds, unlike the cows, could wait, and I
doubted my fellow-workers regarded me as much of a boon to
their efforts. I followed tamely to her little round house, where
she shared a breakfast of porridge with me and spoke her mind.

"Jereth, you know how much it has meant to the Folc to have
Hwyn among us," she said, "but I wonder whether you know
how good this place has been for Hwyn."

"I do know," I said. "She glows like a torch when she speaks
of the things she is learning. I knew as soon as you offered to
teach her that this was the best thing anyone had ever offered
her. I have not been with her long, but I know her life has been
hard; the world outside this valley has been harsh with her. I
know you have been kinder to her than she could ever have
asked, if she dared ask for anything for herself."

"It is not kindness," said Halred, much as I had. "Everyone
who teaches must dream of having such a student. I love Day
and Night dearly, and they are fine, quick-witted girls, but
Hwyn—Hwyn is something else entirely. You know that she
should be a priestess. It is a crime against the gods that no one
ever taught her till now. She may be old to begin, but she is making up for missed time quickly."

"I know," I said. "She is a marvel: no one need convince me
of that. I think I knew it before anyone did."

"But even she cannot take in a lifetime's training in a fortnight," Halred said. "On this bleak journey north, who will teach
her? How will she become all she is capable of becoming?"

"Good Mother," I said, "I see all this, and feel it more deeply than I can say. But if you think Hwyn's plan to move north began with me, you are mistaken. Hwyn leads and I follow. I know what a marvel she is, and I follow as the tide follows the moon."

"And yet I know you have much influence with her," Halred said.

"Do you?" I laughed. "I know no such thing."

"I know you have not been happy here," said Halred.

"The Folc have been kind to me," I said.

"That is not the same thing," she said, sensibly enough. "Your discontent weighs on her. But that can change. You will gradually feel more a part of the Folc. And you too have gifts you have never used. You were a priest once, in the Tarvon tradition, like Anlaf—but your vision is larger than his, perhaps too large to be confined in a single order. You might be sent to be the bridge between my ways and Anlaf's. You too could find a place for yourself here."

"Good Mother," I said, "you mistake me if you think I could be so vain as to put my own goals before Hwyn's. If I thought I stood between her and her true path—dear gods, I think I would take poison. What is my life beside her promise?" I stopped, astonished at what I had just admitted, breathless, confused, naked.

Halred touched my face gently, as she had during the Rite of Increase. "Jereth. I am sorry," she said. "I have touched a sore."

I raised an eyebrow. "Isn't that your professional duty?"

The corner of her mouth twitched as if she would have laughed, but her face was sad. "Hwyn is not the only one who has known little kindness," she mused.

"In truth, we are many," I said. "In my darker moods I think all the kindness in the world would hardly fill that bowl you measured blood in. I have found more of it here than in half a dozen great cities I once knew well. And yet you are right that I am ill at ease here; and yet it makes no difference at all. Hwyn has reasons beyond her happiness or mine for what she does. And my happiness is to follow her, wherever her mad vision leads us."

"I have misjudged you, then," Halred said. "I only hope she chooses the right path. I am sorry to have wounded you; in my zeal for your companion, I have not known you rightly. Come with us some afternoon; our circle should not be closed to you."

"I may," I said, though I doubted I would. "Thank you, Good Mother."

I stumbled to the grainfields half blind. I had looked forward to working beside Hwyn, to stealing a little time with her, but I found I could scarcely speak to her, crushed under the weight of what I had just admitted to Halred and to myself, filled to the mouth with all I could not tell her.

That evening Ethwin came again to look for Trenara. I pulled him aside to speak to him a little apart from the crowd. "You lament that you have never left the Hills of Penmorrin, that you may never leave," I said. "But what if there were reason to leave—a noble reason, a quest on which the life of the world may depend?"

He stared at me as blankly as Trenara for some moments. "Is this a game, or are you really asking me?"

"I am really asking you," I said. "Would you have the foolhardiness to leave everything you love behind?"

"Everything?" he echoed. "Trenara?"

"She is safer here," I said. "So is Hwyn. Consider carefully: it is no small thing to leave your heart behind." I thought I saw a resolution forming in his eyes, but I judged the time not ripe. "Speak of it tomorrow," I said. "Now I am going to seek out Hwyn; if you want to look for Trenara, I will be glad of your company along the way."

And so the young hunter and I walked together, following Seeker up the path to the common paddock under a fast-swelling silver moon. But we did not speak, each lost in our own inner storm. When we reached the paddock, Hwyn and Trenara were with Halred and her acolytes, and we could not tease apart that skein to speak to either woman alone.

The next morning in the fields, I seized a moment to ask Hwyn, "Can you meet me later to speak in private?"

She straightened, wiping sweat out of her eyes. "There is but one private place in this valley," she said softly. "Meet me outside it when you are done with the milking. I too long to speak with you alone."

Then we had much work to do under the high sun, and little breath to spare for talk. But now and again, Hwyn would raise her head and look around, straining her weak eyes to find me among the workers.

At night, as I strode along the climbing path toward the Assembly Stone and the Hall of the Dead, Seeker came bounding up past me and I turned to greet Ethwin as he overtook me.

"Well met, friend," I said. "But I must speak with Hwyn alone tonight; you will not taken it amiss?"

"Not at all," he said, seeming to brighten.

"Have you thought about your decision?"

"I am almost resolved," he said. "Can I have until to-morrow?"

"Till the day after," I said.

The two women were waiting for us behind the Assembly Stone. Trenara ran out to greet us, disappearing once more after Seeker, with Ethwin following, leaving Hwyn and me free to slip into the cavern together.

Again Hwyn gripped my hand as we went into the dark, and the familiar pressure of her fingers made my heart ache for what I had resolved to say. "Hwyn, do you still feel the Eye of Night crying to move on?"

"Nothing is clear," she said. "Nothing gives me firm ground to stand on and argue with Halred why I should leave here. And yet in my heart I know what I must do."

"There may be another way," I said. "You have a purpose here, a place as priestess and healer, as I believe you should always have been. But I do nothing here but the chores the smallest child can scarcely spoil. Let me take the Eye of Night on its journey. If I lack your gift for understanding it, still I can at least follow the stars north. Perhaps before the end it will learn to speak to me. Ethwin may come with me, I think: he chafes under his father's rule, and longs for strange places and adventures. He will not be a bad companion. And you can stay here, loved and honored, knowing you have abandoned neither your task nor your calling."

I could see nothing in the lightless chamber, but as I spoke, I felt her fingers tighten around my hand, then release it.

"Jereth," she said, "why do you say this? Do you want to part company?"

"I don't think what I want is the question," I spoke her words back to her.

She was silent a long while.

"If the question still needs answering," I said, "the answer is no."

"Nor do I," she said. "We will leave, and it will be together. Tomorrow we will say our farewells, and the next day we will leave."

"Are you sure?" I said. "If you do belong here, do not let me sway you from your true path. I swore to Halred that I would never do such a thing—"

"To Halred?" Hwyn seized the phrase. "When did she draw this promise from you?"

I said, "She spoke to me yesterday; she thought I had been pestering you to leave. She sees great promise in you, as I do; thank the gods someone sees it who can nurture it well. Let me give you this gift: let me give you yourself. It pains me to see you torn between your journey and your true name, your true soul."

But Hwyn said, "You have already given me myself, and I think you will again and again along the road we travel together. Halred has no right to say my true name is here. She does not know my name, and if I shouted it to her, she would not hear it over the name she wants to give me. And I, too unused to kindness, have let her drown out my name, and the call that is mine alone, with her teachings. How rightly she warned me when I first came here that the hand of a teacher might lie too heavily on me to let me hear my own call! How well she knew herself then, and how foolish I was not to heed her while she still saw clearly!

"My true name brought me to this journey," she said. "Though I may look back with longing on Folcsted, I do not really want anyone to take up my quest in my place—the quest that called me by name, by my true name, from the waters of the sacred pool. I am my journey: you call me back to myself. If I am sorry to leave here, it is only because I cannot live two lives at once: one here, as Hwyn the Priestess, and one on the road north, as—as myself."

"Are you certain?" I said, hardly daring to breathe.

"Never more so," she said. "Come, let us tell Halred we must go."

She led me out of the stone chamber. I felt the presence of the dead and fancied I heard voices—not words, but small sighs only. When we reached the open air and the rising moon, we found Seeker standing guard outside the cave, but Ethwin and Trenara were nowhere to be seen.

"Where can they be?" Hwyn said, peering behind the Assembly Stone.

I had my suspicions, but did not speak of them. Nor did I need to: as we stood pondering, Trenara and Ethwin emerged from the same gateway we had just passed through, a suspiciously musky scent lingering about them both. Her face was unreadable as ever, his full of wonder. Poor boy, I thought, whether he stays here or comes with us, he will break his heart on Trenara like a hull on the insensible rocks. Seeker leapt up at the sight of them, and Trenara, laughing, bounded off with the black dog, Ethwin following as best he could, as Hwyn and I trudged behind.

"How did they enter the cave without our hearing them?" I said.

But Hwyn did not answer, troubled in a different way. "He is not the innocent I thought," she said. "I should never have left them alone together."

"Why?" I said. "He loves her, and if her feelings are less clear, she at least enjoys his attention. What's the harm in it?"

Hwyn looked at me curiously. "For someone who almost vowed celibacy, you take a remarkably benign view of others' yielding to temptation."

"I'm not such a hypocrite as to judge Trenara," I said. "I was never half so beset with that sort of temptation as she is. Besides, when I looked forward to a life of celibacy, I promised myself all sorts of intellectual pleasures to make up for the physical ones I'd miss. Trenara can't have those, and I can't find it in my heart to frown on one of the few pleasures she has."

"But this pleasure can harm her," Hwyn said, and at my blank look added, "Oh, you're a man—you don't think of these things. Listen: Trenara miscarried a child last year on a rough stretch of road. At first, I didn't even know what was happening. She bled oceans, till I thought she'd die. It scared me to death. I hadn't the least idea what to do about it; no one ever taught me those woman's things. I hadn't even noticed that she was with child. I suppose the hard road must have shaken it out of her somehow, and the gods know we have some very hard roads ahead. Ethwin means well, I know, but his loving could kill her. Unless—do you think he would actually marry her and keep her here?"

"I think *he* would in a heartbeat," I said. "Do you think she would stay?"

"I don't know," Hwyn said. "She seems happy here. And yet there's a restlessness in her."

"And she loves you," I said.

"I suppose so," Hwyn conceded. "Sometimes I wish she did not."

When we reached the common paddock, we found Halred haranguing a shamefaced Ethwin for taking advantage of a simpleton. The simpleton in question sat bewildered in the grass, her arms around Seeker. Night and Day tactfully kept their distance.

"But I will marry her," Ethwin was protesting as we arrived.

"Oh, Ethwin, do you think she even knows what you mean when you say that? How can you exchange promises with her, or expect her to keep a promise? You saw how she fared with the oath at the Assembly." Halred looked up from her tirade to see us awkwardly standing by, awaiting our chance to speak. "Ah! There you are at last. Night is passing: already the moon is far above the horizon."

"And the moon is waxing," Hwyn said. "Tomorrow it will be full, and the next morning," she said slowly, "we must go. I am sorry."

"Ethwin," Halred said, "go home now; I must speak to them in peace." With many glances over his shoulder, Ethwin left us, Seeker bounding behind him. When he was too far off to overhear, Halred asked Hwyn, "What is it? Have any new signs come to you?"

"Nothing like a stroke of thunder, nor even like the voice in the cave," Hwyn said, "but I know in my heart of hearts, as I knew where to seek the Eye of Night, that I must not delay its journey much longer."

Halred turned toward me with a stung look. "If after all you told me, you have prevailed on Hwyn to leave—"

"No," Hwyn said, "far from it. He urged me to stay with you and complete the training we began, but his urging only made me hear more clearly the voice calling me onward. I always knew this was not my destination."

"I will not believe it. I studied the signs carefully," Halred said. "You belong among us. I know this land, these people, and I have seen many strangers come and go in my life, and none, not even Paddon, became so easily part of the Folc as you. I cannot believe you came here by chance, a mere diversion from your journey."

"Perhaps it was no accident. Perhaps the gods sent us here, one of their unexplained acts of mercy," Hwyn said. "Nonetheless, it does not follow that they meant us to stay forever."

"Forever is a long time. But your work here is scarcely begun," Halred said. "You may not understand all you have sown here. It is not only the land's bounty that has increased, but our own open-handedness. While you lie among the flocks to bless them, they are kept in the common paddock as one flock; had you not begun working in the fields, they too would be partitioned. You have helped revive the generous old ways. If only you stay till harvest, the Folc will have time to become used to these ways, and the old customs will take root again. No one will go hungry while another has food to spare. But if you leave so soon, all this will be forgotten."

"I have gone hungry in sight of plenty, and I know how much you stand to lose," said Hwyn. "But you, as priestess, can best see that this season of wonders is not forgotten. I dare not stay to remind them. The Rite of Increase itself has hastened the day of hatching; I must go now and find the place."

"Don't you see? This is the place!" Halred cried. "You said yourself that the Eye of Night had never increased the yield of the land in any other place. The Eye of Night belongs here; this is where it will come to birth."

"You don't know what you're calling down on your land," said Hwyn. "Not for nothing is the Raven's Egg feared. The land of its birth must suffer the pains of birth."

"We are strong enough for it," Halred said. "Who has borne greater suffering than we have?"

Hwyn shook her head. "The well of suffering is bottomless; do not be too quick to claim you have drained it. I know this is not the place."

Halred's mouth tightened a moment. Then she sighed, "If there is nothing I can say to persuade you, I may as well let you sleep. You will have a hard journey the day after tomorrow; you will need all your strength to cross the mountains. I will meditate into the night, and pray that we all see clearer in the morning."

I went home to the house of the Red Oak Clan, dark and silent under moonlight, and was startled by a movement under the eaves: Guthlac pacing uneasily back and forth across the doorway like a dog across the sheepfold gate. "You're up late, cousin," he said.

"And you, my Lord of the Red Oak," I said.

"There's something restless in the land tonight," he said. "You may laugh, but I feel it in the soles of my feet. I felt it when the first of the lean years began, and again when you and your friends appeared at our Assembly. And I feel it now."

"We must leave," I said, "the morning after tomorrow."

"Ah, of course," he said, "This—this time of wonders could not last long. Well, my mystery is solved, and I will try to sleep now. So should you, traveler." I followed him into the dark hall. "We will miss you," he added softly.

"We will never forget your welcome," I said, and then was silent, lest I wake the sleepers all around.

10

THE ENTRAILS
OF THE MOUNTAIN

The next day passed quickly in work and in farewells as word spread among the Folc that we would leave the following morning. Even those we scarcely knew paused in the day's work to lament our parting or wish us well on the road ahead. A farewell celebration was hastily thrown together for the evening, with hymns of thanks, spiced ale from the Linden Clan's stores, and song and dance. It was to begin at the lakeside, drift to each clan's house in turn, and end in a grand procession to the common paddock where we would spend a last night with the flock.

Though we knew we would need sleep before our journey, we never wanted to let the festival end. The Folc's love of song was at its height and we, sure that we would not easily find such a spring of music again, drank it in thirstily. But another kind of drink silenced us at last; dizzy and drowsy with spiced ale, we lay down by the beasts, grateful for the steadiness of the earth and hopeful that our turn to watch would not come too soon.

It never came. It puzzled me to wake to the morning rain and find that the sheep had already been driven away; only the priestess, her acolytes, and my companions remained. But this did not trouble me much; I guessed that a kind conspiracy of the Folc must have plotted to let us sleep and gather our strength for the road.

Seeing Hwyn sprawled near me, still sleeping despite the rain, I reached to touch her shoulder. "Hwyn, it's daylight," I said. "The morning after the full moon. Time to travel on."

One eye half opened lazily, and I almost laughed at the sight. Then Hwyn's hand flew to her chest; she gasped, and sprang to her feet. "Sky-Raven's Bones!" she cried. "It's gone!"

"What?"

"The Eye of Night is gone," she said.

Suddenly I noticed that Halred had been watching us from a little distance away, her face expectant but calm. As I looked her full in the face, she said in warm tones, "What seems to be the matter?"

There was something too innocent in that question; she had been standing near enough to hear Hwyn cry out. Hwyn seemed to feel it, too. She fixed her eye on Halred and said, "Where is the Eye of Night?"

"What do you mean?" said Halred, a touch too calmly.

"It was in my pocket when I went to sleep," Hwyn said.

"Are you saying it is not now?" said Halred.

"If anyone came near me in the night, if anyone else knew where I kept it, please, tell me now," said Hwyn. "I don't like what I must conclude otherwise."

"You're overwrought," Halred said. "You don't know what you're saying. The stone must have slipped deeper into your clothing, or you put it in another pocket, and now, in the anxiety of parting, in your uncertainty whether you do right, you imagine it is gone. Look again."

"Did you think I could believe that?" said Hwyn. "Did you think I might not notice, even for one waking moment, that the Raven's Egg had been taken from me? Even my dreams cried out. Why did I sleep so heavily? Did you know that I had not slept an unbroken night since I first touched it? What drug did you mix in that last cup of spiced ale we drank just before we slept?"

"How dare you!" Day started toward her, hands clenched. I jumped up to stand by Hwyn's side, putting a protective arm between her and the acolyte. Trenara, last to wake as usual, raised her head from the ground, saw us braced for a fight, and started to cry.

Halred held up her hand to check her acolyte's movement. "Peace now. There's no need for hasty actions. Hwyn, if you are sure the talisman is missing, then I can well understand your suspicion, but it is misdirected. Search me, if you doubt my word."

"It is not on your person," said Hwyn. "If it were, I would know."

"Well, then," said Halred, "you do not have it, and you know I do not. But we know the land still blooms and the flocks you slept among still flourish. I would say, then, that the Eye of Night has not left us: it has gone into the land, become part of all these living things. The end of your quest has come: the Eye of Night has reached its destination, awakened to its new life."

"No," said Hwyn.

"What makes you so certain it cannot be?" said Halred.

"I know what I know," said Hwyn. "You yourself said I have my own way of knowing; when did you stop believing it?"

"Your knowledge is still young," said Halred. "I am doing my best to guide you."

Hwyn shook her head. "Good Mother, I understand well why you would do what you must have done. Neither of us could be sure what would happen to this blooming land, these flourishing fields, when the Eye of Night left. But I know the Eye of Night better than you do, and I can promise you one thing: if you imprison it, you will pay the price in tears of blood. A fortnight's prosperity must seem little after three years' anxiety, but it came to you freely and must be yielded as freely as it was given. Hoard it, and you hoard your own destruction."

"You underestimate the blessing you have brought to this land," said Halred. "You said once that the Eye of Night was a living thing waiting to be born. I doubted you at the time, but now I see it is true. Look around you now! All is being reborn: the land, the flocks, the customs of the Folc, and you yourself, growing toward your rightful place as a priestess among us."

"No," Hwyn said again. "This is not the place that calls me by name. Tell me what you have done with the Eye of Night and let me go, for your own people's sake, if not for ours."

"What do you know of the good of my people?" said Halred.

"I know what I brought among you, which you dared not even name before them. I know its power."

"You are still green in the ways of power," said Halred. "You will learn better—"

"I am not so green as you claim—and you once knew this; you said you would not only teach me but learn from me. How, then, can you treat me like a fool at a festival, to be distracted with sweet stories while my pocket is picked?"

Halred drew herself up to her full height, towering over Hwyn. "I took you in when you had nothing and made the Folc accept you. I shared my home and food with you. I healed your friend of his wounds and began teaching you the lore no one had bothered to teach you before. What have I done to deserve your distrust?"

Hwyn was silent a while. "We owe you more than we can re-pay," she said. "It pains me to distrust you again, after having trusted you more than anyone but Jereth. If I have accused you wrongly, I am more sorry than I can say. But you must admit that appearances are against you. Only you knew where I kept the Eye of Night; only you and your acolytes were with us when we woke. You could easily have drugged us—and we were certainly drugged, to sleep through the taking of the Raven's Egg and the driving out of the flocks. Your motive for taking the Eye of Night is all too strong—a noble motive, one that might well soothe a tender conscience over such a small matter as a few words not true by worldly standards.

"I cannot be sure that your love for truth is as strong as your love for your people," Hwyn said. "But I can trust your devotion to the goddesses you serve. If you swear by the Bright Goddess and the Hidden Goddess that you had nothing to do with the Eye of Night's disappearance, neither taking it nor helping another to take it, I will retract my words with humblest apologies and beg your counsel to find it again."

It was some time before Halred spoke; but when she did, it was in a voice as hard as the bones of the mountain. "I asked no oath of you when you first told me your story."

"And I told you no lies," said Hwyn. "Nor do I lie now: the Eye of Night will leave here, whether by my hand or another's. Even if it is bound by necromancy—even if I die trying to un-bind it—this land cannot hold it. And better for you and this land if I bring it away before it feels the walls of its prison."

She swept past Halred, and Trenara followed, tears running down her face. I followed too, but not before I had seen the stricken look on Halred's face, as though she might almost have called Hwyn back. She did not, however, come after us.

When we had passed beyond earshot of the sheepfold, rain pouring down on us like Trenara's tears, Hwyn said, "Dear gods, this is the last thing I expected. And with this rain, I can scarcely trace the path she must have taken. What can I do now?"

"You found the Eye of Night once, though it was hidden be-neath a stronghold. You freed it though it was tangled in the bonds of necromancy," I said. "You will free it again."

"Will I?" said Hwyn. "Will it not think I have abandoned it, and abandon me in turn?"

"Where should we look?" I said. We were instinctively moving downhill toward the fields, but that was only habit.

"To tell you the truth," said Hwyn, "what frightens me most that I ought to sense its presence, as I sensed it from afar when journeyed toward Kelgarran Hall—but I do not. Oh, gods! Do you think—you don't think she's telling the truth, and it really as gone into the land? Have I accused her unjustly?"

"Do you believe that?" I countered.

Hwyn stopped in her tracks and shut her eyes for a second. Not really. It—it's a beautiful story, yet it doesn't ring true. But can bring no firmer reason against it than that."

"Did you have a firmer reason to look under Kelgarran Hall or the Eye of Night?" I said.

"Well, I—I knew the House of Kelgarran had long been powerful, more powerful than seemed quite right. But there are many owerful houses. No, it was all dreams and the shadows of reams, promptings from a source I could not name."

"Well, then," I said.

"You mean I should trust those inner promptings again," she aid. "But at the moment they lead nowhere."

"Be patient," I said. "It must be a shock, losing the Eye of ight. Your senses may need time to recover."

She nodded, and was silent.

"To answer your question," I said, "no, I did not think Halred might be telling the truth. She looked ill at ease, like someone ho dislikes lying but is trying desperately to brazen it out. And he has, as you say, too strong a motive to put this story forard."

"She does," said Hwyn. "Why was I so trusting?"

I smiled. "In the last stage of our journey, you rebuked yourelf for being too slow to trust. It's not easy. Is there anyone we an still trust to help us?"

"Ethwin and Paddon—I think," said Hwyn. "But Ethwin will e away in the wilds now, impossible to find. And I would hate to ake Paddon our first ally. He's a foreigner here, as we are. If he Folc doubt his loyalty, he may lose yet another home."

"Guthlac will be in the high pastures by now," I said. "But hen he comes back, I think I would trust him. He could charge lalred before the Assembly."

Hwyn shook her head. "Halred is two of the nine voices in

the Assembly—and she's too good at swaying others to her side
Remember how easily she gathered supporters when we firs
came here? Besides, even those that disagree with her may mak
trouble for us when they find out I'm the Night-Bearer. Nc
Jereth, I'm not bringing this before the Assembly if I can help it
Whatever the Folc may say, the Eye of Night must leave here—
and every instant that it is imprisoned risks all their safety."

"All right, then," I said. "So it's up to us. Where would yoı
put the Eye of Night if you'd stolen it to make the land fertile
Bury it in the fields?"

"If it's only that, I'll be relieved," said Hwyn. "She'd have
hard time keeping any sort of necromantic circle undisturbed iı
the furrows. If it's there, we can dig it up and leave."

"Good. We may as well look, then," I said. We started down
hill, skidding on mud as the rain coursed down over us. "It was
clear night," I grumbled. "Where did the rain come from?"

"It rained after the Rite of Increase," Hwyn reminded me.

"The water in the darkness," I mused. "The Eye of Nigh
must have power over water. You don't think she dropped it iı
the lake, do you?"

"No. Then she'd lose control of it forever—unless she know
some way to dredge it up off the bottom," Hwyn said.

"I'm a pretty fair swimmer, but I couldn't see myself fishing
up a stone from the lake-bottom mud," I said. "If it were in th
lake, it would have gone into the land—or at least the water—fo
good. And I have a hunch you're right: Halred would not want
so irrevocably out of her hands."

"Buried in the earth would be better," Hwyn mused. "Yoı
could always dig it up again if you wanted its power somewher
else—or if you realized that crazy little woman was right afte
all, and it didn't belong. I hope it's there. Can you see the field
from here? Is anything out of the ordinary?"

"It's raining too hard to see clearly," I said. "Besides, th
other changes didn't happen at once. It might take another nigh
to manifest itself in the land."

"I suppose so," Hwyn said. "Still, it nags at me that I don'
have any sense that the Eye of Night is nearer than it was whe
we started."

"Do you think we're going the wrong way?" I said.

"It's not that I have a sense of moving away from it," she said
"I just don't sense it anywhere, as though it were in anothe

world. It's frustrating, like losing my eyesight all over again. The only power I can feel anymore is that constant air of strangeness from the mountain itself, from the Hall of the Dead." She stopped suddenly. "Jereth, what a fool I've been!"

"It's there," I finished for her. "The ghostliness of the cave is masking the Eye of Night's own ghostliness."

"It must be," said Hwyn. We reversed course and began struggling back up the muddy slope. "Upright God defend us! That cave is the likeliest place for necromancy in all Penmorrin."

"But you've foiled necromancy before," I reminded her. "You'll prevail."

"I'm not so sure of that," she said. "You don't know what it took to free the Eye of Night from Lord Dannoth's spells. It was a near thing, and I'm not sure I could do it twice. And the danger! Even if she's used no binding circles, I'm not sure what the Eye of Night will do to the ghosts we both sensed in that cave. It's too great a risk for all three of us. You'd better take Trenara to a safe place and wait for me."

"No," I said. "Rather, you guard Trenara while I go. With the Gift of Naming, I can keep the ghosts from harming me, even make them tell me where the Eye is hidden. And I hope you trust me by now not to hoard the Eye of Night for myself when I find it."

"I do trust you," said Hwyn, "but this is *my* task. I am bound to the Raven's Egg. It knows me, and I hope it still trusts me. And its absence is like a hole in my heart. I want to go. I must go."

"Very well," I said, "but not alone. I will go with you to speak to the ghosts."

"Then who will guard Trenara? We have lost our chief friend in this place."

"Who will blame Trenara for what we have done?" I said. "She's probably safer without us. And we have not lost all our friends."

"The herdsmen and Ethwin are far off—"

"But Girnhild will be in her kitchen," I said. "Can't we trust her?"

Hwyn considered. "I think so. All right."

When we burst into the kitchen of the Red Oak house, Girnhild and Godrun were stirring a pot of lukewarm milk and rennet over the hearth to start a cheese, while Wylf sat at the churn and a little band of children played on the floor. But at the sight of us—Hwyn panting with exertion, Trenara weeping—the children stared and pointed, the old woman jumped up, Godrun put a hand to her mouth, and Girnhild whirled around, spoon in hand, scattering drops of milk all over. "What's happened? What's the matter?"

"My Lady Girnhild," said Hwyn, "I scarcely know where to begin. I must ask you to trust us in a very strange matter, and if our places were reversed, I'm not at all sure I would be inclined to trust."

"Don't make a long story of it," said Girnhild. "Tell me, and I'll see."

"The thing I carried with me into the Hills of Penmorrin, the thing that has brought healing to this land, was taken from me in the night," Hwyn said.

"What thing? Tell me plainly," Girnhild said.

"The Sky-Raven's Egg," said Hwyn, "the Eye of Night."

"Gods on the Wheel!" cried Godrun; the other two women simply stared, eyes wide, mouths open. Only the children and Trenara, who had joined them playing on the floor, showed no signs of alarm.

"I swear by all the gods that I mean no harm to this land or to any of the Folc," said Hwyn. "I'm sorry I kept this secret from you, but it was not from malice. There are dark legends about the Sky-Raven's Egg in this country, and when I showed it to Halred she warned me not to speak of it. When the wonders began, I told two others what I carried, but not where I kept it. I would have spoken of it in the Assembly, but Halred silenced me."

"And now she has it?" Girnhild guessed.

"Not on her person," Hwyn said. "But I suspect she has hidden it—probably in the Hall of the Dead."

"This grows worse and worse," said Girnhild.

"What will you do?" said Wylf. "Pour out the ashes of our ancestors to search for the—the thing you have lost?"

Hwyn stood silent a moment, as if daunted by the image. "I hope it does not come to that," she said at last. "I have come to love this land, these people. It would grieve me to do you any dishonor. But I will do what must be done to free the Sky-Raven's Egg. It is a living thing with needs of its own, and today it needs to move onward."

"And this thing—the Sky-Raven's Egg—this is what brought new life to our land?" Girnhild said. "I thought it was supposed to bring the world's end."

"It may, if it is not set free," Hwyn said. "It is not evil, as some would have it, but it does not bear imprisonment meekly."

"I scarcely know what to tell you," Girnhild said. "We could bring this before the Assembly—"

"I would rather act now, before the Raven's Egg feels itself caged," Hwyn said. "But I must see to Trenara's safety. She is used to traveling with me, but I cannot take her into a lair of ghosts to wrestle with forces as great as the world. And unless I am utterly mad, it is the world at stake here. So I have come to ask you to guard Trenara while Jereth and I seek the Sky-Raven's Egg—and to give her a home if we don't survive.

"I know how extravagant my request is," Hwyn continued. "I am asking you to take the word of a stranger against your own priestess and the legends of your people and common sense itself."

"Not against common sense," said Wylf. "I have known Halred for good and ill all her life. She is a kind healer and a wise priestess, but the love of power is strong in her; she holds two of the nine voices in the Assembly, and sways as many of the rest as she can. And you brought a thing of great power, a temptation greater than any she had seen before. No, my girl, it makes all too much sense. She would not let so much power slip away." Wylf sighed. "I don't like it, but I believe you."

"It *is* like her, I grant you," said Girnhild, "and however strange it is, your story rings true. Such power to heal in a healer's hands is a great temptation. And yet—who were the two others, the ones who heard of the Raven's Egg but did not see it?"

"Paddon and Ethwin," I said.

"Ah," Girnhild mused, "Paddon would not want to touch the uncanny thing, and Ethwin is too open-handed to keep it to himself. I'm afraid we are left with Halred—and the Hall of the Dead." She fixed Hwyn with a stern look. "What will happen when you take the Raven's Egg out of its hiding place—and out of this land? Will all we have gained be lost? Will the tomb of our ancestors crumble?"

"I wish I knew," Hwyn said. "But I am as sure as I can be of anything that if I don't take it away, we will all suffer for it. For days the Raven's Egg had been crying to leave, till I dared not ignore it. Now it has been taken by force, perhaps imprisoned, spellbound. I first found it in a hall where it had been spellbound thirty years; when I took it away, the hall crumbled and its lord died in agony. If I take it soon enough, if it does not become cankered in the heart of the mountain, much suffering may be saved. Or it may not. I wish I knew," she said again.

"I confess I don't like inviting an outlander to search our tomb," Girnhild said. "Can no one else bring the Raven's Egg out of hiding?"

"If I fail, I hope someone else can do it," said Hwyn. "But the attempt will be perilous. I at least have done something like this before, and Jereth has the Gift of Naming, so our chances are best—unless the one who hid it undoes her bindings willingly."

Girnhild frowned for a moment. Then she said, "Go, then, and the gods go with you. Let Trenara stay with Godrun and the children; I will escort you at least to the mouth of the cave, lest any try to bar your entrance."

"Thank you," said Hwyn, "and may the gods reward you."

"Gods grant I have chosen right," said Girnhild. "Let's go, before I change my mind."

We were not out the door before Trenara, who had been playing with a puppy in the midst of a knot of children, noticed that Hwyn was leaving her. Abandoning the dog, she rushed at Hwyn, weeping, and flung her arms around her: "Don't leave me!"

"Hush, Trenara," Hwyn said, pushing her back. "You'll be safe here. You can't come with us; I couldn't protect you there. I'll be back soon. Stay here just a little while with these good people and the puppy. It won't be long."

Godrun scooped up the puppy in one arm, despite the protests of the children, and brought it to Trenara, putting her other arm around Trenara's waist. It was a clever ploy, the sort of thing I would once have used to distract my little brother and sister, but it was not enough. In the end, it was only with some force that Hwyn detached herself to leave.

"I'm sorry, Trenara," she said, almost in tears herself. "Forgive me. It will not be long."

Girnhild took a moment to shake her finger at the puppy— chiding, "Who brought that filthy creature into my kitchen?"— before shepherding us out toward the Hall of the Dead. The rain continued weeping down on us, the mud squelching under our feet as we trudged silently to the cave.

Beyond the Assembly Stone, Girnhild stopped short with a cry of surprise: "Edwach! What are you doing away from your flock? And Drict, why are you standing here like a stone?"

"Mother Halred set us to guard the tomb," Drict said.

"Guard it! When has it ever needed guarding?" said Girnhild. "And Edwach, when have you and Halred ever agreed on anything?"

"We agree that increase is better than blight; that is only common sense," Edwach said. "She said the travelers had gone mad, that they would steal the holy things from the Hall of the Dead, breaking our hard-won prosperity."

"The travelers brought that prosperity," said Girnhild. "Don't meddle in things you don't understand. Halred is using you."

"Would you let them plunder our ancestors' grave?" said Drict.

"I would let them take away what they brought," said Girnhild. "You know they brought something; do you know what it is? And if you do not, don't be so quick to judge what they do with it. They say it will turn against us if we hold it too long, and I think they know it better than Mother Halred does, having traveled with it. Let them pass, by order of the Headman."

"Ha! Guthlac is in the far pastures," said Edwach.

"Do you think he will gainsay me when he comes down?" said Girnhild coolly.

Neither man said he would, but neither showed any sign of moving from the entrance, till suddenly the mountain shook itself like a wet dog and an inhuman moaning came from inside the cave.

"Gods preserve us," Hwyn said, "it's begun."

"Come on, then," I cried. Drict and Edwach had stumbled away from the entrance; before they could regain their balance, I took Hwyn's hand and leapt into the darkness.

The heart of the mountain was beating hard, a deep drumming that I almost felt rather than heard, stirring the stone floor of the cave. I took a few shuddering steps forward, then did not have time to cry a warning when I found myself plummeting through empty space, deep into the mountain, Hwyn's hand still clutched in mine.

The shock of finding the ground missing beneath us was nothing beside the wonder of landing on my feet, breathless but unhurt. I looked all around me, but could see nothing; the light of the cave mouth was gone. "Are you all right?" I panted.

"I think so," Hwyn said. "Unless, of course, that sudden fall was death, and we're now two of the ghosts of the cave."

"I can reassure you on that point," I said. "Your very corporeal fingernails are digging into my hand."

"Sorry!" Hwyn said, and began to unclench her grip.

"Don't take your hand away," I said, "or I'll be lost in the dark. What happened to us?"

"Tremors in the earth," said Hwyn. "One of the signs of the Troubles. I hope Halred felt it."

"That was no earthquake," I said. "I've never been known to fall like a cat with my feet firmly under me."

"What do you mean?" said Hwyn.

"I don't think we've fallen at all. At least, not in the normal sense of the word."

"So it wasn't the stone that gave way," Hwyn said, "but reality itself."

"Fortunately for us," I said. "If we'd lost the light in a rockslide, we'd be waiting to suffocate or die of thirst."

"If this were a rockslide," Hwyn countered, "I'd be afraid for our lives—but not for the world."

There was not much to be said to that. "Which way shall we go?"

"Forward?" she said.

"Why not?"

But a mere step forward brought us to a solid wall where no wall had been. If we'd had any lingering belief in a rockslide, the wall would have been enough to obliterate it. The stone surface beneath my hands could not have come about by accident: it was too regular, too unbroken to have been formed by falling rocks. The rough surface under my hands was covered with curving grooves and clusters of bumps and dents that seemed to form some pattern. "The walls are carved, I think."

"Yes," Hwyn said, running her hands across them. "Grapevines, like the wall of a vintner's shop. See?" she put my hand on one of the clusters. "Grapes."

"If you say so," I said.

"If only I had the Eye of Night to light our way!" she said.

"If you had the Eye of Night," I said, "there'd be no need to be here at all. But shall we go onward?"

"All right," she said, tugging my hand. "This way."

We inched along for what seemed hours, the curving grooves under our hands offering no clear landmark to track our progress. At last a grayness grew to my left, beyond Hwyn; we shuffled toward it a little more rapidly. As the light grew, something in the air disturbed me.

"Do you smell something?" I said. "Something in the air smells wrong."

"It doesn't smell like outside," Hwyn said. "No flowers, no hay. Probably a shaft in the stone, far from the open air, or a chamber with a lamp."

When we reached the mouth of the tunnel, the light blinded us for a moment. We stood blinking and rubbing our eyes before we opened them to find ourselves standing out on the hillside, the Assembly Stone before us. Blood ran down the stone, lurid in the light of a huge red sun. But this sight was not what most disturbed me.

"Do you see?" I asked Hwyn, afraid to put into words what I saw, lest I make it real.

"Why is the land black?" she said.

"It looks scorched, burned to the roots," I said. "There's no grass, no crops, no living trees as far as the eye can see. Could fire have consumed the land so utterly in the little time since we were last here?"

"You have not been here before," said a voice behind me.

We turned as one, glad to take our eyes from the charred land even for the sight of a gaunt, rangy ghost with the startlingly light eyes of the Folc, a river of blood streaming from his slashed throat.

"Where are we?" said Hwyn. "Isn't this Folcsted?"

"Did you blunder in here without having heard of the Entrails of the Mountain, the Paths of Mystery?" laughed the ghost. He looked a little like Guthlac, a big rugged man in a red tunic. A hammered-gold oak leaf, stained with blood, hung from a leather thong about his neck.

"Dirnlac of the Red Oak," I said, "we are strangers in this land. Answer us clearer than that: by your name I charge you to speak."

"Find your own true name, half-Tarvon. How did you ever come into *that* order?" grumbled Dirnlac. Nonetheless, he answered as he was bound: "The Entrails of the Mountain wind through the dreams of the dead and the living, the deep night-thoughts that catch hold of us and will not release us. The initiates of the Hidden Goddess can open these paths at will. To others, in the normal order of things, they are closed. But on the darkest day of the year, others may enter these paths. Some stumble in like fools and are protected in their simplicity. And others, neither quite fools nor quite wise, may wander confused, trapped in their own imaginings."

"Are we not still in Folcsted on St. Arin's Lake?" I said.

"You are and are not. You are in its dreams," Dirnlac said.

"Why are you here?" I asked, curious after all I had heard. "You died three hundred years ago, before the Red Oak Clan lived in this valley. This was not your home."

"True, this was not my valley," said the ghost, and pointed past us to the gateway in the mountain and the Assembly Stone beyond it. "But I died on that stone.

"Times were hard among my people then, and some of our young men were caught raiding livestock from the Valley of the Linden. The Headman of the Linden sent a message to me, as Headman of the Red Oak, that unless we gave him two goats for every one the boys had tried to lead away, he would cut their throats like beasts for the slaughter.

"If we had given him what he demanded, we would not have had even a breeding pair left, and my people would have starved. So I brought my message back: a Headman's life is worth a herd of goats.

"It was not a true sacrifice: the Rite of Increase requires a willing victim sprung from the land, not a prisoner from over the mountain. And yet it was true sacrifice, for I handed myself over in exchange for my people. My blood marked the Assembly Stone for years, and the Folc of the Linden feared to gather here. Their land did not increase, and the one who ate my heart sickened on it, but my people survived and grew strong in their hardship. And I remain here in the Entrails of the Mountain, in this image of the valley where I died, unable to leave, pinioned between hatred and love."

"Will you ever break that deadlock?" I said.

"I await some deliverance that is scarcely a shadow of a dream in this place of dreams. But my plight is not what you came to learn."

"No," I said softly, "but your story moves me. May the gods send you your deliverance! But first tell me: is the Eye of Night here?"

The ghost's eyes widened. "Who are you that ask of the Eye of Night?"

"You haven't answered my question. Do you know where it is? Much depends on our finding it."

"Much indeed," said the ghost. "It is not in my private labyrinth of hate and love, linden and oak. But the other paths in the Entrails of the Mountain are locked to me."

"How can we find those paths?" I said.

"How can I tell you?" said Dirnlac. "I am caged. But you may find the way in time. None are trapped here but me and my enemy."

Just then a rushing down the passage announced the coming of another ghost, a powerfully built man in sheepskins, brandishing a gleaming sword. "Who despoils my tomb? Dirnlac, what rats have you brought into this sanctuary?"

"If you would fight, Feoward, fight with me, not with these children," said Dirnlac, his own sword bright in his hand.

"Dog of the Red Oak, how many times must I kill you?" shouted the second ghost. Their swords rang together, and the clash seemed to split the mountain around them.

We fell through solid stone, and when we regained the ground beneath our feet, neither the battling ghosts nor the mouth of the cave were anywhere to be seen. Blackness surrounded us again.

"Pity they're gone," Hwyn said, "or rather, pity we're gone so soon. He seemed to know something about the Eye of Night; I would have liked to ask him what he knew."

"I know," I said. "I should have gone straight to the point instead of asking him about himself. But I was curious."

"So was I," Hwyn admitted. "The Folc are a strange people. How did they come to be one after such wars, such cruelty?"

"In three hundred years, even great hatreds may die," I said. "But if I go on asking all these old ghosts for their stories, we will wander lost in these paths of dreams, neither wise enough nor foolish enough to find our way, as Dirnlac warned. Whose dream have we fallen into now, I wonder?"

"It's a narrow pass," said Hwyn. "I can reach both walls at once. There are no more carvings."

"It seems to widen a little in this direction," I said, feeling around me. "Do you mind if we go this way?"

"Let's go," said Hwyn, catching hold of my tunic as we began our creeping progress through the darkness.

We came to a vast, cold chamber lit from a crevice above our heads through which the wind moaned like a thing in pain. Curving paths spiraled down to the central pit of the chamber, where a tall clay urn stood, marked all over with a pattern like leaves or spearheads.

"A funeral urn," I said. "Should we look closer?"

"I'm afraid so," she said, starting down the path. "I don't relish the thought of being up to the elbows in someone's ashes— still less in the grim sort of spells you might bind with them—but with my senses confused, I can't be sure it's not buried there."

"Wait for me," I said, following her.

"Of course," she said. "How could I open it without you?" The urn was taller than she was.

"We're not going to open the urn at all, if I can help it," I said, overtaking her. "I'm going to speak to the ghost."

"You can do that? You don't have to wait for them to show themselves?" Hwyn said.

I was not at all sure I could, but by the time she said this, I was too deep in it to answer her. I knelt before the urn, arms open in prayer. "Rising God, protect us against the pull of death, the hand of the grave, the weight of old anger, and the burden of old sin," I called aloud. Then I rested my palms and forehead against it, searching for a name amidst the ashes. For a long while, it eluded my grasp; some distant part of my mind was grateful that Hwyn was wise enough to keep silent while I sent my mind deeper into the shadows of this burial place. The bones of many were mingled here, their names tangled together in my mind. At last one name rang clear in my mind, and I spoke it aloud, sealing the bond: "Nidrad of the Linden, hear my call, answer my question."

"I am here," said a voice behind us. "What would you ask?"

I turned and saw a tall warrior, sword at his belt, face painted pollen-gold. The wound in his chest was small, a mere discolored slit in his simple tunic of green wool, but it was directly over his heart. Suppressing the urge to ask when the Folc had been warriors, what battle he carried the sword for, and who had made that precise little wound, I asked instead, "Where is the Eye of Night?"

But the ghost laughed. "Ask me a question I can answer, Tarvon Priest. Your Gift of Naming can't draw water from a dry well."

"Do you know what I mean by the Eye of Night?"

"The Sky-Raven's Egg," said Nidrad. "Some say its coming will be a sign that our time of waiting nears its end; what will follow, I do not know. Nor do I know where it is, save that it is not here."

"Ask whether Halred has been here," said Hwyn; but before I could ask or the ghost could speak again, we were falling through the dark to another cave, another version of the Hall of the Dead.

This time we did not land in utter darkness. A soft green light filtered through leaves into the mouth of the cave. "What's this?" Hwyn said, turning irresistibly toward the splash of green.

We pushed aside branches to clear a path to the world beyond, and it seemed we would never be done pushing them aside. "I swear new branches are growing while we push away the old ones," I grumbled.

"They are," said a voice behind me.

I was growing used to this. "Arvath of the Linden," I said without turning my eyes from the strangely fecund greenery, "where is the Eye of Night?"

With a lean arm, he swept the branches aside to show us a valley soaked in green, sated with green, vines across every house, corn tall as trees in the fields, pond-weed floating on the surface of St. Arin's Lake. "Why should I tell you?" Arvath said. "I have all I need now. Even in the waking world you have left behind, they are beginning to have all they need. But you come to take this thing from our mountain. Why should I help you?"

"Because, Lord Arvath of the Linden," I said, turning to face him full on, "I hold your name, and whoever does not follow his name loses it. Answer me, or go nameless into the emptiness before the world was born. Where is the Eye of Night?"

"It is not here," Arvath muttered sullenly.

"Tell me all you know of it," I said. "*All.*"

"The priestess of the Bright and Hidden Goddesses passed

though this path in the night, carrying a great mystery. The land bloomed and flourished as she came. That, I think, is the mystery you seek. Why would you take it from us?"

"If the land is flourishing," said Hwyn, "why does the air smell rancid?"

The ghost had no answer. I glanced back out at the landscape and watched the burgeoning greenery creeping across the surface of the pond. Indeed, the summer sweetness of the air had turned sickly. "This cannot last," I said. "You must know that, if you spent your life on this land. Where did Halred go with this mystery?"

"Deeper," the ghost said. "Deeper than I may go. That is all I know. Two are approaching who may know more. Let me go now."

I glanced at Hwyn, and she nodded. "Very well, then. Go in peace, Arvath of the Linden."

As he vanished, I became aware of a movement in the dim tunnel beyond.

A tenor voice came from the darkness, "I heard you were a scholar, but I did not know you were a priest, Traveler."

"Who's there?" I peered through the gloom. This was no ghost; the voice, moreover, seemed familiar.

"No true names here," he said. "Things listen here that cannot be trusted. I am a priest of the Rising God, like yourself." With that, Anlaf stepped out of the shadows, followed by Night.

"I'm no priest anymore," I said.

"So you say," said Anlaf. "But the gods seem not to be done with you. I was wrong to oppose you in the Assembly. You have the Gift of Naming."

"And you?" I said.

I thought I saw Anlaf smile through the green gloom. "In theory I should; my teaching was passed down from a long line of disciples of St. Tarvi. But I've never put it to the test. You, on the other hand, seem quite at home with the Gift, for one who claims he's no priest."

"I've had more than one chance to practice," I said. "But why are you here? And what do you know of our errand?"

Night spoke then. "We know something is not right: the balance of the world—oh!" For the first time, she took in the view from the cave mouth. "Hidden Goddess! Those branches—I can *see* them growing, crowding each other, choking each other.

It's—it's what I've been trying to say: we've gone too far; the balance is lost. And I know now my teacher was wrong."

"Not in everything," Hwyn said softly.

Night looked at her in wonder. "Do you defend her, even now? No need, sister. I did not mean her teachings were wrong: only this one thing, the thing she has taken from you to safeguard our land. It must not stay here."

"Do you know where it is?" Hwyn asked.

"No," said Night, "but I can guess. It must be in the deepest of all the Paths of Mystery, in the mountain's heart. And that is deeper than I have ever gone, for I am not yet fully initiated. But I know some of the paths, at least. When I heard that you had disappeared in the cave—that the Entrails of the Mountain had opened out of season and taken you—I feared you would be lost, swallowed up, for I knew Halred had not told you about these paths. I knew the ghosts would be stirring, so I looked for the Priest of the Rising God—"

"And met me on the way to the cave," said Anlaf. "Girnhild had summoned me when you disappeared. Fortunately, you are not so unprepared for this place as we had feared."

"Have you come to help us?" Hwyn said. "Will you let us take the Eye of Night away with us?"

"I *insist* you take it away," he said. "The land, like a grafted tree, is struggling to refuse what has been thrust upon it. I don't understand it, but even a Tarvon's curiosity must yield to the need of all things to take their proper name, their proper nature. By its nature, this thing does not belong here. Cut away the graft and let the tree heal."

Still choosing the side opposite Halred in every quarrel, I noted inwardly; but I kept silent, too glad of any help to quibble.

"I will lead you as near the Heart of the Mountain as I can," Night said. "After that, we must all hope for a lucky fall. Along the way, this place will come to know you: it will tease you with things drawn from your hearts. Remember what you have come for and pass on. Now link hands, and I will look for a gateway."

We progressed in an awkward chain away from the creeping branches, holding hands like orphanage children on an outing. After a time the acolyte said, "I feel something. This may be the way. Be ready." We fell, then, but not with the violence I had grown to expect. We were again in a lightless corridor, the walls of smooth, uncarved stone.

"That's odd," said Night. "This isn't the path I expected."

"Where are we?" said Hwyn.

"I don't know," said Night. "Should I try again?"

"You said you don't know the chamber where the Eye of Night must be hidden," said Hwyn. "We may be on the right path. Let's see where it leads."

We followed it to a great chamber of stone lit with a single candle on a tall stand of brass. "Who was here to leave that candle burning?" I said.

"Maybe my teacher. Maybe no one at all," said Night. "These are dreams, you know."

In the circle of weak light around the candle, I could see old iron-bound chests, the largest as long as my arm, rusting away with age. "What are these?" I said. "No ashes of the dead are here."

"I don't think the Eye of Night is here," Hwyn said, "but we may as well look."

The first chest we opened held armaments: short swords and a small round buckler of ancient style. The hilts of the swords were richly patterned with twisting designs like the tangled path we were traveling. The blades, however, showed they were no mere ornaments: notched, scarred, stained, the swords had been used hard. The leather buckler, too, was scarred and pitted with battle, the emblem on it scarcely recognizable as a wolf's head, teeth bared.

"The weapons our forebears carried in the war with the Kettrans, before the migration," Night said, holding a sword up before the candle flame to stare at the deadly thing. "How finely they are made! We have lost this art, here in the mountains."

Hwyn opened the second chest and gasped. "Look: it's beautiful." She drew out a harp graceful as a swan, balanced it against her shoulder experimentally, ran her fingers across the strings. The bright, clear sound was startlingly alive in that place of old dead things. "I guess that proves it's just a dream," she said wistfully. "It could never be in tune if it were real. Ah, but I've always wanted one of these. I think I could teach myself, if only I had the chance. It seems so natural. What a pity to leave it mouldering in a cave!"

"Take nothing with you from these caves," said Night, "save what you brought, and what was taken from you. Remember why you came, or you will be lost." With a sigh, she put away the snake-patterned vambrace she had been studying.

Reluctantly, Hwyn put the harp away, and I too repressed a sigh of disappointment, for it would have been a pleasant thing to have with us on the long journey ahead.

Meanwhile, Anlaf was rummaging in the third chest. "Look at these: the books of St. Arin, lost in the days of our forefathers. So much learning!"

"My good priest," said Night tentatively, "we cannot—"

"Of course I won't take them away—just bring one of them into the light for a moment," he said with an avidity I recognized. "Fascinating!"

"We really must go," Hwyn said, "and take the false graft from the tree—remember?"

When at last we left the chamber, we found that the path that had led us there had disappeared. The corridor that opened before us was different, carved with smooth, undulating lines.

"I don't suppose we could take the candle?" I said.

Night shook her head, so we stumbled off into the darkness again.

After a time, even in the darkness, I sensed something that made my heart lighten. The air seemed different, fresher, more *right* somehow than it had in hours or years. "We must be near an opening," I said. "I can smell the fresh air."

"It smells strange to me," said Anlaf.

The floor had softened, giving under our feet in a way I found familiar, comforting. The clean scent of the air, moist and briny, lifted my spirits. As soon as there was light enough, I quickened my pace and moved forward, desperate to be outside. Hwyn panted to keep up.

What I saw at the cave's mouth was impossible: the long stone houses of the Folc were still there, but instead of the contained blue of the lake, the hillside path led down to the sea. White waves crashed on a jetty, spray leaping skyward as it hit the stone. Farther off, I could see a stretch of level beach strewn with fishing boats. "Ah, Hwyn, if only we had the Eye of Night already! We must find it and bring it here. It's just as the Speaking Stone foretold: a journey by sea. From here, I can take you anywhere."

"This is a dream," Hwyn said, but I was already on my way

down to the water, ignoring the others calling behind me. I was where I belonged at last. The shoreward crash and seaward hiss of the ocean, regular as a heartbeat, filled my ears, leaving room for no other voice. The downward path seemed easier than ever before, and I was careening downhill like a kicked pebble when someone coming up the hill toward me caught my arm, stopping me short.

"I thought we'd find you here!" cried Ethwin, his genial face beaming.

Remembering myself at last, I turned to stare. Trenara stood beside him, holding onto his arm.

"Rising God protect us," I said. "What are you doing here?"

"This is your place, isn't it?" said Ethwin, unperturbed. "One of the places you've seen in your travels?"

"Not exactly any one port, but a bit of this, a bit of that," I said, "and a bit of the land of the Folc. Do you mean this came from me?"

"It must have," said Ethwin, leading me back up the hill. "It's never been here before. I've never even seen the sea before. What a lot of noise it makes!"

Hwyn met us on the way and fell in step beside me. "Sky-Raven's Bones! You gave me such a scare, companion. I thought we'd lost you. And you—" She paused, as if suppressing the urge to call Ethwin and Trenara by name, "My friends, you are real, aren't you?"

"They're not ghosts," I said.

"My Lady," Hwyn said, "I asked you to stay in the house, where it was safe."

"I missed you," said Trenara.

We met Anlaf and Night on the ridge by the cave mouth. "St. Arin's fingerbone!" Night swore. "Is every innocent in the valley traipsing through the Paths of Mystery today? You, Traveler," she said to me, "you mustn't run off like that. You could be lost forever. And you," she turned to Ethwin, "what possessed you to bring the simpleton here?"

"She insisted on going after her friends," said Ethwin. "I came along to protect her."

"A gallant thought," said Night, "but think what you're doing! You could both have been lost here."

"Lost?" said Ethwin with a look of utter bewilderment. "In the mountain? I'm no outlander. I've been up and down these paths since I was six years old. Not this seacoast, of course—Jereth must have brought it here—"

"No true names," hissed Night. "There are ghosts!"

"Oh, you're right. I guess they wouldn't take so well to the outlanders," said Ethwin easily. "With me, of course, it's different. Most of them are my ancestors, the lords of the Linden. They know me."

"Are you saying," said Anlaf, his eyes round as platters, "that you have been coming at will into this—this labyrinth of tombs and worlds, untutored and unguided, for most of your life? Chatting with ghosts, coming and going as you please, all alone?"

"Not always alone," Ethwin said, his eyes sliding toward Trenara. "Why? Is it forbidden?"

"It's impossible!" wailed Night. "How many paths have you found?"

"I lost count years ago," said Ethwin. "But today, this is a new one. I wonder if I'll ever be able to find it again."

"And when you've been to one of these paths, can you usually find it again?" Anlaf said.

"Of course I can," said Ethwin. "I only thought, since this place is Jereth's, really—"

"Eth— *Cousin*," Night stammered, "do you have any idea how much time, how much study it took me to learn to do that?"

Ethwin gaped at her. "I thought everyone could do it. Don't all the couples go into the mountain on their wedding nights?"

"Into the outer tomb, yes; not into the Paths of Mystery," said Night.

"That you could even open the Paths of Mystery in this season is a wonder," said Anlaf. "That you could find your way about them, without teaching and without trouble, is like lightning from a clear sky. My lad, if we'd had any idea, the priestess and I would have been vying for the privilege of teaching you."

Ethwin looked a bit queasy at that thought. "What's so hard about it? It's like stepping between rocks to cross a stream. You look for one that will bear you and shift your weight into it."

"Rest assured," said Night, "it's not so easy for the rest of us."

"You've been given a great gift," said Anlaf. "When we're safe in the daytime world, I would very much like to hear more about your travels here."

"In the meantime," said Hwyn, "your gift could be the saving of all of us, friend. You said you knew many of these places in the mountain, the Paths of Mystery. We think the Eye of Night may be in the deepest of all these hidden places."

"The Heart of the Mountain," said Night.

"Do you think you can find that place?" said Hwyn.

Ethwin considered. "There was a place I found only recently, quite by accident: a chamber with no door. I've only been there once. It seemed different from all the other chambers, somehow: almost alive. Yes, I think that may have been the place."

"Could you find it again?" said Hwyn.

"I think so," he said.

"Let us take your hands," said Night, "so you won't lose us on the way."

And so we linked hands again, all six of us, and easy as a thought, Ethwin stepped forward and pulled us after him into a chamber without a door, deep in the mountain.

Was this the Heart of the Mountain? The beating of the heart was there, a dull thrumming noise from below that I felt in the soles of my feet. Without a crack or crevice even as large as a pore, nonetheless there seemed to be a soft sighing of wind in and out of the chamber, bearing the scents of the living world: the fresh dark earth of spring, the tang of sea air, the dried herbs on Halred's wall, the coarse odors of the paddock, the telltale musk that had clung to Ethwin after he had been with Trenara in these underground pathways. Was this stone or flesh we stood on? Ethwin was right: the place was alive.

In the center of the room, a small stone table—perhaps I should say an altar—held a few objects left almost haphazardly, like the possessions of one who died suddenly, leaving the house in disarray. A small, gleaming sickle-blade lay on a corner of the table. Beside it, a rough clay cup with four handles, somewhat misshapen, stood half full of a liquid that fell in slow drops from some unseen source above us, the musical *plink* of the drops a treble counterpoint to the deep drumming of the heartbeat.

Beside the cup stood an odd-shaped bowl of dark wood, like a long boat tapered equally at prow and stern. A promiscuous assortment of seeds, from the tiniest grains to long green acorns, lay in the bottom of the bowl. Nested upon them were three small bones like fingerbones, an arrowhead that seemed to bleed into the bed of seeds, and the Eye of Night, which illumined the whole chamber with a sort of pale moonlight.

"Gods be praised," breathed Hwyn, "it's *not* a Circle of Power."

"It's the Mysteries," said Night, half hiding her face with one hand, palm outward—but with gaps between her fingers, as if uncertain whether to hide her eyes or stare. "How can we take back the Raven's Egg? I am uninitiated; we all are. I cannot touch the Mysteries."

"Have no fear," Hwyn said. "Your part is done: this task is mine."

"But you are not—"

"Peace. I will touch nothing but the thing I came for," Hwyn said. She stretched forth her right hand slowly, speaking in gentle tones. "I have come back for you, my child. I will care for you as I promised. Come with me." Delicately, she picked up the white stone between her bony forefinger and thumb, disturbing no least seed in the bowl.

For a time she held it against her heart, light leaking out between her fingers, her face bright with joy, eyes closed. Then she slipped it back into the breast of her shift. "It's done." Only then did I realize that it was not the only source of light in the room: the silver sickle, the cup, the bowl, even the seeds themselves shone from within.

"We should go," Hwyn said to Ethwin, who stood holding Trenara's hand, light eyes shining, dreaming awake. When he did not respond, she tugged his sleeve. "Friend, we should go."

"Ah yes," he said, rubbing one eye like a wakened sleeper. "Link hands. I will find the path."

This time the traveling seemed to take longer, like the slow waking of a heavy sleeper. For a long time I felt nothing but Hwyn's hand in my right one and Night's in my left. Then I felt solid rock beneath my feet and saw a glimmer of light ahead of me, the mouth of the tunnel. Trenara and Ethwin stepped out at once, and we followed eagerly, hungry for the open air.

The view that met my eyes made me jump back in alarm. There were long stone houses, sure enough, and two round priest-huts, but they were dilapidated, the lime-wash nearly gone, a crumbled chimney here, an entire wall fallen there. What was more, they were in the wrong places. Even the sun seemed in the wrong place on the horizon. No lake filled the bottom of the valley, but a stream rushed down a canyon, threading between the lower hills in the distance. There was no sign that it had rained at all.

"This is not the path, my friend," I said. "It's another dream-vision of the valley, with the lake drained and the houses in ruins."

Ethwin laughed. "No, Jereth, it's just the other side of the mountain. I thought you might not want to argue with the Nine Voices of the Folc whether you should be allowed to take away the Raven's Egg."

"That is wise," said Hwyn. "Thank you a thousand times."

"This is the Valley of the Red Oak," Ethwin explained, "abandoned long ago when the surviving Folc drew together. I stay here sometimes when I'm hunting northwest of the village, and I keep a cache of supplies in the house nearest the stream. You can wait for me there while I go back to Folcsted to fetch your things."

"You are a wonder," Hwyn said. "I can't thank you enough."

Anlaf stepped toward us, oddly hesitant. "This is farewell, for us," he said. "We did not meet well. That is—I judged you too harshly when you first came. Hwyn, I sensed something uncanny about you, and I thought you a necromancer, come to drink power from the dead. I feared to allow you among us. I see now that I was wrong."

"Why, what have you seen?" Hwyn said.

"If you had entered the Hall of the Dead seeking power, I doubt your dreams would have been as innocent as the harp that appeared to tempt you," Anlaf said. "And you did not try to take anything else with the Eye of Night, though you might easily have called it an honest mistake."

"How did you do that?" said Night. "You didn't move a seed when you took that stone. I watched you very closely, and I don't understand."

"Easy as taking a coin from a merchant's purse without making the others clink," said Hwyn, smiling ruefully. "This was a task for a thief—and I have been one at need."

"Whatever you have been," Anlaf said, "you proved your worth today, and I am sorry I doubted you. And Jereth, I hope that if you come again to Folcsted, you can tell me of your teaching and your travels. May the gods go with you."

"Thank you," I said, and Hwyn added, "May the gods be with the Folc."

Night smiled down at Hwyn. "We will never forget you, you know."

"I expect not." Hwyn grimaced. "I left Mother Halred with such scathing words. How I wish I had not! She taught me so much—even this, even this was a teaching. She did not, after all, lock up the Eye of Night in a magic circle; she placed it safely where I would have found it when I finished training for the priesthood—in her eyes, when I would have been ready to be trusted with it. It was kindly meant, I am sure. Will you tell her—not exactly that I'm sorry, because I had to do this, but—I don't know—"

"I will tell her that you remember her teaching kindly," said Night.

"Thank you," said Hwyn. "And thank you for coming to look for us. I will never forget you either. You'll be a wonderful priestess."

"Do you think so?" said Night, looking sheepish. "I'm sorry—I— We were so jealous of you, Day and I!"

"Were you really?" Hwyn said. "Gods on the Wheel, I've never been so flattered. Bless you. Be happy."

"And you," said Night, "will you be happy?"

"As a fish returned to the water," said Hwyn.

"Godspeed, then," said Night.

They disappeared into the mountain, and my companions and I started down the weedy path to the house by the river, shading our eyes from the slanting beams of late-afternoon sun. We passed a long house with only half a roof, another with a great section of wall in rubble. About halfway down the path stood a covered well; we lifted the cover, found a new rope on the old iron ring inside, pulled up the bucket, and drank.

"Sky-Raven's Bones! I've been so overwrought, that's the first I've realized I didn't drink a drop all day," said Hwyn. "Or eat, for that matter."

"We had a feast last night to last a week," I said. "But I was thirsty. If someone in the seacoast world had offered me a dipper of water, I might have been lost."

"Do you miss the sea so much?" Hwyn said.

I smiled ruefully. "I don't know why I dreamed of the sea. Every nightmare I have ends with the shipwreck, the drowning. And yet the scent of it lightened my heart before I could think what it was I smelled. It was home. But I'm sorry: I nearly lost the way. I should have remembered our quest."

"I had almost forgotten it in this world," Hwyn said, "till you woke me."

"And will you look back in regret on the dream you left behind?" I said gently. "You would have been a wonderful priestess, yourself."

Hwyn shook her head. "Like you, I think, I would have chafed at obedience, at order. I did not belong under Halred's tutelage—at least, not for long. This road is home for me. I meant what I said to Night: I am where I ought to be, where I want to be. I might have liked being a priestess, but I would rather be the Night-Bearer—claws and all, as Paddon would have it!" Her lopsided mouth stretched in laughter. "Gods, what ideas people have of me. Imagine Night saying she was jealous of me. Whatever for?"

"Don't you know?" I said. "You were Halred's favorite, her most brilliant pupil." We reached the house by the water; it was indeed the best of the lot. A small corner of slate roof had fallen, but had been thatched in, no doubt by Ethwin. Most of the shutters were still intact, flecked with the remains of red paint; the faded red door still swung on leather hinges, letting us in to a wide, echoing hall, empty save for a few broken benches, a cauldron on the hearth, and a huge oaken chest.

"I know Mother Halred saw something in me," Hwyn admitted, tugging open a shutter to let in the ruddy light of sunset. "But there was so much I couldn't learn! I could never learn to read, and so much of the rest depended on it. When she held open that mouldering old book and pointed at something on the page, it was like staring at a cloud of flies in the firelight that wouldn't stand still. I couldn't see where one rune-staff ended and the next began."

I wondered how to respond, whether sympathy would sound welcome or insulting. I had never been sure how little she saw; certainly she compensated well enough with touch that it was rarely apparent. In the cave, she had read the walls with her fingers when I had been blind.

"Let me try something," I said. I went to one of the broken benches, drew out my knife, and cut four rune-staves in the wood: Hail, Will, Yng, Night.

"What are you doing?" she said.

"Come here and see," I said, then winced at my choice of

words, but she did not seem to mind. She came, and I took her hand and placed it on the first rune-staff.

"That's Hail," I said. " 'Hail and harsh weather make a hard rune,' or so they taught me as a child. Can you trace it again on my palm?"

Hwyn ran her finger down the trails in the wood that formed the first rune-staff, then easily reproduced them on my hand.

"Not so hard, eh?"

She laughed. "And what good will this be? For books written with a very sharp pen?"

"For messages cut in beech-trees," I said. "The beech-tree is the book-tree, ever since the Rising God brought the rune-staves up from under the earth on the bark of the first beech-tree. There must be many beech-trees on the road ahead of us."

We had covered the bench with rune-staves before Ethwin arrived with our things: our packs, the cook-pot, the fishing-net and line, my cloak and Trenara's. "There's a water-skin in the chest," he said, "and some smoked meat. You had better take them. It's rugged land to be traveling without food or water, even in summer. There's a sheepskin you can have, too. You're going north, and I see only two cloaks for the three of you. I can easily get another one in the blood-month, before the cold."

"Aren't you coming with us?" I said.

Trenara put out her hands to him silently. He took them and stood looking in her eyes, silent as his lady.

"You would be a fine companion, Ethwin," Hwyn said. "You're a good man and I know you would always protect Trenara. If you need to go home first and bid your parents farewell, we can wait the night here; it's late for travel, anyway. If you need to ask us any questions, you have well earned your answers: we would have been hard-pressed to recover the Eye of Night without you.

"You have a great gift," she continued. "If I have left that for last, it is not because I underprize it. I am still amazed, too amazed to quite know what to say about it. But if you had no special ease in the spirit world—if you were simply what I thought you before, a good-hearted young man, skilled with the bow, who loves one of my companions—I would still say, come with us if you choose. But only if you choose.

"I don't understand your gift. I won't pretend to know whether you were meant to use it in Folcsted, among your people, or on the hard road north with us. But I believe every gift comes with a calling, and when you are truly called, there's joy in following. Consider carefully: are you called onward to the north, or back to the Folc?"

Ethwin held her gaze a long while before turning his face to the ground. "I am the only son my mother has left. My brothers all went away; I cannot." He took Trenara's hands again and kissed them one by one, then pressed them to his heart. "Trenara, if I were my own man, I would beg you to stay and marry me. But my father would not be kind to you."

"Come with us," Trenara said, tugging at his tunic. "Come, Ethwin."

"I wish I could, my love," he said. "Farewell. Be happy."

He embraced her, and I looked away, abashed. Then, leaving her arms long enough to throw open the oaken chest, he took out the things he had promised: the water-skin, the sheepskin, and the bundle of smoked meat wrapped in fragrant herb-leaves. "Take these, please."

"Are you sure you can spare them?" Hwyn said.

"Of course. What's to stop me from killing game for meat and pelts, curing the hides, making bedrolls or water-skins as I need? They are nothing to me. I will be angry if I find them here when I come again. I would not want Trenara to be hungry or thirsty in the wilderness, or her friends to freeze in the north without a cloak."

"May the gods be good to you, Ethwin," said Hwyn. "You are a wonder."

"My friend," I said, "you have saved our lives and our quest, and we owe you everything. I wish you were going with us. I wish there were something we could give you in return for all your kindness."

"You've given me a story I can tell again and again, till everyone tires of it but me," he said. "And a seacoast in the mountain's inner paths—gods, I never expected such a thing. Be well. The river is the source of the Ferend: they say it leads to the lowlands. Follow it, and you will not be lost. Farewell." We clasped hands warmly. Then he turned to Trenara again, pulled her close, and held her long.

"Come with us," she pleaded again.

"I can't, my love. Farewell," he said.

"Trenara," Hwyn said gently, "do you want to go back with him, and stay with him?"

Trenara looked from Hwyn to Ethwin and back again. "I go with Hwyn," she said softly.

"Farewell. Be happy," said Ethwin.

He kissed Trenara one more time. She watched him till he disappeared into the swift-falling twilight of the hill country. We sat in silence a long time, ruminating.

"The moon will be just past full tonight," I said to Hwyn. "Should we move on?"

"Let's stay here till morning," she said, "in case the poor boy changes his mind."

But Ethwin did not return with the sun. In the morning we filled the water-skin, took up our bundles, and went our way: the same three travelers on the road that was our home.

11

THE FEAST
OF THE TURNING GOD

As summer ripened into autumn, we made our way slowly north, spending a few days on the roads and then a few in whichever town or village we found in our way, earning food for the next stage of the journey. We harvested oats in the blazing days of late summer, then rye, then barley, then wheat, then black grapes and tart early apples, then the sweeter apples of full autumn.

Though the lowest of the farmhands, we ate well in all these towns, where few hands gathered what many had sown. The flood of refugees, haunted and reticent to speak of the apparitions that drove them southward, continued even as the fruit ripened on the tree with none to gather it. We might have thanked the ghosts for our comfort: the hardships of Kreyn receded like a half-forgotten nightmare, for we never lacked work while the long harvest season lasted in any abode of the living. With so many gone, and with many landed gentry loading caravans for the south, our share of the harvest was greater than it might have been in quieter times. After a few of these harvest-days of nut bread, stewed apples, and dark, malty porter, Hwyn looked a little less brittle, and I in my cassock a little less like a skeleton in a sack. Trenara looked as sleek and content as a cream-fed cat.

Between towns, too, we fared well, following the roads when we might and Hwyn's dark sense when the road vanished into pathless wilderness—or when it seemed more perilous than wilderness itself. On the old north-south trading road we met solitary travelers, bands, and whole caravans heading south, none at all heading our way. When they saw us striding northward toward them, some warned us of plagues or wars or ghosts in the towns they had just quit. Others refused to speak to us, making the warding sun-sign of the Bright Goddess against misfortune or the key of the Upright God against the madness that surely drove us. We sang all the louder when they did. We avoided the plague-sites and war-zones when we could, but marched on squarely to the ghost-haunts—at first because I believed my Gift of Naming would defend us and Hwyn felt we might have some mission to perform there, but eventually, simply because these towns always proved harmless to us. The ghosts, it seemed, only haunted those who belonged to them. In their wake, there would be empty beds for us to sleep in, work for us to do, and food for us to eat.

North of the Dark Eye Lake, we saw the first of the deserted towns: the houses stripped bare of everything that could be carried away; the temple an empty husk; the grainfields choked with weeds. We went from house to house, but found neither a living soul nor a ghost. In the monastery, books had been left abandoned in their embossed cases; I toyed with the idea of taking one, but reflected that they had given their prior owners no insight into whatever had driven them away.

We filled our packs with potatoes dug up near a peasant's cottage and nuts gathered in a burgher's garden, and we spent the night in dusty featherbeds in what must have been the lord's palace. Then we hurried on, not haunted but strangely unsettled by the silence, glad to find the next town still populated. Of the fate of the town we had passed through, they knew nothing: "No news from the south," they said, "in a year or more, till now." They welcomed our hands in the fields, but would say little to us, holding apart from the mysterious vagabonds moving in the wrong direction, against the tide.

We did not stay long, and in the next few towns spoke less about where we were going and where we had been. We took to entering walled towns through the north gate to attract less suspicion.

Once along the road, in sight of the spires of a city, we came upon two warriors in gilded armor, lying entwined, each man's sword in the other's breast, the earth around them dyed red by their death-wounds.

"The crests on their shields are identical," I noticed.

Hwyn nodded. "Brothers? Or pretenders to the same name?"

"They're not telling," I said. "I could speak to the ghosts—"

"No," Hwyn said, "I don't think there's anything for us to do here."

We walked wide of that town, though it forced us to wander the pathless forest, eating beech nuts and ground-cherries and the watery pods of wood sorrel, sleeping under the bushes or in hastily made shelters of branches. The nights had grown chilly and, for me at least, wakeful; while Trenara and Hwyn curled together against the cold as unthinkingly as kittens, I hung back, embarrassed, awkward, and cold. I wished they would invite me closer, and feared that if they did, I would not know how to take it.

In time we found new signs of human presence: bloody strips of venison left on a tree branch, the hunter's offering to the crow, an old tradition I had read of but never seen before. We tracked the hunter carefully, anxious not to miss even the poorest human habitation. The trail led to another chain of dwindling, anxious villages and towns strung along the ghost of a road, full of uneasy rumors of a doom coming down from the North, full of gossip of those who would leave next or remembrance of those who had left for the southern regions of which they had no news. Once we followed a path that looked well trodden, only to find no town but the smoking ruin of one. Most of the time, however, we found a little life, poised on the brink of vanishing southward.

After a succession of these dying towns, each more hopeless than the one before it, we were pleasantly surprised one bright cold morning, emerging from the woods, to stride past well-kept orchards and tidy barns, and see ahead of us on the path a knot of people and two wagons, headed north.

We ran faster after that little caravan than we had run from the guards of Kreyn. Coming abreast of a plodding oxcart on which three children sat atop a load of apples, we stood panting till we could draw breath enough to introduce ourselves. Both the children and the grown people who ringed the wagons turned to stare at us in undisguised curiosity, but without the scowls of suspicion we had come to expect.

"Good morning, fellow-travelers!" I cried as soon as I could speak again. "What brings you on this northward road?"

A bigger boy of ten or twelve who walked beside the cart stuck his fist in his mouth to mute his laughter. The oldest of the grown men ranged around the wagon said, "Blessings of the day, strangers. And who are you that don't know what day this is, or where we're going?"

"Or where we are, for that matter," Hwyn added. "We are traveling players, the Lady Trenara's own troupe."

"Ah, players!" cried a rosy-faced young woman with a blond braid over each shoulder and a baby on her back. "Just the thing for the festival."

"The festival!" I said. "We lost count of days on the road. Is it the Feast of the Turning God already?"

"What, isn't it cold enough for you?" said the man who had spoken first, a broad-faced, blond man of about forty or fifty with dirt under his fingernails. "Yes, traveler, it's the feast already. We're headed into town to take these apples to the fair and see some of the dancing. You may come with us, and if you'll sing for us, you're welcome to taste the wares. I'm Alcorel the apple grower; these are my wife, Beri," he gestured to the older of the two women beside the cart, "my sons, Ador and Alb, my daughter-in-law Vel, and my grandchildren, whose names scarcely matter as they answer to nothing at all, these days. What should we call you?"

"I'm Jereth," I said. "These are Hwyn and the Lady Trenara. And we will certainly travel along with you and sing for you. But tell me first, what town are we coming to?"

"Did you not even know that?" said Alcorel. "This is Berall, the domain of Lord Var, and a finer town you won't find in all the North. You must have traveled far indeed to wander into towns without knowing their names."

"Traveling is our livelihood," Hwyn said, "learning a song or story in one place and taking it where it will seem new and wonderful. But so many towns in these parts stand empty that we could scarcely find anyone to tell us what lay ahead of us."

"Towns with no heart are easily broken apart by the Troubles," said Alcorel.

"Does Berall have a heart, then?" I said.

"Lord Var is our heart," the farmer said. "In the old days, before he had the crown, when we were at war with Myrcwold, he fought at the front of his father's army—not like the Myrcwold prince, hiding in the pavilion, content to let others risk their lives. When raiders came from the wastelands north of us, he rallied all the countryside to unite, and again he faced the foe before us all. He reminds us that this is a land worth loving, worth defending. And he is a friend to the people: when the mood takes him, he will go among the crowd and pick out plain folk to be invited to his table as his guests, sharing the feast with the great. Such things are not to be found everywhere, and so we will never leave Berall. Whatever the time brings, while Var reigns, we will not be shaken."

"Bold words," said Hwyn, "and they call for a bold song. What shall we give them, Jereth?"

" 'King Haylwin's Victory,' perhaps?" I suggested.

"Oh, yes, just the thing! Your version has more verses: you begin and I'll follow," she said, so I filled my lungs with the crisp frost-touched air and launched into the historical ballad we'd often sung to while away long plodding stretches of road. We sang the glories of King Haylwin, who routed the Kettrans from the North Country, made his throne in Larioneth, and established justice throughout the land, if minstrels were to be believed. We counted the ranks of overwhelming foes, mounted our defense, snatched victory from the jaws of defeat, and finished to such applause that we knew we could not stop after one song. Hwyn began a threshing-song, scooped up three small apples from the cart, and began to juggle.

And so when the faint cow-path we traveled gave way to the cobbled streets of Berall, our act was already under way. Alcorel and his family made no move to reclaim the apples Hwyn juggled; instead they guided us, still singing, to the Berall fairground, where they positioned us like sentries in front of their stall and sold apples to everyone who came to listen. From time to time, when we grew hoarse, they would offer us each a mouthful of tangy cider from a jug kept behind the stall.

We found ourselves in the thick of a thriving north-country market town—once nothing to remark on, but in these times of

Troubles, practically a miracle. Clean-lined timber houses with steep-sloping roofs, many with brightly painted shutters and a few with real glass windows, stood in orderly ranks to the north of the square. Craftsmen's shops on all sides were neat and cheerful, decked with garlands and red-oak leaves for the holiday. In the spirit of the day, their fresh-painted signs hung upside-down, for the Turning God is also the Upside-Down God, lord of reversal and change, the only figure painted head-downward on icons of the Four Great Ones on the Wheel.

The people who milled in and out of these shops seemed as well kept as the houses. Most, like Alcorel's clan, looked like prosperous farming folk, their hands roughened with work but their clothes displaying some of the little luxuries of a fortunate year, like fur-lined boots and hoods or the brightly dyed kerchiefs that fluttered like pennants about the women's windblown hair. Other comforts of prosperity were for sale around me: nut pastries at a confectioner's stall; elderberry wine and stronger spirits at a vintner's shop; ointments against windburn and discreet little vials of face-paint sold from a lively old woman's cart. All these kept up a busy trade. I was surprised to hear it was the first day of the festival—usually trade must wait for the second, after the most solemn rites are done—but I was in no mood to disapprove: it was so good to see a city where normal life survived the Troubles.

We had our share of this prosperity: onlookers, reckless with ale and high spirits, filled my cup with coins so quickly that I almost needed to be a juggler myself to stow the loot in my pocket before the cup overflowed. *That will serve us well,* I thought, feeling the wind's icy fingers steal between the tops of my worn boots and the bottom of my threadbare cassock and cloak. Hwyn had Ethwin's sheepskin tied about her thin frame, wool inward, but even on her small body it left too much unprotected. Winter would come down swiftly in this land, and we all needed new clothes to withstand it as we continued northward.

Heartened by the applause and the coins, we gave the people of Berall a bounty of our own: sea chanteys and shepherds' airs, holy hymns and ribald catches, sharp satires and sweet songs of love, buoyant drinking songs and laments. They devoured it all, keeping us at it till, tired and hoarse, we begged off to gather our strength and make a few purchases of our own at the stalls we'd been eying all day. My pockets were heavy not only with this day's song-money but with unspent wages from harvesting along the road, and I was resolved to lighten them.

"I'm not saving this money to buy illusions from ghosts in the empty towns," I said to Hwyn.

She nodded her agreement. "Or to be stolen by the next pickpocket, right here in Berall. You're right: it's no use being prudent now. We're better off carrying clothes on our backs than money in our pockets."

We went straight to the clothiers' booths and spent a long time deciding what we could best get for our money. Trenara was hardest to buy for: we could not afford clothes befitting her station, but would attract suspicion if we dressed her in commoners' clothes. Hwyn settled on buying her a muff for her hands and warmer stockings to wear under her thinning finery, as well as having the lady's boots patched, along with mine and her own. I thought these things should suffice: northern-born Trenara had complained of heat, damp, fatigue, and hunger often enough along the way, but never of cold, even when Hwyn and I woke blue-fingered and miserable. It was Hwyn that needed everything she could get against the cold.

Walking along the rows of stalls, I scanned the faces of the sellers for one that seemed to look with troubled compassion at Hwyn's bony figure and threadbare shift. A kind-eyed woman showed us a gown of thick amber wool made for a delicate child. "The girl died before she could wear it—Hidden Goddess be gentle with her," she said. "I have to sell the gown for less now—this hooded cloak as well, too small for most of the folk that buy from me."

Hwyn regarded them with a solemn eye, but stroked the soft wool of the dress appreciatively. I asked the price—a merciful one indeed—and paid the money before Hwyn could have second thoughts about getting them both.

"Will we have enough left for your things?" Hwyn said.

"I'm sure I can find something," I told her. "And besides, we can sing again tomorrow."

"I don't have clerical garb," said the seamstress, looking at me questioningly—and indeed, by then it must have been half apparent that the cassock was a remnant of some abandoned life.

"I left the Order last spring," I told her. "I just haven't had money for new clothes till now."

"Then I may have something for you," the seamstress said. "Used, but not badly. Beanpole-shaped, like you. I was going to rework the cloth into something else—not much call for such a long narrow tunic—but you might save me the work. Here, take a look." The moss-green tunic and breeches she showed me were all she promised: only gently worn, and about my size. They were plain, sturdy, homespun garments, but they seemed a forbidden luxury: the first colored clothes I'd had since I'd joined the Order. After paying down the coins, I stood admiring them a while.

"Well, what are you waiting for?" Hwyn said. "Put them on." She'd already slipped her new dress on over her old one and slung her cloak over her shoulders.

"Not over this," I said, gesturing at my clerical garb. "It's the festival of change, and it's time to bid farewell to Brother Jereth of the Tarvon Order." I turned to the seamstress. "Is there anywhere I could change my clothes without scandalizing the whole square?"

She smiled, and improvised a tent with a length of homespun over the back of her cart. I folded my long limbs beneath it for enough time to scramble into the breeches, out of the cassock, and into the tunic. Emerging in my new finery with my old cassock in my hand, I noticed a one-legged beggar eying what I carried, his own tunic more battered and threadbare than even Hwyn's old shift. I held the garment out to him: "If you want it, it's yours."

The beggar smiled his thanks, and I felt a weight lift from my shoulders as he took away the last frayed remnant of my ties to the Tarvon Order.

"Come on, let's see the new Jereth," Hwyn called. I hurried over to her, stooped so she could look me in the eye, then, caught by a sudden impulse, lifted her up and whirled her around like one of the festival's Turning Dancers.

"You *are* a new man," she laughed. "I've never known you to dance before. I approve the change! But let's find some morsel to eat and drink before the evening rites begin."

We scarcely had time to buy a couple of handfuls of nuts when the hunting horns of the festival began sounding, calling the people to the temple court. We hurried along with the crowd, munching the bruised apples Hwyn had been juggling all afternoon and looking forward to a more substantial meal later.

In the temple court we found the traditional fire of chaff well ablaze. The sacred clowns—men dressed as women, women dressed as men, or adults of either sex masked as babies or beasts—capered about the bonfire, taunting the people who passed them to throw something in: their riches, their wisdom, their safety, their old way of life. Most of the people passed by; some threw in wax tablets on which they'd written what they wanted to burn. A few threw coins in the fire: a grand gesture, I suppose, but I thought it foolish. If they wanted to unburden themselves, they could throw the money at a beggar and let him get a hot meal with it.

But the clowns would not have known what to do with a beggar. "I can't taunt *you*," one said as Hwyn passed. "You have nothing."

"That's what you think," said Hwyn, and threw in her apple core. Trenara and I did likewise, more to be rid of them before the rites began than for any other reason. But then, many things in this festival were without reason. I had never understood this feast day or its lord, the Turning God. He is Lord of the Harvest: why then do the priests chant that he is struck with each stroke of the flail, ground with each turn of the millstone, crushed with each grape pressed to wine? As we celebrate the god's bounty, why do we await the Procession of the Reaper and fall flat to earth as he passes, mown down by the scythe?

It is sin to slight any of the Four Great Ones, and I would tell myself this every harvest to resign myself to these rites. Whatever we may profess, most of us feel drawn to one side of the Wheel, repelled by the other. Halred was unusual in this: most priests schooled in the lore of more than one Great One worship a god and goddess adjacent on the Wheel, offering only distant courtesy to their opposites. I had entered an order devoted to the Rising God, lord of justice, law, understanding, and light; I understood little of his irrational opposite on the Wheel.

I mulled over these things as we waited among the crowd, mocked by the sacred clowns. They were not, I thought wryly, very good at this task. They spared some of the worshipers most ripe for satire: the merchant who hung near the back of the crowd so he could go back to his selling as quickly as possible; the well-dressed man who kept his hands fixed against his bulging pockets as he passed the fire, as though he feared his coins might jump in of their own accord. Perhaps there was a place for me at this festival, after all, I thought: teaching these complacent, well-fed people to mock. I remembered how in Annelon, when I was an acolyte, one of the Turning God's clowns had mocked my abbot, aping his stiff posture and those prim little maxims that punctuated his every speech, till the abbot was as red as the wine they spilled out for blood later in the rites. Everyone should be fair game at this feast.

The sound of a hunting horn interrupted my thoughts, and soon enough we had to clear the way for the Hunt: men dressed as hunters and hounds who race through the crowd and seize people here and there as prey. They set headdresses of deer-antlers on their heads and gather them on the altar, where they must lie prostrate while the hunters sing the Mourning of the Prey. The meaning of this pageant and its place in the harvest festival is never explained, like so much else in this gloomy rite full of images of death: a strange way to celebrate the harvest that brings promise of life through the winter!

I was lost in these thoughts when I heard Hwyn gasp and realized that one of the hunters had snatched Trenara. The lady accepted the antler headdress as if it were just another holiday treat of new clothing and went docilely along with the masked man. Hwyn struggled to follow her through the crowd, but I caught her arm firmly. "Hwyn, no. She'll be all right, and we'll find her afterward."

Hwyn nodded slowly, and I breathed more easily. However warm our reception, the last thing we needed in a strange town was to fight with priests and respectable citizens during a holy rite. Moreover, Trenara herself showed no signs of distress as she lay among the other antlered victims, listening to the wailing voices of the singers. When it ended, the hunter had to lead her down from the altar, or she might have stayed there resting. I tried to follow her movements, but the Procession of the Reaper was next, and after we got up off the ground, I found I had lost sight of her in the crowd.

We waited without her, casting our eyes about for her as the priest told one of the many contradictory tales of the Upside-Down God: how, captured by foes and hung upside-down from a tree, he saw things nobody sees straight on. Finding he knew something his captors could never grasp, he laughed aloud, and the laugh of their captive, the laugh of a god, sent his captors trembling till they could not hold him. The things he saw are the Secrets of the Upside-Down God, which all his priests seek. They cannot know these secrets, but in the seeking, they believe, there is wisdom.

By the time the clowns dispersed the crowd, Hwyn was agitated, pacing about desperately in the shadowy twilight. "Where can she have gone?"

"Don't worry," I said. "For over a year, she's followed you through cities and woods and mountains and the haunted lands of the North. I doubt she'll let you slip from her grasp."

Just then, Alcorel the Apple-Grower came toward us, beaming. "There you are, players! I scarcely recognized you in your new things—a great improvement, I must say. I wanted to thank you; I've never sold so many apples in one day as I did today, with your song drawing everyone in the festival to my cart. Let me take you to an inn and buy you a good supper in return."

"Thank you," said Hwyn, "but we need to find Trenara. She was snatched by one of the hunters, and now I can't find her."

"Ah, she'll be back soon. The hunter must give the prey a cup of wine in the temple after the rite," said Alcorel. "We'll move closer to the temple to see her on her way out."

Hwyn acquiesced, so we made our way as well as we could through the crowd, wading against the current of people leaving the temple courts for snug homes or warm inns.

"The god's own luck is with me today," Alcorel said, "to have met you players on the way into town."

"In all the towns we've played, we've never been received so warmly as here in Berall," I said. "This town must be hungry for song."

"We don't get many traveling players nowadays," Alcorel said.

"Not even on the great feast days?" Hwyn said.

Alcorel shrugged. "Players are transients; they put down shallow roots. It takes plain, steady farming folk to endure in the shadow of the Troubles. No offense meant," he added quickly. "I suppose there's a poor harvest for minstrels in a land half empty; no doubt you'll be turning back southward when the festival ends."

Hwyn turned to him, smiling as sweetly as her twisted face allowed. "No, friend: our road lies north. We traveling players want to find the last town—the one most in need of song to lift the spirits. Only there will we stay the winter."

"But this *is* the last town," Alcorel said. "Everything north of Berall is deserted. I thought you knew that."

Hwyn and I looked at each other open-mouthed. There was still a long road between us and Larioneth. We'd hoped to cover half that ground before the snows blocked the path, but we hadn't reckoned on journeying into winter through an empty land without hope of bread or shelter.

"Have the Troubles reached so far?" Hwyn gasped.

"Everywhere in the North but here," Alcorel said. "Lord Var has kept them at bay."

"Perhaps we should stay after all," I said. "We'd better sing well; if our welcome here cools, it's a long cold road ahead of us."

"Keep it up, and we'll never want you to leave," Alcorel said.

Just then I saw green-clad hunters emerge from the temple, escorting festival-goers with drinking-horns in their hands. "Look," I said, "there's Trenara at last."

She came toward us, leaning on the arm of her huntsman, a tall slim man with a red leather mask under his green hunter's cap. The hunter's head inclined toward her as if they spoke confidentially. She reached up to touch his masked face, and he removed the mask and hat to reveal an elegant high forehead, piercing gray eyes, and a strong jaw with a blond beard.

"By the Name of the Turning God," said Alcorel, "that hunter was Lord Var!"

"Indeed?" I said, peering at him as he approached us. He was not so young as I had first thought—older than I, perhaps forty—but his vigorous bearing would probably make him seem half youthful even at twice the age. He wore no mark of rank, dressed exactly like the other hunters for the rite. He had no noticeable retinue, unless the Hunt had been composed of his men. If this were a lord, he wore it as lightly as Guthlac of the Red Oak in his tiny domain in the hill country.

"He seems well taken with your Lady Trenara," Alcorel said, as the gold head and the dark one again inclined together companionably.

Hwyn frowned and threaded her way through the crowd toward Trenara. I followed as well as I could, and Alcorel came after us.

"My Lady," Hwyn began when she was near enough to tug Trenara's sleeve, "are you well? We were worried about you. Come with us: Alcorel has promised us a good hot meal."

"We will dine with Lord Var," Trenara said, then turned to the lord. "These are Hwyn and Jereth."

"Players for the festival," I said, bowing showily.

"Players? Excellent! We so rarely have any new ones in Berall," Lord Var said. "My Lady Trenara, will you bring your minstrels to my hall for the feast?"

Trenara nodded in her slow, dreamy manner; the way he followed the gesture with his eyes, I could see that he read volumes into it, as I once had.

"Your pardon, Lady," Hwyn said tentatively. "Surely you will not forget our promise to the farming folk who led us to this town, Alcorel and his family?"

"They may come too," said Lord Var. "This feast day calls for a hall full of revelers! Come with us, all."

Some of the hunters and hounds of the rite then shed their masks and reclaimed swords from a temple guard, transforming themselves into Lord Var's retainers. Alcorel ran to tell his wife to come quickly; Hwyn and I, with nothing else to do, followed the Hunt to the hall, she reluctantly, I eagerly. I could see that Lord Var was a far cry from Lady Goldifer; as he passed, the people did not kneel, but smiled and called warm greetings, and some of every station—plain men of the soil, craftsmen, merchants—were invited to join our procession to the great hall for the holiday meal. I went along with a lively step, eager to find out more about this lord so well loved by his people—and eager for the feast.

But in Berall Hall we were greeted at the door by Var's steward, who seemed disinclined to celebrate the feast of reversal in the traditional way. In Swanroad, even in my father's house, there would have been a Beggar King in the seat of honor, while the head of the house poured ale for the laborers. But Var's steward put us each firmly in our place, escorting Trenara to a chair near the head of the table, gesturing the peasants to seats below the salt, and waving us players off to the harpist's corner. From there we watched the steaming trenchers carried to the table, smelled the spices in the stew and the crisped fat on the roast boar, but saw little hope that they would ever come our way.

Var's household bard, whose name I never did learn, stood by with his harp and air of injured dignity, looking daggers at me and Hwyn. Certainly he cut a better figure than we did, robed in russet silk, his harp gilded. Remembering Hwyn's dream in the Entrails of the Mountain, I expected to see her eying the harp with envy. But she seemed distracted, distant.

When Var called out, "Well, players! A song, for the Turning God's sake!" Hwyn cast an anguished look in my direction. I did not know what was wrong, but understood the plea in her eyes. I addressed the harpist in my butteriest tone of flattery: "We strolling players give place to our better: noble harpist, will you begin?" Looking somewhat mollified, he played a virtuoso piece full of difficult trills and turns, and played it quite well indeed, but without passion, as though he were merely polishing the silver.

As he finished his piece he gave me the strangest look—I might almost have thought it a look of pity. I struck up a lively tune, and then Hwyn began to juggle apples and pears from the table, but her rhythm seemed amiss, and she did not sing. When the song finished she caught the fruits neatly, but without her usual flair. She seemed preoccupied. "Hwyn, are you well?" I whispered to her as sparse applause echoed on the stone walls. "I don't know," she said slowly.

"Good sir," I said to the servant who'd been pouring wine at table, "my friend is ill. Could she have some water?" The harpist had begun to play again in his cold academic style, and was still playing when the servant returned with a chipped clay mug of water. Hwyn, sitting on the floor, raised her head from her hands to thank the man and take a few sips. She looked bewildered—in fact she looked more than ever as she had when I first saw her and mistook her for a simpleton. "Should I make our excuses?" I whispered. She shook her head.

The last notes of the harpist died away and Lord Var called for another song. Starting suddenly to her feet, Hwyn began to sing a song I did not know, her clear, warm voice echoing through the room, and even tossed the apples into the air: one, two, three. And one, two, three fell to the ground, as I had never seen them fall before. The song stopped. "Bones," she murmured.

"Hwyn—you're ill. Rest yourself and I'll take over," I said.

"There are bones under me! Dead bones! This hall is founded on them!" she shouted, "Founded on murder!"

"What!" roared a guard, and Var turned blazing blue eyes upon her.

"You built this hall of them. Brick by brick, bone by bone, castle and tomb. Your sister: dead, murdered. Murdered for your dominion. Her blood flows from your table!" Hwyn screamed. "You can't keep her buried!"

The guard strode up to us. I wrapped my arms around Hwyn fiercely. "Pay her no heed! She means no harm to the lord. This will pass. It is only a fit, poor child, no fault of her own." But that did not deter the guard. I renewed my pleas: "Have pity! Can you blame her for her affliction? She can't help being mad." But the guard seized her shoulder. As he did so, Hwyn cowered closer to me, frightened but not too frightened for one last stratagem. Somehow she'd gotten into one of my pockets: the Eye of Night had passed into my keeping. I recognized it without even being able to touch it: it seemed to burn its way through my garment to my skin, to my very soul. I knew what she'd done not by the sudden heaviness of my pocket but by having to repress a sudden urge to start shouting about Var's sister's bones. That stone had power indeed—and if it called so strongly to me, how much more to a seer like Hwyn? All this passed through my mind in an instant, as the guards dragged Hwyn out of my grasp against both our wills. "It's a mistake!" I screamed. "Can't you see she's no traitor, only mad?"

"It is the mad that bring our troubles on us," Lord Var pronounced. "They bring the ghosts and the earthquakes. They bring the Troubles of the North. We may pity them, but not soften: we are duty bound to destroy them."

"NO!" I hurled myself at the guards. One of them brought a cudgel down on my head and I dropped like a windfall apple.

12

MADFOLK, MAGES,
AND PROPHETS

I awoke in the gutter, my head sorer than all the ale in Swevnalond could have made it. It seemed they'd thrown me out, but not imprisoned me, nor—I checked hastily—rifled my pockets. Thank the gods for small miracles! The Eye of Night was still there, as were a few small coins I might well need. But our packs and what little food we had bought were still in Berall Hall, and I scarcely dared think where my companions were.

I rose unsteadily and looked around me. It was early morning. Berall Hall towered over me to the left; to the right, the streets were beginning to fill once more with carts of harvest goods and care-worn northerners hoping to lighten their hearts at the festival. It was not hard to choose my course from there. The hall seemed unlikely to welcome me back, but in the town I might find Alcorel or one of the passersby who had applauded us yesterday, and might like us enough to be willing to help us.

I walked as though dreaming, silently, through the streets. People glanced at me, then looked quickly away. My heart sank into the pit of my entrails. The only eyes that would meet mine were the painted ones on icons of the Upside-Down God. In this festival time, his image was everywhere: falling, falling, never to quite hit bottom. He seemed a strangely hapless figure. Drawn alone, he was usually hanging by the foot from a tree branch like a tortured prisoner, but smiling as though unaware of his plight. In the Divine Wheel with the other three Great Ones, he sometimes still appeared with a rope on one ankle as though bound to the Wheel and its turning—though it was said that he himself, as the Turning God, started the Wheel's motion and with it time, birth, and death. In other images he simply fell unrestrained, unprotected, helpless, plunging toward a doom always inevitable but never realized.

The stories told of him were as uncomfortable as his icons. I had heard that he tired the other gods with his constant questioning till they sent him to roam the earth in human form. Here, still, he questioned everything, discomfiting kings and rulers and priests. At last, his own high priests, charging him with blasphemy, captured him and hung him by the foot from a tree to be beaten with flails, mocked, and spat upon. But the weight of the god hanging from the branch was more than the weight of the world; with the roots of the tree as a fulcrum, he had turned the world upside-down and made the World-Wheel turn.

Some of the stories say the Hidden Goddess rescued him from his bondage, cut him down, and caught him when he fell. Some say he never escaped, and is still bound to the World-Wheel, still mocked and beaten, still turning the world with his weight.

The god's images unsettled me as much as they always had. Still I stopped to contemplate an icon hanging on the side of a house—a particularly stark image, half naked and covered with whip-weals, still unaccountably smiling—and I murmured to that inverted, inscrutable face, "If one prisoner can help another, then help her now."

As the market-square filled with people, I spotted faces familiar from the previous day, but no one greeted me. Instead they seemed to veer away from me, as though afraid my misfortune would jump onto them like fleas. In front of an inn, I saw Alcorel, and quickened my pace to greet him—but without much hope. When he bolted into the tavern to avoid me, I was scarcely even disappointed.

At last I saw down an alley a one-legged beggar in a gray cassock, who half-smiled at me, his clear gray eyes not averted from mine. I followed him down to a rank corner behind a stable. "Will you recognize me, brother?" I asked.

"You must have fallen far," he said, "to call a beggar your brother."

"I'm accustomed to calling any man in that garb my brother," I returned.

"Fair enough," he said. "But I doubt you'd dispute that you've fallen far—despite your order's reputation for argument. You're muddy as a frog; spent the night in a ditch, no doubt, and never washed that wound on your brow. Come with me. You need looking after," said the stranger. So I followed him to a little makeshift shack, scarcely enough to keep the wind out. "My name's Jereth," I said.

"I'm Vokh," said the beggar. "Here—" and he moistened a rag with water from a bucket near the door, and washed the dried blood and dirt from my brow.

"Thank you," I said. "You're kinder than I've merited. I give you my old clothing, and you receive me when no one else will. Will the law be after us both now? What will this kindness cost you?"

"I'll be all right. No one will notice me—they haven't in years, so why begin now?" Vokh said. "But your little comrade—now there's a desperate case."

"Ah, yes," I said. "It seems the whole town knows my troubles."

"News of such an uncanny performance naturally travels fast. She's taken the surest route to the gallows that Lord Var's rule provides. You're a stranger in these parts, so you don't know what means our lord has used to keep order. He's found a way, he says, to turn aside the Troubles. You see, he believes some people call the Troubles to themselves: madfolk, mages, prophets. Kill them, and the Troubles lie quiet in Berall. The people mostly don't complain, because as he promised, we've had peace. But that peace is cruelly purchased, as you know well enough by now."

"Where is Hwyn—my friend? She's not—they haven't already—"

"She's in Var's dungeon," said Vokh. "They can't hang a criminal during the feast days, lest it offend the god. That gives her three more days. Beyond that, don't raise your hopes. She's run afoul of Var's law in every possible way: if she meant what she said about his sister's death, then she's a rebel and so doomed; if not, then she's mad, and also doomed; and if it should be true that Var murdered his sister—why then she's a prophet, most dangerous of all, and most certainly doomed."

"Gods have mercy, what can I do?" I dropped my head into my hands, irritating the sore. "Will they at least allow me to visit her?"

"I can find out for you," Vokh said. "You wait here. Don't let anyone see you until I come back."

Suddenly I remembered my other companion. "What of the Lady Trenara? Is she also a prisoner?"

"People say she is still Lord Var's guest, not blamed for the defects of her servant. But they say she does nothing but cry."

"She cannot be safe there," I said. "The lady is not what she seems. She—"

"No." Vokh cut me short. "Don't tell me what or who she really is. Don't tell me what Hwyn is, or why you are here, or where you are going. My debt is to you, not to your friends or to whatever fool's errand brought you into this pitiless town. I don't want to know whether you are all traitors, prophets, or lunatics. I know too much already—I know that your Hwyn spoke true, and that you all bear a heavy weight of secrets. I don't want to share that weight. If I can slip in unobserved—and I may, for beggars are common enough at Var's gate—I will ask the lady to meet you outside town. If I cannot, I will conceal you as long as need be, then wish you good fortune and send you on your way."

"That's already more than I could ask," I said. "Knowing what you do—the truth of Hwyn's sayings—you must have been close to them once, Var and his sister. I am not the only one to have fallen far."

Vokh put a finger to his lips. "No more. Let us both keep our counsel." He left me then and I, still weak from injury, slept till he returned.

I woke to a blast of wind as the door opened and shut. I raised myself and made room for Vokh on the sleeping pallet, which was all the furniture he had. He propped his crutch on the wall and sat down next to me. "The news is as good as may be expected," he said. "There's no warrant for your arrest. The townspeople may shun you, but you can probably move about and even ask to visit your jailed friend without landing in the same trap. I couldn't get to see the other one, the Lady Trenara, but I've heard of no further stir at the hall, so it seems that whatever she may have to hide remains hidden."

"There's no sign that the lord might soften toward Hwyn—that my lady might prevail with him to spare her?"

Vokh smiled sadly. "I am sorry."

"I must go see her now, if I can," I said. "You've been kinder than I deserve. I wish I'd given you something of real value. Will you have this?" I offered my cloak.

"No, brother," Vokh said. "I couldn't accept it. Why, I'd be accused of stealing it from some clothier's stall! Go now to your friend. Will you be back?"

"No," I said. "I would not link you to our trouble. And trouble there will be, for I will not abandon her."

"You're a bold man, Jereth. May the Turning God grant you a better turn of fortune."

"And to you," I said, "may he bring good harvest." I hastened to leave, before he could notice the coins I'd left in the sleeping pallet, the last remnant of the previous day's bounty.

The guards at Berall Hall were not put out at my request to visit a prisoner. The dungeon, it seemed, was easy to enter, if rather harder to leave. As the door clanged closed behind me I wondered if they ever meant to let me out—and what would happen to the Eye of Night if they did not. I reached into my pocket to finger the mysterious stone, reawakening that sense of panic I'd felt when Hwyn first slipped it into my pocket. Touching the Eye, I seemed to see around me bricks of human bone mortared with blood. The reality that greeted my earthly senses was scarcely less gruesome. The damp air reeked of excrement and sickness, so that I hated to touch anything in that foul place. And yet I had to keep one hand on the wall lest I lose my step. It was midday, but light barely penetrated Var's dungeon. As I hesitated, a voice pierced the darkness: "Jereth? Is that you?"

"Hwyn!" I hastened toward her, and to my relief found her running toward me, not shackled or chained.

"I recognized your footsteps," she said. "I'm so glad to see you. When they hit you on the head I was afraid...Jereth, you *are* a visitor, not a prisoner?" she asked anxiously.

"Yes, I'm all right, Hwyn, but worried sick about you. They say that madfolk and prophets are both condemned to hang in this evil place. *That* is how Lord Var keeps the Troubles at bay and earns the love of his people."

"So I gathered," she said. "In a sense the lord's right," she mused. "I did come to Berall carrying the Troubles. They lie curled up inside the Sky-Raven's Egg, awaiting birth. Var can't kill the Troubles by killing me, but he hasn't chosen the wrong victim, this time. I am everything he fears."

"He will not buy peace with your life," I said grimly.

"That is certain," she said. "Be warned: if strange signs attend my death, the danger will be greater for you and Trenara. Jereth, my friend, you should never have come. I gave you the Eye of Night for a reason. Take it, and finish my quest while you still can. You have been a great friend to me, better than you'll ever know, and I will treasure this farewell in my heart, but—"

"I'm not saying farewell," I said. "I will either get you out of here or die with you, making all the Trouble for Var that the gods or the powers of earth or the unquiet dead will put in my hands. Whatever it takes, I will do. You're not shackled, thank the gods for small mercies. Now if only I can find a weakness in this cell—" I walked to one of the barred windows, above Hwyn's reach but not mine, and would have pushed against the bars had I not seen the feet of a guard march past.

"What will you do? Break it down with your head?" she said. "Even if you could, what then? There are guards all around the stronghold. No, Jereth. You would accomplish nothing but to lose the Eye of Night and your own life—and I will never consent to that. Besides," she said, her voice dropping to a whisper, "someone has to save Trenara. If Var finds out she's simple—"

"Has it occurred to you that Trenara may be protecting herself in the best way possible?" I retorted. "Has it occurred to you that for her, to be charming and demure may be a better defense than sword and shield? Has the thought ever crossed your mind that you may be the one who most needs rescuing, because only you refuse to protect yourself?"

"Why do you always think you can protect me?"

"What do you expect me to do? Leave you here to die?" I raged.

Hwyn was implacable. "There is no other way. You have done enough to prove your friendship to me, and it will ease my parting to know that you did not forget me. But there is no hope for me now. Go, and the gods go with you."

"No," I said. "We are not so powerless, not now. I have the Eye of Night: what can withstand it? We saw with our own eyes how it shook down Kelgarran Hall."

"And we saw what it does to those who wield it for their own purposes. No, Jereth. The Eye of Night is not ours to command."

"Then why not see whether it has any commands for us?" I said. "Touch the stone, and see where it leads you."

"I did," Hwyn said. "It brought me here. Maybe this was meant to be. Maybe, like the ghosts at Kelgarran Hall, I'll be more powerful dead than alive."

"*No*," I said.

"Jereth, think: how else could it end? I knew long ago that this was a journey to death. You read the prophecy yourself."

"I did, and I told you it had two meanings," I said. "Besides, you admitted yourself that you were never meant to see that prophecy. Maybe this is the reason: so you would not give up the struggle too soon."

"I never expected to survive this quest," she said. "Don't mistake me: I'm grateful for your care for me. I know your noble nature makes it hard for you to leave me this way. But I chose my quest and all its dangers. Leave me with what I have chosen. The only things you can do for me are to save the Eye of Night, Trenara, and yourself."

But I said flatly, "You can't make me leave you."

"Why won't you listen to reason?" she cried. "You told me once that you would be ashamed to turn me from my quest. It is your quest now: follow it, or all I have ventured my life for will be lost. Why can't you understand that? Why can't you do what I ask when the stakes are highest?"

"Don't you know?" I said. "Haven't you guessed?"

At her silence, I spoke more slowly, choosing my words carefully so she could not mistake my meaning, "Hwyn, is it possible you've traveled with me all these months without noticing that I'm far over my head in love with you?"

She did not speak, and in the gloom of the dungeon I could not see her face. The silence struck me like the slap of a wave driving me under. Still, I had already broken open my heart and might as well pour out the rest. I went on: "I don't expect you to feel the same way about me. I can't ever be to you what you are to me: that flash of unearthly brightness across the dull prospect of a life without revelation, without purpose. You are my Firebird, to follow without reason, without reservation, for once I knew you, I could never be the same, never return to a safer life untouched by mystery without feeling an unbearable loss. I love you as you must love the Eye of Night, which called you out of your old way of life into a journey of peril and wonder, and for which you are content to die. I don't ask you to requite my love, and if it pains you to hear of it, I will be silent. I only beg you, don't ever ask me to leave you."

When the echoes of my voice died down, I could hear her sobbing.

"Hwyn, forgive me," I said. "I should not have burdened you

with this confession. Let me be as I was before, your friend, your follower—even your servant—"

"Hush, Jereth," Hwyn said. "Don't you understand? Of course I love you, my true companion. What else could I do? But you—can you really— Oh, gods, Jereth, don't say such things out of pity!"

I reached out blindly in the dark to touch her, then knelt to wrap my long arms around her and press her to my heart as I had yearned to do. I felt her respond with the same desperation I felt inside me, her face against my shoulder, her bone-hard fingers clutching me as if she would never let go. "Hwyn, my heart," I said, "I have ached for this so long. I was never whole till now. Oh, gods, I can never let go of you."

"Why did you never tell me till now, when we have so little hope left?" she said.

It is little hope now; it was no hope a little while ago, I noted to myself, my heart racing. "I thought you knew. I thought I had all but told you. In the mountains I was trying to tell you. Why didn't you give me any encouragement?"

"What encouragement could I give to a love you never spoke of?" Hwyn said, clutching me tighter than ever. "How was I to know what you meant, till you told me? Of course, I knew you cared for me—you were always so kind—but I thought it was in a brotherly way. It is so long since I gave up hoping that love of this sort could ever be for me. Why didn't you tell me plainly?"

"At first I thought you might be in love with Warfast," I confessed.

"Warfast!" she cried indignantly. "Jereth, I explained that already. It was the Eye of Night that wanted him."

"Then I thought, when you were Halred's acolyte, that you meant to be celibate. I knew she had no husband, and I noticed that though many men watched Day and Night, none seemed to court them."

"I never thought of celibacy as a choice," Hwyn said. "My face has kept me celibate all my life. How should I dream you were trying to speak of love? You sent me away once, and once proposed to leave me!"

"What do you mean? When?"

"First when you were wounded, you sent me away. Then in Folcsted, you offered to go on without me."

"Hwyn, as the gods hear me, those were the hardest things I

ever did. I sent you away when I thought I would die, and did not want you to risk your life guarding a doomed man in a barren land. And when I offered to take the Eye of Night alone and leave you in Folcsted, I was offering you my life, Hwyn: my whole chance of happiness in exchange for yours, to live maimed so you could be whole."

She gripped me tighter than ever and shook me a little. "Never do that again, do you hear? Never!"

"No," I said, "I was wrong. I see that neither of us can be whole without the other. Can you see now, Hwyn, what you do to me when you tell me to accept your death and leave you?"

"I left you," she whispered, "when you bade me in the name of my quest."

"You came back," I reminded her. "You were scarcely gone when you came back with willow bark to ease my pain. And though I must leave soon, I will be back. Gods grant I can bring you some hope of freedom."

"What hope can there be for me now?"

"Not much, maybe," I said, "but maybe the gods have not abandoned us. I have the ghost of a plan."

"What plan?"

"I can't speak of it now," I said. "If it succeeds, I will tell you."

"No, Jereth," she said maddeningly. "You must take away the Eye of Night, or far more than my life will be lost. Do not think you can save me; I have never expected to live long, not since I first got the wounds that mar my face. Don't risk your life guarding a doomed woman in a nest of enemies."

"Do not think you can spare my life by sending me away," I told her. "If you die on the third morning, I will die with you. I will sooner give the Eye of Night to a beggar than leave without you. I'll come back screaming of Var's sister's bones and be hanged with you."

"Gods on the Wheel," Hwyn said, "how you frighten me!"

"As you frightened me," I said. "Hwyn, don't you understand how I need you? If I had not met you, where would I be? I would have gone back to the monastery and realized that I had come full circle without hope of change. Then I might well have hanged myself on the nearest tree with the hempen belt of my cassock. I was dead when you found me. Did you not see that?"

"No," Hwyn said, "I was lost in my own needs. I saw that you were kind and brave and something beyond that: a seeker, one who is not content to see as others see. I knew you were sad, but in my selfishness I thought you could never be as terribly lonely as I was. I never thought you could need me as I needed you."

"Did you need me, then?" I asked.

"Can you doubt it?" she replied. "Have you ever noticed how often people shrink from me, how they avoid touching even my hand? When we were in the rudderless boat, I began to cry, and you put a hand on my shoulder. It was like discovering food or water for the first time, something I had always been starving for and never known how to name. Do you remember how you woke to find me weeping, during the Feast of the Bright Goddess? It was because I was sure you would leave me once you came to your senses."

"And then you would not tell me why," I said, "and I quarreled with you, because I thought you didn't trust me. What an oaf I was! How strange it seems now! But, my beloved, the gods have brought us together, and I will not despair. I will go now and try what I can to save you and Trenara without losing the Eye of Night. Trust me."

She turned her face toward mine as though to answer, but before she could speak, my lips found hers and all words were lost. I left shaken, knowing I had more to lose than I had ever had in my life, and only a desperate gamble of a plan to preserve it all from destruction.

When I left the gloom of the dungeon, the low red light of sunset almost blinded me. It was the autumn of the day, and thus the hour to gather at the temple in honor of the Turning God. The more pious festival-goers were leaving the market, and I followed them to the northern rim of the town where the temple lay. Most of the people still hung back in the marketplace, more for the chance of squeezing one last bargain out of the day than for any festivity. All in all, I thought, this festival was little distinguishable from a successful market-day. There were, as Alcorel had told us, few players to stoke the feeble flame of merriment. Small wonder, if Var had been killing lunatics for years. In the shadow of coming winter, who's to lead the dance but madfolk? Who sings in hard times but a fool?

At least in the temple court, some semblance of holiday reigned. Four priestesses sang and beat drums while acrobats performed the traditional Turning Dance in front of the temple.

But one of the priestesses kept falling behind the beat as though her mind were occupied elsewhere, and the acrobats looked more tired than they should. It was only the second day of the festival, but already its spirit seemed half extinguished.

After the evening prayers, I walked away from the temple lost in thought. Once I imagined I saw Hwyn among the crowd in the temple court, and I half laughed, half grieved to see how hope could trick my senses. I prayed I was not similarly deluded in my half-conceived plan. In the meantime, I scrounged a pauper's meal of fruits and sweets fallen from the carts of vendors, and drifted toward the fields that encircled the town, now gleaned of their crops and deserted for the winter. The sky darkened from deep blue to black. Under the cover of darkness I picked a place in the far fields, barely within the walls of Berall, for the task I had in mind.

What little I'd read about necromancy during my studies at the monastery was a warning against its use, not a handbook of the methods; but like any scholar, I'd heard the usual rumors of its practice. Perhaps the rumors would prove wrong, and nothing would happen. But I had to try.

In the dust I traced a figure like a wheel with twelve spokes, then marked the end of each spoke with a small stone I had gathered at the roadside. In the center I placed the Eye of Night. The autumn wind nearly took my words away from me, or perhaps it was fear that made my tongue falter as I spoke words of binding, dangerous words: "By the power of the World-Wheel, by the Eye of Night, by my name, Jereth son of Garmund, and by yours, Lord Conor Kelgarran, I call you to this place."

There was a storm within the circle as the ghost of Lord Conor Kelgarran appeared glowering over me, his chest drenched with the blood of his death wound. "What fool dares meddle with powers beyond his strength?" As he looked closer, his expression turned to amazement. "You! Tarvon priest, I thought better of you. If the torment of my soul does not move you, could you not at least be warned by the downfall of Dannoth? Do you expect to escape his fate?"

I replied, "In a moment I will break the circle and set you free. I have no wish to keep you bound. But the one who freed you from long bondage is in prison now awaiting the gallows. If this news does not move you, then do what you like with me. My name is Jereth son of Garmund: use it to bind me or kill me for all I care." With that I swept a hand over my crude magic circle, erasing part of it and breaking the bond that held Conor. "Conor of Kelgarran, I release you!"

The specter vanished and I thought for a time that I had simply lost him. But then I was aware of a presence, and when I turned, there he was beside me, sitting on the ground like an ordinary field hand tired out with swinging the scythe. His death wound was no longer visible; I began to wonder whether he controlled its appearance and used it for dramatic effect.

"Jereth son of Garmund, you're a fool," he said, a hint of a smile playing at the edge of his mouth. "Now tell me the troubles."

So I told him as much as I could explain of Hwyn's quest, of our travels since leaving ruined Kelgarran, of her untimely burst of prophecy in Berall Hall, of Var's dreadful edict and Hwyn's imprisonment. "She is doomed to hang as soon as the festival ends, three mornings hence. And she seems resigned to it. I almost feel she's trying to make a sacrifice of herself, crying prophecies to enrage a powerful lord and lose her life. She says the Eye of Night brought her into prison, and it may be where she's meant to be."

"What can I say against it? She may be right," Lord Conor said. "She may be some sort of mage, and they can be more powerful dead than alive. I have seen such things happen. She may be completing this task of hers in the best way she knows, and you, trying to save her, may be hindering her." I recoiled, but he only shrugged and spoke again. "But all the same, you love her, don't you, and nothing much matters beside that, does it?"

"Has everyone seen through me except Hwyn?" I said. "And yes, I love her, and no, nothing else much matters, and I'd be likely to throw away the whole quest for half a hope of saving her, if it weren't that she'd never forgive me."

"Well, I like you the better for it. *Someone* should love her. Still, I must say you've become everything the good people of Berall fear most: not only do you carry the Sky-Raven's Egg, packed full of Troubles, but you've used it to summon a ghost to this peaceful town. You've gambled high for this parley. What is it you hope I can do?"

"Give Var the fury you held back from Dannoth," I said. "I've seen your power."

"It's waned since spring," the ghost said. "I am less a part of this world than I was when you met me, more ready for whatever lies beyond. My brothers have reconciled themselves and left this earth; only I remain, and not for long, I think."

"Why are you the last?"

"More sins to atone," the ghost said dryly. "But even I will soon be done. My power to affect this world is fading. Much of it was spent in your escape from Kelgarran Hall. If you were hoping I could shake Var's fortress to the ground, you'll be disappointed."

"Maybe," I said, "but perhaps you could shake his mind. Suppose you appear before him and convince him he is mad. Then he will no longer dare hang strangers for madness."

"That may not necessarily follow," Conor said. "But I will do all I can. She may be right to accept her doom, and you wrong to prevent her, but I have always preferred to be gallantly wrong. I will appear to Lord Var as appallingly as I can, and then I will slip through the house in secret and see what I can learn that may help you."

"Could you seek out the Lady Trenara and ask her to meet me by the scullery door tomorrow evening? She may be in danger there."

"I'll look for her."

"What shall I offer in return for all your aid?"

"Invite me to your wedding." Lord Conor grinned. "And next time you need me, leave the Eye out of it: call, and I'll answer." With that, he was gone. I pocketed the Eye of Night, carefully brushed away all traces of the Circle of Power, then found myself a meager shelter from the wind in some hedges. The weather had turned colder, a foretaste of winter. Wrapped as tightly as possible in my long cloak, cursing the loss of my provisions in Berall Hall, I wondered if it were possible to sleep in such cold and wind and still wake in the morning—yet I did both.

When I visited Hwyn again the next day, I told her I'd asked a friend to exert some influence on her behalf.

"What friend do you have in this town?" Hwyn demanded. "The apple grower? I wouldn't expect him to have much influence on Var."

"No, not Alcorel," I said. "I doubt he'd even look my way now. I mean a friend of yours. Conor."

"*Conor?*" She started away from me. When she could speak

again, she whispered, "Good gods, Jereth, what have you given him?"

"Nothing," I said. "I think he loves you almost as much as I do."

I left at twilight, after the hunting horns had announced the beginning of the evening rites. As casually as possible I walked past the scullery door to look for Trenara, then faded back a bit into the trees, facing the footpath behind the building to avoid the appearance that I was watching the hall. No one appeared. With my cloak over my face, I went up to the scullery door and begged bread from a servant, but glimpsed no familiar face behind the door. At last I heard a voice at my ear, Conor's voice. "Don't turn to see me: I'm not visible. Just walk to some secluded spot and I'll tell you what I know." So I slipped down alleys and cow-paths till I reached the hedge where I'd slept the night before.

"Haven't you the sense to come in from the cold?" Conor demanded. "There's a disused shed not far down the lane. You'll turn blue out here."

"I didn't last night," I said, but followed his directions to the shed. Inside it I saw Conor sitting on the dirt floor at the ghostly semblance of a fire, which gave off no heat but at least lent the shack light and some meager portion of cheer.

"I spoke to the Lady Trenara, but she wouldn't come," Conor said.

"Perhaps she couldn't hear you," I said.

"Oh, I'm sure she did. She fastened her eyes on me the whole time, but when I'd finished speaking she just smiled and shook her head."

"There's no understanding her," I said.

"Why?" objected Conor. "You of all people should understand. Hwyn is in Berall Hall, or at least under it. Trenara follows Hwyn, and so as long as Hwyn remains there, so does Trenara, come peril or peace. There's nothing she can do for her, but the demands of loyalty have little to do with practicalities— for Trenara or for you, Jereth."

"Then Hwyn had it backwards," I said. "The only thing I can do for Trenara is to save Hwyn: if that succeeds, Trenara may depart on her own with a gracious farewell, as she did in Kreyn. But I fear that rescue may be a long way from success. If anything had happened to Var, some news would surely have leaked out during the day."

"I'm afraid you're right," Conor said. "The work's not prospering. What good is it to haunt Var? He's already haunted. His chamber is lousy with ghosts. How can I drive him mad? He is already mad; what more can I accomplish?"

"How do you know he's mad?"

"It is well accepted that a man who speaks to ghosts where none exist is mad. Even so, a man is also mad who sees ghosts and never speaks to them."

"Are you sure he sees you?"

"He sees all of us. His eyes follow us—a physical response too instinctive to suppress—but otherwise he ignores us."

"Does that make him mad? Some would say that makes him sane."

"Would you? Imagine yourself in his position. Imagine that I and my brothers thronged round your bed at night, plus a few deceased members of your own family and some gruesome specters who charged you with their death, every wound visible, each of us warning or cursing you by turns or in chorus. How long could you avoid responding? Wouldn't you try to seek some means of either satisfying our demands or banishing us? If you were determined not to answer our accusations, would you not at least cover your eyes to shut out the grisly sight? Var does nothing. He is mad, I tell you, as mad as a man would be who, surrounded by living folk, never spoke to a one of them."

"Maybe," I said, "but he's sane in the eyes of the world, never betraying himself with a word or gesture. All the same, I can hardly believe what you tell me. If Var is, as you say, lousy with ghosts, a veritable lodestone for the spirit world, how can he condemn Hwyn and dozens of harmless lunatics for attracting ghosts to Berall? What ruler would issue an edict against himself? It makes no sense."

Conor scowled. "Here we see the defect in the education of Tarvon priests: you're trained to expect too much logic in the world. It's neither just nor logical for a haunted man to condemn the haunted. And what of it? I remember King Elion of Kettra, Elion the Stern. A fierce moralist, Elion: he decried adultery as an offense against law and nature. Not only must adulterers die, but the hapless offspring of their unions he also doomed to death. Dozens of bastards and accused bastards died in his lands before some benefactor to the realm lodged an arrow-point in the king's throat. Among Elion's possessions was found a letter written by his mother on her deathbed, confessing to twenty years' intimacy with a horse-breaker who was Elion's true father. Elion had kept that letter all through the years when he called bastard children born traitors, unnatural monsters, the spawn of darkness.

"Var is another Elion. He must kill ghost-seers and lunatics to prove that he is not what he knows he is. He cannot retract this sentence of doom, for to admit the smallest whisper of self-doubt is to lose all: his lordship, his life, and the icon he thinks is himself. To admit doubt is to admit guilt: first and last, the blood-guilt of his elder sister Ruva, the heir to the rule by Berallian custom, who showed signs of madness even in childhood, and died in what was called a riding accident. No more can his faithful followers afford to doubt him: they would then face the guilt of having bound up his prisoners and built his gallows. The lie of Var's wisdom will not shatter easily: too many need to believe it true."

"There's not much hope, then," I said. "Maybe I should call on his sister?"

"What for? If she could do any more than she's already done to shake Var out of his senses, she would do it without the urging of a passing vagabond. But there's one among the living you'd best see," Conor said, "someone who's shown interest in Hwyn. Could Hwyn have a sister?"

"I don't know," I said. "She doesn't like to speak of her past. For all I know of her family, she could have hatched from an egg."

"This woman is enough like Hwyn to be her sister. She hasn't asked about her outright, but skulks about the castle listening for news. I followed her through town to the north square by the temple, where she sells fine cloth and lace from a cart. I didn't catch her name. She seems to be a stranger here and wary of the townsfolk. You can probably find her in the morning."

"What two strangers can do against the whole town I don't know," I said. "But where else can I turn? I'll look for her tomorrow."

"And I'll return to Var," Conor said. "Sleep now."

13

THE BOND OF A NAME

I could not sleep much, too filled with forebodings to rest. I had only a day left to save Hwyn or take up her quest without her. I knew I was no warrior, to kill the tyrant who imprisoned her; no fire-tongued leader, to rouse the populace against him; no master thief, to cheat the bars that bound her. Together, we might overpower one guard at the prison door if luck favored us, but there was never just one; against the whole company of guards, we could do no more than die with some travesty of honor against the company of guards. And if Hwyn and I both died, who would complete this crazy errand of hers?

At dawn I rose, sore and befuddled with fatigue, to seek the north square of town. With the festival nearing its close, the merchants did not scramble so early in the day for places in the square; most of their best wares were sold, and most of the townspeople had lost interest in what remained. I saw wagonloads of vegetables and carved wooden toys, a shoemaker and a blind beggar setting up shop, but no seller of fine cloth and lace. Later, perhaps, I might have more luck. Passing the time, I strolled to the temple grounds, where a girl was sweeping fallen leaves off the Turning Dancers' platform. There was not much to do here. There had been a dawn service marking the festival's last day, but it seemed I was too late for it; already people were leaving the temple. Scanning the little knot of temple-goers, I saw a familiar figure in a gray hooded cloak stride past, head down, as though she did not want anyone to meet her eyes. I darted after her, breathless. Only when I was close enough to lay a hand on her shoulder did I dare whisper, "Hwyn? Can it be you?"

She looked up in astonishment and I realized my mistake. The eyes that met mine were bright blue, and normal; Hwyn's were dark gray and crossed.

"So sorry!" I exclaimed. "I took you for a friend. Of course you're not Hwyn."

"But I am," protested a voice somewhat deeper than my friend's. "Who are you?" This, then, was the woman Conor had promised I'd find. A sister to Hwyn? Maybe; but then again, perhaps only a sister in misfortune. Like my Hwyn, this woman was most distinguished by a stunted body and crooked face, a face broken at nose and jaw and badly mended.

"My name is Jereth," I said. "I thought you were my friend Hwyn, a traveling player like myself; but it was foolish hope that made me think so, for she is in prison."

"Yes, I've heard of this double of mine," the woman said. "I would like to meet her. Indeed, I may have some idea who she is. Come with me to my lodging, and we'll talk. My name, as I said, is also Hwyn: Hwyn the Weaver." I fell into step beside her. When we reached the inn where she was staying, I adopted her habit of ducking my head to avoid recognition, lest I be spotted as the man thrown out of Lord Var's hall. No sense causing trouble for my new acquaintance before I heard what she had to say. We reached a back chamber where she'd stashed her wares: fine, gauzy fabrics for ladies' veils, intricate lace, embroidered linens. "Is this all your handiwork?" I asked.

"Much of it is," she said. "I used to have a partner. Pity I'm not trained to a homelier craft; there's little call for such airy finery in the shadow of winter, in a cold land, in the Troubles. But that's beside the point; you didn't come to buy linen. If you'll help me set up my shop this morning, I'll answer your questions—and give you some breakfast. You look like you need some."

Knowing no other source of help, I nodded my assent. As she unwrapped a parcel of bread and cheese and divided it in two, I asked, "What do you know of my friend?"

"I know a story Deor told me—that's my husband, dead and lost now. We were parted for a while when I accompanied my lady into exile, and Deor came looking for me all across the land. He says he had false hope thrust upon him once in the town of Gwilth: there he saw a woman who looked marvelously like me—only worse, from his description—another runt of the litter, like me, with blond hair and a damaged face. He ran toward her, calling my name; when he realized his mistake, she told him she'd be Hwyn if it would make him feel better. In fact she liked the name so much, she said she'd keep it. That's your friend, isn't it? The cross-eyed one?"

"Yes. In fact, I've heard that story too," I said. "She remembered him fondly, that man who first called her Hwyn. She'd

wanted him to come with her, but he wouldn't. I guess he found
the real Hwyn in the end. Strange chance that the two of you
should come to Berall at once."

"More than chance," she said. "The name is a bond. I've been
looking for her. I know more about your friend and your journey
than I care to speak of here, in a common inn where all the world
may pass by listening. I may know enough to be of some use to
you." By this time we'd each had our share of bread, cheese, and
water, all slightly stale. Hwyn the Weaver rose and shouldered a
parcel of cloth bolts. "Now if you'll help me about my business
in the morning, I'll go about your business in the afternoon."

"We don't have much time. She won't live beyond tomorrow
unless someone can save her."

"I know," said the weaver. "But I haven't decided yet what's
best to do. If you have a better plan, go off and set to it. But if
not, then come with me. Sell my wares for just a few hours while
I weave and think."

I had no choice but to trust her. I helped her pack a cart with
wares, harness a horse to it, and drive into the square. There I set
about work I had not done in years: haggling with customers
while keeping an eye trained for thieves among the buyers.
Strange that the weaver could think in peace while a stranger
sold her wares, one whose honesty and good sense were both unknown quantities to her. Funny, too, that she'd happen to pick a
merchant's son for the task. I'd never liked it, but I was about as
good at it as a man can be while worrying whether all that he
lives for will last another day. When I stole a glance at the
weaver, her face looked solemn, lost in thought, while her hands
darted to and fro on a small hand-loom.

At midday the dancing began in the temple court. "I've decided," Hwyn the Weaver said simply, so we closed up shop and
drifted off as though to watch the dancing, but instead went back
to her inn. We left the packed wagon at the inn, but the weaver
saddled the horse, climbed a stile to mount, and rode from there
while I walked alongside. "When we reach Berall Hall," she told
me, "I am your friend's cousin, and I have just learned of her
plight."

"What do you mean to do?" I said.

The weaver shook her head. "I can't tell you that. Trust me:
you have no one else."

"Gods," I said, "you *are* like her. Why are you so much like her?"

She shrugged. "Maybe blind chance. Or maybe the strange plan of the gods that I should play a part in these mysteries you are caught up in. I was born with the first rumors of the Troubles, thirty years ago; maybe I was born for this. And then again, maybe even the gods had no notion of what we would do with the fates—and the faces—they gave us. It matters little now: all we can do is make the best use we can of what we are." She gestured with her head toward the gate of Berall Hall looming just ahead of us. "Hush, now. The time has come for deeds, not words. Do as I bid, and I will not fail you."

At the stronghold gate I discovered that arriving on horseback wins some respect even for the kin of a prisoner. It helped, too, that beneath her rough traveling cloak, the weaver was nobly dressed, no doubt in clothes of her own making: a moon-white shift covered by a full-skirted surcoat, deeply dyed with indigo and artfully embroidered with curling vines and clusters of red grapes. As a well-to-do artisan visiting some disgraced poor relation, she was helped off her horse and assured of its safety by one of the guards. They even seemed to shut the dungeon door behind us without the customary self-satisfied clang.

As we descended into the gloom, I discovered another subtle difference between this Hwyn and the one I knew. Unlike my Hwyn, half blind and accustomed to compensating with sound and touch, Hwyn the Weaver stumbled in the dark prison, needing my hand to steady her on the stairs. But by the time we reached the bottom, her eyes had adjusted enough to recognize her double. "Look at you," the weaver marveled, "no wonder Deor took you for me. No wonder he called you by my name."

"So *you're* Hwyn," my Hwyn said, then asked, "Deor—is he in Berall, too?"

"No," Hwyn the Weaver said softly, "killed in battle a year ago."

"I'm sorry," Hwyn said. "He was a good man."

The weaver nodded. "He died as he lived. We supported Maethaldor of Troeth against her uncle's usurpation, and lost. He died defending her, and I've been in exile ever since."

"The world outside Troeth is wide, and most of it more comfortable than Berall. What brings you here, Hwyn the first?"

"You, of course," said the weaver in a hoarse whisper. "Did you imagine you could take my name and give nothing in return? At the time you met Deor, I was a paltry fortune-teller, able to tell lovers whether their sweethearts were faithful and such stuff—divining little more than a sensitive ear and a taste for gossip could uncover without magic. I wove weak love-charms into handkerchiefs and veils to sell to eager maids and neglected wives. After you took my name, I felt myself flooded with your power, your knowledge. I became a seer of real gifts, a treasured counselor to my lady."

"Surely you haven't come all this way to thank me," my friend said, "or to gloat over the reversal of our fortunes."

"No," said Hwyn the Weaver, "I have come to repay you. Do not be afraid." She bent and whispered in Hwyn's ear, and I saw my friend's face go as still as death, her eyes vacant, her unspeaking mouth half open.

I had been standing aside to let the two Hwyns have their say, but now I came between them, catching my friend as she slumped earthward, then seizing the other one's sleeve with my free hand. "What have you done to her?"

"Nothing! I'm trying to save her," she hissed, "*if* you'll allow me. Listen! She's not hurt, only entranced. I've ordered her by her name—her true name, which I learned when she took mine—to let go control of her body until dawn."

"Why?"

"Because she'd never let me do what I'm going to do," the weaver said. "I know her. I know her quest, too, and all that depends upon it. She must not be stopped here by a narrow-minded lordling and a herd of frightened burghers. Or by her own talent for self-sacrifice. I must take her place." The weaver threw off her cloak and began undoing the lacing of her surcoat. "I'll need to trade clothes with her—at least the outer layers. Could you loosen her gown? Hurry: there's no time for modesty. If the guard looks in we'll all be lost."

"But what will become of you?" I said.

"I'll tell them Hwyn bewitched me and took my clothes, and then you stole my horse and helped her escape," she said. "The innkeeper will back my story. By that time I'll expect you two to be far away. I only ask that you let my horse go free after the first day's journey, so he can find his way back here. There's food in my saddlebags; you'd better keep those. I can get more at the inn."

"What if they don't believe you?" I said. "I don't like to think I'm sacrificing one of you for the other."

"*You* are sacrificing nobody," Hwyn the Weaver said. "You have no choice whatsoever in this matter. You men can never seem to understand it when you're not in charge." I thought this unfair, since all my life I'd done little but follow, but this was no time for petty arguments. She continued: "You can't stand in for your companion, as I can. You can't break this prison down. If you know a better way, speak now." I had nothing to say. I helped undress and redress the limp, doll-like body. Finally she wrapped my Hwyn in her cloak. "Say she fainted," blue-eyed Hwyn suggested. Gently she pressed Hwyn's dark-gray eyes closed. I shuddered—it looked like what you do to a corpse— but when she handed the unconscious woman into my arms, I could just barely feel a stirring of breath from the passive body. "Now, who could tell us apart?" gloated the weaver.

"I could," I said, "even if your eyes, too, were closed. Your mouth is a little shorter, your eyebrows a little more arched. But I think few others would notice. Gods grant they believe your story while you still live!"

"If they do not," she said, "then I will die, but the world will live—a good bargain, I believe. But don't despair of me yet. I still have a few tricks in store. Now be swift."

I shifted the sleeper on my lap so that I could free one hand to take Hwyn the Weaver's deft one. "Gods be with you," I whispered.

"Gods help you; your task may be harder than mine. Go now," she said.

I turned away to climb the stairs, holding my Hwyn firmly in my arms. "Sir," I called to the guard, "let us out! My lady needs air." He peered through the grate while my heart pounded. "To see her cousin in such a place, the shock was too much for her," I said. "For pity's sake, let her out into the air." I tried not to sigh audibly in relief as he let us out. Another guard approached with the weaver's horse. I tied Hwyn to the saddle so she would not fall, and prepared to mount behind her when the Lady Trenara came upon us. "Here, my Lady," I said, struggling to contain my astonishment, "will you ride with her?" She nodded and passed me something she'd had under her cloak—my pack, the one I'd left at Berall Hall. Then I held the stirrup steady as Trenara mounted. She held Hwyn as gently as you please, and I took the horse's reins to lead them away from this place of doom. Not until we were well away from the town did I dare speak: "Trenara, are you all right? Did Lord Var hurt you?"

"He hurt Hwyn," she said indignantly, tightening her protective clasp.

"She'll be all right now," I said, hoping I was right—about both Hwyns. "It was clever of you to leave just when you did. And I'm glad you remembered the pack." Trenara smiled blissfully down at me.

We pressed on into the woods north of Berall, north of all human settlement for all I knew. The interlacing pine branches that parted before us and sprang back behind us were as welcome to me as the sight of the town had been a few days earlier. I would not feel safe until the woods had closed around us like a merchant's fist around a coin. No doubt any huntsman could follow our trail, but I knew none of the arts of covering it, so the wisest thing I could do was to keep moving until we were farther north of town than any of the craven folk of Berall would care to pursue us.

The setting sun drenched the woods in blood-red light and then was gone. Still I led the horse through the darkness under a meager sliver of moon, half hidden by branches. I stumbled on roots and rocks, wishing for Hwyn's night-sense to guide me, envying the surefooted horse that followed me. Finally in the depths of the night I fell, and could not convince my tired limbs to right themselves. The horse, free of my tyrant grip at last, bent to crop some grass by the roadside, then strayed farther off the path with Hwyn and Trenara still on its back. I crawled after it just a little way; then I heard the music of the brook. "Perfect!" I rasped, dry-throated. With the last of my strength, I crept to the bank, stuck my face and hands in right beside the horse, and drank. I must have walked for nearly twelve hours since my last meal, but for that moment, at least, the water satisfied me.

I think I dozed a minute on the bank before I looked up again at the horse and its burdens. Then I staggered to my feet and reached out to grasp the stirrup. Trenara had fallen asleep in the saddle, bent over Hwyn. I shook her awake and helped her dismount. She stared about her, bewildered, for a few moments, then knelt to drink from the stream as I untied Hwyn from the saddle and laid her on the mossy bank. Remembering the weaver's last kindness, I unbuckled the saddlebags and dropped them to the ground. Then I went anxiously to Hwyn.

She was still limp as a rag doll. At dawn, the weaver had said, the trance would end. I was not sure how far the night had advanced; it seemed I had been walking forever. Then for a while I leaned on my arm in the grass beside Hwyn, stroking her forehead, chafing her hands, looking for signs of life. But soon fatigue overpowered anxiety, and I drifted off to sleep, still holding her.

A familiar voice and a gentle touch woke me. "Jereth," Hwyn said, "where are we?"

"Hmm? I don't know," I mumbled groggily. "Nowhere."

She laughed a little, but hesitantly, as though still afraid. "Nowhere, indeed!"

I blinked and came a little more awake. "Well, nowhere with a name, most likely. We're in the wilderness north of Berall. The other Hwyn saved you."

"I know that part," she said. "I was awake in the trance—at least at the beginning. I saw everything until she closed my eyes, and even after that I heard a good deal until I fell asleep in earnest. I still can't believe she was willing to risk her life for me. What did I ever do for her but steal her name?"

"Strange," I said. "It seems you of all people should understand her: she is like you. After all, she understands you: she understands your vision. That's why she chose to save you."

"She understood what I need to do as well as anyone can—as well as I can understand it myself. But there was another way for her," Hwyn said. "She might have taken my place in the quest, and not in prison. She could have borne my name, with the Eye of Night, into the North."

"That was not her way," I said. "And don't forget that I still had the Eye of Night—still have it even now." I drew the white gem from my pocket and presented it to Hwyn.

"No—keep it," she said. "I must go back. I cannot let another woman die for me." She sat up abruptly.

"Hwyn!" I seized her wrist and forcefully pressed the Eye of Night into her hand. "Which one of us needs to learn to listen to reason? Your double chose this risk. Don't waste the chance she's given you. Think! It's morning already, the morning after the festival. We are a long night's journey from Berall. By the time you can reach town, her fate will be sealed. Besides," I added, "don't give up all hope of her escape. I left her busy devising plans, and Conor of Kelgarran busy stirring up trouble in Berall Hall."

"So you said. I've been wondering ever since you mentioned him: how did you get that angry old ghost into the melee?"

"The Gift of Naming has many uses. And besides, he still remembers you with gratitude." I doubted she'd approve of the risks I'd taken with the Eye of Night, so I left it out of the story for the time being. "I called on Conor to drive Var mad. He told me the lord is crazy as a nightmare already, if he could only be made to show it."

"That I'll believe," Hwyn said. "But it will take strong proof of his madness to turn his loyal followers against him. I don't hold out much hope for brave Hwyn—the real Hwyn, I mean."

"She always seemed to sense your presence," I said. "Do you have any instinct about her situation now?"

Hwyn closed her eyes for a moment, then shook her head. "I feel as though a curtain had been drawn over my senses. I don't think she wants me to know." She settled down again full length on the moss, lying close to me, and I carefully put an arm around her.

"I'm afraid for her too," I said, "but still glad beyond measure to have you here, alive and free and as safe as we can expect to be while the journey lasts." Then I brushed back a strand of pale yellow hair from her face and kissed her. Her mouth responded warmly, but with my arm I could feel her trembling. I backed away. "Do I frighten you?"

She looked back at me in amazement. "Then I didn't just dream it—what you said to me in prison. When you said you loved me."

"Is it so hard to believe?"

"Of course. Look at me!" she said.

"Look at me," I returned. "A scrawny weakling with dirt-brown hair already going gray. Does it matter to you? I hope not. Anyway, I *am* looking at you. I see a face full of scars. I see someone who's been hurt, battered, brutalized." I shook my head. "If I could get my hands on whoever did this to you—"

"Never mind. He must be dead by now," Hwyn said, turning away quickly. I had touched a sore spot.

"Hwyn—listen," I said. "I only wanted to say this: when I look at you, I see someone who's been hurt and learned courage, learned compassion. It's made you brave, but it hasn't made you harsh. That's why you're beautiful."

"Romantic fool," she laughed, abashed. "But it's worth three days in that awful hole just to hear you say these words. If I'd never been in prison, would you never have told me?"

"I'd have told you. But it would have taken longer," I said. Just then a sudden sound—a crunching sound—made Hwyn look up in surprise.

"Trenara?" Hwyn leapt to her feet, seeing the Lady Trenara sitting on the stream bank, eating an apple she must have put in her pocket at Berall Hall. "Trenara! You're safe!" The lady dropped the apple core, ran to Hwyn, and hugged her. When she could breathe again, Hwyn said, "Jereth, how did you rescue her?"

"I didn't need to," I said. "As I guessed, Trenara knew how to take care of herself. She left Berall Hall without warning just as we made our escape. She even brought one of the packs—we lost the nuts, but we still have the tinderbox and cooking-pot."

"Splendid!" Hwyn hugged Trenara back. Meanwhile, I wasted no time in opening Hwyn the Weaver's saddlebags and raiding her stores of dried fruit and salt meat to rally our strength for another long walk.

When we took up our journey again, Hwyn walked close to me, while Trenara skipped on ahead. The horse, untethered, had run off during the night, and we plodded afoot again.

"I wonder if they'll even dare pursue us from Berall," mused Hwyn, "when they see that our tracks lead northward, to the land of ghosts and earthquakes."

"After the hospitality of the peaceable townsfolk, I say welcome, ghosts!"

"Careful," Hwyn said, "they may be listening for your invitation." But just then I could think no ill of ghost-kind. I remembered my friend Conor of Kelgarran and Var's unfortunate sister, and mouthed a silent prayer that the Turning God would bring them good harvest.

14

THE LAND OF TROUBLES

An old soldier that my father once hired to guard his cargo told me that most of war is waiting around for something to happen. In the same spirit, I could tell you that most of following a mystic quest is tramping tired and footsore through unchanging landscape. After the miles between us and Berall quenched our fear of pursuit, for a long time our journey was simple, a slow, monotonous trek through ankle-deep brown leaves in a silent forest.

As the autumn nights grew colder, we took to sleeping in the milder midday, knotted together for warmth and comfort. We would wake in the chill of twilight to walk ourselves warm by moonlight or starlight or, on cloudy nights, by Hwyn's night-sense; at first the shadowy forest nights seemed full of hidden menace, but after a while they became routine. A low, broad stream flowed northward for many miles, giving us a road to follow, a bright band of silver under moonlight. The smell of moldering oak leaves made me sneeze, but for a long while nothing else happened to interrupt the long riddle game Hwyn and I played to amuse ourselves.

"I saw a strange spectacle," Hwyn said. "It had three eyes, six legs, and heads by the dozen. What was it?"

"Hmm." I pondered her words a while, turned aside to sneeze, then walked on a bit, thinking. "*Heads* must be a pun."

"That's not an answer," she teased.

"I know, I know. I'm coming to it. *Eyes* might be a pun as well."

I could see a smile tugging at the corner of her mouth, but I wasn't sure whether it meant I was getting warmer or colder. I shuffled "eyes" and "legs" and "heads" around in my mind till I said, "I have it: a beetle on a potato atop a heap of cabbages."

"Oh! Do beetles have six legs?" Hwyn exclaimed.

"That wasn't the answer?"

"Well, I guess if they do, it fits," she conceded.

"What was your answer, then?" I said.

"A one-eyed farmer leading a donkey-cart full of cabbages to market," she said.

"One-eyed farmer! That's not fair," I said.

"How is it not fair?" Hwyn challenged.

"You know," I fumed. It was not fair because Hwyn should know that I would never joke about being one-eyed in the presence of someone who was as good as one-eyed herself; but the same inner barrier that would have kept me from hitting on the answer forbade me to explain myself. "Oh, never mind," I said, when it was clear that she did not understand.

She shrugged. "I allowed your answer was as good as mine, so it hardly matters whether the question was fair or not. Your turn to ask."

"All right," I said. "I'll need to think about this one. I'm running out of riddles."

"Take your time."

I sneezed, cursed the moldering leaves, and scowled ahead of me. Trenara walked before us, her hood thrown back, her dark curls tossed in the wind. I watched her movement, graceful as a sail on a distant ocean, and gathered my thoughts. Hwyn kept silent beside me, breathing deep draughts of the forest air that did not trouble her nose as it did mine, stretching her shorter legs to match my stride.

At last I said, "I have one. Ready?"

"Ask away."

I chanted,

> "I can always be found in my bed but never resting,
> "Always in motion but never traveling,
> "Never silent but never speaking,
> "Always cold at my heart but never freezing. What
> am I?"

Hwyn was silent for just a few paces along the leafy ground before she answered: "The sea."

"Gods alive! I thought that was a hard one!" I burst out.

Hwyn doubled over laughing, clutching my arm as if she could scarcely stand. "It would be, certainly, if anyone else were asking it," she said when she could speak clearly again. "But whenever I don't know what you're talking about, it has something to do with the sea. The first rule of the riddle game is to know who's asking."

"This is what comes of playing too long with the same riddler," I said. "We need another player."

"True," Hwyn said. "Trenara, do you know any riddles?"

Trenara turned and gave us one of her long, solemn looks full of portent.

"She *is* one," I said. "I have a riddle for us all: where are the fabled horrors of the North? I haven't seen a ghost since Berall—and I summoned that one."

Hwyn raised an eyebrow. "Watch what you call to yourself—you with your Gift of Naming! This is no tranquil place."

"Why, what do you see that I miss?"

She unlaced the first bit of her surcoat and pulled the Eye of Night from her breast pouch, holding it up to the moonlight.

"It's larger," I said. When I'd first seen the stone, it had been no bigger than a robin's egg; now it was big as a hen's egg, and a large one at that.

"Heavier, too," Hwyn said. "I've felt it swell these last few days."

"I could carry it for a while," I offered.

"No," she said, returning it to its place in her garments.

"I only wanted—"

"—to help. I know, my love," she said. "It's not that I don't trust you."

"Why, then?"

She raised an expressive hand, open, empty, a gesture of helplessness.

"I know," I sighed. *"There are some things you can't tell me."*

"I'm sorry," she said, but revealed nothing else. We plodded on in silence, watching Trenara dance ahead, then twirl gracefully back, one hand on a sapling straight and slim as herself. Hwyn smiled, then. "Another riddle for us: why is Trenara so lighthearted here?"

"She comes from the North," I guessed. "Maybe this land seems familiar to her, comforting."

"Trenara," said Hwyn, "do you remember this land?"

"Yes," Trenara said. "We've been here for days."

We looked at each other and shrugged, then fell as silent as the moonlit forest around us till I sneezed again.

"The leaves are still bothering you?" Hwyn said.

"It's still autumn, isn't it?" I grimaced. "And those are still oak leaves."

"I thought in time you'd get used to it and stop sneezing."

"Apparently not," I said. "In time the snow will cover them. Hopefully, before then we'll come upon different sorts of trees. I didn't have this problem in the beechwood. Do you have another riddle for me?"

"I'm ransacking my memory," she said. "I think I'm running out."

"Haven't you been making them up?"

"Some of them," she said. "But I'm running out of ideas, too. You made up that last one, didn't you? The sea?"

"Yes," I admitted. "Not very successfully."

"How did it go again? I should remember it in case we meet another riddler. No one would guess it coming from me. It was a good one, really."

"Oh, stop pitying me!" I said, laughing. "I lost fairly."

"No, I'm serious. What was it again? 'Always in my bed—' "

"Look: a town," I said, pointing ahead through the lacework of branches at the thatched roofs just visible in the valley beyond.

Hwyn shook her head. "You know I can't see what you're pointing at. I'll take your word for it. But that's great news! I hope there's something edible left in the kitchen-gardens. The saddlebags are getting empty."

We hastened toward the houses ahead, eager for the brief comfort of a roof over our heads and a wall against the wind. But as I neared the clearing, I seized my two companions by the arm to pull them into the partial shelter of some brush. "Shh! I saw movement ahead."

"Fine place to meet wolves," Hwyn whispered as I peered cautiously out from our shelter. "Not a branch within climbing distance."

We'd come upon a wolf-pack once during the journey; for a man who'd never climbed trees as a boy, I thought I'd managed to get the knack of it wonderfully fast that night. But Hwyn was right: even at my height, there were no accommodating branches to be seen. Nonetheless, I was not too alarmed: the movement I'd seen had not looked like wolves. I stuck my head cautiously out of the thicket and peered on ahead. As I did so, Trenara broke away laughing and dashed on ahead before either of us could stop her.

"Hidden Goddess!" Hwyn swore under her breath. "There's no keeping her safe."

If there were any wild beasts ahead, they now had no doubt of our whereabouts. We rushed out and followed Trenara into the clearing.

I saw clearly before me, then, no wolves, but a clear, dusty path between gleaned fields and a farmer pushing a wheelbarrow of late vegetables toward the gray walls of the town. We careened downhill at full speed and walked between the wintering fields, staring about us. Smoke came from the chimney of every farmhouse we passed. Plowmen and oxen toiled along some of the gleaned fields, breaking them up for the new seed.

When we reached the gates, the sentry neither responded to our hail nor delayed us, staring dully out into the moonlight. We shrugged and went on into a bustling town. Tradesmen led loaded carts of wares through the wide gates; smaller peddlers pushed wheelbarrows of goods. Women clustered about the well, filling buckets and talking. Children ran and screamed in front of the houses until their mothers leaned out the windows to hush them. It was all so normal that it astounded me.

"Alcorel swore no one remained to the north of Berall," I said. "Here we see life undisturbed."

"Not quite undisturbed," Hwyn said. "Have you been traveling so long by night as to forget the ways of daylight? Who plows a field by night, or goes to market by moonlight? Why have they taken to the darkness?"

"Well," I said, "you told me the Troubles are the fall of night. Maybe this is how they've learned to live with them."

Hwyn raised an eyebrow. "A better way of meeting the Troubles than Lord Var's, to be certain. Let's find out."

We caught up to the farmer with the cart of vegetables and called a warm greeting. He took no notice, plodding ahead as steadily as before.

"Rude," I muttered.

Hwyn said, "We'll go to the market-square. They can't ignore us if we're buying."

So we followed the farmer and his cart, certain he would lead the way. But before we reached the marketplace, a familiar sound captured my ears. "There's a shipyard in this town! I'd know that noise anywhere."

"Can't be," Hwyn said. "Does this look like the seaside to you?"

"Maybe the stream joins a river on the other side of the town," I said. "Though I grant you it's strange. The lay of the land seems wrong. Besides, it would be foolish to build a town between two rivers where they join—that's flood land. It doesn't make sense. But I can hear the sailors' chanteys—no inlander sings like that."

"Lots of workmen sing at their jobs."

"But not that song," I said. "Besides, I could swear I smelled the sea. I must at least look."

I turned down an alley toward the shipyard sounds, and Hwyn followed me. As we passed, a burly man turned the corner suddenly and collided with me head-on.

"Sorry," I said, "I didn't see you in time." But he never looked at me. Instead, he kept on walking straight into Hwyn and almost through her without once breaking his stride, as though we weren't there. She tripped on his leg and just managed to catch herself on her hands, or her face would have kissed the ground. I cursed the man to his back, but Hwyn, uncharacteristically calm, looked thoughtful as she got to her feet. "Jereth, I've got the strangest feeling these people don't see us, don't hear us," she said.

"What could do that to them? Sorcery?" I said.

"Maybe."

We came out on the other side, and sure enough, it was a shipyard. I breathed in the smells of sea air, fish, and the pitch they were using to tar a broad-bottomed fishing boat. It all looked familiar—too familiar. I was certain I'd seen it all before. Of course I'd seen thousands of boats tarred in my lifetime—but I felt I knew every knot, every peg in its hull, every movement of the workers, every stray cat prowling the shipyard, every dead fish lying on the dock.

Farther down the dock, men were unloading a cargo ship, a great three-masted galleon, taking down baskets of exotic fruits and loading them onto carts. As the carts passed by us, Hwyn tried to stop one after another of their drivers, but none of them saw her. At last she turned back to me. "No use. As far as we're concerned, they're blinder than I am," she said. "What is that they're carrying?"

"Oranges," I said. "An Iskarrian fruit; it's too cold to grow them in Swevnalond. They're a bit tart, but quite good once you get used to them."

"It seems unlikely we can buy or beg a meal here," she said. "As long as we're invisible to them, I might as well take something."

Even months after our mishaps in Kreyn, I was still uncomfortable with Hwyn's thievery—once a priest, always overscrupulous. Still, I hardly felt justified rebuking her; our stores of food were small, and the road ahead hard. So, keeping uneasy truce with my conscience, I ignored Hwyn as she strolled off toward the unguarded baskets of fruit waiting to be loaded on the wagons. But eventually my eyes turned to the galleon they were unloading, noting the unusual height of its aftercastle, and a lightning bolt went through my head. "Hwyn, wait!" I shouted, "stop!"

"Jereth, I was going to leave payment," she protested. "I still have a penny or two of Hwyn the Weaver's in my pocket."

"Hwyn, listen to me!" Three sailors turned to look at me as I called out. "Don't eat what they're carrying! *Those are dead men!*" Hwyn froze; the fruit she'd picked up dropped from slack fingers.

Just then one of the sailors pointed at me: "Look! Isn't that Garmund's son? The one washed ashore alive?"

"Hey, survivor!" another called, "what are you doing here? You've still got flesh on you."

Now it was my turn to stand paralyzed, my nightmares taking shape around me in waking life. At last I felt Hwyn's arm around my waist. "Jereth, let's go," she said. "We'll find Trenara and leave this place."

I nodded and followed numbly. At last I spoke: "That ship they were unloading, the Sea-Bird, went down seven years ago. It was my father's. All those sailors, my mother and father, my brothers and sister-in-law and uncle, even the baskets of oranges, everything on that ship sank beneath the sea—everything but me. They don't *feel* like ghosts, but they can't be anything else."

"Then this is the land of the dead," Hwyn said, "which we walked into alive. No wonder they asked you what you're doing here. We don't belong here. We'll soon be gone."

"I thought," I said slowly, "that they were asking me what I was doing still alive."

"No," Hwyn said softly, her arm tightening around me.

Back in the market-square we found Trenara dancing. A crowd had gathered about her, laughing and clapping their hands. Her every movement expressed perfect grace; her face was lit with ecstasy.

"Well, this land of ghosts doesn't bother her," I said.

"No," Hwyn breathed, gazing ahead spellbound. She approached one of the onlookers, tugged at his sleeve, then, receiving no response, elbowed in front of him. I threaded through after her, so that we stood together in the midst of the throng. "Look," she said, "these people can't see or hear us. They can't even *feel* us. The sailors you knew saw you, but they couldn't see *me,* could they? I'd have gotten away with that fruit easily."

"We're the ghosts here," I said. "They're solid enough to our touch. We're insubstantial, only visible to special people, to people who knew us."

"Then why," Hwyn asked, "can all these people see Trenara?"

I had just opened my mouth to reply when one of the onlookers, a burly, weathered man of about fifty, confronted Hwyn: "Hey! Little flea on a rat's tail, what are you doing loitering in the market-square? Didn't I send you after water?" At the sound of his voice, I saw her face freeze. Before I could react, he seized her with massive hands and dragged her out of the throng.

I struggled to push my way out after them, calling ineffectually, "Hey! Let her go!" But the crowd blocked my way, and my shoving did not even seem to bother them. Still, I trusted that Hwyn could defend herself a little, even with her size so much against her, until I came to reach her. I knew she had a knife, and I had seen her draw it, though I was not sure it would be any use against a man already dead. But Hwyn offered no more resistance than to drag her feet, cowering away from the man. He hauled her along like a sledge. With a clout of the fist to the side of her head, he shouted, "Good-for-nothing bastard! Is this the way you mind me? Is this how you repay me and mine for the food you take out of our mouths? Loitering along the way, watching the players in the marketplace instead of doing what I told you? I'll make you sorry you ever heard of players. I'll play a fine tune on your skull."

"No!" she gasped, limp with terror, as I had never seen her, even in a fetid dungeon awaiting her death. "Please, stop, Grandfather!"

Grandfather? The man was beating her like a drum. His meaty fist looked almost as big as her head, and to judge by the knotty muscles on his thick neck he might be a blacksmith, strong enough to bully draft-horses. And I had the dark suspicion that the Hwyn he saw was even smaller than the woman before my eyes: in his ranting and cursing, he seemed to be speaking to a child. But her weakness did not soften him. He might be a ghost, but he seemed in no way insubstantial. If the man in the alley, ghost though he was, had tripped Hwyn, this one could hurt her. What's more, I could not bear to see Hwyn so afraid, so broken. I squirmed through the crowd to catch up with them.

Coming within reach of the man at last, I grasped him by one iron-muscled arm. He neither saw nor felt my touch, but it did not matter: I had him. I had teased his name out of the tangle of ghosts' names in this place of the dead.

"*Del, son of Devon,*" I cried, and he turned to me, seeing and hearing me for the first time. "By your name I command you: let go of her." He dropped her helplessly. "I banish you, now and while I live, from the presence of your granddaughter. By your name and my own, Jereth son of Garmund, I seal your banishment." The man disappeared: he melted away between my fingers, while I was so intent on holding him that I lost my balance and fell in the dust. Hwyn, still shaking, came to help me off the ground. I put my arms around her and sat holding her a while.

"What have you done?" she said, her voice a hoarse whisper, as if she still feared her grandfather would find her by her voice and punish her for daring to speak.

"I bound him by his name." I stroked her hair; her body was still tense as a bowstring.

"And by your own," she said. "Gods protect you, by your own name."

"I should have banished him forever, and not just for my lifetime," I said. "I should have sent him to the scorched valley where Dirnlac of the Red Oak nurses his anger."

"Jereth, my love, my life, you must know by now that you will pay the price for sealing that bond with your name."

"Never mind that, beloved. Nothing less would do. How

could I leave you at his mercy? I've seen you face death with a steady hand and a bold word on your lips. I've never seen you so frightened before."

"I'd become like a child again," she said. "It's what I've always feared: that at any moment, in any place, my grandfather could come back for me. I scarcely dared speak of him for fear the words would bring him back, or change me back to the helpless thing I was in his grasp."

"Where were your parents, then? Dead? Or were they as bad as the old man?"

She laughed then, bitterly. "My parents? I never knew my father. My mother was something like Trenara—only a little different, more mad and less simple. At least she had sense enough to run away from home to St. Fiern's Town before I was born. There, they think fools and lunatics are holy: they write their ravings onto oracle-sticks and use them for augury. Better yet, they take care of them, feed, shelter, and cherish them. As a madwoman's daughter, I seemed to inherit some of that sanctity; I was fed, sheltered, and cherished as well. I lived most often with the midwife who looked after my mother, or in the temple of the Hidden Goddess, where the priestesses used to teach me chants; but I was at home everywhere. Every house in St. Fiern's Town was my home, every child my sister or brother. A place was set for me at every table. I could even rebuke my playmates' parents for beating them, and they would heed my words. It was a marvelous childhood!

"But one day my grandmother, no doubt meaning well, came to bring back her lost, moontouched child into the care of the family; and to my harm, she discovered she had a grandchild as well. She bundled us both, unwilling, back to Tarn's Ford. Back to my grandfather.

"Till then, I had never lived like other children. I had never had to account for my comings and goings. I had done chores to keep my friends company, not because anyone said I must. I was unused to being ruled; Grandfather was unused to being gainsaid. And I was too young to see trouble coming until it was upon me. I couldn't understand why he kept beating me. When I asked, it only made him more furious. Once, he struck me so hard on the side of the head that something burst in my eye; it's been turned off course ever since. He broke my nose and jaw. He did unspeakable things to me. He made me the deformed creature I am today, unrecognized when I returned to St. Fiern's Town, mocked by children, shunned by all, never to be loved by anyone but you, who must be a saint or a blind man to see past my horrible face."

I didn't know what to say to her. I rocked her in my arms as though she were a child.

"My mother," Hwyn continued, "ran away again soon after we reached Tarn's Ford. I don't blame her; she couldn't have done anything for me anyway. No one could defend me—until you, who have entered a bond with your name only to guard me from him."

"Never mind," I said. "It's all right. It's rare enough that I can do the least thing for you, you who carry the world's burden in your breast pocket. Now let's leave while we still can. If Trenara doesn't follow us, then we'll know she belongs here."

Hwyn allowed me to help her to her feet and lead her along the outskirts of town. "If I'd had my wits about me," she said as we left the marketplace, "I'd have asked my grandfather why he recognized Trenara. He was watching her, you know. I'll never get a clear answer from her."

"It doesn't matter," I said. "He might sooner have answered me, since I held his name, but it was hardly the first thing on my mind at the time." The northern gate was already in sight when I heard a voice calling my name. When I started to turn, Hwyn caught me by the shoulder.

"Don't," Hwyn said. "Don't listen. There's nothing good for us in this town."

"I have to," I said. "It's my mother."

Turning, I saw both my parents standing some distance away. "*Jereth,*" my father shouted, "why did you leave us? Why did you let us go down? You just watched me as I went under; couldn't you have stretched a hand in my direction?"

"It wasn't like that," I said. "You were well out of reach. The waves were high as a house. If I'd let go of that scrap of the hull to swim toward you, neither of us could have reached it again alive. Is that what you want? Would you rather have me dead, too? A clean sweep, the whole crew, the whole family, dead on the ocean floor?"

"You never tried to save anyone but yourself," he said. I turned from him to my mother, absurdly seeking pardon; her face unreadable as ever, she only said my name once more: "Jereth."

"I'm sorry," I said hopelessly. In front of me the ground seemed to open and then surge. I felt myself tossed up and down on the waves once more, saw them all but swallowed up in the sea; no way for me this time but to give in, try to do what I hadn't seven years ago, play the hero's part, give my life: better that than to live with myself as a coward for another seven years. I dropped off the edge of the board I was floating on, and plunged into the tumult. But something held me back; I seemed caught in rough claws. I struggled until I heard Hwyn's voice, and realized that it was her bony hands holding me back. She was standing on dry ground; only I was on the sea, tossed almost out of her reach as she struggled to hold on. "Jereth! For the gods' love, for mine, don't go!"

"I let them drown once! I can't again."

"What use could it be to throw your life away? What good will it do them if you die? Who could possibly demand that?"

I gestured mutely at my father, who seemed frozen in the moment of drowning.

"Garmund!" she called—but he didn't respond. "Why doesn't he hear me?"

"You need the Gift," I said. "Only I could banish them—but I can't. Now I must go."

She locked her arms around me with all her strength. "If you throw yourself in now, I'll go with you. Jereth, these people aren't drowning now; they drowned years ago. You can't save them. You couldn't have saved them then. Look how far they are, and how high the waves. You can't blame yourself. You weren't to blame."

"How can I be sure?" I cried. "How do you know? What makes you think I didn't play the coward's part seven years ago?"

"Because I've led you into the dungeon of Berall Hall, the abodes of ghosts, and a desolate wasteland, and I've *never* seen you play the coward's part anywhere," she said. "You've even risked a binding with your name—a binding for *life,* which will do no more good if you drown yourself now."

Someone came, then, between me and my parents, walking over the waves as though she could not see them: the Lady

Trenara. "Let's go now," she said. Under her feet, the waves had turned to sand. Looking over her shoulder, I saw my parents alive, sitting in their favorite chairs on the balcony of our old home overlooking the sea.

Hwyn had not let me go. "Jereth, I need you now, *alive,* in the present day, not holding on to a long-lost time, to a moment's decision made when you were scarcely strong enough to hold on, let alone swim to anyone's rescue."

"I can't stop wondering whether I chose wrong. I wanted to live so badly."

"It's not cowardly to love life," she said.

Now it was my turn to laugh bitterly. "In the past seven years I've done everything but love life. I've been eaten away inside like a rotten tree."

"Eaten away by useless guilt," Hwyn said. "There's no use hanging back here. Life, and all the good you can do, lie beyond that gate. Now come with me."

Just before we passed through the gate, I turned to Hwyn. "You saw everything," I said. "You saw the shame I've been carrying for seven years. Can you still—"

I broke off, but she finished for me. "Of course I still love you, Jereth. Now let's go."

Trenara had already gone ahead of us out of the gate. Hwyn and I followed, clinging to each other, slowly but steadily leaving our dead behind us.

15

TREMORS IN THE EARTH

I guess it's fish from now on," Hwyn said glumly as we ate the last of the dried apples and salt meat from Hwyn the Weaver's saddlebags. We'd meant to make them last longer, living mostly on fish from the broad stream we followed, but the best-made plans don't wear well in the wilderness. For the past two days rain had pounded down; there was no dry wood I could burn to cook the fish I could catch, and we were not yet hungry enough to eat them raw. We'd forgone food as long as we could bear, but the rain did not subside, nor did any place of shelter appear in the day's travels.

"There's about a handful of barley meal left," I said. "Other than that, it'll be whatever we can find on the way." In other words, fish—varied at times with bitter boiled acorns or the tasteless, starchy roots of thistles, delicacies I'd never dreamed I'd try. There was small game in abundance, and even herds of deer where the woods thinned, but neither Hwyn nor I had ever learned to hunt or trap. So the meat to be had was not for us, and we expected to reach the rim of the world sooner than the next town where we could buy bread.

Hwyn scowled. "Wouldn't it be funny if we escaped the sword in Kelgarran Hall and the gallows in Berall only to starve to death in the empty North, the quest undone?"

"No," I said flatly, and sneezed, for the leaves were still bothering me.

"It's wet here," Trenara said needlessly.

"Yes, Trenara," I said. "Can you walk some more?" She nodded and I turned to Hwyn. "And you?"

"We may as well. I doubt any of us could sleep." So we got to our feet again and staggered onward, cold and tired. It was the most miserable day of our journey since our escape from Berall, and it did not comfort us to consider that things could easily be worse, because soon enough they would be. Winter was at hand.

As we trudged on through the mud, keeping the rain-swollen stream just barely in view to guide us, I paused a moment in astonishment. "Hwyn, do you hear music?"

"No," she said. "You do?"

"I thought I did," I said. "But this wind snatches away every sound except the drumming of the rain."

"Maybe you heard me wishing we were singing for our supper in a nice dry tavern," she said, and we were able to laugh for at least a moment.

Sometime later the rain abated to a trickle and the wind ceased its howling. It wasn't yet dry enough to tempt us to stop and rest in the mud, but we breathed easier, straightening backs that had been crouched forward against the wind. I turned to Hwyn. "Are you still dreaming of singing for our keep?"

"Hmm?"

"Because I can hear it again, clearer than before. The music,"
I explained. "Can't you?"

"No. Where do you hear it?" she asked. I pointed to my right,
across the flood. She shook her head. "Pity. If there's another human being in this wasteland, I want to see. But there will be no
crossing that stream for days."

"Do you think there's really someone there?" I said.

She shrugged. "You're the one who heard it."

"I do hear it. But who would be out playing the flute in the
pouring rain? I must be losing my mind."

"I thought that was settled long ago," she said, "when you decided to come with me."

When the rain stopped at last, we practically dropped down
where we stood to sleep on the ground, wrapped in our cloaks
and heaped together for warmth. It was night, and we'd grown
accustomed to sleeping by day, but we were in no state to be
fussy.

Toward dawn I woke, shivering. The mud had frozen during
the night. I forced my eyes open and checked anxiously, reassuring myself that the two sleepers beside me were breathing. Then
I would have pressed closer to Hwyn and slept again—but I noticed that the sound of my dreams had continued into waking
life. I could hear it again, the sweet round tone of the flute playing a tune I knew well. Gingerly I raised my head and looked
around, but there was no one in sight. One thing, however, had
changed: the musician was definitely to the west of us, on our
side of the river. It all fit then: the bizarre image of a flutist
calmly playing in the rain-drenched wilderness. No earthly being had crossed the flood in this weather to haunt me with an old
tune. I knew beyond doubt, then, what musician serenaded me,
and why Hwyn's sharper ears detected nothing. He played for
me. I knew this musician, but I did not know what I would say to
him.

Straining my ears to hold the song, I did not expect to fall
back asleep, but I did. When I woke again it was gone. I told
none of this to Hwyn and Trenara, weighing my feelings pri-
vately. The day passed in commonplace worries: how close
dared we go to the stream, now swollen over its banks and powerful with its new weight of water; how far dared we stray from
it lest we lose direction; what would we eat until it could be

fished again; where would we sleep. In the night I listened for the flute half in hope, half in dread, but finally in vain.

The path eased for a while: frozen ground tired our feet less than treacherous mud, and thickets that had offered scant shelter from the rain were tolerable shields against the wind. We discovered a grove of nut-trees, perhaps the remnant of an orchard, and gathered as many as the squirrels had left us. Trenara wandered off into the woods to eat some evil-looking whitish berries off a low shrub, and when we realized she hadn't poisoned herself, Hwyn and I also picked our fill. "They're good," Hwyn admitted, surprised. "Have you had these before, Trenara? What are they called?"

"Berries," Trenara answered patiently.

We sang as we traveled; it made the land seem less lonesome. I taught Hwyn the song I'd heard in the night, forgetting for a while both the dangers ahead and the darkness behind my memory of that music. But it could not last: on the fourth day after the storm, the wind began to snatch my song away, and snow blurred our view of the path ahead.

"There's higher ground over that way," I said, pointing away from the river. "Maybe we could find a dry cave, or at least an outcropping that would give a little shelter."

Hwyn agreed, so we trudged uphill, notching trees along the way to mark our path back to the river. The hill rose sharply beneath our feet. Scrambling upward, Hwyn tripped on something to land on her hands and knees. She shrieked, and I rushed over to help her before I realized that it was a cry of excitement, not pain. "Jereth, look! These flat stones I tripped on—they're a stairway!"

"Are you sure?" The snow hid them, but when I groped in the snow with freezing hands, I admitted that the arrangement seemed too regular for anything natural.

"It must lead to something," Hwyn said. Dusting the snow off her hands and knees, she started upward, and Trenara and I followed eagerly. Sure enough, at the crest of the hill stood a stone house, its shutters hanging off at their hinges, obviously disused and therefore ours for the taking. The door yielded easily. Inside we found what looked to us like luxury: a wood floor half covered by a moth-eaten rug, some broken chairs and footstools under a thick coat of dust, a northern-style closet bed, like a long cupboard with slots cut in it for breathing, and a broad fireplace with a massive cauldron that must have been too big for the owners to take away with them when they fled the treacherous north. I brought in snowy branches from outside and set them by the hearth to dry while I started a fire with some ends of broken furniture. We melted snow in the cauldron for much-needed baths, and more in our own cooking-pot to boil our meal of acorns and whiteberries.

"This was a lovely home once," Hwyn said. "Imagine a lamp on the table, curtains at the windows, fresh bedding, embroidered cloths on the walls to hold the warmth in. These northern houses could be very comfortable." She tossed a twig into the fire, experimentally; it sputtered a little but caught soon enough. "In fact, it's still a good home."

"We could winter here," I suggested, feeding the fire a good-sized branch. "I could fix the shutters so we wouldn't be bothered by the draft. There are doubtless other houses nearby—a deserted village, most likely—and tools may have been left in some of them. We're close enough to the river to fish, and in time we might even learn to hunt. When the snow subsides a bit we could look for the remains of a vegetable garden. We might find some root plants still growing, something we could live on. We can survive here till spring more easily than anywhere in the north. Then when the ice thaws we can finish the journey."

She smiled a little, but hesitated to speak, staring into the fire until her smile disappeared. "I'd love to, Jereth," she said. "But I don't know if I can wait. The Eye of Night may not let me."

"We won't do the quest any good if we freeze or starve to death in the wilderness," I said. "The Eye of Night has waited at least thirty years; can't it hold out until spring?"

"What you say seems reasonable enough," she said, "but the Eye is rarely reasonable. All the same, I'll try to stay." She looked away from me, into the flames again. "Of course, even if I leave, you could stay here with Trenara until spring."

"Don't be ridiculous." I slipped my arm around her shoulders. "I haven't come this far to abandon you." We sat holding each other, neither of us saying anything, both of us fearing the journey to come.

We swept the cobwebs out of the closet bed; there was no bedding left in it, but it was still probably the most comfortable sleeping place in the room. We let Trenara have it and bedded down on the floor in our cloaks. Hwyn was asleep almost before we lay down. But as my eyes drifted closed, a thread of music insinuated itself into my consciousness. I sat upright, rubbed my eyes: the music did not fade. In fact it seemed closer now, louder. It might be just outside the window. I stood and groped my way to the window, pushed the dangling shutter out of the way, and strained my eyes against the dark. There was a glimmer near the trees. There, illuminated by a thin-strained trickle of moonlight through the clouds, or by some kind of ghost-light, was my younger brother, my favorite by far, Saeverth. Oblivious to the snow, he sat under a pine tree, playing his end-blown Magyan flute, the one I knew had drowned with him on the way back from Iskarron. He tilted his head back a little, seeming to notice me at the window, but did not speak or even stop playing.

"Saeverth!" I called, but he took no notice. "Saeverth, won't you speak to me?" Suddenly my face flushed hot and my throat tightened. "Saeverth!" I called a third time, "you of all the drowned have no call to haunt me or reproach me with your death. By all the gods! I didn't even see you go under. What could I have done for you? Your death is *not* on my soul. I never did you harm. Do you grudge me my life?"

He stopped playing and stared at me. "Once you liked to hear me play." He turned and started away, the ghost-light flickering between branches. Suddenly remorseful, I dashed from the window to the door, threw it open, and ran out into the snow without bothering to put my boots back on. "No! Wait!" I called, but he was gone. Bereaved anew, lost in that old intermingling of grief and guilt, cursing my temper and the snow that froze my feet, I turned back to the house.

Hwyn stood in the doorway, silhouetted by the hearth's glow behind her. "Jereth, what's the matter? I heard you shout. Was someone here?"

"Yes and no. My brother," I said.

"Your brother who is—"

"Dead," I finished for her. "Yes, like the rest of my family, drowned in the wreck of the Sea-Bird."

"Another of those accusing ghosts? Don't follow them. They haven't the right."

"No, Saeverth is different," I said, following Hwyn back into the house. We sat at the hearth again, stirring the embers to warm ourselves. "He wasn't accusing. But I didn't understand that until too late. I'm afraid I've driven him away."

"Why? What did he say?"

"Very little. Mostly he just played that flute of his, the throat-flute as they call it in Magya. I thought, at first, that he was haunting me, following us through the wilderness for days, playing the same tune."

"That music that I couldn't hear," she said, understanding. "You didn't want him to leave you now."

"No, but I knew it too late, too tied up in my own self-blame to realize that he didn't blame me." I stared unseeing into the fire, remembering the body washed ashore after the storm, bruised and blue-lipped. I hadn't wept for him or for any of them, but I remember sitting long hours on the sand clutching that battered remnant of him, seeing nothing before me. The fisher families, accustomed to drownings, came finally to pry him from my hands and pull me away from the rising tide, and I neither resisted nor quite acquiesced to their rescue.

"He'll return," Hwyn was saying to me. "If he's followed you for four days, he won't give up now; he'll be back. We can wait here, at least a little while. Not even the Eye of Night can be so unreasonable. We all need rest and shelter."

I nodded absently, still looking into the fire. She took my hand. "Tell me about him."

"He was the youngest, six years younger than I. We weren't always close. He had a twin sister who was naturally the closest to him. But she died of a sudden fever, quite young, and when I saw how desolate he was without her, I started to look after him. Before long, we were inseparable. He was the cleverest of us: he knew all the stars we sailed by when most boys were just learning to count their fingers. He learned the language of Magya so well that, but for his light eyes, he might have passed for a native. And he'd have been the one to have with us this summer, singing for our keep: Saeverth and his flute were almost famous from port to port." I stared into the flames again. "He was seventeen years old when he drowned."

"You miss him," Hwyn said.

"Yes," I said, "of all of them, he's the one I still look for."

"He'll be back," she said, stroking my hand. "I'm sure he will."

"Even if he doesn't return," I said, more to convince myself than Hwyn, "at least I've seen him. He's there somewhere, and he hasn't lost his touch at the flute. That's some comfort. If he didn't seem exactly content, he looked no less so than in life."

"I wonder if they're all out there—the dead," Hwyn said.

"Who knows? All we're taught—that they return to the lap of the Hidden Goddess—is too poetic to exactly mean anything or exclude anything."

"Well, the North is her land," Hwyn said. "Maybe they belong here."

"Well enough for them," I said. "They need no shelter from the cold." We sat silent a while, hearing only the soft crackling of the fire and Trenara's rhythmic breathing. The red glow of the flames seemed to shine through Hwyn's pale hair. She was staring into the fire with an expression I could not read. I leaned closer, slipping an arm around her, taking comfort from the warmth and solidity of her body in this land of ghosts. She leaned against me trustingly; it seemed strange that we had ever distrusted each other, ever been apart.

For a short, blissful time we made the house our own and did not speak of leaving. In the days we fished for our sustenance, or scavenged nearby houses and barns for anything of use: a half-broken axe, a covered pot for carrying fire, a blanket not too badly moth-eaten. We found old vegetable gardens and dug up roots to eat, often coarse and unsavory, but better tasting than thistles and more filling than fish. In one of the houses we even found a cask of strong, old wine; it lent a dash of festivity to our meals, a little flavor to our food.

In the evening we sang by the fire; Hwyn was making a ballad of the tragic tale of Dirnlac of the Red Oak, singing a few lines, then appealing to me for a word or two when the flow of inspiration seemed blocked. We sat awake long into the night after Trenara was in bed, talking of everything and nothing. Hwyn asked me, "Whom did you love before me? There must have been someone; a sentimentalist like you doesn't live thirty years with his heart closed."

I laughed, embarrassed. "There was no one important. Growing up at sea, I didn't meet many women except the prostitutes at the ports—and they didn't appeal to me. Month after month seeing no woman but your mother or a boatload of whores—it can make a boy awkward with women, and gods, how awkward I was! And ashore, I was too much under my father's thumb to meet many girls—except the ones I met on his terms, the daughters of solid merchant families, decked out like bait to snare profitable alliances in a way that would have made the Bright Goddess unattractive."

Hwyn laughed. "But you must have liked someone. Come on, I won't be jealous—after all, this was before you knew me."

"All right," I said. "There was a shipbuilder's daughter at Bellen that I liked well enough; I thought she liked me. She had a pretty singing voice, though it was nothing to yours. She liked riddles, as you do. She had a soft heart, and filched from her father's strongbox to give to beggars. But I was dragged out of my dreams to a long trading voyage with my father, and when I came back to look for her, she was married. I pined a while, and wrote some poetry of more than the usual awfulness."

"Oh, good," Hwyn teased. "Tell me some of it."

"Not till you tell me your true name," I said, stopping her mouth for a while. At last I asked, "What about you? Whom did you love?"

"With my face, can you doubt you're the first?" she said.

"But you must have liked someone," I turned her own protest on her.

"All right then," she said. "But it was ridiculous. I spent two years pining for Mavan, the second son of King Evan Tyrnos."

"You knew Mavan of Tyrnos?" A book of Mavan's poems had found its way to the Abbey of St. Tarvi a couple of years before.

"I was King Evan's court fool," she said. "His court was a dazzling place, strange enough to impress even someone from St. Fiern's Town. There were never less than a dozen bards there, not just skilled harpists but wisdom-drinkers and riddle-spouters of the old school; Mavan was learning their sublime lunacy, and it made him—interesting." She smiled crookedly on that word, then said, "Was there ever anything sillier than a deformed jester composing love songs to a prince? Of course it wasn't funny to me then; I saw my situation as hopelessly tragic, relished the feeling, and put it into verses, like yours, of more than usual awfulness. I was young enough to think sitting at his feet would be enough for me. I'd hoped, at least, that he'd keep me in his service after the old king died, but neither of the brothers did. So I took my broken heart to St. Fiern's Town and washed pots in a pilgrims' inn, searching the travelers for some sorcerer that could change my face—until gradually I began to forget what

made Mavan so desirable other than his utter untouchability."
She laughed, then. "Suppose I'd had my wish, become beautiful
by sorcery, and caught the prince's eye: what would I be now? A
cast-off mistress, I guess: too lowborn for a bride, and too old at
thirty to distract him anymore. Some wishes are better left un-
granted."

"I can't see you standing for such treatment," I said. "Let's
say you found a sorcerer, sold all your possessions for a spell,
and became more beautiful than Trenara. You'd have gone back
to the court of Tyrnos, unrecognized but well noticed. I could see
Mavan coming by stages to admire first your beauty, then your
wit, and lastly your heart; and I could see you enjoying his attention—for a while. Then you would remember how easily he
could ignore both wit and heart when your face didn't match. In
the end, you'd have refused him."

"I'd like to think you're right," Hwyn said. "That's what I'd do
now. But I was scarcely more than a child, then, and I scarcely
knew myself except as a lonely girl trapped behind a monstrous
face. I didn't know my strengths yet. It's terrible to be young.
People forget that."

"I remember," I said. "And like you, I'm glad not to have the
life I would have chosen then. Had I married the shipbuilder's
daughter, I wouldn't be where I am now—"

"In a leaky house in a snowy wasteland, on the road to the
heart of the Troubles?" Hwyn said.

"That's right," I said. "Don't you know that this is the best
time of my life?"

"Is it?" she said. "Gods, Jereth, what a strange man you are!"
But she said it smiling.

"Hwyn," I said, "marry me. I meant what I said in the dungeon of Berall Hall: I was never whole till I met you. It is as if I
had always been searching for you, without knowing what I
sought. I have followed you from summer into winter, and for all
we have suffered, I have never been so happy before. I could
never be so alive with anyone else as with you. Let me belong to
you, heart and body. Let me love you as you deserve to be loved.
Let this be our wedding night."

"You really mean it!" Hwyn exclaimed softly.

"Why do you always find it so hard to believe what I say? I
love you. And I have ached to touch you, Hwyn. I want to know
all of you. I want to caress you in every place someone has hurt

you. Let me begin tonight. Our time may be brief: on the road, we may freeze to death in a matter of days or starve in a matter of weeks. Why should we wait? Let's exchange promises before the gods right now, and proclaim them publicly when we reach a town with a temple—if we live so long. What do you say, my love, my life? Will you marry me?"

"There's nothing I'd rather do," she said, too slowly, too sadly for me to think it meant yes. "But not now; not until we reach the end of the road. I love you with all my heart, and though I can scarcely believe even you could love my body, I have longed for your touch as well. But the journey ahead will be too hard for me to risk traveling pregnant, and I wouldn't know how to avoid it if we started living as wife and husband. Trenara miscarried on an easier journey—and she's younger and healthier than I am. But I promise you, beloved, if we finish this journey alive, I will certainly not refuse you."

"You'd better mean what you say," I said. "I'll hold you to your promise if I have to crawl from the grave to do it."

On the fourth morning the sun broke through. The snow still spread over the land, great wet clumps of it sliding off the tree branches at intervals to drench anything below, but otherwise it was as fair a day as any we could hope for between there and Larioneth. When I awoke, Hwyn was already sitting at the window, its shutters thrown open, staring out at the brilliant white land under the sun, her hand pressed against the pouch over her heart where she kept the Eye of Night. Wordlessly I slipped my arm around her shoulders; she turned from the window to me. "Look," she said, "has it ever been so bright?"

"It almost hurts the eyes," I said.

"I wish it were spring," she said, "instead of a little teasing lull before winter. Still, we should enjoy this while we can." But she didn't look as though she were enjoying it.

I thought of asking her whether we were staying or going, but decided instead to wait for her to say the dreadful words, *we must go*. But for that day, at least, they remained unsaid. We spent the day laying aside provisions: roots from the gardens, some mushrooms that had grown in the partial shelter of a half-wrecked wooden house. I tried to preserve some fish by smoking it. Hwyn said little, but looked uneasy. From time to time she touched the burden near her heart, and I felt my own heart sink.

For the next night and day, I felt something building like a wave against a dam, ready to break.

In the night she woke screaming. I reached out, only half conscious, to calm her with a touch, but instead her panic flowed into me, waking me fully.

"I dreamed I was filled with fire," she said, "burning from inside, until there was nothing left. Even my name was burned. And when I had been consumed, I looked down at the world from somewhere outside my body, and saw only a scorched wasteland."

I stroked her hair, waiting for the sentence of doom that I knew would follow.

"I'm sorry," she said. "I don't know how to tell you, but—"

"I know," I said. "It's time to move on."

"I'm sorry. You didn't see your brother again. And I'm sorrier that we have to move on at all: we could have spent a fine winter here. But it won't let me rest." Through the fabric of her clothing, her fingers closed about the round stone.

"I know," I repeated. "It's all right. The Eye of Night drives us; I accepted that when I chose to follow you. Besides, my brother never told me to wait for him."

The day dawned clear and bright. We cooked a small breakfast over the fireplace, woke Trenara, and tried to savor the pleasure of eating indoors once more before leaving all shelter behind. Then we packed our bundles, with the fire-pot and other things we'd salvaged from the empty houses, and set out toward the river again. There was small need to regard the trees I'd carefully notched: we could follow my footprints in the snow where I'd gone down to fish the day before. But before we'd covered half the trail to the water's edge I heard it again—the ghostly music.

"There!" I said, pointing ahead and to the left, where I heard the playing.

"What?" said Hwyn. But I ran toward the sound without stopping to explain myself, aware only by the footsteps and hard breathing behind me that my companions were following. I thought I glimpsed a splash of color through the trees like my brother's crimson cloak, and I dashed after it before it could disappear—but to no avail.

There was a sound like sharp thunder, and the sky split open as the ground beneath me gave way. Then I was falling, falling, unable to touch anything solid or see anything that made sense. Trees upside-down, trees sideways bewildered my eyes. No longer desperate to reach my brother, I tried with all my powers to find my two companions. At last my flailing hand met another and gripped for dear life. For a moment that grasp was all I knew for certain in the world. Then I found myself still and wet and cold, lying in the snow holding tight to the Lady Trenara's hand while her other arm enfolded Hwyn.

"I nearly lost you both, chasing the ghost through the woods," I said. "It was foolish. I'm sorry."

"You're all right," Trenara kept saying in a soothing tone, whether to calm me, Hwyn, or herself, I was uncertain.

Hwyn, half hidden by Trenara's cloak, lifted her head groggily and said, "Yes, I think we're all right. We've survived our first earthquake."

"Not my first," I said. "I was in Iskarron once when the mountains shook; it destroyed most of the fine glass we'd been hoping to sell. But this was different." Releasing Trenara's hand, I rose to my knees, then cautiously stood, brushing snow off the front of my clothes, breathing deeply, enjoying the way the earth stood still. Then looking about me, I was astonished. "Wait! This was no earthquake."

"What do you mean?" Hwyn demanded, as she and Trenara disentangled themselves to stand.

"Look around you," I said. "What can you see but snow? There's no rocks or earth dislodged on top of it anywhere. And the snow's lying as evenly as before—not piled high anywhere, not shaken out of place. This land didn't shake: only we felt the tremors."

"Like the Entrails of the Mountains," Hwyn mused, picking snow and pine needles off her clothing—and paused, noticing suddenly what she was doing. "Look—Jereth, you're right. Look at this," she said, holding up a spring of pine. "While I was falling, I clutched at the branches—pine branches. But we're in a birch grove now."

I nodded. "Not a pine tree in sight."

"Where have we fallen to?" Hwyn said. I shook my head, unable to venture a guess.

"I caught you when you fell," Trenara said softly. "Were you afraid?"

"Yes, I was afraid," Hwyn answered her. "Were you?"

"Not I!" laughed Trenara, and she started forward. We wandered in amazement among trees that bore none of my knife-marks, in land that held none of our footsteps. We could not find the stream.

"What can we do?" I said.

"Keep going north," answered Hwyn, looking around a tree-trunk for the mossy north side. We walked through a seemingly endless day, quenching our thirst with snow when we needed it, until the snow melted and our boots sank into mud. Toward evening we found a few whiteberries growing in the underbrush and ate them, as much for thirst as for hunger. By the time we collapsed from weariness in a half-dry, shallow cave, we had still found no stream.

The cold had abated while we slept. As we walked under brilliant sunlight, we slipped off our winter cloaks and carried them over our arms. We found a stream at last, not flowing north like the one we'd followed, but good enough for our thirst. As I filled the water-skin, I heard Hwyn gasp: "Gods! I can't believe it." I looked up sharply and followed her gaze to the Lady Trenara, basking on the stream bank in her shift, which stretched over a distinctly rounded belly.

"Trenara," Hwyn said, "are you with child?"

Trenara looked up perplexed, saying nothing, but the answer was evident.

"Trenara," Hwyn tried again. "You look as though you're going to have a baby."

The lady smiled, patted her abdomen, and said, "I know."

"Is it Var's?" I wondered aloud. Trenara shrugged. But Hwyn said, "Unlikely. It would hardly be so visible by now. It could be almost anyone's—Ethwin, Lok, that young Kettran that was killed in Kelgarran Hall, any of a hundred and one men that looked longingly at her anywhere on the journey. But that hardly matters. What are we to do? She should be taken somewhere safe."

"Where?" I said, "To Berall, where we could all be killed? And how? We don't know how we got here, never mind how to get back. Till spring there may be no safe place for any of us. But I wouldn't lose hope for Trenara. She seems to have a knack for surviving."

"She does," Hwyn said. "Like my mother."

The other mysterious fool. Of course. "Like your mother," I

agreed. "But she's not your mother; nor is she your child. You can't protect her. She won't let you. And you have enough to guard, carrying the Eye of Night."

"You're right, of course," Hwyn said. "There's nothing I can do. Well, it had better be true that fools are the gods' favorite children, because I don't know who else can possibly take care of her."

Trenara's condition worried me, too, but I had already had too much experience worrying about what couldn't be helped; I refused to let this new difficulty preoccupy me. At least now the traveling was easier, mostly downhill, and the weather strangely mild, out of keeping with the season. But for some reason we could not fathom, we were worn out with traveling before the sun had even passed noon. Finally we gave in to lethargy and settled on a mossy bank to rest. "It must be the unaccustomed heat," I murmured as I drifted to sleep.

I woke to a strange sensation, a sweet smell at once familiar and unfamiliar, echoing a memory I could not place. I felt refreshed as though I'd slept for hours, but it was still midday. Hwyn and Trenara were still asleep, so I let them lie there, taking the time to explore our surroundings. Venturing into the trees, I was careful to mark my trail, lest I lose my companions in this strange land. When I returned, Hwyn was staring around her in puzzlement, while Trenara toyed with something in the grass. "Ah, there you are," Hwyn said. "I feel so strange here. I suppose I shouldn't complain when winter's given us a respite, but the heat's almost addled my brain. It feels like summer."

"It is summer," I said, and showed her the wild raspberries I'd gathered in the hood of my cloak while she slept.

"What is this place?" she whispered. "Have we fallen out of winter?"

The afternoon's travel, once again, seemed endless. The warmth that had seemed such a gift that morning began to feel burdensome. We took off layers of clothing and carried them over our shoulders, sweating where the parcels touched us. "I feel as though we've walked farther today than in all the days since we left Berall," I told Hwyn.

"Maybe we have," she said. "How long have we been here?"

"Less than a day," I said.

"And how long was that day?"

I stopped in my tracks. "Forever," I said finally. "One day.

How can you measure a day except by itself?" I smiled: "A riddle: how long have we known each other?"

"Five or six months," she said. "I've lost count."

"Maybe," I said. "Or maybe forever, since it includes this endless day. Or maybe not ever, since I don't know your true name."

"You know it, but you know it not," she said, "and I want desperately to tell you, but would die sooner than tell you now, though you already know it and have spoken it; and those are my riddles for you." So I was left once again unanswered—intrigued, frustrated, annoyed at her for holding back on me, afraid I had prodded a wound in her by asking for her name yet again, afraid of what it was she dared not tell me.

We lacked nothing but answers in that untimely summer country. Everything grew there: blackberries, strawberries, mayapples, mushrooms. The ponds and streams teemed with fish. Even we seemed infused with life: Hwyn's ragged blond hair grew abundant, my beard almost too thick to trim with my old knife. And Trenara's pregnancy seemed to burgeon out of season, like the mayapples. The abundant life here was welcome relief from the deadness of winter—but it felt unstable, uneasy. The heat became oppressive, like midsummer, and the day wore on as we walked and slept and woke and walked again under the untiring sun.

Watching Hwyn walk in the sunlight, her face half hidden by shining hair, I wondered if this fertile country might have power to restore to her the vitality a harsh life had denied her: could her body, like her hair, grow unseasonably here? Could the soft air hold any healing ointment for her scars? How would she look without them? How might she have grown up if she'd had enough food and care? What would the lines of her face have been without the marks of her grandfather's fists? Her eyes, without the violent blow that had disturbed their orbits, would look solemn instead of demented. And her face—without its distracting lopsidedness, would it be dominated by those serious eyes, or by the mobile, humorous mouth? Would I even recognize her, healed? I tried to picture it in vain. It was no use wondering: these marks of ill-use she would carry till death, and it was well that I had grown used to them. I should know from my own experience that some wounds never heal.

When at last the sun slunk down near the horizon, we saw the walls of a town glow red in the slanting light. "You know," Hwyn said to me as we approached the gate, "since we left Berall we've found human houses only twice, and both times ghosts were nearby. Maybe we'll see them here."

"Maybe," I said, fighting to keep my hopes in check. The gate of the town was unguarded, and beyond it no one was to be seen. But the moment we passed through I could hear, faint as the memory of a dream, the music echoing off the stone walls. I turned to Hwyn to tell her, but to my surprise she spoke first: "Jereth, is that the music you've been hearing?" Trenara seemed to hear it too: she said nothing, but had begun to dance in time to the melody.

"Yes," I said. "He's here. Why can you hear him now, when you couldn't before?"

"It may be we're in his country now," Hwyn said. "You fell here following him; maybe you need to see him here, on his own ground. You lead the way."

The town began to change before my eyes to a coastal town, not my hometown of Swanroad but one of the many ports I used to know, whose names and features had long since blurred together in my mind. I turned toward the sea by instinct, part of my mind knowing that we were miles inland, part knowing that, in this land of ghosts, that fact was no more stable than a cloud passing over the sun. Soon I heard voices: sailors calling to one another to time their movements as they hauled at a rope; and from another part of the pier, rough unpracticed voices shouting out an old seafaring song to the sounds of a Magyan flute and a gittern. Turning a corner, I found them: my brother sitting on a coil of rope, the gitternist on a barrel, amusing the sailors. Saeverth looked younger than he had when I last saw him—perhaps twelve. I pushed boldly into the knot of listeners; as in the ghost-town where I'd seen my parents, no one noticed me but the one who knew me. His eyes met mine, and he raised his eyebrows as though to let me know he saw me. I glanced back at Hwyn and Trenara, who still hung back at the edge of the crowd. Hwyn nodded to me. "Go on. We'll stay close."

When the song was done Saeverth smiled at me, made some excuse to the gitternist, and pushed his way through the crowd toward me. Reaching me at last, he put a hand on my arm, which fell straight through my solid flesh, leaving only a prickling chill. "Do you remember the hideaway?" he whispered.

The hideaway was not in the town I saw around me; it was home in Swanroad. In fact, it no longer existed even there: storms had changed the shape of the dunes the very winter after we'd claimed our stronghold there. But I knew that if Saeverth led me, we would be there anyway, so I nodded and followed him, across wharves and over dunes, to a place concealed by a rise of sand, the place where we'd hidden from the world, from our father, one summer long ago. I looked back to make sure Hwyn and Trenara had followed us, and I saw them waiting close by on a rise of sand. Reassured, I turned back to my brother seated beside me. He looked older now, maybe as old as he'd been when he died. "I've been thinking about what you said the last time we met," said Saeverth.

"I'm sorry," I said. "I didn't understand."

"But the question was a fair one: do I grudge you your life? I don't think so. But I do envy you, if that's any different. I wasn't ready to die; after seven years I still haven't accepted it. Yes, I definitely envy you—but then, I always did," Saeverth said.

"You envied *me?* Whatever for?"

"You were the only one of us that seemed to have a mind of your own and, occasionally, the courage to show it," he said. "Father didn't own you the way he owned everyone else."

I had to laugh. "You can't mean me, little brother. Don't you remember? Saeverth, when Father died I was twenty-three years old and still his bondsman, with nothing of my own but a book of poetry in the Old Tongue—"

"And your soul," Saeverth said. "You belonged to yourself. Garholt was Father's son and I was Mother's, but you were no one's pet, no one's favorite—except mine." My brother grinned. Then he fixed me with that piercing look of concentration that he'd always brought to a difficult lesson, a new language, an intricate passage of music to be learned. "In some ways all that happened was only right. You were the most fit to make a life for yourself alone."

"No. You were so full of promise," I reminded him.

"Everyone said so," Saeverth admitted. "But I was timid, afraid of angering Father, afraid of being left alone. You thrived alone. I'll never forget how you escaped at seventeen, slipped away as we embarked for Magya and weren't missed until we were well at sea. That was bold! Then, two years later, quite by chance, we stopped at Bellen to replace one of our ships, and found you apprenticed to the shipbuilder."

"Yes, I'll always remember," I said, "the look on Father's face when he saw that the shipwright's boy was his own son. I thought I was safe in my indenture—I was pledged to serve the shipbuilder another five years. But Father bought me like a slave and dragged me back home to Swanroad, and that was the end of all my independence."

"At least you had two years," said Saeverth.

"They were good ones," I said. "I should have brought you with me."

"I wished you had," Saeverth said. He looked young again, as young as he'd been when I left home.

I tried to imagine what it would have been like plotting our disappearance together, bringing a younger boy with me through the disreputable backstreets of port towns where I'd hidden myself; seeking work for two instead of one. I was as uncertain as I'd been thirteen years ago whether I could have managed for both of us. All the same, regret stirred my heart. "I'm sorry," I said. "I nearly did ask you to come with me."

"But you couldn't be sure I could handle it," Saeverth said.

"I was so uncertain of myself," I said, "that I couldn't tell anyone, afraid one word against the plan would change my mind."

"You knew I would have been afraid," Saeverth said. "You were always more daring."

"You were young," I said. "If you'd lived longer, in time you'd have rebelled too. But at any rate, it's strange to hear you say I belonged to myself—and then to bring up this story, of all things, to prove it. Don't you remember how it ended? Father bought my indenture. You said he didn't own me, but for the last four years of his life he literally did."

"And does that kind of owning matter now?" Saeverth said. "Here you are, as far from his world as you could be. Tell me, what did you do with the family fortune?"

"I gave it to the Tarvon Order, where I spent more than six years after the shipwreck," I said. "They founded an orphanage with it."

"Good!" said Saeverth. "Do you know what the rest of us would have done, had one of us been the sole survivor? Garholt would have kept Father's business going, just the same as ever, and been ruled by the old man long after he died. He'd already married the sort of woman he was expected to marry; the rest was bound to follow. Me, I'd have sold everything, boats, house, and all, and tried to live on the sale until some other plan occurred to me. Most likely I'd have run out of money and had to indenture myself. Mother would have held on to everything, preserving inviolate the memory of a great man that Father never was. And you? You gave it all away. You broke free."

"Not quite free," I said, as all the anguish of guilt and doubt that had haunted me for seven years came flooding into my mind, and my father appeared.

"There you are!" he called, striding over the ridge of sand, "hiding out like a couple of thieves. No one in my house should have anything to say that I can't hear."

"This is not your house," I said, looking back at him as steadily as I could. "Your house is hundreds of miles away, and seven years in my past."

"You gave it to strangers," my father said. "Once we were gone, you never looked back, did you?"

I could no longer meet his eye. Looking away a little, I saw Hwyn coming toward me, followed by Trenara and a dark-cloaked figure I thought I recognized. Taking courage from the sight of friends, I turned back to face my father. "I did what I needed to live."

His eyes narrowed to the sarcastic slits I remembered so well, as he prepared his retort. But Saeverth cut between us. He looked older now, maybe as old as he would have been had he survived. Reaching out to Father, he said, "Be at peace," and touched him on the shoulder.

As they touched, a clap of thunder sounded and everything disappeared. Earth and sky trembled and gave way. When they stilled at last, I found myself, Hwyn, Trenara, and no one else, sprawled in the snow by the riverside, the sun just sinking behind the pine trees. No town was in sight.

"Here we are again," Hwyn said, once again brushing snow off her clothes. "I guess we couldn't expect summer to last much longer. What did your brother do, just at the end?"

"He touched my father and told him to be at peace," I said. "I wish he would be. I wish I could be." I told her, then, all I'd been speaking to my brother about: how I'd run away from home and seized a brief taste of freedom, only to become my father's slave in law and in fact.

"What a hard man your father was," she said. "When we saw him in that ghost-town, haranguing you out into the waves to drown, it gave me the chills. How you grew up with any heart at all, raised by such a man, is the world's wonder."

"I wasn't really raised by him," I said. "For the most part, I was raised by a long series of tutors—each one cast aside in turn by my father as inadequate. But they were wise, and some were gentle. I knew the whole world was not cut of my father's cloth."

"Why didn't you ever tell me this story?" Hwyn said. "I would have understood you better."

"Why didn't you ever tell me of your grandfather?" I said. "I had to bury the past deep, for fear it would come back. But I should never have made Saeverth a part of what I thrust away from myself. I should have known he wouldn't condemn me. It's not in him."

"He loves you," Hwyn said quietly.

"I know," I said, pausing to take Trenara's cloak and my own out of my pack before the cold bit too deeply into our bodies. Then I said to Hwyn, "That was Conor with you in the ghosts' town, wasn't it?"

"Yes," she said. "He told me some alarming things about what you were doing in Berall to rescue me."

"I knew you'd disapprove," I said, "when I used the Eye of Night."

"And your own name," Hwyn cut in. "Do you have any idea what a risk you were taking? Jereth, you could have lost your life, or your name itself."

"Do you think I cared?"

"No," she said. "That's what worries me."

16
THE JOURNEY
INTO WINTER

We had reached the stretch of road we'd always feared. Now, toiling northward through ever-deepening snow, we scarcely had strength to speak against the wind.

When the stream we followed joined another to form a river, I tried to build a small boat for us to travel more easily, but the broken axe I had picked up in the deserted village was a poor tool for the job, and my hands were stiff and clumsy with cold. There could be no question of cutting planks; the best I could manage was a crude dugout with bits of log lashed to each side to stabilize it. It did not serve us well: toward the end of the first night's travel, a sharp spur of rock tore off the lashings. Without the logs on each side to steady it, the dugout capsized, drenching us to the bone and sending me fishing in icy water for our gear.

Sitting cold and wretched on the shore, our only clothes soaked through, we debated whether it was worth trying to lash the dugout to a new pair of logs. In the end, we decided that since we were already wet, we might as well try again with stronger taproots for lashings. We used that miserable tub until the river snaked eastward and Hwyn declared that it was time we left it, angling north again, into the wind, into the Troubles. At least thirst was not a worry, even after we left the riverside: there was always plenty of snow we could melt for our drink. We were thankful we'd brought a pot to carry fire; it was heavy, but without it we'd have gone for days without a dry place to catch a spark in a handful of twigs.

We still lived on fish: small streams and pools abounded where I could break the ice with my axe to catch the day's meal. When food was scarce Hwyn and I, by tacit agreement, gave the biggest portion to Trenara, whose pregnancy was so far advanced that we wondered how we could have ignored it so long. Still, even Hwyn no longer fretted over the lady's condition, intent only on hanging on. The wind had burned some of the pity

out of us; and besides, Trenara herself seemed singularly uncon-
cerned.

Traveling was bad, but resting was almost worse. Often, finding no cave to shelter us, we huddled in the underbrush like animals, heaped together without modesty to make the most of our
bodily warmth. After years lamenting my celibacy in the Tarvon
Order, I could almost have laughed to find myself sleeping in the
arms of two women—one that I loved, and the other splendidly
beautiful—too cold, tired, and sore to have a lusty thought
toward either of them. Still, the warmth of their bodies at rest
and the sight of them walking beside me were the only cheer to
be had in that harsh land. My brother's flute did not sound for me
again, in this land where nothing sang except the wind.

The snow drifted up high above our boot-tops, soaking our
feet. At times Hwyn struggled up to her waist in the stuff. But it
took a few days of torment, her small body lost in the drifts, wet
to the skin, before she would surrender enough pride to let me
carry her over the worst spots.

One evening, dividing another fish supper in a snowy copse,
Hwyn poked at her share listlessly. "Fish! What wouldn't I give,
right now, just to have a simple piece of bread."

"Or cheese," I said, tasting the word on my tongue before I let
it go into the night air. "Or ale."

"Stop," she said, "I can't stand it."

"You started," I reminded her.

"I know," she said crossly, poking the fish again. After staring
at it a while, she said, "You know, it's strange, but after talking
about food, I don't feel like eating. Who wants this piece?"

The next morning she was violently ill. "Sky-Raven's
Bones!" she swore, painfully trying to wipe her mouth with
snow, clinging to whatever dignity was left her. "What's the matter with me?"

"Fever," I said; a touch on the forehead was enough to confirm it. "And here we are with no shelter but the trees. If we
could only find a dry cave! But at any rate, there's no staying
here. I'll carry you." This time she didn't bother to argue. She
wasn't heavy—none of us had had much to eat lately, and only
Trenara was mysteriously still gaining weight. But I was doubly
burdened, carrying the provisions on my back and Hwyn in my
arms, not daring to give much baggage to pregnant Trenara. All
we needed, just then, was for her to give birth before her time.

I found no shelter. When I could walk no more I set down Hwyn and the baggage in the least uncomfortable spot I could find, where at least the bushes blocked the wind a little. I had saved a fish packed in snow from my last catch, so I boiled it with snow in the cooking-pot, divided the fish with Trenara, and gave the broth from the cooking-pot to Hwyn to drink. She could scarcely digest even this. Choked by fear for her, I could say nothing, reaching out mutely to clasp her to me.

"My love," she murmured. "Thank you. And I'm sorry."

"Never mind that," I whispered back to her. "Just please, please, survive."

When she had fallen asleep, I wrapped my cloak around her, then wrapped myself as best I could in the trailing ends, enclosing her in my arms, using my body to shield her from the cold. Trenara, on Hwyn's other side, threw one slender arm over us both, and darkness took me.

I awoke to cold and pain and the sound of Hwyn's ragged breathing, still alive. I kissed her forehead, waking her. She smiled a little. "Where are we?"

"Who knows? Still on the earth, not buried in it. Still in the godforsaken North. That's all I know. Let's move on before we freeze." I moved away as gently as possible, stretched my cramped limbs, and sat up. Trenara, lying curled up on her side, rubbed her eyes and then rolled backward, placing a hand on her belly, reacting to a sudden movement within. Then, slowly, she righted herself.

"Can you walk, do you think?" I said to Hwyn, reaching out a hand to help her up.

"I'll try," she said. She noticed, then, for the first time that she was wrapped in two cloaks, hers and mine. "Jereth—" she said, pulling at the extra one, but her voice caught, and tears spilled down her cheeks.

"It's all right," I said, bending to touch her face, feeling hot tears on my chapped hand. She wrapped my cloak around me once again, indignantly.

"It's not all right," she said, burying her face in the front of my tunic, clasping thin arms around me, shaken by sobs.

We set out again under a pale crescent moon, on snow disturbed only by the tracks of animals. Hwyn walked for the first leg of the journey, but when I stopped by a riverbank to fish, she fell asleep right there in the snow before I even had supper for us. I had to wake her to offer her some of it. "Try to eat," I told her. "You need to take something, or the next wind will blow you away." She took it reluctantly, and ate little. What she needed was bland food, gruel or bread, things as inaccessible to us now as the choicest delicacies on the Emperor of Magya's table. After we'd eaten I packed our things, gave the fire-pot to Trenara to carry, and slung the rest on my back. Hwyn took a few faltering steps, then swayed and grabbed me for support. "I can't—" she said. So I lifted her and carried her from there forward.

"Gods," she said, "I'm so much trouble. What did I ever do to deserve you?"

"Everything," I said.

Through the night I plodded forward as best I could, every muscle in my back screaming a protest against the double burden I carried. I bit my lip to silence myself, knowing that any complaint would hurt Hwyn. I looked for shelter, but none could be seen in the shadowy forest, so I had to be content to follow the north star and hope that some cave or empty house lay ahead of me. Just before dawn, the silence of the woods was broken by a man's gruff voice: "Give her to me." He appeared from nowhere in the clearing before us, lanky and pale, almost handsome but for his cruel eyes. He repeated, "Give her to me. I have a score to settle with her—don't I, Hwyn?"

"No!" I said. In my arms I could feel Hwyn shrinking away from the sound of his voice.

"There he is. I should have known," she murmured. I didn't wait to hear more: I turned away, hurrying back the way we came—but he was before us again. "Go away," I said, sifting thoughts for his name, distracted by fear. "You have no claim on us."

"But I do," he said. "The highest claim: my life. A life for a life."

"Jereth," said Hwyn, barely audible, "I killed that man." Then to him, she raised her voice as well as she could manage: "I'm sorry I killed you: I only wanted to frighten you, but I was too frightened myself to hold back."

I had his name in my mind, then, and would have used it—but Trenara strode between him and me. He looked at her, breathing,

"No," backing off sharply, wailing aloud, "NO!" She raised her hand as though to touch him, and he was gone.

"Trenara," I said, "what did you just do?"

"Nothing," she said. "He only saw me."

"He knew Trenara," Hwyn explained to me. "He used to sell her. Why he was afraid of her now, I don't know. Why, Trenara, for the gods' love?"

"He saw who I was," was her only answer.

I started down the path again, too weary to puzzle over our latest visitation. "Jereth," Hwyn said, "I told you I killed a man. Aren't you going to react to that?"

"I know you," I said. "I trust you. You didn't take revenge on Dannoth when it was offered to you. If you killed someone, you had a reason."

"He was beating Trenara," Hwyn said, "and I thought, this time I'll fight back, for all the times I didn't fight my grandfather. I only meant to scare him, make him drop her, and flee. What I didn't realize was that it takes the strongest fighter to do that, to leave the fight with your enemy still alive and capable of retaliating. Once I started, I was fighting for my life."

"If you're waiting for someone to blame you," I said, "you're talking to the wrong man."

"I know," she said. "But it's a fearful thing, to kill someone."

"It's over now, and long past," I said.

"Long past it is," she said. "But some things in the past—as you know well enough—are just never over."

"Well, there's one comfort," I said. "Always before, the ghosts have been near deserted houses. We may find ourselves a real hearth to sleep by—if we dare use it."

"Oh, we'll dare," said Hwyn. "The ghosts can do no worse to us than the living."

I pushed on, hopeful, as the sun rose to my right. Still the lonely wilderness stretched on ahead of me. It occurred to me that, even if we'd been near a town, we might have passed it on either side. Hours passed, and clouds gathered. The chill sank into my bones. I had been carrying both Hwyn and the pack for hours without rest, and my back was one long cramp. At last I could go no farther. Without a word to either companion, I set Hwyn down gently, threw off the pack, stretched out in the snow, and was asleep before either of them could even ask me what I was doing.

I must have slept a few hours before Hwyn shook me awake. "Jereth! It's snowing again. Wake up!" I shook my head, my eyes still screwed shut. "Jereth, come on. We'll die if we stay here."

I sat up, rubbed my eyes, and looked around. "Where's Trenara?"

"I don't know. I dozed off, too. She must have wandered off alone."

We shouted after her until we heard her answer: "I'm here." When we followed the sound, we found her leaning on a square stone pillar carved with four directional symbols: sun for south, moon for north, eastern key, and western vine. To either side of the pillar we could see a long swath cut out of the forest—tangled with saplings and brush, to be sure, but clear of full-grown trees.

"A road," I breathed. "Gods be praised! It must lead to some town."

"And it's going north," said Hwyn.

Our hopes were not disappointed. Toward evening we found a deserted cottage at the roadside, and broke years' worth of cobwebs to enter it. By then the air was thick with snow. I took in wood for a fire, but had to leave it to dry while I burned the broken remains of a cradle and chair the inhabitants had left behind. Over this fire I cooked the few small fish left from my last catch. This time, Hwyn took one eagerly—but seconds later was doubled over in the doorway, retching in the snow outside. I helped her up and brought her back in to the hearth. As she huddled dangerously close to the fire, which seemed to have no power to warm her, I noticed the sharp outlines of bones under her windburned skin, and terror welled up in my chest like a wave waiting to break.

"I'll forage in the morning," I promised her. "I'll look for something more fit to eat. Fish is no good for a disordered stomach." She nodded, but I doubt she set her hopes on it. What could I promise? I'd be lucky to find acorns or thistle-roots. The two women fell asleep curled together on the hearthstones, as I kept vigil, waiting to banish any hostile ghost by its name. I watched the two sleepers, Trenara childlike, at ease, Hwyn restless, stirred by fever-dreams. Wearily I rubbed my burning eyes with my fists, unable to weep, afraid to seek refuge in dreams. When I uncovered my eyes, there was a guest in the room.

It was a slender young woman with long, chestnut hair clutching something in one arm. There was something at once familiar and out of place about her hazel eyes. She smiled at me—decidedly at *me*—somewhat shyly as she came in, but went first to Trenara, laid a hand on the woman's belly, and looked content at what she felt. Then she crouched over Hwyn and, for a few moments, watched her sleep. A grieved look crossed her fair face, and she touched the sleeper gently. I felt confused, mistrusting any phantom that approached Hwyn, but seeing nothing but sympathy in her gestures. Then she stood, and I saw for the first time what she was carrying: a doll. A memory slid into place. "Anverth?" I said.

Beaming, she stepped toward me, changing in an instant to the child I remembered, the sister who'd died so young. "I'm so glad to see you," I said, reaching out to touch her—but of course, my hand met nothing. She looked sad for a moment. "It was good to see you grown at last," I said, "and so beautiful." Smiling, she took on her adult from again and crouched on the hearthstones near me. Her hand swept my forehead like the caress of a breeze, and I fell into dreams.

I woke to dim gray half-darkness, perhaps at dawn. My companions still slept near the dying embers of the fire. Quietly, I tugged on my boots and ventured out the front door. Snow swirled down, and the wind cried like a living creature. Bracing myself, I stepped out into the wind and went as far as I dared go lest my tracks be lost under snowfall, but I found nothing of use: no stream where I could fish, no whiteberries, nothing edible growing in the ruins of orchards around the other deserted houses. When I returned, the women still lay curled together by the hearth, but Trenara was stirring in her sleep.

"What?" Hwyn murmured groggily, rubbing her eyes. "Oh, Trenara, it's only you." They sat up slowly. "You and the baby, that is. I felt it kicking. Doesn't that wake you?"

Trenara only gave one of her slow, reflective smiles that seemed to mean everything and nothing. I shook the snow off my cloak, set down the fresh branches I'd brought for the fire, and crouched beside them. "How are you feeling?" I asked.

"A little better. I must have slept a week," Hwyn said. Then, as if to belie her words, a shudder came over her, and her face turned ash-gray. She lurched to the door, clutching her gut, and doubled over retching from an empty stomach. I helped her up off the threshold, pulling her gently indoors. The pressure in my chest rose to my throat, so that I could scarcely speak. She leaned against me, her face turned down. At last I recovered my voice. "Rest now. That's all you can do. Later you may want to eat; I'll try to find something." I could feel her body shaking, or maybe I was the one trembling.

"No," she said at last. "I can't eat, and I don't have time to rest. I have to move on."

"Hwyn, it's snowing," I said.

"I saw," she said. "I'm sorry. We have to go now."

"Sorry?" I said. "You must be mad! You can hardly stand, let alone travel. It's colder than Var's heart out there, and I haven't even found anything to eat."

"I'm sorry about that for your sake and Trenara's; for my part, it hardly matters. I know how insane I must sound, but the Eye of Night was burning in my dreams all night. The time is near. I can't afford to wait."

"How can you travel? The wind is from the north; that means against us all the way. Even here, out of the wind, you can hardly walk to the door."

"Can you bear to carry me a little longer?"

"NO!" I shouted, startling Trenara to her feet, while Hwyn stared stubbornly back at me. "I will not murder you by taking you out into the cold. You can't make me do it. We have good shelter here, and we're staying until you're stronger."

"*Jereth, look at me!*" Hwyn shouted back with more force than I thought she had left. "Listen to me! In here or out there, I'm dying. If we don't reach our destination in time, I will die for *nothing*. Do you understand now? I haven't come this far to fail in the last stretch."

Something exploded in me then, searing my brain. If I could have wept it might have released some of the blinding fury I felt. But instead I snapped back at her, "If you're strong enough to argue, then maybe you're strong enough to walk. No chain binds you; go where you will, but don't ask me to carry you. Kill yourself if you must, but don't make me do it for you."

"Fine, then!" she shot back. She grabbed the pack and went hobbling out into the storm, followed by the bewildered Trenara. I doused the fire in the hearth, snatched up the rest of our things, and stalked out after them, slamming the door behind me. It took only a few of my longer strides to pass Hwyn. Without speaking I grabbed the pack roughly from her. One of its straps tore, and she cursed shrilly. Stone-faced, I slung it over my shoulder on its

one undamaged strap and carried it in silence, hating myself, furious at Hwyn. The snow continued.

We'd not gone a mile when Hwyn fell face-down in the snow.
With a wordless cry of pain I dropped the fire-pot and swept her
up into my arms, relieved to see that she responded, holding on
with desperate force.

"I'm sorry. I'm so sorry." I kept saying.

"It's all right," she murmured reflexively.

"Nothing's all right," I said. "This is tearing my heart out,
piece by piece. Hwyn, if you died I'd lie down next to you and let
the snow cover us both."

"No," she said. "You mustn't do that. Promise me you won't
do that."

But I could promise no such thing. Instead I carried her,
letting Trenara take the fire-pot, while the pack on my shoulder
hung crazily from its one strap—like us, barely hanging on. I realized, then, how naive I'd been to think that we were traveling to
anything but death, walking northward into the winter. Even
when we reached our goal, who would there be to take us in
from the storm and tell us we'd done well? A ghost? Before or
after reaching Larioneth, we'd all starve or freeze, and it was unlikely that I would be lucky enough to be first. I wondered if I
would have to bury all three—my love, the lady, and her child. I
wondered if I would have the strength, if it came to that, to finish
Hwyn's quest without her.

Once during the day's march, I had to stop to ease my aching
back. I set Hwyn on her feet and sat on a boulder that jutted out
of the snow at an angle. Hwyn came to put her arms around me,
and I rested my head against her, holding her around the waist.

Without my having to speak of it, she rubbed the muscles that
ached along my neck and shoulders. "Will you be all right?" she
said.

"Only as long as I have you," I said. "You know I could never
go on without you. I'm not strong like you."

"You are strong," she said.

"I don't want to be told I'm strong enough to lose you."

She was silent a long while, as if searching for some word of
comfort that would not seem a transparent lie. At last she said,
"Remember in the mountains, when you offered to take on my
quest for me? You would have gone alone into the North on a
quest you scarcely understood, carrying me in your heart as your

only comfort, not even able to tell yourself that I would know you did it for love. You were my strength then. Be strong for me again, I beg you. I will not die easily; I will not leave you easily. Do not despair easily—even if I die. Much depends on you."

I looked at her solemn, wind-beaten face, and could say nothing. What could I ask of her? She could no more promise to live than I could promise to calm the wind or dry the ground for a campsite; and here I was, plaguing her for a promise she could not make as I had plagued her for the secrets she could not bear to tell. "Forgive me," I said at last.

"For what? For loving me too much?" She smiled weakly.

I kissed her slowly, my heart tight, afraid this might be the last kiss. Then I picked up the pack, and lifted her again to travel on.

Toward midday the snow subsided and the clouds thinned, allowing a clean, cold light to shine from no particular point in the heavens. The forest, too, had thinned. With the veils of snow and branches taken from my eyes, I thought I glimpsed movement through the trees. "Look," I said, "to the left and ahead. Something's moving."

"What is it?" Hwyn twisted in my grasp for a better view.

"I don't know. It might be a ghost—or a wolf. I'd feel safer viewing it from a less exposed position. Trenara, come on, let's hide." As we crept in among the brush on the other side of the road, a sudden flash of movement made me clutch Hwyn in shocked reflex. A stag leapt across the path and dove for the cover of brush on our side, its flailing heels barely missing our heads where we crouched, hearts pounding, waiting for whatever beast had sent the stag into desperate flight.

The curtain of branches was broken, then, by a tall, proud horse. At the sight of us cowering in the bushes, its rider reined it to a halt and peered down at us, uncertain. She was a tall, dark-haired woman, as proud-featured as her mount, a bow in her hand, a quiver at her back, and a boar-spear at her side. "You're not ghosts, are you?" she said at last.

"No," murmured Hwyn, "but we will be soon without help." I didn't think the huntress had heard her response, so I repeated it for her. Two more riders reined up near her and fixed us with the same look of astonishment. "Where do you come from?" one of them asked.

"That's a long tale," I said. "I met these two in Kelgarran; we've traveled together from there."

"You came from the South," the woman marveled.

"And what are you? You're not ghosts, surely?" I asked.

One of the riders, a burly, thick-bearded man, laughed warmly. "Have you ever known ghosts to have a moment's doubt whether or not you're alive? We are three of the Holdouts of Larioneth, and we have seen no living travelers from the South since before my memory."

"Larioneth," Hwyn breathed. "Gods be praised!"

"Please," I said, "for the gods' love, if you have some place of shelter, take us there quickly, and we'll answer your questions there. We are nearly dead with cold and hunger, and Hwyn here is ill."

"Come, then," the woman said. "Ride with us, and welcome. I am Syrc, and these are my brothers Hart and Hauvoc."

"You are of Larioneth?" Trenara asked, stepping out of the trees. Syrc nodded her assent, and Trenara announced, "I am the Lady Trenara of Larioneth."

"Hidden Goddess!" swore Syrc, "It's the Returner." She slipped down from her horse to kneel at Trenara's feet. "My Lady, will you ride with me?"

Trenara nodded. Syrc rose and held the stirrup while she mounted, then swung back into the saddle with her. Meanwhile, the burly man reached down to take Hwyn from my arms. "Ride with me, child. You'll be safe, I promise. I may look like a bear, but I've bitten no one yet." I helped her into the saddle in front of him. "You're warm!" she exclaimed. "We've met no one but ghosts since the Feast of the Turning God."

Hearing the voice of a grown woman emerge from his tiny passenger, the man took a better look at her. "Why, you're no child! A thousand pardons, Lady."

"No lady either—just a common woman," Hwyn said, "and no need to ask pardon. I'm well used to the mistake. I'm called Hwyn, but if you'll take me indoors by a fire, you can call me child all you like."

I rode with Hauvoc, a wiry adolescent with proud, dark features like his sister's. Along the broad road they went abreast, clearly expecting no other riders to approach. Soon we were out of the forest, passing snow-covered fields and meadows. I saw ahead vaguely, gray against the gray sky, a circle of tall, massive stones standing upright. "What are those stones?" I pointed. As we passed them by, I saw Hwyn, on Hart's horse, shift to squint at them.

"That is our Sky-Temple," Hauvoc said. "Have you no such thing in the South?"

"I have never seen anything like it," I said, but some memory nagged at my mind, telling me that this might not be wholly true. "Are there other Sky-Temples in the North?"

"I don't know," the boy said. "I've never been anywhere but Larioneth. I thought every town must have a Sky-Temple, as well as an Earth-Temple, the kind like a round house. You do have those in the South?" I told him we did. "The Sky-Temple must be a northern kind, for the goddesses. The goddesses have always been close to this land," he said proudly. "But of course, it's not the Sky-Temple we're using now. Not even we Holdouts are crazy enough to dance outdoors in winter."

The gates of the city rose before us, glittering with a bluish sheen even under the dull light of a cloudy day. We passed through unhindered, no guard in sight. Then we saw Larioneth in all its splendor. The high turrets of the great hall, cut in just such sleek shapes as the wind might have sculpted out of snow, gleamed blue-black wherever they were not white-mantled. Carved shapes of heroes and beasts jutted out over the doorways, their details half hidden by snow, enticing the eye. Beyond Larioneth Hall stood a temple resplendent with colors, painted with gods and saints, stars and trees, flowers and strange beasts. Even ordinary houses, with their steep-pitched, snow-swept roofs, were as gracefully shaped as the crests of waves. "Do you have any idea," I said to Hauvoc, "how beautiful this place is? I've been all up and down Swevnalond, Kettra, Magya, and Iskarron, but never have I seen such a city."

I couldn't see his face, bent over the horse's neck, but I could picture him beaming with that half-charming, half-exasperating arrogance of adolescence. "You haven't begun to see Larioneth," he said.

We circled the hall to arrive at the stables in back. There a big, light-haired man ran up to Syrc. "What's this? Back so soon? And riding double? Was a horse hurt?"

Just then Trenara turned to face the man, and he saw it was a stranger. "Who's this?" Without waiting for answers, he held the stirrup for the women to dismount. He gripped Syrc's hand even after she was steady on the ground.

"Kernan," she said, "call a council. We have guests. Listen," she continued, her voice rising, "they've come all the way from Kelgarran. And more—this woman told me she's the Lady Trenara of Larioneth."

The man's jaw dropped, and for a few seconds he could only stare blankly at Trenara. "My Lady—if this is true you are as welcome as spring will be." Then he turned back to Syrc. "I'll take care of the horses. It's your news: you go in and tell them. I'll join you soon."

We followed Syrc to the back entrance of the hall. Hart carried Hwyn gently, but once we were indoors I asked him if I might take her myself. He placed her carefully in my arms, a flash of understanding in his eyes.

They led us into an ample room with an enormous, blazing hearth and a massive table. Its walls rang with high-pitched laughter as two small children ran to catch Hart around the legs, squealing "Uncle Hart!"

Hauvoc, casting a sardonic glance over such childish commotion, tossed another log or two onto the fire and beckoned to us to come warm ourselves. We needed no urging. When we were warm enough to notice anything of our surroundings but the fire, I saw how rich a place we'd come to. The table, carved with a pattern of leaves and acorns edged in real gold leaf, seemed to cover more ground than the whole House of the Red Oak Clan. This must have been the feasting-hall of a great lord, with plenty of room for his kinsfolk, war-band, guests, and a veritable city of servants. Some of the wealth of those days was gone—where once silver goblets must have stood I saw cups of clay, wood, and tin. But splendor remained: among the earthen cups gleamed a silver candelabra, and on the walls, intricately woven tapestries sparkled with gold thread and blazed with scarlet and purple. Our rescuers wore nothing of silk or gold, nor any emblem of rank, but they were clearly at home in this palace, tossing their wet cloaks over the richly carved backs of tall chairs to dry.

"Rand!" Syrc called, and in ran a child older than the two we'd first seen, a serious-looking girl of about ten with Syrc's dark hair and aquiline nose. "There's news," Syrc told her, "I need you to get people together. Do you know where Harga is?"

"She's at Brin's house," the girl said. "He fell on the ice and his ankel swelled up as big as his head, almost."

"We need her here," Syrc said. "Find her first. If she can't come at once, tell her to send Dara; but it's herself that I want. Then ride to all the houses you can and call a meeting." Then she pointed at us, huddled by the fire. "You see those people?" Seeing us, the girl stared wide-eyed at the first strangers she'd seen since her birth. Syrc told her, "Those are the first travelers to come to Larioneth from the South since I was a child. And one more thing—you needn't tell the others yet, but I want you to know first. That dark-haired lady," she pointed to Trenara, "is the Returner." Rand took in Trenara with solemn eyes. Then Syrc gave her a quick pat on the shoulder. "Now go get Harga. Wear your hood!" she called after the girl, who took off like an arrow, "I don't want you taking cold just before the festival." She watched the girl disappear, then shouted down the hall in the other direction. "Ash! Come see!"

"Coming!" answered a woman's voice down the hall. A big-built, auburn-haired young woman bustled in. "Hart told us. Where are the guests?"

"There, by the fire, warming themselves," said Syrc.

"Standing slumped on the hearthstones? They look so uncomfortable. Where's your sense of hospitality?" She came toward us, dragging a couple of armchairs, and seated Trenara in one almost by force, saying, "I'm Ash, Syrc's sister. Have you had anything to eat?"

"Not since yesterday," I said, helping Hwyn into the other armchair.

"I'll get something in a minute," she said, and on the way out complained, "Syrc, you think of everything but food. They're sitting there starving!"

"Food's your job," Syrc said. "I sent for the healer; one of them's ill, if not all of them after that journey. And I've called a full council. Everyone should know."

"That means more food," Ash said with single-minded practicality. "I'd better get working." She didn't even ask our names or where we'd come from until she returned with a loaded tray: mugs of hot cider, steaming barley soup, and warm, crusty bread. "I wish it was better stuff. This was all I had ready," Ash said above the din of voices rising with the news of our coming. "It's plain food, but at least it's warm."

"It looks wonderful," I said.

Hwyn drew in a long breath full of the scents of food. "Bright Goddess! It's *bread*," she said in almost the same tone Syrc had used to say, "It's the Returner." "I haven't seen it in so long I don't know if I remember what to do with it."

"Well, I remember," I said, eagerly breaking off a chunk of it. "Hwyn, how's your stomach? Can you eat?"

"I'll certainly try," she said. "The soup and bread should go down easily enough."

"If they don't, I can fix you some porridge," Ash offered. "And I'll see about getting you some cushions and a blanket. If Syrc's determined you're to stay awake for the council, sick or well, at least you should be made comfortable."

I thanked Ash and told her, "You may have just saved our lives." She grinned and hurried back into the kitchen to prepare for the coming crowd. To Ash, the food might be plain fare, but to us it was a rare feast. Hwyn ate a little, cautiously; Trenara and I ate a lot; and life returned gradually to our worn bodies and tired spirits.

The room filled with people, noisy, curious, joyful. They were not, like the Folc, obviously one family, one stock. They were of all kinds, big-boned or delicate, ruddy or sallow, blond as Kettrans or black-haired as Magyans. Most seemed fairly young, although I saw a few gray heads among the crowd. Their hands were rough with work and weather, their clothes old but adorned here and there with embroidered vines or flowers that held a fraying cuff or hem together. And all seemed as much at ease in the great hall as the hunters who had brought us there.

Hauvoc soon returned, shyly offering Hwyn and me a cushioned seat made for two. He took our muddy cloaks and replaced them with clean blankets, then hovered protectively around us. I thanked him and asked, "What's happening here?"

"Legend," he said. "One of the House of Larioneth has returned. This day was foretold to our people—though I, for one, never believed it till now."

I probed, "Syrc seems to be a person of power here."

Hauvoc grinned. "Then it's not just the little-brother's-eye view that makes her so?"

"Is she some sort of chieftain or elder? Will she decide what's to be done with us?"

The boy laughed. "We have no chieftain, no elder, no leader of any kind—unless, perhaps, this hunt has brought us one. We Holdouts are sworn to follow no one but the one who returns, the only one of the House of Larioneth who cares enough about the land to come back to it in the Troubles. There she sits," he gestured grandly toward Trenara. "As for Syrc's power, how could we ignore anyone who can shout like that?"

As though to prove his point, Syrc threw back her head and called in a ringing voice: "Listen my friends, my kinfolk! Let the council begin!"

The rumble of conversation quieted. "Harga's not here yet," an old man pointed out.

"Harga's the first to know every secret in Larioneth," a plump, florid-faced woman grumbled. "Let her catch up when she gets here. I'm bursting to know what's happened."

"Syrc, you haven't called us here just to show us your latest strange catch from the hunt?" a young man said.

"I doubt it," said the old man.

"Not exactly," Syrc said, flashing us a wry look.

"Til, are you blind?" another young man said. "Don't you see those three strangers on the hearth? Who are they, Syrc, and where did you get them?"

"We *did* find them in the hunt," Syrc said. "My brothers and I were chasing a stag when we saw these three travelers near the old South Road. At first I thought they were ghosts, but they shivered in the cold; the dead don't do that. So we stopped to speak to them, and one of them, the tall woman, gave us her name: the Lady Trenara of Larioneth!"

Half the assembly sprang to their feet; one man fell to his knees; two people on the far side of the room jumped on top of the table to get a better look at Trenara, while others behind them chided them for blocking their view. Trenara, hearing her name, stood and accepted the attention as though she had been born for it—and it seemed she had. But one man—the one called Til—said, "How do we know it's true?"

"Who else would brave the painful road north in this weather, all the way to Larioneth?" countered Syrc. "Who else but the Returner?"

"Apparently, two others did," Til said. "Who are they? Do they claim to be nobles of Larioneth as well?"

"No," I said, standing to be seen among the crowd.

"These are Jereth and Hwyn," Hauvoc said. "They come from—where did you say? Kelgarran?"

"Not exactly. We met in Kelgarran," I said, "but I came from

Swanroad in the southeast of Swevnalond, and Hwyn from St. Fiern's Town in the west."

"Can you attest to this woman's claim? Is she really of the House of Larioneth? Did you know her family?" Til pressed.

"I believe she speaks the truth," I said, "but I have no proof of it. She had no family when I met her."

"If you didn't know who she was," an older man asked, "why did you follow her?"

"I didn't," I said. "I followed Hwyn." Uncertain how much to reveal, I tried to catch Hwyn's eye, looking for some signal; but she only looked sleepy, worn out with illness and travel, relaxed in the unaccustomed warmth and safety of these strangers' hearth. So I was left to my own judgment. I continued, "I met her when I had nowhere to go. She offered me friendship and a direction: north. I liked her well enough to follow her. Trenara had been traveling with her before I met them, for reasons of her own; whether she came here to claim a throne or to find her lost childhood was not my concern."

"What about you—Hwyn, is it?" the older man said. "Can you bear witness that this lady is truly of the House of Larioneth?"

Hwyn roused herself languidly. "Not I," she said. "I met her on the road north, and became her companion by accident. I've known people of every station, and I'm sure of this much: manners like hers don't thrive in a farmhouse or a tradesman's shop. She's a lady, no doubt. She seems at home in the North. More than that . . . ?" she turned her hands up, as if to say, "who knows?"

"Ask the lady herself," the red-faced woman suggested. "Lady, can you prove who you are?"

Trenara stood silent a while; I thought she would never know how to respond. But at last she said, "This place knows me. The land knows me; it knows who I am."

"Of course," said an old man, the one who'd spoken up at the beginning to point out that someone wasn't there. "The land knows its ruler. It wouldn't matter, would it, whether she were of the old line, if the land didn't know her. And if it does know her, she's our Lady no matter whose daughter she may be."

"What do you mean, Per?" said Til. "What if the land knows her? How can we tell?"

Per considered his question a while. "Its ghosts would know her."

"What should we do, then? We can't just wait here till one comes by," Til said.

"I could call one," I suggested.

All eyes turned to me. Hwyn said sharply, "Jereth, don't you dare use your name again."

"I won't this time," I said, "only the ghost's name. I wouldn't need to bind the ghost, just call to it. They're common as snow here, anyway, and not shy of being seen. It shouldn't be hard."

"How?" Syrc asked.

"The Gift of Naming," I explained.

"Ah! A Tarvon priest?" said the one called Per.

"Almost," I said. "I left the Order without vows, but the Gift stayed with me. Shall I try it?"

Per nodded. "Look for someone who loved this land, someone who loyally served the House of Larioneth."

"All right," I said. "I'll need quiet." The room stilled. I closed my eyes and let my mind slide away into ghost-dreams until it touched a name, Lancar the Horseman. His name was sacred even in my homeland; I knew him as the great, sad hero of the North who sacrificed himself for a faithless lord. Carefully, gently, I spoke the name aloud, feeling and treasuring Lancar's stubborn, misplaced love and loyalty. When I opened my eyes he was there, as strong-featured and handsome as any of the stubborn northerners gathered at council. He inclined his head to me in courtesy but not deference, then favored Hwyn with just such a slow, sad smile as may pass between fellow-sufferers of the same affliction. Then he turned to Syrc—with what expression I could not see, but it moved her visibly. Then, turning at last to Trenara, he knelt before her and kissed her slender hands. Doubt fled the room like a banished spirit. Everyone except Hwyn and me fell to their knees.

The hoarse voice of an old woman broke the spell. "My old bones!" she said, coming in the doorway, "What's this? Syrc sent for me, and she doesn't fetch me without reason. Who's sick?"

"Harga!" one of them chided, "the Returner has come, the Lady Trenara of Larioneth! Look at her, she—"

"—is great with child, near her time by the look of her, and traveled through the forest on foot, if I heard rightly," Harga cut in. "Don't just gawk at her; she needs care. And Rand said someone was sick. Let me through!" She pushed unceremoniously past Trenara's subjects, paying the ghost of Lancar little more heed than the rest. He noticed her, however: rising, he laid a spectral hand on Harga's shoulder, just such a gentle pat as Syrc had given to Rand. Then he was gone. "Which of you is ill? You?" the healer demanded of Hwyn, who nodded. "Come with me." With that she herded us out of the stunned assembly, leaving the other Holdouts of Larioneth to digest their wonder without us.

17

THE HOLDOUTS
OF LARIONETH

If I'd thought Syrc the commanding voice of the Holdouts, I had not reckoned on Harga. As she led us through the hall, a broad-shouldered man followed her and put a hand on her arm as though to ask her something, but she cut him off. "Hern, I want water heated for herb baths. Three of them. Get Syrc to help you; it will break her out of this awestruck stupor. If she values these guests, she may as well make herself useful to them."

"Harga—" he said, a protest or a question abandoned unformed. She hurried us past him and he retreated, abashed.

"As you've no doubt grasped by now," she told us hurriedly, "I am the town's healer, Harga. I should have been here sooner, but I was setting a bone, and afterward, my own old bones wouldn't let me move any faster. So they had you sit on display while they held council about you, instead of letting you rest and warm yourselves."

"They did seat us nearest the fire," I said, "and Ash brought us food."

"Ash has sense," Harga conceded. "So does Syrc, sometimes, but not today. She's a hothead, that girl; anything her heart seizes on, she won't let go for good sense or bad."

"Is Syrc your daughter?" I found myself asking.

Harga laughed abruptly, as though caught off guard. "Ha! She should be. But no, she's not." We arrived then in a cramped, cluttered room, partitioned with an embroidered curtain that might once have adorned a queen's bed. Its walls, like those of Halred's hut, were covered with bundles of dried herbs, mingling their perfumes through the room.

Harga set to work examining each of us in turn, all the while asking when we'd last eaten, what, and how much; how far we had traveled, how fast, and under what conditions; and on and on, until she knew more about us and our journey than anyone in Larioneth, despite missing the council. She took Hwyn behind the curtain and ordered her to undress for closer examination. Then I heard the healer say, "Will you stop clutching that pouch and let me examine your chest? I'm not going to rob you."

"I know that," Hwyn said wearily. "I'm not guarding it against theft. I trust you. But please try to trust *me* when I tell you I have my reasons for needing to hold this close."

"Either the fever has twisted your brain," Harga said, "or you've brought a thing of power into our house. I think it's only fair you let me see what it is that you fear to put down for even a minute."

"I've almost been killed for it; small wonder I'm loath to uncover it," Hwyn said. "But I couldn't hope to stay long in this house without revealing it to someone. If it turns you against me, then that must be my fate." I could not see but clearly imagined the white stone being unveiled. I heard Harga gasp. "The Eye of Night," Hwyn said. "The Sky-Raven's Egg. It is alive, and it needs me to care for it, to keep it warm. I am bound to it, and it is bound to Larioneth—like the Troubles."

Harga let out her breath slowly, as though she'd just remembered to breathe. "Another mystery," she said at last. "Well, hold it if you must, but hold it out of my way. You owe me an explanation, but I won't trouble you for it till you're stronger. So you'll have to recover quickly—do you hear?"

"I'll try to oblige," Hwyn said.

"Now breathe deeply," Harga ordered. "Good."

When she'd finished examining the three of us, the healer declared, "Why you're alive at all after a trip like that, I can't fathom. The gods must have walked by your side."

"If so," I said, "then St. Ligaiya spoke true: they are no easy comrades."

"Did you ever doubt it?" Harga said with a knowing smile. Then she checked herself: "Ah, but what right have I to sound wise about your journey? I did not suffer through it. It must have seemed to you, starving in the snow, that the gods had cast you away. But I think you have little to fear now. You're made of strong stuff, all of you—even Trenara's baby." She sent Trenara back to the council to be fussed over by the Holdouts, and offered Hwyn a strong-smelling drink she'd brewed over the fire. "Take this: it will make you sleep off the fever." Hwyn hesitated, and Harga said, "Still distrustful? I promise you, I know what I'm doing. You southerners have always thought the North a land of spell-chanters and poisoners. You forget," she said, "the great school of physic that flourished here, the greatest in all Swevnalond. I was well trained there; I know what can heal you."

"I know," Hwyn said. "I have heard of your school, and I trust your knowledge. But a sleeping-draught—I don't want to die in my sleep."

"You won't die," Harga said.

"Is that a promise?" Hwyn smiled grimly, and at Harga's silence, she added, "Please—would you leave Jereth and me alone for a moment? I will drink then."

Harga nodded silently and left the room. I took Hwyn's hand. "I'll be here," I said. "I didn't come this far to leave you now."

"I hope I can say the same," she said. "But I am weak now."

"You need rest," I said.

"There is so much I haven't told you. I wish I could tell you now, but I'm afraid it's still not safe," said Hwyn.

"Don't you trust me, even now?"

"Of course I trust you, Jereth. But as Halred once told me, knowledge can either help you or hinder you from doing what must be done. I don't want to tell you things that will stand in your way, like that scrap of prophecy that almost made me despair. But there is one thing I must tell you that I would rather not speak of, for it will hurt you. I leave you with a burden. If I die, you must take the Eye of Night from me before my body is cold."

"Don't speak so!"

"I'm sorry," she said, but her eyes, locked on mine, were unyielding. "I wish I didn't need to speak so grimly. I wish I could promise to live. But you must be ready to carry on in my place, if I fail."

I bowed my head. "I will," I told her. "I promise to keep your trust. But I don't know what must be done with the Raven's Egg, now that we have taken it to Larioneth."

"You will know," she said, "if the task falls to you. It will tell you. Haven't you felt its power already?"

"I have," I said. "In Berall, it almost made me shout treason along with you. Have no fear, then. I will not fail you."

"I know you won't," she said a bit sadly. Then she drank the potion, and I held her until she was asleep.

After I'd watched Hwyn breathing rhythmically for some minutes, Harga came in softly. "She'll sleep all night, most likely. She needs it."

I nodded. "It's been hard for us all, but hardest for her."

"You could use some rest yourself," Harga said, "though I doubt you'll want to sleep now; you'd be wide awake at night. What will you do while Hwyn sleeps—go back to the council with the lady?"

"No," I said. "I want to stay with Hwyn."

Harga scrutinized my face, then Hwyn's. "You're not kin, I think. Is she your wife?"

"Not yet," I said. "She promised to marry me at the end of our journey. But now I don't know if she can keep that promise. She told me this morning that she was dying. I don't dare leave her now. I don't want to return from council to find—" The words stuck in my throat. I began again: "—to find I've lost her. What I'll—what I'd do without her, I don't know."

"Don't lose hope," Harga said. "She's in less desperate straits than she was this morning. You've reached a safe place, with not the worst of healers to care for her. Besides, a woman stubborn enough to make that journey in winter is too stubborn to die easily."

"I hope so," I said, and for a while we were silent. Harga left the room abruptly, without saying anything. When she returned, she said, "I've asked them to make up this room for the two of you. There's enough space for a trundle bed, and I'll be close enough to be there if Hwyn needs me, but not too close for privacy."

"You're so kind to us," I said. "I feel like an impostor. After months of vagrancy, sleeping in temple courts in the towns, or under hedges in the wild, we reach the end of the road to be treated like saviors, all because a companion neither of us sought fits into a legend."

"Ah yes: I was hoping to ask you about just such matters," Harga said. "To the others here, you two are the Lady Trenara's followers—but that's not what I see, and it's not how you see yourselves, I dare swear. When I interrupted the council, you two were the only ones not on your knees to her. You didn't cross the wasteland for her."

"If you think you're speaking to the leader now," I said, "you're mistaken. She sleeps before you."

Harga nodded. "As I thought. And of course, those youngsters in the council paid her the least heed."

"She wasn't saying much," I said. "Either she was too tired or hadn't worked out whom to trust. Possibly both."

"I'm dying to question her, of course," Harga said, "but I had to let her sleep. I know there's greater things at work here than the return of the House of Larioneth. What brought you here? It's bound up with that stone Hwyn carries, isn't it? The Eye of Night?"

"That's Hwyn's tale to tell," I said. "There is much that I don't understand. She keeps some secrets even from me. And besides, I don't think she understands it all herself."

"If you don't understand it, why did you follow her?" Harga asked.

I smiled. "Do you know the Magyan legend of the Firebird?"

"I've read it," Harga said.

"You don't ask the Firebird to explain itself when it flashes across your life," I said. "You follow, or spend the rest of your life wondering. Following her, I have had everything the legend promised: poverty, peril, hardship, trouble, wonder, and a joy I would never have known. And no shadow of regret."

"You talk like a book-learned man," said Harga. "What were you before you followed her?"

"Lost," I said. "Disillusioned. I'd been initiatied as a Tarvon priest, but left the Order without vows. Their neat solutions to every problem, their orderly scheme of life with a place for everything, didn't seem to fit the upside-down world I knew. Either the Order was wrong or the world was wrong, and I'd come to consider the Order, and all order, part of the problem."

"So instead you followed Hwyn to Larioneth, where not even the seasons can be counted on to keep their order," Harga said. "We had two summers last year. The year before, two winters."

"We stepped into summer a while on the way here," I said. "I'm not sure for how long. The sun never set, but that day seemed an age."

"That happens here sometimes," she said. "Once a hunting party disappeared for a month, and when they returned they swore it had only been a day. Time is not to be trusted in the North." She smiled ruefully. "I suppose, then, it matters little that the Lady Trenara can't tell me when she conceived her child."

"She did seem to gain weight suddenly in the summer country," I said. "When we found ourselves there, Hwyn and I hadn't even realized Trenara was pregnant. By the time we left, we couldn't have ignored it with our eyes shut."

"I couldn't glean from her who fathered the child, either," Harga mused. Her eyes narrowed. "You didn't have anything to do with that?"

"Certainly not!" I said. "For all I know, she was with child before I met her. It could have been—" Suddenly realizing the weight of what I'd nearly said, I clamped my mouth shut.

But it was too late. "Who?" Harga demanded "It could have been who?"

"I don't know how much you want to hear," I said. "You have your legend, your Returner; will you accept all I may say about this icon?"

"Tell me and be done," Harga said. "I'm an old woman; I have no icons left without cracks or stains. I like them better that way, in truth. Say on."

"All right," I said. "I was going to say that the father of Trenara's child could have been anyone. She is simple."

"I know *that*," Harga said impatiently.

I looked at her with new respect. "It took me longer than that to see through her fine demeanor," I said.

"A man *would* be distracted," Harga said. "Go on."

"When I met Hwyn and Trenara they were already traveling together," I said, "so I didn't know Trenara in her old way of life, but I can easily believe what Hwyn told me. She's at once too high-bred and too simple to work; she had no family; she had no caution. What could she live on but her beauty?"

"You're saying she's a prostitute," Harga said. "Well, that explains some things."

"She wasn't selling herself while she traveled with us," I qualified, "but it seemed any man that pleased could lead her where he chose. Hwyn was always trying to keep her out of trouble, but that wasn't easy."

"I'm surprised you brought the lady along at all," Harga said.

"We didn't. She followed us. Or rather, she followed Hwyn," I said. "We couldn't shake her. We would have loved to leave her someplace safe, but she wouldn't stay. Hwyn had defended her once from a brute of a bawd, and the lady became attached to her. So Hwyn, being what she is, felt obliged to keep protecting her."

"Being what she is," Harga mused. "A protector of the weak? A would-be hero? Perhaps a hero already."

"She is that and more," I said. "She must recover. I am not the only one that needs her."

"Don't lose hope," Harga said. "Rest now. It's all you can do."

We spent the night in the healer's room, moving Hwyn to a child's trundle bed that the others brought in; for once, her smallness made things easier. On the larger bed behind the curtain, I slept deep and long—so soundlessly that I almost wondered whether a little of that strange draught had been added to my food.

When I woke, close to midday, I hurried to Hwyn's bedside to find her sleeping peacefully, her color a little closer to what it should be, her breathing easy. Someone had left clean clothes for us that were not ours; our own travel-stained ones had been taken away. I dressed in the russet tunic and breeches they'd left for me, and ventured out quietly into the hallway, finding no one. After pausing to look out a window into the glistening white day, I returned. Someone had left jugs of water and mild apple wine, the sort given to children, with two clay cups. I mixed some for myself to drink. When I turned to Hwyn again, she was stirring.

"How do you feel?" I said, moving to take her hand.

"Hungry," she said. "That's good, I think."

"That's wonderful," I said. "I was so frightened for you. But you look better now."

"I feel better," she said. "Journey's end has brought us to a good place. Is that fresh bread I smell down the hall?"

"I'll find out for you," I said. I had no trouble finding the kitchen; following the warm scent of baking to its source, I could have found it with my eyes closed. After alternating fish and starvation for so long, it was like a sweet dream.

The kitchen was enormous, built to furnish food for a royal household big as a village, plus all the myriad guests of feasting-days in more prosperous times. No kings had feasted their retainers in Larioneth Hall for years, but the cavernous hearths, the formidable spits, the ponderous cauldrons showed no signs of disuse. From one end to the other, fires burned and pots bubbled. At a sturdy table in the center of the room, a red-knuckled adolescent girl sat washing vegetables and handing them to Ash to chop. Near them sat Harga, warming her hands around a mug of hot cider and talking. Before one of the fires, Rand and a slightly older girl sat side by side, each carving something out of wood. From time to time they paused to compare handiwork, talking in soft, giggling girlish voices. Two smaller children amused themselves spinning a pot-lid on the floor. And in an alcove under a window the Lady Trenara sat engrossed in conversation with a thin, white-haired man whom I remembered seeing at the council. As I stood in the door, the lady looked up at me, smiled broadly, and called, "Jereth! There you are."

"You're awake!" Harga said as I stepped in to greet first Trenara, then all the rest. "How is Hwyn?"

"Better, I think. Hungry," I said.

"Good," Harga said. "I think Ash can cure that."

"There's porridge and stewed apples," Ash said. "The bread will be ready soon, too. Rand and Taryant, will you give him a hand? I'm up to the elbows in onions." The two girls by the fire left their carving, fetched a broad tray, and showed me where to find bowls and spoons. They ladled out generous portions of steaming food for me and Hwyn, then insisted on carrying the tray to our room themselves. At the door they lingered shyly, half in, half out. From her bed, Hwyn peered back at them with almost the same wary expression.

The bigger girl stepped in, set down the tray on a little table and, twisting her red hair around one finger, said, "I—we—my name is Taryant, daughter of Trista. This is Rand—"

"Daughter of Syrc," Rand added. "I was at council yesterday."

"I remember you," Hwyn said.

"We wanted to meet the Far-Travelers," Taryant said.

Hwyn smiled then, seeming relieved. "We thank you for your welcome," she said in a tone ceremonious enough to match the girls' gravity, extending her damaged hand to each in turn.

"We haven't properly met," I said to Taryant. "I didn't see you at council. I am Jereth son of Garmund, and this is Hwyn."

"Hwyn daughter of who?" Taryant asked, and I listened curiously to see whether Hwyn would reveal anything. But Hwyn answered, "Daughter of no one in particular," with a wry expression.

"That's like my mother," Rand said. Taryant looked embarrassed, and the girls retreated toward the door, shy again. We thanked them for the breakfast, and then watched as they fled back to the kitchen.

"It's terrible to be young," Hwyn laughed. "To be cowed even by the likes of us!"

"It may not be just the children," I said. "We're special here, creatures of legend: the Far-Travelers."

"Well, the name fits," Hwyn said. "We've come as far as the north edge of nowhere. Which just turns out to be a very good place to be."

After we'd had our fill of hot food, Harga bustled in. "I see you've survived my potion," the healer said tartly, then put a hand on Hwyn's forehead. "No fever. Good. And I take it your appetite has been restored." She gestured at the tray emptied of food.

"Thank you a thousand times," Hwyn said.

"Never mind that," said Harga. "Breathe deeply now—good. All seems to be well, or at least, nothing wrong that a few days' rest won't cure. Maybe now you can begin answering some of my questions."

But just then Rand burst in: "Harga—my mother—she's hurt." After her came a bulky knot of people: Hart and Kernan, supporting Syrc, who leaned one arm over each man's shoulders, hobbling on one foot. A large tear in her skirt was edged with blood.

"What happened?" Harga said.

"She was gored by a boar," Hart replied.

"It's not so bad," Syrc panted. "You should see what I did to the boar. Hauvoc and Hern are cleaning it. Why don't you go help them, Rand?"

"I'll stay here," the girl said stolidly.

The two men set Syrc down on a high-backed bench, and Harga crouched in front of her, folding back the huntress's skirt to reveal a messy leg wound.

"I should have known I was too close to the brute," Syrc said. "But I got him."

"Show-off," Hart teased gently, "you just had to beat me to the kill again."

As Harga cleaned the wound, Syrc flinched, and Rand looked queasy. The bandage Harga pressed to the gash turned red. Shaking her head, the healer threaded a needle to stitch the skin closed.

"Rand," Hwyn said, "would you help me to stand? I think Harga must need this bed. Come, you look about my height; I could lean on your shoulder."

"Go, child," Syrc ordered, and Rand obeyed. She took hold of Hwyn hesitantly and helped her out of bed. They were indeed of a height, though oddly matched otherwise: the strong, comely child and the worn, scarred woman. As they moved clear of the bed something tumbled from Hwyn's pocket to the floor, something Hwyn would never have let slip unintentionally. Rand gasped: "Oh! What is it?" First Hart, then Kernan, then Syrc turned and stared down at it until Hwyn gently detached herself from Rand's unneeded support, picked up her treasure, and held it out for all to see. "The Eye of Night," she said simply, giving one of her slow, sly, crooked smiles to Rand and me, and then to the other open-mouthed Holdouts of Larioneth. Only Harga remained undistracted, intent on her task. Syrc seemed to have forgotten her pain, transfixed by the strange gem that shone with the cool glow of moonlight. "So beautiful," breathed Syrc, as Harga poulticed her wound in silence.

"Did it fall from the stars?" Kernan gasped.

"It fell from her *pocket*," Rand said almost indignantly. "I don't understand. Such a gem—you wouldn't carry it carelessly, like a shell you picked up on the beach. You wouldn't put a thing like this in a torn pocket, or forget it was in your lap, and let it fall."

"Clever girl," Hwyn said. "You're right, of course. I didn't drop this by chance."

Harga finished binding Syrc's wound. "Well, traveler," she said, "I see you've decided to give us some answers, after all."

"That I have," Hwyn said. "I didn't plan it quite this way, but I knew I needed to tell sooner or later, and it seemed that at the moment we needed a distraction."

"You staged that like a master player," I laughed.

Syrc was laughing, too. "I wanted something to distract the girl, yes. But I think I've got more than I bargained for."

"Mother!" Rand protested.

"You *were* fretting, Rand. And see? It's all right, now. Dare say I'll be dancing by festival night." Syrc tried to rise, grimaced a little, then sat again. "Far-Traveler, if we're to hear the whole story of this moonstone of yours, then I'd like my sister and Hauvoc to hear as well. Do you mind if I call them in?"

"Per should hear," Harga cut in. "He's a scholar, wise by book-learning and by years. He may know something of use to you, or to us all in this time of portents."

"Good. Call them together. Bring whoever should hear," said Hwyn.

In the end we gathered in the warm kitchen, setting the two invalids, Hwyn and Syrc, in high-backed chairs at the hearth. Rand and Taryant slipped shyly in together; Hwyn beckoned them closer and they sat on the hearthstones at the foot of her chair. I sat beside them on the floor and leaned back against Hwyn's chair; she smiled down at me, eyes gleaming with anticipation. Trenara and the old scholar, Per, drew their seats closer; Hauvoc, his clothes still blood-spattered from the boar-carcass, stood by his sister; Ash and her young assistant Tresanda hovered around with warm bread and hot cider for everyone. Last of all Hart returned with a moon-faced, black-haired woman and what seemed a cloud of children. "My wife, Modya," he explained to us as they settled themselves, each holding a child.

Hwyn took the Eye of Night once more from her breast pouch and held it out for all to see. "Let me tell a story: much of it you will know already, but I think some will be new to you. In the beginning of time, when the world was new, the gods grew the sun in a secret chamber below the earth, meaning to send it skyward to light the world when it was full grown. But in the night, seeds had taken root on earth, and living things had grown. The gods feared that as the sun passed the earth, making its way to the sky, its heat would burn the new shoots, leaving the earth barren. So the Sky-Raven, older than Earth and greater, spread her wings over the earth, shielding it from the fire of the sun. The sun scorched her wings, but the Sky-Raven held her place, sheltering the earth, until she burned to death, just as the sun cleared the rim of the world. The fire of her immolation shines red in every sunrise and sunset, even now, countless ages after her sacrifice. This much you know: the story is told each winter on the Night of the Hidden Goddess. But there is more:

not all was lost in the burning. I hold the Sky-Raven's Egg, hidden since the earth was new, revealed to us in a time of Troubles."

"The prophet Evrel wrote of the Sky-Raven's Egg," Per said. "But she said it was hidden far from sight, in the heart of the earth or the depths of the sea, and that were it moved, the earth might lose its heart. Whatever power moved it from its resting place must be great indeed. But why have you drawn it forth? Have you considered the price?"

"They were mightier than I who drew it from the heart of the earth," said Hwyn, "and whether we are all now paying the price of their pride, or whether our Troubles are only the waning of an age, I do not know. Long ago, some mage coaxed it forth from hiding—and died for it, no doubt. Since then, it has passed from hand to hand. Its holders wielded it for their profit until its power shattered them. For thirty years or more it was held by the House of Kelgarran; it upheld their might and prosperity. It was there that I found the Sky-Raven's Egg, freed it from the bonds of necromancy, and brought it away with me. As I took it away, Kelgarran Hall fell in ruins."

"Thirty years in the House of Kelgarran," mused Per. "I wonder if the House of Larioneth held it till then. Thirty years ago, in the height of their dominion, they were struck down by plague and calamity. Perhaps they, too, had drawn their power from the Sky-Raven's Egg, and fell when they lost it."

"It may be," Hwyn said, holding the Eye of Night against her breast as though it might whisper its story directly to her heart.

I noticed that Per did not bother to ask Trenara, sitting at his side, whether the Sky-Raven's Egg had been in her family's keeping. He knew, then, that it was no use asking her. Instead, Per addressed Hwyn again: "If all who hold this treasure die for it, as you say, why have you brought it here? Don't you fear their fate?"

"I do not wield the Eye of Night," Hwyn said. "I hold it, but I do not hold it bound. Since I broke the magic circle in Kelgarran Hall last summer, the Sky-Raven's Egg has been free—free to grow."

"Save for a moment's time," I interrupted, "when I used it, against Hwyn's will, to try to rescue her from prison. If there is a price for that binding, I have not paid it yet. But it was only bound a few moments, no more."

Hwyn looked down at me with troubled brow and passed a hand gently across my hair. Then she resumed her explanation: "The life within this egg has grown since I freed it. I have followed its commands and brought it where it wished to go: here, to the northern end of the world. What I do with it here depends on its own demands. The future is still dark to me. But I think the Sky-Raven's Egg has come here to hatch."

"What will be born from this egg?" asked Per.

Hwyn shook her head. "We will see when it comes."

"This thing you bring us spans the ages of the world, from its birth to this moment," Per continued. "Is this the end of the world?"

"I do not know." Hwyn closed her eyes. "If it is, then I doubt burying the Eye of Night could have forestalled it. I'm afraid—I may need to ask your forgiveness for what I have brought you. But I did the only thing that seemed right to me. Nothing can be bound forever. Whatever lies within this egg cried out for freedom, so I freed it. If it is good, this land has need of it; if it is evil, let us confront it bravely together—for I could seek no braver comrades-at-arms than you, who dared remain all these years in the Land of Troubles. But I do not believe it is evil. I cannot believe it."

"Let others fear this hatchling: I will trust it," Syrc spoke up indignantly, sounding almost like Rand. "The Sky-Raven sheltered earth in the beginning of time. I will trust its child. The Returner is here; one promise to us has been kept. But we were promised three things more: strength from the earth, friends from the South, hope from the sea. The strength we feel within us; the friends," she gestured toward us, "have come. The hope will come as well. I have no fear, though the world's end be at hand."

"I too will trust," Per said. "No good has come from holding this spirit bound. You can hardly do worse by releasing it than the lords of Kelgarran by binding it. In this land, too, we have seen the dangers of binding spirits against their will. King Isenmund of Larioneth, the chronicles tell us, bound the spirit of a rebellious wizard, and thought to protect the land by keeping him prisoner. But the spirit ate Isenmund away from inside until it looked out from his eyes and commanded his body. Thus a dead wizard ruled this land and wreaked long-stored wrath upon it till a Tarvon priest set him free. The ghost went in peace, then, and left his vengeance incomplete. To imprison a spirit may be prudent, but never wise," he concluded. "I have questioned you sharply, Hwyn, because I needed to know that you were not another Isenmund. Now I see I have nothing to fear. Whatever you bring, welcome." And the old man went to Hwyn, took her thin, rough-skinned hand, and kissed it in courtly fashion.

Tears sprang to Hwyn's eyes. "Thank you," she said hoarsely. "You're too good, you're all too good to be true. I must have dreamed you. But do you understand what it is you welcome?"

"No," Per said quietly. "Nor do you understand what it is you bring. We can only trust."

"You are a brave people," Hwyn said.

"In the last town we traveled through," I added, "they would have killed us at a glimpse of the Eye of Night. They nearly hanged Hwyn for prophesying, even without it. Prophets, they said, bring the ghosts and the Troubles."

"Those that feared ghosts left Larioneth years ago," Harga said sharply.

"The people in Berall, killing prophets and lunatics, managed to hold back the Troubles. But you've learned to live with them," I said. "How?"

"We've learned to love our ghosts," said Modya, flushing slightly.

Kernan nodded. "We've learned, too, to save seed for a second planting in case the seasons turn backward. We've learned to hunt any nameless beast that appears in the woods, so long as it doesn't speak. We've learned to bend with the wind, to survive anything."

"It's Harga's doing," Syrc said, "and Per's. Without them we'd have fallen apart, wandered away, or died. There wouldn't *be* any Holdouts but for them."

Harga laughed, and looked downward, embarrassed. Per's keen blue eyes were on her. "Well, Harga, it was you that called the first council."

"I did, didn't I," she said. "Well, why not? I was the one who had to watch the worst of the suffering. I had to do something." She turned back to me and Hwyn. "Twelve years ago was the last and largest migration out of Larioneth. The city was unpeopled almost overnight. Perhaps a hundred of us were left—and far fewer lived through the winter. All the other healers in town—curse them for cowards!—had fled south. I was left scurrying from one house by the sea-cliff to another in the woods, half the time arriving too late, as survivors lamented that they hadn't known where to find a healer when a healer could have done something. I saw the young and the old left uncared-for, the sick dying because they had no neighbors to help them. Dying even of petty illnesses, when a dipper of water might have saved them, had there been anyone to bring it. Before that first winter was over, I knew we needed to pull together or we'd all die." Her eyes touched Syrc and Hart, then rested on Ash. "I sent children—Ash was one of them—through each section of the city looking for people, to bid them all gather at the temple on the next full-moon night. And when I came to the temple myself an hour before dark to wait for them all, I found Per."

"I'd moved into the temple," the scholar explained. "The priests who had kept it were all gone. So, too, were my Brothers and our pupils. My school was too far out in the woods for an old man alone. When Harga's young messengers called for council in the temple, people came to ask me about it, thinking I must have started it. I thought it a gift of the gods; I'd never have been able to bring everyone together myself."

"All the same," Harga laughed, "you made us the Holdouts."

"I made the *name,*" Per said. "I thought that with a name, we might make people proud of staying."

"It did," said Syrc. "Since then, save for two felons we exiled, no one has left."

Harga continued the story. "We found the castle as empty as the temple, so we moved in, thirty of us. The rest moved closer in to the center of the town: the most prosperous families had left, so there were fine houses for the taking. What was left in Larioneth, we decided, was our common inheritance. We resolved to share our goods and our labors. We apportioned tasks to each according to their talents. And we swore to have no lord, ever, except the Returner of the House of Larioneth."

"I meant to ask about that," Hwyn began cautiously. "Your loyalty to the royal house—it has outlived many years of hard waiting. To hold your hearts so, after so long—they must have been glorious."

"They were a bad lot," said Harga. The younger Holdouts, Hauvoc and Tresanda, looked shocked, but Per only smiled sardonically, and Harga continued. "Present company excepted, of course," she said, peering about for Trenara—but the lady had already drifted away after a knot of children running races into the great hall. "But most of them were degenerate, weak as rotten wood; they were the first to leave when the Troubles began. The Plague hit them hard, I'll grant you; knights in their prime lost all strength; queens went barren; princes were born moontouched, mad, or deformed. The king tore his eyes out at something he saw that no one else could see; his own brother killed him to silence his ghost-ridden ravings, and fled the land. One by one, the lords of the land fled their curse as fast as their fine horses could carry them. Not like the Old Days—then, if the land were blighted, the king would take the curse upon himself and do what was needed, even to dying for the land."

"That was done more than once," Per confirmed. "Three hundred years before my birth, Haylwin of Larioneth sailed to the world's rim and never returned. And before him, Avar the Kin-Slayer offered his blood in the center of the Sky Temple: he atoned for his crime to save the land."

"Such kings died centuries ago," Harga said. "Our king and lords saved themselves. We owe them no homage. But we were promised one that would love the land enough to return to it in its bleakest hour."

"It was the prophecy of Creyusa," Per explained, "a priestess of the Hidden Goddess who died the year of the First Migration. With the House of Larioneth fleeing like birds in autumn, Creyusa told us, 'Let them go. One will return, the only one worth your allegiance. In the darkest time, in the dead of winter, one will return, bringing an end to your hardship.'"

"And one has returned," Ash said, smiling in the direction of Trenara, who had settled herself at the far end of the kitchen, where she patiently allowed two of Hart's children to play with her hair.

"Is she—" I hedged a bit, afraid to give offense, but insatiably curious. "Are you sure of her? We ourselves know little of her, despite long companionship."

"You saw Lancar bow down to her. You named him yourself, and know he was no impostor," Per said.

"And so our companion is a legend," Hwyn said. "Is she all you hoped?"

Syrc suppressed a giggle; even Per seemed ready to laugh. "We've noticed she's simple," he said, "if that's what concerns you. Ah, well, at least some of us have. Til, I think, is still too ashamed of having doubted her to have noticed any real flaw in her. But I've had a good long talk with her and I assure you, I'm undeceived. I was, I confess, a bit disconcerted."

"I like her this way," Syrc said bluntly. "The others can think as they choose, but I—I think this is perfect. You see, if the only ruler we're to have is an—a—a simpleton, then the gods must mean us to go on as we've been, deciding all things in council amongst ourselves, expecting no other guidance. It's a way I've come to love. I once thought it would come to end with the Return, but now I see I had nothing to fear."

"Ever since Trenara joined me," said Hwyn, "I've been looking for a safe home for her, a place where someone would care for her as she is, so that I could journey freely into the dangerous lands ahead. Little did I know that her safe haven lay at the end of the road."

"I marvel she made it so far," Harga said, "defenseless and even pregnant. You two must have taken good care of her. I'm of one mind with Syrc: I too once feared the Returner, and grudged the oath to support even a very hypothetical sovereign. But the Lady Trenara is welcome to me: a gentle ruler, indeed!"

"I think I may know her lineage," Per said. "Not the highest in the royal house, if I guess right. There was a cousin in a cadet branch of the king's family, one of the first to leave Larioneth, with a moontouched daughter of ten or twelve years old. They disappeared from Larioneth twenty-eight years ago."

"You're not suggesting that Trenara's forty years old!" I laughed.

"Oh, no, of course not," Per said. "I think she must be the daughter of the child I remember, named for her, and inheriting her frailty. But how she knew to come back to the land of her forebears, the gods alone know."

"However she came, I'm glad of it," Syrc said. "We'll have plenty to celebrate on the Night of the Hidden Goddess—and here I am, too lame to dance!"

"We lost track of time in the journey," Hwyn said. "When is the festival?"

"We're not always sure of time ourselves," Per said, "But we've fixed on the next full-moon night, and the half-moon was last night."

The days till the festival passed swiftly. I had work to do: since hot food and rest had cured all that ailed me, I felt that like the Holdouts, I should do my share of labor. So on my third morning in Larioneth I rose before dawn and followed Ash's husband, March, down to the wharf where the fishing boats awaited us.

"Whatever else you foreigners bring, it's good to have another fisherman," March said. "Since my father died we've been shorthanded. You are used to the ocean, aren't you? It's different from river-fishing, of course."

I assured him that the sea was no stranger to me.

"Good," he said. "Grim and Til usually sail with me—but maybe this time we can patch up the old Gull's Cry and go two by two. Til's a fair hand at fixing boats—"

"I was once, myself," I said, and as Grim and March put out to sea, I hurried to join Til patching together an old boat, one of those flat-bottomed clinker-built fishing boats that seem the same in every land. It had been hard hit by its last voyage, but not beyond repair. Soon enough we had the Gull's Cry in order, and Til and I set out.

"I thought you were a landsman," the young fisher said, adjusting the angle of a sail. "They said you'd been in the Tarvon Monastery in Annelon."

"I wasn't born in a monastery," I said.

Later, returning to land with our haul of fish, Til spoke suddenly. "I misjudged you. I seem to be doing a lot of that lately," he laughed. "I thought a priest would be no help on a boat—"

"Ex-priest," I corrected.

"—but you sail like you were born on the sea."

"I was," I said. "I come from a long line of sea-traders. People in my family lose their balance on dry land, not on shipboard." After all those years, the old family joke tasted strange in my mouth. "I knew the ports of South Magya better than the rooms of my parents' house—I spent more of my childhood there. I've sailed to Iskarron in a tempest, when everyone from the captain to my little brother, seven years old then, had to lend a hand to keep the ship afloat. Even when I ran away from home I was too sea-crazy to realize that my father wouldn't find me inland: I stuck to the coast, and was caught."

"And yet you left it for an inland monastery." Til shook his head. "Who drowned?"

I whipped my head around to glare into his bland face and deceptively lazy blue eyes.

"I'm sorry," he said hastily. "I've touched a nerve. That was clumsy. I should keep—"

"No, you were right," I said. "Everyone drowned. My whole family, the whole crew, everyone but me. You don't always misjudge, Til."

"No wonder you left," Til said softly. "I'm sorry."

After that Til was a friend. In a few days' time I had more friends among the Holdouts than I'd made in six years in the Tarvon Order, and Hwyn felt more at home there than she had even in Folcsted. Each day I would come in from the sea, achingly cold and smelling of fish, to find Hwyn by the fire with Syrc, two invalids unused to rest, exercising their well-matched wits while they waited for their bodies to heal.

"I left such a piece of flesh behind in that hunt," Syrc would complain, "that I scarcely needed to leave any offering of the boar's."

"I hope you left it anyway," Hwyn would retort. "It seems your flesh was too tough for the boar. How could spirits get their teeth into it?"

Sometimes, too, Rand and Taryant would hang about Hwyn in fascination, and one day she began trying to teach them to juggle. "Don't toss too high!" she was chiding as I came in that evening. "Keep an even pace. You might try singing to yourself to get the rhythm. That's what I do." By the time I'd washed the fish-smell off myself, she sounded more pleased with her pupils. "Good. You have deft hands. You'd make fine pickpockets, both of you—though I doubt your neighbors would appreciate it if I taught you that skill."

"What's a pickpocket?" Rand said.

And Syrc laughed. "Little enough it would matter. We haven't used money since before these girls were born."

"Really?" Hwyn said. "Then what's this halfpenny doing behind Rand's ear?" It was a simple sleight-of-hand trick from her days as King Evan's jester, but enough to make the girls laugh when she pulled the coin out of Rand's dark hair. But as she held out the coin for the girl to take, I could see Rand's eyes directed, instead, to the stump that remained of Hwyn's little finger, and her solemn, curious expression overtook all laughter. "What happened to your hand?" she asked.

"Rand!" chided Syrc.

But Hwyn answered her. "This is why I shouldn't jest about teaching you to pick pockets. My finger was cut off for thievery when I was about Taryant's age. I was lucky, they told me, not to lose my whole hand—but I only took a small sausage, so they only took a small finger."

Rand, properly horrified, gaped silently.

Taryant demanded, "They did this to you for a *sausage?*"

"It was a bad bargain, I guess," Hwyn said. "I might have been more cautious, but I hadn't eaten for two days."

"Then why wouldn't someone give you food?" Rand asked.

"Because I didn't have this," Hwyn said, deftly drawing the coin from Taryant's pocket and producing it once more. "Not everywhere are there people as kind as you Holdouts."

"Even Larioneth was like that once," Syrc told the girls, "before the emigrants left. Before the Troubles."

Syrc was not alone among the Holdouts in relishing life amid the Troubles. Til and March and Grim all agreed their lot was better than their fathers' had been; they'd been poor before, and disregarded, and now no one in Larioneth was either. Yet it was a hard life in many ways, I could tell. The folk I saw were mostly young: life was short, hard-won, in a land of long winters and shifting realities. Those that survived were strong—and none stronger, Harga told me, than Syrc. "Syrc's name ought to be Anvil," the healer said, "because you can hammer at an anvil without mercy, but it's only the hammer that breaks."

As if to prove Harga's words, Syrc was chafing to be out hunting before her wound had even a day to heal. Only the promise of the coming festival—and the dancing she refused to miss—restrained her. I could sympathize. I was caught up, myself, in all the excitement of preparation. In the Tarvon Order, and in much of my part of the country, the Night of the Hidden Goddess was a solemn occasion, but here in the North, where darkness nearly crowded out the winter day, this longest night of all called for wild celebration. After six years in an ascetic order and a journey full of privation, my appetite was whetted for the feast. Hwyn too seemed almost giddy with anticipation. As the hours of slanting sunlight dwindled and the moon swelled to fullness, the very earth seemed to hold its breath like a child awaiting a present.

18

THE NIGHT OF
THE HIDDEN GODDESS

As the full moon shone through the eastern forest in a deep blue twilight, we joined the procession to the temple, bearing our evergreen boughs. Hwyn, outdoors for the first time since our rescue, pressed close against me, but she was not shivering, and smiled up at me.

"It's a beautiful night," I said to her, and it was: the air was clear, and the snow glistened in the silver moonlight.

"It should be. For 'the morning may never come,'" she said, quoting the words of the midnight rite.

"Hush, that's for later," I said. I silenced her with a kiss, bending down as she stood on tiptoe to reach me.

Ahead of us, Hart and Hern, Til and Grim solemnly carried a great log for the fire that must not die tonight. Behind them Trenara held a position of honor, escorted by Per, who acted as priest. He was, like most scholars, devoted to the Rising God and the Bright Goddess, the beacons of light, revealers of knowable truth; but no other priest remained in Larioneth, so all rites fell to his charge. Behind him walked Harga, and we followed her, taking our cue from her actions in this unfamiliar northern variant of the ancient celebration.

When the bearers of the log reached the temple they walked straight forward into its dark interior. The torchbearers who had flanked our procession hovered outside, but the rest of us went in, groping our way in the dark, into an open space that offered no handholds. I kept my hold on Hwyn, trusting her night-sense to guide us.

After the sounds of shuffling feet were silenced, a woman's voice, clear as flame, pierced the darkness, singing, "Holy the night, holy as day! In darkness life dawns." Then seventy-odd Holdouts and Hwyn and I sang it back to her three times, until I felt a shiver that was not of cold.

At last the torchbearers entered; they ringed the room, and

the singer proclaimed, "Holy the night, holy as day! Through the night the fire endures." Then as we sang after her, the torchbearers moved through the crowd to the center of the temple and lit the great tree-bole on the hearth. I saw then, by its light, who the singer was: the kitchen-girl, Tresanda, who had scarcely seemed to talk. Her voice was almost as fine as Hwyn's. She sang again: "Holy the night, holy as day! Through darkness, life endures." As we repeated after her, the torchbearers moved back to the rim of the circle, where they set the torches in wall sconces.

I could see, then, by the flickering light, the rich painting that ringed the domed ceiling, the four gods on the World-Wheel: the Rising God, clothed in the dawn; the Bright Goddess, clothed in flowers, arms open to embrace the world below her; the Turning God, bound at one ankle but crowned in vines; and the Hidden Goddess, her face turned away as always, curtained from view behind a waterfall of black hair. She leaned on one arm, reaching upward with the other toward the center of the circle. Behind her an owl peered around at us, and near her outstretched hand a raven flew. At the hub of the Wheel was a smoke-hole for the hearth below.

Tresanda sang, "Holy the night, holy as day! From darkness all was born." Then the Holdouts—and we travelers after them—turned to the north, to the image of the Hidden Goddess, and knelt to her. Trenara, I noticed, needed to be prompted in this. But moments later, when those who had borne the torches began circling the room, hand in hand, gathering worshipers into the dance, Trenara melted into them as though she knew the steps in her sleep. Soon we were all linked hand in hand and the steps came even to me with uncanny ease. Concentric circles rotated against each other as Per chanted,

> "Four Great Ones gird the earth:
> Revealer of riddles, the Rising God;
> Bright Goddess, bringer of joy;
> Turning God of time and change;
> The last and first lives in shadows,
> Unseen wonder, womb of lives,
> Hearth of the dead, the Hidden Goddess,
> Giver of rest and grower of seeds,
> Life unwithered, winter's hope,
> Whose hand stretches to the hub of the world."

There was more, of course; some I knew well, and some was new to me. For the most part, the words blurred in my mind. I was conscious of Hwyn's hand in mine and her rich strong voice raised in the responses we all sang, ringing above the rest; of Harga, on my other side, treading the measure with a grace that surprised me; of the hypnotic rhythms of the dance; of all of us, eyes shining and faces flushed, linked one to another by the hand, daring together to dance winter into Larioneth. When Per chanted the prophecy I'd first heard by the fireside: "Strength will come from the earth, friends from the south, and hope from the sea," I seemed to feel the promised strength rising up into me, into all of us. Looking at Hwyn, I saw her head tipped back, her eyes half shut, her smile, stripped of irony, as wide as the breadth of her heart.

At the end flagons of wine circled through the crowd and we all drank, wishing each other health and joy as we passed the cup. Then we flocked back to the hall for the feast—that is, all save those whose turn came first to tend the fire.

Larioneth Hall had seemed splendid to me when I first entered—as, indeed, any warm room would have seemed—but now it was twice as brilliant, with costly candles squandered for this nightlong celebration, and precious ornaments from the hall's treasure-troves, little moons and stars of silver and crystal, hanging everywhere to reflect the light. Evergreen boughs hung over doorways, scenting the rooms. In the great hall were piled more dishes and cups than I could readily count—some of clay, some of wood, and a few of gold. They'd all be needed, for everyone alive in Larioneth would be dining here tonight. To that end, a quarter of the crowd disappeared into the kitchen and put themselves at Ash's disposal to make ready the feast. But Trenara, Hwyn, and I, as honored guests, were told in no uncertain terms to sit and wait.

Instead we followed a flock of children who promised to show us the best rooms of the castle. By the light of Rand's lantern, we saw tapestries of strange beasts: dragons and hippogryphs, winged women and goat-hooved men; we saw gilt carvings as subtle and delicate as the finest needlework; we saw one room nearly covered by the largest looking-glass I'd ever seen. In that glass I saw a stranger: thin to be sure, but not spindly and meager as I knew myself; rather, weathered and hard-looking as the old sailors I remembered from my youth at sea. Hwyn laughed to see me gaping at myself. "I've changed so," I explained.

"No," she said, "you are the same man I met this spring, only more so."

Lastly, blushing a little, the children showed us what must have been a private chapel, notable for an elaborate rendition of the Bright Goddess on the ceiling, entirely nude. Such icons were common enough in the south, and indeed the only kind you saw in Iskarron—but in this cold land, nudity was not so readily associated with joy, and seemed more crazy than titillating, even to the boys in the group. There were icons on the walls as well: the Rising God leaping skyward, the Upside-Down God hanging from an oak tree. I was surprised not to see the Hidden Goddess, until I realized that the floor was tiled with the pattern of a dark hand, or the shadow of one. The Unseen held us in her palm.

When we rejoined the others, the feast had already started. All the bounty this harsh land offered was spread at table: boar and venison, fowl and fish, soups and stews, crusty loaves and browned pancakes with stewed apples. There were sweet cakes for after the meal, and plenty of cider and ale at all times. Hwyn and I eagerly helped ourselves to everything but the fish—of that, we said, we never wanted another mouthful in our lives.

There were presents, too, when the feast was done—even for Hwyn and me, who had nothing to give the others. They gave us fine brooches, treasures of the House of Larioneth. When Syrc fixed on Hwyn's brooch, Hwyn wept for joy, and we embraced everyone within reach. Trenara was given a circlet of gold and crowned solemnly as Queen of Larioneth. Around her neck they hung a silver pendant with the crescent-moon emblem of her noble house. She did not weep, but laughed. Then the music and dancing began.

The Troubles must have been good for music: there were more competent singers among the Holdouts than a remnant of a hundred souls, barely clinging to sustenance, had any right to expect. There were instrument-players, too: harp and drum carried most of the tune, but late in the evening Til took out a throat-flute just like my brother's, and I stopped singing to listen, lost in thought. Hwyn came and put her arms around me.

"You look haunted," she said.

"It's all right," I said. "This is the night for ghosts."

It was, indeed. Watching some children play in the hall, I noticed by some odd chill in my spine that one of them was a ghost. I turned to Hart, who stood nearby watching with what I suppose must have been my expression when I heard the familiar flute-voice. "Your sister?" I whispered.

He nodded. "Lind, the one my last daughter is named for. I'm glad to see her happy."

"I know," I said. "I saw my sister like that, on the way north." Suddenly I thought, in the corner of my eye, that I could see Anverth, too, among the knot of children—but before I could be certain, she was gone. "You have made peace with your ghosts, in truth, I see."

"Some of them," he said. "Who can make peace with them all? Only a saint."

"You're all saints here, to me," I said.

He laughed. "You scarcely know us! But you are kind, *friend from the South,*" he said, quoting the words of the rite. "It is you Far-Travelers who bring the blessings of this night to us."

"I am no saint," I said. "But Hwyn—"

He nodded, and said nothing. Then Modya swept him into a dance, and I returned to Hwyn's side. We sang and danced a while with the others; Hwyn at last had the chance to show off her Ballad of Dirnlac of the Red Oak, to great effect. The Holdouts were moved by the story, and the more eager singers among them asked her to repeat the words so they could learn them. As she began again, I thought I saw the ghost, Dirnlac himself, sitting on the floor behind Tresanda, listening with an expression of purest wonder. I would have spoken to him, asked him how he had escaped his prison, but I did not wish to interrupt the song, and when it was done, he faded from view. Before I could speak of it, Til began playing a dance-tune and Hwyn pulled me into a dance. We were ungainly dancers, especially together, with our awkward difference in height; but we felt safe among the Holdouts, who were too kind to laugh at our clumsiness. We soon tired ourselves out, and slept a time to save our strength for the midnight ceremony.

In the deep of the night we went forth to the temple without song, without sound, without torches, but carrying soft deerskins slung over our backs. These we spread on the temple floor, making a circle around the fire. The children remained behind, and the younger adolescents and a few adults kept watch over them. The older, more solemn congregation of midnight sat cross-legged on the skins, holding hands in a quiet circle.

At last Per spoke: "The morning may never come."

"Hope survives in the darkness," we replied.

There was no singing this time. Tresanda was absent, probably still too young for the midnight rite. I saw that Til, sitting nearby, had his flute, and other musicians had brought harp and drum, but for now they were still. The time had come for tales of the darkness: of things unknown and beyond our fathoming; of suffering and compassion; of loss and the blind hope that helps us bear it; of the Hidden Goddess and her saints. Per stood and bowed to the north, but instead of beginning the first tale himself, he said, "Hwyn the Far-Traveler, tell us the story of the Sky-Raven."

So Hwyn told again the same story she'd told at the hearth of the sheltering darkness that saved the world from the sun's fire. Though we had all heard it before, we had never heard it like this, in the middle of the longest night with a relic of that ancient sacrifice in our midst. All listened breathlessly. Hwyn's hand was near her heart as she spoke, clasping the Eye of Night through her clothing as if to guard it from the fire before us.

When she had finished, Per told the tale of one of the Hidden Goddess's saints: "The Hidden Goddess gave St. Fiern of Etar eyes for the unseen. In the trance of the goddess, the saint could see through a mountain to the gold in its heart, through a man's face to his intentions, through time to the roots of things, through things as they are to things as they might be or ought to be. And for a time she was glad to give counsel to all that asked. Kings sent messengers, queens sent their maids, merchants sent their bondsmen to ask on their behalf what the saint's wisdom foresaw. And common people, too, when they might leave their work, came asking her to see what was dark to them. And in time she grew to feel herself a prisoner of her gift, answering all callers, seeing for others but never for herself. So she withdrew to the hills outside Etar until she found a small, still pool, and she gave the light of her eyes to that pool for all people. And thus the Mirror of St. Fiern was formed. All who look into it may see with Fiern's eyes—if they have the courage to bear what they see there. St. Fiern herself lived the rest of her days in darkness;

the light of her eyes was gone and she was blind. But they say that in the darkness she learned to sing, and was content."

There followed a long story that I had never heard before a northern legend, it must be: "Lew was the fairest-made, brightest-eyed young man of his generation, and this was his misfortune, for his beauty caught the eye of his half-sister and she burned for him unlawfully.

"This might have been her misfortune alone, but she was a necromancer and a magician, familiar with the unquiet dead and learned in the secret arts of influences and forces in the world. Bold in her power, she asked outright for the love of Lew's body. When he shrank from her, she cursed him that if he would not have her, no daughter of womankind would have him. And her words were fulfilled. After that, all women shrank from Lew, handsome as he was, as they would shrink from the touch of incest.

"As the years went by and the mage did not relent, Lew's loneliness turned to frenzy. He began to haunt the temple, praying hours upon hours to the Bright Goddess for a woman who was the daughter of no woman before her.

"She who delights in the work of her hands could not long resist this prayer. The Bright Goddess made for Lew a woman of flowers, not born but grown in the rich soil of the southern islands sacred to her worship, and shaped with her own fragrant hands. So that the woman might live as a human creature and not merely as the green things of the earth, the goddess gave her a name, Eorthwyn, which in the Old Tongue meant Joy of the Earth.

"The Bright Goddess sent Eorthwyn to Lew and whispered in her ear, 'This is the man you shall love.' And because the gods' words have such power in our hearts and our bodies, Eorthwyn no sooner looked on Lew than she knew she needed him like soil for the roots of her soul. As he stood praying before the image of the Bright Goddess in the temple, she ran toward him, calling his name.

"As Lew saw this woman come toward him, her breath like the exhalation of a flourishing garden, her skin soft as rose-petals, her hair abundant as summer, her eyes full of tenderness for him, he felt that at last he had come alive. They were married at once, and wherever they went together, flowers sprang in their path.

"Their first year together was like the golden age in the childhood of the world. And yet no such childhood can last. When they had been married two years, Lew asked Eorthwyn when she would bear him a child. 'My brother has only been married a year, and he has a child already; surely ours will come soon?'

"'I am petal and leaf, not flesh and blood,' Eorthwyn said. 'How should I bear you a fleshly child? The blossoms spring at my feet as we walk, is that not enough for you?' It was not enough; yet Lew was silent, keeping his thoughts to himself.

"He had his consolations, for Eorthwyn loved to sing, and no bird ever sang more sweetly. No one hearing her song could feel sorrow or pain. Lew loved to call her before the people to sing during festivals, at the wedding of a neighbor, at the welcoming of a neighbor's child, and in the spell of her voice, he would forget the sorrow of their childlessness. And she, longing to please him, delighted in this power.

"This solace served them well until Lew's beloved father died. As he stood weeping over the grave, there broke into his grief a sound that drew him beyond sorrow, beyond shame: Eorthwyn was singing, and he could scarcely help but dance.

"'Eorthwyn, this is not the time,' he said wearily, but she did not listen.

"'Eorthwyn, for the gods' sake, be quiet,' he said, but she caroled on joyfully, heedless of the stares of their neighbors.

"'Eorthwyn, enough!' he shouted, and struck her across her blossomlike face.

"'How dare you strike me!' she cried.

"'How dare you mock my father's funeral with merriment!' he replied.

"'I was singing for your comfort, and for the comfort of all those who were weeping. What is the harm in that?'

"'My father is dead, and I have just buried him! Why should I not weep?' Her bewildered stare confounded him. 'What is wrong with you? Have you no heart?'

"'Of course I have none,' she said, 'thank the goddess who made me! Otherwise I would be growing old now as you are, my hair losing its color, my skin losing its freshness. I would be dying little by little as your father did, instead of growing new flowers with the spring, fresh from year to year. Why do you not understand? I am not flesh and bone, but leaf and flower. What should I want with a heart?'

"'Well, you shall no longer have mine!' Lew shouted. Then he turned south, as though he could have shouted to the rim of the world, and cried to the Bright Goddess, 'Take back your gift, oh Goddess! What good is a woman of flowers to a man of flesh and blood?'

"And Eorthwyn, fearing he would kill her, ran from her husband. She dared not seek sanctuary at the temple where she had met Lew; instead she took refuge in a cave sacred to the Hidden Goddess. There she opened her hands in prayer: 'Oh Wise One, what is there in me that makes all people hate me?'

"'It is not what is in you, but what you lack,' answered the Hidden Goddess. 'Take heart. Trust me. Hide in my womb and I will do what can be done.' A new fissure opened in the back of the cave, and Eorthwyn crept inside.

"Into the cave, then, came the Bright Goddess herself. 'Sister,' she said, 'what have I done? How can I answer the prayer of my suppliant without doing harm? Should I take back the name I gave and let my ill-made creature return to the flowers she was? I am loath to unmake a soul I have made, and Eorthwyn has done no wrong by any law she can understand—nothing to deserve death. Yet she cannot live among humankind.'

"'My sister, my sister,' said the Hidden Goddess, 'why did you begin the work without me? When did one of us alone ever bring forth anything half as good as the work of all our hands together? A woman should not be made of flowers: gut and gristle, blood and brain and bone, sweat of desire and pain of birth, all these make a woman.'

"'And thought of the brain, and dream of desire, and will of the heart,' said the Bright Goddess. 'I know now my mistake. But Eorthwyn is made already, and I would not deprive her of what life she has.'

"'She is but half made,' answered the Hidden Goddess. 'Let me have the rest of her making.' So the Bright Goddess kissed her sister and assented.

"Eorthwyn lay in the womb of the Hidden Goddess until, in the darkness, her petals faded into feathers, her stalks hardened to hollow bones, and she flew out of the secret place as an owl.

"Still she flies the night, fearing the sun. The people who hated her as Lew's wife still shun her, eater of vermin, bringer of ill omen. And yet she is happier than before: now she has hope.

"From the entrails she eats, a heart is growing within her.

And in the darkness, she is learning to feel. Some day, she will be human.

"As for Lew, he too, in time, sought the shrine of the Hidden Goddess, which he had neglected before. 'What shall I do?' he said. 'I have done wrong to blame Eorthwyn for her making, which was my choice, not hers. But must I be punished with a lifetime of solitude? I cannot live with Eorthwyn, nor can I marry any woman born of womankind. What I long for is not for me. Is it my fate to be forever alone?'

"And the Hidden Goddess responded, 'It is good that you are here. You have been too long away from me. Stay among my priests, serve me, and learn my mercy: for I am not born of womankind.' And he remained with her in the Order of Hope, till death united him with her forever." So the tale ended.

There were other stories, of course, but I sat long pondering this one, and missed the ones that followed. The story both drew and repelled me. I was startled to hear it in the temple, in a solemn feast; it seemed blasphemous to say that the Bright Goddess had done wrong, or that the Hidden Goddess had taken a human paramour. Yet it reminded me of Halred of the Folc and the Rite of Increase, celebrating the work of both goddesses together, light and dark bringing forth life. Maybe even in blasphemy there could be a hidden truth: not that the gods do wrong, but that we wrong them in our worship, wanting to see only light or only dark, only rising or only falling. I thought of the god that had always troubled me, the Upside-Down God, and wondered what the Rising God could not have done without him.

When I came out of my reverie, I realized that they had already begun the Rite of the Dead, speaking the names of those they mourned that year, sharing the grief and the honor of their memory. This part of the ceremony, at least, was familiar to me. I listened solemnly: the names of the dead were many. When my turn came to speak, I told them of Ennes, slain in Kelgarran Hall on the night that had changed my life; and I recalled the names of the four guards of Kreyn killed by their old comrades, mourned by their enemies. I spoke, too, of my brother Saeverth, dead these seven years but still an open wound in my heart.

In her turn, Hwyn surprised me by naming our enemy Dannoth of Kelgarran, without judging him, without according him less honor than the other dead. She spoke, too—hesitantly—of Hwyn the Weaver. I wondered whether the weaver were truly dead; I wondered whether my companion knew.

As we spoke the names and praises of the dead, drums beat at the rim of the circle, while a solitary flute lamented. When the last of the congregation had named her lost ones, the whole crowd of us swept to our feet, moved the deerskin mats to the edges of the room, and began a slow dance round the hearth. Pricked by the Gift of Naming, I turned around to see another circle turning behind us, a dance of spirits. Somewhere in that ring, Saeverth was dancing. I wanted to run to him, but I dared not break the circle. When harp and viol joined the music, and the tune broke into full-bodied song, the ring of dancers dropped hands and I turned back—but could not see him. The ghosts had vanished—at least to the eye. Somewhere around or in us, I felt, they were still there.

Letting my brother's spirit go, I clasped Hwyn's hand and let myself be carried along by the dance. We stumbled, confused in following, as the pipes trilled faster and the steps grew more buoyant, but some spirit of the night seemed to guide us, for all our awkwardness, into our rightful place in the wheel. Near us we saw Trenara dancing, for all her bulk of pregnancy, light-footed as a child, graceful as a ship in smooth waters.

We danced till the riotous pipes subsided again to slow sighing, and cups of wine were passed from hand to hand. Two by two we drank and gave drink to each other with the words, "The morning may never come." A hush was over us; we'd all known those words since childhood, and repeated them every year since we came of age, but who can speak them in the flickering torchlight of the temple, in the dead of night, the longest night of the year, and feel no tremor of the spirit? Even Trenara remembered those words and spoke them with that tone of profound gravity that had so deceived me when I first met her. I took the cup first from her, drank with her, and then passed it to Hwyn with the same shivery greeting. By and by I shared the cup with Harga and Per, Hart and Modya, Syrc, Til, and others I could not name. When there was no cup in our hands we embraced, clinging to each other as though in defiance of all life's losses, while the words echoed round: "The morning may never come."

My pulse quickened at the sound. In the Tarvon Order, these words would have marked the end of the rite, except for the nightlong vigil to keep the fire burning. But here in the North, I had heard tell—and I began to believe it, as the music rose again to a heady reel, and the Holdouts put aside their goblets to stamp and spin in a wilder dance—those words might sometimes signal one night's license for wild carousal and coupling, each with all as the night's mood took them. As the dance swirled to ecstasy and the music to passion, I saw gentle Hart leaping madly near the fire, his shirt half unlaced. Syrc, I noticed, had left the dance to recline on the skins in the corner—and she was not alone. It seemed the rumors had been true. Now I admit that a year before, weary of my Order's discipline, I might have warmed to the suggestion. But that night I had other plans. As the revelers leapt and shouted, I swept up Hwyn in my arms and whispered close, "Come away with me!"

She kissed me and whispered, "Yes." Arm in arm, giddy with drink, we threaded our way through the surging crowd of revelers, out into the night.

The full moon was high over the turrets of Larioneth Hall. We scurried as best we could through the snow, half laughing, to the kitchen door, and let ourselves in. The sleepy adolescents standing guard over the children watched us enter without any sign of surprise. Two wet cloaks thrown over chairs in the kitchen seemed to tell me we were not the first couple to slip away home. Undetained by any question or greeting, we swept down the hall to our bedroom, the healer's room, and clapped the door shut as though we thought ourselves pursued. There in the shadowy moonlight Hwyn leaned on the door panting, laughing. I caught both her hands in mine, pressed them to my heart, and looked searchingly into her moonlit eyes.

"*Yes,*" she said.

"You haven't even heard what I'm asking," I said. I knelt before her. "Hwyn, my heart, will you marry me tonight, here, and proclaim it publicly tomorrow?"

"Yes. I said yes," she laughed. "How many times should I say it?"

"As many times as possible. I've waited so long for it."

"Then yes again. Yes! I love you," she said.

I kissed her, long and slow, taking my time as it seemed I never had before—always hurried on, stealing time when Trenara was distracted or asleep, snatching moments when we were not too tired and sore to feel a whisper of delight, each moment hemmed in by traveling and worries of traveling. At last we had time, all that longest night of all nights. I felt Hwyn lean into the kiss, into my arms. When at last we moved apart, it was just far enough that I could murmur into her ear, "I love you, heart of my heart. I have no ring to give you—but I could knot some of my hair into one." I laughed. "It's grown long enough, since the summer country." And so, with trembling fingers, we cut locks of our hair with my knife and twisted them into rings, Hwyn's pale gold for my hand, my earth-brown for her thin finger.

"And now?" Hwyn said.

"There's one who should witness this," I said. "I promised Conor—"

No sooner did I speak his name than he was there, dressed in lordly splendor, his wound not visible. "Well, friend, you keep your promises in startling ways," he said to me, and to Hwyn, "I wish you joy." As well as he could, insubstantial as he was, he made as though to kiss her hand. Then he stepped back from us, and I spoke to Hwyn the words that had been on my tongue for so long: "Before the Great Ones of the World-Wheel and before this witness, I offer you, with this ring, my heart and my body, my home and my goods, my love and my loyalty, as long as we live."

"I accept you," she said, her flute-voice betraying a slight tremolo, "and give in return, with this ring, my heart and my body, my home and my goods, my love and my loyalty, as long as we live. And longer, if it were possible to promise that," she added. Then we slipped the rings of hair over each other's fingers and kissed.

"I wish you joy," said Conor again, but his face looked almost sad as he faded from view, leaving us alone.

I held Hwyn's bony hands between my own: the wounded one, with its shorn stump of a finger, and the one now marked with the ring. "The morning may never come," I said softly, "but this night is the center of my life. Holy the night! For the first time in my life, I understand those words."

We kissed again, Hwyn pressing her thin body against me. I could feel her heart, fast and frantic as a bird's. "And now—" she said again, haltingly. "My heart and my body, I offered you. But I—I almost don't know what to do."

"Nor do I," I whispered. "But together—let us step into the unknown."

"We always do," she said. "That's what I love you for." I lifted her gently off her feet and carried her to bed.

We were old for bride and groom, I know. We were old enough, almost, to have been planning a daughter's wedding. But my youth had been spent in a celibate order, and Hwyn's simply in loneliness. The dance of this night was new to us. Our coming together was awkward, gentle, careful of each other's wounds, of bodies and spirits too often and too easily hurt. Ah, gods, but it was the loveliest thing in my life. And when at last we could do no more than curl together and sleep, we slipped into dreams so tightly twined around each other that I thought we would never come unknit. I can never understand how it happened that I woke alone.

19

THE END OF THE WORLD

It was not yet dawn when I woke to find Hwyn gone. At first I thought the night of joy had been a dream. After a moment's doubt, I decided she had only gone for water, and would be back soon; but all the while my heart misgave me. Unable to rest, I pulled back the curtain and sprang out of bed to grope about searching for flint and steel to strike a light. But in the moonlit dark, I saw enough: she was not there, nor were her shift, overdress, boots, and cloak. All thoughts of comfort left me. She had not put on her cloak to go down the hall to the scullery or the privy; she had gone outside. This could mean only one thing: the time had come for the Raven's Egg to hatch.

Without a moment's delay, I threw on my clothes and bounded through the hall. All were asleep, tired out from the festival night; there was no one to ask which way she might have gone. Where would she go? Hwyn had never said more than that she must bring the Eye of Night to the North, to Larioneth. And now we had reached Larioneth; the great hall was its center. What might her destination be, if not here? The temple?

I went out into the snow and started toward the temple. The revelers would still be there, I thought, or at least those charged with the last hours of the vigil. At least she would not be alone. But why did she not wake me, unless she chose to be alone?

That thought stopped me in my tracks. I remembered, then, how Hwyn, riding into Larioneth, had turned to peer at the ring of gray stones: the Sky-Temple. "Of course!" I shouted aloud, and spun about to rush in the opposite direction, away from the scene of the revels, out beyond the walls of the town. My progress was slow: here, no path was cut in the snow to make the way easier. But I was certain, now, that I was right: everything in me said so. I remembered the feeling of familiarity that had struck me at the first sight of the Sky-Temple: a premonition? And then another image struck my mind's eye so forcefully I almost lost my footing: the Eye of Night encircled in twelve stones, my makeshift Wheel of Power. I should have known! I redoubled my efforts.

The sun had not yet peered over the horizon, but the moon was still high, and a pearly half-light on the horizon presaged the coming of dawn. By this ghost-light I could half perceive the shapes of the standing stones, and at my feet in the snow—was that another trail of footsteps, joining mine? "Hwyn!" I shouted, though I knew the wind would carry my voice away from her.

Suddenly there was a crash like the cracking of a world, louder than thunder, louder than the earthquake that had shaken us from winter into summer. From the Sky-Temple rose a shadow, black against the gray sky; and as it rose, it grew. Black wings swept across the sky and covered it utterly, swallowing even the pale foretaste of the sun. There was no sun, no moon, no stars. There was no morning, no twilight, no predawn gray. There was only darkness.

I stood in the middle of an open plain as though I were in a sealed hold or a tomb, enclosed in blackness, afraid to move forward, as though I expected to strike painfully against the wall of dark. "Hwyn!" I called. No one answered. I could see nothing. Blindly I crept forward, a half-step at a time, to where I thought I must have been headed. Between me and the Sky-Temple, I knew, was clear, level ground. If I could only keep my direction—I staggered on for what seemed an endless journey, gradually daring to move faster, calling Hwyn's name at intervals as I went. At last I collided hard with a standing stone, almost too relieved at discovering a landmark to mind the force of the blow. "Hwyn!" I called again.

"Jereth," the answer came, a soft moan. My heart contracted painfully.

"Hwyn! Where are you?"

"In the center," she said weakly. "Lying in the circle's center. Can't—can't you see me?"

"No. I see nothing," I said. I dared not walk toward her, sightless as I was, for fear of stumbling on her, so I dropped to all fours in the snow and crawled, groping ahead of me with one hand before I moved. "I'm coming," I said.

"I thought it was my eye that had failed," she said.

"No," I said. "Night has fallen. Are you near?"

"Here," she said, not so far ahead of me now.

As I crawled toward her, I noticed that the snow under my hands and knees thinned and then disappeared, and the ground even grew warm. "Hwyn, what happened? Was this—did you plan this?"

At that moment my outstretched hand touched her body. She let out a helpless cry of pain. Hastily I drew back.

"Gods! What have I done?" I cried. "Oh, Hwyn! What's happened to you?"

"Jereth—I—I'm sorry," Hwyn murmured absurdly, panting as though with exertion, as though the effort not to scream again exhausted her strength. "I didn't mean to—to drive you away. I—I'm hurt. I—Jereth, I'm dying now."

"*No!*" A choked whisper: it was all I could say.

She spoke on, breathless and stammering but insistent. "I know it will hurt but I want you—I want you to hold me while I die."

"Oh gods! Hwyn, I don't want to hurt you again, I—I'll do this as carefully as I can. Where are you hurt?"

"My chest. Here—lift me by the shoulders—" One hand reached out and found me. I reached carefully to take both her shoulders without touching her chest, to lift her as gently as possible; but by her sharp intake of breath, I knew it pained her. Still, I managed at last to settle her more or less comfortably in my arms.

"Thank you," she panted. "I love you."

"Hwyn, you're not going to die," I said. "I'll take you back to the hall. Harga—"

"No," she said simply. "You can't see. By the time you find your way—no, Jereth. Let me stay here in peace."

"But—"

"It's no use, love," she said. "The morning may come—but I will not see it."

"Then neither will I," I said.

"You must," she returned. "You will be needed."

"For what?" I said bitterly.

"I don't know," she said. "Maybe—maybe to correct what I have done. It is so dark! I never imagined it so dark. I—I wonder—was I wrong?"

"No," I said. "Hwyn, don't say so. You always knew—"

"Not now," she said. "My truesight is gone."

"Hwyn, what happened? What hurt you?"

She was a while catching her breath before she could answer. "The Eye of Night has hatched," she said. "I felt it, ready, when I woke in the night. That—that's why I left your side. I knew—I had to bring it here." She paused for breath.

"What happened? What did it do to you?"

"It was filled with fire," she said. "It burst with a force like lightning, and it—the force of the blow—" She paused to gasp for breath, and I waited, scarcely daring to breathe myself, lest I miss her faltering words. "Part of the shell was driven through my chest. And the fire—it burned me."

"Through your chest— It was still in your breast pouch, then," I said. "*Why?* Why didn't you leave it at a safe distance? Why couldn't you hold it in your hand, at least, away from your heart?"

"It needed me," she said, more steadily than before. "The warmth of my body to kindle its fire. The pulse of my heart. Maybe even my life."

"*It needed you.* What if it did?" I retorted. "What kind of creature could feed on your life like that?"

"I don't know," she sighed. "It may be—I may have done wrong."

"No. Hwyn, no," I recanted desperately. "Don't mind me; I never understood this quest. You *must* have done right. You were—you have always been so wise. You knew—" Suddenly a new thought struck me like the crash of a wave, hard and merciless on the rocks. "Hwyn, you knew it, you knew this would happen, didn't you? That's why you wouldn't let me carry the Eye of Night, toward the end. You knew."

"I expected something of the kind," she said wearily.

"And did you know when I was making the breast-pouch for you, that I was helping to kill you? Dear gods, if only I had died first!"

"No, Jereth, my love, you did nothing wrong. You did nothing to hurt me, and everything to help me. The breast-pouch made no difference."

"No difference? A shard through your chest, no difference?"

"It would have made no difference if I'd left the Eye here and run away, Jereth," she said. "I was doomed. I sealed my fate the night I met you."

"What do you mean?"

"When I found the Eye of Night in the magic circle," she said, "it was bound with the names of the lords of Kelgarran. To break the binding, I had to replace their names with my own."

"Oh, no. Oh, Hidden Goddess, no," I groaned, remembering how insistent Hwyn had been against my using my own name in bindings—seeing how she had protected me, unprotected herself.

"The Eye of Night was enclosed in my name," she said. "I had no more hope of surviving its hatching than—than if it had been closed in my flesh."

"Oh Hwyn, my heart, my life!" I moaned, rocking her gently. "How can I live if you do not?"

"I wanted you to live," she said slowly, her voice down to a hoarse whisper. "I—Jereth— As best I could, I tried to keep you alive. I love you so. Maybe—maybe I should not have let you love me. It—it was a little cruel, because I knew. I knew I could only die."

"That love was the saving of me, Hwyn my soul, my saint," I said. "I love you so desperately."

"I know. I'm sorry and I'm glad," she said. "Without you— A person can only take so much loneliness. I needed you. And with you I have been happy, even starving and cold and stumbling through the snow toward my death."

My eyes burned with tears I could not shed. "Oh, why can't I save you? Why can't I die with you?"

"Jereth—I'm sorry."

"There's been so little time," I said. "We were scarcely together. There's so much you haven't told me. Not even— What is your name?"

"Can't tell you," she murmured. "It is broken. Shattered, with the egg."

"Oh, gods. Is there no mercy anywhere?"

"But you guessed it," she said. "You named me right. That first morning. When we sailed."

"What?"

"You named me," she sighed.

"What did I say?" I pleaded.

No answer came.

The land was very still. The only sounds in my ears were my own ragged breathing and frantic heartbeat.

"Hwyn?"

I loosened my hold on her with one hand to caress her face. "Hwyn, speak to me, please." She did not respond. I clutched at her wildly, almost as I had in the night, in our brief night of pleasure. When my hand fumbled against her wound, she did not cry out. My last hope died.

There rose from my throat a wordless, senseless cry, the raging of a beast that can roar but not weep. I thought my heart would split. I thought the world would crack. But nothing happened, and that was worst of all.

Nothing happened, except that my body shook, and my unseeing eyes seemed to be bleeding, bleeding fire, bleeding life out of my soul, as the hot harsh tears I had dammed up since childhood burst forth. It hurt to weep, as though the tears were too big for my eyes. In a confusion of grief and pain and shame, I sat in the center of the Sky-Temple clutching her poor torn body, clutching the wreck of all I loved. How long I sat there, I do not know; there was no sun or moon to mark the time.

At length I was disturbed by a light. My eyes were closed, but such was the shock of it after utter darkness that I swear I saw it through my eyelids. I opened my eyes, and was at first too dazzled to see the figure carrying the torch. "Who is it?" I said, in a voice that scarcely seemed to be my own.

"I," said a voice I knew.

"Trenara?" Slowly, my eyes adjusted to the torchlight. It was the lady indeed. "Trenara," I sobbed, "look— What's happened, I can hardly tell you. It—it's Hwyn. Hwyn is dead."

The lady planted her torch in the earth, crouched beside me, and slipped her arms gently around the body I held. Her touch was as soft as compassion. She bent to kiss Hwyn's cold brow, then slid away, only holding one lifeless hand. Then at last she spoke: "Alas, my faithful traveler! I come too late for farewells. You have gone too swiftly before me."

Was this Trenara? I gaped astonished. I must have been mistaken. Peering through the unsteady torchlight, I looked into her face—Trenara's face, there was no doubt—and felt, for the second time, a veil fall from my eyes.

"Goddess," I said, "why didn't I recognize you till now?"

"Peace, child. Your Gift of Naming did not fail you," she said. "But come: I have slept too long. Years, long dark years. And in the last hours I walked in dreams in my own land, with you and this saint. Come, bear her with honor to the hall."

Too stupefied to argue, I followed. I noticed for the first time that Trenara shone with a radiance not lent by the torch. She cut the darkness as a ship's prow cuts the wave. How had I ever been deceived? She was different, and yet oddly the same as ever, with the same thoughtless grace like an animal moved only by instinct. Even the inhuman glow of her body, which I had never seen before, was strangely familiar, as the Sky-Temple had been familiar. But I did not set my mind to this riddle. She ordered me, "Come," and I came, too weary to resist, too weak to choose my own path. Hwyn lay in my arms, a trifling small burden, as though half her weight had departed with her soul. Hwyn who had never been still, even in sleep, always full of quick and nervous motion, now lay limp and unresisting as a doll. With every step I took, every motion to which she did not respond, I rediscovered her death, a dagger of ice in my heart.

We reached Larioneth Hall's back kitchen door, the one that was never bolted. Trenara stood aside as though it were beneath her to open the door for herself—or as though she still expected Hwyn to lead the way. I would not put down Hwyn's body to grasp the door handle. Instead I kicked the door, surprising myself with the gesture, with the anger lying just beneath the surface of my grief.

The door opened and Ash appeared, holding a lantern. "Jereth! What's happened?" she began, then saw what I carried.

"Hwyn is dead." It came out as a sob.

Ash pulled me indoors without another word and, with her usual instinct for giving people whatever they most needed, she wrapped her arms as far as she could around me and Hwyn together, pressing us to her breast, saying nothing, for no words could console me.

I heard Trenara step in behind me; from among the people who'd been with Ash in the kitchen, I heard gasps and shouts of amazement.

March's voice broke out above the scattered sounds. "My Lady—what *are* you?" Even Ash, then, released me to stare past me at the lady.

I looked over my shoulder at Trenara, who stood silent and radiant as ever. "Oh, Trenara. She is the Hidden Goddess," I said indifferently, and sank into one of the kitchen chairs, rocking Hwyn's body in my arms, as though she were a sleeping child that might wake again.

Around me the Holdouts of Larioneth were falling to their knees again. I would not. Goddess though she was, Trenara had not saved Hwyn, and I was not impressed with her divinity. She spoke to her followers now in the sweet musical tones that had beguiled me when I first met her, but I shut my ears against her.

In the firelight of the kitchen I could see Hwyn's wounds clearly for the first time, the ugly burns covering her chest, the bloody passage that a shard had made through her body. She had been right: there had been no hope of healing. Scar upon scar and wound upon wound: such had been her life. There was no part of her small body that did not bear witness to suffering. And I had dreamed that I could mend those hurts, caress away the memory of pain. But pain had been her destiny; she had been marked for it, like an animal consecrated to sacrifice in the old days. I could do nothing for her. In the end she went off alone to die, protecting me, surrendering herself. I had not saved her.

A hand touched my arm. "Jereth, let me see her."

It was Harga. I loosened my grip enough to let her examine Hwyn's wound, feel desperately for a pulse, and shake her head. "I'm sorry," she said. "I had hoped it might all be a mistake. I—I hope she did not suffer much."

"She died in pain and doubt," I said, "wondering if she had done wrong. I—I had never seen her in doubt before. It was—it was merciless, the Eye of Night. She nurtured it and it destroyed her. Left her with nothing, not even the sense of having done right. Not even her name."

"Oh, my child," Harga murmured, a mere comforting noise, while she wiped away my tears and stroked back the hair from my face, as though I were one of Ash's babies. I had never seen her gentle before, and it almost unnerved me. I was still weeping uncontrollably, though some child-self in the back of my mind continually expected to be beaten for it. It might have been a relief, at that—simple physical pain to drown the horror.

"I want to die," I whispered.

"Hush now," Harga crooned meaninglessly, awkwardly half embracing me with one knobby-boned arm. "We're here. We won't leave you."

They did not leave me, the Holdouts. The hours that followed were a succession of reassuring touches, old arthritic hands and young sinewy ones, all tender with an affection I had never earned from them; warmth, as someone drew a blanket over my trembling shoulders; meaningless voices, a hushed babble of comfort nearby, and farther off, the purposeful speech of council led by Trenara's silvery voice; but no meaning, no meaning anywhere, except my loss. *I too have lost my name,* I told Hwyn silently: *I had one, when you called me and I followed you. Now I am no one.* My mind heard nothing else. Once, with the same gentle touch as all the others, someone moved to take the body from my arms, saying something or other, I cared not what. I snatched her back: "No! No one shall take her from me!" They retreated, and I contracted farther around her, clutching the ruin of my hopes, clutching despair.

After a time someone put a cup to my lips and, drained dry with weeping, I gave in and drank. I slept, and in my dreams she was alive again. I was calling her, calling a name I could not hear and could not remember once I had spoken it.

I woke calmer, if it can be called calm when a man's heart is dead. I was still clutching Hwyn's body so hard I could scarcely straighten, cramped around her.

The council was dispersed, but it seemed they'd kept a vigil over me, like the vigil for the fire in the temple. Syrc was with me. When she saw I was awake, she moved toward me slowly, carefully, saying nothing, but looking gravely into my eyes all the time. She knelt, took Hwyn's hand, and kissed it. The gesture touched me; it opened my sealed heart. "Syrc, what shall I do?" I whispered.

Before speaking, she moved cautiously and covered my hand with hers, as though the touch would ensure that I accepted what she said in good will. "Friend," she said, "if we cannot comfort you, let us mourn with you."

She paused, and I nodded, waiting for her to go on.

"Little though we knew Hwyn, we had begun to love her too, though not with the great love you have for her. I—I grieve for you, Jereth. But I also mourn Hwyn as a friend—if I may say so."

"You *were* a friend to her," I said. "She'd never had many. She— I'm glad that—" I could not go on. I was weeping again, ready to slip back into unreason, into the haze of pain.

Syrc's grip on me and the hold of her dark eyes remained steady, grounding me to earth. "We want to honor her," she said. "We—we talked it over, but I don't think you heard or understood. There is a custom, a rite reserved for the most honored dead, for heroes: to build a lordly boat for them and launch the body on the ocean, sending them in state to the rim of the world or the embrace of the waters. We want to do that for Hwyn, as for the greatest of heroes. She gave her life for—for *hope*, for the North, maybe for all the world. It is only her due."

I nodded, not trusting myself to speak again.

"Til says you know something of shipbuilding," she said. "Do you want to build the boat? He'll help you, or simply give you what tools you need, as you prefer."

"I'll build it," I said. "That will be fitting."

"Good." Syrc nodded, then hesitated a while before she spoke again. "When you're ready, I—I will take her to be washed and dressed for the funeral." By the time she finished I could hear the tears in her voice.

"Did you come for her once before? Was it you that I pushed away?"

"Yes," she said.

"I'm sorry. I just couldn't—couldn't bear—"

"I know," Syrc said. "It's all right."

I built the boat with as little help as I could manage, rusty though my shipbuilding skills had to be after all those years in the Tarvon Order. It was not very seaworthy, with a showy swan-curved stem and stern, and a low freeboard that would be too easily overwhelmed by the waves; but it was adequate for its purpose, a rudderless boat for her second ghost-driven journey into the unknown. It was a reliquary, a throne for the remains of a saint: one of those who bear the gods into this world. For this reason, I adorned the high prow and stern with rough paintings, icons of her glorious deeds: stealing the Eye of Night; confronting the ghosts in Kelgarran Hall; traveling northward, bent against the wind; lying wounded in the center of the Sky-Temple, a sacrifice, though for what cause I knew not. I was not deft with the paintbrush, but the vague images I drew seemed fitting to me, my clumsiness with the brush masking the damage to her face, blurring the memory of pain. Almost in despair, not knowing anymore if it meant anything, I painted a last icon on the sail, the Great Wheel of the Gods: the Rising God, yearning upward, seemed unable to quite reach the Bright Goddess above him, her arms open in mercy, like Ash, offering comfort he could not attain. To her right, the Upside-Down God smiled his mad grin, diving downward. At the bottom, for the Hidden Goddess, I painted no image of Trenara, but the shadow of the Sky-Raven spreading its wings over the world. As I added the last strokes of the brush to the icon, I felt a presence at my shoulder. There Trenara stood; how long she had been watching me, I did not know, but she smiled, stretching a hand toward my work as though to touch it, but stopping short of the fresh paint. Then she circled the boat, admiring in turn each of the four rough icons, nodding her approval silently.

At last she put a hand on my shoulder and guided me into the great hall. I did not want her guidance, but she was going where my heart led me, so I had no choice. We walked together to the bier where Hwyn's body was laid, dressed once again in the other Hwyn's embroidered gown. It was her best garment, travel-worn but still splendid in its crafting, and fitting, in more ways than one. Fitting that she should be buried in her clothes and in her name, now that her own had been torn by the hatching of the Sky-Raven's Egg. I knelt by the bier, cradled Hwyn's head in my arms, and wept yet again. Some time later I noticed that Trenara, facing me across the bier, was also weeping.

"Why do *you* weep, Goddess?"

"Don't you know?" she said in such a feeling tone, such a forlorn haunting sound, that I almost relented, almost regretted the harshness of my question.

Almost, but not quite. "No," I said fiercely.

"I have as good a right to mourn as you," Trenara retorted, matching my fierceness. The Holdouts standing around us drew back a pace.

"What right?" A memory turned in my mind: I remembered how Hwyn had spoken of her mother, the holy fool. "Were you her mother?"

"Only in the sense that I am your mother as well, and the world's," she said. "I gave birth to it before time."

"Ha! Fine neglectful mother you are."

"If I am that," she said evenly, "then why am I *here?*"

I could not answer that riddle, but I was not to be won over. I turned my face away from her. All the while that I argued with their goddess, the Holdouts had been staring at me in horror, awaiting a response, awaiting, perhaps, retribution. I did not care. I turned again to face her, challenging: "You sacrificed her! You have no right to weep for her. Her death was just part of your plan."

She didn't flinch, didn't drop her gaze, didn't even blink. She only said very softly, "I have no plan."

Syrc came between us, nothing afraid of the goddess, for all that she'd been the first to kneel to her. "It's time," she said, so surely that we all forgot time had stopped in this endless night. "Come, Jereth. The other fishers are bringing your boat to the shore. Now we must carry Hwyn's body in procession. The people will follow us." She took one corner of the bier, I another, Hart a fourth of the bearers. Led and flanked by torchbearers, we marched toward the sea with a slow drum beating and Tresanda keening somewhere behind me, singing a lament, in that sweet high voice that was almost as good as Hwyn's but never, never so dear to me. Outdoors, beyond the shelter of the city walls, the torches' light was strained thin, all but swallowed by darkness, with little to send the beams back to us in the open expanse of the shore. The torchbearers led us to a long pier stretching out into the ocean, a finger pointing north to the Rim of the World. Upon its boards we stepped fearfully, mindful of the dark waters on both sides. It had never been meant for use in such utter blackness. But half the funeral procession held torches or lanterns, and in the patches of light around them we were able to creep cautiously to the far end of the pier. There the fishermen moored the boat I'd made, and we set Hwyn gently down inside it.

Trenara claimed the right to speak first. I did not mind, so long as the last turn was mine. "This night," proclaimed the goddess, "we send forth a great saint who died in the darkness so that others could come through the darkness alive. If you have any hope in this night, it is her gift. Honor her for that. She gave herself to my quest, knowing full well what it would cost her. Such a generous heart should never be forgotten." And Trenara took off the silver crescent pendant they had given her at the festival, and fastened it around Hwyn's neck.

Next Per spoke: "We were promised hope in dark times: strength from the earth, friends from the South, hope from the sea. Now we commit one of those friends to the sea. May the Hidden Goddess—" he turned suddenly to Trenara, and seemed to pause, disconcerted, seeing the flesh-and-blood face of his formulaic invocation—"may all the Four Great Ones keep her in their care, and may we always keep her in our memories, so long as we have tongue to tell the tale or pen to write it."

Syrc would have deferred to me, but I motioned her to proceed. She spoke little, uncharacteristically. "Hwyn was my friend," she said. "I am grateful for that. She was the strongest soul I ever knew."

Fourth and last, I spoke. "Hwyn was all they say, and more than any of you can say, more even than I can say who knew her best, but never knew her true name. That name is lost now: she sacrificed it with her life for the hope she saw amid the Troubles. All that she was—which was most precious—" the tears began again, and my voice shook, but I gathered breath to speak through it, "—all of herself, she sacrificed: for the Hidden Goddess, for me, for all of you. Whether she did wisely I cannot now say. I know nothing—I never knew anything—except that she—" tears choked me, but I forced myself to go on, "—of all things that touched my life, she was most beautiful."

Then I turned from the crowd to the boat moored beside me where Hwyn lay. "Hwyn, my heart, in the morning we would have proclaimed our marriage vows before the people—but that morning, now, never comes. Nonetheless, I have married you with ring and promise, heart and body. And I have not followed you so far to abandon you now." With that I lowered myself slowly into the boat, careful not to unbalance it. I had made it to hold us both, but the disparity of our weights made it difficult to keep the craft upright. But not for nothing had I spent my childhood at sea. I found my balance, unfurled the sail, and untied the mooring-rope. "Thus I began this journey, and thus I end it. To the world's end or the sea's bottom, I go with you."

I heard a chorus of voices cry "No!" and "Stop!," Trenara's among them. Then came the splash of a body cutting the water. Before we were well clear of the dock, the swimmer reached the boat and pulled himself up on the edge. "Jereth, don't," panted Til. "Come back to us."

"Til—"

"Gods, but I'm cold," he sputtered. "Come on! Or I'll freeze to death, and you'll have that on your conscience to the world's end."

"Til, I'm sorry, but you shouldn't have swum out," I said. "It's kind of you, but it's no use. You can't help me. Please, let me go." But he'd already retied the mooring-rope to the boat.

"Jereth, you can't do this!" called the Hidden Goddess, her musical voice filled with a cold fury I hadn't known she possessed.

"Why not?" I shouted back. "Wasn't there once a custom to send one of the living to the world's rim with a dead hero as an offering? An offering in exchange for the dead—to bring the hero back."

"*We* never demanded that," the goddess proclaimed. "We never asked for that offering. It was human custom—"

"Because human hearts demand it," I said, "when we cannot accept unjust and untimely death. Command what you will, a man cannot live when his heart is dead. You may stop me from sailing to the world's end, but you can't forbid me to die." As I said this, I held Hwyn's body in my left arm, leaning half over her; my right hand gripped the knife I always wore at my belt. I set the hilt against the bottom of the boat beside Hwyn, the point against my heart so that, embracing her, I could lean into the knife and die.

"*She* would forbid it," Trenara said, and I knew without looking that she was pointing at Hwyn.

I let the knife clatter to the bottom of the boat. "You are cruel," I said, "to torment me so with the truth." Then I picked up the knife again, speaking once more only to the dead. "Because you forbade it, Hwyn, and for no other reason, I will not send my body with yours. But a part of me goes with you to the world's end." With that I made a slash across my left forearm and let my blood spill out onto her breast. "May I soon follow." Then I allowed myself to be hauled back up onto the pier. Held back from the edge by kind, imprisoning arms, I watched the rudderless craft carry her off into darkness.

"Gone. She's gone. What can I do?" I cried. No one answered, but Hart and Til, who'd been holding me back from the brink, tightened their grip on me. Til was wet as a flounder and shivering violently. "Til, I'm sorry," I said. "You'll catch your death. I never meant—"

"It's all right," he said. "Come on." I put my cloak around him—he resisted at first, then gave in—and I let them lead me home.

In Larioneth Hall, Ash and her helpers started warming fish stew and pancakes left from the feast to feed the mourners—not the traditional generous funeral dinner, but just enough to keep strength up. Food had to be doled out cautiously, for no one dared guess how long it might be before there was light to hunt by. But I excused myself from the meal, saying I wanted to sleep. They let me go uneasily, but they'd taken my knife away, and there was no other blade left in the room I'd been sharing with Hwyn, so they gave me my way.

But when I was alone again, the door shut against any who might have consoled me, I did not sleep. I stumbled through the darkness to the bed where Hwyn and I had shared our one night of joy, but I could not lie down on it. I wrapped the blanket around myself, dropped to the floor, and sat leaning against the bed brooding till my back ached.

There was a timid knock on the door. "Come in," I said indifferently.

The candle they carried dazzled me a moment. "Your fire's gone out," Hart said, and Syrc groped her way to the grate to light what remained of the fuel from the candle flame. I thought they had come to coax me out into the great hall with the others, but they shut the door instead, set the candle on the bedside table, and drew near me, even sat on the cold stone floor as I did.

"Do you mind if we sit with you a while?" Syrc said.

"No," I said listlessly. "I mean, thank you. Everyone's been so kind, but I—it's no use, I just can't bear it, and no amount of kindness—I'm sorry, I must seem terribly ungrateful, but—"

"No," Syrc said, "We understand. That's what we came to tell you, that we understand. I mean, not really *understand,* of course, because no one really understands, do they? It's all inside you where no one can see, no one can touch. And it's not the same, it's different for every loss. People always say 'I know how you feel,' but they don't know, do they? You know? Do you understand what I'm trying to say?"

"Yes," I said, seeing her with new clarity, for her disclaimer had convinced me, as no assurances could, that she did understand. I touched her shoulder. "You've been here."

"In a way," Syrc said, trailing off to silence as though weighted down by memory.

"Then tell me, please, how did you go on?"

"That's just it, isn't it?" said Hart. "Sometimes it seems harder for the ones that have to go on living. But we wanted to ask you to live. And we thought if we told you our story, you might think we had some right to ask."

"We haven't spoken of this in years," Syrc said, "and everyone in Larioneth knows better than to speak of it, for I won't hear my parents' names spoken; I struck the last man that uttered their names in my hearing."

"They left us," Hart explained, "with the crowds that left Larioneth."

"It was fifteen years ago," Syrc said. "They went south without us. Sent us down to the seaside to dig clams and were gone when we returned, taking most of their household goods with them, but leaving the baby crying in his cradle. I don't know what they thought we could do without them. I don't know if they *thought* at all."

"Syrc was fifteen then, and the oldest," Hart said, "so most of the burden fell on her."

"Maybe they thought I was old enough to manage," Syrc said. "Well, I didn't manage. There were eight of us when they left. Four died, almost before the dust of our parents' footsteps had settled on the road south. The little ones caught fever, and I didn't know how to care for them. They—they just seemed to dry up, burn up. Three of them died within a week—my sisters Byrne and Lind, my brother Aern. And after that, my first brother, Ord—" she stopped, choked, but this time Hart did not offer to continue for her. After a heavy silence, Syrc went on: "He was the one between me and Hart. We were almost twins, nine months apart, companions and rivals from the cradle. Well, Ord—after the three little ones died, he—Hart and I found him in the barn. Hanging. He hanged himself. We—I was so angry at him, I—oh, gods."

I took her hand. She didn't tremble or show any sign of weakness, except to grip my hand painfully tight. After a time she spoke on: "Yes, I was angry at him, furious. I still am: he deserted us. But I wasn't so different, myself."

"We both admitted," Hart said softly, "that we'd thought of doing the same. Both of us."

"And we agreed then and there that we wouldn't," Syrc said. "We swore a solemn oath to each other not to—not to do what Ord did, for each other's sake, and for Ash and Hauvoc, who needed us."

"They don't know about this," Hart said. "At least I think they don't; maybe the ghosts have told them. We buried Ord in secret. We told Ash that Ord had gone looking for our parents, that we'd tried to stop him but he wouldn't listen to reason. She was young enough to believe us. And Hauvoc was just a baby."

"It's a wonder he survived," Syrc said. "He must be made of iron."

"You kept him alive," Hart told her. "I remember. You wouldn't give up."

"Not I." Syrc smiled. "You were always better with children than I was. But you see," she said to me, "it doesn't matter who. We both had to live for Hauvoc, for Ash. They needed us. And now we need you."

"What for?" I said. "Me, I was never anything but Hwyn's companion. You have the goddess now."

"Of course," Syrc said, "but she is beyond us. Wonderful she may be, indeed—but we can't understand her."

"Neither can I," I said.

"Of course not," Syrc responded. "She is the Unknown." She said it so simply that I was quite overcome with the force of it. I'd been underestimating Syrc—a dangerous error, as Harga had warned me—believing she deferred to me for lack of discernment, too easy-tempered to notice any defect in me. Clearly I'd judged her unjustly; she saw much that I, in my pride, had refused to see. I listened, humbled, as she continued: "We cannot know her. But we can know you. And you, too, are part of the

romise: 'friends from the South.' We need you, Jereth. You
ust not waste your life; you must not waste that promise."

Hart added softly, "I know you would have died for Hwyn, if
ou could. But it's not so simple as that. I used to dream I could
o that: buy back the children's lives with mine. Probably Ord
reamed that, too. But you can't do that; you can't die for her; he
ouldn't die for the children."

"But you can live," Syrc said, "for the promise. For us all."

"I owe you at least that much," I said. "I don't know what sort
f joker god would fulfill a promise with me: a lifelong failure
ith a talent for losing everything I have. I am no prophet, no
ero. But what I can do, I will. I'll try not to fail you."

"You won't," Syrc said.

I almost laughed at her earnestness. "Why you should have
uch faith in me, I can't fathom. I keep expecting everyone to
rn against me. All I do is argue with your goddess. Doesn't it
hock you?"

"Which of us hasn't reproached the gods in silence?" Syrc
aid. "You are only too honest to hide it; and I am at least too
onest to pretend it shocks me. Besides," she added, "it doesn't
eem to shock *her*."

I let them lead me back to the great hall, to the circle of com-
assionate faces. They set food before me and I ate submissively.
fter a time the goddess entered the room; her dark eyes on me
ad the insistence of a call. I rose from my seat and crossed the
om to her, head held high. Then I knelt to her for the first time,
ot in worship but in supplication.

"I need not sail to the world's end to ask you, Goddess: why
id you refuse me? Am I worthless even as sacrifice? For the last
me, will you take my life in exchange for my saint's?"

"I told you," she said, "we never asked for that sacrifice."

"Didn't you accept the blood-offering in the Hills of
enmorrin?" I challenged her. "It was your touch, wasn't it, that
ade the land bloom after we worshiped you with song and with
lood?"

"The song woke me a little to my true nature, when my saint
ang my call to the buried seed," the goddess said. "And the
lood made me weep for pity. I tried to catch you when you fell."

"Then why, why didn't you have pity on Hwyn?" I asked. "I
hought you loved her."

"I do," she said. "Trust me. What I can do, I do."

"But you've done nothing," I said. Then, more quietly, "Are you saying it's not in your power? Are you not a goddess?"

"You yourself named me," she said. "My power is yet to be seen; what I may do, I cannot say. I am not the Rising God to answer your riddles. I am the riddle. I am the Unknown. I offer everything but promise nothing. Will you refuse the offer for the dream of a promise?"

"Lady," I said, "I want nothing except what you have not offered: to return my love to life. But if I cannot have her back, at least tell me what I can do to finish her work, so the hope she served will not die as well. She said that if the task ever fell to me, I would know what to do. But I am as lost as I ever was."

"Not so lost as you believe," she said. "You were right in one thing: you will offer yourself at the world's end; that is your part in this breaking of the age. Build a new boat for yourself and me, and we will sail together to the rim of the world."

"How should I build it?"

She shrugged. "You are the shipbuilder, not I."

"I am a two years' apprentice, and a decade out of practice."

"You will know how to build it, and you will know the way to sail," she said. "Only you could make this journey, Jereth son of Garmund. Whoever would sail to the world's rim must set all life behind him and make for the emptiness beyond the world. Who else could set his back to the world so well as you?"

For a while I only stared at her cold impassive face. "You—you wanted me broken," I said. "You needed me in despair. You needed Hwyn dead and me bereft. How can I follow you? How can I trust you?"

"That is your riddle to resolve," she said. "You must find a way. You will need to trust me."

"Why should I?"

"Because you can only trust me and hope, or distrust me and despair. You will never find the certainty you seek," the goddess answered.

I shook my head. "Never mind. Trusting or not, I will do as you say. I have nothing to lose, nothing I value: life or name, home or goods, heart or body." I rose from my knees, weary, aching, but certain that only Harga's potions could make me sleep. "I can't trust you. But I can build your boat and try to sail it. And if it drowns us—" I shrugged, turning away, "I warned you I was incompetent."

I worked for what should have been days, but was still the same unchanging night. When I grew so bone-tired that my hands fumbled and fouled the work, I let Harga drug me to sleep, and endured the fresh grief of waking from dreams of Hwyn to the remembrance of loss. I needed the rest to restore me, for the work was hard. The craft did not come easily to me, nor did the seasoned boatmen among the Holdouts venture any correction of my methods. Everyone assured me that I knew best. It maddened me. I was working on half-remembered teachings of twelve years ago, filling the gaps with pure, uninspired guesswork. I was not at all certain I did right. My only comfort was that I didn't care if I drowned in my bad handiwork—except that the Holdouts were counting on me to make this journey, whatever it was for. I couldn't fail them. But how could I succeed?

Til worked silently beside me, lending a hand wherever I needed it, docilely following my instructions—though I would have been more thankful for his criticism—and treating me with the sort of pained reverence usually reserved for the dying. When we'd finished tarring the bottom, I said, "Well, it's done, for good or ill."

"It's done," Til said more positively. "All it needs is the sail—and a lantern, for this journey."

I was not so sure; I wondered whether the yard were too long to manage, whether the rake of the stempost were wrong. Something looked odd about it; either that, or I had been staring at the thing too long to see it straight. But I sighed, "Let's get them, then, and test this tub to see if it sinks or swims."

"It'll swim," Til said. "There's nothing wrong with this boat. What are you afraid of?" Then he caught himself. "Gods! Listen to me: what do I think this is, a ferry-trip across the salt ponds?" He put a hand on my shoulder, and spoke quietly: "Jereth, I couldn't do what you're doing, sailing out into that endless darkness without a sight of land or a star in the sky to guide me. I couldn't face it."

"Just as well," I said. "You heard why this journey is mine: because I'm so lost to life that I can set it all behind me and steer for the cold of the unliving as though it were my guiding star. You shouldn't be able to face it. No one should."

"All the same," Til said, "If I had any courage, I'd join you. I ought to. You're sailing for all of us; it doesn't seem fair that you should go alone."

"The Hidden Goddess will be with me," I reminded him.

"And isn't that alone?"

We went looking for Grim's wife, Mara, who had offered to fix a sail for me, in the great hall. People clustered there and in the adjoining kitchen for warmth and light, saving firewood and tallow by banding together instead of kindling separate fires in their separate chambers.

"Mara," Til called as we entered the room, "is the sail ready? We'll be needing it."

"Here it is," Mara said.

Near her, Trenara sprang to her feet. "Is the boat finished?"

"It's done," I said. "It's time now to test its seaworthiness."

"It will be seaworthy," the goddess said, implacable. "We must go now."

"You haven't even looked at it!" I protested.

"Never mind that. It will carry us. No time for tests: we must leave at once."

"*Are you mad?*"

Her silvery laugh rang through the great hall; it chilled me to the heart. "Maybe! You have known me longest—have you ever known me otherwise? But we have no time to lose. The hour of birth is near, and what I hold in my womb must not be born in these lands. It comes from your world, but your world cannot bear it. Come!" she said, gesturing about her to the Holdouts gathered around, "bring lanterns and gear for the journey, and see us off."

So they brought lanterns and oil, ropes and gear, and everything we might need, and followed Til and me as we brought the boat down to the sea. For this launching there was no ceremony, but the people who had saved my life, first from the cold and then from myself, came in as great a throng as for funeral or festival. They paid final homage to Trenara, their queen and goddess, and begged her to remember them. "You are my children, my beloved," she said. "How could I ever forget you?" Some kissed her hands; other, bolder souls embraced her. And many came to bid me farewell with a warmth that surprised and touched me. I remember Syrc clasping me fiercely, as though she never meant to let me sail; Hart half crushing me; Rand

ayly offering a good-luck token, one of the gilt stars they'd
ung up for the festival; Ash bringing food. Harga, her face lined
a worry, told me, "Take care of yourself, for a change." Over
er shoulder I could see that Syrc's eyes glittered with tears. I al-
ost felt I was present at my own funeral. As we said our
arewells, we all heard the crashing of waves gone wild in this
uding time, felt the cold spray, saw the water lapping too high,
most topping the pier. But none of us spoke of it, as though our
ords alone would make the danger of the journey real.

Just as I was about to embark, Til caught me in a tight em-
race. "Forgive me," he muttered, "for not sailing with you."

"Don't be absurd, Til," I said. "You saved my life once; that's
nough. Just don't forget me."

"I'll keep the lantern lit for you on the point," he said. With
aat we pushed off the boat, and the Hidden Goddess and I sailed
way into the darkness. The torches glimmered a while behind
s, calling forth an answering glow from the waves, but I could
ot spare a look of farewell on that last sight of human habita-
on. One hand on the tiller and the other on the sheet, I turned
way from this last vestige of comfort and took on the dire invis-
ble waves. For a time it seemed that if we capsized, I would
carcely know it, for I could see neither sky nor sea and, dizzied
y the waves' tossing, scarcely knew up from down. After a time
ay sense of balance adjusted and I snatched a glance behind me,
ut the Holdouts and their torches had vanished into mist; in all
ae world, the lantern hanging from the mast and the ghostly
low of Trenara's face were the only lights. With no stars to steer
y, all I had to guide me was the vague sense of life and warmth
ceding behind me. Ahead was the cold emptiness I had been
ailing toward, without knowing it, for years, maybe for all my
fe, losing pieces of myself all along the way. Suppressing a
hiver, I lashed the tiller in place, lest my resolve might fail me
a this last stage of a thirty-year journey into darkness.

The wind rose, and our little craft bucked and leapt on the
aves. I struggled desperately with the sheet, and was surprised
o meet Trenara's hands on the rope, working with me.

When we'd fastened the sheet to the belaying pin and had
me for a breath, I said, "I didn't know you were a sailor."

"You know me little," Trenara said.

"Can you blame me?" I said. "After all the time you played

the fool, leaving Hwyn and me to guess and wonder and try t
keep you out of trouble—"

"That was no play-acting," she said.

"What do you mean?" I asked, but was interrupted by a wav
slopping over the gunwale into the boat. I bailed frantically, the
adjusted the sheet again, for the wind had changed somewha
When I felt more confident of staying above the water's surface
asked again, "What do you mean, it wasn't play-acting?"

"When I chose to come into this world," the goddess said, "n
one earthly body could contain all of me, so two bodies wer
prepared: the one you know as Trenara of Larioneth, and the Ey
of Night. Both parts were bound together, inseparable in healt
or harm. Now the Eye of Night, as you know, was harmed: im
prisoned, bewitched, pent up like a caged bird in a magic circl
that kept it from growing, from fully living. So was my mind
imprisoned, moonstruck, stunted, confined. One could not b
whole when the other was harmed. Thus I became a fool."

"But—but you are a goddess!"

"Yes," she said, "as I was all along, even when I could no
dress myself. Think of that! You wondered why you did not know
me at once, why the Gift of Naming failed you. It did not. Yo
knew me: the moment you looked in my eyes you knew all I was
And you refused to know it."

"I—I refused?"

"Of course. Who could blame you? Who could bear to know
that the world lay in the hands of an idiot?" She laughed, bu
there was sorrow even in her laughter. "For so it was, then. An
it would have driven you mad to acknowledge it."

"That it would," I said. "But how—how could you be s
marred? You, a goddess? Who could have power to harm you?"

"Mortals, at times," she said, "have more power than they be
lieve, and we gods, less." The wind shifted, and we had ou
hands full a while, too absorbed in our task to speak. But whe
we'd steadied our course she spoke on. "You think of us as invin
cible, untouchable: four puppeteers pulling the strings of the
world, pulling you here and there, now and then cutting the
strings of one you loved for some cruel caprice of our own. Bu
we are no such thing."

The wind toyed with us another while, and it took some diffi
cult tacking to keep our prow headed north, the distant memory
of life astern. But I did not forget, the whole time, what we'

been speaking of, and when she knew I had an ear free for anything but the wind, the goddess continued. "Four potters spun the earth on a wheel, and only later found the flaws in the vessel we had shaped. By then, in our eagerness for life, we had filled it with oceans and lands, with living things growing on the lands and swimming the seas. It was too late, then, to spill the work and start afresh, planning a flawless vessel in calmer moments. We had acted hastily, but it was done: we would not destroy what we had created. And yet the flaws were grave, and the whole would crack if nothing were done and the Wheel kept up its turning. So from time to time one of us enters the Wheel to work from within, perfecting what we began, saving it from dissolution. Each in turn, throughout the ages of the world, must be born into our own creation to give what we have to give, each according to our nature. The Rising God would bring some new knowledge to light, or establish justice through law; the Bright Goddess would build something; the Upside-Down God would give his life. I give birth."

"To whom—or what?"

"It is not in my nature to know," she said. "I do what I can." Waves crashed around us, but her fine musical voice somehow stood out amid the din; I can still hear it. "And if in the confusion of storm and darkness, one woman, most precious to you and to my own heart, slipped through my fingers, I grieve for the loss."

Tears blurred my eyes, but it hardly mattered, for there was little to be seen. By the Hidden Goddess's voice I knew that she also wept. "I have misjudged you," I said. "I'm sorry."

"Everyone does," she replied.

"But I berated you openly, in front of those who loved you, in the harshest terms I could devise!"

"And do you think I could hate you for that?" said the goddess. "You still have much to learn, my child. My ways are not human ways, nor do I judge by human measure. I know you taunted me to rouse my wrath against you, to make me strike you dead for your insolence. Is that not true?"

"You see through me," I said. "You know too, I suppose, that you punish my presumption more truly by keeping me alive."

"But my aim is not to punish you," said the goddess. "Indeed, I love you more even than those that bowed to me. You were kind to me when I was weak; you did not flatter me when I became powerful. You loved my saint with all her beauty invisible, hidden. No more than I, do you judge as others judge or love as others love. You turn other men's measures upside-down. The wonder, Jereth, is that you were ever a priest of the Rising God, when you have lived most of your life as a disciple of the Upside-Down God. You have been falling toward me all your life. You even tried to trick me into taking your life: his own most desperate stratagem."

"The Upside-Down God—" I mused, "I never understood him."

"Does a fish understand the sea?" said the goddess. "He comprehends you, nonetheless."

"He is your consort?" I asked, drawing on one of the many traditions.

"My lover? My brother? My father? My son? You have no words for what he is to me, what we all are to each other, we four that encircle the earth. But deep beneath words, you have known something of that love."

"Yes," I said, "I think I have known that love. Do I not presume greatly in saying so?" She rested a hand gently on mine where I held the tiller, and gave no other answer.

I asked, "Since you know my love and my grief, tell me, Goddess, how long must I live?"

"Long enough to complete the work your beloved began," she answered.

"That is what she asked of me," I said, "to complete her work, or correct it. She wasn't sure in the end if she had done right. After all she'd given—her life, her name—she feared she'd done wrong."

"She followed her quest with absolute fidelity," said Trenara. "She held nothing back."

"And in the end, she could not even be satisfied with her own work, for all it cost her," I said. "It was doubt that crushed her spirit in the end; the doubt seemed harder than the dying. It seemed so cruel, so unjust." The goddess showed no sign of anger, but neither did she answer me, or justify herself. I pressed on. "Why was she chosen for this quest, this sacrifice—she who had suffered so much already?"

"She herself chose this quest," said the goddess. "Nothing less would satisfy her. She sought me, though she did not know me when she found me. She was looking for the Eye of Night when she found me, not knowing we were one and the same. And when she defended me from the man who used and sold me, she chose again, though she knew not what she chose," the goddess continued. "She chose not to try to use my powers, but to give my own back to me, to set me free—all for the sake of common compassion, the same compassion she would have offered to any other suffering creature, or to the world, had she known it was in her power to heal it. She chose; and though in some ways she chose in ignorance, it was nonetheless a true choice, the same she would have made if she had known everything."

I nodded mutely; this was the Hwyn I knew. However greatly I loved her, I could no longer cling to the fantasy that I or anyone else could have saved her from the fate she had embraced—not without breaking her will; not without destroying her name, her soul.

"And yes," added the goddess, "I chose her as well. Bound and bewildered as my mind was, I still recognized in her what I needed: the kindness of her heart and the power hidden in her name. For that I followed her."

"The power of her name," I echoed. "You knew her name, didn't you? Why don't you ever speak it?"

"I don't answer riddles," the goddess said, "I create them. And beyond that: do you imagine that you would be happier if I told you her name? Do you think it would give you peace?"

"It might," I said.

"Tarvon Priest," she said, "what peace can the name bring you unless you learn it for yourself?"

I was not sure what she meant by this question, but I had no leisure to puzzle it over. Wind and waves together rose against us; I thought the boat would be turned bottom up, and we travelers spilled out like the sodden dregs of herbs at the bottom of one of Harga's brews. There seemed to be as much water in the boat as beneath it. I fumbled with the sheet and wrestled with the tiller, wondering desperately whether it made any sense to pray when one of the Four Great Ones was in my boat with me, bailing. After what seemed an eternity, there was enough calm to let me ease my cramped hands for a moment, chafing them together for some shred of warmth. I turned to my companion to find her holding back the waters with her hands. She seemed larger than before, more luminous, less human than I had ever seen her.

"We are near the Rim of the World," she said, "and I am returning to myself. Soon I will leave this boat and send you back alone."

"Where will you go?" I said, but her answer was snatched away by the wind. Overhead, I seemed to see the sky torn and hanging loose like the edges of a damaged tent; from the rent in the sky, wind rocked us, driving us back from our goal. I let out the sail, tacked, and was amazed and grateful to see how close to the wind my haphazardly constructed little boat would sail. We neared the rim again, neared the tear in the sky, and met its resistance again. The sky looked strangely close, and it seemed petty and foolish to fuss with the sail when the sky itself was too torn to hold back the wind. On impulse I leapt up and, to my own amazement, caught the torn edges of sky at the end of the world.

I hung there, half disbelieving what I'd done, and looked down at my boat below, perched across the edge of an abyss, where the waves broke off like the edge of a table. The sky quaked, pulling me both ways at once. I strained against the pull to force the two parts together. Then for some minutes the universe was only darkness and pain and an animal reflex to hold on, not to fall. There was nothing else; I could scarcely remember why I needed to hold on, to stay on this rack, but something in me refused to let go.

I could not reason out a better plan; I could only hold on, and scarcely that. I felt my heart would soon burst, my breastbone crack under the strain. I remembered Hwyn, pierced through the heart by the fulfillment of her quest; I remembered the Holdouts in their unsheltered northern land, who would bear the brunt of this wind if I did not fight it for them; and I held on.

Hands stronger than mine grasped my wrists, plucking me down from the sky. I tumbled, dazed, into the boat. When my head cleared, I looked up to see Trenara standing where I had hung—standing on the sea's bottom, up to her waist in waves, hands raised above her head, holding the sky together. "Jereth son of Garmund," she said, "did you think you could be one of us on the world's rim—one of the gods, holding sky and sea together? How long did you think you could hold on?"

"More presumption," I gasped, when I could speak at all.

The goddess drew breath to respond, but before the words left her lips, her face contorted in pain, and the only sound she made was a long groan of agony.

"It pains you too?" I said fearfully. "Do you bear pain here for all ages?"

She shook her head. "The pangs of birth," she panted. "Hurry away!"

"But—there's so much you haven't told me," I protested. "What must I do now to finish the work?"

"Leave here!" she commanded. "Leave at once, or the waters of birth will drown you."

"But—"

"You will know what to do, my child," she said. "Go. Live to tell the story." She grimaced in pain again, but mastered it. "Go now. You tried to bear my burden, and for that you have my blessings forever, Jereth of World's End. Now farewell." With that, she drew a long breath and blew on the sail, spinning the boat around, driving me back from the Rim of the World, back toward the faint trace of life I had left far behind me. The last I saw her, shining far off on the horizon, she looked almost like a silver tree with its roots in the ocean and its branches in the clouds. Then the storm broke, and I saw her no more.

It broke from behind me, driving the boat before it crazily fast. It unleashed torrents of frozen rain to hammer down on me, nearly filling the boat with ice. It blew the lantern down from its perch to smash on the icy deck, flames flaring a moment as though the boat might catch, then dying in the damp, leaving me sightless on the wild sea. I thought of Hwyn, so sure in the dark, and wondered what she would do in this situation. There was a brief flash as lightning stuck the mast. Then there was nothing.

20

DRIFTWOOD

I woke to a crashing headache and the sound of the sea and the smell of fish cooking. And something else, something I never thought to awaken to again: light, a soft glimmer along the horizon. "*Dawn!*" I gasped, sitting up cautiously. "It's here!"

"Yes: the morning has come after all," said Conor of Kelgarran.

He sat in the stern of the boat, calmly roasting a fish over a small fire on a long splinter of wood that must have been part of the mast, because pieces of the mast lay everywhere. The sea had grown almost calm, though clouds still veiled the sky.

"Lord Conor," I said, "what are you doing here?"

"Bringing you in to land," he said. "Here, take this fish, and I'll take up the oars again. I'm glad you had the sense to tie them, so they weren't washed overboard."

"You've been guiding the boat?"

"Since you lost the lantern, and consciousness. Yes. I've done it before, you know," he said. "I sailed about a little in my youth."

"You saved my life. Again."

"You're welcome," said the ghost dryly. "Now take this fish off my hands. You need it to keep your strength up; I don't. The fish is real; luckily you had some nets among your gear. The fire, I'm afraid, is an illusion. Kindling a real fire on a wet deck and keeping it contained once I'd started it—all that would be well beyond my powers now."

"So the fish only seems to be cooked?" I said, taking it from him, relishing the illusory heat in my chilled fingers before taking a bite.

"That's right," he said, taking the oars and moving carefully to the bow. "The illusion should at least make it palatable. The bread you brought with you would be more comforting, I guess, but the ocean took it."

I was almost hungry enough to eat it without the illusion. I wondered how much time had passed since my last meal in

Larioneth Hall. I'd said I never wanted to taste fish again, but I attacked this one eagerly. When I was done, I said, "Thank you. You keep turning up when I need you."

"I couldn't leave you alone, after what I saw," Conor said. "When you last summoned me—when I witnessed your wedding—I saw the expression on Hwyn's face. In my time as a ghost I've come to know that look." He sighed. "Whoever wears it is not far from death. Jereth, I'm sorry. I know how you loved her."

"And you tried to warn me once, back in Berall," I remembered. "But this time you said nothing."

"I knew you'd learn of it soon enough. Why spoil your fleeting hour of happiness?" Conor said. "Besides, Hwyn knew. I was sure of that. Either she would tell you herself, or she withheld it for a reason."

"She withheld it," I said, "to shield me. But I suppose you know how it happened."

"No," he said, "I only know what I saw that moment." So I told him everything that had happened. Conor listened sympathetically and did not interrupt, keeping up a patient rhythm with the oars.

When I had finished the narrative, I said, "And so Hwyn sacrificed everything—all she had, all she was—and I still don't understand what it was for. What did Trenara give birth to? Was it a new sun? Was the old one dying? What new life has risen out of the night?"

"That I don't know," Conor said. "But the world seems changed; it feels different."

"You haven't seen Hwyn, have you, in the ghost-world?" I asked, voicing at last my greatest fear. "You—I guess you can't have seen her. She is nameless. She—isn't."

Conor gave me a look of tortured compassion. "I wish I could reassure you," he said gently. "I can't confirm your fears either. In this time of confusion I don't even know where my own brothers may be. All I know is that the time when ghosts walked the North is ending, and I soon must go."

"Where?"

"I don't know even that much," Conor said. "But something calls me, calls me away. When you reach the shore, I will not be with you. I was scarcely allowed to show myself now, under this new dawn."

"But you came anyway," I mused, "as you have always come for Hwyn and me."

"I took an interest in you bold fools," he said. "No, more than an interest. Better call it love."

"I always thought you loved Hwyn," I said.

Conor nodded, smiled. "And you too—my son," he muttered, half embarrassed. "I wonder if you might really be my grandson, at long remove."

"I doubt it," I said, and then remembering the history I'd learned, added, "I thought you had no children?"

"None by my own wife," he said ruefully.

"I wish you *were* my father," I said.

Conor rested the oars and put a spectral hand on my shoulder. It seemed I could almost feel it. "No you don't," he said gently. "I was terribly neglectful of my own bastards; and then the one I acknowledged was murdered by the usurper. But I know what you meant. And I thank you."

I wanted to clasp his hand in return, but that would only emphasize the distance between us, Lord Conor a ghost, insubstantial, myself still alive and solid. So I said the only thing I could think of to touch him. "As long as I live, I will keep alive your story."

He grinned, and might have said more, but something caught my eye ahead of us.

"Look: land!" I said.

"I must leave you soon, then," the ghost said.

"Farewell," I said, "and thank you. Wherever you are going, may it be good to you."

"Godspeed," he told me. "Jereth, my lad, take courage. You still have more to suffer. Do not despair." With that he vanished, leaving me alone in a half-ruined boat. I took up the oars myself and discovered how weary I still was, scarcely able to fight the current with such puny weapons. To think I'd believed myself strong enough to hold the sky together! Well, Syrc would enjoy the story, I thought, if only I could win my way to land to tell it all.

The sun had risen up under the clouds: a gray day, but so bright to my unaccustomed eyes that it made my head throb. Nonetheless it revived my spirits to row toward a visible destination, to see the daylight returned, to know that life would go on after all. Not for all; not for the best, the one I most loved—but some life would go on. Morning followed night, and night followed morning, and stories followed the deaths of heroes, bearing them into new ages. I had not Hwyn's gift of inspired lyric, but I could do one thing she couldn't: I could write. Someday I would write her story, and lame though my words might be compared to hers, they would outlast her sweetest songs. The voice fades; the parchment remains; thus we mortals struggle with time, preserving the dry husk of what was vibrant and vital. The best, the worthiest passes away; we must be content to preserve the remnant of former glories. The worthiest passes away; the least worthy survives, as I did.

By inches I neared the shore. The storm must have been wild indeed, for the coast was changed beyond recognition. I wondered how long I had lain unconscious, how much of the gale I had missed. Perhaps I had been driven off course to the uninhabited lands farther east or west along the northern coast. Still, it seemed best to go ashore to try to find my bearings, and perhaps something I could fashion into a makeshift mast and sail, before setting out to follow the coast back to Larioneth. Avoiding a rocky point beneath a towering cliff, I rowed around eastward to a low, sloping beach. There I landed and dragged my boat up the sand. But no—not up the *sand*, for it was no sand I found underfoot, but black soil, planting soil. Farther from the sea, the parallel tracks of the plow still marked it. It was a field lying fallow for winter, half swallowed by the waves. This could not be Larioneth, where the farms lay south of the town, away from the sea. And yet it was not quite desolate, as most of the North had been: had this field not been tended as recently as summer, weeds would have overtaken it. Where could I be?

At the top of the rising land I left the boat and trudged forward through what seemed more and more clearly to be wintering grainfields. After passing an orchard, I saw the walls of a town. I hastened toward them; they were high and forbidding, too plain to be the sculpted walls of Larioneth. Seeing no opening, I circled around looking for a gate, and found myself atop the cliff I had seen from my boat. There I found a gate facing the sea. It was shut, but a watchman called down from the guard-tower: "Greetings, stranger! Did you come from the sea?"

"Yes," I said. "I set sail from Larioneth in the Longest Night, and meant to return there. I seem to have been blown off course in the storm. What town is this?"

"Welcome to Berall," he said. "Come in; we have been waiting for you!"

"Berall!" I shouted. "Impossible! Berall is inland."

"This *was* inland, until the storm," said the watchman. "Didn't you know? The sea must have taken the whole north country. We are an island now."

"The *whole* north country? Larioneth? *Sunk beneath the waves?*" My right hand, jammed in my pocket against the cold, clenched spasmodically, closing on something hard and sharp: the gilt star Rand had given me as a token. I clutched it, driving the points into my skin, as though the pain would drive from my mind the words I heard. "It can't be!"

"But it is. Thank the gods that those ghosts drove everyone south before the deluge," said the watchman.

"Not everyone," I gasped, "not the best of them. Oh, Hidden Goddess! How could you abandon them?—your children!"

"What are you saying?" the watchman called.

"Another city—a better city than this—the bravest, best people in the world," I cried. "Larioneth! Oh gods! What is the good of this new dawn? Why did the sun rise at all?" I thought, when Hwyn died, I had suffered the worst; I thought I could fall no lower. But this was worse, infinitely worse. Hwyn had at least chosen her fate, accepted a death that had meaning to her when she accepted it, if not amid the pain of her last moments. A hundred Holdouts, drowned by the storm, had not chosen. Ash's children had not chosen. They had died for nothing. And now Hwyn too had died for nothing, for worse than nothing, for a force that could break loose and drown a hundred brave souls. The waters of birth, Trenara had warned, might drown me; why had she given no warning to them? Either she was as cruel a goddess as I had thought her when Hwyn died, or stupider than she had seemed when she couldn't lace her own tunic, *criminally* stupid for one who held the world in her care. Something might have been worth Hwyn's sacrifice; nothing could be worth this carnage. If this were the new world to rise out of the Troubles, I wanted no part of it. I turned away from the gates of Berall, back to the sea.

"Wait!" called the watcher. "Where are you going? Hold on, I'll open the gate. We've waited so long for you. Your coming was foretold: we were promised hope from the sea."

"So were the Holdouts of Larioneth," I shouted back, "and it drowned them." Then I turned away again, ran to the cliff's edge, and dove.

For what seemed ages I was falling, falling endlessly, as though I would never hit bottom. Then the water struck me like a giant's fist and I knew no more.

I awoke face-down on the low beach, muddy and frigid and still alive. That last fact galled me the most. My head throbbed; my boots were swamped in wintry water; and nothing between the two extremities felt any better. The sea had washed me ashore like driftwood but soon enough, I thought, it might pick me up again and draw me down with the rest of them, down where I belonged. But then I noticed the damp soil far above me on the slope, the waves barely lapping my feet where they trailed close to the water. The tide was going out. I would have to swim into it. I made a motion to push myself up off the ground and was paralyzed by a spasm of pain that seemed to echo through my whole body. I didn't know it then, but both my arms had been broken on the rocks, and one leg as well. I could not move. The ocean lapped teasingly at my feet, but it was retreating from me.

"You!" I shouted to the impervious ocean, "You've taken everything I loved; why won't you take me?" There was no answer. There was never any answer. I lay shivering in the mud, waiting for the cold and my wounds to give me the deliverance the sea denied me. Hours passed, and the waves shrank back from me as from contagion. The arm folded under me lost feeling; in the other, a fire raged. From the corner of my eye I saw a jagged edge of bone piercing my skin. I shut my eyes and clamped my jaw against a wave of nausea.

"Look!" a voice cried after a time. "A man on the shore. It might be—"

"Is he dead?" said another voice. I kept my eyes shut, kept still, hoping they would pass by. But the voices neared.

"So much for our hope from the sea," said a third voice. "Dead. Like all other hopes."

"No, wait," said the first speaker. "I think I saw him move—a slight shiver."

"The wind stirring his garments," said the third man—they were all men's voices, deep and resonant.

"It can't hurt to look," said the second one. Then I felt a pair of hands, shockingly warm, on my shoulders. I steeled myself not to respond, but it was no use: he must have felt the tension in my muscles. "Come quickly! I think he's alive," he said. Then with the greatest delicacy he tried to turn me face up. Even that was too much. The skin around the broken bone tore farther, and against my will I cried out.

"He is alive—barely," he said to his companions, and to me, "I'm sorry."

"Leave me," I whispered, then gathered more breath. "Please, leave me," I said again, my voice still weak, as though drained in one cry.

"I didn't mean to hurt you," the man said. "I'm sorry. It couldn't be helped. The healer will come soon, I promise." Then, turning to his companions, he said, "One of you go for the healer, quick. He might die."

"*Let me die,*" I groaned. "Please, if you have any mercy, leave me here. By tomorrow I'll be past suffering."

"Hush now," said the man who had turned me over. "You're past the worst of it. The healer will bring something for the pain."

"Should we move him first?" said one of the others. "Is the tide coming in?"

"Out," I said. "It's going out, gods curse it."

"He should know," said the other. "He came from the sea."

He said it in such a tone of reverence that even through my anguish I had to laugh. "Yes, I came from the sea. I was trying to drown myself. How does *that* fit your prophecy?"

"Then you did not come in that boat?" said the man closest to me. "You must have; you can't be from Berall, with that accent."

"I came in the boat," I admitted.

"Then you *are* the one promised, the hope from the sea," he said. "Claron, please—the healer, while there's time."

"I'm going," Claron said.

"No," I groaned. "I beg you, leave me to die. I will not trouble you long; a day at most, and perhaps then the sea will deign to accept me. Or if you pity my suffering, give me a quick death with a knife."

"He's raving," said one of the men.

"He's feverish! No wonder," said the other. "He's been lying here cold as the north end of nowhere. What have I been thinking of?" Gently he spread his cloak over me.

"I am not raving!" I cried with all the strength I still had. "If you knew what reasons I have to hate my life— It was not enough to be widowed on my wedding night. No, I was not wretched enough till the bravest and kindest people that ever lived, the Holdouts of Larioneth—a people so much greater-souled than your miserable town that if they had come to Berall, you would have killed them for envy—all of them, down to the most defenseless child, were cast to the bottom of the sea. And for what? To prepare a new day for *Berall*? For the most accursed of all towns ever built on the slaughtered bodies of saints and innocents? And for *this* I sailed to the world's end—to come to Berall?"

"*You sailed to the world's end?*"

There was wonder in the man's tone; it defeated me. "Believe that I rave," I said wearily, "or believe that I speak true. What does it matter? I accomplished nothing there. All in vain, all for nothing. Let me die now. I can offer you no hope."

"Gods have mercy," breathed my would-be rescuer. "What is to be done? You cannot die. You are sent by the gods."

"The gods are mad," I said, "and I am dying."

"Hush, now," he said, and pulled the cloak up where it had fallen from my throat. It alleviated the cold, but not my misery. "Try to rest," he said. "Askol will be here soon. He will heal you."

Too weary even to speak more, I shut my eyes.

I must have slept, because I was unaware of the healer's arrival until a sudden storm of pain assailed my arm. I cried out, and he stopped what he was doing.

"Ah—so you're with us, traveler," he said. "You should have stayed asleep."

"I should have died," I told him. "I was trying to die. If you mean me any kindness, please, kill me."

"Gods forbid!" he said.

"Why save a life that is hateful to me and useless to you?"

"Hush now," he said. "Don't speak nonsense. I'll have to finish tying the splint now; it will hurt, but less so if you lie still." There was a sharp tug at my arm, and for the next minute I was too overcome with pain even to protest. "There now. The worst is over. Let me give you something to make you sleep."

"I beg you, please, give me enough so that I never wake."

"*No*," said the healer. "Should I break the vows of my calling?"

"Then I'll have none of it, nothing for the pain," I said. "What are these wounds to the ruin of my world? A curse upon this town! When we came here seeking a livelihood, you would have killed us; now I would die and you force me to live. A curse upon Berall, of all towns most accursed!"

"He is feverish," they said to each other nervously as they shifted me onto a litter with trembling hands. When they put a flask of palliative to my lips, I spat it out angrily. As they carried me to town, I cursed them in every language I knew.

There followed weeks of fever and delirium, when I lived half in dreams. At times I forgot time and place, calling the people who sat by my bed Hwyn, or Harga, or even Mother. At times I ranted to the Hidden Goddess, demanding answers. At times I remembered where I was and what I had suffered. Then I would refuse all nourishment, determined that if I could not drown I would starve. After that the dreams would overtake me again, soothing me with the forms and voices of those I had lost, or tormenting me with old horrors. I found myself again clinging for dear life to a broken scrap of the Sea-Bird, lifting Saeverth's cold body from the sand, hearing Hwyn's last ragged breaths as she died in my arms. At other times, I thought the gods stood over me in a circle, all talking at once, demanding something of me that I couldn't understand. "Speak sense to me, or be quiet!" I shouted at them. "Tell me what to do and I'll do it, but tell me plain; don't keep me spinning in circles trying to hear just one of you right." The Upside-Down God grinned mockingly; Trenara turned her back. All the while I burned and froze, fever and chills, but it seemed to me to be the fire in the Eye of Night and the frigid Berall seacoast that should never have been a coast. The room spun like a potter's wheel and some ghost played hammer-and-anvil with my head.

After uncounted days, I regained my senses. Dreams came only with sleep, and all the grief that had driven me over the cliff-edge filled my waking time. I refused food more steadfastly. My stomach cramped and knotted in protest, then gave up. My head throbbed, awake or asleep. I gritted my teeth and waited for death. I didn't know whether to pray to the gods; I didn't know whether they cared. I prayed to Hwyn, my saint, without hope that she existed anywhere anymore; I prayed to Conor, old sinner-saint that he was, and to my brother Saeverth; I prayed to the spirit I'd summoned in Larioneth, Lancar the Horseman, a greater fool than I and happier, more fortunate in his misplaced devotion, for he had only lost his life, while I had lost all hope. Let him pray for me; dear trusting soul, he was always a believer.

They brought me food, the people who tended me. I shut my eyes and mouth against it. They pleaded with me to eat, but I did not listen and scarcely heard. I slept most of the day, and more with each day's growing weakness.

But I couldn't shut out the smells of food, which followed me even into sleep, into hungry dreams. At last one morning I awoke half crazed by the fragrance of a simple bowl of porridge left on a bench by my bed. I rubbed my eyes and looked around just long enough to see that no one was with me. No one would know I had weakened. I reached eagerly for the spoon, succeeding only in knocking it off the bench and away across the floor. Too weak to get out of bed and look for it, I dipped my hand into the porridge bowl and scooped some clumsily into my mouth. Then I realized what I'd done: I'd abandoned my resolve, broken faith with the dead, forgotten all my loss, for nothing but an empty belly and the smell of porridge. Sick with shame and weak, weak as a baby—I blush to speak of it—I found myself once again unable to do anything but weep.

Thus my nurse found me. I turned away from her, but not soon enough. "You're weeping!" she said. "Tell me the trouble."

"Don't inquire into my shame," I said, sounding barely alive, as perhaps I was.

"No shame," said the nurse, "Tears are the start of healing, as my mother used to say."

My father had had a different saying. "Not for me," I said. "For me there can be no healing. I should have died by now. I weep for shame to think I am so weak as to try to feed my body, when in a little more time I might have joined all those I loved."

"You tried to eat? I knew you would, if I left you! Oh—I'm sorry," she said, for I covered my face with my hands, overcome by shame. Light fingers encircled my wrist. "Forgive me; I do everything wrong! What can I do for you? How can I help you?"

"It's not your fault," I said. "You've done nothing wrong. The fault is mine. But it's hard to die of starvation; my will is too weak for it. At least my arms have healed. If you would only give me a knife, and leave me—"

"Gods forbid!" she gasped, just as the healer had.

"Then you cannot help me," I said.

I was shocked, then, to hear a stifled sob. I looked up at her for the first time, but now it was she who covered her face, hiding her tears. I propped myself up unsteadily on one arm, reached out carefully to touch her. "Don't cry, please. What am I to you, that you should care what I say? An ungrateful stranger you should have left out in the cold. Why waste your tears—"

"Don't you know?" she said. "All the elders, the whole town is waiting for your recovery. They thought I might—might make you want to live, so the curse would be lifted from the town—"

"Is that what worries them?" I laughed. "That I cursed the town when they found me and would not let me die? I doubt the gods heed *my* curses or blessings, but very well: if any curse settled on this town at my word, I take it back. I take all curses upon myself—what are a few more, that I should notice them? My life ended on the Longest Night. My body just hasn't the sense to die with my heart."

My nurse looked me full in the face and I noticed for the first time that she was only a girl, about fifteen, with the clear forthright eyes of youth. "You must live," she said. "You are our hope, the Hope from the Sea promised by the mad prophet Areyn in the time of the persecution. You are a great saint—"

At that I had to laugh again. "Your people are sadly mistaken in their saints," I said. "I am flotsam cast up by the sea, which swallows the grain and leaves the chaff. Tell them to save their reverence for those that didn't return."

"And who were they?" said the girl, crouching near me as though not to miss a word, her startling blue eyes all attention.

"First there was the woman called Hwyn, a great prophet and saint, though unrecognized."

"Hwyn—the prophet—she was hanged here, after the Feast of the Turning God, before the Sickness came and the persecution was stopped! No wonder you cursed this town," the girl said.

"*Hanged here?*" I said in momentary confusion—then remembered Hwyn the Weaver. "Oh. That was an impostor, a woman who took her place to save her life. Another great saint dead. Another crime on Var's bloody hands. They are both dead, then—both the women called Hwyn, both saints rejected by this town's wisdom."

"We will repent it," the girl said gravely. "Do not abandon us. We need you."

I studied her face, young, earnest, strained with the weight of the message entrusted to her. I noticed at last, life-weary as I was, that the girl was strikingly beautiful, her elegantly tapered face framed by glossy golden-brown hair, her lips rose-petals, her body graceful. "Child, why was it left to you to persuade me?" I said, suddenly suspicious.

She blushed—beautifully—under my scrutiny, so that I dropped my eyes not to give her more discomfort. "They said—" she began haltingly, "they thought I might make you want to live. The elders thought so, I mean. They said if—if you took a bride of this town, you might be appeased with us, and remain. So they gave me to you—"

"What a hideous idea!" I exclaimed without thinking. "Gods! What hateful men this town breeds! Who—" Then I stopped, seeing the girl had shrunk back, hiding her face. "I'm sorry, lass, I—my anger's not at you. It's for your sake. Even if I were not just widowed and still in mourning, I could never accept it. Why—to bind a lovely young girl like you to a bitter old wreck like me—it's monstrous! How old are you?"

"Fourteen," she said.

"Do you realize I am more than *twice* your age?" When she showed no surprise, I added, "I suppose after what I've been through, I look even older." Suddenly I realized that it wasn't only moral revulsion I was feeling: the mouthful of porridge I'd taken had hit my stomach, which, unused to the intrusion, rebelled. "Excuse me," I managed to mutter before turning to the opposite side of the bed, hanging my head over the edge, and losing what little I'd eaten. There was a taste of blood in my mouth.

Without flinching, the girl got a wet rag and reached out with it to wipe my face. I caught her hand, took the cloth, and did it myself. "I'm sorry," I said. "You shouldn't have to see this."

"Do you think I've never seen the like before?" she snapped. "Did you think they sent me to you only for an ornament? I had to watch my whole family die of the Winter Sickness. If I have to watch one more, well, I will outlive it!" She was cleaning the floor with a vengeance as she spoke. Her face was turned to the floor, but I could almost feel the reflected sparks from her eyes. It was her first show of temper, and healthier for both of us than all her earlier forced gentleness. I was properly chastened. By the time she stormed back to me, after meticulously cleaning the soiled rags and her hands, I'd come to my senses.

"Forgive me," I said. "I've been acting selfishly, as though no one had ever known loss but me."

"I didn't mean—"

"Yes you did," I said, "and it was the best thing you've said since I awoke. And it tells me we have something in common: we are both sole survivors."

"Was the Winter Sickness in your land too, then?"

"Not sickness," I said. "My family's merchant vessel was shipwrecked years ago; they all drowned but me. And now that Larioneth is sunk under the ocean, I am the sole survivor again."

"I couldn't survive a second time," the girl said with sudden heat. "I'd die with the rest. I couldn't bear it." Suddenly she seemed to grasp what she herself was saying, to see it anew. Her eyes widened, then narrowed. "That's what you were trying to do."

"Yes. But I was wrong," I said. "I forgot a promise I made to the dead—or rather, not forgot, but judged wrongly that their death had released me from the promise."

"What did you promise?"

"To try to live," I said, "to do what needed to be done. You were right to be angry with me: I had no right to die while I still might do something."

"Then you *will* help us!" the girl said eagerly.

"Don't pin too much hope on me." I smiled ruefully. "But I'll do what I can." I tried to sit up; my head responded with a sharp stab of pain, and I rubbed it a while. "What's your name?"

"Renn daughter of Rebarrin."

"Mine is Jereth son of Garmund. I am a merchant's son, sometime shipwright's apprentice, sometime novice in the Tarvon Order, sometime minstrel, field hand, and beggar. I have been a failure at everything, even suicide. I'm at your service, if you are foolish or desperate enough to want it."

"You were a minstrel?" Renn seized on the phrase. "You played at the Feast of the Turning God?"

"Yes," I said. "You remember me?"

"I thought I recognized you! Your voice, that is; you some-times sang in your fever-dreams. The elders said I was mis-taken," she said gleefully. "I heard you at the festival. I listened for hours. You sang harmony with a funny-looking, cross-eyed little woman. There was another woman with you too, dark and quiet and very lovely." She added more softly, "Was that your wife—the one you mourn for?"

"No: the other one," I said, and winced in anticipation of a tactless adolescent response.

The girl raised her eyebrows, blushed deeply, and was silent for a few heartbeats. When she spoke, her voice was calm and quiet and serious. "She must have been extraordinary."

"That she was," I said.

"No wonder you were so shocked when I told you about— what the elders planned for you and me."

"Don't tell me you would have accepted it," I said. "Tied for life to a ruin like me!"

Renn shrugged coolly. "You are a saint. I might have liked being married to a saint—almost like being a priestess."

"But you are already a priestess," I said without thinking, and then realized that I knew it was true as certainly as I'd known the names of the ghosts who escaped from the Eye of Night. "That is your true work, your true self, Renn daughter of Rebarrin. You don't need to marry holiness. You surely don't need to look to me for it. If the elders of Berall had any sense, they'd turn to you for answers—never to me. You are their priestess; I am refuse cast back by the sea."

"How do you know?" she cried, hopeful, perplexed, and then, almost angry. "If you are nothing, refuse, as you say, how do you know what I am?"

"The Gift of Naming," I said. "I was in the Tarvon Order once. It no more makes me a saint than having been a merchant once makes me rich now. But I am not wrong about you, Renn. And if the elders insist on seeing me as a creature of legend, then tell them—tell them I consent to live, and to live *here*, for your sake only, not for theirs."

"I can't tell them *that*," she said. "Think how it would sound!"

"Then I'll tell them myself," I said. I swung my feet out of bed and tried to stand, only to find myself in a heap on the floor. For several seconds I could only hold my head, waiting for the room to stop spinning. Renn silently helped me up; it mortified me to discover how heavily I had to lean on her. I noticed for the first time how bony I was. "Gods," I said, "I'm a corpse."

"You haven't eaten in weeks," Renn said sharply. "What did you expect?"

I didn't answer. I was shaking, and I could see that my weakness frightened her, for all her cross words.

"What's the use?" she grumbled, setting me back in bed with practiced gestures. "You starve yourself till you can't eat, and now you'll probably die anyway and leave us in this fix—oh, gods, what am I saying? I'm sorry. I'm so sorry."

"Never mind," I said. "What you say may be true. But I doubt it. I've sailed to the world's end and back alive. I was alone and unconscious on a damaged boat and didn't drown. I dove off the sea-cliff and broke both arms but not my neck. I washed up on the shore, just hurt enough not to be able to throw myself back in the ocean. It would be an odd joke of the gods if I died the moment I stopped pursuing death."

"You think the gods have been keeping you alive?"

"Someone or something has," I said. "Either they're not through having their sport with me, or there's something I'm meant to do."

"You have a task here," Renn said. "I know it. Rest now; I'll thin out the porridge so you can eat. I'll return soon."

I thanked her, then lay back in bed, looking up at the ceiling—and broke suddenly into helpless laughter at what I saw there.

Renn spun back to stare at me in alarm. "What—what—" she sputtered, then oddly, "*Who are you?*"

"That's a strange question," I said. "My name is Jereth, as I told you. I rather thought you'd ask why I was laughing."

"Why were you laughing, then?"

I gestured at the ceiling. "Night after night I dreamed the gods crowded around me, scolding me. And there they are—painted on the ceiling!" They were marvelously lifelike, and the Hidden Goddess, her back turned as always, could almost have been modeled on Trenara, the arc of her spine graceful as a young tree. "So much for the notion of inspired dreams: I was only making the most of my surroundings. I'm in the temple?"

"Of course," she said. "Where else would we house a saint?"

"I wish you'd stop calling me that," I said. "Now tell me, what made you ask who I was?"

"When you laughed like that," she said, "you looked just like *him*." She pointed to the western quadrant of the dome, to the icon of the Upside-Down God with his sardonic grin and his mirthless, haunted dark eyes. I stared back into those eyes, not knowing what to say.

Renn brushed a hand over my forehead. "I'll return soon," she said, and left.

21

JERETH OF WORLD'S END

Renn soon returned with the porridge, watered down and re-heated. After convincing her that I could feed myself, I took a spoonful of it, cautiously waiting to see if it stayed down.

"How do you feel?" she said.

"Strange," I answered, swirling the spoon around in the bowl, delaying. "Tell me about yourself, Renn."

"There's not much to tell," she said.

"Have you always lived in this godforsaken town?"

She nodded, seemingly unaffected by the epithet. "My father kept a shop on Westmarket Lane, not far from here. He was a wheelwright. We all helped out: my mother, my brothers and sisters, and I. There were five of us. I was the middle child—the hub of the wheel, as Father liked to say ..." she trailed off. "Then eight days after the Feast of the Turning God, the Winter Sickness came ... and now I'm alone. The elders let me live in the Temple because it was empty, after the priests fled ghost-ridden, so I was here already when they brought you in from the water. The elders thought it fitting." Her eyes, which had wandered away when she spoke of the Winter Sickness, traveled back to me. "Why do you want to know about me?"

"Why not? You're the only friend I have in Berall. Unless—"

"What?"

"There was one man who was kind to me. I wonder if I can even find him—if he is alive, after the winter, after the sickness you speak of. A beggar named Vokh. He lived in a makeshift shack somewhere south of the marketplace. I'll look for him when I'm stronger."

"I'll look for him," Renn said. "If he's still here, I'll find him, I promise."

"You promise much," I said. "I can promise so little in return."

"So you say," Renn said. "But you say, too, that you sailed to the world's end and back, alive. If you can afford to despise such a feat as that—" she lifted an eloquent hand, palm up. Then, her expression suddenly young, natural, she asked, "What did you see there? Could you see beyond the rim, or is it dark?"

"Everything was dark; it was the Longest Night," I said. "But let me start at the beginning." She acquiesced, and I began telling her all the whole story, beginning with my pilgrimage. It was slow in the telling: I was still weak. I paused now and then for another mouthful of food, and Renn asked many questions, diverting me from the main path. I thought I would soon tire, but instead it seemed to strengthen me, telling my story to a sympathetic ear, letting loose all the impressions of a year that had been the crown and the scourge of my life. I began little by little to feel more human than I had since Hwyn died. Renn hung on every word, and I left nothing out except my fleeting attempt to hold the sky together; gods alone knew what her hagiographic imagination would have made of that.

Toward sundown we were interrupted by the entry of a group of men, well-dressed, gray-bearded burghers, looking like any of the merchants my father had known, except a little worse for a winter's strange fortunes. "How goes it with our guest?" they said. "Will he speak to us?"

"I don't know," Renn said. "He brings heavy accusations against this town: he says we have killed saints and innocents. He says that when he was last here, he was not welcome, and he would never willingly have returned. We must answer these charges and not take them lightly, for he is a great saint, Jereth of World's End, who traveled with the Hidden Goddess to the Rim of the World."

"I am no saint," I interrupted. "I did sail to the world's rim, as Renn says, but gained no wisdom there. What I saw and heard, Renn must interpret. She is obviously a priestess; after six years in the Tarvon Order, I can at least recognize a true calling. I will tell her all I know, and that is probably all the good you'll have of me. It's Renn I'll tell my story to, mind, not to any of you elders—and least of all to Lord Var, that murderer of prophets."

"Var no longer rules," said one of the men.

I sat bolt upright in bed. "Since when?"

"Eight days after the close of the autumn festival—after the last of the executions, when they hanged the prophet Hwyn— Var went mad. After that the ghosts came in, angry, howling for vengeance, and the plague soon followed. We didn't know what to do with Var; he'd run afoul of his own law, and the sentence of death he himself had established. But he was our Lord, and we loved him; how could we condemn him?"

"What became of him, then?" I asked.

"He is a prisoner," the elder said, "the only one, now. Did we do wrong? What should be done with him?"

"I suppose he should go to St. Fiern's Town," I laughed grimly. "They like madmen there."

"How should he reach it? The land is flooded," said the elder.

I realized then, with a shock, that he took my answer seriously—that he had asked me as I had asked the Mirror of St. Fiern what to do with my life. *Suppose I'd said, "Kill him,"* I thought, barely suppressing a wicked laugh. But then a new realization shocked me harder: the answer I'd given carelessly, flippantly, not expecting it to matter, was *right*, right in ways I hadn't considered when I spoke. Var *should* go to the Mirror of St. Fiern, look in it, and see the truth he'd hidden from. He should do penance at the shrine of a saint of the Hidden Goddess, whom he'd thwarted, and the Turning God, whose festival he'd defiled—and Fiern had been devoted to both. He should go as a pilgrim, humbled. I hadn't meant any of this—yet I'd hit upon the truth.

"My Lord?" said the elder. It took me a while to realize that he meant me. "How should he travel? All our roads south are cut off by the flood."

"By sea, of course," I said. "Why, the pilgrimage has become almost too easy!"

"We have no knowledge of the sea," said another of the elders, "and no oceangoing vessels. We are lost to all we knew. That is the last and most lingering of our curses: we are an island now."

"And you call that a curse?" I laughed. "Iskarron is all islands, and richer than any part of Swevnalond. But I see I have work in Berall after all—not in the temple, but on the shore. I am not the best shipbuilder or sailor you could hope for, but I'm the best you have. As soon as I'm well I'll make a boat to send your Lord away for you—and good riddance, I say."

"And you, you who came from the sea according to the prophecy—will you be our Lord henceforth?"

I choked.

"I know you are angry with this town," said the elder. "The gods are angry with us, too. You can amend what is wrong with us."

"No," I said. "You are mistaken in me. I am not holy. And Berall has had enough of the worship of lords. Better you should settle things in council together, like the Holdouts of Larioneth, than take another lord and treat him as a god, like Var. That was wrong; but worse yet to follow one who has cursed you, and whom the gods have cursed." I meant myself, but they did not listen to the last part. Instead they said, "We will do as you say. We will follow the example of Larioneth."

When they had left, I turned to Renn. "You called me Jereth of World's End?"

"It seemed to fit," she said. "What use calling you by your patronym in a town where your father is unknown?"

"It's what the goddess called me," I said, "the last time she spoke to me."

Renn put a hand over her mouth and sat stone-still.

I reached out and touched her arm. "I know how you feel," I said. "You're not the only one to have found out today how disconcerting it is to speak truth without knowing it."

"Is that what it's always like—priesthood?" she asked.

I shook my head. "Not for me. In the Tarvon Order, I never felt like a priest. Maybe I just became one today." I laughed at that, dryly: "Today, when all I can do is blaspheme the gods! They have a strange sense of humor."

"You scare me," she said, but in a quiet, level voice that belied her words.

"I'm sorry. I scare myself lately," I said. "But you've had more than enough of it for one day. Go and rest, Renn. I'll still be here tomorrow."

"I sleep here," she said. "I've been nursing you—remember?"

But she did leave for a while to walk alone, and I was asleep before she returned.

In the morning I went down to the sea, leaning on a crutch sturdier than my atrophied limbs, trying not to ask the help of Renn, who stayed anxiously close to me. I swayed a few times, but didn't fall. When I reached the easy slope where I'd landed on the First Morning, I said, "This is where the harbor should be. It's the easiest landing—unless there's another one farther south; this was the best I found where I sailed. We could build a quay over there." I pointed. "And even without it, we could start building fishing boats here. If we brought this plan to the elders, do you think they could find people to help us? Anyone who used to navigate the river, when there was a river, and any woodworkers—plus weavers and sempsters to make sails. Would they agree to it?"

"The elders would be glad of it, and most of the people," Renn said. "But Kelab will complain. This is his field."

"Not much good for planting now," I commented.

"No," Renn admitted. "But he keeps hoping the sea will give it back."

I shook my head. "There's a time to accept your losses."

Renn nodded silently. I went back to planning my shipyard, scratching my thoughts onto the wax tablet I'd brought, limping about from one spar of land to another, then to higher ground to survey the sweep of the bay. Before long I was expounding to Renn on tides and currents, on everything that made the spot favorable and everything we'd have to take care of when we actually launched our boats, falling into a sailor's lingo I thought had died on my tongue years ago. How much of it Renn understood I don't know, but she listened tolerantly, bless her. Very likely she was used to hearing her elders drone away at nonsense, and could let it wash over her, as I used to do with my Magyan tutor. No matter. I was talking to myself, really. For the first time since the Longest Night, I had found something to absorb me beyond regret.

After we trudged back to the temple, I collapsed on the bed at once. "I should take this to the elders," I said wearily, waving the tablet.

"I'll take your plans to them," she said, "if you like."

"Thank you," was all I had a chance to say before dropping off to sleep.

From then on I was blessedly busy. I had boats to build. I had apprentices to train—a horde of them, more than the richest shipwright in Swanroad, from a ten-year-old orphan to a white-bearded, bent-backed farmer whose livelihood lay beneath the sea. They hung on my words, worse than the Holdouts had when I built the boat Trenara had demanded. But this time I minded it less: unlike the Larioneth fishermen, these were truly ignorant of the sea, and my little knowledge meant much to them. Besides, my own hastily built craft had carried me to the world's end and back, so perhaps I knew something after all. I patched my world's end boat, built a few more with the help of my new following, and soon we were hauling in nets full of incautious fish from the swollen sea. We gave the best of the first catch to Kelab to soften the loss of his land. He joined my crew the next morning.

I did not, at first, warm to any of them; in my bitterness I attributed half their compliance to the proven truth that Berallites were a servile lot, easily led and without genius. But I had some companionship beyond my shipyard; for one thing, Renn proved a better friend than I might have expected from her youth, my age, and our stormy first meeting. After the first day, she ceased to be shocked by any of my rantings; on the contrary, she listened with understanding, and I think enjoyed hearing her elders rated as fools—well, so would I, when I was fourteen. I took her equally at her word as she, hesitantly at first, but with ever more confidence, spun plans of a new order, the Sisters of the Dawn, to replace the priests who'd fled in the hard winter. She also had more immediate plans to solace the orphans of the Winter Sickness and those still ailing. She meant to bring them to the temple and assemble her own crew of apprentices to care for them. She'd learned much from the healer during her family's illness, and I harried him into teaching her more. I seconded all her plans, and as the elders feared me, they came around to her ways, until in time it became habitual to them to hear and obey their fourteen-year-old priestess.

She kept up some of the fiction that she was destined for my bride—I suppose it served to drive away more eager suitors. She had an intermittent follower—a boy of about fifteen who lacked neither wit nor heart, and seemed almost as interested in her theological opinions as in her rose-petal lips—but she seemed chary of encouraging him in anything but theology, at least for the time being. Wise girl, I suppose: she was not made to marry young, as my mother had, to be worn away by the demands of an older husband or the needs of a young one until her character was as indistinct as the face of a century-old coin. She needed to grow alone, and she had not Hwyn's marred face to ensure the solitude she needed. She had me instead. That may have been the best service I did her, as a scarecrow for suitors, and if so, I was glad to serve: I could almost be glad of the elders' nonsense, humiliating as I found it, if it helped me repay her kindness.

She tried to find Vokh for me, but everyone denied knowing such a man. After a few days in Berall I searched the back alleys where he had taken me, wounded and outcast, during the autumn festival. In the same shack where he had sheltered me, I found him wasting away with illness and want.

He lay still and shrunken on his pallet. At first glance I thought him dead. Moved by regret, I knelt and touched him, murmuring, "Vokh. Brother." He opened his eyes and stared.

"The minstrel from the autumn festival," he murmured. "Gar— no, Jereth. Are you living, or ghost? Is this my death?"

"I hope not," I said. "I live—and so will you, if I can help it. I have a debt to repay you." I brought him to the temple and cared for him. Renn helped without being asked, eager as she was to begin her mission as healer-priestess.

The next time the Elders of Berall came to the temple to talk at me and receive their answers from Renn, one of them, Aron, stared at Vokh with such a fixed look of shock and dismay that I moved protectively toward my guest to cut short what I was sure would be an explosion of scorn. I began my defense: "You cannot be surprised to see a sick man housed here; Renn has spoken more than once of her plan—"

But Aron paid me no heed. Instead he reached out, as if for a handhold, toward the invalid. "Evokhion? Evokhion the Horseman?" he gasped.

"You would not know me when I came home, maimed, from the wars," said Vokh stiffly. "Why now, Aron?"

"I would not know you—? You came—to me? Are you saying I turned you away?" Aron cried.

"Not in so many words," Vokh said. "But I begged in your sight often enough, these twelve years, in the marketplace."

"Strangers and friends may pass unseeing in the marketplace. Why did you never come to my door, old comrade?"

"Why, I—" Vokh began indignantly—then stopped short. When he spoke again, his tone was softened. "I suppose I was too proud to cry out to old companions, 'Here am I, Evokhion, your disgraced comrade, half dead now and no use to anyone. Give alms to me, for I ride to war no longer.' Instead I waited to see if some passerby would call my name. But who looks a beggar in the face?"

"Vokh, I swear I never knew you returned," Aron said. "Var told us you were dead."

"He would," Vokh said darkly. "He knew where my loyalties lay. But by the time I returned, my lady was dead, and there was none to speak for me."

Aron bowed his head. "It was sorrow upon sorrow that year, as it is again. I never knew you lived to mourn Lady Ruva. But that is past healing. For now, will you let me offer you a place at my table, a bed in my home, as I would have done at once after the war, had you come to me?"

"Only if my newer friend is tired of keeping me," Vokh said. "Jereth, you stand amazed. This mystery is a small thing: I was once a guardsman to the late lord, Voryon."

"The best rider of the guards," Aron put in.

"We two campaigned together many times, till I was demoted to a common horse-groom—for an offense best unmentioned. But when Voryon's army went to war with Tell of Myrcwold's, at the start of the Troubles, I was called to full service again; they needed every able man they could get, respectable or no. In that fight I lost my leg and was left for dead. I might have begged as well there as here, but when I could hobble around on crutches I was stubborn enough to struggle back to Berall. The journey took four years, and I aged at least ten. When I returned, I found the town changed in my absence—the Lord and the Crown Princess dead, the people trickling away southward—and I was much altered. No one knew me; or at least, none would acknowledge me. I knew no work but warfare, and I was unfit for it. And so I became a beggar." He turned to Aron to explain, "And so Jereth found me during the autumn festival. We exchanged kindnesses."

"Vokh sheltered me when I was an outcast," I said. "What I had given him was little enough."

Vokh shook his head. "It was not for an old coat you gave me," he said, "but you looked me in the face when you gave it."

Later, when the elders had gone, I questioned Vokh further. Var left you behind on purpose?"

"Var maimed me himself," Vokh said. "He never meant me to return."

"Was that why you had to return? For vengeance?"

Vokh looked away, then changed the subject: "You told them to take Var to St. Fiern's Town. To let him go free." He laughed. "Var took a less lenient view toward your Hwyn. What mood of mercy hit you?"

"To tell you the truth, I was joking when I suggested the pilgrimage," I told him.

"But you don't take it back," Vokh pursued.

"And you didn't speak against it," I said. "If you think Var deserves death, why didn't you tell Aron what you just told me?"

Vokh shrugged. "Fine friend I'd be, to speak against you when you're taking care of me. Besides—" he half trailed off— "you may know something. They say you came from the sea."

"Don't *you* begin that!" I growled. "But Vokh, you haven't answered. Why did you come back to Berall—to the lord who would have murdered you, the city that disgraced you? When all the world was leaving, why return?"

"Var was not Lord of Berall when I left," Vokh said. "Voryon was almost as bad as his son, but the heir—"

"Lady Ruva," I said, then leapt in the dark: "You and she—"

Vokh held up a hand to cut me short, lest I speak aloud what I had guessed, and tarnish his love's name. "Ruva," he mused, eyes downcast. "I taught her to ride: the champion horseman teaching the young princess. A riding accident, they said later. Not if I knew my craft in the height of my career. She was perfect." He looked up at me. "Mad, they called her. True enough, or she would not have let me become her shame and her deadly danger. Mad, indeed, she was—but splendid. He killed her; and if I had his life in my hands, as you did, he would be dead. But all the same, something in me trusts that you are right."

"It's the local disease." I grimaced. "Don't be too much infected with it."

Vokh steadily gained in strength. What he had needed most was decent food, and I was finally in a position to make sure he had it. When he returned to health, I took him to my shipyard and tried to make him one of my apprentices. I say *tried* for a reason; soon enough I could understand how he'd fallen into begging. "All I know is horses and arms and warfare," he would repeat ruefully. "The best of me was lost long ago." I tried teaching him to mend sails, which I had thought an easy task in my ignorance, accustomed to the life at sea where every man can sew. But Vokh, unaccustomed to working with small things, was hopeless with a needle, and suspicious of what he called "women's work."

I had just resigned myself to the idea that he would never progress beyond sweeping up after the defter workers, when Renn discovered what he could do. I came back to the temple one evening to find that we had a guest: one of my fishermen with a hook embedded in the flesh of his left hand. The fisherman was cursing the hook by more gods, it seemed, than were on the World-Wheel; Renn stood over him, letting him grip her hand so hard she occasionally dropped her priestly demeanor to add to the noise of profanity; and Vokh, a hub of calm in the center of chaos, was silently extracting the hook from the man's hand. He was not a trained healer, but he'd seen enough of battle to have a fair working knowledge of wounds and what could be done for them. As there was only one healer left in Berall, a good binder of wounds was a godsend to the town. Renn was delighted with him, and he with her; he took to her half as the daughter he'd never had, half as a fellow-survivor of cruel fortunes. He soon fell in with her plans for the Order of the Dawn—now to include brothers as well as sisters in its fellowship. And so Vokh, once a hero, later a beggar, was once again honored in Berall.

Things went well. The shipyard flourished. The fishing boats hauled in plenty. Planting began again on lands not drowned and slowly, it seemed, the sea was giving up the lands it had usurped. The bounty of land and sea was shared equally. Renn saw to that—fourteen-year-old Renn who'd been the elders' protégé and pawn, the maiden to be offered up to an angry saint, now a priestess, able to rebuke the rich and hearten the poor. She began to have followers, the makings of an order. There began to be prayer in the temple that was not the prayer of fear. The Feast of the Upright God was a small, timid celebration, a green shoot in a ruin, but the Feast of the Bright Goddess was celebrated with proper gaiety.

The first Feast of the Turning God after the one that had turned

rall into a wasteland was celebrated as a feast of repentance,
ning back from the heedless ways that had reigned under mad
rd Var. Urged to join in the festival as priest, I chose instead the
mi-priestly role of a clown. From behind the mask of some fab-
ous beast, I poured forth scorn on the elders with their full sanc-
n, teased Renn more gently, and embarrassed her suitor till she
as roused to defend him, revealing a warmer feeling for him
an she had ever dared show before. When one of the Huntsmen
proached, also masked beyond recognition, I pretended to mis-
ke him for myself, and mocked Jereth of World's End: that
peless Hope from the Sea who presumed to tell the folk of Be-
ll what to do when he could not govern himself, demanding
erything, satisfied with nothing.

Indeed, I knew that my scorn for Berall had become unfair.
hey had changed for the better, and I did not want to recognize
did not want to love anything that survived after the drowning
Larioneth. When the Feast of the Hidden Goddess came
ain, I refused to enter the temple or join the festivities. I hid
der an overturned boat at my workshop, stopping my ears
ainst the temple bells. Even Renn and Evokhion dared not
ek me out. When I returned to work after the fourth day of the
stival, I was impatient with my apprentices, sarcastic, unjust.
hey held their distance until my mood softened again to the
iet desolation that had become as familiar as my name.

In many ways it *was* a better world born out of the Longest
ight. But it was not for me. Building my boats—doing the
ork I had wanted in my youth, the work my father had taken
om me—I marveled how the gods had finally granted my wish
hen it could no longer gladden me. I loved my work, but it
uld not answer for me the insoluble question of what new
orld could be worth the sacrifice of Larioneth. By day I lost my
rrows in the tasks at my fingers' ends, but my nights were
ven to evil dreams.

There was another insoluble riddle in this wish come true: I
ould not have been able to build what I built. I had never learned
w. I had never learned half the things I taught my apprentices. I
as working on odd hunches about the way the waves would run
ong a certain curve of the keel, or the wind on a certain rigging.
he boat I had taken to the world's end had been good for prentice-
ork, for a craftsman half trained and long unpracticed; it had
ld together through that wild journey, which was more than I

could have expected. But what I made as master-shipbuilder
Berall—that was another thing entirely. I hesitate to praise m
own work, but speak of Jereth of World's End to any shipwright
Swevnalond today, and you will hear what a name those weather
carvel-built craft have won me. There was no earthly reason
should have been able to build them. It was as if I had brought th
skill back from the world's rim.

One of my creations—the first full-rigged ship we made—
had to take the former lord of this land to St. Fiern's Town aft
my second Feast of the Rising God in Berall. Thus I had my fir
long sea-journey since I had returned from the world's end, an
my first attempt to make sense of the altered geography
Swevnalond. But the voyage, this time, went easily. Looking
the tides south of Berall, I had come to the conclusion that th
waters there were not open ocean, but a sound between our i
land and a mainland just out of sight. This proved true, and onc
we found the mainland, it was an easy matter to follow the coas
stopping from time to time to take on provisions at other tow
newly turned ports. We had gold from Var's treasury, and on th
mainland, that still meant something—in the new Berall, co
had become as useless as in Larioneth. But I think the folk w
met would almost have provisioned us for free, so glad were the
to see signs of life in the North. What's more, from the way th
locals regarded me, I think my fellow-travelers must have oile
their generosity with stories told behind my back of Jereth
World's End, the Hope from the Sea.

For all the change in Berall and the new northern coastlands,
found the western coast blessedly familiar. The west had felt th
trembling of the earth and seen the darkening of the sky, but ha
kept their coastline; it seemed they had suffered no terrib
losses. We left our ship in the harbor at Mereford, where it wa
guarded almost with reverence, and completed our journey b
land, a procession that swelled with each town we passed as pe
ple flocked to see the strangers from beyond the northern water

We found St. Fiern's Town still a bustling city, and if its pe
ple responded without undue amazement to the upheavals i
earth and sky, that was to be expected: they had always been
home with marvels. The Order of St. Fiern accepted the lunati
lord, told us we'd done right to bring him there, and offered hos
pitality to all our crew. I thanked them briefly and slipped awa
before my own story could be demanded.

The streets of St. Fiern's Town drew me: a dizzying place, furtive alleys snaking off in unexpected directions, fanciful paintings adorning even the poorest tumbledown houses with the dream-forms of birds and beasts never seen in the waking world. Here, Hwyn had wandered, a child of madness and prophecy, belonging to everyone and no one. How strange to walk these haunted streets, as alone as I had been on my bleak pilgrimage, before I met her. How strange to feel, months after the loss, the near-certainty of finding her just over my shoulder, just hidden by a taller bystander, ready to grab my hand out of the crowd and pull me down an alley to present me with a new song for our performance or a handful of stolen fruit or a kiss.

I must have been looking about wildly, for a stranger stopped to ask, "What are you looking for, pilgrim?"

"Pilgrim? Not this time," I laughed dryly. "Not a pilgrim to the Mirror of St. Fiern, at any rate."

"Lucky for you, then," the man said. "You'd be searching till snowfall. The Mirror's lost underground; an earthquake buried it. But never fear," he added, seeing the shock in my face, "we will find it again. Our strongest are searching the rubble for it; they shift stones carefully and pray. St. Fiern will not hide her eyes forever."

I bowed my head. "May you find what you seek," I said doubtfully.

"And you," the man said, "can I guide you to what you've been seeking so desperately?"

"No," I said, wanting to say more, to tell him what ghost I sought—but my heart was caught in my throat. "No," I murmured hoarsely.

"I might have known," the man said. "You have the eye of those who look for the gods. And you may find them in these streets—but no one can help you."

I looked at him wide-eyed. "Are all the people here prophets?"

"No," he said, "but at least we learn from them. Do not despair. Good journey, pilgrim."

I thought, then, that I ought to rejoin Lord Var's escort at the Lunar Temple, but my feet dragged as I went, my mind grasping about blindly for anything that might set it at ease: *If only I could be at sea already. If only I could be back in my shipyard. If only I could be in Larioneth, lying in Hwyn's arms, and all that happened since then a dream.*

I found myself drawn almost against my will to the place where my adventures had begun, the hill behind the Lunar Temple where the Mirror of St. Fiern had been. *Fitting that I should seek it again now*, I thought: *a lost man to a lost oracle. Maybe now that it's dead and buried, it will at last deign to give me some sign.* And so I crept silently past the temple, avoiding my companions and the Order of St. Fiern, to take the stony path through the hills.

At last I came upon the spot: a barren mess of broken stones where once a spring-fed pool had waited under a willow-tree, now lightning-blasted and dead. I would never have recognized the place without the knot of workers, gray-faced with rock dust, digging gravel or setting their shoulders to huge stones as a priestess in black chanted softly above them. Suddenly the faint drone of chanting was broken by one man's cry of pain and another's shout, "Don't just stand there! Give us a hand or it's on your head when Donerth's maimed!"

I hastened toward them to add my strength to the three men straining at a slipping boulder, and for a while noticed nothing beyond the weight of the stone we struggled against. When at last the stone rested on higher ground and we sat on our heels, panting and sweating, the man who had shouted at me came toward me, holding out his sinewy hand. His somewhat swaggering walk, the muscular bulk of his shoulders, seemed vaguely familiar; his voice left me in no doubt. "Sorry I barked at you. I thought you were one of the work crew, back from an errand. And thanks—" He broke off, suddenly, blinking as if he had just emerged from a tunnel into the light. "I have met you before, haven't I?"

I hesitated to confirm it, given the tone of our parting, but in the end, my curiosity was great, and my desire for self-protection small. I nodded. "You saved me and my companions from the guards of Kreyn. What are you doing here, Warfast?"

He peered at me more closely. "Gods on the Wheel! The prophet, the priest, and the fool. And you're the priest!"

"Not anymore," I said. "I'm a shipwright and fisherman. Jereth, in case you've forgotten."

Just then another worker, farther off, called out, "Warfast, who's that talking to you?" and started toward us, wiping rock-dust out of guileless blue eyes that I remembered well.

"Sky-Raven's Bones!" I said. "Is that Ethwin the Hunter, so far from Folcsted?"

"Jereth?" he shouted, and ran toward me, a spade still in his hand, in a welcome much simpler and warmer than the outlaw's. The two of them retreated with me to a distance from their fellow-workers, as if they were used to each other's company, and the others used to regarding them as a team apart.

"Hidden Goddess!" Ethwin babbled, "Jereth, I scarcely expected to see you anywhere again within the world's rim, let alone here."

"Or I to see you," I said, "so far from the Hills of Penmorrin, and in company with Warfast the—Warfast of Kreyn. How do you two know each other? And why in the Wheel of the World are you here?"

"As for me, need you ask?" Warfast said. "I took Hwyn's advice. Can you really have doubted who won that argument? What an extraordinary little creature. I may have shouted her down in the moment, but her words stuck like burrs to my heart, till I had to listen. I have left my old way of life, and come seeking an oracle to find my new path. How she will laugh, I expect, when she sees how she triumphed!" Then the lurch in my heart must have shown in my face, for the outlaw's eyes widened a little, and when he spoke again, his tone was unexpectedly gentle: "Gods, man, what happened?"

"Hwyn is dead," I said, my voice harsh in my ears. "She died on the Longest of Longest Nights."

Ethwin cried out wordlessly. To my surprise, it was Warfast who put a hand on my shoulder. "I'm sorry," he said. "She was a rare one, to be sure."

"There is none like her," I said.

Ethwin stammered, "Jereth, I—I'm so sorry. I know you loved her, just as I—oh, gods, I remember when you said we should take the quest together, you and I, and leave Hwyn and Trenara safe in Folcsted. But they went, and I stayed, and—oh, gods. Is Trenara safe, or—"

I put a hand on Ethwin's arm. "She must be alive, for the world has not died, nor the grain ceased to send out roots in the earth. She is the Hidden Goddess."

Warfast's mouth fell open and stayed that way. Ethwin

dropped the shovel, which clattered down among the stones. "Oh, gods," he whispered. "Oh, have mercy. What will become of me? I lay with her. I lay with the Hidden Goddess, as a man with a woman."

I kept my grip on him steady, saying, "You were singularly beloved of the goddess, Ethwin. Many men loved her, but you were the only one she asked to come with us. She must have cared for you." His eyes remained round as platters, but at least he seemed to be breathing. I turned to Warfast. "As for you, I seem to recall, she said you had kind eyes."

"Hidden Goddess!" swore Warfast, then checked himself. "Yes. I remember. What a strange thing to say! And she was the Hidden Goddess—the simpleton? What a strange world this is! And Wilgar assaulted her. No wonder he went mad."

"I can see we have a great deal to tell each other," I said. "Will you come with me to some inn so we can moisten our throats as we talk? I think we will go through many pitchers-full in the telling."

"By all the gods on the Wheel, I could use a drink," said Warfast, adding to the bewildered Ethwin, "you too, eh, shepherd boy?"

"But others will want to know this," Ethwin said. "The Order of St. Fiern—"

I shook my head. "I'm done with priests and orders. You tell them if you want. You have both well earned an explanation, for each of you came to our rescue, and aided the Hidden Goddess in the perils of her earthly journey. I will tell you alone; choose for yourselves what you'll do with the story."

"All right, then," said Warfast. "But not now. While the sun shines, we have work to do here. Come back toward the end of the day, and we'll contain our curiosity till then."

"Why should I go? It seemed you needed another pair of hands," I said.

I worked by their side until the sun hung low, and then we found a dark tavern full of inviting scents and slipped into chairs in a corner where we could nurse our ale over long talk undisturbed. I was glad that the gold of Berall enabled me to pay for all we drank and ate, playing host to two men who'd known me as a beggar.

When we were well settled with brown ale, fragrant stew, and fresh bread, Warfast said, "Well, Jereth, will you finally satisfy our curiosity what you meant when you called Lady Trenara the Hidden Goddess?"

"It's a long tale," I said. "But first I want to hear how you two came to know each other, and how you came here. Surely that will be a shorter tale than mine."

"Not necessarily," said Warfast. "But since you've given us drink, we owe you news, at least. I'll begin; Ethwin can eat while I talk, and be ready to bear his part when it comes.

"I was never the same after you and your friends stumbled into our northern stronghold with that magic stone Hwyn carried. None of us were. We rejoined the rest of my troops, but we could never really go back to living as we had: it all seemed empty.

"Lok could not stop speaking of Trenara," Warfast continued, his eyes sliding uneasily to Ethwin, who looked down, shamefaced. "He said he would never love another woman, and he should never have let her go. It was Lok that discovered you had left your water-skins. I let him go after you with them; I even gave him some food to give you; and I said to myself, I will never see him again, for he'll follow that lady to the world's end. But he did not find any of you."

"And we dared not go back," I said, "for fear you had meant your parting words."

"I know," said Warfast. "I'm sorry. I never meant it to end that way, and for a long while I tormented myself with the thought of you three hapless fools dead of thirst in the mountains. But I knew that if Lok had not found you when the trail was fresh, I could not find you when it was cold. Or at least, so I told myself at first, when I still thought we would forget.

"Wilgar was my first worry. He never recovered from having seized that magic stone; he kept slipping off into dream, forgetting where he was. I could not take him on raids anymore; he'd have been butchered. He stayed at the camp like an invalid.

"As for me, I kept turning Hwyn's words over and over in my mind, till I had to admit every word was true. I had long ceased to trouble the Guardian of Day. Where I was, I could only harm the land I had loved, and make a mockery of the Laws of Antir, for which I had sacrificed all I had. The only thing I could do for Kreyn was to leave it.

"I told my men that I had resolved to disband our gang, for the good of the city we had left. I told them I had met a prophet and seen a mystery that would not let me ignore the truth. But only Lok and Wilgar understood, having seen for themselves. In the end we had to fight our way free, for the others would not have let us live, knowing their strongholds. It was only then that I understood what I had done by refusing to flee when my insurrection failed. In the old days, I'd had a band of reluctant outlaws, honest men roused to fight by intolerable injustice; over the years, the best had fallen away and the worst remained, the ones that loved battle for its own sake or for what it could gain them. I had loosed this monster on the land I loved; and I no longer had enough loyal men around me to put it down.

"Far outnumbered, we fled for our lives with little more than the clothes on our backs and the horses under us. We lost our pursuers deep in the Hills of Penmorrin. I had long known there was a tribe of herdsmen somewhere in the hills, for a few of them had come to trade woolen goods in Kreyn when I was young. We kept watch for signs of human presence till we found our way to Folcsted by St. Arin's Lake. There they welcomed us, needing hands for the harvest, which was bigger than they had expected. I was overjoyed to find among them my lost comrade Paddon; he was one of the best of my men in the old days, and his desertion had cut me deep. But we did not lodge with him, for we were adopted into the Linden Clan, brothers to Ethwin, who you see here. Now, lad, it's your turn."

Ethwin nodded and took up the tale: "I told them all about the strange things that happened that summer, with Trenara and Hwyn and you and the Eye of Night. And they told us what they'd seen. They said they'd stay for the harvest, and then when it was done, they'd try to follow the trail of wonders left in your wake. But winter came upon us early, and by the time the work of harvest was done, they could not think of leaving.

"As the Night of the Hidden Goddess approached, Night—you remember her, the acolyte; she's a priestess now—Night had a vision that all the goods of the Folc should be brought to the Hall of the Dead on the first night of the feast, when the Paths of Mystery open.

"At first we doubted her, but night after night, she kept dreaming the same dream. Then Mother Halred persuaded half the Folc, and Father Anlaf most of the others. There was a storm of preparation after that—no time to prepare a proper feast, for we were busy building more wagons to move grain and a new barn to store it in, close to the Assembly Stone. And the flocks had to be driven up the mountain as if it were summer, into the biting wind. But all the while, some said it was a trick of the priests to put all our possessions in their hands."

I raised my eyebrows, and Ethwin read my face right. "Yes," he said, "as you may well imagine, my father was chief among the doubters. None of the Linden Clan's possessions were moved except a few things my mother and I brought in secret.

"Then on the Night of the Hidden Goddess, the Paths of Mystery opened and Halred and Night led us all in, with all our goods. Most of the people had never been in the Paths of Mystery before; they were naming the dead around the Assembly Stone, and the dead appeared around them: it will be talked about forever. We landed in a dream of the Valley of the Linden when it was first settled, in the time of St. Arin, and held the holiday rites there. And Night became a priestess, too, with all the vows.

"After that, people went back to the clan houses for the meal, because we always believed if you eat anything in the Hall of the Dead you will never leave. Of course, there were always a few of us guarding the fire by the Assembly Stone. In the small hours, I was keeping watch with Halred and Night—talking about Hwyn, in fact, and all of you, and the strange events of the summer—when we heard a terrible noise and saw black wings cover the sky. We waited for it to pass, but it just stayed dark, and we couldn't just sit there forever.

"Night and I took torches, lit them in the ritual fire, and went down the hill to gather the Folc together. Halred stayed to watch the Gate of the Mountain for any sign that might guide us. Besides, someone had to be there to calm people when they arrived, and Halred would be best at that.

"When we came to my family's house at the bottom of the valley, we saw that the lake was rising fast, unnaturally fast. We herded all the people and the livestock up the hill to safety, but we lost the grain in the Linden Clan's barn.

"By the time we all reached the Assembly Stone, we could see what Night's dream had meant. The lake was taking the valley; we'd have to stay in the Paths of Mystery till the waters fell again. The grain and stock we had moved there would feed us while we were there, so we would not have to eat the bread of dreams and be lost among the ghosts.

"We lived in the mountain all that Longest Night, lit by the suns of days gone by. When we left, it was for the Valley of the Red Oak, for even by last summer, the lake had scarcely given up any of the Valley of the Linden. Still, they say one day we will live there again, and live well: where the lake has been, the soil it leaves behind is black and rich. And herbs are growing there that no one has ever seen before: Halred, Day, and Night are in raptures studying them."

Warfast cut in, "Lok is studying them too—or maybe studying Night. I'm not sure whether he's turning into her acolyte or her husband."

Ethwin objected, "The priests of the Folc have never married."

"Maybe not," Warfast said, "but many things have changed since the Longest Night. Ethwin, you've left out the crux of the matter. When the Folc had to flee to the Paths of Mystery, everyone was amazed to see Ethwin more at home there than the priestesses. And some of the ghosts there bowed to him, calling him King of the Folc and Lord of the Land."

Ethwin grimaced. "My father loved it, you can well imagine. Halred hated it; she was very put out at the ghosts. And I—gods help me, I don't know what to think of it. I am the great-great-grandson of Arinlaf, who united the four clans of the Folc to save them from dwindling away. He promised to share the headship with the elders of the other clans, each ruling one year in four, so they could live together in peace. Should I undo what he did, putting the other clans under me? Should I make Guthlac of the Red Oak my subject—after all the times I came sulking to his house from a fight with my father, and he made room for me without grudging?"

"The other clans would not submit easily," Warfast told me. "There was dissension and fear. And I, who started a war in my own land, could well warn them what would follow if they fed this blaze. The lad is too noble-hearted to let himself be the cause of strife."

Ethwin shrugged, blushing. "Jereth, you told me once about the Mirror of St. Fiern, and I thought it might answer my questions: Should I be king? And if not, can I even go home again without tearing the Folc apart?"

Warfast nodded approvingly. "I honored the lad for his doubts. I had seen the costs of avoiding such questions—in Goldifer and in myself. And I could not let this boy, who'd never seen a town of a dozen houses, wander lost in the wide world by himself. Besides, I had questions of my own for the Mirror of St. Fiern. I offered to go with him. Odd companions though we may be—a bitter old rogue like me and a fresh-hearted innocent like Ethwin—nonetheless, I have never met a man I could trust more wholeheartedly. I could not ask for a better companion on whatever road the Mirror might show us. But we found no Mirror to ask. And here we are."

"And I am as ignorant as ever," Ethwin said. "I don't know what it all meant, whether I can even go home again."

I considered. "It may not mean anything, but for what it's worth, the Hidden Goddess asked you to come with us."

Ethwin raised his head from his cup, eyes wide. "She did! Oh, if only I'd listened—"

"Now, mind, it may not have meant anything," I repeated. "When she said this, she did not even know who she was."

But Ethwin paid no heed. "I felt I should have gone with you, but I thought it was only my selfish desire to see the world. But I could have been useful. I could have hunted for us all in the wild, protected the women from their enemies. Maybe if I'd been there, Hwyn would not have died."

"No," I said. "Don't even touch that thought. You could not have saved her. Not even the Hidden Goddess could save her."

"Tell us," said Warfast, with a gentleness I would not have expected in him.

I told them all, ending, as they had, with questions: "I still know nothing. What did Hwyn die for? Why were the Holdouts of Larioneth not spared? If the goddess warned the Folc of the coming flood, why should she not warn these people who did her homage and loved her without reservation? Did she herself not know what the waters of birth would do to them? And what did she give birth to at the Rim of the World, in the depths of the sea?"

"Your questions make mine seem small," said Ethwin. "But at least I think you have solved one of mine. The Hidden Goddess would not have urged me away if the Folc needed me as their king. I will not return to my home; at least, not until years have passed and I can expect the madness to have died away. I will stay here, learn from the priests and the other pilgrims, and see which way opens to me."

"And you?" I said to Warfast. "What will you do? Go back to Kreyn?"

"I don't know," the outlaw said. "My heart always turns to my homeland, but I have not been good for it. I will remain here till the Mirror of St. Fiern shows itself, and then ask it my questions. If the saint never shows her eyes again, I will know she has answered no."

"What about you, Jereth?" Ethwin said. "Now that we've met again, will you stay with us to unearth the Mirror? You won't go back to Berall, will you?"

"I have to," I said. "I came here in a ship I built, with a crew I trained, scarcely able to clear the port without my help. They will never reach their home without me. I can't leave them to fend for themselves. But I'm overjoyed to have seen you again, alive and well after the Longest of Longest Nights. I hope you find what you seek; and I hope it answers you better than it ever answered me."

I lingered with Ethwin and Warfast while we stayed in St. Fiern's Town, and treasured their company. And yet, strange to say, I felt impatient to return to my ship, and relieved when the Order of St. Fiern told my crew it was time for us to leave. Only when the familiar bother of keeping a ship afloat filled my mind did I breathe easily. Even on board, I fretted over the slowness of our return, as though I had left a kettle boiling or a task undone; uneasy until we brought the ship in to the Berall harbor, which people had already begun to call Jereth's Landing. I ought to have longed to stretch out my stay in St. Fiern's Town, where I had found friends, but every time I talked to Ethwin the thing I could never tell him burned in my mind: that I was not sure whether to love or hate the Hidden Goddess, after all that had happened, all the losses that could never be justified. Besides, the dead Mirror buried in the earth made this pilgrimage seem as bleak as my first, when I had seen nothing but darkness.

When I had foreseen the Longest Night.

Somehow it did me no good now to know the vision had been

ue. An unreadable prophecy is worse than none. Only Hwyn
ad been able to read it for me; without her, I was once again as I
ad been, uncertain where to go or what to do, driven onward by
vague sense of unfinished work, hounded by unquiet dreams.

The dreams, at least, she could not have helped me with. The
pirit who haunted me was not one she could face in life. Del
on of Devon—her grandfather—grumbled ceaselessly in the
dge of my consciousness. I tried ignoring him as the idle pro-
uction of my brain, but he was too insistent to be my own
ancy: why should I dream more of him than of my own father?
At last, as Berall prepared to celebrate the Feast of the Upside-
Down God, the second anniversary of its downfall, I too faced an
unwelcome necessity. I could not ignore the ghost. On the eve of
he festival, alone in a gleaned field at night, I summoned him.

He didn't appear in a cloud of fire, but he almost might as
vell have done so. "What do you want of me?" he raged. "Why
lo you hold me here, conjurer, ruffian?"

"I might ask the same of you," I said, "when dreams of you
nake sleep a curse to me. Why won't you leave me?"

"Leave you? It's you that bound me. But by all means, take
he high ground, priestling: banish me, summon me, come be-
ween me and my kin—"

"And a good thing I did come between you," I countered,
growing hot in the face. "Someone had to protect her."

"Protect her! Where is she, then? Dead, I'll wager. Lost
omewhere in the North. She *must* be dead: else you would be
vith her, and I would not be near you. Fine work *you* did, pro-
ecting her," he snorted.

He hit so close to the heart that at first I could make no an-
wer.

"What did you want with Yana anyway?" Hwyn's grandfather
demanded, "a pawn for your sorceries?" I knew that he meant
Hwyn, and at the same time, I knew that it was *not* her name.

"I loved her," I said.

"Love! You led her to her death somewhere in the barren
North."

"What do you care? You used her, beat her, broke every bone
n her face—"

"Should a man not discipline his own flesh and blood? And
now she needed it—wild as she was, idiot child of an idiot."

"She was a prophet, old man," I said wearily, "one of those that the gods ride hard. If there is a new world around us, she died in childbirth of it. And I was only her follower."

This time it was the ghost who could not speak.

"Leave me now," I said. "You have no need to haunt me for your granddaughter's death; she chose her own way."

"I don't haunt you. You haunt me," said the ghost. "I am bound—bound to your name. Did you forget?"

Bound to my name? Of course! The truth struck me ungently, full in the face. Hwyn had warned me there would be a price. I had not forgotten, but neither had I understood what I was doing, for all her warnings. Still there might be some advantage in the accident. "If I hold you bound, then—I command you, tell me your granddaughter's true name."

"Yana daughter of Anya. She had no other," said the ghost. He did not know it, then.

"How did you know she was dead?" I asked.

"You banished me from her presence. While she traveled with you, I did not see you, though I felt your name like a leash at my throat. When all the dead moved onward, I could not follow them, for your name stopped me. I was drawn to you instead."

"Then you do not know where she is?" I scarcely dared ask.

"How could I? I am banned from her sight, bound by your name."

I closed my eyes. He still hovered before my sight, under my eyelids. What a fool I was not to have grasped it! I had conjured with my name twice, once to call Conor to Berall, to strike at that town and its lord; and once more to banish Del son of Devon. In the end I had bound myself to Conor, to Berall, and to Del. The bond to Conor had become one of friendship. My bond to Berall had drawn me to it against my will; some of it might have been released when I told Renn that I revoked my curses, but enough had remained to keep me here when my heart was so far away. My bond to Del, more than all the others, had remained and festered like a wound continually galled, never cleaned or poulticed.

"Del son of Devon," I said, "by your name and my own, I, Jereth of World's End, son of Garmund the Sea-Trader, release you from all bindings and forgive you all quarrels between us, by aid of the Rising God, giver of the Gift of Naming. May your name return to you. Be free."

When I had spoken the last words he faded from sight—without forgiving me his captivity, without conceding the smallest particle of his conviction of righteousness, but that did not matter anymore: I too was free. I turned toward the roofs of the town. "People of Berall, I release you from any bindings and any curses I have not yet released, in my name, Jereth of World's End, and with the help of the gods." Then I walked down toward the sea and sat on the sand, feeling strangely empty.

The sea rushed in, the sea rolled back. The roaring of it struck my heart like a blade. Against my will, the realization broke on me that I loved the sea—that after all it had done to me, all it had taken from me, I still always crept back to it like a faithful, beaten dog. It held my birth and my life and my beloved dead; it held the birth-waters of the Hidden Goddess; and I was not big enough or strong enough to go on hating it. But my anger—at the sea, at Del son of Devon, at Berall, at the gods themselves— had been such a solid thing to hold onto in the shipwreck of my life that I did not know how I could survive without it. Ashamed of my own weakness—as if the emptiness in my heart must show in my face—I did not want to meet another human creature. Instead of returning to the temple, I stretched out on the sand beside my cruel lover, beside the sea. In time I slept.

22

THE LEAVINGS

OF THE SEA

With my mind cleared of the ghost of Del son of Devon, I was free to dream of other things. I saw myself sailing a bright sea beneath a low wintry sun, the spray at the bow as cold as loss, my hand on the tiller unshaken though my heart pounded. *I am awake at last,* I thought to myself as darkness fell and the moon rose to its zenith, then swelled to cover half the sky. Under the weight of its new fullness it sank to the horizon before me, and I sailed into the moon.

I awoke, as I had once before, on the empty beach, alone with the sea. "I must sail," I said to it, as though I expected it to respond, to roar agreement or debate my resolve. "I have set Berall free; I too should be free now. I must leave here. I have too much to find, and none of it here. Take me away."

At that moment, I had no clear idea where to go, though one formed in me as I harangued the insensible waves. At first I only knew that the weight on my soul that had anchored me was lifted. It was a burden painfully lost. "I can live without her," I confessed to the sea; though my heart bled, though I hated myself for those words, I was too old in the ways of this life to doubt their truth. I had already mourned Hwyn for longer than I'd known her. I had lived with loss before, and I would again, till my heart grew as tough as a plowman's palm. "I can live without her—but not without the gods, as I have since I landed here. I will find them. I will ask them *why*. Let them answer me or destroy me."

I gave Renn only a censored version of this resolution. "I will leave on the eve of the Longest Night and sail north to the Hidden Goddess. Maybe she is the least likely of the four to answer me—she refused once before—but she said she loved me, and there is hope at least in that. Besides, I know where to find her. If she has no answer for me, let her send me to one of her kin."

"Let me go with you," Renn said. "I want to see the Rim of the World. As a priestess, I *should* seek it. Besides, you'll need help."

I shook my head. "You are all kindness. But your people need you now, priestess. And besides, you could not go where I am bound. To reach the North of North you must turn your back on life—and you, dear lass, are as full of life as St. Bridwen's Day in a year of plenty. I could never reach my goal with you aboard."

Vokh's offer was more circumspect. "I don't want to slow you down. I'm no sailor, as you well know. Still, to see you go off alone—it seems mad, unnecessary—"

"It *is* mad, most likely," I said, "and therefore necessary. This is just the sort of journey to be taken alone—and not the sort to be taken with any vestige of sanity. Turn your back on life, the goddess said, and sail for the empty space beyond. Last time only the goddess herself was in the boat with me. This time, who knows but she may join me again?"

"You *will* return, won't you?" Renn asked.

"Have I ever deserved that you should care whether I come again?" I mused. "Never mind: you are like the Bright Goddess, and give where there is no deserving. For you, I will try to return with an answer, if I find one. If I don't find it, I will go on seeking, and not bring my despair back to a place that has seen too much sorrow. Not that I have any intention of giving in to despair; one of the four corners of the world must hold an answer."

In the end they knew they could not detain me. Besides all the nobler purposes I claimed, I was anxious to be gone before the Feast of the Hidden Goddess stirred memories too painful to be borne. As winter approached, I appointed the best of my apprentices master of the shipyard in my absence and tried to prepare him to continue work without me. I built and provisioned a new craft for my journey, designed for one alone, a single-masted boat with a deep cutwater not easily turned from its course. To its mast I nailed the gilt star from the feast at Larioneth, once a good-luck token, now a token of all I had lost, of the reasons for my anguish and my quest. At last the time came to flee. Before the evening bells announced the first rite of the festival, I was safely out to sea, out of earshot. In the hands of the wild waters I found not precisely solace, but an ache to fill the empty place in my heart. I was content.

Perhaps for that very reason, I could not reach my destination. I sailed for days, for weeks, marveling that the way that seemed so short when I last traveled it should prove so long. Still, I did not at first doubt that I could succeed. After all, there was no knowing how long my first journey had been, in the Longest of Longest Nights with no sun or moon to mark the time, in the numbness of loss, in the unearthly presence of the Hidden Goddess, and in the unconsciousness that had swallowed much of my journey back. It might have been slower than this. Still, other things seemed wrong: I was astonished to see, three weeks' sail north of Berall, a smoking mountain rising from the sea, far to port. Some days later I saw a snow-covered island to starboard. Surely these were new. There had been nothing north of Larioneth in the old days—and I was sure I had traveled long enough and fast enough by then to be north of where Larioneth had been. Still I turned neither west nor east, but kept my prow trained on the northern star, my heart steeled for the darkness beyond it.

Time passed; my food ran out; still I pressed onward, certain by then that the world was larger than it had been. I caught fish and ate them raw; I caught rain and was grateful even for snow to quench my thirst. But at last came a storm from the north that did more than fill my rain-barrel: it drove me inexorably backward, away from the object of my quest. I lost all my sails battling it, and at last even my rudder broke from the sheer force of the wave against my desperate efforts to choose my own course.

My boat drifted, aimless, a toy of the waves, for uncounted time, under a storm so thick I could not tell day from night, much less follow the stars. Still some inner compass told me I was drifting southward, ever southward, refused by the North of North. At last the waves cast up my crippled boat on a sandbar. When the rain subsided I could see the shore an easy swim away. It did not look like Berall; it must be another part of the new northern coast. I saw something on the hills above the coast that looked like human habitation. With nothing to lose and not a dry inch of me left to soak, I braced myself against the crushing cold and swam.

When the shallowness of the water forced me to stand, I looked up the hillside to see a little knot of people descending toward the sea. One of them, seeing me, let up a shout; there was some commotion among them; then after a bit one of them broke from the group and ran toward me. My stomach turned over—I had been welcomed so eagerly from the sea once before, on the bitterest day of my life. Still, there was nothing to be gained by hanging back with my feet in ice-cold water. I continued on out of the ocean's embrace and stood on the shoreline, waiting.

When the first runner drew so close I could see his face, I too cried out: "*Til?*"

"Jereth?" In a matter of moments I was seized roughly and spun about, danced about. "I told them it was you. It had to be you. Who else would come down from the North?" Til crowed, and before I could catch my breath again, Grim was there, and March, all the fishers of Larioneth, with Ash coming after them, a child clinging to each hand. "Jereth the Far-Traveler!" she cried, releasing the children's hands to embrace me. They were all embracing me, and I was clinging to them as to life itself, now that I found I wanted life after all.

"You're alive. Dear gods, you're still alive," I babbled, and they sounded as dazed as I.

"You're alive," Ash said, as if in echo. "You must come inside. My sister will be so glad."

"I knew you were alive," said Til. "You had to be."

"They told me you were drowned," I said. "They said the whole North Country was sunk in the sea."

"Who said so?"

"The watchman of Berall," I said.

"Berall!" scoffed Til. "What did they ever know about us? What did they know about anything?"

"But I sailed right past you—right over you, it seemed. I thought there was nothing left of Larioneth. I thought you were all drowned in the Longest of Longest Nights, a sacrifice for the new world to come."

"We thought you were the sacrifice," March said, "given up to the sea for us."

"I kept up hope," Til said. "I kept a lamp burning to guide your ship—at least, till the Feast of the Turning God. Then I gave up. But now you're back."

"And he's wet as a flounder," Ash said, coming to herself enough to start mothering everyone. "Come indoors. I'll heat up some porridge from breakfast, and let you warm up by the hearth." She broke away to call to her children. "Hros! Hild! Come on back!"

I turned to see that the two children, with their parents distracted, had run out far from their sheltering gaze, *right across the surface of the water.* The waves tossed them up and down but did not cover their feet, though they had run far out to sea, nearly halfway to the sandbar. My mouth fell open and stayed that way as Ash herself stepped lightly onto the water's surface to fetch them back.

March, seeing my consternation, put a steady hand on my shoulder. "Fear not. We are the same friends you left behind— only a little changed."

"Are we above the water or under it?" I stammered, when I could speak at all. "Did my boat sink in the storm to bring me here?"

"You would know best," Grim said. "You have been elsewhere; we have only been here. All we know is that the Longest of Longest Nights, and the storm that followed it, came and went, and we still live—stronger than before."

I was still trying to fathom it when we reached the great hall. There Rand and Taryant, engaged in fixing one of the ancient carved chairs, gasped to see me, and Rand went off calling,

"Mother! Mother! Come see!" I hastened after her, eager to see Syrc, who had been a friend to me and Hwyn from the moment she found us. I would not have expected it, but I had enough room left for astonishment to be a bit surprised to find her sitting in the warm kitchen with a child of about a year old asleep in her lap.

"Daughter of the Longest of Longest Nights," she explained, when she had gotten over her shock at seeing me alive. "There were four conceived in the night, all born during the Feast of the Turning God—a good omen, we thought. Hauvoc and Dara had one; they're married now."

"And you?"

She shook her head. "I've never lacked helping hands with the children—that is, with *my* children—as I did with my brothers and sisters. I'll be fine—and the better for seeing you, Jereth the Far-Traveler. Why, you keep looking at the baby as though she were a greater wonder than yourself, just returned from the world's end."

It was true; I stared at the child as though I'd never seen one before. "I never thought to see new life here again. I thought you were all dead. I cursed the gods for you—for the children of Larioneth. And you're safe. And your children, even—lives brought forth out of the great darkness." The sleeping child looked as thoughtlessly graceful as Trenara, her head lolling against Syrc's strong arm. She had a thatch of dark hair like her mother's, but no one's heritage could yet be traced in her features. She might be anyone's daughter. "What do you call her?"

"I hope you don't mind," Syrc said. "I've named her Hwyn." At that I had to wrap my arms around them both and hold them a while.

Before I knew it we stood in the midst of a council of the Holdouts, convened as speedily as the one that had taken place the day Syrc had discovered us in the snow. As before, Harga was the last to arrive, complaining of her aching bones. Seeing me, she seized me, kissed both my cheeks, and said, "Welcome back, son. The year's treated you hard: you look almost as old as I feel."

"You haven't changed," I said ruefully.

Without a trace of embarrassment, Harga turned to her people. "All here? Good. Let's begin."

I wanted to question the Holdouts, to learn how they had survived, how they had been changed; but they were many and I
only one, and they overpowered me. I had to tell my whole tale
from the Longest of Longest Nights to that morning before they
would tell me anything. They drew all my story from me on a
silken cord of warm concern, and I told them more than I had
ever told in Berall: all the words of the Hidden Goddess that I
could remember; my escapade at the world's rim, trying to hold
the sky together; my shock on arriving in Berall; my descent into
despair. When I told of my suicide attempt, I asked Syrc and
Hart's pardon for breaking my promise to them; they dismissed
my failure with comforting words. With their encouragement, I
came at last to the present. "I sailed out again looking for the
world's end to ask the goddess why—why she demanded your
sacrifice; why you all had to die. And now, without reaching my
goal, I have found out that it was not so: you were not sacrificed.
Except that I see you changed in ways that make me wonder
whether I am among the living or the dead, mortals or
demigods."

"We are mortal enough," Harga said. "Per died last summer—you will remember him; he was a wise man. The rest of us
still have our colds and sprains. But as you say, we are changed."

"We thought you had been sacrificed for us," Syrc said. "You
went out, and after a time the sea came in—but it came as a
friend, took us by the hand. We are the Sea People now. We
thought you had made peace with it for us, died so we might
live."

"Not I," I said. "It must have been Hwyn. But I still don't understand. You are the Sea People—what does that mean?"

"Only this: we cannot drown. The waves bear us up," Hart
said.

"It's no small boon to a fisherman," added Grim.

"I wish you'd been changed with us," Til said. "In the summer
you'll see what fun it is. You will stay to see, won't you? You
should stay with us always, now."

I smiled ruefully. "I don't know. I'm a shipbuilder; what use
am I here?"

"After all that you have seen and suffered along with us, did
you think we would only ask how you could serve?" Til responded.

"Peace, Til," said Harga. "A man may not want to be idle, though his friends are willing to keep him thus."

"But even we may have some use for boats, in time," added Hauvoc. "We've never tried a long journey over sea. If able-bodied walkers want a wagon on land, the Sea People may well want ships to travel far."

"Why, where would you go?" I asked, startled that any of them might think of leaving Larioneth now, after the storm and the danger were past.

"Everywhere," said Syrc.

"This power must have been given to us for some purpose," said shy Tresanda, startling me. "It can't be just for us. I'm going to the mainland to see what I can do."

"Me too," Taryant put in.

"Even I'll go, as soon as the little one is old enough to travel," Syrc said.

"I suppose we'll all go for a while and return," Hart said. "I'll never love another place as much as Larioneth. But I feel the call. I think we all feel it."

"For so many years we looked for the Hope from the Sea," Syrc said. "But we *are* the Hope from the Sea: hope for others, somewhere out there. It must be true. This power wasn't given just so we could have ocean dances at the midsummer festival."

"Ah, you should see it, Jereth," Til said. "I wouldn't leave till after midsummer. It can't be missed."

"I'll stay till then," I decided. "Afterward, if anyone means to see Berall, they can come with me. I promised two friends there that I would return with answers, when I had them, if I could. And now I have them. What new world could be worth the sacrifice of Larioneth? Larioneth was not sacrificed: it *is* the new world. And what was born of the Hidden Goddess in the darkest night? New lands and new oceans, as at the start of the world."

They lodged me once again in their great hall as their honored guest of whom nothing was required. Their easily given friendship was a joy, as ever; but idleness wore at me, as Harga had guessed. I set my hand to any task I wouldn't spoil—cooking, for one, was swiftly forbidden, but at least I could help with menial tasks, until it shamed my hosts' sense of hospitality to have their guest scrubbing greasy pots. I tried to write the first bits of this saga, scratching my first formless thoughts on wax tablets. But I worked slowly, still groping with unanswered questions. I might have some answers, but still somehow, the story seemed too unfinished to commit to writing. Would it ever be finished before I died? I set it aside in despair.

More and more I found myself with Syrc; she did not hunt much now, for little Hwyn could not be carried on a hunt, and protested any separation as though it were the world's end. She worked at little tasks here and there, like me; and like me, often found herself idle, either too well liked or too little trusted outside her usual trade to be given much to do. Sometimes in mild weather we would wander out beyond the city walls on the excuse of digging clams on the beach or finding whiteberries in the wood. We would walk for hours, talking or silent, with little Hwyn toddling beside us or sleeping in a sling that hung from Syrc's shoulders. Toward winter's end, as we strolled over the hills with little Hwyn, asleep, bound securely to her mother's hip, Syrc surprised me by saying, "When you return to Berall, perhaps I should go with you."

I wasn't sure what to say to that. "That's kind of you. I—I— Do you mean—"

"Never fear: I'm not proposing marriage," Syrc laughed, then grew more solemn. "I think we can understand each other. There was only one man I wanted, and he's been at the bottom of the sea since Rand was a baby. I'm too stubborn to be consoled with another, and if my flesh has demands of its own, it can be satisfied with one Feast of the Hidden Goddess each year. And you—"

"There was only one woman, and only one Longest Night for me—and that is all," I said. "But you are a good friend. We do understand each other. I'll be happy to travel with you."

"If you can be happy at all," Syrc qualified, her tone gentle. "I've watched you. Your heart has not come out of shadow."

I hunched my shoulders. "It's a defect in me. I have always been like this—except for a few hard, blessed months with Hwyn."

The baby, hearing her name, blinked and looked up a bit, then fell back asleep. Syrc bowed her head. "Have you spoken to her since— I mean— You used to speak to ghosts."

"Hwyn— She may—" I could not say it. "That wasn't even her name, you know. I never knew her name. She wouldn't tell me—though she used to tease me with the riddle that I knew it, and knew it not."

"But you had the Gift of Naming," Syrc said. "Or was that lost at the world's end?"

"No," I said. "But when—when she lived—the Gift was never meant to reveal the names of the living. And after—" again it stuck in my throat. "Hwyn may not even be a ghost now. Her name was broken when the Eye of Night hatched."

Syrc stared in horror. "So all this while—whenever we leave you idle—you search and find no answer?"

I shook my head. "I have not searched."

Syrc stopped in midstride. "Not searched!" she echoed impatiently.

I shrugged.

"How can you stay in torment, not knowing, and never even look for her?"

"Because if I search and don't find her, I'll know," I said. "What could I do then? How could I live?" She had no answer for me; we did not speak of this for the rest of the day.

But after an unquiet night I woke just before dawn, turning it over in my mind. I wrapped myself in my cloak and crept out, down to the seashore, where the waves murmured prophecies I could not understand.

"She always insisted that I knew her name—that I had spoken it," I told the sea. "Why would she tease me with that riddle if she didn't mean me to solve it, to call to her? She knew her fate far in advance. But at the end, she said her name was broken, irrecoverable. And, oh! she was unreadable, a riddle herself: a mystery, like the Mirror of St. Fiern, whose visions only make sense too late, when the battle is done and the dear comrade is dead."

Suddenly I jumped to my feet and smacked my forehead, crying, "Mirror of St. Fiern!" Oh, gods, for the thousandth time, what a fool I'd been! In my memory, I could hear myself saying on our first day's journey together, "You are the Mirror of St. Fiern to me." That was her name. It had to be. "Mirror of St. Fiern," I repeated, marveling.

The sea came in; the sea went out. I heard no other answer.

"Will you take me now?" I called to the sea. "Now that I have forgiven you, solved the last riddle, and released the last binding, will you take me away from my sufferings? Will there be, even at the world's end, any peace for me?" I walked toward the sea, spiraling down toward an inlet where I knew the slope was easier, a perfect doorway to the waters. "Come: drown me or carry me anywhere. I am a rudderless boat. I know no destination, nor will I try, any longer, to guess whether I should live or die. Choose for me. Only don't leave me becalmed, without change, without hope."

Ahead of me, at the water's edge, I saw some flotsam on the beach, more leavings of the drowned lands cast up by the sea. We found those at Berall, too: everything from broken chairs to the jeweled comb of some long-dead princess washed ashore. But as I drew closer I realized that this flotsam had a human form: a small body, thin and pinched, with ragged light hair.

"Hwyn! Hwyn!" I shouted, running toward her. But as I ran, the body seemed to change shape, like water pooling into new form. It stretched and grew in my sight: limbs long, hair luxuriant, flesh rosy with health. The figure stirred and sat up, wrapping her arms around her knees: a woman with wheat-colored hair, eyes dark as storm-clouds, and a round moon-face that I had never seen before. She wore only a crescent-moon pendant.

"You're not Hwyn," I said as I neared her.

"But I'll be Hwyn if you want me to," she smiled wryly, and there was something familiar about the smile. But it lasted only a moment. "Jereth, why do you shrink back?"

"How do you know my name? Who are you?"

"What? Don't you know me?" she said. "You named me yourself. Has it been so long?" She crept closer. "You are much changed. How many years has it been?"

Well might she ask. My hair was bone-white. "Only two. Grief aged me. Oh, gods, this is foolish! I have never seen you before. You are not Hwyn."

"What, am I so changed?" Suddenly she looked down at her hands. "My finger! It grew back. But that's a small thing. What more? But of course: it seems I can see so clearly, better than I have seen since childhood. My eyes are straight, aren't they?" She touched her face with both hands. "My face—what's become of my face?"

"You're beautiful," I said.

She burst into tears. Remorseful, I took off my tunic and offered it to her. "You must be cold," I said. She slipped it on. I was cold, too, in my shirtsleeves, but it hardly mattered.

Soon I was weeping too. She noticed, and took her turn to accuse: "Now I begin to think you are not Jereth—Jereth who never wept, who could not weep, not even when I lay dying."

That cut me. "I wept after you—after Hwyn died. I wept till my eyes burned. I wept oceans." The tears flowed faster and she, pitying in turn, reached out as if to brush my tears away—but hesitated, a few inches from my face.

"I don't know anymore how to touch you," she said. "You don't know me anymore, not without my scars. Oh, why did I have to be changed!"

I took both her hands and rested my face against them, feeling torn. They were the hands of a stranger—yet who but Hwyn could wish to be scarred, disfigured, rather than healed beyond recognition? "I want to believe," I said. "I want it so badly that I can't believe. How can I believe this? Hwyn died in my arms. I held her body, still and cold, and touched the cruel wound in her chest, and my heart died. How can I dare to trust my wildest hopes?"

"You can *only* trust," she said. "You will never find the certainty you seek."

"*She* said that to me!" I cried, "Trenara said that."

"*Trenara?*" she exclaimed.

"The Hidden Goddess."

Her mouth fell open. "Was Trenara the Hidden Goddess? Sky-Raven's Bones! What a fool I was!"

"And I," I said. "And here I am: confused as ever. And cold. You're cold too. Come inside."

"I don't want to see the others yet," she said, though her teeth chattered.

"There's a boathouse a little way up the shore. We can be alone there."

We walked there in awkward silence, not touching. She was almost as tall as I, and surely stronger, glowing with life and vigor. When we found my cloak on the sand, she ignored my offer of it and wrapped it about me with a firmness that might have been Hwyn's—but with a stranger's hands.

"Do you still doubt me?" she asked as I kindled a fire in the boathouse.

"I don't know what can set my mind at peace," I said. "Hopes are such liars."

"So they are. And I was a thief and a liar—did you love me less for it?" she countered. "Ask me something only Hwyn would know."

I considered a moment, then asked, "What was between us after we left the temple on the Longest Night?"

"The Eye of Night was between us," she answered, "for even when we lay together as wife and husband, I would not take off the pouch I had hung round my neck, so that we had to make love around it, like the gods around the world. Are you answered?"

I sighed. "No other mortal would know that. But the Hidden Goddess might. And she has deceived me before."

"*Trenara*," Hwyn repeated in an exasperated tone. "I might have known! It seems—it seems I almost knew," she marveled. "And yet I lay in her womb and did not know her."

"What child knows its mother? What fish knows the ocean?" I said. "I too almost knew. But I could not know, as I cannot know you."

"Curse it, Jereth, you named me! Twice, now: once long ago, and again today."

"Not Hwyn," I said. "Mirror of St. Fiern. But Mirror of St. Fiern might be a stranger. I traveled half a year with a woman called Hwyn, and loved her, and lost her. But you— Are you immortal? How old are you? Have you lived since Fiern's day?"

"No," she said. "I was born in St. Fiern's Town—how long ago I'm not sure, for no one counted my birthdays for me. Some thirty years ago, I think, or a little more—I always thought you and I must be the same age. And the whole crazy mouthful, Mirror of St. Fiern, was the name my lunatic mother gave me at birth. At least I think she was behind it; I can't remember her calling me anything but 'Baby' or 'Little One.' But in St. Fiern's Town, her words would be taken as oracle; I think that she must have uttered the name that the midwife hid from me. This midwife, my Little Mother as I called her, only told me that I had a name of power, which she would tell to me when I was old enough to keep my own secrets. I think she was a mage, for I never knew her name, either; the people only called her 'Midwife.' If I had stayed there, maybe she would have trained me in the secret arts.

"But before Little Mother judged me old enough to be trusted with my true name, my grandparents bundled me back to Tarr Ford; not liking the nicknames I had been used to, Wren a Nightingale, they called me Yana, after a daughter of theirs th had died. When I returned to St. Fiern's Town as a woman, found that my Little Mother had died and my mother could n be found. I did not know my true name till I dove into the Mirr of St. Fiern and it told me.

"No sooner did I have a name than I had a quest, formless first, but gradually taking shape: my calling to free the Eye Night. That is why I told you in Folcsted that my name lay on th road ahead of me: the journey and the name were one. But own the name publicly would have made its power vulnerabl so I used the nicknames people had given me: Wren or Nighti gale, Riddle or Patch, Midge or Half-Pint or whatever strange called me, short of vulgarities. Then on the road I took the nam of Hwyn the Weaver, and kept it till death."

"She is dead now," I said.

"I know," she said. "I saw her, brave soul, in the womb of t Hidden Goddess."

It was too much to take in. "Is that where you've been?" said. "Then she gave birth to the dead?"

"Yes," Hwyn said. "To think of all the times I tried to prote her from getting pregnant."

"And you said she miscarried once," I remembered. "De gods, what was lost?"

"I don't know," Hwyn said. "I tremble to imagine. It scar me now to think of the importance of a thousand small things did—feeding Trenara, lacing her boots, making her keep h clothes on. If I'd known what I did every day, I might not hav been able to go on."

"What you did know was more than enough," I said, sti overwhelmed by the admission, now more than two years ol that Hwyn had walked open-eyed into death. "But I don't unde stand. Were you walking by her side and in her womb at once?"

"Not quite," Hwyn said. "I am the last buried and the fir born. I was almost too late—but I had to be almost too late, carry the Eye of Night to its destination."

"The first born," I mused. "There are many, then?"

"Many and more than many," she said. "The dead lie waitir under the sea."

stared at her a few moments. "I know," I said, astonished
a myself. "I've felt them there." A commotion of names that
hovered just beyond the edge of my consciousness suddenly
d my mind, as a whisper can fill an empty temple. "Dear
s, why didn't I hear them before this? Their names. So many
es."

Mirror of St. Fiern put a hand on mine. "Do you believe in
now?"

"Almost," I laughed.

And she laughed in return, dryly. "Almost. Jereth, it's so like
that I could shake you. You named me yourself—and the last
g in the world you can trust is your own judgment. Give it
then. What if you don't know who I am? You never did—but
followed me, nonetheless, to the world's end."

And that was so like the woman I knew that I pulled her to me
kissed her mouth. She clung to me; the strangeness of her
ch, the unaccustomed size of her hands and length of her
s, still bothered me, but something began to triumph over
bt in me.

"Hwyn, my heart," I murmured, "my life. Can it really be
? I have longed for you so."

"You know me," she said. "Close your eyes. Don't look. Who
you think is speaking in your ear?"

"Why did you leave me to this uncertainty? Why didn't you
me your name—even when you married me?"

"I dared not," she said. "You had the gifts to learn to use it.
Gift of Naming was strong in you, beyond even the custom
our Order, though you left without vows, and might not have
n expected to keep the Gift at all. It was so strong that you
ght have entangled yourself in all my bindings and drawn on
rself the doom I had bound to my name."

"You mean I might have managed to die with you."

"Or in my place," Hwyn said. "It might have fallen either
."

"You know I would gladly have done either," I said fiercely.

"I knew that," she said. "And if you had, who would have
ed me back from the dead?"

That silenced me for some time.

"I almost lost it all," I confessed at last. "I tried to die, more
once. Once at Hwyn's—at your funeral. And again—" and

with that I told the whole story of my journey to the world's e
my landing in Berall, my despair, my second journey. Hwyn
tened solemnly, gripping my hand all the while.

"I'm sorry," she said when I had finished. "I thought I
protected you. But instead, you were sacrificed, much more t
I. My suffering was brief, but you—you were made like
Upside-Down God, falling ceaselessly, never to reach the b
tom, never to rest."

"It's all right," I said. "I was falling toward you. I've be
falling toward you all my life, like the Upside-Down God to
Hidden Goddess." Suddenly the rightness of it struck me, a b
that nearly unbalanced me. "Sky-Raven's Bones!" I swore
Hwyn. "At the risk of sounding blasphemous—what are we,
and I?"

"We are human creatures," said Mirror of St. Fiern, "an
us, the gods are born anew."

She was right, of course: she always led the way, and I follow
when I could. It was as Hwyn proclaimed: strange as it seem
from two such hapless vagrants as ourselves was born an age
marvels, a world made new.

That was thirty years ago. That age is passing now, as it m
for the world cannot often bear such upheavals—even if they
the tremors of joy. Everyday life will return. Our children's c
dren will say we were only legends, but I record here—for th
that may believe and those that may cherish a little hope withi
larger doubt—that the Sea People and the Sea-Born were r
and known to me. Ninety-nine Sea People of Larioneth trave
to other shores and worked wonders, rescuing ships in dan
fighting tyrants and oppressors. And three hundred and thirty
the dead were reborn from the sea, bringing wisdom from
yond the world's rim, a race of prophets, priests, and poets,
my beloved. I know them all, for I was keeper of their nam
charged with calling each one at the hour of need, in the pl
that needed them. That was all I did: it was they who worked
wonders, carrying the sad world I had known into a new age
wisdom and justice. My wife says I am one of the Sea-Born,
that my knack for shipbuilding is one of the gifts brought b
from the world's end, but that is only a lover's partiality. I
never quite dead or quite reborn. I am not one of this age's m

ls; I have been privileged to see and touch them, and that is
ough.

This age must pass, I know: even our wisdom will be forgot-
n; even our justice will be corrupted; even the Sea-Born will
e in time, and I too will die, so that none will be called from
e sea for another age of the world. But something of hope will
main even in the legend of them, even when no one fully be-
ves it any longer. And for all these things that will be lost
ain—and for all the unnamed dead not called back from the
a—I can only trust, like my patron the Upside-Down God, al-
ys falling, never certain, but always in hope. May he bring me
last to good harvest.

ABOUT THE AUTHOR

JLINE J. ALAMA studied medieval literature at the University of chester, where she earned a Ph.D. in English, searched for Grail in *The New York Times On Disk,* and learned a lot ut snow, beer, and procrastination. Her Sapphire-winning ry "Raven Wings on the Snow" is in *Sword and Sorceress III,* and her work has appeared in *Marion Zimmer Bradley's ntasy Magazine* and *A Round Table of Contemporary hurian Poetry*. She writes grant proposals for New York undling, a children's services agency, and lives in New Jersey h husband Paul Cunneen and cat Crichton, both of whom are y supportive.